The Decimation Trilogy

Richard T. Burke

Contains the full-length novels:

Decimation: The Girl Who Survived
Termination: The Boy Who Died
Annihilation: Origins and Endings

Other standalone books by Richard T. Burke:

The Rage
The Colour of the Soul
Assassin's Web

The Decimation Trilogy

Richard. T. Burke

First Printing: 2022
ISBN: 9781916141735

www.rjne.uk

For Mum and Dad

Thanks for everything

Even though the future seems far away, it is actually beginning right now.

Mattie Stepanek

Book One

DECIMATION: THE GIRL WHO SURVIVED

1

Monday 3rd January 2033

She sensed the contraction approaching like a breaker bearing down on a beach, and then it hit, engulfing her, crashing through in an implosion of bone and muscle. It seemed as if every sinew and tendon in her body was being stretched to its limit.

"Just try to relax," the midwife said, her voice muffled by the white surgical mask that hid the lower part of her face.

"You've got to be bloody jok—"

"Breathe, Antimone," the girl's mother interrupted, her face also partially covered by a mask. She brushed a stray strand of hair from her daughter's cheek.

The girl fought through the pain and forced herself to exhale through gritted teeth. Just when she thought she could bear it no longer, the tension eased as if somebody had loosened a band around her stomach. The white material covering her nose and mouth felt damp as it clung to her skin.

The midwife glanced at her watch. "That was three minutes. I think we need to get her to the operating theatre." She strode across the small white room and through the open door.

Antimone turned her head to the right and met the anxious gaze of her father. He clasped her hand between his own, and she realised her fingernails had been digging deep into the flesh of his palm. She smiled gratefully at him, and he gave a gentle squeeze in return. The harsh ceiling lights reflected from a tear forming in the corner of his eye.

"Don't worry, Dad, it'll be alright," she said although she knew it wouldn't.

"It's just so damn unfair," he began, but before he could continue, the midwife returned to the bedside.

"The porters are coming now, and they'll take you to the operating theatre. I know we've been over this before, but you know what'll happen next?"

Antimone stared out of the window at the dark clouds scudding across the pale grey expanse of the winter sky. This would be her last glimpse of the world outside. Her eyes slid across to a poster on the opposite wall. In the picture, three remarkably healthy-looking patients in hospital beds surrounded a cartoon representation of a sneezing man who seemed far more unwell than any of them. 'Always Wear a Facemask' read the caption beneath, followed by the text 'Germs Kill'.

The midwife raised her voice. "Antimone, you know what's going to happen next?"

"Yeah, yeah," Antimone snapped. "You're going to put me to sleep, cut me open and take the baby out. Oh, and I'm never going to wake up. Is that about right?"

A flicker of irritation crossed the midwife's face before she forced a tight-lipped smile. "We'll try to make you as comfortable as possible."

"They're only trying to help," the girl's mother said.

"Okay, I know," Antimone said. "I'm sorry."

The midwife stepped outside the small room, leaving the father, mother and daughter together, each counting down the seconds until the inevitable conclusion.

"We'll look after the baby as if... well, as if it were you," her mother said.

"I know you will," Antimone replied. "Just don't let him get anyone pregnant."

Her father made a sound that started as a laugh but turned into a sob.

A metallic clanking noise drew their eyes to the door. Two porters dressed in pale green overalls entered the room pushing a narrow hospital trolley. The midwife followed a couple of paces behind.

The taller of the two consulted a clipboard. "Are you Antimone?" he asked, pronouncing it An-tee-moan.

"It's Antimone," her father replied. "Like the metal."

The man stared at him blankly.

"An-tim-oh-nee," her father repeated, stressing each syllable.

"Nice name. Okay Antimone, if you could just pop yourself off the bed and onto this trolley, please."

Antimone made no attempt to move. The man turned to his colleague in confusion. "Is she...?"

The midwife intervened before he blundered further into the minefield he was laying for himself. "She's paralysed from the waist down, so you're going to have to help her."

The man's face turned a bright crimson colour as he consulted the clipboard once again. "I'm s-s-sorry."

The smaller man took charge. "You're her parents, right?"

Antimone's mother and father responded in unison.

"We'll put a sheet underneath her, then slide her over."

He manoeuvred the trolley alongside the bed and applied the brakes. Meanwhile, the midwife unfolded a sheet and laid it out, adjusting the girl's position until she lay on top of it. In one swift movement, they transferred Antimone across. The taller man, his cheeks still glowing with embarrassment, removed the brakes and raised the sides.

"Another one's coming," Antimone said.

"Okay, we'll wait here until it passes, and then we'll move you," the midwife said. "Don't fight it, just let it come."

Within seconds, another contraction enveloped her. Her teeth ground together as she tried to ride the wave, her head thrown back. She groaned in agony. It was as if she was trapped in a machine that was testing the breaking point of the human body. Just as she felt she was about to snap, the pressure lessened.

"Jesus," she muttered. "What a way to die."

The midwife consulted her watch. "That was less than three minutes. We need to get her to that operating theatre quickly." She led the way as the two porters wheeled the trolley along a corridor interspersed with numbered doors every few metres. Her parents hurried behind. They turned two corners before arriving at a room labelled 'Operating Theatre 3.'

The midwife addressed Antimone's parents. "I'm afraid you're going to have to wait outside during the procedure. It's time to say goodbye now."

Antimone's mother bent over and hugged her daughter. "I love you so much."

"I know, Mum."

Her mother could no longer hide her tears as her father embraced Antimone one last time. "You know we both love you. We couldn't have wished for a better daughter."

"I love you too, Dad."

"You can watch through the viewing window if you want," the midwife said, leading Antimone's distraught parents away.

Antimone brushed the tears from her eyes with the back of her hand. Despite the presence of the two porters, she had never felt more alone in her life. They pushed the trolley on which she lay through a set of double swing doors. A woman wearing a dark blue operating theatre gown, a light blue hairnet and a white surgical mask separated from the other two doctors and crossed the room. She consulted the clipboard and smiled down at Antimone.

"I'll be putting you to sleep. We just need to get you ready for the surgeon."

The porters turned away, the taller of the two giving Antimone a self-conscious wave.

The anaesthetist positioned the trolley beside a rectangular platform covered in a green sheet and applied the brake. The two men halted their conversation, one moving to Antimone's head, the other to her feet. On the count of three, they transferred her to the operating table.

The woman removed Antimone's surgical mask. In its place, she slipped on a black mask connected to a beige-coloured box by a snaking corrugated pipe.

"Let's just pop this on. We'll let you know before we turn on the gas."

Antimone inhaled the smell of rubber and strained her senses to detect any change in the air hissing through the tube. The woman raised Antimone's hospital gown, exposing her distended abdomen.

A door to her left opened, and a man dressed in blue surgical attire entered backwards, his gloved hands extended in front of his body. He stopped by the operating table and peered down at Antimone through a pair of large, plastic-framed glasses.

"The name's Martin," he said. "I'll be the lead surgeon today. In a second, we'll put you to sleep, and this will all be over."

A surge of adrenaline made Antimone's heart beat faster as the full implication of his words sank home: over, as in dead. Her life was moments away from ending. Despite coming to terms with her predicament, now that the time had arrived it was all happening far too quickly. When her mother had given birth, it had been a joyful experience. Now pregnancy was a death sentence.

A faint hissing sound joined the beeping and humming of the assorted machines. Antimone's eyes darted across the room in panic, attempting to identify the source. She sensed dampness on her face and stared up at several evenly spaced, white, circular plastic boxes on the ceiling, each of them emitting a fine mist into the room.

"Nothing to worry about, just anti-bacterial spray," the surgeon said. "We need to keep everything germ-free in here."

The woman who had fitted the black mask moved back into Antimone's line of vision. "Right, we're going to put you to sleep. Start counting aloud backwards from ten."

"Ten, nine…"

This isn't happening. I'll wake up in a second, and it'll all be a bad dream.

"Eight, seven, six…"

A sickly-sweet scent invaded her nostrils. She experienced a brief sensation of nausea as her vision greyed out.

"Five."

Antimone sensed the approach of another contraction but was unconscious before it took hold.

***

One of the assistant doctors painted yellow-brown liquid across the lower part of Antimone's stomach. The surgeon peered down at the stained skin and nodded his approval.

"Cauterising scalpel please," he said, holding out a hand expectantly.

Grasping the instrument like a pen, he made a confident incision horizontally across her abdomen. Like a well-oiled machine, the surgeon lifted his hand away as the doctor swabbed away the small quantity of blood that welled from the cut.

"Spread the incision," the surgeon said, using his left hand to open the wound from his side of the operating table. On the opposite side, the doctor used a metal instrument to pull back the layers of skin and muscle and expose her uterus. In his other hand, he held a suction tube that hissed and gurgled as he inserted it inside the cut.

"Making the incision," the surgeon announced. With a steady stroke, he drew the scalpel towards him in a straight line.

"Okay, we're in. Let's bring the nipper into the world."

Both men used their hands to ease the baby's head out. Within seconds, they grasped a slippery, screaming bundle of life and handed it to the doctor who had been waiting patiently at the side.

"A boy," the man announced, although none of those present in the room paid any attention.

The surgeon waited until his assistant had clamped the umbilical cord, then severed it. The third man cleaned the baby and placed him in an incubator.

The anaesthetist looked up from the readout on her machine. "She's flat-lined."

The surgeon glanced up at the wall clock. "I see no point in attempting resuscitation. Call it at two forty-eight. There's nothing more we can do for her." He began the job of suturing the open wound.

The row of stitches extended across a quarter of the incision when a repetitive chiming sound filled the room. The doctor closest to the flashing terminal strode towards it. "I'll get it." He swept a hand across the front of the screen.

The image of a woman's head occupied the display. "Mr Martin and Dr Carlson are wanted in operating theatre one as soon as they're free," she announced. "Emergency C-section."

"It sounds like we're needed elsewhere, Dr Carlson," said the surgeon, addressing the anaesthetist. He turned to face the two male doctors. "One of you can finish up in here. The other can assist me next door." He strode away without waiting to see who volunteered to join him.

The two men stared at each other. "I'll sew her up," said the doctor who had assisted Martin during the procedure, "but it all just seems a bit pointless when the pathologist is only going to open her up again."

"I know what you mean," the other said, "but the dragon will fire you if you don't follow procedure. In any case, the girl's parents may still be watching through that window."

"Good point," the doctor said turning back to the lifeless body. "See you later. Have fun."

***

The blue-gowned medical staff departed, leaving Antimone's body lying on the operating table. The doctor hurriedly completed the stitching job before rushing away to his next call. The faint hum of the machines was the only sound in the room. A thin film of moisture from the inactive atomisers in the ceiling coated every surface.

A cough and then a low groan broke the stillness. The fingers of Antimone's left hand twitched. Her head moved first to one side and then to the other. She sucked in a lungful of air but couldn't seem to satisfy her body's unconscious craving for oxygen until finally she was forced to exhale and draw in another deep breath. Sensations crowded in on her as she began the painful return to full consciousness. The reek of the anti-bacterial spray filled her nostrils and stung her throat as she inhaled. She ran the fingertips of her right hand down her arm, the skin feeling cold and clammy. Instinctively, she brushed her hand against the outline of the bump that had been a feature of her body for the past few months, but snatched it away as she sensed the rough edge of the stitches through the thin hospital gown.

Slowly her thought processes ground into gear. She moved her elbows back and tried to raise her head, but the excruciating pain as she tightened her stomach muscles forced her to lie back. Once again, she probed the edges of the incision. *The baby's gone. Why am I still alive?*

In a rising panic, she inspected her surroundings.

"Help! Someone, please help me!" she croaked, her throat muscles still sore from the exertions of the labour.

She lay back, trying to goad her oxygen-starved brain into action. Her eyes scanned the deserted operating theatre. *They think I'm dead. It could be hours until somebody comes. I've got to get help.*

Steeling herself, she shifted her elbows backwards for a second time and raised her torso. She almost passed out from the jagged shards of pain ripping through her abdomen, but eventually manoeuvred herself to a sitting position. Spots of blood appeared on the front of the hospital gown where it touched against the rushed stitches. Using one arm to support her upright posture, Antimone used the other to slide her left leg until it was dangling over the edge. She paused for breath, allowing the agony to subside before repeating the process with the right leg. With excruciating slowness, she shuffled her body forwards. It was over a metre to the floor, far higher than she would have attempted under normal circumstances.

"Here goes," she muttered as she edged her bottom over the rim of the operating table. Her toes touched the ground, but as she passed the point of no return, she couldn't stop her momentum and pitched forward. She tried to break her fall but still smacked her head on the white, plastic-coated floor.

For several minutes, she lay motionless, dazed by the blow. Finally, she moved her right hand and probed her forehead, which had borne the brunt of the impact.

"Christ, that hurts," she whispered.

Using her arms, she dragged herself across the floor, centimetre by centimetre, with frequent pauses for rest, until she found herself up against the door. A thin smear of blood trailed behind her. She attempted to push the door open with one arm but couldn't budge the heavy mechanism. She had no more luck when she used both hands. Rather than achieving the desired effect, she found herself pushing her own body backwards. In frustration, she rolled onto her back and closed her eyes. Within seconds, exhaustion overcame her, and she was asleep.

A sudden bumping against her head awakened her. Her brain struggled to make sense of her surroundings before she recalled where she was. Somebody was entering the operating theatre.

"Hang on," she croaked, "I'm trying to get out of the way."

The door stopped moving, and the sound of low voices filtered through. She shuffled her body out of its arc.

"Okay, you can open it now," she called.

The door opened a few centimetres, and a head peered tentatively through the gap.

"Who the hell are you?" the man asked. His eyes tracked the smeared blood trailing from the operating table to where Antimone lay. "My God, you just had a baby, and you're alive? Nick, get in here and call Mrs Baxter. This one's alive."

A second man entered the room, pushing a trolley. "Yeah, right. Nice one."

The smile vanished from his face when he took in the girl lying at his feet and the patchy, red streaks across the floor. While the first man tended to Antimone, the other rushed to the wall-mounted terminal and swept his hand from right to left in front of it.

"Call Mrs Baxter," he said in a trembling voice.

After a few seconds, the irritated expression of a man in his mid-twenties with jet-black hair, and a narrow face filled the screen.

"I'm Nick Jenkins from the mortuary. I need to speak to Mrs Baxter urgently."

"Mrs Baxter is busy. What's it about? If it's something to do with overtime or working conditions, take it up with Personnel."

"No, it's nothing like that. Could you please inform her that the woman who just gave birth in operating theatre three is still alive?"

"Alive? Are you sure? If this is some sort of practical joke, there will be serious consequences."

"I'm telling the truth. She's talking to my colleague right now. We came in to pick up the body and found her on the floor."

"Wait right there. For Christ's sake, don't touch anything... In fact, don't move at all."

The display went blank.

Part One: Origination

2

9 ½ months previously

The woman lay back against the cold brickwork and closed her eyes. She was twenty years old but would have struggled to answer had she been asked her age. Her brown hair was straggly and greasy. She couldn't remember when she had last washed it, or any other part of her body for that matter. Her face might once have been described as pretty, but a life on the street had hollowed out her cheeks and etched dark shadows beneath her eyes. Her body was angular, all sharp corners and jutting bones, due in the main to the starvation diet she had endured for the last few weeks. She wore a grimy pair of blue jeans and a thick green woollen sweater that was several sizes too large. On her feet was a pair of tattered trainers, which she wore sockless.

Her home, if it could be called that, was the alley in which she currently sat. If the weather was good, as it was now, she occupied the space between the two large industrial waste bins. When it rained, she would often take shelter inside one of the brown plastic enclosures if the stench from the contents was not too much to bear.

The sole purpose of her life was to consume the next fix of 'Chill Black', a narcotic that, for a few brief moments, generated a sensation of immense pleasure and allowed her to ignore her woeful existence in the real world. She was prepared to do pretty much anything to obtain a supply of the small yellow pills. She had frequently sold her body although she drew the line at unprotected sex—even in her drug-addled state, she knew that one simple mistake could cost her life as it had her mother. Recently the flow of men willing to overlook her poor physical condition had dried up, and she was forced to resort to begging and stealing to feed her habit.

She opened her eyes and fingered the small pill, rolling it between a grubby forefinger and thumb. Placing it in her palm, she stared at it in hungry fascination. She savoured the moment, the build-up before she popped it in her mouth. Another user—it would be inaccurate to refer to her as a friend—had taught her that she could prolong the mind-blowing high by placing it beneath her tongue. She found it amazing that this small yellow capsule held the power to transport her to a place where nothing else mattered.

In the rare moments of clarity between the highs and the subsequent lows, she contemplated seeking help. She had led a relatively normal home life until her mother had fallen pregnant six years earlier and then, like every other expectant mother, had died in childbirth. Her father had lost his job soon afterwards and had been unwilling or unable to cope with looking after a new baby. He had offered the child up for adoption and in the following weeks had descended into an alcohol-fuelled depression. When his anger turned towards his remaining daughter, she had moved out. Initially, she had stayed with friends, but when she wore out her welcome, she turned to a life on the streets. From there it was a short and painful trip to where she now found herself. As a consequence, there was no parent to whom she could turn, and the authorities would only send her on a rehabilitation course, after which she would, more than likely, end up back in the same situation.

She delayed the moment of gratification, prolonging the anticipation ahead of the oncoming rush. She was about to lift the pill to her mouth when a shadow passed in front of her. Lifting her head, she saw a smiling man wearing a pair of blue overalls. The man was well-muscled, with blond hair and piercing blue eyes. For a moment she wondered whether this was part of the trip, but when she glanced down the pill was still in her hand.

"What do you want?" she asked in confusion.

"I'm here to help," he said, still smiling. Although his English was perfect, he spoke with a slight accent.

"I don't need any help," she said, her voice hardening.

"But I think you do, actually." The man took a pace forwards and held something up to her neck.

There was a short hiss, and she experienced a sharp stinging sensation. The man stepped backwards and studied her carefully. A feeling of light-headedness swept through her as she stared at him blankly. His blue eyes drew her in.

After thirty seconds had passed, he spoke again. "You want to come with me, don't you?"

The girl nodded, although it felt like somebody else was moving her body on her behalf. She rose shakily to her feet and took a tentative step towards him.

"My van's just over there," he said, gesturing vaguely behind him. "It's comfortable in the back. I think you should lie down there."

"Okay."

He led the way to a white van and unlocked the rear doors. On the floor were a pile of blue mats.

"There. Why don't you have a nice relaxing sleep? You're feeling a bit tired, aren't you?"

"Yes," said the girl, clambering into the back and lying down. She curled up into a foetal position and closed her eyes. Within seconds, she was unconscious and breathing heavily.

The man slammed the van doors and locked them. He returned to the driver's seat and pressed a button on the dashboard.

After a brief pause, a male voice crackled over the internal speakers. "Yes, what is it?"

"I've got one. I'll be back in about forty-five minutes."

"Okay, we'll be ready."

The man started the vehicle and inched his way out of the alley onto the main road.

On the ground, between the two bins, lay a small yellow pill.

3

Sunday 4th April 2032

Antimone Lessing raised her right arm and extended it backwards behind her head. She repeated the exercise on the other arm, all the while the music booming in her ears. She wore her brown hair in a ponytail that draped over a bright yellow, long-sleeved training top. Her legs, dressed in a form-fitting black material, were bunched beneath her body in a kneeling position suspended above the lightweight frame of her racing wheelchair.

The only other girl in the group of athletes sat beside Antimone on the damp grass and leant forwards until her nose touched her outstretched leg. Erin Riley had little in common with Antimone other than their shared interest in athletics. Neither girl was popular, but for different reasons. Despite her athletic physique, Erin was not physically attractive with her thin fly-away hair and bland features. She tried to ingratiate herself with her fellow pupils by trading gossip but instead had earned a deserved reputation for being indiscrete.

Antimone, by contrast, owed her lack of popularity to being different from her peers. The wheelchair was one aspect of it, but the fact that her parents could barely afford to send her to Oakington Manor even on a scholarship didn't go unnoticed by her classmates. The majority came from privileged backgrounds and held a casual disregard for money. They intuitively identified Antimone as an outsider and maintained a distance.

Five metres away, a boy, a man really, was performing a similar set of warm-up exercises on his calf and thigh muscles. Max Perrin was a little over six feet tall, maybe six two, she estimated. His hair was a close-cropped golden brown. He wore a designer training top and a pair of baggy training pants. On his feet was a pair of high-end athletics shoes. Every few seconds, an illuminated pulse swept along the red stripe on the side of each shoe.

Three other boys warmed up a few paces away, flashing jealous glances at Max as he flirted with two attractive fifteen-year-old girls. The taller of the girls wore an expensive-looking, pale green T-shirt and a short, pink skirt. The skirt seemed to possess a life of its own, fluttering up and down in waves even though there was no wind. The control system carefully coordinated the movement to ensure that it preserved her modesty at all times. Antimone had heard about these so-called 'Marilyn' skirts but had never seen one in action.

Seeing the impact the billowing skirt was having on the group of boys, and not to be outdone, the second girl, who wore a similarly skimpy but conventional white skirt, tapped the nail of her little finger with her thumb. A gasp rose from the small group as a hole seemed to open up through her midriff and expand in size. The ragged edges exposed her internal organs and lent the image a gruesome reality. The girl flashed a smug smile now that she was the centre of attention and leant forward to whisper something in Max's ear.

Antimone rolled her eyes. Max Perrin was good-looking and from a wealthy family. He used those assets to his advantage when it came to the opposite sex. As far as athletics went, despite an over-confidence in his own abilities, he ranked only slightly better than average. That didn't stop most of the teenage girls at the school from lusting after him. *But two at the same time? Didn't they have any pride?*

Antimone's gaze meandered past another group of three boys and two girls perfecting their sprint starts and settled on a boy practising his run up for the javelin. He looked faintly ridiculous as he charged up to the white line identifying the end of the runway, simulated a throw and juddered to an abrupt halt.

A voice rose above the thrashing beat. "Antimone!"

Antimone glanced up at her coach and noticed his lips were moving. She realised everybody was staring at her. She tapped the fingernail of her right middle finger with her thumb, and the music ceased abruptly. "Sorry, Coach. What did you say?"

John Marshall was approaching retirement and had taught Physical Education at the school since its inception ten years earlier. He insisted the students addressed him as 'Coach' at training sessions. He was a no-nonsense teacher with a background in the military, but beneath the brash exterior he was conscientious and genuinely cared about the progress of his pupils. At this particular moment in time, however, he did not appear impressed.

"Look, when you're at the track I expect your undivided attention. I don't give up my afternoons so you can daydream during my sessions."

She opened her mouth to speak, but he interrupted before she could apologise. "Two hundred metres at three-quarters pace followed by two hundred metres warm down. Six reps, please. The same applies to all of you."

Antimone groaned inwardly. She loved the big occasions, the important races, the roar of the crowd, but training was just so boring—and often painful. *But six repetitions?* She must have really upset him. It was clear from the scowls on the faces of her fellow athletes that they blamed her for the harsh instructions.

Seeing her lack of enthusiasm, the man nodded towards the track. "Come on. Let's get going. You won't improve if you don't put the effort in. And turn on your logger, Antimone. I want to study the pattern of your push." He turned his focus to the two girls still flirting with Max. "I take it you ladies aren't training today. Maybe you could cheer on your champion from the stands."

Max smirked as the pair sauntered across the track, swaying their hips in an exaggerated manner, aware that every eye was upon them. The arrival of the sprinters down the home straight spoiled the effect, forcing the girls to hurry to avoid being trampled underfoot.

"Hey, fancy going out sometime?" Max asked, turning to Antimone.

"Um… maybe," Antimone replied in confusion, unsettled by the question. Despite her ambivalence, the thought of how it might improve her image to go on a date with him sprang to the forefront of her mind.

"Thought so. The problem is I don't fancy going out with you," he said with a sneering laugh. "The trike queen wants to go out with me," he announced, draping an arm around one of the other boys.

"I only said maybe," Antimone replied hotly, but nobody was paying any attention.

The coach clapped his hands and turned back to the group. "Come on, I haven't got all day. Is this a fashion show or a training session?"

Antimone propelled her wheelchair towards the white start line slashed across the ochre surface of the running track, her face still burning, and frustrated that she had let Max get the better of her. Tapping the nail of the little finger on her left hand, she navigated the menu structure with no need for the audio cues whispering in her ear. She selected the logging option, and a green light illuminated on a panel located just behind the front wheel. She fitted the helmet resting on her lap and pulled a pair of protective gloves from the pockets in her training top, then slipped them on.

At first glance, the racing wheelchair resembled a tricycle with a single wheel at the front and the back two wheels canted inwards, but it was hand- rather than pedal-powered and lacked the handlebars of a traditional cycle. The in-built sensors and data logger allowed her coach to analyse in detail the timing of her propulsive stroke and suggest ways to race faster whilst at the same time consuming less energy. At the level of competition she had attained, every millisecond counted and could make the difference between gold and silver medals.

Her talent was first identified when, as a skinny thirteen-year-old, barely a year after the car accident that had left her paralysed from the waist down, her father had taken her for a trial at a local athletics club that catered for disabled athletes. During a four hundred metre race, despite having no training and using an obsolete wheelchair, she had thrashed her more experienced opponents, leading from the start and winning by over ten metres. Within weeks of that race, the trustees of the prestigious private school, Oakington Manor, had offered her a sports scholarship. There was no way her parents would have been able to cover the extortionate fees without financial assistance, but the generous bursary covered tuition costs, leaving them only to find money for incidental expenses such as the school uniform—and the gear for wheelchair racing. Now, one month short of her sixteenth birthday, those in the know were touting her as a potential Paralympics medal winner in the eight hundred metres event.

Out of instinct, Antimone looked across to the stand. She knew her parents were not there, but it was an ingrained reflex. A group of six adults sat together at the front towards the centre, chatting and paying no attention to the training session. As her eyes swept along the rows of seats, her gaze came to rest on a man standing by himself at the far-right end. Besides being the only person on his feet, what struck her as odd about him was his black woollen hat. It seemed totally incongruous amongst the expensive attire of the other wealthy, well-dressed parents,

The coach's voice drew her attention back to the track. "Let's get going then."

She grabbed the circular metal bar that rimmed the wheel and propelled the chair forwards, accelerating with several powerful shoves. Settling quickly into a steady rhythm, she guided the vehicle between the stark white lines. She rounded the bend, and as she approached the end of the straight, she reduced the stroke rate, allowing the chair to coast down to a slower speed.

"Hey! Don't just slow down suddenly like that. I nearly ran into the back of you. You need brake lights on that bloody thing." Max jogged alongside, glaring angrily at her. Antimone maintained her focus on the track, doing her best to ignore him.

When they arrived back at the starting point, Max surged forwards and cut ahead of her, two of the others following a few paces behind. Antimone delayed her acceleration as she steered the chair into the third lane. Max glanced behind him, grinned and moved out to block her progress. Antimone swung out into the fourth lane and then the fifth, accelerating as she did so. Max and the other boys ended the bend in a line across the track, Antimone now out in the sixth lane.

By the end of the fifth lap, the rest of the group were tiring and had dropped back by twenty metres, leaving Antimone and Max leading the way. Perspiration trickled down her face, and her biceps felt like they were on fire as she moved into the curve. Max drew alongside and matched her pace even as she increased her push rate. As the straight ended, Antimone slackened the power of her strokes, and her speed slowly reduced. Rather than decelerating, Max continued to maintain the same pace into the next bend until he was five metres ahead. He glanced over his shoulder.

"Not tired are you, trike queen?" he gasped between breaths, lengthening his stride.

Antimone knew that she shouldn't respond, but his smug expression goaded her on. Despite her aching arm muscles, she accelerated once more, maintaining the distance between them around the curve. As they reached the start of the straight, she allowed the chair to drift out into the second lane and applied the power to close the gap. The separation gradually reduced. Three metres... two metres... one metre. Ten metres short of the finish line they were neck and neck, both determined to cross first.

Antimone drew on her last reserves of strength and put everything into one final shove. As she did so, a droplet of sweat splashed onto the shiny metal ring, and her left hand lost a small amount of grip. The difference in torque between the two wheels was minimal, but it was enough for the chair to veer sideways and cross the line separating the lanes. Her left wheel caught the outside of Max's right foot.

The effect on the wheelchair was insignificant, but the contact sufficed to disrupt the boy's stride pattern. For a second it looked like he would keep his balance, but a couple of paces later, arms wind-milling, he pitched forward and crashed to the ground. Antimone shot across the line and quickly brought the chair to a halt. By the time she had turned around, Max was sitting on the floor cradling a gashed knee. Blood dripped from a long graze on his left arm.

"You stupid cow," he screamed. "You did that on purpose." He examined the shredded material of his training pants. "These cost over a grand. You're going to pay for a new pair."

"I'm sorry," she muttered. "It was an accident." She looked up to see the coach hurrying over.

"Are you okay?" he asked the prostrate boy.

"The stupid bitch tripped me deliberately."

"Max, watch your language. What were the pair of you thinking? That was supposed to be a warm down, not a damned race."

"Sorry, Coach," Antimone mumbled.

Erin sidled up beside her. "Nice one."

"I didn't—"

"Jack, go and get the first aid kit," Marshall said, addressing one of the boys who had formed a semi-circle around Max. The boy hurried away across the track.

"Antimone, come with me." He strode away from the group without looking to see whether she was following. When they were twenty metres away and out of earshot, he swivelled and thrust his face towards her.

"What the hell were you playing at? I know it was an accident, but Jesus, why can't you do what I ask? Anything like that happens again and you find yourself a new coach. Now I suggest you get out of here while I sort this out."

"Sorry, Coach," she said, but he had already turned away and was heading back to the group where Jack had returned carrying a green medical box.

Antimone slipped off her gloves, unclipped the helmet and placed it on her lap. She shivered as the perspiration on her arms and upper body cooled. For the second time that afternoon she was furious at herself for being drawn into a confrontation with an idiot like Max Perrin. Blowing out her cheeks, she steered the wheelchair towards the changing rooms, giving a wide berth to the small crowd clustered around the injured boy. The parents had all come down from the stand. Two of the women glared at her as she rolled past.

Keeping her eyes downcast, she propelled herself down the tunnel. She approached her locker and the conventional wheelchair a few paces away. She opened the door and flung the helmet and gloves inside. Grabbing her bag, she turned the key then banged the grey metal with the palm of her hand. "Damn!"

She tossed the bag onto the other wheelchair and undid the straps securing her to the racing chair.

A voice came from behind her. "Do you need any help?"

Antimone whipped her head around. The boy, who had been practising the javelin run-up, stood in the doorway, a wry smile on his lips.

"No, I can manage," she replied tersely.

"Jason Baxter," he said, extending a hand.

"Antimone," she replied, aware of the sweatiness of her palm.

"Good race," he said after a short pause, the smile remaining.

"If you say so. Coach didn't appreciate it, though. It wasn't supposed to be a race."

Jason laughed. "Always good to see Max Perrin being taken down a notch or two. So, did you intend to trip him?"

Antimone stared back in silence.

"Okay, a bit of a sore point, I see," Jason said, the smile fading. "I'll take that as a no then."

He watched as she used her powerful arms to transfer herself from one chair to the other.

When she had finished, Antimone looked up. "Do you still want to help?"

Jason nodded.

"In that case, could you put the racing chair in the storeroom for me, please?"

She followed as he wheeled it down the corridor. She didn't like asking for assistance, but it was difficult to move one wheelchair while seated in another.

He tried the door, then turned back to her. "It's locked."

"Oh, sorry." She fumbled inside the bag that now rested on her lap. She tossed the key to him and watched as he secured the racing machine.

"Here you go," he said, handing the key back.

"Thanks."

The only way to leave the stadium was to retrace their steps to the running track and depart via the main gate. Several metres short of the tunnel, a group of three people, silhouetted by the bright light from the archway, approached from the opposite direction.

"Look, it's the cripple," Max said, hobbling forwards, supported by a boy at each shoulder.

Antimone and Jason moved to one side to allow the three to pass, but Max shrugged off his two helpers, limped over and stood before them, blocking their path. "You really shouldn't have done that," he said with a sneer.

Jason stepped in front of Antimone and glared at Max. Face to face, Antimone realised that Jason was a few centimetres shorter than the other boy, but what he lacked in height, he made up for in upper body strength. "Big man, threatening the girl in the wheelchair. It looked like an accident from where I was standing."

"No, the bitch was sore that I didn't want to go out with her, and she was getting her own back."

Jason gave a snort of derision. "Frankly, I think she's got better taste than to go out with you. Now get out of the way."

Max made no attempt to move.

Jason turned to Antimone. "Come on, we're leaving," he said, barging past Max. The injured boy staggered and leant against the wall for support. Antimone followed a short distance behind as they emerged into the stadium.

"You're going to regret that," Max shouted to their backs.

They passed through the main gate without speaking.

"I can look after myself, you know," Antimone said eventually without looking at Jason.

"I'm sure you can," he replied, glancing down at her, "but it doesn't hurt to have a bit of support from time to time. Anyway, I wouldn't worry about him—he's all bark and no bite."

"I'm not worried."

They stopped opposite the pedestrian crossing that traversed the two-lane road. "Okay—um, where are you heading? Do you need a lift?"

"No, I've got my own transport, thanks." This wasn't true, but Antimone wasn't in the mood for conversation.

"Well, I'm just over there. Listen, I'm having a birthday party next week. I wondered if you'd like to come."

Antimone glanced up sharply. "You know I can't feel much down there, right?"

Despite his attempts to mask his surprise, an expression of shock flickered across Jason's face. "Okay, well thanks for the information, but I had kind of guessed that. It was only a party invite, not an offer of marriage. I'll see you around then."

She immediately regretted her harsh words. "God, I'm sorry. That came out all wrong. I'm just a bit shaken up by that whole Max thing. I'd like to come to your party."

"Good. Are you sure about the lift?"

Antimone relented. "Um… okay then, why not? Thanks. Are you going to be able to get the wheelchair in?"

"Yeah, no problem. It's one of my mum's company vehicles. Plenty of room."

"What does your mum do?"

"She runs Ilithyia Biotechnology, you know, on the edge of Northstowe. I think that's one of the reasons I'm not Max's favourite person. His dad works for my mum. Anyway, the car's just over there."

Without thinking, Antimone set off in the direction he was pointing. A bright flash accompanied the screech of brakes. Time seemed to stand still as she flinched before the impact that never came. She turned to her right to see a man mouthing insults at her through the windscreen of a small white car with a blue dome affixed to the roof. The car had stopped with under a metre to spare.

The man wound down the window. "What the hell do you think you're doing? I nearly had a bloody heart attack. You'll definitely be getting a fine for that, you fricking moron. Look where you're bloody going."

The car waited while Antimone completed the crossing to the central reservation, then moved off, the electric motors humming softly, the man still shaking his fist at her. Antimone raised two fingers in return.

Jason hurried across to the paved area at the centre of the road and stood beside her. "You certainly believe in living life dangerously, don't you?"

"I didn't see him."

"No, but luckily he saw you. I think he might be right about getting a fine, though—I saw the flash go off."

"No, I don't think so," she replied, a slight tremble in her voice. "It took my picture, but the database will tell them I'm disabled. They're pretty lenient with disabled people."

Despite her seemingly calm outward appearance, Antimone's heart was racing. Memories of the accident which had paralysed her flashed through her mind. The circumstances had been remarkably similar, walking out into the road without looking, not hearing the approach of the electric vehicle, the screech of brakes. The only difference, in this case, was the improved reaction time of the computer compared to that of the human driver. She clamped her hands onto the arms of the wheelchair so that Jason wouldn't notice the shaking.

Jason made a point of looking carefully to the left before stepping out to complete the crossing. When they reached the far side, he turned to face her.

"I have to say there's certainly never a dull moment when you're around."

4

Monday 5th April 2032

The hubbub of conversation died down and was replaced by the scraping of chairs as the members of the cabinet rose to their feet to welcome the Prime Minister. Andrew Jacobs, or 'AJ' as his friends and colleagues knew him, was in his early forties and was a vigorous man who somehow found time every day to fit a thirty-minute jog into his busy schedule. His rapid advancement in politics was largely down to his attention to detail and his single-minded approach to any problem he encountered. He was also a consummate negotiator who more often than not got what he wanted through charm and a smile. His film-star good looks and witty repartee had led to a popularity rating far greater than that usually attained by a premier nearing the end of his second term.

He wore a tailor-made suit and a blue tie as he stood at the head of the table. "Please sit down," he said, waiting patiently until everyone else was seated. "I'd like to introduce you to Rosalind Baxter, the CEO of IBC, that's Ilithyia Biotechnology Company for those of you who don't know."

He nodded to an aide who opened one of the tall wooden doors to admit a smartly dressed woman, wearing a white blouse together with a matching green jacket and skirt. Her blonde hair was styled in a trendy bob and framed an attractive face. The bright red colour of her lips was in stark contrast to the paleness of her cheeks. She was two weeks short of her forty-sixth birthday but looked at least ten years younger. She exuded an air of confidence as she strode across the room to stand by the Prime Minister.

"I've asked Mrs Baxter, or should I say, Rosalind, to join us today to brief us on her company's progress towards finding a cure for this terrible virus. As I'm sure you're all aware, this disease is the most pressing crisis this country has ever faced. Rosalind, over to you."

"Thank you, Prime Minister. Before I start, I'd like to go over the background, just in case any of you are not up to date with the facts."

She clicked the button of a small device she held in her hand and a three-dimensional image of a blue sphere, with an array of protruding spikes, appeared, floating above the long wooden table.

"This is the Orestes virus, so-named after the character from Greek myth who killed his mother, Clytemnestra. The first case was sixteen years ago. Since then, we believe that it has infected every single person on the planet. We still don't know where it originated, but we have good information that it was probably somewhere in central Africa. As I'm sure you're aware, it has no discernible effect on either men or women—that is, until a woman gives birth. At that point, something triggers a change in the virus, causing it to suddenly become extremely aggressive and destructive, attacking the mother's brain and vital organs. For those of you who have not witnessed the effects first hand, the final stages can be particularly traumatic. For that reason, these days we generally anaesthetise the mother and perform a caesarean section to spare both her and the family any unnecessary suffering."

"Mrs Baxter, you're not telling us anything we don't already know." The speaker was the Secretary of State for Health, a grey-haired man in his mid-fifties, wearing the standard attire of dark suit and blue tie. "Please get to the point."

She picked up a glass of water and took a sip before continuing. "My company has analysed statistical data for the United Kingdom's population, and we have performed some projections on the way the numbers are likely to change over the coming years."

Another click, and a graph replaced the image of the virus.

"This graph shows the population of the United Kingdom for every year since the start of the century and the projected population from now until twenty fifty if no cure is found. As you can see there was a sharp dip around twenty seventeen when the virus first broke out. This was exacerbated by a sudden increase in drug-resistant bacteria at about the same time. Together, these two effects mean that our population is currently being decimated every six years, and I use the term in its literal meaning of one in ten. One of the biggest issues, however, is that even if we find a cure now, one that's a hundred percent effective, the population will continue to decline because the proportion of women of child-bearing age has shrunk drastically."

"Yes, Mrs Baxter, I think we're all aware of this," the Secretary of State for Health said. "What we want to know is what you're doing about it."

Rosalind Baxter smiled thinly. "I was just coming onto that. The Orestes virus is a very tricky customer. Just when we think we're getting close to a solution, it mutates. The rate of mutation is unprecedented compared to any other virus we've ever seen, and that's the main factor making the development of a treatment so difficult."

"So, what you're saying is that you're no closer to a cure than you were this time last year?" said the same man, drumming his fingers on the table.

"Well, I wouldn't say that," she replied. "We have a better understanding of the virus' mechanisms for reproduction, and we are developing several unique approaches to counteract it."

The Chancellor of the Exchequer, a dark-skinned woman of African-Caribbean descent, impeccably dressed in a black dress and wearing matching pearl earrings and necklace, spoke. "How much money did your company receive in government grants over the past year, Mrs Baxter? Actually, let me tell you.

My figures indicate it was a fraction under one billion pounds. Does that sound about right?"

"The figure for the last financial year is nine hundred and eighty-three thousand. What is your question?"

"Practically all our scientific research budget is going towards finding a cure. So why, Prime Minister, are we pumping such huge sums into the coffers of this woman's company when there is little or no appreciable progress? Surely, she must demonstrate that this money is not being frittered away. There are several multi-national research efforts on which I believe these funds would be better spent."

Several sharp intakes of breath rose from around the table, followed by a number of whispered conversations.

Andrew Jacobs waited for the disturbance to settle down before he spoke. "I'd like you all to remember that Mrs Baxter is here as a guest today. The questions you raise deserve to be answered, and I expect Mrs Baxter to do so in due course, but that was not the purpose of today's discussion. I want to move the conversation on to ways in which we can counteract this dramatic reduction in population. Do you have any ideas, Mrs Baxter?"

Rosalind cleared her throat. "I understand from my colleagues in the medical community that considerable research effort is being expended on artificial wombs. All the papers I have read indicate there are several insurmountable problems, and a breakthrough is fifteen or twenty years away at the earliest. By then it may be too late. This country is going to need as many fertile women as possible in the future to rebuild the population. There are certain chemicals that can be put in the water supplies to skew the proportion of female to male conceptions in those women who do fall pregnant. Likewise, there are other chemicals that increase the likelihood of multiple births. If a woman is going to die anyway, she may as well give birth to triplets or quadruplets instead of a single infant. It's even better if all the children are female."

A stunned silence occupied the room before the Chancellor spoke again. "That's a pretty callous attitude. What's more, if the public discovered we were secretly putting drugs in the water supplies, we'd all be lynched. We have enough trouble with campaigners objecting to Fluoride in tap water. Voters would never agree to something that radical."

"Drastic times call for drastic measures," Rosalind Baxter replied, "and the voters don't necessarily need to know. There are no simple solutions to this crisis. It's scientifically possible and my company could assist with the implementation."

"I'm sure you could," the Secretary of State for Health said, "no doubt at huge expense to the taxpayer."

Once again, several whispered conversations broke out.

Andrew Jacobs rose to his feet. "Ladies and gentlemen, I'd like to thank Mrs Baxter for joining us today. We'll pause for some refreshments, and then we'll continue the debate. Thank you, Mrs Baxter, for sparing the time from your busy schedule."

He shook the woman's hand, then accompanied her to the tall wooden doors. He paused as he rested his hand on the ornate handle. "Thanks for coming in Rosalind. Some interesting ideas. I'll be in touch."

He opened the door and stood back to allow her to pass. Her heels clicked across the highly polished oak floor. Her aide, who had been waiting outside the cabinet room, hurried along beside her.

"How did it go, Mrs Baxter?" he asked.

"Pompous, arrogant pricks," she said as she stormed towards the guarded entrance.

5

The girl opened her eyes. Her first observation was that she was no longer in the alley. Her mind immediately turned to the yellow pill. She had been holding it when… when… The memory refused to surface. She held up her hand to her face and blearily inspected it. No, the pill was definitely not there. She sat up quickly, realising that she was lying in a bed with crisp white sheets and a thin blue blanket. The acrid scent of body odour no longer filled her nostrils—somebody must have washed her. She was dressed in a loose white gown of some sort. A quick check confirmed she was not wearing any underwear.

She sprang from the bed and stripped the upper sheet back. She inspected the mattress, but there was no sign of the small capsule. She fell to her hands and knees and peered beneath the metal bed frame, hoping to pick out the yellow colour against the white plastic floor covering. Maybe she had swallowed it, but if that was true, she had no recollection. Maybe this was all part of the trip, but it didn't have that other-worldly haze that was a common facet of the experience.

"Shit," she muttered.

With the absence of the pill confirmed, she scrutinised her surroundings. As far as she could determine, she seemed to be in a windowless hospital room. The biggest clue was the pervasive antiseptic medicinal smell.

There were two closed doors leading off the room, both coloured white, one incorporating a narrow rectangular window at head height. She padded over towards the windowed door first and was unsurprised to find it locked. A red light shone out from a small white box affixed to the wall beside the doorframe. She peered through the glass pane onto a featureless white corridor containing another three identical-looking doors. Similar white boxes were mounted beside each door, electronic card readers she assumed. Beneath each window frame was a black three-digit number. They were numbered consecutively from 221 to 223.

She turned her attention to the second door. When she twisted the handle, this one opened to reveal a cramped windowless bathroom containing a sink, toilet and shower cubicle. She focused back on the main room. The bed appeared to be typical of those found in a medical institution, and the walls were a bright white colour. Beside the bed was a cream coloured, metallic bedside cabinet on wheels. A quick check of the interior proved it to be empty. The harsh ceiling light illuminated a space devoid of any decoration.

Where was she? How on earth had she arrived here? She cast her mind back. She remembered how she had scraped together enough cash to buy one of the yellow capsules from the scruffy, rat-like man who operated his business from an alley, not unlike her own. She recalled the sense of anticipation and the feel of the pill rolling between forefinger and thumb. But then what? Maybe it had been part of a bad batch, and that was causing her amnesia. Perhaps a passer-by had discovered her in the alley and called the emergency services. But in that case, why was she alone?

A thought occurred to her. Maybe somebody was monitoring her remotely. Her eyes swept the ceiling, but the glare of the light made it hard to detect the presence of a camera. She returned to the small window and banged on the door with the flat of her hand.

"Hey! Is anybody there?"

Silence.

"Hey! Open this bloody door!"

She continued to shout and hammer at the door until her voice was hoarse, and her hand ached. She shuffled back to the bed and sat down, staring around the room at the featureless walls. With rising frustration, she raised her legs from the ground and shoved them against the cabinet. A resounding crash filled the room as it toppled over. Encouraged by the sound, she rose to her feet, placed her hands along the sides of the frame, lifted it and tipped it onto its side. The noise was not quite as satisfying, the mattress absorbing much of the impact.

She surveyed her handiwork before once again returning to the door. The corridor was still empty. If somebody was watching her through a hidden camera, they weren't overly concerned by her demonstration of petulance. Dejectedly, she trudged back to the toppled bed, pulled the mattress away and laid it flat. She dropped onto it and curled up on her side, her arms around her knees.

An electronic beep disturbed her repose. She sat up and saw a balding man wearing a white medical coat and carrying a clipboard enter through the windowed door.

"Ah, I see you've rearranged the room," he said, a thin smile on his lips.

"Where am I? What am I doing here?"

"Both good questions. You're in a secure facility undergoing treatment for your addiction."

"I didn't ask for any help."

The man stared at her for a moment before continuing. "Well, technically we don't need your assent. You were discovered unconscious in an alley, suffering the after-effects of a bad batch of..." He consulted the clipboard. "Ah yes—I believe the street name is Chill Black. Under the terms of the Misuse of Substances Act, twenty thirty-one, we can hold you here indefinitely for your own good."

"You can't just keep me locked up in this fricking shithole."

"Ironic that you should call this place a shithole after the alley in which you were found, but the truth of the matter is that we can keep you under our care until we determine you're well enough to leave."

"How long will that be?"

"Well, young lady, that depends on how cooperative you are, but I would estimate several weeks at least in your current state. Why? Do you have any pressing engagements?"

The girl folded her arms but remained silent.

"Do you want a hand sorting out the bed?" he asked.

"No. I haven't slept in a bed for over three years. Why the hell would I start now?"

"Do what you like. We're only trying to help you get better. Please note that we are monitoring you, and we will restrain you if we believe that you may be a danger to yourself."

The girl glowered at him.

"Somebody will bring you food in a few minutes," he added, strolling towards the door.

He halted at the entrance and turned back to her. "Enjoy your stay."

6

Saturday 10th April 2032

Antimone took a sip from her drink as her eyes roamed the room. The house was beginning to fill up as people arrived. Jason had invited eighty-five guests to his birthday party, although he had admitted that some were there at his mother's request, including Max Perrin. Apparently, she did not wish to risk alienating important contacts by excluding their children from this celebration.

As Antimone had predicted, no threatening letter had arrived as a consequence of the near miss with the car a week earlier. She had been more worried about her parents finding out than by any prospect of a fine. Following the accident which had placed her in a wheelchair, they had been overly protective, and she was glad to have avoided what would have been a difficult conversation.

She had done her best to avoid Max since the fateful training session, although that was not always possible given that they attended some classes together. There had been no major confrontations, but there had been a number of low-level incidents, which she attributed to him. One morning she had attempted to open her locker only to discover that the keyhole was filled with glue. Another morning, the outline of a huge penis had been drawn on her locker door. The most sinister was a drawing that had appeared on the wall of the female toilets, depicting a girl in a wheelchair with a noose around her neck. As the only wheelchair student at the school, it was fairly obvious to whom the graffiti referred. That last episode had drawn the attention of the school authorities. Following a brief and inconclusive investigation, there had been no further problems.

Since arriving she had chatted briefly with Erin Riley, but the other girl soon lost interest and wandered over to another group to collect the gossip around which her life revolved.

Antimone sensed a presence behind her, accompanied by a whiff of expensive perfume. She spun her wheelchair around to discover Jason's mother, elegantly dressed in a fashionable green dress with a black belt cinched around her narrow waist. Her assistant, a slight, narrow-faced man with thinning black hair and wearing a dark suit, stood a pace back.

"It's Antimone, isn't it?" the woman said, extending a hand. "It's a pleasure to finally meet you."

Antimone took the delicately manicured fingers in her own and was surprised at their coolness. "It's nice to meet you too, Mrs Baxter."

"This is my assistant, Julian Stefano."

Antimone shook hands with the man. By contrast, his handshake was warm and sweaty. She wanted to wipe her palm on her cream coloured trousers but resisted the temptation.

"I've followed your athletics career with great interest," the woman said. "It's fantastic that the school has offered a bursary to an up-and-coming Paralympian such as yourself. In fact, I'm sure you're aware that my company is a major contributor to the scholarship fund."

"Yes, Mrs Baxter. I'm very grateful for the opportunity."

"Oh, please call me Rosalind."

"Okay. Well, thanks very much… um, Rosalind."

"Can I get you a refill?"

Before she could reply, the assistant spoke. "I'm sorry, Mrs Baxter, but I've got Dr Perrin on the line."

"I'll catch up with you later, Antimone," Rosalind Baxter said as she strode away, her offer to replenish Antimone's glass already forgotten.

Antimone turned back to face the window and tapped a fingernail to start her favourite album playing in her ears. Soon the driving beat had her nodding her head in unison. She stared vacantly out at the carefully manicured gardens as she allowed the music to wash over her.

The reappearance of Rosalind Baxter on the stone-paved area by the back door drew her attention. The assistant was nowhere to be seen, but she was deep in conversation with a scruffy looking, bearded man wearing a black woollen hat. Antimone paused the playback as the man pointed a forefinger at Jason's mother and shouted something at her. There was something familiar about the man, but at first, she couldn't place him. She racked her brains trying to jog loose the recalcitrant memory. Then it came to her—she had seen somebody wearing similar headgear in the stand at the athletics stadium just before the training session last week. Was it the same man? He didn't look like a parent, but there was always the possibility that one of the pupils had an eccentric father. And what was the argument about?

At that moment, two muscular men dressed in matching grey suits emerged from the house and took up positions, one on either side of Jason's mother. The man jutted a finger at her, but then took a hurried step backwards as the two men advanced towards him. Rosalind swivelled on her heel and re-entered the house, her face a mask of fury. The two grey-suited men hustled the third, bearded man through the gate that led to the front of the house.

Antimone was jolted from the drama by a bang on the back of her wheelchair. She spun around to see Jason staring down at her, a grin on his face.

"Something exciting going on out there?" he asked.

"Um, no, not really," she replied after a moment's hesitation.

"Why don't you come over and join us?"

"Sure," Antimone said, smiling.

Jason studied her, pondering his next statement. "I guess it's hard joining in a conversation at a party when everybody else is standing up."

The comment caught her by surprise. The observation was correct, but she hadn't expected Jason to be so perceptive. "Yeah, I suppose."

"Tell you what, why don't we go over to the sofa? At least then we'll be at the same eye level."

"Okay."

Jason led the way across the room and through the doorway into a lounge that was big enough to accommodate the whole of the ground floor of Antimone's house. He clapped a couple of boys on the back and accompanied them, and the girls they were chatting with, to a huge red L-shaped sofa arrangement in the corner.

When everybody else was seated, Jason said, "I'll just get something to drink. Back in a sec."

Antimone sat in silence as the other four resumed their previous discussion. She was relieved when Jason reappeared carrying a large glass bowl containing a red-coloured liquid and a ladle. "Fruit punch? Strictly non-alcoholic. The alcohol only comes out when my Mum's disappeared."

Antimone smiled and watched as Jason topped up her glass. After serving the others, Jason refilled his own glass, dipping it directly into the bowl.

"To the next sixteen years," he said, standing up. The rest of the group echoed the toast, and the conversation flourished as Jason played the part of the perfect host, ensuring that everybody joined in. Antimone began to relax and was soon engaged in good-natured banter as Jason gently teased one of the other boys who fancied himself as a good footballer.

"I'm just going to get a refill," Jason said, getting to his feet and retreating with the empty bowl. This time, Antimone joined in with the exchanges in his absence. He returned carrying the topped-up container. He quickly replenished his guests' glasses and sank back onto the sofa.

Antimone took a sip of the second batch. It tasted slightly different to the first, but she put it down to the contents being mixed in different proportions. After a couple more mouthfuls, she felt dizzy. "Zu haven't putz alclol zin tish, has zu?" she asked. Her tongue felt too big for her mouth. Jason shook his head, but he too seemed to be struggling to speak.

Antimone closed her eyes, only dimly aware that all conversation in their corner of the room had ceased.

***

"Wow! Somebody must have spiked the drink."

Antimone groaned and opened an eye. Max Perrin was standing a few paces away, staring down at her.

"It's probably your first taste of alcohol, eh, trike queen?"

"Piss off, Max," she replied, running a hand across her face. A headache was pounding behind her eyes, and she felt bile rising in her stomach. She belched.

The sweet scent of the fruit punch repeated on her, and she immediately felt better. The others, including Jason, were sitting where she had last seen them, all still unconscious. She glanced at her watch. She had been asleep for just under an hour.

Ignoring Max, who stood with a half-smile on his lips, she wheeled herself across the room and through the doorway. The body of the party seemed to have gravitated to the garden, judging by the raucous laughter and music coming through the back door. She was at the bathroom door when she heard the sound of breaking glass. Antimone stopped and cocked her head. At first, she thought somebody must have dropped their drink. The throbbing beat continued from outside, but the sounds of merriment had died down.

A shout accompanied the tinkle of more falling shards. She pushed through the door into the garden. A large group of people were staring towards the side of the house.

A man's voice rose above the music. "Hey! Stop!"

One of the two grey-suited men she had seen earlier with Jason's mother clambered through what she could now see was a shattered ground-floor window and set off at a sprint across the lawn. He headed towards a wooden gate embedded in the well-tended hedge, leading into the adjoining field. The man barrelled through the partially open gate, leaving it swinging on its hinges.

Several people ambled in the direction the man had taken and craned their necks to peer over the hedge. A couple tentatively approached the gateway. Somebody had turned off the music.

"What happened?" Antimone asked a girl, standing a few paces away.

The girl dragged her attention away from the unfolding scene and glanced down. "Well, a chair crashed through the window, and this man sort of climbed out and started running towards the gate. Then these other two, they came out of the window after him and shouted for him to stop. They all ran into the field."

"Who was the man, the first one I mean?"

"Dunno. I've never seen him before. He had a beard and this funny black woolly hat. I think the other two were security or something. I saw them when I arrived."

Before Antimone could ask any more questions, a woman's voice rose above the hubbub. "I'm sorry about that, everybody," Rosalind Baxter said. "There was an intruder, but my people are dealing with it. Please carry on and enjoy yourselves. I'll get somebody to sweep up the broken glass."

The buzz of conversation increased, and the music restarted although at a lower level than previously. Antimone turned to thank the girl, but she had already wandered off to join a larger group. Antimone resumed her trip to the bathroom but bumped into Jason as she entered the house.

"What's going on out there?" he asked.

She ignored the question and asked one of her own. "Did you spike the drink?"

He appeared shocked. "No, I'd never do that."

"So, if you didn't, who the hell did?"

Without waiting for an answer, Antimone made her way across the hall. When she reached the bathroom door, she turned back to Jason.

“I’m calling my parents, and then I’m going home.”

7

Monday 12th April 2032

"Damn. Well, thanks for letting me know, Nigel."

Rosalind Baxter put the phone down. Another test failure. She allowed herself the luxury of staring out of the huge plate-glass window onto the well-manicured gardens surrounding the Ilithyia facility. A gardener was digging in one of the flower beds filled with a colourful array of spring flowers. The man glanced up, perhaps sensing that someone was watching him. Rosalind turned back to her computer monitor, even though she knew there was no way he could see her.

She swept her hand across the screen, manipulating a column of figures. A pulsing red dialogue box disturbed her concentration. It seemed to hang in mid-air a few centimetres in front of the display. The text indicated her secretary wanted to talk to her, so probably an incoming call. She sighed. This was the part of being in charge of a company that she hated the most. There was never enough time to concentrate on anything without being disturbed.

She snatched up the telephone handset. "Yes," she snapped.

"I have the Prime Minister's office."

"Okay. Put him through."

There was the faintest of clicks. "Hello, this is Rosalind Baxter. How are you Prime Minister?"

A female voice that was clearly not that of the leader of the country replied. "Please hold for the Prime Minister."

Rosalind rolled her eyes. This overt display of one-upmanship irritated her, the implication that his time was more important than her own. *I earn at least twenty times his paltry salary*, she thought. For a moment she considered putting the handset down. *Then he would have to wait for me for once.*

She was still toying with the idea when the familiar, well-cultured voice of Andrew Jacobs came on the line. "Sorry to keep you waiting, Rosalind."

"No problem, Prime Minister." *It's not as if I've got anything better to do.*

"So how are you, Rosalind? And please call me AJ."

"I'm fine. And yourself?" *Not that either of us really cares about the health of the other.*

"Fine, fine. Thanks for coming in last week."

"It was my pleasure." *As if I had a choice.*

"About that. I'm under a lot of pressure to reduce the funding your company receives. Certain members of the cabinet believe we might get better value for money by diverting it to our American friends."

That bitch, the Chancellor of the Exchequer. "You know as well as I do AJ, that of all the biotech companies in the world, we are the closest to finding a cure. We've already done it once, which is more than anybody else has achieved. No other organisation has even come close."

Fifteen years ago, Ilithyia Biotechnology had still been a small business on the Cambridge Science Park when the development of a prototype treatment had catapulted the company into the limelight. During the next three months, the value of the company's stock rose by several thousand percent, making the shareholders, including Rosalind Baxter, hugely wealthy. The company had relocated twice since then, finally settling in a purpose-built facility at the edge of the new town of Northstowe. Even after the virus mutated and the drug lost its effectiveness, the flow of research grants had continued and now accounted for a sizeable proportion of its revenue.

"Be that as it may, Rosalind, we can't keep pumping money in with no sign of progress."

"Look, Prime Minister. We're close to having an answer, one that works for more than a month or two. If you cut our funding, you'll be jeopardising the world's best chance at a solution to this problem." *And you'll cripple Ilithyia's stock value.*

"I hear you, Rosalind, but there's a limit to how much cash we can provide without any concrete results."

"So, what are you saying?"

"I know this sort of work takes years, and I'm happy to fight your corner—at least for the time being—but I need evidence that these funds are being put to good use. There are those in the cabinet who still support you, and I can hold the doubters off for nine months, maybe a year, but after that, I'm going to struggle to finance your company without positive results."

Good to know the money I transfer to those accounts in the British Virgin Islands every month isn't totally wasted then. "I appreciate your support AJ. I'm confident we'll have something by then."

"I hope so, Rosalind. Do keep in touch. And good luck."

"Thank you, AJ, I…" Rosalind trailed off as she realised she was talking to a dial tone.

8

The electronic lock beeped, drawing the girl's attention to the door. As it swung open, she jumped to her feet and took a pace towards the balding doctor. He still hadn't told her his name.

"Hey! Why haven't you brought me any food?"

"I'm sorry," replied the man. "I should have told you sooner. We did some tests on the blood we took when you arrived, and we need to perform a minor operation. Unfortunately, you can't eat for several hours before a general anaesthetic."

The anger on the girl's face changed to concern. "What operation? What's wrong with me?"

"Like I said, it's a minor operation. We just want to take some more samples to confirm that your treatment's going according to plan. The procedure can be a bit painful, so it'll be less unpleasant for you if we do it while you're asleep. It'll all be over in half an hour or so, and then you'll be able to eat."

"What are you going to do to me?"

"We're going to insert a probe inside you and extract a small sample of material."

"Are you going to cut me open?"

"No, nothing like that."

"So where exactly are you going to insert the probe? Down my throat or up my arse?"

"Um, the second of those," said the doctor, looking slightly uncomfortable.

"Great. So, you cop another good look at my fanny."

"Look, I see naked bodies every day of the week. It's just part of the job. You're no different—I've seen it all many times before."

"Not mine, you haven't." The hint of a smile touched the girl's lips. "But I bet you wouldn't mind having my undivided attention for an evening with both of us naked." The smile turned more lascivious. "If you let me out of here, I would do anything you wanted. I can be quite... um... accommodating when I put my mind to it."

The arrival of two orderlies wheeling a hospital trolley spared the doctor a response. "Just pop yourself on there and lie down."

The girl ambled sullenly to the trolley and lay down as instructed. As soon as she was on her back, each of the orderlies grabbed an arm and fastened it to the *frame with a strap. She struggled briefly against her bonds. "Hey! Why are you tying me down?"*

"Just a precaution in case you get any ideas about making a run for it."

Once they had secured her arms, the two men turned their attention to her ankles. When they had securely restrained her, they raised the sides and wheeled her through the door, the doctor following a couple of paces behind. As they travelled down the featureless white corridor, she swung her head from side to side, trying to garner any clues as to where they were holding her. In the week she had been here, this was the first time she had been outside her room. Was that a face at the small window of one of the numbered doors? She couldn't be sure in the short time before one of the men obstructed her view.

They turned a corner and approached a door labelled 'Operating Theatre S1'. The girl passed through the swing doors into a brightly lit room where a woman wearing a blue medical gown, hairnet and white surgical mask stood beside a machine covered in indicators and dials. "I'm just going to slip this over your nose," she said, placing a black mask linked to the machine via a corrugated tube on the girl's face. "Start counting backwards from ten for me."

Almost immediately, a sickly-sweet smell filled her nostrils. She fought the encroaching darkness for a second or two, but was soon unconscious.

The doctor, who had by now also donned a hairnet and mask, entered the room pushing a wheeled cabinet on which rested a syringe connected to a long rounded barrel. He raised the girl's gown up until he had clear access to the lower part of her body, then carefully inserted the plastic tube and slowly depressed the plunger.

"Nice fanny," he muttered under his breath.

9

Sunday 25th April 2032

"I want to practice sprinting this afternoon," John Marshall said, addressing the group of five. Antimone was the only girl—Erin was suffering from a cold—and also the only wheelchair athlete. "Let's do eight reps of one hundred metres sprint pace followed by one hundred metres jog. I want to see some effort today. Let's see you really push it around those bends."

Max had still not returned to training, even though it was over three weeks since his fall. There had been no further incidents following the party, and she was hopeful he had finally put the accident at the track out of his mind. He had even been moderately polite on a couple of occasions in the past week, acknowledging her and calling her by her real name when they crossed paths.

In contrast, it seemed that John Marshall had still not entirely forgotten the episode. While there was no major change in his behaviour, he was far more distant and business-like in his dealings with Antimone. He had discussed the results of the analysis taken from the data logger with her, but it felt like he was doing it more out of duty than through goodwill. She had tried to follow his instructions to the letter, but she had the distinct impression that there was a lot more work to do to restore her good standing with him.

She glanced over towards the javelin runway. There was no sign of Jason. She had questioned him the day after the party about the spiked drink, but he remained adamant he had not been responsible. She had kept her ears open, hoping to hear rumours of who the instigator was. Surprisingly, the school grapevine was quiet on the subject. In any case, she didn't need the distraction of any romantic involvement, what with both exams and trials for the British Paralympic team coming up in the next few months.

A wave of nausea swept over her as she placed the helmet on her head, tightened the strap, then slipped on her gloves. She had not been feeling well all day and put it down to the onset of the cold that was doing the rounds. She directed the wheelchair to the start line, waiting for a nod from the coach to begin. When it came, she surged ahead, rapidly accelerating as she entered the bend. At the end of the curve, she allowed the chair to coast down and tried to recover her breath. Within a few short seconds she reached the start of the next bend and once again propelled herself forwards.

By the time she had completed the second lap, she had built up a lead of over fifty metres over her fellow athletes, but the queasiness had increased to the extent that she had to stop and pull over onto the grassed oval at the centre of the track. She leant forwards and retched. A thin stream of mucus dribbled from her mouth, and she spat on the grass to try to remove the aftertaste.

"Not working you too hard, am I, Antimone?" Marshall said, strolling over.

"No, I'll be okay in a sec, Coach," she replied, spitting again.

"If it's not hurting, it's not doing any good."

"Yeah, I know." She glanced over to see that the rest of the group had nearly caught her up.

"Come on. Halfway. Two more laps," he shouted as the four boys approached. "Let's see you really put some work into those sprints."

As soon as they had passed, Antimone edged out onto the track and accelerated. She finished the bend in the fourth lane, five metres behind the pack, pulling wide to avoid any recurrence of the collision with Max. The last two laps were sheer agony as she pushed her body despite the bouts of nausea that seemed to creep up on her as she coasted between sprints.

Finally, she joined the rest of the group, all of whom lay on the ground, panting for breath. Once again, her stomach heaved, and she spat out a mouthful of foul-tasting vomit. This appeared to set off a chain reaction as two of the other boys copied her example.

The coach sauntered towards the athletes, a faint smile on his lips. "Good session ladies—at least so far. There's nothing to be ashamed of with a bit of puking. Just make sure you stay warm. We don't want any strained muscles. We've worked on your stamina, so we're going to do some weight pulling next to improve your power."

The two boys who had retained their stomach contents rose to their feet, grinning down at their vomiting training partners.

"I think they must be suffering from morning sickness, coach," one of them said.

"Nah," laughed the other, "not possible. I reckon they're all virgins."

10

Thursday 20th May 2032

Antimone unlocked the blue front door and propelled herself into the hall of the small detached house. It occupied a plot at the end of a cul-de-sac in a modern housing development at the edge of the town of Northstowe.

Her parents had bought the property shortly after the award of the scholarship at Oakington Manor. The house was a short bus ride from the school, but her father's commute to his place of work at an engineering company on the south eastern side of Cambridge had increased by half an hour compared to their previous residence.

Her mother, who had trained as a primary school teacher, had already lost her job prior to the move due to the drastic decline in pupil numbers resulting from the Orestes virus. She was now retraining as a nurse at Addenbrooke's Hospital to the south of Cambridge city centre. Both parents left for work long before she caught the school bus, but they had taken the afternoon off so that they could be at home to greet her when she returned home on her sixteenth birthday.

The sound of whispered voices came from the lounge. As Antimone pushed open the door, an out of tune rendition of "Happy Birthday" burst out. Her mother proudly held a cake topped by a forest of lit candles. Halfway through the song, the candle flames merged together, and her mother had to put the cake down to avoid singeing her hair. The melody petered out as her father hurriedly knelt down to blow out the blazing mass.

"I told you to place them further apart," he said to his wife when they were finally extinguished.

"My hero," she replied. "I've always wanted a big, strong fireman to look after me."

Laughter rang around the room as Dominic and Helen Lessing bent down to hug their only daughter.

"I thought I was supposed to blow out the candles," Antimone said.

"I can relight them if you want," her mother replied, "but we should probably call the fire brigade first."

"On second thoughts, maybe not."

"Who'd have thought it?" her father said. "My little girl, sixteen years old and all grown up."

"Let's sit down," her mother said. "We've got some presents for you."

A pile of brightly coloured parcels on the coffee table drew Antimone's gaze. She followed her parents as they crossed the room and settled onto the blue-coloured sofa.

"Here's one that I think you'll like," her mother said, picking up a small bright green package wrapped in a red ribbon.

Antimone undid the ribbon and tore the paper off. She lifted the lid of a blue, hinged box to reveal a pair of earrings in the shape of the five Olympic rings.

"They'll go well with the gold medal around your neck in September," her mother said, leaning over to hug her daughter.

"I've got to be selected for the British team first, Mum," Antimone replied.

"Yeah, but you'll breeze the final selection race," her father added. "You've only got to finish in the top three to guarantee your place and your times this year are faster than anybody else in the country by several seconds."

"Thanks for the support, Dad, but I've still got to do it on the day."

"I've every confidence in you."

"Oh, that reminds me," her mother said. "I was talking to one of the doctors today—"

"Not a handsome one, I hope," her father interrupted.

"As I was saying, I was talking to one of the doctors who's a specialist in spinal injuries. He said that there have been some exciting breakthroughs in repairing spine damage, with stem cells and the like. It's all a bit experimental, but he said that he might be able to get you into one of their programmes if you want."

The smile disappeared from Antimone's face. "So, one minute you're talking about me racing at the Paralympics and the next about me walking again."

"But you can do both," her mother replied. "After that court case last year where the man received treatment and regained the use of his legs, he was allowed to continue competing in the Paralympic wheelchair races."

Antimone sighed. "Yeah, but none of the other athletes want anything to do with him. What is it they call him? A Fake-Olympian? He may have won the court case, but once you start letting able-bodied people take part, there'll be loads of people giving it a go. Before you know it, the genuinely disabled won't get a look in."

Her mother's face dropped. "I thought you'd want to walk again, but if you're happy to stay in that contraption…"

"Helen, let's change the subject," her father said. His expression brightened as he picked up a shiny red package and handed it to Antimone. "This one's from both of us."

Antimone removed the paper, uncovering a rectangular shaped plastic box.

"Go on then, open it," her mother said, the earlier conversation seemingly forgotten.

Antimone inspected the contents and pulled out a wristwatch with a large black dial.

"It's the latest in health watches," her father said excitedly. "It measures pulse rate, blood sugar levels, time of the month, if you know what I mean, and so on. It even tells the time. Try it on."

Antimone slipped the gadget over her wrist and tightened the strap. The black face illuminated to display a clock face reading five thirty-two and a 'Calibrating' message at the centre of the dial in green text. After four or five seconds, a heart icon appeared in the top left corner with the number fifty-two to the right of it. A yellow exclamation mark flashed in the top right.

"Look, your heart rate's fifty-two beats per minute," her father said. "That's pretty low, but you are a well-trained athlete after all. I don't know what the yellow symbol means, though." He picked up the box and removed the instruction card.

"Why do they always have to make the text so small?" he complained, squinting at the tiny letters. "Ah, here we go. Press the button in the bottom right quadrant."

Antimone did as he suggested and depressed the sliver of black plastic that protruded from the body of the watch. She stared at the message displayed in the centre but remained silent.

"What does it say then?" her mother asked.

"Um—it—it can't be right. It says I'm pregnant."

"What?" her father said, jumping to his feet. "Let's have a look at that."

"You haven't..." began her mother before tailing off.

Antimone rubbed the back of her neck. "Oh, don't be ridiculous. Of course not."

"It must be faulty then," her mother said. "I'll take it back tomorrow and get a replacement."

"Bloody cheap crap," her father added before realising what he'd said. "Actually, bloody expensive crap. Look, we can exchange it for something else if you want."

"No, it's okay, Dad," Antimone said, chewing a fingernail.

"Why don't I try it on?" suggested her mother. "It might give us a clue as to whether it's faulty or not."

Antimone slipped the watch off her wrist and handed it over.

Helen Lessing tightened the strap and inspected the dial. "Heart rate eighty-five but no exclamation mark."

"That's a bit fast," her husband replied.

"Well, I'm a bit bloody stressed," she snapped. She clicked the same button that Antimone had pressed, but the only things to be displayed were her blood sugar level and a green tick. A quick consultation of the manual revealed that the tick was an indication she was not in her fertile window.

The room descended into silence, the unopened presents forgotten on the table.

11

Friday 21st May 2032

The following morning, Helen Lessing was ready to leave the house before seven o'clock. It was too early to phone in sick, but she had every intention of letting her employers know she was feeling too unwell to work as soon as the reception staff arrived. She had persuaded Antimone to accompany her on the trip to Cambridge city centre, where she had originally bought the watch. The plan was to depart early enough to beat the morning rush hour and be there by the time the electrical goods store opened at nine o'clock.

The previous evening, she had grilled her daughter about her sexual activities despite the vociferous protests. It was only when Antimone screamed at the top of her voice that she had not even kissed anybody in the last six months, let alone had sexual intercourse, that her mother finally relented. "It must be faulty, then," she had stated as if announcing a court verdict, reluctantly accepting that her daughter was telling the truth.

"Call me when you know anything," Dominic Lessing said as the two women departed the house into the dull grey morning. Helen helped Antimone enter the small red autonomous car, collapsing the wheelchair and placing it in the boot. She selected their destination on the central navigation screen and waited while the onboard computers performed their start-up checks. After a few seconds, the vehicle exited the short driveway and smoothly edged onto the quiet residential street. They sat in silence, each lost in their own thoughts as it navigated itself along the already busy roads towards the Grafton Centre car park.

"Let's have breakfast at one of those coffee bars while we're waiting for the shop to open," Helen suggested when the car announced it had reached its destination.

"I'm not hungry," Antimone said, but her mother insisted she needed to eat something. They found an empty table at a Coffee Station restaurant and ordered a hot drink and a croissant each.

"It's got to be faulty. There's no other explanation," Helen said, grasping her daughter's hand across the table.

"Yeah, I know, but I'm still allowed to worry, aren't I?"

Time dragged as they watched the minute hand slowly edge around the clock face. At ten to nine, they left the coffee shop and began the short journey to the Gadget Gangsta store where Helen had bought the watch the previous week. As they arrived, a man dressed in matching red trousers and shirt was busy raising the security shutters.

"We'll just be another minute or two if you'd like to wait," he stated cheerily. He completed the task, then held the door open for them, smiling brightly. "How can I help you?"

The man seemed puzzled as Helen explained their problem. "I have to say these watches are pretty reliable," he said, "but if you want to try another one, I'll just go and fetch one."

He hurried away to the stock room and returned a minute later carrying a box identical to the one that rested on the counter. "Here, put this on."

Antimone slipped the chunky black watch over her wrist and adjusted the strap. The dial displayed the calibration message. This time, the heart rate read ninety-two. Her eyes homed in on the top right corner where the exclamation mark had appeared. Nothing. She exhaled loudly and turned the watch face so her mother could see. Helen's pallor turned an ashen white as her eyes met her daughter's. In confusion, Antimone glanced down a second time and spotted the flashing yellow icon.

"Oh Christ," she said in a low whisper.

The man's gaze flitted between mother and daughter. "Um, on rare occasions I have heard of… um… inaccuracies with this type of technology. You could always go to the chemist for a more reliable test. So, do you want to return it, keep that one or take the original?"

He had barely finished speaking when Helen said, "We'll keep it," snatched up the empty box and hurried towards the door, pushing her daughter's wheelchair from behind. Under normal circumstances, Antimone would have objected violently to being pushed, but her mind seemed to have turned to mush, and she allowed her mother to propel her forwards.

"Okay, well have a—" The man stopped when he realised he was talking to a closing door.

Helen hurried along the concourse past the brightly coloured shop fronts until she spotted a familiar green cross. Several customers and staff watched in interest as mother and daughter raced down the aisles. Finally, they came across a shelf stacked with five different brands of pregnancy test kit.

Helen grabbed one of each, dropping them on Antimone's lap and rushed towards the checkout. She quickly retrieved the boxes, placed them in the scanning area, then waved her card at the machine, not even bothering to check the amount. No sooner was the transaction confirmed than she tossed the selection of kits back to her daughter and swept out of the store.

"Mum, wait," shouted Antimone. Her mother stopped pushing, her breathing coming fast and ragged. "Just calm down. We need the loos. They contain little sticks that I need to wee on. Look there are some toilets over there." She indicated a corridor with a large sign above it. "And by the way, I can push myself."

"Okay, sorry. Shall I carry some of those?"

"No, I'm fine. Just make sure I don't drop any."

Antimone guided the wheelchair into the ladies toilet area. She found a stall reserved for the disabled, and both she and her mother hustled inside. As she transferred herself to the seat, her mother opened one of the boxes with fumbling fingers and handed a tester to her daughter.

After losing bladder control as a consequence of her injury, the surgeons had fitted Antimone with an implant that warned her when she needed to urinate and controlled the flow using fingernail sensors. She tapped out the correct combination and held a strip in the stream.

"It'll say on the display," her mother said, her face a mask of tension.

Both mother and daughter studied the indicator at the end of the short white stick. Within five seconds, the word 'Pregnant' was clearly visible.

***

The small vehicle pulled into the staff car park at Addenbrooke's Hospital. They had tried another pregnancy kit, just to be sure, but the result was the same. Helen Lessing had contacted a work colleague and arranged to visit her employer's maternity department to get a final confirmation and an estimate of how long since conception. She was still struggling to come to terms with the fact that her daughter had no inkling how she had become pregnant.

"But you must have some idea," she said in exasperation.

Antimone sighed. "Mum, if I knew, don't you think I'd tell you? It's not the sort of thing I'd be likely to forget, is it?"

"When we know how far along you are, that might give us a clue. Let's just pray it's less than four weeks."

Silence fell between them as they hurried down the brightly lit corridor. No sooner had they entered the maternity reception area, than a woman in her early fifties with greying hair tied back in a ponytail and wearing a blue nurse's uniform rushed over to greet them. Her face was etched with concern.

"Thanks for doing this, Angie," Helen said.

"No problem." She stared down, but Antimone avoided her gaze. "I just hope… Anyway, follow me, and we'll start the tests. So, you have no idea how this happened?"

Antimone shook her head. The nurse glanced towards her mother for confirmation.

Helen shrugged her shoulders. "Apparently not."

"We'll need to take a urine sample. I'll take a blood sample too, just in case. We should have the results in about half an hour if I rush them through."

The nurse led them to an examination room containing a single hospital bed. A door opened into a cramped bathroom. "I just need you to wee in here," she said handing a small plastic container to Antimone. "Just screw the lid on when you've finished."

"Do you need any help?" Helen asked.

"Jesus, Mum. I think I can pee in a jar."

When Antimone returned to the room, she handed the specimen bottle over. The nurse wrote on the label, then asked her to roll up her sleeve. She fitted a rubber tourniquet just above the elbow, then inserted a needle and withdrew a vial of blood. Once again, she recorded the details.

"That's it," she announced brightly. "I'll take you back to the waiting room, and we'll have the results shortly."

***

Antimone glanced at her wrist before remembering she was no longer wearing a watch, having removed it to try on the one given to her for her birthday. Instead, she turned her attention to the large clock dial on the wall. It was now forty minutes since they had left the examination room. Her eyes roamed across the room. Only two of the seats were occupied. On one of them sat a woman with long dark hair who appeared to be in her mid-thirties and was clearly pregnant. She was engrossed in the display of her phone, her fingers performing intricate manoeuvres above the screen. The other seated a woman with mousy shoulder length hair, leaning forward, her head in her hands. It wasn't clear from her outline whether she was pregnant, but her demeanour told another story.

Antimone and her mother both looked up sharply as the sound of footsteps signalled the nurse's return. Her face gave nothing away.

"Sorry, that took a bit longer than expected. Let's go back to the examination room."

Antimone's heart hammered in her chest, and her breath came in short bursts as she propelled herself along the corridor beside her mother. This must be how a prisoner felt before learning whether the judge was about to pass a death sentence.

The nurse closed the door and turned to face mother and daughter. Helen rested an arm on Antimone's shoulder.

"I'm sorry to say, but you're definitely pregnant. Unfortunately, the tests indicate that you're six weeks along, which means it's too late to consider a termination. I'm really sorry."

Antimone gasped. A rushing sound seemed to fill her head. Her ears burned, and her face felt flushed. She had only nine months left before she died—no, less than that—seven and a half months.

"Are you absolutely sure?" Helen asked, her voice quivering. "Can you run the test again?"

"I already ran it twice, which is why it took longer than I said it would. Do you need some time alone? I can arrange counselling if you'd like."

"No," Antimone said. "I want to go home."

12

Friday 21st May 2032

The policewoman peered sceptically at the father, mother and daughter who sat before her on the other side of her desk. Karen Atkins, or Kat as her friends and colleagues knew her, was a senior investigator for the Maternity Crimes Unit, more commonly referred to by its abbreviation, MCU. The division was established to investigate allegations of rape and to put a stop to the activities of the backstreet abortionists who offered their services when the government-appointed health professionals announced that a pregnancy was too far advanced to operate. Kat professed a particular hatred for the charlatans and criminals, who in practically every case, ended up terminating the pregnancy but also killing the patient at the same time.

The unit had been formed eleven years earlier, and she had been appointed to her position following a successful career in the Metropolitan Police Service. After more than a decade of seeing the depravity wreaked upon women by men, many of whom still professed to love their partners, Kat thought she had seen it all, but encountering a victim who had no recollection of the crime was a new one for her.

She wore her straight brown hair just over her ears, although at the age of fifty-one, its uniform colour owed much to the contents of a bottle. The room was a couple of degrees too warm, which caused the collar of her white shirt to chafe at her neck and the black skirt to feel sweaty around the waistband. She adjusted her position on the chair and resumed her questioning.

"So, let's go back to the beginning again. You're six weeks pregnant, but you've no idea who's responsible?"

Antimone shook her head. "No."

"And you can't remember how it happened?"

"No, but I think it must have been when I was at a friend's party."

"When was the party?"

"It was the tenth of April, just under six weeks ago."

"And whose party was it?"

"Jason Baxter invited me. He's the son of Rosalind Baxter. She's the owner or something of this big biotechnology company."

Kat made a mental note. She knew exactly who Rosalind Baxter was. Rich and powerful people generally wanted to protect their privacy in situations such as this and were often prepared to flex political or financial muscle to ensure it happened. This case would have to be handled sensitively.

"So, what makes you think you got pregnant at the party?"

Antimone paused before replying. "Well, um… a group of us were sitting in the corner—I mean I was in the wheelchair, but the others were sitting on the sofa. Jason went to get a refill for the fruit punch and shortly after that… um, I couldn't get my words out, and then I fell asleep."

"So, you think the drink was spiked?"

"Yeah, it looks like it."

"You never mentioned that before," Dominic Lessing interjected.

"Please let her continue," Kat said. "Do you know if it had any alcohol in to start with?"

"No, I don't think so, but after he came back, it tasted slightly different."

"In what way?"

Antimone thought for a second. "It's difficult to describe, but there was a bit of a funny taste to it."

"Was anybody else drinking alcohol?"

"No, I don't think so. Jason made a joke about only getting the alcohol out when his Mum wasn't around."

"So, his mother was at the party?"

"Well, I saw her when I arrived, but then she received a telephone call and left the room."

"And afterwards?"

"I eventually woke up about an hour later. All the others were still asleep on the sofa. I think it must have happened while I was unconscious."

"Why are you only telling us this now?" interrupted her father angrily.

"Sorry Dad," Antimone replied, "I didn't think it was important—well at least not until I found out I was pregnant."

Kat raised her hands. "Mr Lessing, please let your daughter tell me what happened."

"Well, I was feeling a bit sick and wanted to splash water on my face so I started heading towards the bathroom. Then I heard a shout outside, so I went into the garden and saw one of Mrs Baxter's security guards jump out of a broken window and chase after a man who was running away."

"Did you see the man: the one being chased?"

"No, but somebody told me he had a beard and was wearing a woollen hat of some sort. I think I saw him arguing with Mrs Baxter earlier."

Kat scribbled on the pad in front of her, preferring the old-fashioned pen and paper method of taking notes. "And you don't know who this man was?"

"No… although I think I may have seen him at the athletics track."

Antimone continued to explain about the training session and how she thought she had seen the same bearded man in the stand.

"What happened next at the party?" Kat asked.

"I phoned my Mum, and she came to collect me, then took me home."

"Okay. Well, we'll need an official statement, and I'm going to talk to Mrs Baxter and her son. We'll also take a blood sample so that we can do some paternity tests. I know it's not much of a consolation, but we're going to find the person who did this to you."

Kat walked around the desk and shook hands with Antimone and her parents. "I've got your details. I'll be in touch in the next day or two. Thanks for coming in."

She waited for the door to close, then returned to her chair. She picked up the phone and dialled a number. After a few seconds, somebody answered.

"I've got an interesting one here."

13

The girl winced as the needle slipped into a vein on the inside of her elbow. She had been scared of needles since the age of four when a staphylococcal infection had resulted in her being hospitalised and hooked up to a drip containing powerful anti-bacterial drugs. Even now she could remember her childhood terror when the doctor first inserted the shiny needle. What had helped to sear the memory in her mind was the trauma of the nurse ripping off the anaesthetic patches afterwards, two from each arm. Ironically, they had been put in place to numb the area where the needle would be inserted but had been left on for so long that each one came away attached to a rectangle of skin.

The balding doctor filled two vials with blood, then positioned a small wad of cotton wool over the puncture wound and told her to press down on it. He placed the two small tubes on the bedside cabinet and affixed a piece of surgical tape to hold the cotton wool in position.

"That wasn't so bad, was it?" he said, not looking at the girl as he wrote on the labels.

"What do you need it for?" she asked.

The man waited until he had finished writing, then turned to face her. "You know we took that sample a few weeks ago? Well, we're just checking up on something. How are you feeling anyway?"

"Actually..." The girl paused for a second, deciding how to answer. "I've been feeling a bit sick the last few days."

The doctor frowned and sat down on the bed. "About that. There's something I need to tell you. I'm sorry, but I've got some bad news."

The girl looked up sharply. "What? What's wrong with me?"

"We think you're pregnant. This blood test will help to confirm how far along you are, but it's at least seven weeks."

"How could I be? Seven weeks? I've been here for—what?—five. You're saying I was pregnant when you brought me here? I haven't had sex with a man, proper sex that is, for months and even then, he wore protection."

"Look, I don't know how it happened, but I suspect it was while you were out of it on one of your trips."

"That's impossible. I'm never so far gone that I don't know what's going on in the real world. The drug heightens reality—it doesn't replace it. You're lying."

"I wish for your sake I was, but unfortunately, it's true. I don't know how you got pregnant. All I know is that we went back over the blood tests, and it had already happened by the time you arrived here."

"If I'm pregnant, why have you only discovered that now? I've been here for ages."

"I'm really sorry. We were concentrating on treating your drug dependence. We didn't realise you were pregnant, and you didn't tell us."

"How the hell could I tell you?" she screamed. "I didn't bloody know."

"I'm sorry, it's very unfortunate."

"Unfortunate? You tell me I'm going to die in a few months, and it's fricking unfortunate? Christ, you people. So, it's too late for an abortion?"

"I'm afraid so. After four weeks, the chances of survival are practically zero, and you've already been in our care for five. I know it's not good news, but you're in a place where we can give you the best treatment throughout the pregnancy."

"I still don't know where this place is. Have you forgotten to tell me that too?"

"You're in a state-of-the-art hospital. We have excellent facilities, and we'll make you as comfortable as we can."

"I don't give a toss where I am or what facilities you have. Just get out and leave me alone."

The doctor rose to his feet. "Once again, I'm really sorry to bring you this bad news. I'll be back later to check on you again." He crossed the room to the door, swiped his card at the reader and let himself out.

The girl clambered off the mattress and screamed at the top of her voice. Then, for the second time during her stay, she lifted the bed and hurled it onto its side.

14

Monday 24th May 2032

None of the Lessing family had left the house that morning. Dominic and Helen had phoned their places of work and Antimone her school, all claiming to be unwell. The weekend had passed in a haze as they tried to come to terms with the shocking news they had received the previous Friday. Antimone had gone over in her mind the events at Jason's party, but the only rational explanation was that somebody had raped her when she was unconscious. How could that have happened at a busy gathering? Surely somebody would have noticed?

"I'm making a pot of tea," Helen said, rising to her feet. "Does anyone else want one?"

"Yes, please," Dominic replied.

"Antimone?"

Antimone shook her head. "No, thanks." She had already consumed one cup of coffee and two of tea that morning, and it still wasn't yet ten o'clock.

The doorbell chime echoed through the house.

"I'll get it," came a call from the kitchen. The sound of footsteps preceded the scrape of the heavy wooden door opening.

"Who is it?" Dominic called.

His question was answered when Helen led Karen Atkins into the lounge.

"Can I take your coat?" Helen asked.

Kat shrugged out of the lightweight brown overcoat and handed it over. She wore a black skirt and a matching jacket over a white shirt. "Thanks"

"I'm just making a cup of tea. Do you want one?" Helen asked.

"Yes, please," Kat replied, taking a seat on one of the two green armchairs. "White, no sugar."

"Have you got any news?" Dominic asked.

"Yes, but let's wait until your wife returns. How are you, Antimone?"

"Alright, I suppose," Antimone said. "None of it seems real yet."

"Yeah, a lot of people in your situation say that."

The room descended into an awkward silence as they waited for the tea to arrive. Eventually, Helen bustled into the room carrying a tray on which sat three mugs and a plate of chocolate biscuits. Kat accepted the mug but declined a biscuit, conscious of the tightness of her waistband. When she had handed out all the drinks, Helen took a seat on the opposite end of the sofa to her husband, her hands resting on her lap.

"Well, we've made quite a bit of progress," Kat began. "I spoke at length to both Mrs Baxter and her son and several other guests. I haven't told any of them that you're pregnant yet, Antimone, just that you think you were sexually assaulted."

"And what have you found out?" Antimone's father said, leaning forwards.

"Well, we know the identity of the man who was arguing with Mrs Baxter and who was later seen fleeing through a broken window. His name is Daniel Floyd. He's a convicted murderer who was released from prison three months ago after serving a nominal life sentence."

"What was he doing at Mrs Baxter's house?" Helen asked, concern etched across her face.

"I'm just coming onto that. He was arrested after his wife went missing. The police discovered traces of her blood in the boot of his car, and he was convicted of her murder even though her body was never found. He claimed he had nothing to do with it. The wife used to work as a researcher for Mrs Baxter's company, and he apparently thinks she withheld vital information that could have helped clear him. Of course, she denies it, but it seems he still holds a grudge against her. Floyd and Mrs Baxter also have a bit of history together before he met his wife. By all accounts, they went out for a while just after they both left college, but then split up."

"So, what's this got to do with Antimone's rape?" Dominic asked.

"We have several eyewitnesses who spotted him at the house, including Antimone herself. We still have blood samples on record from the original investigation and from when he was in prison. We ran tests on the blood we took from Antimone last Friday, and we were able to create a genetic fingerprint for the baby. The analysis isn't as accurate as it would have been had we taken material directly from the foetus, but at this stage of the pregnancy that's far too risky. In any case, it's good enough to identify the father with a high degree of probability."

"And…"

"It appears that Mr Floyd is the rapist. There is a very strong correlation between his genetic material and that of the baby."

Antimone gasped and held a hand to her mouth.

"But why would he rape Antimone?" Helen asked.

"We don't know that, but we intend to ask him when we catch him."

"So, you haven't caught him yet?"

"The results only came in this morning, but a warrant has been issued for his arrest. It shouldn't be too hard to track him down because his address is registered as part of his parole conditions. I'm expecting the call any minute."

"So, what's going to happen to him?" Dominic asked.

"Well, obviously he'll be put back in prison, and then he'll be charged with rape. On the basis that there were no witnesses to the act itself, we'll need to rely on the genetic evidence to convict him. And that brings me onto a bit of a sensitive point. I'm assuming that you plan to carry the baby to term Antimone?"

"Why wouldn't she?" her mother asked, a hint of hope in her voice. "The doctors said it was too late for a termination."

"I know," Kat replied. "This situation doesn't happen very often because most women are aware that they've been raped and have the abortion within the first four weeks. There have been a few rare instances like your own when too much time has passed for the mother to survive a termination. Some of those women have the termination anyway."

"What, and die?" Dominic asked in horror.

"I'm afraid so. Some just can't bear to have the rapist's seed growing inside them. Not that I'm suggesting for one minute that Antimone should do that."

"I'm keeping it," Antimone announced firmly. "It's not the baby's fault, and I'm not ready to die yet either."

Kat appeared relieved. "Good. The only thing is, the Crown Prosecution Service will probably want to wait until after the baby is born before they open the case."

"Why can't they prosecute him now?" Helen asked.

"They'll want to take blood directly from the baby to prove paternity, and even then, it often takes six months to a year for the prosecution to build the case. He'll be kept in prison during that time, though."

"I just want to see him suffer," Dominic said vehemently.

"I can assure you, he won't have a pleasant experience in jail. Rapists generally get a very rough ride from both the guards and the other inmates."

"I hope they kick the shit out of him."

"Hmm," Kat said, getting to her feet. "Anyway, I'll let you know as soon as we have him in custody. Thanks for the tea."

Antimone remained in the lounge while her parents saw the policewoman out. They returned to find her reading the screen of her phone.

"What are you looking at?" her father asked.

"Just the details of the original court case."

Dominic peered over his daughter's shoulder at a photograph of an attractive woman, smiling brightly into the camera. It had obviously been cropped from a group picture because a man's arm was clearly visible in the bottom right corner. The image appeared dated, but that was probably due to the fact that it was recorded in two dimensions compared to the more common three.

"She was a beautiful woman," he said.

Antimone didn't respond but scrolled down to read the story. "It says she worked at Ilithyia Biotechnology. In those days it was only a small company on the Cambridge Science Park. He was a physicist working at a research laboratory. Apparently, he phoned the police to say she hadn't come home from work, and he was worried about her. When they checked his car, they found a pool of blood in the boot."

"Does it say anything about why he did it?" Dominic asked.

"No. He used to go out with Mrs Baxter and the police had a theory he still loved her and wanted to get rid of his wife so they could get back together. But it says here that when he was sentenced, he tried to get out of the dock and attack her."

"And they never found the body?"

"A witness said they'd seen his car parked by the river. They used divers and dredged it, but they didn't find anything. He claimed he was at home at the time, sick in bed."

Antimone scrolled down further until she came across a photograph of the killer. In the image, he had short brown hair with a parting to the left and was smartly dressed in a white shirt with a blue tie. His smile seemed unnatural and forced. She attempted to reconcile the picture with her memory of the bearded man she had seen through the window but could not detect any similarities. She shuddered slightly as she focused on his hazel eyes.

"I hope the bastard rots in hell," her father said.

15

Saturday 5th June 2032

Antimone heard the sound of a car door shutting and pulled the curtain back to look out of the window. A slightly built man wearing a dark suit walked around the back of a silver-coloured car and opened the door on the opposite side. *Rosalind Baxter's personal assistant. But what the hell was his name?* His boss' immaculately coiffured head appeared above the roof of the vehicle. She glanced once in Antimone's direction, then murmured a few words to the man. He nodded and got back in using the same door.

The elegantly dressed woman approached the ramp leading up to the front door. A second or two later the doorbell rang. Both parents were out. Her mother was doing the weekly shopping, and her father was at work making up for some of the time he had lost during the past fortnight. Antimone debated for a moment whether to pretend she wasn't in but then propelled herself along the hall.

A concerned expression occupied Rosalind's face as Antimone pulled the door open. "Hello, Antimone. I was so sorry to hear the bad news. Are your parents at home?"

A waft of expensive perfume drifted into the house. Antimone shook her head.

"Um… do you mind if I come in for a second?"

Antimone thought it would be rude to refuse. "Okay."

Rosalind closed the door behind her and followed Antimone into the lounge. "May I sit down?"

Antimone nodded.

Rosalind perched on the edge of her chair and stared at Antimone for a moment before speaking. "I just wanted to let you know how sorry I am that you were um… assaulted… at Jason's party. I feel really bad about it—not that I could have anticipated…" Her voice tailed off.

Antimone had a sudden urge to challenge this woman. "I saw you arguing with him before I was drugged."

Rosalind seemed surprised at the boldness of the statement. "I'm afraid the man's totally delusional. I assume you know his wife used to work for me. He thought I kept back evidence that would have proved he was innocent of her murder, but it's all total nonsense. I told him if he didn't leave, I'd call the police, and I thought that was the end of it. I had no idea he would come back and… well, attack you."

"I read that you used to go out with him."

Rosalind frowned. "That was a very long time ago, and I very quickly corrected my mistake. It's not something I really like to discuss."

Antimone realised that she had overstepped the mark and changed tack. "So, do you know if they've caught him yet? The police said they would tell us when he was arrested, but we still haven't heard anything."

"No, they haven't told me anything either. It seems that he hasn't been back to the address he registered with his parole officer. I just hope they find him soon." Rosalind sat back a fraction. "There was another thing I wanted to talk to you about, but maybe I should wait until your parents are here." She hesitated, glanced at her watch, then seemed to come to a decision. "If I tell you my proposal now, perhaps you can discuss it with your mother and father and let me know your thoughts."

"Um, okay."

"As I'm sure you know, my company has a large facility very close to here. We're working hard to find a cure for this awful disease. I know it can never make up for what's happened to you, but I'd like to offer the use of our facilities when the time comes. There's a hospital on site equipped with all the latest machines. Of course, you'd have a private room and some of the best medical care in the world. If you like, I'd also be happy to include you in one of our experimental research programmes. I certainly can't promise anything, but we're making progress all the time."

Antimone had to admit that the proposal was unexpected. On the face of it, it was a generous offer, but a cynical part of her wondered whether this was all a ploy to prevent legal action, not that they had ever discussed the idea as a family. The real carrot was the hint of a cure.

"Um… Thanks."

"So, you'll discuss it with your parents when they return? Here's a card with my private number on it. Call me anytime."

Antimone took the rectangular card and placed it on the coffee table.

Rosalind stood up, brushing down her grey skirt and smiled. "I've enjoyed our little chat. Don't worry, I can let myself out." She crossed the room and strode along the corridor without looking back, her heels clacking on the wooden planks. Antimone followed a short distance behind.

Rosalind opened the front door, turned briefly and raised a hand in farewell before pulling it shut after her. She descended the ramp and hurried across to the car. Her assistant was still only halfway out of the door by the time she slid in beside him.

"Am I not paying you enough to open doors for me?" she snapped.

Julian Stefano mumbled an apology. He had been taking a call and hadn't noticed her leaving the house until it was too late, but he knew better than to make excuses.

When she had finished instructing the navigation system to take her home, she turned to him with a smug expression on her face. "So, are you going to ask me what happened?"

"Okay. How did it go?" he asked dutifully.

"Impertinent little bitch. Her parents weren't there, but I don't think she'll be a problem."

16

Monday 21st June 2032

The pregnancy wasn't showing yet, but even so Antimone deliberately wore loose, baggy clothing. She waited with her mother and father outside the head teacher's office. Her 'I Level' examinations were due to start the following Tuesday. Part of her had considered leaving school and skipping these tests—she was sixteen years old, after all—but her parents had persuaded her to continue with her studies. As it turned out the hours of revision had been a welcome distraction from her predicament.

Normality was what Antimone craved the most. The initial shock had abated to the extent that it was now little more than a foreboding thought lurking in the back of her mind. Every so often it would creep to the forefront. When that happened, she would descend once again into a dark pit of despair. It was the mundane activities of home life and school work that helped her to maintain an even keel. She worried that if she didn't keep herself occupied, she would give up and descend into a spiral of depression.

She had not attended athletics training since she had discovered she was pregnant. Thoughts of the Paralympics were now a distant dream. By the time October came around, she would be six months pregnant and in no state to compete. She didn't think she could even tolerate watching coverage on the television. It would be a painful reminder of what could have been. Her coach, John Marshall, seemed the most disappointed. It was clear he knew nothing about her condition. Shortly after her return to school, he had cornered her in the corridor and asked what was going on. She had spun out some story about commitments to examinations getting in the way, but her explanation had sounded unbelievable even to her own ears.

The solid wooden door opened and the figure of a tall man, wearing a dark suit and red tie, emerged. Two patches of grey hair, one on either side of his head, framed a bald patch on top. He wore a pair of frameless, rectangular-shaped glasses, the strong lenses exaggerating the size of his eyes. The slightest hint of body odour wafted through the open doorway.

"Mr and Mrs Lessing, Antimone," he said. "Sorry to keep you waiting. Please come in."

Dominic and Helen Lessing rose from the low-slung, red armchairs and followed their daughter across the deep pile of the blue carpet.

Two wooden chairs with black leather seats occupied positions in front of the large oak desk, the surface of which was empty apart from a black computer display and matching keyboard perched on the left side. Framed certificates ringed the walls and sunlight streamed in through the wide, floor to ceiling windows.

"I'm John Weaver," he said, shaking hands with each of them in turn. He had to stoop to shake Antimone's hand. "I think we've met a couple of times before. Do take a seat."

He rounded the desk, sank into the high-backed swivel chair, then leant forwards, his elbows resting on the polished surface. "I wanted to start by saying what a wonderful student Antimone has been but... um... I was shocked and saddened to hear about what happened. I understand they're still looking for the man responsible."

"Thanks," Dominic mumbled. "He seems to have disappeared off the face of the planet, but the police are still searching for him."

"Well, I hope they find him soon. Anyway, there's something else I need to discuss with you today. I know Antimone's scholarship was established to cover the fees until the end of her secondary education, but it is the duty of the trustees to ensure that the funds are used effectively. Given Antimone's condition, I imagine she won't be pursuing her athletics career, and that was one of the major factors in deciding to offer the scholarship in the first place. It also seems unlikely she'll be able to complete the academic side of her education. I feel the other students will find it unsettling to have Antimone sharing the classroom with them in her current condition so it's with regret that I have to inform you the trustees and I have decided we will be withdrawing Antimone's place at this school with immediate effect."

Dominic turned to Helen, who reflected his own shocked expression, then back to the tall man seated opposite. "What? So, you're expelling her? I don't believe this. There are only six weeks of term to go."

Weaver appeared flustered. Antimone noticed that his left hand was trembling until he clamped his right on top. "I wouldn't call it an expulsion, but we do have to consider the welfare of our other students."

"You mean your other *fee-paying* students," Dominic spat. "My daughter is sexually assaulted, gets pregnant through no fault of her own and now you want to kick her out of school a week before she takes her exams in case it upsets your other students. What about upsetting us?"

"Look, I'm sorry, but the board's decision is final. Also, I'm sure I don't have to remind you about the non-disclosure agreement you signed when we offered Antimone the scholarship."

"What, because I might want to tell the press about the despicable actions of this school?"

"Dad, just leave it," Antimone interrupted. "It's not worth it. It's not as if the qualifications will be any use to me, anyway."

"That's not the point," her father said.

"My hands are tied," the head teacher said. "Regretful though it is, there's nothing I can do. Of course, all fees are covered to date."

"Well, that's good to hear," Dominic said, his voice dripping with sarcasm. "I wouldn't put it past you and your friends on the board to send us a bill." He rose to his feet. "Come on, we're leaving."

Weaver came around the desk. "Once again, I'm really sorry. Our thoughts will be with you."

"Yeah, right," Dominic said, turning his back on the man. He strode towards the door, followed by his wife and daughter.

When they had left, Weaver turned the key in the lock and exhaled deeply. He returned to his desk, withdrew a phone from his jacket pocket and selected a number. The call was answered after a couple of rings.

"Hello, it's John Weaver. Can you let Mrs Baxter know that I've told them?"

17

Monday 2nd August 2032

Antimone's phone rang. She didn't recognise the number, but she could tell from the code that it was another mobile. "Identify," she murmured on the off chance that some public database held the details. Two seconds later, the screen displayed a 'not found' message.

"Oh, what the hell," she muttered and pressed the answer button. "Yes?"

"Antimone?" a male voice said.

Her finger hovered over the disconnect button. "Yeah, who's this?"

"It's Jason, Jason Baxter. You're quite hard to track down."

Antimone didn't respond.

"Are you still there?" he asked.

"Yes, I'm here."

"So, how are you? I didn't get a chance to say goodbye when you left school."

Antimone wasn't sure whether Jason was aware of the pregnancy. She figured it was likely that he was because the police had interviewed him, and his mother certainly knew.

"Alright I suppose," she answered tentatively.

"Erin Riley said you'd been expelled."

"Yeah, well, you know what she's like. Let's just say they decided I wasn't worth the cost of the scholarship any longer."

"Bastards. I'll have a chat with my Mum. She's on the board of governors."

"Don't bother. I'm not sure I'd want to go back anyway."

"Look, I'm so sorry about what happened at the party. I had nothing to do with it, but I still feel partly responsible. If you hadn't sat with me and the other guys…"

So, he did know. "It's okay, Jason. I don't blame you if that's what you want to hear." She immediately regretted her harsh words. "I'm sorry. I appreciate the call."

Jason sounded relieved. "So, what are you up to?"

"Oh, you know. Watching vids, listening to music, reading. Nothing much, really. What about you?"

"Much the same. Hey, look. Mum's said I can take one of the cars this afternoon. I was thinking of going to the seaside. Maybe Hunstanton. Do you want to come?"

"Just you and me?"

"Unless you think you need a chaperone."

"It's a little late for that, I think."

Jason laughed nervously. "I'm glad you've still got your sense of humour."

"So, when? Now?" Antimone asked, glancing at her watch. It was already twelve thirty.

"Yeah. I can be round in ten minutes."

Antimone hesitated. She didn't really feel like socialising, but the more she contemplated Jason's offer, the more the idea of getting out of the house grew on her. Both her parents were at work, and she was starting to get bored being on her own. She might not be able to feel the sand between her toes anymore, but the seaside always brought back happy memories. "Go on then, why not? But make it twenty minutes. I need to grab a bite to eat before we go."

"Great. I'll be there around one. Get your beachwear on."

***

The journey took nearly two hours, but Antimone hardly noticed. The car was a far more expensive model than the one owned by her parents and was equipped with a state-of-the-art entertainment system. They spent the first half an hour playing with the various controls as the onboard computers navigated them through the Cambridgeshire and Norfolk countryside. Jason was a witty and entertaining companion, and he soon had her laughing at the outrageous stories of what he had witnessed at his mother's parties.

Eventually, the conversation moved on to parents.

"So, do you see your Dad?" Antimone asked.

Jason suddenly became serious. "I was adopted as a baby. I don't remember my biological mother, and my father apparently died from cancer before I was born. Mum's never really told me much about them. I've always wanted to find out more, but every time I ask, she changes the subject. Either she doesn't know or she doesn't want to tell me."

Antimone was silent for a moment. "I hope you don't mind me saying this, but your Mum doesn't seem like the type to adopt a child."

Jason laughed. "Well you know my Mum. She's so busy she wouldn't have found time for a pregnancy, so getting a readymade baby was probably the ideal solution for her."

"So, what's she like? I've only met her a couple of times, but she seems very… um… serious."

"Mum? If there's one word to describe her it would be driven. For the first ten years of my life, I was closer to the nannies she brought in to look after me. She began to show more interest once I could hold an intelligent conversation with her, but even then, the business always seemed to come first. That's just the way she is. Sometimes I think she's more attached to that little toad, Julian Stefano."

Antimone giggled. "Yeah, he's got a really slimy handshake. It felt like shaking hands with a slug. I wanted to wash my hands afterwards."

"I know exactly what you mean. He's like her poodle. If he had a tail, it'd be wagging every time she spoke to him."

Antimone did an impression of a dog barking as they both descended into fits of laughter.

***

The car navigated itself to a parking spot a hundred metres from the seafront. Jason slipped on his sunglasses, retrieved Antimone's wheelchair from the boot and helped her into it. He was wearing a multicoloured T-shirt that would have looked out-of-place anywhere but the seaside and a baggy pair of beach shorts.

"Let's head towards the promenade," Antimone suggested, the wind tugging a wisp of hair across her face. She wore a tight pink T-shirt and blue jeans but felt slightly drab compared to Jason's garish attire.

"Good idea."

They navigated their way across several roads, following the brown tourist signs that pointed to the south promenade. When they reached their destination, Jason ran on ahead, dodging between the tourists who strolled along the pedestrianised road adjacent to the shore.

"I thought you were supposed to be a wheelchair athlete," he called over his shoulder.

Antimone laughed as she steered around the pedestrians. "I could wup your ass anytime in a straight race, spear boy."

At a point where the beach was at the same level as the road, Jason slowed and allowed her to catch up. "How about here?" he asked.

"Yeah, why not?" She propelled herself onto the soft sand until the wheels sank deep enough that she could no longer move forwards.

"I think the lady's got a problem," he smiled. "Do you want to stay in that contraption of yours or sit on the sand?"

"Could you assist me to the ground, sir knight?"

"Yes, my lady." Jason picked her up, surprised at how little she weighed, and deposited her on the sand. He flopped down beside her. They both stared out in silence towards where the cloudless blue sky met the darker shade of the sea. The tide was on its way out, revealing the wooden groynes that seemed to pen in the holidaymakers like sheep in a field.

After a while, Antimone turned to Jason. "Thanks for bringing me here. I was starting to go a bit crazy stuck at home."

"You're welcome." He placed his hand on top of hers. When she didn't remove it, he leant sideways and kissed her gently on the cheek. She turned her head sideways, and their lips met.

After a few seconds, Antimone pulled back. "I really like you, Jason, but are you sure you want to do this? I'm not going to be around for much longer. We both know how this ends."

Jason took her face between his hands and kissed her again. "I really like you too. I know this can never be a long-term relationship, but I want to get to know you better in whatever time is left. I'm a good listener, and I'm here for you if you need me. So how are you bearing up?"

"Well, it's like... um... it still hasn't sunk in yet. I know I'm going to die in five months or so, but it still seems a long way off. I feel like I'm in a car hurtling towards a cliff, and I know the brakes don't work. It's like I'm still far enough away that I don't need them yet. But when I do... well, I don't know how I'm going to feel."

"I wish there was something I could do."

"Your mother did put me on one of her experimental programmes. One of her doctors gave me some pills, but he wouldn't say what they were. He did warn they might be a placebo, and even if they weren't, the chances of success were extremely small."

"Well, they've certainly got good facilities there. She's always moaning about how much the equipment costs."

"Yeah, it was also part of the deal that I went to her hospital for the birth."

"I'm sure they'll look after you well."

"Anyway, I don't want to talk about that anymore," Antimone said, brightening. "What sort of music do you like? Not that crap you had in the car I hope?"

Jason laughed and dropped a handful of sand on Antimone's lap. "You better be nice to me. Just remember you need me to get home."

"Yeah, that crap music was *really* great," she replied, returning the gesture.

***

The sun was getting lower in the sky. Antimone glanced at her watch. It was just before five o'clock. "We need to think about getting back. I haven't told my parents where I am."

Jason turned to face her. "Do you tell them everything you do?"

"Ever since the accident, they've been a bit over-protective. Anyway, I'll give them a call so it's not a problem."

"Time for an ice-cream before we go?"

"Why not? It wouldn't be the seaside without one."

Antimone brushed the sand off her jeans, and Jason helped her back into the wheelchair. He pushed the chair back onto the firm surface of the road.

"I can manage now," she said sharply.

"Um... I guess you don't like people pushing you."

"Not really. It's like... I don't know... like somebody playing with your hair or something... or prodding you in the back when you're walking to make you go faster."

Jason raised his hands. "Sorry, I didn't know."

Antimone silently cursed herself. She seemed to have developed this habit of pushing people away when they were only trying to be helpful. "Don't worry about it. Look, there's an ice-cream van just there."

"I'll get them. What's it to be? A cone?"

"Yeah, thanks, with one of those chocolate flakes in it if they've got one."

The white van was parked to the side of the pedestrianised road. Jason ran ahead and joined the queue of holidaymakers. Antimone turned her wheelchair to face the sea. At this spot, the promenade was two metres above the beach with stone steps leading down to the sand. She watched as families packed up their belongings in preparation for the journey home.

Her observations were distracted by somebody grabbing the wheelchair handles. "Jesus, Jason. I told you I don't like that."

"It's not your boyfriend, you little whore," said a voice deeper than Jason's. "If you scream, I'll push you over the edge. Come to think of it, I might just do that anyway."

Antimone jerked her head around. A man wearing a pair of large aviators and dressed in a navy-blue T-shirt stood behind her. Even without the beard, she recognised his face instantly as that of Daniel Floyd, the rapist.

"What do you want?" Antimone asked, her voice quivering with fright.

"What I want is for you to tell me why you set me up."

"Set you up? What're you talking about?"

"Give it a rest, alright. Was it that harpy, Rosalind Baxter? Was it her idea?"

"I'm sorry. I don't know what you mean."

"Oh, come on. You can't keep your bleeding legs together, get pregnant and then blame me. Haven't you heard of bloody contraception? It was that boyfriend of yours, wasn't it? I should have known the apple wouldn't fall far from the tree."

Antimone finally understood. "You think Jason raped me?"

"Raped?" the man said angrily. "It didn't look like that to me. I saw him come out of that bedroom looking as if he didn't have a care in the world. You followed him a minute or two later, and you certainly didn't seem distressed."

"What bedroom?"

"Oh, for Christ's sake, I *saw* you. How did you convince the police it was me? They must have done blood tests. Who did you bribe, or was it that witch, Baxter?"

"I—I didn't bribe anyone. I don't remember any of it, I was drugged."

"Drugged? That old excuse. You expect me to—" A shout came from the other side of the road. "You better watch your back," the man growled before he turned and ran.

"Who was that?" a breathless Jason asked. He held a cone in each hand, but one of them had lost the scoop of ice-cream and chocolate flake. "Are you alright?"

Antimone shivered and folded her arms across her chest even though it wasn't cold. "Daniel Floyd," she whispered.

"Daniel Floyd? What, the rapist?"

She nodded mutely.

"Christ, we better call the police."

Jason grabbed his phone from a pocket in his shorts and dialled. "Yes, it's an emergency. Police, please."

As he described what had happened, Antimone spoke in a dull voice. "He said he didn't do it."

"Hang on a sec," Jason said into the phone, then pulled it away from his ear. "What did you just say?"

"He said he didn't do it."

***

Antimone arrived home just after ten o'clock. The curtains twitched, and a face briefly appeared at the window before the front door swung open to reveal her anxious parents. "Let's get you inside," her mother said. Her father strode in the opposite direction to talk to the policeman who had helped Antimone out of the car.

When Jason had made the call, the emergency operator, determining that they were in no imminent danger, had instructed them to wait where they were until assistance arrived. By the time an officer located them half an hour later, Floyd was probably miles away. They had been driven to Hunstanton police station and were questioned separately. Antimone had repeated several times everything she could remember about the man's appearance and what he had said. The police had circulated Floyd's description but admitted they had little hope of catching him with the town packed with holidaymakers. Afterwards, when the sergeant had asked if she wanted to travel home with Jason, Floyd's words echoed through her head. *I saw him come out of that bedroom looking as if he didn't have a care in the world.* Sensing her discomfort, the man had offered to give her a lift, and she had gratefully accepted.

Several times during the journey, Antimone's mobile had rung. Other than a brief exchange with her parents when she told them the police were driving her home, the remainder were from Jason. Until she got her thoughts straight in her head, she didn't want to talk to him and so had rejected his calls. Now the phone rang again and Jason's number appeared on the screen. Reluctantly, she pressed the answer button.

"Thank God. Are you alright?" he asked, the worry in his voice sounding genuine.

"I'm okay," she replied.

"They said they were giving you a lift home."

"Yeah, I've just got back."

"So… um… Why didn't you come back with me? You didn't believe what that bastard said, did you?"

"He said he saw you come out of the bedroom, and that I followed you moments later. Why would he say that?"

"He's just messing with your head," Jason said.

"I don't know. I just need some time to think things through."

"Look, I promise you I had nothing to do with it. You believe me, don't you?"

Antimone ended the call without answering.

18

Tuesday 3rd August 2032

Mother and daughter waited in the interview room at Parkside Police Station in Cambridge. Two cardboard cups of cold tea rested on the industrial grey table. Antimone had allowed hers to cool without touching it and now nervously tapped her finger on the metal surface. She glanced up at the video camera in the corner of the ceiling and idly wondered whether anybody was watching them.

The sound of footsteps echoed down the corridor, and a moment later Karen Atkins bustled into the room, carrying a file under her arm. "Good morning, Antimone, Helen. Thanks for coming in." She opened the file and read for a few seconds before raising her eyes. "It seems you had a bit of excitement yesterday, Antimone."

"Yeah, you could say that."

"I've got your statement here, but I'd like you to go over what happened one more time."

Antimone recounted the events of the previous evening.

Kat interrupted a couple of times to clarify Antimone's words but mostly listened in silence.

"I'd say you were lucky that Jason came back when he did," Kat said when Antimone had finished.

"I suppose."

"Have they caught him yet?" Helen asked.

"No, I'm sorry. At this time of year, the town's extremely busy. He could be anywhere by now, but obviously we'll keep looking."

"Do you think he'll try again?"

"I think that's unlikely, but I'd recommend you take some precautions. Keep the doors and windows of your house locked and make sure you've got a phone handy at all times."

"He said he saw Jason and me coming out of the bedroom. What if he's not the rapist?" Antimone asked.

Kat considered her response before speaking. "The blood tests have been checked. There's definitely no mistake there. He *is* the father of your child. Sometimes rapists blame the victim. You've got to remember this man's a convicted murderer. You can't judge his behaviour by the norms of society."

"He just seemed so—I don't know—angry, I suppose. He accused me of framing him."

"Well, he has got a history of doing that. He claimed he was framed for his wife's murder too. You'd be surprised how many prison inmates protest their innocence despite conclusive proof to the contrary."

"So, you're still convinced he's the murderer?"

"You mean rapist, right?" Kat asked.

"Yeah. Isn't that what I just said?"

Helen put an arm around her daughter.

Kat's gaze alternated between the two. "Yes, I'm still totally convinced he's the rapist."

19

Saturday 25th December 2032

Antimone stared at the pulsating patterns of the lights on the Christmas tree. Her parents had spared no expense to ensure that their last Christmas together as a family was special, but the atmosphere in the house was still sombre. In some ways they were trying too hard. The enforced joviality was wearing thin. The basketball-sized bump sitting on her stomach worsened her mood. The size and shape meant she had been struggling to get comfortable at night.

The last few months seemed to have rushed past. Daniel Floyd was still on the run, and there had been no sightings since the day at the seaside. She suspected that the police had scaled back the hunt for the rapist but had heard nothing officially. Karen Atkins visited once a month to reassure them the search was continuing and that they would catch their man. No doubt the birth of the baby would stimulate a fresh burst of activity, but by then it would be too late for Antimone.

Things hadn't been the same with Jason following the incident at Hunstanton. It was clear he still felt aggrieved about Antimone travelling home without him and her failure to acknowledge his assertion of innocence. He had called twice since, but the conversations had been awkward and stilted, and eventually he stopped calling altogether.

She had struggled to make friends at Oakington Manor, so there had been little contact from her other classmates. The only person who might have fallen in that category, Erin Riley, had also called once. She had started by appearing sympathetic, but Antimone had hung up when she asked what the sex was like.

True to her word, Jason's mother, Rosalind Baxter, had arranged for her to give birth in the private hospital at Ilithyia Biotechnology. The midwife had warned them the contractions could start at any time, and Antimone's father had prepared a holdall so they wouldn't need to waste time packing when that happened. Once a month, Antimone attended the Ilithyia clinic for an examination and to pick up the next batch of pills. Her parents still clung to the hope that she might survive the birth, but she was realistic enough to understand that the odds were infinitesimally small.

"Right," Helen said brightly. She picked up a red, book-shaped parcel, tied with a turquoise–coloured ribbon, from beneath the tree. She read the label aloud, although she already knew what it said. "To Antimone, with all our love, from Mum and Dad."

Antimone accepted the package and ripped off the garishly coloured paper to reveal a book. She turned it over to examine the title: 'The 2032 Delhi Olympics and Paralympics: A Review'.

"We know you couldn't compete," her father said, "but we thought you might find it interesting to look at the pictures."

"Thanks, Mum, Dad." The gift was a reminder of a past life, one that no longer held much interest for her, but she knew they meant well. She had deliberately tried to avoid all contact with the Olympics but had relented when it came to her own event, the eight hundred metres women's T54 wheelchair final. The British girl, whom she had beaten in their last two races, finished just outside the medals in fourth place.

The present giving continued until a single brightly wrapped parcel lay beneath the tree. Most of the gifts Antimone received were frivolous and jokey. *After all, what do you give a girl with less than two weeks left to live?* she thought.

Helen picked up the blue-wrapped package and searched for a label. "It doesn't have a name on it," she said.

"I know, Mum. It's from me to the baby. By the way, I want to call him Paul."

"Oh… um… well, should we open it now?"

"Yes, please. I want you to see it too."

Antimone's mother removed the wrapping and held up a large book with a multi-coloured, patterned cover.

"Look inside," she said.

Helen placed the book on the coffee table and carefully turned over the jacket. Antimone's father sat beside her, staring at the open page. Inscribed in neat calligraphic script were the words, 'To Paul Lessing. Everything you need to know about your mother.' Beneath the writing was a photograph of a smiling Antimone, proudly holding up a gold medal.

"It's a scrapbook. That's what I've been spending my time doing the last few months. Turn to the next page."

Her mother did as instructed. An envelope was taped to the paper. Hand-written on it was the text, 'To Paul, on your first birthday.'

"I've written letters to him for every one of his first eighteen birthdays and one for his wedding day. You're going to have to read the first ones to him until he's old enough to read for himself. Make sure he doesn't open them ahead of time. I've also included a whole load of other stuff, what music I like, the books I've read and masses of photos. I know a lot of it's online, but this sort of tells a story."

Antimone watched as her parents slowly turned over each page. Tears streamed down both their faces.

"Hey, I don't want you getting it wet," she said, smiling.

"What a wonderful idea," Helen murmured, staring at her daughter.

Then she rose to her feet and hurried out of the room, her face in her hands, no longer able to hide the violent sobs wracking her body.

Part Two: Evaluation

20

Monday 3rd January 2033

Rosalind Baxter held the handset against her ear as she hurried along the corridor. "So which patient are we talking about?"

She listened impatiently to the reply. "What? You're sure? The sixteen-year-old girl in the wheelchair?"

The other person responded affirmatively.

"Well, get her down to the basement emergency ward immediately and the baby too, but keep them apart. And Julian, get Grolby to make sure those two goons from the mortuary don't talk about this."

Anders Grolby was Ilithyia's Head of Security. He was a blond-haired Swede who had been with the company for the past eighteen years. He had been discharged from the Swedish army in his mid-thirties after an incident in Iraq when a family of four locals had been shot dead. Fortunately for Grolby, despite the overwhelming circumstantial evidence, there had been no solid witnesses, and he had escaped prosecution.

She stabbed the end call button and waved a key-card at the reader on the wall by a door labelled 'Biohazard—authorised personnel only'. The light on the box turned green, and the electronic lock opened. She barged through and strode down a passageway towards a lift bearing an identical sign. She jabbed the call button, pacing backwards and forwards while she waited for the doors to open. When they did, she hurried inside and stared into the red glare of an iris scanner. A display panel illuminated, and she stabbed a finger at the on-screen 'B' icon.

The floor sank down beneath her feet and a second or two later pressed up again as the lift decelerated. She stepped out into a brightly lit, white corridor. The clacking of her heels echoed as she bustled towards her destination. One of the numbered doors opened ahead of her, and a white-coated doctor wearing a surgical mask emerged. She immediately altered direction to intercept the man.

"Find Dr Perrin and tell him to go to the emergency ward."

"But I was just about to—"

"I don't give a damn what you were about to do. If you still want to be employed at this hospital tomorrow then locate Dr Perrin and get him to the emergency ward in the next two minutes."

The man said something, but she had already turned her back and resumed her journey. She took a left turn, then a right and reached a set of wide elevator doors just as they opened. Two men wearing pale green overalls manoeuvred a trolley through the gap.

On the trolley lay a girl with a white sheet drawn up to her chin. Wisps of damp hair framed an attractive but exhausted-looking face. A bruise was forming on the girl's forehead. Her eyes alighted on Rosalind. "Mrs Baxter," she croaked, then broke into a cough.

Rosalind ignored the girl and picked up the clipboard at the foot of the trolley. Her eyes scanned down the text, then she replaced it.

"Mrs Baxter," the girl repeated.

"Just lie back, Antimone. You're in good hands. We're taking you to an emergency room to make sure you're okay."

"My baby."

"Your baby's fine. We're just checking it over." Rosalind didn't know whether her statement was true or not, but she figured it was better to keep the patient calm.

"Can we…" interrupted one of the men.

Rosalind waved a hand impatiently. "Yeah, get on with it." She trailed behind the two men as they wheeled their cargo down the corridor, then turned right through a set of swing doors. She followed them into a room containing four beds, only two of which held patients. An array of machines sat next to the head of each bed. A nurse who had been sitting at a desk making notes rose to her feet.

"Mask," Rosalind snapped, holding out a hand. The nurse hurried to a dispenser and handed her a surgical mask. "Get them out of here," she said, sweeping a hand towards the occupied beds.

"But these—"

"Why the hell do I always have to repeat myself in this place?" Rosalind snarled. "I said get them out of here. I don't care where you put them." She turned to the two porters. "Get this patient into that bed there."

The two men positioned the trolley beside the empty bed, removed the sheet covering Antimone, then slid her across using the under-sheet upon which she lay. She grimaced at the sudden movement.

The arrival of a bald-headed man wearing a white coat and surgical mask saved the men from Rosalind's wrath.

"Nigel, about time," she said.

"What's going on?" he asked, his gaze following the nurse who was busy disconnecting machines from one of the patients.

"Let's get these other people out of here, and then we'll talk about it."

"Rosalind, these women are seriously ill. If you move them now, they might die."

"Look," Rosalind hissed, "You see that girl on the bed over there? She just gave birth and survived. Now tell me which patient is more important. I don't want any risk that she might get infected."

"My God. You're serious?" His eyes bored into hers, his brain already whirring. Seeing no change in her humourless expression, he whipped around. "You two. Get this one to room two oh eight and the other to two ten. When you've done that, come back and take the machines with you."

He pointed at the nurse who was busy disconnecting equipment from the second patient. "She'll tell you which ones they need."

The nurse completed her task and stood up. "Dr Perrin, what's going on here?"

"I want you to reconnect those two and keep an eye on them. This girl is a high priority, and we can't run the risk of cross-infection. I want you to call Personnel right now and get more nursing staff down so there's cover twenty-four hours a day. They must have the highest level of security clearance, at least an eight but preferably a nine."

"But what's so special—?"

"Samantha," Perrin interrupted, "Please just do as I ask. This is really important."

The nurse smiled tightly. "Of course, Dr Perrin. I'll get right on it."

While the other members of staff busied themselves with their allotted tasks, the doctor strolled over to Antimone's bed and picked up the clipboard which had been transferred from the trolley.

"Hello, Antimone," he said, staring down at the girl. "How are you feeling?" He held her wrist, measuring her pulse rate.

"Like crap," she replied. "Where's my baby?"

Perrin glanced towards Rosalind, who shook her head. "We're looking after your baby, but it's going to be a while until we can bring it to you."

"Why? Is something wrong?"

"No, just routine tests."

"And by the way, *he's* called Paul."

"Of course. I see you've had a Caesarean. I just want to look at the stitches."

Perrin rolled back the sheet and carefully lifted the blood-spotted hospital gown. Rosalind edged closer to inspect the wound herself.

"Hmm," Perrin said, studying the hasty stitching. "One or two of these stitches have popped. We're going to have to do some repair work. We'll give you a local. You won't feel a thing."

"Where are my parents?"

"There's too high a risk of infection at the moment," Rosalind said. "You'll be able to see them in a day or two."

Antimone tried to sit up, then flopped back, her face a mask of agony. "Can't I talk to them? Do they even know I'm alive?"

"Antimone, you need to relax. You've been through a traumatic experience. We'll let your parents know you're okay. Maybe a mild sedative, Dr Perrin?"

Perrin nodded, then strode to a set of cabinets beside the nurse's station. A few seconds later he returned carrying an injection gun, a small glass vial of clear liquid protruding from the top. He held the barrel against Antimone's arm and depressed the trigger. The drug entered her bloodstream accompanied by a short hiss. "This'll help you relax."

Antimone's eyes grew heavy-lidded. "I want my baby," she murmured, but within seconds she was asleep. By now, Rosalind and Perrin had the room to themselves.

"You know what this means, Nigel? Do you have any idea of this girl's value? If we can work out what makes her special, we can finally develop a cure. This company will be worth billions, maybe even tens or hundreds of billions."

"We'll have to get blood from both mother and child and test for the presence of the virus. We'll also need to sequence their genomes. I'll get the tests started right away."

"This has to remain tightly controlled, only the highest level of security clearance. We can't afford for anybody to find out she survived. Not even her parents can know."

"What do we tell them?"

Rosalind pondered a moment. "Well, they already think she's dead, so let's keep it that way. Tell them the child died too, some bacterial infection so dangerous that we had to cremate both bodies immediately. Get one of the doctors who works down here to sign the death certificates. If we give the parents some ashes, they won't know any better."

"She's not going to stop asking to see them, though. That might become a problem."

"What's she going to do? Yes, she'll be pissed off, but she can't get out of here. I'll get Grolby to arrange for an armed guard to be stationed outside her room."

"I'll get a gynaecologist to look her over, somebody we can trust."

"Who did the C-section?" Rosalind asked.

Perrin consulted the chart. "John Martin."

"That old fart. But at least he needs the money. He's an eight, right? We need to keep the circle of people who know about this as small as possible."

"But that stitching was a disgrace. If he did that, I don't want him anywhere near her."

"He might not be the most dynamic character in the world, but as far as I know he's conscientious," Rosalind said. "Find out who did this work then sack them. If it wasn't Martin, get him down here. If it was, find someone else."

"I'll get on it right away, Rosalind. By the way, what are we going to do about the child?"

"Until we've done the tests, keep them separated. I want round-the-clock care. Nobody needs to know what's special about the boy."

"She's definitely not going to like that," Perrin said.

"I suggest we use it as leverage. Threaten to keep them apart unless she behaves."

"Good idea. That should work."

"Let me know as soon as you find out anything. You know, Nigel, this is going to make Ilithyia the biggest company in the world." For the first time that day, Rosalind Baxter smiled.

21

Tuesday 4th January 2033

Dominic Lessing wandered from room to room, more than anything to give him something to do. There were reminders of Antimone everywhere: the colourful snake draught excluder she had given them for Christmas last year, the cushion she liked to lean against when she was sitting on the sofa, the stair-lift that enabled her to go upstairs.

The image of his daughter's stomach being cut open before they removed the baby would be seared in his mind for the rest of his life. He had wanted to rush in and stop the operation, but he knew it was beyond his control. He had read about the agonies endured by women after they delivered their children naturally, the way the virus turned the body on itself, basically turning their internal organs and brains to mush. He couldn't bear to think of that happening to his own daughter and just prayed that she hadn't suffered.

The doctor had held the boy up to the observation window so they could see their grandson. To Dominic he had looked like any new-born child: a scrunched-up face, eyes that couldn't focus yet, fine wisps of hair, mouth open as he exercised his lungs in a high-pitched wail. That first glimpse had been all too short as the baby was whisked away and placed in an incubator.

A counsellor had guided them away before the surgeons had stitched up the incision. The only real consolation the woman could offer was that their daughter's death had resulted in a new life. In many ways, Dominic relished the prospect of the sleepless nights and the endless routine of feeding and changing as a way of distracting him from darker thoughts. Before any of that could begin, though, they had to wait for the hospital to call. The child seat was already installed, the formula milk was piled up in the cupboard, and the crib was assembled in the spare room.

Dominic glanced at his watch once again. Half-past eleven. The midwife had assured them that the baby would be ready to go home sometime this morning.

"Dominic, will you please stop pacing?" His wife sat on the sofa, cradling her fifth cup of tea of the day. "You're driving me mad."

"Sorry, but I can't sit down. Why don't we drive there now? They've got our mobile numbers."

"I think I'd rather wait here than in a hospital waiting room. It's only ten minutes away."

The trilling of the phone interrupted the conversation. Dominic took two swift paces and snatched the handset from its cradle. Helen's gaze followed him expectantly.

"Yes, this is Dominic Lessing. Can we come over now?"

"Problem? What problem?"

Dominic's mouth opened, and his face turned an ashen colour. He seemed to be struggling to breathe. With a moan of anguish, he sank to his knees.

Helen rose to her feet in consternation. "What is it? What's happened?"

Dominic dropped the phone and pitched forwards onto all fours. His shoulders heaved, and he vomited on the carpet.

An expression of terror occupied Helen's face. "Are you alright? What the hell's wrong?"

Dominic raised his eyes slowly to meet his wife's panicked stare. Even without speaking, the depth of his evident despair told her everything she needed to know.

"No. Not the baby?"

The slightest nod of the head. She bent down and picked up the phone, almost as if somebody else was controlling her body. "This is Helen Lessing. Who is this?"

"It's Jennifer Anderson, the counsellor at Ilithyia. We met briefly yesterday. I'm so sorry, Mrs Lessing. The baby's—Paul's—condition deteriorated overnight, a bacterial infection. The doctors did everything they could, but unfortunately, he didn't respond to the drugs. He passed away at just after ten o'clock this morning."

"He's dead?"

"I'm afraid so. On behalf of everybody at Ilithyia, I'd like to offer our condolences on the loss of your grandson."

"But… but he seemed healthy when he was born."

"I'm sorry, I don't have all the details, but I understand the infection began to develop during the night and didn't respond to the drugs."

"But…"

"I know you must be in shock. I'm going to drop by this afternoon, but I felt you needed to hear this terrible news as soon as possible rather than finding out when you phoned the switchboard."

"Um…"

"There is one other thing I need to tell you. Well—ah—because of the nature of the infection we were left with no option but to cremate the bodies of your daughter and your grandson. I'll bring the ashes with me this afternoon. I'm really sorry for your loss. Our thoughts are with you."

"Th-thanks."

Helen ended the call. She walked as if in a trance to the telephone cradle and deliberately placed the handset in the slot.

She turned and stared down at her husband. He lay on the carpet in the foetal position, his face in his hands.

22

The girl lay on the bed. The bump on her stomach was so large that whichever way she turned she could not get comfortable. Even though she knew that giving birth would kill her, in some ways it would be a relief. When she had asked the doctors when it would be, they had been non-committal, telling her that it could happen anytime in the next few weeks. After almost nine months cooped up in this room, she felt like a prisoner on death row.

She knew they were planning something for her. No food had arrived that morning. She wondered whether they intended to perform the Caesarean on her that evening. It would be just like them not to inform her. Her fears were confirmed when the door opened, and the balding, white-coated doctor entered the room accompanied by two orderlies, dressed in pale green overalls.

"Is it time?" she asked, her voice quivering with anxiety.

"No, not quite yet," the doctor said. "We just need to do an examination to see how the baby's doing."

"Why can't you do that here?"

"We're going to use a scanner, and we need you to be completely still, so we're going to give you a general anaesthetic."

"Is something wrong with the baby?"

"No, we don't think so, but given your history of drug abuse, we just want to be absolutely sure. Do you need a hand getting on the trolley?"

"No, I can manage."

She shifted her body around until her legs dangled over the edge of the bed, then shuffled forwards. She sighed when her feet touched the floor, then waddled towards the waiting trolley. The two men helped her up and when she was lying down again, strapped her arms and legs to the frame and raised the sides.

"Is it really necessary to tie me down? It's not as if I'm going to be able to run far, is it?"

"It's just a precaution," the doctor replied, smiling.

One man stood on each side, and they manoeuvred the trolley down the white corridor. This was only the second time she had been outside her room since arriving. Her brain soaked everything in: the doors containing the small windows, the recessed lighting, the smoke detectors on the ceiling, all of it a welcome distraction from the monotony of the same four walls for months on end.

They passed the sign for the first operating theatre. She was just about to ask where they were taking her when they pushed through a set of swing doors *labelled 'Operating Theatre S2'. The arrangement of the room was identical to the one she had been to previously. A woman wearing a blue medical gown, hairnet and white surgical mask awaited her. The girl couldn't be sure, but she thought it was the same woman who had administered the anaesthetic the last time.*

No sooner had the trolley stopped moving than the woman slipped a black mask over the girl's face. "Hello again," she said. "It's just like before. Start counting backwards from ten."

***

The girl opened one eye. Her gaze tracked along the white floor to the featureless white walls. For a moment her sluggish mind refused to function, and a sense of disorientation engulfed her. Her head felt like it was full of sand. She blinked open the other eye and, as her brain engaged, she concluded she was back in her room, lying on her side in bed. Instinctively, her hand moved to her stomach. For a brief second or two, hope flared that the baby had been born and she was still alive, but the presence of the bump indicated otherwise.

"Don't try to move," a voice said from behind her.

She ignored the instruction and tried to face the speaker, but her legs wouldn't respond. With a rising panic, she realised she had no sensation at all below the waist. She lowered her hand and brushed against warm skin, but the touch of her fingers didn't register at all. It was as if she had placed her hand on somebody else's body.

Her heart rate increased, and she felt the baby kick. Her breathing came in ragged bursts, a rushing sound in her ears. Her mouth was suddenly dry.

"What the hell have you done to me?" she gasped, trying to locate the man.

A chair creaked and soft footsteps came around the bed. The bald-headed doctor entered her field of vision.

"Just try to remain still and relax."

"I asked what you've done to me. I can't feel my bloody legs."

"Yes, I'm afraid there was a complication."

"You told me I was going for a scan. How the hell can a scan go wrong?"

"During the scan, we discovered a growth on your spine. While you were under the anaesthetic, we decided to deal with it there and then."

"So now I'm paralysed from the waist down, you bastard," she screamed.

"We hoped that we'd be able to remove the tumour without any side effects, but unfortunately it was so close to your spine that it didn't prove possible."

"You lying sack of shit. I don't believe a word you're telling me. You've lied to me since the day I arrived."

"We only have you and the baby's best interests at heart. Now you need to calm down."

The girl stared at him for a moment, then opened her mouth and screamed. The doctor winced. He fumbled in his pocket and withdrew a small injection gun. He adjusted the settings and stood just out of reach of the hysterical girl.

"I was hoping it wasn't going to come to this," he said.

She drew breath and screamed again. She tried to bat his hand away as he lunged towards her and pressed the barrel against the top of her arm, but he was too quick. He depressed the trigger and sprang back.

The girl's eyes rolled up in her head, and within seconds she was once again unconscious.

23

Thursday 6th January 2033

Rosalind Baxter and Nigel Perrin entered the large CEO's office on the second storey. Rosalind shut the door, then took the chair behind the heavy black wooden desk facing the floor to ceiling plate-glass window.

Perrin sat opposite, clutching a sheaf of papers, silhouetted by a beam of sunlight that broke through a gap in the slate-grey clouds. He seemed ill at ease.

"Too hot in here for you, Nigel?"

"No, I'm fine."

"Still, it's a little too bright for me."

Rosalind pressed a button on her keyboard. "Darken," she said. The light streaming into the room decreased until the glare no longer bothered her. "Stop," she commanded.

"So," she said, addressing Perrin, "what have we got?"

"Well, to start with they're both doing well. We're keeping them separated for the time being, but she's starting to get difficult, demanding to talk to her parents and see the child."

"Keep stalling her for the moment. What about the test results?"

He consulted the reports he held on his lap and placed them one by one on the table. "We've taken blood from both mother and child, cheek swabs, urine and faeces samples. We've also done full body scans." A small mound of documents rested on the black surface of the desk. Several sheets of paper remained on his knee.

"You don't expect me to read all that, do you? What are the highlights?"

"Okay, Rosalind. The virus is still active in both their blood samples. For whatever reason, it hasn't entered the destructive phase in the mother. Urine and faeces don't show anything unusual. We've sequenced the DNA from the cheek swabs on the child, and there's nothing obvious there. I've asked them to repeat the mother's cheek swab. It looks like somebody mixed up the samples."

"I take it you know who that was?"

Perrin nodded.

"Well fire them. If there's one thing I won't tolerate in this organisation, it's incompetence. We pay well above the going rate, and I expect the best."

"Um… okay Rosalind, but it's not easy to find good technicians. She's never made a mistake before."

"I don't care, Nigel. Get rid of her. If you don't want to do it personally, phone somebody in Personnel."

"No, I'll do it," he said in a resigned voice.

"What about the body scans?"

"Nothing unusual in the child's. As you know the mother has a fracture between the T-eleven and T-twelve vertebrae."

"You don't think that's got anything to do with her surviving, do you?"

"I already thought of that, Rosalind. It seems unlikely, but I have instigated an experiment."

"Good. The mother was being treated here before the birth. What did you prescribe her?"

Perrin glanced up sharply. "I did as you asked and gave her the placebo."

"And you're sure none of the technicians mixed up the pills?"

Perrin sighed. "No, Rosalind, I can't be a hundred percent, but the chances are extremely small. In any case, as you know, we always conduct trials on a number of patients, and so far, none of the others has survived." He shifted his weight on the chair.

"Something's bothering you, Nigel. What is it?"

Perrin hesitated. "I told you we discounted the DNA test on the mother, but there was something of note about the baby."

Rosalind leant forwards. "You just said there was nothing unusual in the child's DNA. Make up your mind. What did you find?"

"I meant nothing to explain why the mother survived. What I didn't mention was that we also used it to determine paternity."

"Oh, for crying out loud, Nigel, get to the point."

Perrin placed the remaining sheets of paper on the table. "When we ran the sequencer and analysed the results, I immediately recognised the signature, even though it was many years ago."

"Yeah, that arsehole Daniel Floyd. I have to admit, for all his faults, I never took him for a rapist. He was probably just trying to get back at me, but even so. He wasn't happy when I got the security guards to throw him out."

Perrin stared at her without speaking.

"Stop playing games, Nigel. I haven't got time for this."

Perrin inhaled deeply, then slowly released his breath.

"He's not the one I'm talking about. Daniel Floyd isn't the child's father."

24

Thursday 6th January 2033

Anders Grolby waited at the side of the road, although all of his attention was focused on the screen of the head-up display inside his helmet. A map displayed the stretch of the A14 road where he sat stationary astride his electric motorbike, his feet keeping the lightweight machine upright. A green dot drifted slowly from right to left, approaching the blue icon of a car at the centre that signified his own position. A red dot trailed the green one by a centimetre, travelling in the same direction.

Grolby muttered a series of instructions and studied the scrolling text to confirm the system had interpreted them correctly. Over the course of the next few seconds, the distance between the green and red dots halved. Satisfied that everything was going to plan, he extended his gaze to the grey ribbon of tarmac. The traffic was quieter than usual at this time of day. The schools weren't back yet, and people were probably extending their Christmas break until the end of the week. He had no qualms about causing collateral damage, but the fewer witnesses who were present, the better.

For what he planned, human observers were less of a worry than the electronic eyes of the cameras fitted to all modern vehicles. The bike he rode was a popular model, indistinguishable from the thousands of others, at least to the untrained eye. He had upgraded the motor and battery systems to provide far greater power and range than the unmodified version. The mirrored visor meant that nobody would get a look at his face. He had also disconnected a wire from the vehicle's transponder. If the police stopped him, it would appear as if a damaged connector was the culprit, but the chances of them being vigilant enough to spot the absence of the signal were extremely slim. Even if a camera picked him up, they would have a hard job identifying him.

Grolby consulted the map once again. The green dot overlaid the blue car symbol. He had fitted a tracker the previous evening, attaching the small magnetised disc to the underside of the body where it was parked on the road. They should be visible by now. He surveyed the passing traffic, seeking out the target. There it was, a small, silver autonomous vehicle, two passengers. He had a good idea where they were going. He had tracked them from their house to the local supermarket, and now they were returning home—or so they thought. He pulled out into the traffic and slotted into a gap two cars behind them. If he was correct, they would take the next exit.

This type of work was different to what he had done before joining the company. When he was in Iraq, the rules of engagement had been a major source of frustration. Anybody could tell that half the population would happily kill the infidel invaders given the chance. He could see it in their eyes. They tried to hide it with their lowered heads and subservient body posture, but it was all just a mask for their true intentions.

Whilst on patrol, his contingent had come under attack from a group of insurgents. One of his team had died, and another had taken a bullet to the thigh. As soon as the soldiers returned fire, the attackers melted away. Grolby had recognised one of them as a local shopkeeper. He notified his commander, but after interviewing the suspect, the decision had been made to set him free. Grolby trailed him along the bustling streets to the scruffy house where he lived with his wife and two sons.

When Grolby burst through the door, the man was embracing his wife. The boys, aged ten and twelve, looked up at the blond westerner who had invaded their home. The man turned around and screamed in Arabic at the interloper, gesticulating wildly as he attempted to usher him out. Grolby smiled once then emptied his entire clip leaving the devastated bodies of the father, mother and two boys lying in an expanding pool of blood. The way he figured it, if he killed only the man, the surviving members of the family would have all the motivation they needed to become insurgents themselves. Best to deal with the issue before it became a problem.

During the court martial he had denied ever being at the man's house, and there was no proof other than a couple of eye-witnesses who described having seen a tall, blond, white man fleeing through the dusty alley. In light of Grolby's initial accusation and the sighting of a man matching his description immediately after the incident, the circumstantial evidence was overwhelming. However, his lawyer had argued that the description matched half of the unit and the whole group knew the murdered man's identity. In the end, Grolby received a dishonourable discharge from the army but served no time in jail.

Working for Ilithyia had been tedious at first, but as time went by, Grolby had grown into the role. He had ample budget to put in place the security measures he wanted and was allowed to recruit his own team of like-minded men. Jobs like this one made him nostalgic for the old days in the military. Yes, he could have commanded one of his subordinates to undertake the task, but there was nothing quite like doing it oneself. Now that he was closing in on the target, the jolt of adrenaline and the racing heartbeat brought a smile to his lips.

The silver car indicated left a good two hundred metres before the junction. Grolby twisted the throttle and surged ahead of the vehicle before veering off at the exit. Once again, he muttered instructions into the microphone located inside his helmet. He raced down the slip road and arrived at the roundabout at the bottom of the slight incline just as the traffic lights were turning amber. He accelerated, hugging the inside of the traffic island and leaning into the curve. He reached the opposite side, just over one hundred metres away, as the target drew to a halt at the lights. Turning off the bike, he dismounted and propped it on its stand.

He gave the final set of commands. The distance between the green and red dots on the display narrowed to a couple of millimetres. He glanced up expectantly and grinned as a massive yellow driverless truck appeared at the top of the ramp and began the descent downhill. The sound of the goods vehicle changing gear reached his ears, but instead of slowing down, it increased velocity down the gentle incline.

The traffic lights changed to green, and the small silver car pulled away but not fast enough. By now the truck had achieved a speed in excess of seventy miles an hour as it gained momentum from the downward slope and the straining engine. The blunt nose of the cabin smashed into the slow-moving car, instantly crushing the vehicle to half its original size. For a second or two, the concertinaed body of the car was shunted forwards before the front wheels of the articulated truck lifted off the road, dragging what remained beneath it.

The truck careened across the lanes of the roundabout and towards its centre. For a moment, Grolby thought it was coming straight for him, but the front wheels dug into the soft earth causing it to jack-knife. He felt the tremor through his legs as the goods vehicle toppled onto its side, churning up huge piles of earth and vegetation. The screech of tortured metal accompanied a subsonic rumble, the energy of the sounds creating a deep vibration in his chest and setting his teeth on edge. Chunks of soil and fragments of metal pattered down around him. He dropped to the ground as a wheel from the car flew past like a bouncing bomb, centimetres from his head.

A metallic clang made him flinch. He glanced behind and was relieved to see no discernible damage to the motorbike. If something took it out of action, he would have a serious problem.

After what seemed an age, silence returned to the scene of devastation. Grolby stood up and brushed dirt and shredded vegetation off his black leathers. The truck lay on its side, a great gouge of broken earth trailing behind it. One of its wheels continued to rotate. Amidst all the bent metal, nothing was recognisable as the remains of the car.

He strolled to the cab of the heavy goods vehicle and placed a small, black plastic box on the radiator grill. A metallic ticking sound emanated from somewhere inside the engine as it cooled. He retreated from the wreckage. When he had reached a distance of fifty paces, he withdrew a second unit from inside his leather jacket. A solitary red button was the only feature to break the smooth black surface, and he stabbed it with a gloved finger. Nothing visible happened to the truck, but his head up display flickered for a second or two. The electromagnetic pulse generated by the first box would wipe the memory of all the electronic devices on the vehicle, leaving no evidence of the software he had inserted allowing him to control it. He hurried back to retrieve his equipment before returning to the motorbike.

He mounted the bike and glanced back once more at the twisted metal.

"Jesus Christ!" Grolby muttered to himself. "Now that's what I call a crash."

25

Thursday 6th January 2033

"When are you going to let me out of here?" Antimone asked.

The nurse looked up from the computer screen, then rose to her feet. "That's up to Dr Perrin."

"You can't keep me locked up like this without my permission."

The nurse approached the bed, lifted her surgical mask and stared down at Antimone. "I don't think you're in any condition to be going anywhere, young lady."

"That's a point. When can I have my wheelchair back?"

The woman tutted. "You're not getting out of that bed until the stitches are taken out."

"When's that going to be?"

"They have to be left in for at least five days, so maybe another forty-eight hours."

Antimone sighed. "I want to see my baby and talk to my parents. Do they even know I'm alive?"

"That's—"

"Let me guess," interrupted Antimone. "That's up to Dr Perrin."

The nurse smiled humourlessly. "Yes. You're learning fast."

"Anyway, why can't I see my baby? And don't tell me I have to ask Dr Perrin."

"We don't want either of you giving the other an infection. It's a miracle you survived, and we don't want to risk the health of you or your child."

"I thought breast milk was supposed to help strengthen a baby's immune system. These," she indicated her nipples, "are really sore and they keep dribbling. They're not going to like, burst or anything?"

The woman laughed. "No, I wouldn't worry about that. You'll stop lactating in a day or two. The baby's being fed on artificial milk, but it's every bit as good as the real thing, if not better."

Antimone remained silent for a moment. "Do they know why I survived yet?"

"They're still working on it. That's why you've been having all these tests. I'm sure Dr Perrin will let you know when they find anything out."

"Yeah, I feel like a pin cushion, all the blood they've taken the last day or two. I'm surprised there's any left."

"I know it's uncomfortable, but they only take a small amount—"

"They took quite a lot actually, at least five or six of those little tubes last time."

"Your body soon makes more," the nurse said. "Is there anything you need?"

"Just to get out of here."

"Apart from that."

"Nah. Although a book or some music would be good. When are they going to give back my ear implants?"

"You can't keep those in when you're in the scanner. You'll—"

"... have to ask Dr Perrin," Antimone said, completing the sentence. She blew out her cheeks. Her eyes drifted across the room and settled on the telephone handset resting on the nurse's desk.

The nurse tracked her gaze. "You can't dial out from down here—even mobile signals are blocked, so I wouldn't even think about it."

"So, when is Dr Perrin coming back?"

"Whenever he's ready," the nurse replied. She was on her way to the desk when the swing doors opened, and a middle-aged woman, whom Antimone hadn't seen before, swept into the room. Her hair was tied back in a severe bun, and she could have been attractive were it not for the permanent expression of distaste on her face. She wore a white coat and flat shoes.

The newcomer strode up to Antimone's bed. "They need to repeat a test."

Antimone groaned. "Not more blood."

"Not this time." The faintest glimmer of a smile. "Just a cheek swab. Open your mouth, please."

"What if I don't?"

"We sedate you and take it anyway," the woman said, her face returning to its original disdainfulness.

Antimone reluctantly opened her mouth and allowed the woman to run the tip of the white plastic rod across the inner surface of her cheek. The medic removed the stopper from a transparent tube, dropped the sample inside, then resealed it.

Seconds later she had departed, leaving the doors swinging in her wake.

26

Thursday 6th January 2033

Jason took the stairs two at a time. He rarely came to his mother's place of work, but Julian Stefano, the little toad, had called and said his mother urgently wanted to see him. He could have taken the lift to the second floor, but after the Christmas and New Year break, he decided he could use the exercise. Her personal assistant wouldn't say what it was about, just that his mother needed to speak to him face-to-face. A car had been sent to pick him up and dropped him off outside the front entrance.

He strode along the plushly furnished corridor, past the original oil paintings hanging on the wall, his feet swishing against the deep pile carpet. The place seemed quiet, but it was a quarter to one, so people were probably still on their lunch breaks. He reached the door bearing his mother's name and thought about knocking. He decided against it. His mother's secretary occupied the outer office and would let her know he had arrived.

He pushed the door open and stuck his head in the gap. The secretary's desk was empty. Presumably, she was on her break. The inner office door was partially ajar, and he detected the sound of muffled voices. He crossed the floor, the heavy carpet masking the approach of his footsteps. He raised his hand to knock but halted as he recognised the familiar voice of his mother.

"Where is the little bastard, Julian?"

"He should be here by now. Do you want me to find out if the car's here yet, Mrs Baxter?"

Jason took a step back. His face flushed, and his ears burned. *Was he the subject of the conversation?*

"Yes, and if the little prick has arrived, get Grolby to locate him and bring him up here."

A rapid sequence of beeps signalled the start of a telephone call.

"Yes Anders, it's Julian. Check whether Mrs Baxter's son is here, and if he is, please escort him up."

So, they were talking about him.

Several seconds passed while Stefano listened to the Head of Security.

"What? You've tracked him down? Excellent news. Where is he?"

Jason's heart sank. *They knew he was here.*

More silence.

"I don't know Bedford that well. What, near the railway station?"

They were obviously discussing somebody else, but who?

"Okay. Don't do anything for now. I'll discuss it with Mrs Baxter and get back to you. And like I said, bring the boy up here when you find him. Bye."

"What was that about?" his mother said.

"Grolby's managed to track Floyd down. He's hiding out in a derelict building in Bedford. What do you want to do about it?"

"Good question. Well, we know he's not the rapist, but he'd still make an excellent scapegoat. I assume the police don't know his whereabouts yet?"

"No. We could just make an anonymous call and tip them off."

"Hmm. I want to think this through. I'll talk to my son first, then let you know."

"Do you want me to go and look for him, Mrs Baxter?"

"Go on then, Julian. He must be here by now."

Jason thought about slipping away, but part of him wanted to find out what this was all about. In any case, Anders Grolby would know by now that he had arrived and would be looking for him. He ran back to the door, pulled it open, then spun around as if he had just come in.

Stefano appeared shocked to see him there. "Your mother's waiting for you."

Jason strode towards his mother's inner office, aware of the man's gaze on his back. He didn't bother to knock and entered, shutting the door behind him.

His mother looked up sharply. "Jason, about time."

When he showed no sign of taking a seat, his mother stood up. "Sit," she said, pointing at the chair.

Jason reluctantly settled into the visitor's chair. "What's this about, Mum?"

Rosalind paused, gathering her thoughts. She remained standing and leant forwards, her hands resting on the surface of the desk. "Do you know how much this company is worth, Jason? The nearest billion will do."

"I don't know. Four, five billion?"

"Close enough. And what do you think would happen if it became known that the CEO's son was a rapist?"

Jason's mouth opened, but no sound came out.

His mother's face flushed apart from two white patches on her cheeks. "After everything I've given you," she screeched, "what the blazes do you think you're doing raping that girl?"

"I… I," stammered Jason.

"What? Did you think the police would just forget about it when the baby was born? How could you be so bloody stupid?"

"But…"

"She was in a wheelchair, for Christ's sake. What the hell were you thinking?"

"But I…"

"Jesus. I can't believe you would do this to me."

"But I didn't."

"Don't lie to me. You've done enough damage as it is. I have a good mind to turn you in myself and see you rot in prison for the next fifteen or twenty years."

"Mum, I didn't do it."

"DO-NOT-LIE-TO-ME. There's no doubt. I double checked the results. You're definitely the father of that child."

"But there's a warrant out for Daniel Floyd."

"They're incompetent tossers. I just hope they don't study the baby's blood samples too carefully."

"Seriously Mum. If I did it, I don't remember anything about it."

Rosalind's glare pinned him like a butterfly to a board. "How can you not remember raping a girl?"

"Somebody spiked the drink. I woke up on the sofa an hour later. I swear to you, I know nothing about it."

"If you're lying to me, I'll drag you down to the police station myself."

"Honestly, Mum. You must know I'm not like that."

"I don't know a thing about you anymore." Rosalind finally sat down. "What a bloody mess."

"So, the baby's been born? Antimone's dead?"

"Yes."

"Shit."

Jason hung his head. Several moments of silence passed while they each considered the implications of what they had learned. "I'll turn myself in," he said.

"You'll do no such thing."

"But you just said I'm definitely the father."

"You are, but that doesn't necessarily mean you're to blame."

"I don't understand."

"Think about it. That bastard, Daniel Floyd, has been plotting his revenge for years from that prison cell. What better way of discrediting me than by making my son look like a rapist?"

"But I don't see how he could have done it. How could a stranger wander through a party without anybody noticing him?"

"I don't know. But he was definitely in the house."

Jason took a sharp intake of breath. "Unless…" He ran the theory through his head. The more he thought about it, the more plausible it became. "I think I know who might be behind this."

He explained his suspicions to his mother.

When he had finished, she stared out of the window, deep in her own thoughts. "I suppose it's possible, but we have to keep this between us until we have proof."

Rosalind turned back to Jason. "I need you to go downstairs and get some tests done."

"I don't understand. What tests?"

"Just do as I say, Jason. Go to the Medical Diagnostics department and wait there. Somebody will come and get you."

Jason stood up to leave.

Rosalind waited until he had left the room, then picked up the phone. She explained what she had learned. "I think he's telling the truth. He was drugged when it happened. He's on his way down to Medical Diagnostics. I want full blood, DNA, body scan—in fact, the same as the girl and the child. Maybe there's something there to explain how she survived, and we need all the facts. He doesn't know they're alive, so keep it that way."

"Oh, one more thing, Nigel. There's something else I want to talk to you about. Come up to my office once the tests are underway."

27

Thursday 6th January 2033

Nigel Perrin paced in front of the desk. Every few seconds he glanced at his watch. In his hand, he held a ballpoint pen, which he clicked in and out several times a second.

Rosalind Baxter stared at the column of figures but found it impossible to concentrate. "For Christ's sake, Nigel, sit down. And stop that damned clicking. You're driving me nuts. He'll be here in a minute."

Perrin returned the pen to his jacket pocket and lowered himself onto the leather-bound chair. He leant forwards and tapped his hands on his knees. Rosalind sighed. The tapping was almost as distracting as the clicking and the pacing.

"Oh, sorry," he said. Rising to his feet again, he crossed to the window. His eyes roamed the barren flowerbeds, slashes of black against a background of green. He put his face against the glass, straining to get a glimpse of the path leading to the entrance, but the angle was against him.

A knock at the door broke the silence.

"Come," Rosalind said.

Perrin spun around expectantly but seemed to deflate when Julian Stefano's bespectacled head appeared in the gap.

"Do you have a moment, Mrs Baxter?" He held up some pieces of paper. "I just need some signatures."

Rosalind beckoned him in and snatched up a pen. "What are these for?"

"Letters of condolence," he replied. "The first one's for the Lessing family."

Rosalind signed the letter without bothering to read the content.

"This one's for Nick Jenkins, the guy from the mortuary. He and his wife were killed two days ago when an out-of-control lorry ran into the back of them. A terrible shame. The letter's to his parents."

Rosalind scrawled an illegible mark above her printed name. "Most unfortunate," she said, without a hint of irony. "Is there another one?"

"Um, no. Were you expecting something else to sign?"

"No, that's okay, thanks, Julian. Is there anything else?"

"No, Mrs Baxter. Let me know if you need me for anything."

The slightly built man left the room, closing the door behind him.

"I know you like him, but he gives me the creeps," Perrin said, turning back from the window.

"I don't *like* him," Rosalind replied, "but he is very efficient. I know what you mean, though." A thin smile crossed her lips. "He is a bit creepy."

Perrin returned his attention to the glowering winter sky, lost in his thoughts.

A second knock at the door, this one more tentative.

"Where's my bloody secretary?" Rosalind muttered. "Come," she said in a louder voice.

Max Perrin shuffled into the room, his face a mask of trepidation. He seemed shocked to see his father glaring at him from beside the floor to ceiling glass.

"You asked to see me?" Gone was the cocky confidence.

"The Lessing girl," Rosalind said.

The colour drained from Max's face.

"You didn't have anything to do with her getting pregnant, did you?"

The boy glanced towards his father. The older man frowned and provided no offer of support. Max turned back to Rosalind and swallowed hard. "Er…" He remained mute, acutely aware of the two pairs of eyes boring into him.

"For God's sake, it's a simple question," Perrin senior yelled, although the boy's delay was all the answer he needed.

"Um… I…"

"Tell us what happened, Max," Rosalind said.

"I didn't mean for her to get pregnant," he gabbled. "She deliberately tripped me. I was injured for weeks. I was just trying to get even."

"Go on," his father said in a menacingly low voice. "What did you do?"

"You'd talked about those drugs that make you, like, do things that other people say. I was in your office, and I saw this sort of little bottle. I looked it up on the Internet and realised it was some of that stuff."

"I've told you before, Nigel, dangerous drugs like those need to be kept locked up," Rosalind said.

"Go on, Max," his father said, ignoring the admonition.

"I put it in my pocket and took it home. It was a few days before Jason's birthday. At the party, I poured it into the fruit punch just before he picked it up. I didn't expect it to do anything."

"So, what happened?"

"Well, I followed him back to the group of them sitting on the sofa. They all seemed, like, spaced out. I didn't know whether it was the drug so I told one of the boys to kiss the other, and he just, like, did it, snogged him right on the lips."

"And…"

"So, I told her to follow me to the bedroom, the one on the ground floor, and she pushes herself along behind me. I told her to take her top off, and she does it, just like that. Then I said to take everything off, but she couldn't do it in the wheelchair, so I put her on the bed. Next thing I know, she's lying there naked. I took some pictures."

"Where are they?" Rosalind snapped.

"They're still on my phone," Max replied.

"Did you show them to anyone?"

The boy shook his head.

"Nigel, when we finish in here, get Grolby to delete them permanently." She turned back to Max. "What did you do then?"

"Um..."

"You didn't..." his father began.

Max lowered his head.

"You raped her?"

He nodded.

"Jesus Christ," Perrin senior bellowed. "What the hell were you thinking? I raised you better than that."

"His brain wasn't doing the thinking," Rosalind said drily. "Did you wear protection?"

"What do you mean, like a condom? Yeah."

"So, let me guess. After that, you went back to the group and got Jason to have sex with her too?"

"Yes."

"What did you tell him?"

"I dunno. I think I just told him to shag her, or something like that."

"What, while you watched?"

"Yes."

"I don't fricking believe this," his father said.

"But he didn't have a condom?" Rosalind asked.

Max shook his head. "I didn't think she'd get pregnant, what with her being in a wheelchair and all that."

"So afterwards, you tell them to get dressed and forget everything that's happened?"

"Yeah. Jason went back first. It took her a bit longer to put her clothes back on, and then I had to put her back in the wheelchair. I waited until they'd gone, then waited a few minutes and followed them back into the room. When they woke up, I pretended I'd been affected too."

"Unbelievable," his father muttered.

"Well, that explains a lot," Rosalind said.

Several seconds of silence passed.

"So, what happens now?" Max asked.

"You go down to Medical Diagnostics and get some tests done while your father and I discuss what to do with you."

"Medical Diagnostics? I don't understand."

"Just do as you're bloody told," Perrin senior bellowed.

"Okay, I'm going."

"We haven't finished talking about this. Now get the hell out of here."

"What about my phone? You said about deleting the photos."

"Give it to me now."

"It's biometrically locked, though."

"We know where to find you if we can't unlock it."

After his son had departed, Perrin retrieved his own phone from his shirt pocket. He made a couple of calls, then turned back to Rosalind. "I'm really sorry about all this. I had no idea. I remember the vial going missing from my office. I thought Grolby had taken it."

"Hmm. Your son does seem to have a problem understanding the concept of proportionate response. Well on the bright side, if none of this had happened, we would've missed this opportunity."

Perrin removed the pen from his pocket and began clicking the tip in and out again. "So, what do we do now?" he asked.

28

Thursday 6th January 2033

Jason emerged from the MRI scanner changing room, still trying to come to terms with what he had learned that day. Somehow, he had been manipulated into raping Antimone and making her pregnant. Now both mother and child were dead. Maybe Antimone had subconsciously identified him as the rapist, and that's why she had pushed him away. A heavy dread enveloped him. Even though he knew he was a victim too, a deep sense of guilt pressed down on him. Whether intentional or not, his actions had caused Antimone's death.

Surely the police would eventually identify him as the child's father. But why were they still chasing after Daniel Floyd? It didn't make any sense unless they really were as incompetent as his mother had suggested. There had been one obvious suspect, and they seemed to have latched onto him without considering the alternatives. As far as he could remember, the police had never requested a DNA sample from him. How would he be able to prove his innocence if they ever did test him? Any evidence was long since gone.

If his hunch was correct, all of this stemmed from the incident at the track. He found it hard to believe that Max Perrin would go to such lengths just to get even for what was obviously an accident. The guy was a bully and would have interpreted Antimone's actions as a direct challenge to his perceived status. But to rape and effectively murder her? Maybe he was wrong after all, and Floyd was somehow behind it.

As Jason passed an open doorway, a flashing red light at floor level caught his attention. He retraced a couple of steps and stared down. A man sat with legs extended, his face and body obscured by the angle of the walls. On the man's feet was a pair of blue trainers with a familiar illuminated logo. If they were originals, they were hugely expensive, and there was only one person he knew who could afford such an item. Jason read the nameplate above the door: 'Medical Diagnostics—blood tests.' Less than an hour ago he himself had waited in this same room to have a blood sample taken.

He stuck his head around the door and confirmed the person's identity. That could mean only one thing. His suspicions had been correct. The likelihood of Max Perrin undergoing the same test on the same day by coincidence was tiny. Jason felt his ears burning, and his breathing quickened. With no thought as to what he was going to do, he strode through the doorway and stood in front of the seated boy.

Max raised his eyes and a flash of fear crossed his face. In that moment, Jason knew with certainty that Max was responsible for administering the drug and everything that followed. He reached forwards and grabbed his surprised classmate by the lapels of his designer jacket. He hauled him to his feet and shoved him backwards.

Max crashed into the wall. The chair he had been sitting on skittered across the floor.

"You bastard," Jason growled. He shot out his hand and dragged the other boy upright. His fist drove into Max's stomach. Max doubled over, gasping for breath.

Jason seethed with pent-up rage and frustration. "You're a fricking murderer."

Another blow slammed into Max's face. Two more followed in quick succession as Max attempted in vain to fend off his attacker.

Jason was unaware of the shocked expressions of the other patients or the running feet behind him. He launched a vicious kick that connected with Max's midriff, but before he could strike again, strong arms wrapped around him and hauled him away.

"Call security," a voice from behind shouted as Jason struggled to free himself.

"Alright, alright, I'm stopping." Jason allowed his muscles to relax and sensed a corresponding loosening of the grip on his arms. Without hesitation, he once again hurled himself at the other boy. His foot smashed into Max's nose with a satisfying crunch of cartilage.

This time, the two men who had been caught by surprise wrestled him to the ground. Seconds later they wrenched his arms behind his back and bound them together with a plastic restraint.

A tall man in a brown uniform stood over Jason.

"I'll take him to the security office. You better sort the other one out."

29

Friday 7th January 2033

Antimone inspected her new surroundings—monotonous white walls, a cream-coloured floor and no pictures or decorations of any kind. The only window in the small room was a small rectangle at the top of the door leading onto the corridor. Another door led into a cramped bathroom containing a toilet, sink, and shower. A white plastic chair with metal legs occupied the shower stall. The facilities were a definite improvement on the emergency ward where she had to be helped with even the most basic bodily functions.

Earlier that morning, an orderly had turned up with a battered wheelchair and despite her protests, had insisted on pushing her to her new quarters. They had passed along a featureless corridor with sequentially numbered doors, all of them starting with a two. The wheelchair was a clunky, old model, nothing like the lightweight one she had arrived at the hospital in, but at least she had regained her mobility.

They had even returned her ear implants and music player to her. It was the loud song booming in her ears that prevented her from hearing the door open. The first she knew about it was when a nurse entered her field of view carrying a tightly wrapped bundle. Antimone stopped the thrashing beat and focused all her attention on the object in the nurse's arms.

"Is that…"

"Yes, Antimone, it's your baby."

Antimone reached out to accept her son. Clasping him to her chest, she stared down at his tiny face. He stirred slightly, one eyelid opening a fraction then shutting again. He pursed his lips before settling back into an expression of contentment. *I never thought I'd meet him. He's perfect.*

She glanced up at the nurse, tears of gratitude in her eyes. "Thank you."

"I'll leave him here for a couple of hours. I've brought this in case he needs feeding." The nurse pointed to a pushbutton on the side of a plastic bottle filled with a white liquid. "Press that button there, and when the green light comes on, it's warm enough. Is there anything else you need?"

"No, I think I'll be alright."

"Well if there is anything, just shout or wave your arms. I'll be keeping an eye on you." She gestured towards a small black circle in the ceiling, obviously a camera and microphone. "I'll be back in a second with a cot."

The woman strode to the door and waved her access card at it. Antimone's eyes remained focused on her child, but out of the corner of her eye, just before the door closed, she picked up the outline of a uniformed man sitting in a chair in the corridor. Evidently, she was still a prisoner.

She studied the baby's face, the wispy, light brown hair, the button nose and the delicate eyelashes, imprinting the features on her mind. She raised a finger and gently touched an ear. The size of her hand seemed to dwarf the diminutive head. Her fingertips caressed the scalp, marvelling at the warmth and the softness. Strange to think this tiny, defenceless creature would turn into an adult one day. She watched in fascination as the child's fists clenched and unclenched. A sensation akin to déjà-vu swept over her, a sudden revelation that she was studying an extension of her own body as if she and her son were one entity.

The return of the nurse pushing a wheeled crib disturbed her moment of reflection. This time, the woman left the door open.

"If you need to put him down, slide the side down like this, place him inside then raise it again. Got that?"

Antimone nodded.

"Right I'll leave you to it."

The doorway revealed a better view of the guard. He wore a brown uniform and sat impassively, facing away from the entrance.

"What's he doing there?" Antimone asked.

The woman glanced behind her, then faced the girl once again. "Him? Oh, just a precaution."

"What? To keep me in or to keep somebody else out?"

The nurse smiled but didn't answer the question. "I'll see you in a couple of hours." She was halfway across the room when a muffled scream originated from the direction of the corridor. The baby tensed suddenly, flinging both arms out sideways.

The woman quickened her step and closed the door.

Antimone glanced down to see a pair of unfocused eyes staring upwards, the pale blue irises contrasting against the black dots of the pupils.

Seconds later, the baby's mouth opened, and a high-pitched wailing sound erupted.

30

Nigel Perrin stood outside the girl's room, peering through the small window. "Have the contractions started?" he asked.

The midwife took her turn at the glass. "No, I don't think so. She's just hysterical. Since the operation, we've had to keep her restrained. Even though she has no use of her legs, she pushed herself off the bed a couple of times. We had to tie her down for her own safety."

"So, you've no idea what started this latest episode?"

The woman paused for a second. "I think it's just a culmination of things—being stuck in the same room for nine months, losing her mobility, being heavily pregnant. I think the kindest thing to do would be to do the C-section now. The baby's about due in any case. You don't honestly think severing the spinal cord is the answer, do you?"

"We won't know for sure until she gives birth—but no, I don't. If it was that simple, hundreds would've survived. As you know, there've been no verified accounts of a woman living through childbirth for over fifteen years."

"Still, it seems cruel abducting these women and making them pregnant."

Perrin turned sharply to the midwife. "You're not getting cold feet are you, Rose? We only take subjects with a low life expectancy in the first place, drug addicts and prostitutes. Think of all the women leading constructive lives and contributing to society who die in childbirth. The ones we take are just throwing their lives away. If we want to find a cure, we have to do this sort of work. If somebody doesn't come up with a solution and quickly, the whole of the human race is finished. At least this way, they're being productive."

"Yes, you're right, Dr Perrin. I just wish it wasn't necessary. So, what're we going to do about her?"

"I agree with your suggestion, Rose. I'll sedate her now. While I'm doing that, can you organise a surgeon to do the caesarean?"

The doctor opened the door and entered the room. The woman strapped to the bed craned her neck to identify the intruder. "Are you going to untie me, you bastard?"

"No. I'm sorry, but it's time."

She struggled against her bonds, pulling first one way then the other, her breath coming in frantic gasps. "No, no, no. Leave me alone."

Her eyes followed the doctor as he moved to the head of the bed. "No-no-no," the syllables blending into each other.

As he approached, she opened her mouth, filled her lungs and screamed. The cords in her neck stretched taut like ropes. Her wide-eyed gaze tracked him as he pulled out the injection gun. A deep intake of breath. Another shriek. The short hiss of the instrument. A final "No," almost a whisper, then silence.

The tension vanished from the woman's muscles. Her body seemed to sag back on itself.

"Sleep well," the doctor muttered.

***

Nigel Perrin coughed as the stench of the anti-bacterial spray filled his nostrils. It was like standing in a thin, drizzly, chemical rain.

John Martin drew the electronic blade of the cauterising scalpel towards him. "Spread the incision." He raised his eyes, frowning. "I said spread the incision."

"I'm sorry," Perrin said from the opposite side of the operating table. "It's a while since I've assisted during surgery. Twenty years at least, I reckon."

"Use that instrument to pull the wound apart so I can get to the uterus," the surgeon snapped.

"Oh, right." Perrin fumbled with the metal instrument.

"No, the other way," Martin said in mounting frustration.

The doctor adjusted his grip and used the tool to separate the edges of the cut.

"Good. Keep it like that."

Another smooth stroke and the wall of the woman's uterus parted.

"Okay, we're in."

Martin reached inside the deep gash in the patient's belly and eased the baby's head out. Using his other hand, he grasped the body and guided it into the harsh light of the operating theatre. The midwife stepped forwards to accept the child, and within seconds the boy was exercising his lungs in a reedy wail. She severed the umbilical cord, clamped it and placed the infant in an incubator.

"I'll sew her up," the surgeon said. "If there's any chance she might survive, we better do a good job."

Perrin ignored the implied insult, although he was happy to allow Martin to complete the work. "Check her pupillary response," he said to the midwife.

The woman raised an eyelid and shone a bright handheld torch at the exposed pupil. "Very little dilation," she reported.

The anaesthetist, a man in his early thirties, peered closely at the readouts of his instruments. "Heart rate erratic," he called. "She's crashing... That's it, she's flat-lined."

The surgeon glanced up from his work. "It doesn't look like this one's going to survive Dr Perrin. Do you want me to attempt resuscitation?"

"No, don't bother. It was always a long shot." Perrin focused on the anaesthetist. "But I need you to stay with her for at least an hour, just in case."

The man groaned. "Whatever you say, Dr Perrin."

"And check her core temperature before you record the time of death, just to be absolutely sure."

The room fell silent.

"Right, I've finished here," the surgeon said.
Perrin inspected the neat row of stitches. "Thanks, John."
He turned back to the anaesthetist.
"Just remember, we thought the girl who survived was dead as well."

31

Friday 7th January 2033

Karen Atkins sat impatiently in the reception area at Ilithyia Biotechnology, studying the contents of the beige folder. Glancing at her watch, she noted that she had already been waiting for twenty minutes, and there was still no sign of the Chief Scientist, Nigel Perrin. She was about to approach the receptionist for the second time when a bald man wearing a white lab coat burst through a set of doors marked private. He halted and surveyed the room before his gaze alighted on Kat. He navigated the rows of chairs and stuck out a hand.

She rose to her feet. "Are you the Chief Scientist?"

"Yes, I'm Dr Perrin. What can I do for you, Ms…?"

"Atkins, Karen Atkins, but everybody calls me Kat. I'm an Inspector at the Maternity Crimes Unit. Is there somewhere we could talk in private?"

"What's this about?"

"Oh, I'm just checking up on some results from a woman and her baby who died here recently, an Antimone Lessing."

"Do you know how long this will take? Only we're very busy at the moment."

"Well, that depends to a certain extent on the answers to my questions but probably no more than a few minutes."

"Right. Well, follow me."

The man retraced his footsteps and upon reaching the door held up a card to the electronic reader. A short beep and the red light turned to green. He pushed through the door, holding it open for her. "Just down here."

He marched down the corridor, Kat following two paces behind and struggling to keep up. He entered a room on the left, the lights automatically ramping up in brightness as he crossed to a chair facing the doorway. He gestured to a seat on the opposite side of the polished oak table, then sat down.

"Nice facilities you have here," Kat said, studying the framed prints and expensive looking furniture.

The doctor removed a ballpoint pen from his pocket and began clicking the tip in and out. "Yes, well you've got to set a good first impression in business. So, what can I do for you?"

"Could you start by telling me a little about the work you do here?"

"Like I said earlier, I'm very busy just at the moment so I'll keep it brief. We have a research centre and a private hospital at this site. Most of what we do is targeted at creating drugs to treat the Orestes virus, and the majority of our patients are pregnant. I'm sure you're aware that we developed a cure a few years ago, but then the virus mutated, making it ineffective."

"So, how's the research going? Are you close to finding another cure?"

The doctor returned the pen to his jacket pocket and stared across the table. "I can refer you to our PR department if you need background information on the company, but you'll find pretty much all of it on our website."

"Okay, maybe I'll take a look when I get back to my office. So, do you run experiments on pregnant women?"

Perrin frowned. "The patients who come here do so of their own accord. We make no promises, but we do offer them experimental treatments that aren't available elsewhere. As you know, getting pregnant these days is a death sentence if it isn't terminated within the first four weeks. We're doing our best to make sure all that changes in the future. Anyway, as I just said, you can download all this information. You mentioned a specific patient. What did you want to know about her?"

"Yes, Antimone Lessing and her son Paul. I understand you treated them here."

"We treat thousands of patients a year. I certainly don't remember them all."

"Well, this girl was sixteen years old and in a wheelchair. The reason my department became involved was because she claimed she'd been raped."

Perrin scratched his head. "Yes, I do remember her. As I recall, the baby died of a bacterial infection."

"Yes, very sad. I met the girl and her parents several times, a nice family." Kat withdrew a couple of pieces of paper from the folder. "We requested that your company provide a blood sample from the child, mainly so we could identify the rapist."

"Was there a problem with the sample? I'm sorry, there's nothing much I can do about that. Both mother and child were cremated."

"So, you do remember them."

"Well… yes, as a matter of fact, I do."

Kat raised her eyes from the printed sheet. "There was an oddity. Our analysis shows no evidence of any infection. Don't you find that strange? From what I understand, the child died within twenty-four hours of being born."

"Do you mind if I look at that?" the doctor asked, extending a hand.

Kat passed the report over and studied him as his eyes ran down the page.

He handed the sheets of paper back and met her gaze. "It's not that unusual, really. New-born babies are at risk of all sorts of infections. The blood sample would've been taken soon after birth, so there's a good chance either the child hadn't yet been infected, or the bacteria levels were too low to detect."

"But it doesn't reflect well on your hospital if he picked up the infection here, or you failed to spot that he was already infected."

The doctor's eyes narrowed. "We go to great lengths to prevent infections. For example, this company made a large investment in anti-bacterial mist systems in all our operating theatres two years ago. You wouldn't find that in the majority of National Health Service hospitals. You must know that a lot of these bugs have resistance to anti-bacterial drugs. Sometimes there's just nothing we can do."

"But still, to go from no evidence of infection to death within what, just over twelve hours, you've got to admit it's strange."

"Like I said, infections can take hold really quickly, particularly in babies where the immune system isn't fully developed."

"I asked our expert, and he said the same thing, except that he thought the timescale was extremely short."

"What can I say? He's right, but all cases are different."

Kat rose to her feet. "Okay, well thanks for clearing that up. I'll let you get back to your work."

Perrin shepherded her out of the room and back towards the main entrance.

"Thanks for your time," she said, shaking hands.

He watched until she had left the building, then withdrew his phone from his pocket. He dialled a number and waited. The ring tone repeated six times.

"Yes."

"Hello, Rosalind. I've just had a chat with the police about the blood samples we provided for the child. It seems they might not be quite so incompetent after all."

32

Friday 7th January 2033

Jason Baxter drew back the curtain and stared out of the window. The car headlights dazzled him, but a second or two later the curving drive returned to an inky blackness. As his eyes accustomed themselves to the dark, the vehicle's interior light came on, and he recognised the silhouette of his mother. He watched as she got out, reached in to grab an attaché case, then slammed the door behind her.

She hadn't returned home the previous two nights and had refused to accept his calls. His heart rate increased as he anticipated the forthcoming encounter. The key turned in the lock, and he picked up the lightweight virtual reality glasses, slipping them onto his face. The clicking of her high heels approached but didn't stop. He knew that the light beneath the door revealed his presence, but she had chosen not to talk to him. Not a good sign.

He heard the kitchen door open and the click of the light switch. For a moment he contemplated going out to greet her but thought better of it. He was still wearing the glasses when the footsteps returned along the hall, and the door opened. His mother stepped into the room clutching a glass of red wine.

"Hello, Jason."

"Hello, Mum."

Rosalind took a sip and stared at her son. "Have you eaten?"

"Yeah, I did a frozen pizza in the oven. What about you?"

"I'm going to make a salad—after I've had another of these." She lifted her glass. "You can't beat a Chateau Margaux. It's not a seventeen eighty-seven, but it's not bad. What are you doing?"

Jason removed the glasses. "Oh, you know, just watching a film." He tracked his mother's gaze to the headset, noted the absence of a green light and realised she had caught him in a lie. She drained her glass, turned on her heel and headed back through the open door without speaking. Jason fidgeted on the sofa, wondering whether he should follow her.

Several minutes later, she reappeared carrying a tray containing a plateful of salad and a half-empty wine glass. She crossed to an armchair, sat down and ate her meal, perching the tray on her knee.

Jason waited patiently until she had finished. "Everything okay at work?"

Rosalind nodded. "Really busy. Never a quiet moment. I should have called to let you know I wasn't coming home. I slept at the office the last two nights. Sorry about that."

Jason shrugged. There was nothing unusual about his mother staying at work overnight, but it was unlike her not to call. Rosalind rose, placed the tray holding the empty plate on the coffee table, then returned to her seat, clutching the glass to her chest. The silence built between them like an invisible barrier.

Jason leant forwards. If she wouldn't speak, he would. "So, you heard about the… um… incident at the hospital?"

His mother stared down as she swirled the contents of the glass, then raised her eyes. "I assume you're referring to the thing with Max. Yes. I can't say I blame you."

"What about Max?"

"He'll survive."

"That's not what I meant. What's going to happen to him?"

"Nothing. Unfortunately, there's no evidence. If we go to the police, they'll discover you're the child's father and… well, like I said, there's no proof you were drugged."

"So, he's just going to get away with it?"

Rosalind didn't reply. She drained the glass, then stood up. "I'm going to get a refill."

Jason sat back on the sofa, his mind whirling. She knew about the assault, but why had they been testing Max? It must mean their parents believed that both boys had something to do with Antimone getting pregnant. What puzzled him was the reason for the tests. Why the interest in the blood and DNA samples and why the scan? Something else was going on that she wasn't telling him.

Rosalind returned to her chair with a full glass.

"So, what will happen about Daniel Floyd?" he asked.

His mother's eyes were slow to find him. He realised that she must have been drinking before she came home.

"He's a convicted murderer. If the police catch him, he's only getting what he deserves."

"So, you're not going to let them know they're after the wrong man?"

Rosalind glanced up sharply, spilling a drop of wine on her dark skirt. "No," she said, brushing the liquid off. "If I knew where he was, I'd tell them."

But you do know, Jason thought.

"I'm off to bed," his mother said, rising to her feet. More wine sloshed from the glass onto the carpet. "I'll see you in the morning."

"Are you working tomorrow?" he asked.

"I'm not planning to," she said, but both of them knew that meant very little.

"Good night, Mum."

"Good night, Jason."

33

Saturday 8th January 2033

Antimone stared at the face reflected back in the mirror. The previous evening a technician had unscrewed the fixture from the wall and lowered it to the correct height for somebody in a wheelchair. Beneath each grey-blue eye was a crescent-shaped dark shadow. She hadn't slept well since she had arrived. In the darkness, a sense of claustrophobia built up inside, the featureless white walls seeming to close in on her. Her breathing became tight and the thudding of her heart echoed in her ears. Only when she turned on the lights did the panic subside. During the last two nights she had slept with them on but had woken up every few hours, disturbed by the unfamiliar illumination cast by the ceiling panels.

Her gaze moved down her face. The faint tendrils of broken blood vessels adorned the top of each cheekbone, the after-effects of the contractions. A prominent blackhead occupied a position just above her left nostril. She applied her fingernails and forced out the small black dot. Instinctively she reached out a hand to grab the antiseptic face cleanser she always kept by the sink at home, only to find it wasn't there. Old-fashioned soap would have to do on this occasion. Another item to ask for when the nurse came.

She washed and dried her face. Leaning forwards, she ran a finger over her cracked lips. The atmosphere down here was warm and dry. Every morning she woke up with a raging thirst. She added lip balm to her mental wish list.

Her dark hair was tied back in a ponytail. She brushed a stray strand behind her ear, her eyes drawn to a small vein pulsating at her temple. She pressed it in then released it, studying the way it fluttered briefly before resuming the rhythmic pulsing. Her heart beating, something she hadn't expected to be the case a few short days ago. In the months before the birth, she had often wondered what it would be like to be dead. No sense of feeling, no thoughts, just like being asleep except with no prospect of ever waking up. The hardest thing to come to terms with was the idea of the world carrying on without her. In a sudden epiphany, she understood the urge to reproduce and have children. It was about part of a person continuing after they died. Without that, death would be a permanent ending.

The beep of the electronic lock disturbed her moment of reflection. She swivelled the chair around and headed into the main room. A nurse shuffled in carrying a tray containing Antimone's breakfast, a breezy smile on her face.

"How are we today?"

She had only uttered four words, but already she had annoyed Antimone.

"*I'm* okay," Antimone replied, glancing behind her to emphasise the point. "I don't see anybody else here, though."

"Somebody's in a bad mood this morning, aren't they? Didn't you sleep well?"

Antimone wanted to snatch the tray out of this smug woman's hands and fling it against the wall, but the smell of bacon and hot coffee was making her hungry. "I think you might be bad tempered too if you were stuck in one room, twenty-four hours a day with no sunlight."

"These lights provide the same spectrum as the sun," said the nurse, setting the tray down on the bed.

"You don't get it, do you? It's driving me mad being cooped up in here."

"But you do get to see your baby, don't you?"

"Yeah, but it's boring as hell the rest of the time."

"I wish I had the time to sit around and do nothing. You've got your music and reading material. What else would you be doing?"

"Jesus Christ," Antimone muttered, shaking her head. "You really think it's okay to keep somebody locked up in a tiny room as long as you bring them food and books and let them listen to music?"

"Well, um…"

"You must lead a really boring life if you think this is fun."

The nurse flushed and folded her arms. "I'm doing my best to help you, but if you'd rather I didn't."

Antimone's lips twitched with a slight smile. "I appreciate what you've done for me, but I'd just prefer to be elsewhere."

The nurse seemed mollified. "By the way, my name's Rose. Is there anything else I can get you?"

"Um… Thanks, Rose. Actually, is there any chance you could get some face cleanser and maybe some lip balm?"

"I'll see what I can do. Any chemicals, medicines or things like that, I need to get Dr Perrin to sign off first."

Antimone shrugged. She glanced towards the open door, spotting the legs of the guard seated in the corridor. "Has he been there all night?" she asked.

The nurse looked perplexed for a second, then turned around to see what Antimone was looking at. "Oh, him. Yes, I think so, or at least one of his friends."

"You never answered me last time. Why is he there?"

The nurse hesitated. "You'd have to ask Dr Perrin or Mrs Baxter. They don't tell me that sort of thing. That reminds me. Mrs Baxter said she'd be popping in to see you later."

"Oh, right."

"Well, I best be off. I'll bring Paul round in half an hour or so. He's a pretty baby. I'm sure he'll break a few hearts when he's older."

"If he ever gets out of here," Antimone muttered.

34

Saturday 8th January 2033

Jason yawned and examined the dial of his alarm clock. Nine thirty. He flung the sheets back and slipped his feet into a pair of brown moccasin slippers. There was a silence about the house that suggested he had it to himself. His mother had said she was not planning to go to work today, but that meant nothing. Over the past fortnight, she had seemed more distant, spending less time than usual in the house, almost as if she was avoiding him. He still couldn't get the overheard conversation out of his head. What had she called him? A little bastard and a prick.

She was certainly not the most affectionate of people. As a young child, she had kept him at arm's length, relying on nannies and au pairs to look after him. Apart from a perfunctory kiss at bedtime, she had demonstrated very little warmth towards him. He could still recall his abiding childhood wish to be hugged by her, but it rarely, if ever, happened. When he turned thirteen, she explained that she had adopted him. She was reticent in providing details about his birth-mother. She told him his father had succumbed to cancer, leaving his pregnant mother to fend for herself. When his mother died in childbirth, Rosalind had agreed to adopt Jason. Over the years, Jason had pressed her to describe his biological mother, but she always replied that she hadn't known the woman well. She had even refused to let him know her name, saying she would tell him when he was older.

Over the last year or two, he felt they were becoming closer. He sensed that he still came second after the company, but at least they had shared some interesting conversations. She had even discussed some key business decisions with him and seemed pleased when he offered his opinion. During the past week, the longest discourse they had exchanged was in her office. By the time he woke up, she had long since departed for work. On the occasions when she had returned home at night, such as the previous evening, it was usually late and mostly, she was uncommunicative.

Jason wondered whether she still blamed him for getting Antimone pregnant. For the past two nights he had lain awake until the early hours, worrying about the future. It was clear that someone had drugged him, but where was the evidence? The only person who truly knew what had happened was Max, and he wasn't about to confess. The big question was what to do about it. He could go to the police and tell them the whole story, but Max would only deny it. And if his mother wasn't speaking to him now, he could only guess at what her reaction would be if he handed himself in.

One thing was clear, though: she intended to let Daniel Floyd take the blame. The man had certainly been in the house and had at the very least been trespassing. Why was he there? Apparently, nothing had been stolen, but he didn't trust his mother to be truthful if something had gone missing. On top of that, he was a convicted murderer, so did it matter if he took the rap for another death? The more he thought about it, the more it gnawed at his conscience. It was hard to feel sympathy for somebody who had slaughtered his own wife, but the man was innocent of Antimone's rape. But what could Jason do about it?

As he rolled that question around in his head, probing it like a sore tooth, an idea came to him. He didn't know whether his mother had revealed Floyd's location to the police yet, but if she hadn't, he could warn the man to expect a visit. It wasn't a complete solution, but it would at least give Floyd a fighting chance of evading capture and help to salve his feeling of guilt.

But how to contact Floyd? Ideally, he wanted to remain anonymous, but that was impractical. He knew the approximate location, a derelict building close to the railway station in Bedford. He could travel there by train, find Floyd and alert him. How the man would react was anybody's guess, but he relegated that concern to the back of his mind. Maybe he could get some answers of his own, perhaps find out what Floyd was doing in the house and what he was searching for.

There was obviously some prior history with his mother, but she had always been reticent on the subject. He had read about Floyd's court case on the Internet and discovered that his mother and Floyd had studied the same course at Cambridge University. According to the report, they had even been boyfriend and girlfriend for a while. His mother never talked about that phase of her life and deflected any questions on the matter.

Jason padded along the hall to his mother's room. He pushed the door open and was greeted by a waft of expensive perfume. "Mum," he called, sticking his head in the gap. The curtains were drawn and the king-sized bed was made. Feeling like an intruder, he crossed the scarlet-coloured carpet to the en-suite bathroom. He rapped his knuckles on the solid wood and called her name again. No reply. He edged into the fully tiled wet-room. The scent of perfumed soap and shampoo assaulted his nostrils, but it was empty. He closed the doors behind him and retreated back to the hall.

He descended the stairs and was unsurprised to find the kitchen deserted. As expected, there was no sign of a note. He opened the dishwasher and inspected the contents: a plate flecked with toast crumbs, a coffee cup and a knife still smeared with butter. It seemed that his mother had eaten her customary breakfast and returned to work. For a moment he toyed with the idea of phoning the hospital to be sure but decided against it. After all, where else would she be?

He poured himself a bowl of cereal and sat at the island in the centre of the kitchen. What should he do? What would Antimone want him to do? The right thing was to hand himself in to the police and tell them the whole story, but he wasn't quite ready to take that step yet.

"Damn it," he said, dropping the spoon into the bowl. His mind decided, he hurried upstairs and got dressed.

35

Saturday 8th January 2033

Antimone glanced up as the door opened. Rosalind Baxter entered the room, wearing a matching pale blue jacket and skirt. Antimone switched off the music, her gaze following the woman as she strolled across the floor.

"Hello, Antimone. How are you feeling today?"

"Bored," Antimone muttered. "When are you going to let me out of here?"

"We still need to run some more tests, make sure you and the baby are okay."

"He's called Paul."

"Yes, I know. I have a question for you, Antimone. Do you know how many women have survived childbirth in the past fifteen years or so?"

"I'm guessing none."

"That's right. In all that time, not one single woman has given birth and lived. Do you know how special that makes you?"

"Yeah, but I don't feel very special at the moment. Why are you keeping me a prisoner in here?"

Rosalind smiled, but it didn't reach her eyes. "You're not a prisoner. You're here so we can look after you."

"So why is there a guard outside my door?"

"This is a classified area. We need to make sure no unauthorised people are wandering around."

"Okay, but why is he sitting outside *my* door?"

"It's just a convenient spot. He can see the whole corridor from there."

"Hmm." The tone of Antimone's voice indicated her scepticism. "So why can't I speak to my parents?"

"We've told them you're doing well, but we can't risk any possibility of infection."

"That doesn't mean I can't talk to them, though."

"I'm sure it's been explained to you. The work we do down here is very commercially sensitive. For that reason, we don't allow calls to outside lines. Mobile phone signals are also blocked. You'll be able to see them in a few more days."

Antimone folded her arms. "Well, that's a load of crap. Are you telling me you can't arrange a telephone call?"

Rosalind's expression hardened. "You should've checked the contract you and your parents signed. We agreed to give you the best care available, but in exchange you gave us exclusive rights to your genetic makeup. You also gave us permission to choose the treatment we felt most suitable for your condition. What we have decided upon is to keep you in total isolation."

"But I didn't expect to survive."

"We didn't expect you to survive either, but that doesn't change anything. It's our decision as to how we treat you."

"So how long is this going to last?"

"Until we're ready to discharge you, and we still have a huge amount to learn, so I'm not going to put a timescale on it."

Antimone frowned. "You're saying you can keep me here as long as you want?"

"Yes."

"But I have human rights. We studied that in Ethics at school. You can't just lock me up against my will."

Rosalind sighed. "Look, Antimone. Do you know how many women have died since this virus first started? Let me tell you. Across the globe, it's tens if not hundreds of millions. And amongst all those millions, you are unique. Do you have any idea how important you are?"

Antimone shrugged. Rosalind fixed her with her blue-grey eyes and continued. "Unless we find a solution in the next five or ten years, mankind is doomed. Already the birth rate has declined to something like a twentieth of what it once was. There aren't enough children being born to maintain the species. But *you* contain the answer. Somehow *you* survived. Think about the lives you can save. It's no exaggeration to say that you could be the person who saves the human race. Isn't that worth a few days of your time?"

"I still don't see why I can't talk to my parents."

"Look. We can do this the easy way or the hard way. At the moment we've provided a wheelchair, we allow you to see your son several times a day even though it's extra work for the nurses, you have music to listen to and books to read. Now imagine life stuck in this room with none of those things. Think what that would be like."

"So now you're threatening me?"

"No. I'm just saying how things could be. I hope you realise how important it is that we determine why you survived and agree to cooperate. For whatever reason, you've been given a remarkable gift. Don't you think it's right to share it with the rest of the planet?"

"Okay, I'll tell you what. Let me speak to my parents, and I'll let you do what you like without complaining or anything."

The two females stared at each other in silence.

"Well?" Antimone asked.

The ring of her mobile phone spared Rosalind from having to answer. She withdrew the device from a pocket inside her jacket and held it to her ear.

"Yes, Nigel. What is it? I'm a little busy at the moment."

She listened while the voice on the other end of the line spoke.

"You've what?"

Antimone heard the tinny voice say something else but could not distinguish the words.

"Excellent news. I'll be with you right away."

Rosalind clicked off the phone and put it away.

Antimone glared at her. "I thought you said mobile phones don't work down here."

"My phone is different," Rosalind said, turning around and heading for the door.

36

Saturday 8th January 2033

Jason stepped from the train onto the platform at Bedford station. A handful of people hurried towards the exit. He followed the general flow and waved his phone over the reader to open the barrier. A cold wind infiltrated his blue winter jacket as he descended the steps outside. He looked both ways, attempting to identify any buildings that gave the appearance of being derelict. A row of trees obscured his line of sight. The only structure of which he had an unobstructed view was a nine-storey block of flats. Faded text extended along the brickwork above the ground-floor windows, but the lettering was no longer decipherable. Whilst it seemed a little run-down, the curtains in the windows and the furniture on the balconies indicated that people still lived there.

He passed a taxi rank of autonomous vehicles as he crossed the car park. A residential road led straight ahead, but all the properties seemed to be in a good state of repair. He debated with himself whether to knock on one of the doors and ask if the resident knew of any abandoned properties in the immediate vicinity. Instead, he decided to investigate further before approaching the locals. Glancing to his right, he spotted a green and yellow sign, just over a hundred metres away and headed in that direction. As he drew closer, his eyes picked out the words, 'Service, Tyres and Batteries'. Maybe the owners would be able to give him some hints as to where to look.

The reception area ran parallel to the pavement, but when he pushed against the door, it was locked. Glancing down at the notice above the handle, he read that the business was closed on Saturdays.

"Damn," he muttered under his breath.

Ahead, the straight road ended in a roundabout. He strode along the pavement as the cold winter wind ruffled his hair. On his right, he passed another local business. A sign painted in a variety of pastel shades read 'Low-Cost Printing', but the lack of internal lighting indicated that it too was closed.

On the opposite side of the road, an elderly man traipsed along behind his dog. The man shuffled forwards, his face barely visible between a black woollen hat, a thick, slate-coloured scarf and the upturned collar of his coat. The dog, a small, brown animal with pointed ears, ranged ahead at the full extent of the lead, vigorously sniffing the wall of the adjoining property.

Jason waited for a gap in the traffic, then hurried across and approached the man. "Excuse me."

The dog gave a high-pitched growl, then sensing that the stranger was not a threat, lifted a leg and urinated before resuming its analysis of the wall. The man took a step backwards, dragging the dog away from a particularly interesting scent. "I'm sorry, I don't have any change."

"Right. I don't need change."

A pair of rheumy eyes inspected Jason. "Well, what do you want, young man?"

"Well… um… I was wondering if you know whether there are any derelict buildings near here."

The man scratched his left ear. "Derelict buildings?"

"Yeah."

"You're not one of those squatter types, are you?" the man asked, looking Jason up and down. "You don't look old enough."

"No. I'm trying to find a… friend."

"So, your friend's a squatter then?"

"Look, it's a long story. This friend of mine moved recently, but he didn't leave a forwarding address. I remember him saying that his new house was near a derelict building close to the railway station."

"No new houses here, you know."

"No, it wasn't a new house. It was an old house, just new for him."

"The railway station's over there," the man said, pointing.

"Yeah, I know. I just came from there."

"What's your friend called?"

"Um… Daniel. Why does that matter?"

"I don't know anybody called Daniel," the man replied.

Jason shook his head. "Never mind. Thanks for your help." He had taken a couple of steps when the man mumbled something from behind his back. Jason turned to face him. "I'm sorry, I didn't catch that."

"The old sorting office is derelict."

"Sorting office?"

"That's what I said. It must be what, five years ago, no… nearer ten I should think. They moved it all to Milton Keynes, been empty since then. No call for letters anymore. It's all this new email rubbish. Can't use a computer to save my life."

The dog approached Jason and sniffed his shoe. Jason bent down to stroke it but hastily removed his hand when it growled.

"Oh, don't mind Billie," the man said. "He's all bark and no bite. Thinks he's a Rottweiler."

"Um… okay. How would I get to the sorting office?"

The man pointed. "Just the other side of that road, but it's all locked up. I don't know where your friend might be living unless it's somewhere along here."

"Thanks," Jason said. "I'll try that."

"You must want to find him badly. Owes you money, does he?" The old man cackled, his laugh turning into a hacking cough. He raised a gloved hand and waved to Jason before resuming his shuffle along the road.

"Have fun and good luck," he called.

37

Saturday 8th January 2033

Rosalind strode down the brightly lit corridor, her heels clicking on the white linoleum floor. She reached a door labelled ‘Chief Scientist’ and turned the handle without knocking. Behind a large wooden desk sat Nigel Perrin. A frown creased his forehead, and his fingers clasped a pen that he clicked in and out in a rhythmic pattern. “Couldn’t you knock for once? You nearly give me a heart attack every time you do that.”

A smile twitched on Rosalind’s lips. “I’ve got to keep you on your toes, Nigel. So, what’s the big news?”

“Come and have a look at this.” He returned the pen to his pocket, jumped to his feet and rounded the desk. Grabbing one of the visitor chairs, he dragged it with him, placed it next to his own swivel chair and invited Rosalind to sit.

She crossed the room, her eyes sweeping over the framed certificates and photographs that lined the walls. She and Perrin featured on the majority of the images, smiling alongside a selection of politicians and celebrities. She had never understood the need to display the trappings of fame like this, an unspoken statement that the well-known personalities were somehow more important than the people who did the real work. It occurred to her that she could probably afford to buy most of these people ten times over. Unfortunately, the Public Relations people insisted that famous faces had to be present at the big occasions.

The doctor moved his seat to the side and angled the monitor to direct it towards the visitor’s chair. “Can you see that okay?” he asked as Rosalind sat down.

She nodded, her eyes drawn to the three-dimensional display. “What am I looking at?”

Perrin could barely contain his excitement. “You know we had to re-run one of the tests?”

“Yes. As I recall, a technician mixed up the samples, and you fired her.”

“Well, it seems that we sacked her unfairly.”

Rosalind turned her head sharply to the doctor. “That’s not going to be an issue is it?”

“No, no. She received a generous pay-off, and I gave her a good reference. She won’t be a problem.”

“Okay, you better explain then.”

Perrin turned his attention back to the screen. "Right. Well, as you know, we took blood samples and a buccal swab from the inside of her cheek. We ran both samples through the DNA analyser. So, this is the blood sample." He jabbed a finger and a three-dimensional graph floated a few centimetres in front of the monitor.

"So, what am I looking at?"

"There's nothing particularly special about this. But here…" He gestured to the display as if beckoning the data to come out. "Here we have the sample from the cheek cells."

The original graph reduced in height, and a second one appeared just below it.

Rosalind squinted and leant forwards. "Are these supposed to be the same? They look totally different. Are you sure they didn't mix up the samples again?"

The doctor grinned. "Not possible. I personally took another blood sample and cheek swab just to be absolutely sure. There's no mistake. They're both from the girl."

Rosalind frowned. "That doesn't make sense. How can one person have two different…? Oh, hang on. She's not a—what do you call it? You know, a —"

"Yes," Perrin interrupted. "She's a chimera, and what's even more interesting is that the DNA from the cheek cells is male."

"What? So, the blood cells have different DNA to the cheek cells?"

"We need to do more analysis, but here's what I think happened. When her mother got pregnant, two eggs were fertilised, making one male and one female foetus. As they developed, something went wrong, and somehow the two foetuses fused together. Basically, the female foetus absorbed the male one, but some of the male cells remained and were incorporated into the female."

"But what about rejection? Wouldn't the female's immune system attack the male's cells?"

"Apparently not. You've got to remember that they share the same parents, so they're likely to be genetically close in the first place. It also depends on when the merge took place. If it was early enough, the immune system wouldn't have had time to develop yet and would recognise both sets of cells as the body's own."

"So how rare is this?"

"I did some reading. There were a couple of well-reported cases twenty or thirty years ago. In one of them, a woman offered to donate a kidney to her sick son. When they did a compatibility match by taking a cheek swab, they told her she wasn't the mother. As you can imagine, that came as quite a shock. It had been a home birth, so there was no chance that the child had been mixed up with another at the hospital. They confirmed it by testing her other sons, none of whom matched the DNA taken from her cheek either. When they ran the blood, they found a different set of markers that were a match for all the sons."

"So, she was a chimera?"

"That's right."

"But how rare are they?"

"From what I've read, male-female chimeras are incredibly rare. It's difficult to know what proportion of the population are chimeras because they don't tend to display any overt sign of their condition. Apparently, it's quite common in fraternal twins when they share the same portion of the placenta. Each twin can incorporate the other's blood marrow cells, so they can even end up with two different blood types. If I had to hazard a guess, I'd say for the male-female variety, maybe one in eight hundred million or more."

Rosalind pulled an earlobe, deep in thought. "Okay, so let's say she's a chimera. How come she survived?"

"Well that's a different question, but it's got to be more than a coincidence. I'm guessing that something in the foreign cells prevented the virus' normal reaction to the changes that take place in the mother after childbirth."

"Could be. I don't need to tell you how important this is, Nigel. If we can work out what those cells are doing, we can create a cure."

"I know, I know," Perrin said, shifting on his seat. "I'm well aware of the implications. The first thing we'll have to do is identify the disposition of the different cell types. That's going to mean taking a lot of samples. It's going to be pretty uncomfortable for her."

Rosalind stared at the doctor. "And? What's one girl's discomfort compared to saving the human race?"

"Yeah, I know, but one of the nurses was saying that she's becoming less cooperative, wants to talk to her parents."

"Not a chance. If they find out she's alive, we won't be able to hold onto her. There'd be all sorts of awkward questions to answer. I spoke to her earlier today, threatened to remove access to her son and to withdraw things like the wheelchair and the music. I don't really care if she likes it or not. We're going to do what's necessary to develop this treatment."

"Of course, Rosalind. It's just easier if she cooperates."

"Oh, I think she will. By the way, how are we going to discover whether the boy had anything to do with her survival?"

The doctor scratched his bald head. "Good question. Maybe we make her pregnant again, this time by a different father."

"Hmm. I don't like the idea of waiting another nine months."

"We could always deliver the child early, say at six months. In fact, if you don't care about it surviving, any time after about six weeks would be fine to test the hypothesis."

"Good point, Nigel. Let's wait until we know more, but that's not a bad idea."

"We're going to require more test subjects. I better tell Grolby to find some."

"Yes, do that. One other thing, Nigel," Rosalind said. "I want you to keep all of this to yourself. Make sure that all samples are destroyed. I don't want any of the workforce knowing what's going on."

"Um… okay, but that's going to slow things down a bit. All the ones who work down here are on the highest security clearance. Don't you trust them?"

"Look, Nigel, it's all about degrees of trust. Would you leave ten or a hundred billion pounds lying around, just waiting for somebody to walk off with it? If one of our researchers were to learn about a cure, the temptation might be too great, especially given what it would be worth. Grolby's got the security pretty tight around here, but this takes it to a whole new level. I'd rather delay things if it means that we reduce the risk of losing out to a competitor. You can use other staff to help you, just ensure they don't get too much of the overall picture."

"Fair enough," Perrin replied. "I'll get on it right away. Have you decided what to do about the boys? Max hasn't been sleeping, worrying about what you might do. Jason gave him quite a going over, although from what he told us I think it was justified."

"Tell him not to worry. I'm not going to jeopardise the future of this company just to save a low-life like Floyd. Tell Max to keep his mouth shut. I'll get Grolby to give the police an anonymous tip-off. Do you see any problem with that?"

"No, no problem at all."

38

Saturday 8th January 2033

Jason walked in the direction the man had indicated. At the roundabout, a tunnel led beneath a flyover to a locked gate. A sign on the gate read 'Bedford Network Rail'. He hurried across the road and peered through the bars. Railway tracks cut through an area of open ground. Patchy grass and weeds poked up through the industrial landscape. A large, red brick building emblazoned with the text 'Bedford Depot' dominated the scene. Twisting his head to the left, he could just about make out a four-storey structure, although at this distance it was impossible to determine whether it was derelict or not.

Jason followed the pavement in the general direction of the building, his view blocked by the elevated roadway. After fifty metres, the ramp had descended, and he obtained the first glimpse of his target. A Royal Mail icon still adorned the beige-coloured structure. A high fence surrounded it, but the broken windows suggested that there was a way past, at least for the local vandals. This could well be the location that Grolby had mentioned. It certainly met the vague description he had overheard. The problem was how to get in. Whilst the surrounding fence was scalable, he could hardly do so in front of the steady stream of traffic rolling along the main road.

As Jason strolled past the tired-looking facade, he spotted a narrow alleyway running down the side of the structure alongside the barrier. He waited for a gap in the flow of vehicles, then crossed the busy highway. The alley provided access to the rear of a row of terraced houses. Backyards and garages, many of them with paint flaking off the woodwork, backed onto the narrow strip of concrete. More fencing blocked off the end, but alongside it stood a low storage shed with white doors. A paved footway switched back on itself and led to the back gate of one of the properties. A metal handrail divided the two opposing directions of the path.

Jason ambled down the alley, his head down. When he reached the shed, he glanced around and confirmed nobody was paying him any attention. If he could get on the roof, he could drop down into the fenced off area. There was no certainty that Floyd was even hiding here, and for a moment he questioned the sanity of the decision to warn the man.

"Ah, sod it," he muttered.

He placed one foot on the handrail and pushed himself up. On the first attempt, he lost his balance and dropped down. He repeated the process and this time maintained enough stability to jump the short distance to the shed roof. His stomach bore the brunt of the impact as he landed on the sharp corner.

"Shit."

The flat roof creaked ominously but held his weight. He pulled his legs up, crawled forwards then lowered himself down inside the delivery office compound. Feeling exposed standing by the railing, Jason sprinted across the open space to the side of the building. Most of the windows were broken, but heavy metal bars blocked the frames, making it impossible to gain entry. He followed the wall away from the main road and came across a door. He twisted the handle, but it refused to budge. A second door was also locked. He rounded the corner and crept along the end of the structure. Glancing up, he spotted an empty window frame, just above head height, that did not appear to be protected by bars. Jagged shards of glass rimmed the aperture. He would cut himself to ribbons if he tried to get through. If there was no other way of getting in, it might be worth reconsidering.

He turned the next corner, his hands brushing against the dusty brickwork. Seeing no means of entry through the windows, he proceeded to another door. That was locked too. He was about to resume his search when an area of freshly splintered wood around the lock caught his attention. This one had been recently forced open. There was no handle, so he dug his fingertips in between the door and frame where the material had been prised loose. A splinter embedded itself beneath his fingernail.

"Damn." He snatched his hand away and delicately withdrew the thin sliver. A small spot of blood welled up, and he placed the injured digit in his mouth. More gingerly, this time, he applied both hands and attempted to lever the door open. No movement at all. Somebody had definitely come through here in the recent past judging by the fresh state of the exposed timber, but they had obviously used a tool to crowbar their way in.

Jason lowered his eyes to the ground and searched for a suitable implement. His gaze settled on a rock about the size of his hand. He bent down and picked it up, but when he held it to the frame, he realised that it was too big. He dropped it and sighed in frustration. As he surveyed the wall, he spotted a corroded metal sign, the lettering long since eroded away. Four rusty screws secured it. He retrieved the stone and banged it down on one of the protruding screw-heads. The sharp thud sounded incredibly loud over the swish of passing traffic, and he scanned the surrounding fence for observers before studying his handiwork. The end of the screw was bent at an angle. Another blow and it dropped loose with a metallic tinkle.

He repeated the process on the second screw-head and after three strikes had reduced it to the same state as the first. One side of the sign now sat slightly proud, held only by the two remaining fasteners. He levered the plate backwards until it separated from the brickwork in a shower of dust.

He returned to the door frame and slipped the flat piece of metal in the spot where somebody had gouged the wood away. He pressed against the lever. The base of the door made a scraping sound, but there was no perceptible movement. He flung himself at the improvised tool, and this time, a crack opened up. Three more shoves and the space between door and frame was large enough to obtain a grip. He inserted both hands through the gap and pulled, but the timber had warped and resisted his efforts. With increasing frustration, he placed a foot against the wall and heaved backwards. Finally, the door surrendered and screeched open.

A damp, mouldy smell assaulted his nostrils. He slipped through the opening and yanked the handle towards him. The door closed most of the way, but a thin sliver of light remained around the frame. He tossed the faded sign on the floor. A loud clang reverberated through the cavernous space. If there was somebody here, Jason had certainly announced his arrival.

He surveyed the hangar-like building in the dim illumination that leeched through the narrow, barred windows. Grey tiling extended outwards in a zig-zagging pattern. Dark shadows indicated where machinery or shelving had stood. In several spots, dampness had lifted the tiles, spoiling the symmetry of the lines. Rows of fluorescent tubes hung by chains from the high ceiling every few metres, but they had probably remained unused for years. Even without the aid of artificial illumination, he could see that the entire space was empty.

Jason waited for his heart rate to slow, then strolled across the tiled flooring, his footsteps echoing in the vast room. There was no evidence of anybody living here and no place to hide. Maybe Floyd was hanging out in the multi-storey building at the front of the structure. Set in the grubby beige wall at the far end were two green doors. The first was locked, but when he pulled the second, it opened. Glass fronted offices lines both sides of a corridor that led towards another green door. Jason crossed the grey linoleum, glancing into the empty interiors as he passed. Still no sign of habitation.

He reached the door and turned the handle. It moved a few centimetres before sticking. He applied his shoulder, and it juddered open the rest of the way. He found himself in what was once a large open-plan office. The carpet was a tatty dark-grey colour, the indentations of furniture still visible in places. Once again it was deserted. He inspected the glass-fronted offices that ran around the edge of the room, but all were empty. A short corridor led to male and female toilets. A quick search showed no sign of recent activity.

He retraced his steps and passed through a set of double doors into what must have been the reception area. The curved desk bearing the Royal Mail logo still occupied its place in the centre of the tiled floor. Two sealed lifts and another pair of swing doors were set in the wall adjacent to the wide staircase that led up. Jason pushed through the doors. He emerged into what was a carbon copy of the first office area, but a quick survey proved this to be equally empty.

He was beginning to suspect that he had made a wasted trip when a muffled scraping sound reached his ears from above. Maybe somebody was here after all. His heart thudded in his chest as he returned to reception and headed up the stairs. The staircase turned back on itself and led to a space with a lift on one side and toilets on the other. An archway opened into an even larger room with individual offices extending along each of the side walls. The same dark grey-coloured carpet covered the floor.

Jason figured the time for stealth was long since over. "Um, Mr Floyd?" he called, a slight tremble to his voice. A cloud of steam rose from his mouth in the frigid air. If Floyd was here, he must be hiding in one of the offices. "Mr Floyd?" he called again, louder this time.

He held his breath and strained his ears. No reply. A sharp bang and the sound of something rolling across a hard surface broke the silence. He spun around. His eyes darted around the dilapidated interior. Nothing moved.

He headed to his left and pushed open the first office door. Empty. He worked his way along the row. All of them were deserted. Maybe it was just a rat he had heard. The thought of their scaly tails made him shudder. A sudden movement at the periphery of his vision caught his attention. The cord for a raised blind shifted in the air entering through a shattered window.

He tried to calm his frayed nerves and traversed the room. He tried the first door on the other side. A half-full black plastic bin bag occupied a spot in the far corner. Jason widened the top and peered inside. The rancid stench of rotting food wafted out. He wrinkled his nose and turned away. There was no way to know how long the rubbish had been there, but judging by the condition of the banana skin he had spotted, it couldn't have been more than a few days.

Jason pulled the door handle towards him, eager now to inspect the adjoining offices. The door slammed into his midriff, knocking him to the ground and winding him. Before he could recover, a figure barged into the room and knelt on his chest.

The man clamped his left hand on Jason's throat. His right grasped a long-bladed knife. The tip quivered less than an inch from Jason's eye. "What are you doing here?" he growled.

Jason wrenched his gaze from the knife and towards the man's face. "I..."

The blade touched Jason's cheek. "How the hell do you know my name?" The man paused and frowned. "Shit, it's you. The Baxter bitch's son."

Jason made a choking sound. He raised a hand, trying to loosen the stranglehold. "I can't..."

Floyd's grip slackened slightly, but the razor-sharp edge remained in place. "How did you know I was here? Spit it out or I'll start cutting."

Jason drew a deep breath and coughed. "My mother's Head of Security found you."

"How did he do that?"

"I've no idea. I overheard them talking on the phone."

"So, I'm going to ask you again. What are you doing here?"

"I... I came to warn you."

"Warn me? Warn me about what?"

"The police are coming."

An expression of incredulity crossed the man's face. "You came here to warn me that the police know where I am?"

Jason tried to nod, then thought better of it. "Yes," he rasped. "Look I can't breathe properly. Can I at least sit up? I'm not going to run away. If I wanted to turn you in, I would've already done so."

"Okay, empty your pockets. You're not carrying any sort of weapon, are you?"

Jason shook his head. He withdrew his house keys, wallet and phone and placed them on the floor.

"Lean against that wall," Floyd said, releasing his grip. Jason shuffled backwards until he felt the hard surface against his back. He rubbed his throat.

"Don't try anything. I don't want to redecorate the place with your blood. Am I clear?"

Floyd picked up Jason's belongings. He flipped open the wallet, inspected the contents, then tossed it back on the ground.

"Okay, so you discovered where I was hiding, and you decided to warn me. You haven't told me why."

Jason stared up at the bearded face, the black woollen hat, the grimy skin. "I know you didn't rape the girl."

Floyd fixed him with a glare. "Go on."

"My mother was going to let you get arrested for it."

"So why should you care?"

"Well… um, I don't know. It's just not right."

"Yeah, life's not fair, and I should know. So, do you know who the rapist really is?"

Jason hesitated. "Um… no, I don't."

"But you know it's not me?"

"Yes."

Floyd scratched his chin. "I don't believe you, but we'll come back to that. When are the police coming?"

"I've no idea. I found out two or three days ago. All I know is that my mother knows you're here."

"You say you want to help me, and yet you waited all that time before warning me? I could be banged up in a prison cell by now. Why did you leave it so long?"

"I'm not sure. I had a lot on my mind."

Floyd looked down at the busy main road, then turned back to Jason. "Do you have any idea how long it took me to discover this place? And now you want me to move on your say so?"

"Look, do what you like. All I'm telling you is that they know where you are. Why does my mother hate you so much, anyway?"

"Your mother and I go back a long way. I don't think the vindictive cow has ever forgiven me for dumping her. Not that I owe you any answers."

Silence settled on the small room. Floyd stared at the winter sky, deep in thought. Suddenly he tensed. "Shit, it looks like the filth have arrived." He whirled to face Jason. "I knew I shouldn't have trusted you. You've brought them right here."

Jason shuffled sideways to increase the distance between them. "I already told you—if I wanted to turn you in, I wouldn't have bothered talking to you. I'd just have told them where to find you."

"Maybe." He turned back to the window. "Well they're here now, and they've come in force."

Jason rose to his feet and stood beside Floyd, surveying the empty car park and the road beyond. Three white vehicles were parked in front of the entrance gates. As he watched, people emerged from the cars. One of the men approached the gates holding a large pair of bolt-cutters.

Floyd hurried out of the room and into the adjoining office. Seconds later he emerged carrying two bulging plastic bin bags. "If you don't want to get arrested, I suggest you follow me." Without waiting for a response, he rushed towards the staircase. Jason needed no second invitation. He snatched up his own belongings and trailed the other man down the stairs. When they reached the ground floor, Floyd retraced Jason's route into the huge hangar-like building. However, instead of going to the door Jason had used to gain entry, he headed to one at the far end. He drew back the bolts, pulled it open and darted out into the overcast afternoon.

He sprinted ahead to a gap between two buildings, apparently towards a dead-end. The area ended in a low single storey structure. He tossed the two bags onto the roof, then shimmied up a drainpipe after them. Keeping his head lowered, he ran up the shallow incline and then down the other side. Jason followed a short distance behind. The pair dropped down beside some adjoining shrubs.

Floyd stuck his head around the corner of the building. Satisfied that nobody was there, he turned to Jason. "Thanks for the tip-off. Give my regards to your mother… actually, on second thoughts, don't bother." He took two paces, then hesitated. He spun around and studied Jason's face for a moment before coming to a decision.

"Have you still got your phone?"

Jason nodded.

Floyd held out his hand. "Unlock it and give it to me."

Jason held the lozenge-shaped device up to his eye and stared into the camera. When it beeped, he handed it over.

"I'm adding my number," Floyd said, tapping at the keys. "If you have any more tip-offs, call me. It's under the name F."

He tossed the phone back.

Jason opened the contacts list and found the entry as Floyd had indicated. When he looked up again, the man had disappeared.

39

Saturday 8th January 2033

Karen Atkins surveyed the dingy grey carpet and shivered in the frigid atmosphere.

"Jesus, I wouldn't want to live here," she muttered.

The uniformed policeman who was carrying a black bin bag of rubbish towards the stairs looked at her questioningly. "Eh?" he said.

"Oh, nothing," Kat said. "Where's your sergeant?"

The man pointed in the direction of one of the abandoned offices. Kat thanked him and strolled to the door he had indicated. She stepped inside to find a tall man in a dark blue uniform staring out of the window with his back to her. The man whirled around at the sound of footsteps behind him.

"Ah, you must be Karen Atkins," he said, taking a step forwards. "Mike Knowles." He extended a meaty hand and crushed hers in a powerful grip.

"Hi Mike," she said, subconsciously rubbing her knuckles. "Everybody calls me Kat. So, what have you got?"

The man frowned. His hair was brown but flecked with grey and receding at the temples. A thin layer of stubble ran from cheek to cheek. It was a large face, but all the elements were in proportion. A typical policeman's face, thought Kat. "Well, somebody was certainly here recently. There was a bag of rubbish, a couple of books, a comb."

"Yeah, I just saw one of your men carrying an evidence bag out."

"We'll check everything for fingerprints. We should be able to confirm pretty quickly whether it's your man or not."

"So, you don't know yet if he was living here by himself or not?"

"Like I said, the fingerprints should tell us that, but all the signs are that he was alone."

Kat paused for a second. "I take it you've searched the entire building?"

The sergeant held her gaze before replying. "We may only be the local police, but we do know what we're doing."

"Um… sorry," Kat replied. "I wasn't trying to imply…"

"Right," the man said, relaxing slightly. "As luck would have it, we did have a drone up this afternoon. Unfortunately, it was quite high to cover the whole of the town—the cuts, you know. I'm having one of my men examine the footage now."

"So, you'll be able to see when he left and where he went?"

"Yeah, but the resolution probably won't be good enough to identify him."

"Okay. Can you let me know as soon as you hear anything? How did you know to look here?"

"Anonymous tip-off," the policeman said. "The caller knew Floyd's name and described the location perfectly, which is why we took it seriously. It came from an unregistered mobile, but we do know it originated from somewhere around Cambridge."

Kat stared out of the window, deep in thought, before turning back to the sergeant. "Isn't that a bit strange? If the call came from Cambridge, the person must have been hanging onto the information for a while. It's not as if the informant spotted our man and called it in straight away."

"Yeah, it is weird, but I'm not sure what it means. Maybe they thought about it before calling us."

"Have you tried to trace the phone?"

"I've got one of my men looking into it now, but I don't hold out much hope. If whoever it is doesn't want to be identified and is savvy enough to use an unregistered phone, they're unlikely to leave it turned on."

"But if that's the case, it doesn't sound like your average law-abiding citizen, does it? I mean, who's going to buy a mobile and then throw it away after one call?"

The policeman ran a hand across his stubble. "Let's see what the trace turns up, but it's a good point."

"Do you mind if I have a look around?" Kat asked.

"Sure, do what you like, but I'm sure I don't have to remind you not to touch anything."

It was Kat's turn to roll her eyes. "Don't worry, Mike, I may not be the local police, but I do know how to treat a crime scene."

"Touché," the policeman said, grinning.

Kat returned the smile, turned around and left the office. She walked a few metres and stuck her head inside the next door. Another policeman was photographing something on the floor in the far corner of the room.

He glanced behind him. "Can I help you?"

"Karen Atkins, Maternity Crimes Unit. What have you got?"

"Hi. It's a comb. It may belong to the suspect. I'm just about to bag it."

"Yeah, your sergeant mentioned it. Anything else?"

The man shook his head. Kat thanked him and returned to the large open-plan area. She looked inside each of the rows of offices but discovered nothing out of the ordinary. She had just about decided that there was nothing further to see when the sergeant strode across the room towards her.

"Kat, glad you haven't left yet. You'll want to hear this. I've just heard back from the drone unit. They saw two people leave the premises shortly after we arrived."

"Two people? Are you sure?" Kat asked.

"Yeah, they used one of the doors out of the old sorting room."

"Sorry, where's that?"

He pointed in the direction of the staircase. "You know, the big long building tacked onto the back of this one. They came out together and climbed over the roof of one of the outbuildings. Then they split up."

"Do you know where they went?"

"One of them headed back towards the station."

"Do you know which train he caught?"

"It's difficult to say. The main entrance is under cover, so he disappeared from view when he went in. If we check the footage carefully, we may be able to work out which platform he came out on and from that, the time of the train, but it's going to take a while. Remember what I said about the drone being high up."

"Damn. Isn't there CCTV in the station?"

"Hmm. There should be, but from past experience, it's often on the blink."

"What about the other man?"

"Unfortunately, he headed away from the city centre and out of the drone's camera range."

Kat scratched an ear. "Any cameras on the ground along his route?"

"Maybe, but in the current climate, there's not been much investment in that sort of thing. We'll check it out, but don't expect anything quickly."

"He's a slippery bastard, this one, but it looks like he's not working alone."

"Yeah, it's galling to get so close and let him slip away again."

Kat sighed in frustration. Suddenly she shot out a hand and grasped the sergeant's arm. "Hang on. You said one of the two people went to the train station. Isn't it possible that he arrived by train too? If he did, you could backtrack his movements and work out what train he travelled on."

"The drone's only up for three or four hours at a time. They generally don't fly at night, but if he got here in the last couple of hours, we'd be able to tell when and where he came from. I'll get my team on it right away."

"Thanks," Kat said. "You've got my number."

40

Saturday 8th January 2033

Jason opened the door and entered his mother's outer office. The lights came on as he crossed the threshold. Her secretary was not at the desk, but that was hardly surprising on a Saturday evening. He approached the door leading to her inner sanctum and knocked. No answer. He stuck his head inside the room and saw that it was empty. Typical. He pulled his phone from his pocket and double checked the message.

Fancy going out for a meal tonight? Meet me at the hospital at 6pm. Mum.

He tapped out a reply.

I'm here. Where r u?

His mother was probably in a meeting. He typed out a second message.

I'll wait at hospital reception.

Jason strolled along the corridor towards the stairs. Despite the exertions of that afternoon, he would still have felt guilty if he had taken the elevator. He trotted down the staircase taking two steps at a time and emerged into the reception area. Even at this hour on a weekend, medical staff bustled to and fro, like worker ants around sugar.

A solitary receptionist wearing a headset pressed a button on the screen in front of her. "Just putting you through." She turned her attention to Jason and smiled brightly. "Hello, sir. What can I do for you?"

"Um… I'm here to meet my mother, Mrs Baxter."

The smile dropped a notch. "Right. I'll try her office."

Jason opened his mouth to explain that she wasn't there, but the woman had already placed the call.

"There's no reply. Do you want me to page her?"

"No, don't bother. I just wondered if you knew where she was. I'm supposed to meet her at six."

The receptionist glanced up at the large illuminated display above the entrance. 18:10. "I'm sorry, I don't have your mother's schedule, but if you'd like to take a seat, I'm sure she'll be along shortly."

"Thanks." Jason turned and ambled towards a row of blue-coloured armchairs. As he did so, he spotted a middle-aged woman in a blue nurse's uniform staring at him from a few feet away.

She took a pace forwards. "Did I just hear you say you're Mrs Baxter's son?"

Jason nodded.

"Oh hello. It's nice to meet you." She extended a hand. "My name's Rose."

The skin of the woman's palm felt rough and dry.

"I've just seen your mother with Dr Perrin," she said. "They're in the basement lab. I can take you down there if you want."

"Um… sure, thanks," Jason replied.

"Okay, follow me," the woman said, heading in the direction of a set of double doors labelled private. She waved a card at a box on the wall and barged through. She led the way down a corridor to another door carrying a large yellow warning sign. 'Biohazard—authorised personnel only.' Once again, she used the card to gain access and pressed the lift call button.

"Is it safe down there?" Jason asked, a worried expression occupying his face.

The woman looked puzzled for a second until she realised what had drawn Jason's attention. "Oh, yes," she laughed. "Don't worry about that. You'll be perfectly alright."

A ping announced the lift's arrival, and they stepped inside. Rose stared into the red light of the iris scanner and selected the basement level.

"I never even knew this was here," Jason said as the floor sank away.

"Yes, this is where a lot of the sensitive work takes place," Rose said. "All very hush-hush, but then again, you are the boss's son."

The doors slid apart to reveal a featureless white corridor. The illumination cast by the diffuse ceiling lights was so bright that Jason had to shade his eyes.

"Yes, it is a bit dazzling, isn't it?" Rose said as she guided them past several numbered doors. They turned a corner and encountered a guard wearing a brown uniform sitting outside one of the rooms. "Hi Tony," she called. "Just taking Mrs Baxter's son to see her."

The man waved a hand but didn't reply.

"It's just at the end," Rose said, pointing.

"Um, Rose," Jason said, slowing down. "Is there a loo nearby?"

"There's a Gents just there. I'll wait for you here."

A strong perfumed scent hit Jason's nostrils as he entered, in stark contrast to the medicinal smell in the corridor outside. He relieved himself at the urinal, then stood by the white marble sink and examined his reflection in the mirror. The cold winter air had coloured his cheeks a rosy hue. His hair looked like he had just got out of bed, several patches sticking out at odd angles. He rinsed his hands under the tap and smoothed down the stray tufts. He used the dryer, then pulled the door towards him.

As he exited into the corridor, a movement to the right drew his eye. The end of a hospital trolley emerged from the room outside which the guard was sitting. A body lay on top, covered by a sheet. Jason half expected the head to be covered too, but it wasn't. He only gained the briefest of glimpses, but he instantly recognised the face of the patient. *It couldn't be. She was dead. His mother had told him so.* Yet her eyes were open, staring at the ceiling.

Two orderlies wearing green outfits followed the trolley out, partially obscuring his view. An arm moved. The person lying on the stretcher was definitely alive. The two men turned the corner and disappeared from sight, pushing their cargo before them.

Jason stood slack-jawed, staring after the departed trolley. The nurse's voice dragged him back to the real world. "It's this way. We don't want to keep your mother waiting."

Jason stumbled towards her as if in a trance.

"Are you okay?" she asked. "You don't look well."

"I'm fine," he replied, but his face felt flushed, and his ears were burning.

Rose resumed her route, a worried frown creasing her forehead. Reaching the door labelled 'Chief Scientist', she knocked loudly.

A voice inside shouted, "Come."

She turned the handle and held the door open for Jason. "Your son was waiting in reception, Mrs Baxter. I thought I'd do you a favour and bring him down."

Even as she said the words, she realised from the shocked expressions on the two people's faces that she had made a terrible mistake.

41

Saturday 8th January 2033

The pen tip clicked in and out at an alarming rate. "Jesus Christ, Rose. What were you thinking? You know about the security precautions. We have them for a purpose."

The nurse's chin quivered. She looked like she was about to burst into tears at any second. "Sorry Dr Perrin. I… I thought—"

"That's exactly the problem. You didn't think."

"But he's her son. I thought it would be alright to bring him down here. I was only trying to be helpful."

"Look," Perrin said, attempting to control his temper. "We have several women being held down here against their will. What do you think would happen if he discovered what we were doing? The boy's sixteen, for heaven's sake. Would you tell your teenage son something like that?"

"I haven't got a—"

The doctor slammed the pen down. "Jesus, Rose. Are you winding me up deliberately?" He glared at her across the desk. Now, she did start crying. She pulled a handkerchief from a pocket in her uniform and dabbed at her eyes. A series of mewling whimpers emerged from beneath the square of cotton.

Rosalind and Jason Baxter had departed a few minutes earlier. Perrin knew from the paleness of the CEO's face and the vivid red spots on her cheeks that she was struggling to maintain her composure. He had been unfortunate enough to witness several meltdowns over the years and had offered to handle this situation, knowing that if left to Rosalind, the nurse would be unemployed by morning and also probably on Grolby's to-do list. He debated with himself what action to take. The easy option would be to fire Rose on the spot. She had committed a grossly irresponsible breach of security and could have no complaints if they sacked her. In her favour, she was actually a good worker and would be hard to replace. That, and the fact that she knew too much. What she said next would help him to decide.

"So, did he see anything he shouldn't have?"

Rose lowered the handkerchief and sniffed loudly. "Um, like what?"

Perrin frowned. "Are you being deliberately obtuse, Rose? Do I have to spell it out? Did the boy see anything he wasn't supposed to?"

"Oh, you mean like one of the patients?"

"Yes, that's exactly what I mean."

The nurse hesitated for a moment. “No, I don’t think so. We were only in the corridor for a second or two.”

Perrin’s eyes bored into her. “You do realise that the sixteen-year-old girl, Antimone, was his girlfriend?”

The colour fled from her face. “His girlfriend?”

“Look, Rose, you’re really stretching my patience. Antimone Lessing was Jason Baxter’s girlfriend. You just led him right past her room. Now did he or did he not see anything?”

“N–n–no,” she stammered. She met the doctor’s gaze for a second, then stared down at her feet.

“You better not be lying, Rose. Are you sure?”

A quick glance up. “No, he definitely didn’t see anything.”

The doctor relaxed slightly. “Good.”

Another sniff from the nurse. “So, is Mrs Baxter going to fire me?”

“I’ll have a chat with her in the morning. Just make sure you stay out of her way. Are you working tomorrow?”

She nodded.

“Okay. You’re going to take a couple of days off, starting immediately, as holiday of course. There’s been a breakthrough in developing a cure, so hopefully she’ll be in a good mood over the next week or so. I can’t make any promises, but I think I can persuade her not to do anything too drastic.”

Rose buried her face in the handkerchief again. “Thanks, Dr Perrin. I really appreciate it. I was only trying to be helpful.”

“Yes, I know, Rose. Now I suggest you go home. Have a good break, and when you come back, for heaven’s sake, do as I said and keep out of Mrs Baxter’s way.”

Perrin watched as the nurse got to her feet and shuffled towards the door, her body language a picture of dejection. He waited until he had the room to himself, then walked around the desk and made sure that she was not standing outside. He returned to his seat and stared at the phone for a second or two. Placing the handset to his ear, he spoke Grolby’s name. A click and three rapid beeps. The sound of a ring tone. Another click as somebody answered.

“Grolby here.”

Perrin remained silent, wrestling with his thoughts.

Grolby’s voice again. “Is anybody there?”

“Sorry, Anders. It’s Nigel. It’s nothing. I dialled your number by mistake.”

42

Saturday 8th January 2033

A burst of raucous laughter erupted from the corner of the restaurant. Three suited men and their expensively dressed partners were sharing a table and by the sound of it, several bottles of wine. La Cordonnerie was one of the most expensive places to eat in Cambridge, but in spite of this, always had a long waiting list. However, when Rosalind Baxter's personal assistant had called about a reservation, a table for two miraculously became available.

Jason sat across from his mother, studying her as her eyes ran down the menu. The journey had passed mostly in silence. Throughout the drive, she had remained engrossed in the screen of her mobile phone, but he could tell by her uneven breathing and the slight tremble in her fingers that she was still seething with anger. As they neared their destination, she had finally emerged from her fugue-like state and had asked him about his day. He had been deliberately vague, implying that he had not left the house.

The aroma of French cooking made his stomach rumble, overlaid though it was with the scent of his mother's perfume. Rosalind dropped the folded menu on the tablecloth, and within seconds the waiter was standing beside them, pen and pad at the ready. Neither of them ordered a starter, Jason choosing the pan-fried duck and his mother a tuna salad.

Rosalind ran a finger down the wine list. "Ah, a Chateau Margaux, twenty twenty-five. Not a bad vintage. I'll have a bottle of that, please. Do you want a drink?"

Jason shrugged. "Water's fine, thanks."

"I thought we should go out to celebrate," she said. "I know I haven't been home much recently, but we've made an exciting breakthrough. We might finally be on the path to a cure."

"Good," Jason replied. "Is that what happens in the basement?"

Rosalind frowned. "The work that goes on down there is top secret. I know that nurse meant well, but she should know better than to bring unauthorised people down there, even if you are my son."

"Anyway," she said, brightening, "Back to school on Monday. Any more thoughts about what you might want to do for a career?"

"Well, obviously something related to science with the subjects I'm studying, but I'm not really sure yet."

The arrival of the waiter holding a bottle of wine interrupted the conversation. He presented the label to Rosalind. She nodded her approval, and he withdrew a corkscrew from a pocket in his jacket before removing the cork. He poured a small amount into Rosalind's glass and waited while she took a sip.

"That's fine," she said, putting it down.

The man half-filled the glass with ruby-coloured liquid. He turned to Jason. "Would Monsieur care for some wine?" he asked.

"You're sixteen now," his mother replied on his behalf. "I think you're old enough for a glass."

Jason was not unaccustomed to the taste of alcohol, but on the few occasions he had tried it, he couldn't really see what all the fuss was about. At his age, it was more a case of conforming with his peers, but he wasn't about to go into that with his mother. "Yeah, okay," he said.

The waiter smiled and poured the wine, barely covering the bottom of the glass. He placed the bottle in the centre of the table and draped a napkin around the neck.

"Now, where were we?" Rosalind asked once the man had departed.

Jason stared at his mother for a moment before replying. "I know she's alive. I saw Antimone this evening."

Rosalind froze, the wineglass halfway to her lips. Slowly, she returned it to the table. The tinkle of cutlery and the muffled conversations of the other diners seemed to increase in volume to fill the silence.

Finally, she spoke, her voice a low whisper. "Jason, you don't know what's going on."

Jason leant forwards. "But you told me she was dead. You lied to me."

A flush rose from Rosalind's neck. "I did it to protect you."

"So, she's the breakthrough that you mentioned?"

The pinkness had extended to her cheeks. "The less you know about this, the better."

"But you're not denying that she's alive?"

The silence stretched longer this time. "Yes, she survived the birth, and she's being cared for at Ilithyia."

"But she's my friend. Jesus, I'm the father. You let me think I was responsible for her death. Did the baby survive too?"

An expression of anger flashed across Rosalind's face. "Keep your voice down," she hissed. "You might be the child's father but, as we both know, you're not culpable when it comes to the pregnancy. Unfortunately, the child died."

"What happened?"

"A bacterial infection is what happened. Now I don't want to talk about this here."

It was Jason's turn to display his anger. "So, when are we going to discuss it? You hardly ever come home these days."

Red blotches formed in the centre of her cheeks. "I don't answer to you."

"Would you rather I discussed it with the police?"

Rosalind pushed the table back and stood up, wine sloshing from her glass and staining the tablecloth. The sudden movement drew glances from the other diners. "Right, we're leaving." She strode towards the bar at the entrance and entered into a low conversation with a man in a bowtie standing by the till. She withdrew her phone from her purse and waved it at the reader, then stormed out onto the pavement without checking whether Jason was following. Her fingers jabbed at the screen of the phone and within a few seconds their driverless car drew up alongside. Almost before the vehicle had stopped moving, she extended a hand and yanked the door open. She climbed in and slammed it closed behind her.

For a moment, Jason thought she was going to drive off without him, but the car remained stationary. He crossed to the far side, opened the door and clambered in. He buckled himself into the seat on the opposite side from his mother. She stared straight ahead, a vein throbbing prominently at her temple.

Finally, she turned to face him and spoke, ice dripping from every word. "You do not talk to me like that… ever. Am I clear?"

Jason remained silent, his heart thudding in his chest. He had never pushed her this hard before.

"Am I clear?" she repeated, raising her voice.

Jason met her eyes, nodded, then looked away.

"There is more going on here than you can possibly imagine," she said. "Yes, Antimone survived the birth against all expectations. It was nothing to do with any treatment that we gave her. It seems that she has some natural immunity to the virus. Now, think about it for a minute. Millions of women have died since this virus first emerged. Your friend, Antimone, holds the key. Think of the lives that could be saved. Now, knowing all that, do you think she could just saunter out of the hospital and resume her life? Of course not. Apart from being hounded by the press, she'd be a target for every religious nutcase and lunatic who thinks it's a punishment from God. What's more, she'd be top of the kidnap list of every foreign power trying to develop a cure of their own.

"Keeping her survival quiet is the best thing that could happen to her. When we've found a way to treat this disease, she'll no longer be such a big story. She'll just be one of many women who have survived giving birth. But that means we have to keep the fact that she's alive a secret. If news gets out, she'll be in danger, and the chances of finding a cure will be reduced. You can see that, can't you?"

Jason hung his head, then glanced at his mother. She fixed him with her gaze. "I suppose."

"Good. I'm glad you understand, but you mustn't mention this to a soul. As far as you're concerned, she's gone. Just forget about her."

"I assume her parents know she's still alive though?" he asked.

Rosalind hesitated for a moment. "At the moment, no. I don't think that's something they'd be able to hide, so it's best for Antimone if we keep things that way for the time being."

"So, you're just letting them think their daughter's dead when she's actually alive and well?"

Rosalind sighed. "Like I said, until we work out a treatment, it's the best thing for her. That's all we're thinking about."

"Did she ask about me at all? Does she know I was the one who made her pregnant?"

Rosalind's tone hardened. "Look, Jason, didn't I just say that you have to forget about her. She still thinks it was Floyd who raped her and no, she hasn't asked about you. She's still grieving for the loss of her baby."

"Alright, I'll keep it to myself, but I want to talk to her," he said, a note of belligerence entering his voice.

Rosalind folded her arms and fixed him with an angry stare. "Haven't you listened to a word I've just said? You have to put her out of your mind. Pretend she never existed. It's for her good and your own—and the future of the human race. Now I don't want to hear any more about it."

"But Mum."

"Enough."

Jason wanted to argue with his mother. Even though he had been under the influence of mind-altering drugs at the time, he still felt partially responsible for Antimone's death. Learning that she was alive had lifted a huge weight off his mind, and the fact of the matter was that he enjoyed her company. He still hadn't come to terms with his feelings concerning the baby's death. Technically the child was his son, but there was no real emotional attachment. Now that he knew Antimone had survived, he desperately needed to see her, but it was obvious that his mother had no intention of allowing that to happen. There was nothing to be gained by prolonging the argument, but he was already planning how to circumvent her mandate.

"Alright then," he said. "I'll do what you say."

43

Sunday 9th January 2033

Antimone coughed. Sharp, shooting pains sparked through her body.

"I didn't see him," she mumbled through cracked lips. In her mind she heard the squeal of brakes, the car still hurtling towards her. A quick sideways glance, the shocked face of the elderly male driver, everything happening in slow motion. The force of the impact, limbs tangled together, the surface of the road rushing up to greet her, then darkness. Then the sudden inrush of agonising pain, unable to draw breath, the panic as her muscles refused to obey her commands.

"I can't move. No!" Her head thrashed from side to side, the sheet clenched between her fingers. She tried to open her eyes, but they felt gritty, the eyelids gummed shut. Hysteria bubbled up inside her before first one, then the other blinked open. Her gaze traversed the white ceiling, the featureless white walls and the door with the small window. The realisation grew that she was in the hospital room, lying on the bed.

She felt like a herd of elephants had trampled her. The slightest movement sent a cascade of agony rippling outwards. Her head throbbed, and her throat felt as if she had swallowed a set of nail files. Her lethargic brain attempted to make sense of the excruciating sensations. Slowly it came back to her. They had told her they were going to perform a series of tests, but the after-effects were way beyond anything she had expected.

With slow, microscopic movements, she raised her right arm and stared at it blearily. A white dressing was affixed to her wrist, another on her forearm. A grid of brown plasters covered the limb at regular intervals. She lifted her left arm. It was a carbon copy of the right. With trembling fingers, she picked at the edge of one of the plasters and peeled it back to reveal a small circular incision. A scab had started to form, surrounded by a circle of inflammation.

She touched her face, feeling the outlines of at least six more plasters. A tight sensation drew her fingers to her scalp. Her fingertip brushed over bare skin, then the surface of another plaster. Her delicate probing revealed a regular pattern of sample points across her skull. All her hair had been shaved off, leaving her totally bald.

Whilst the plaster-covered wounds felt tender and there were more of them, the dressings were the main source of the throbbing pain enveloping her body.

She picked at the surgical tape securing one of the white squares. She winced as she slowly lifted the gauze material.

The electronic beep of the door lock interrupted her efforts. A nurse entered and strode towards the bed. She gently took hold of Antimone's wrist and placed it back on the sheets.

"Glad to see you're finally awake," she said, "but that's not a good idea. Those dressings need to be kept on for a few days. If you take them off now, you'll be risking infection."

The woman had greying hair tied back in a ponytail. She wore a pale blue top that extended to just below her ample waist, and dark blue trousers. Her face was round and ruddy coloured. Her chin blended into her neck.

"What the hell have you done to me?" Antimone asked, her voice coming out barely more than a whisper.

"I'm sure they told you what they were going to do beforehand, but you probably weren't paying attention. They've taken a series of skin biopsies. That's where the plasters are. The white dressings cover the sites where they took bone marrow samples. They shaved your head to prevent hair getting in the wounds."

"They said they were going to do some tests," Antimone rasped, "but they never said anything about drilling holes all over my body and shaving my hair off."

"I can give you some painkillers. That should help. You'll feel a lot better in the morning."

Antimone groaned and closed her eyes.

"I'll be back in a sec." The nurse bustled out of the room, closing the door behind her as she went.

As soon as she was alone, Antimone picked at the dressing again. She lifted the edge to reveal an angry looking circular wound, several millimetres across. If what the woman had said was correct, and there was no reason to think otherwise, they had drilled through the skin into the centre of the bone to extract a sample of the marrow—and not just once, but all over her body. No wonder the pain was so intense. For the first time in her life, she was thankful she had no sensation in her legs. Gingerly, she pressed the surgical tape back into place.

She glanced up as the nurse re-entered the room, carrying a bottle of pills.

The nurse crossed to the small shower room and returned a few seconds later with a glass of water. She shook out two tablets and passed them to Antimone. "Here, you'll feel a lot better after a couple of these but no fiddling with the dressings. After all you've been through, we don't want you succumbing to a bacterial infection, do we? You're far too valuable for that."

Antimone accepted the pills, placed them in her mouth and washed them down. She drained the glass and handed it back. "Can you get me a refill?"

The woman retraced her steps and watched as Antimone drank a second glassful. "Okay now?"

Antimone nodded. "Thanks."

"Is there anything else I can get you?"

"No." Antimone sank back onto the pillow with a groan. The sharply focused stinging sensation on her back told her they had taken samples from there too.

"You've been through a major procedure. I suggest you try to get some sleep. If you need anything, just shout. I'll be keeping an eye on you through the monitor."

Antimone closed her eyes and remained immobile, waiting for the pain to subside. As she did so, something the nurse had said kept repeating in her head. *You're far too valuable for that.* In a burst of insight, she realised that was how they saw her—a commodity to be bought and sold. They weren't interested in her wellbeing or that of her son. It was even possible they had no interest in preventing countless thousands of women from dying in childbirth. It was a business. Everything was geared to making money. They could have asked for her help, and she would willingly have offered it, but instead they had kept her a prisoner and performed experiments without her permission. They had refused to allow her to speak to her family and then threatened to withdraw her few remaining privileges if she didn't cooperate.

As the thoughts spun through her head, another realisation came to her. Nobody other than the hospital staff knew she was here. If they had lied to her about the medical procedures, could she trust them to inform her parents that she was still alive? Surely her mother and father would have insisted on visiting her by now or, at the very least, talking to her on the phone. If nobody knew she had survived, they could keep her here and perform whatever experiments they wanted until they had all the answers. And once they had their answers, what then?

Her scalp prickled with anxiety as the implications of her situation hit home.

How far would they go? What would they do with her when she was surplus to requirements?

44

Wednesday 12th January 2033

Jason stared out of the window of the coffee shop as two nurses walked past on their way home. Neither of them was the one he was looking for. It was just after six o'clock in the evening. He had been sitting here for three hours and was beginning to question the wisdom of his plan.

The last few days had passed in a blur. He should have been excited about returning to school and meeting his friends after the Christmas break, but he couldn't get the conversation with his mother out of his head. He had told her that he would forget about Antimone, but he had no intention of doing so. Several of the teachers had commented on his distracted state of mind, mistaking it for a lack of enthusiasm following the holidays.

He had pondered his options but kept coming back to the same conclusion. He desperately wanted to talk to Antimone but didn't want to alienate his mother. There was no way he could sneak past the security measures designed to keep people out of the basement laboratory a second time. Even if he did manage to get down there, a guard was stationed outside her room. The chances of being detected were too high, so where did that leave him?

The only plan he could conjure up was to ask the nurse who had escorted him there previously to take a phone to Antimone so that they could at least have a conversation, even if it wasn't face-to-face. He had therefore bought two cheap phones and had programmed into each of them the number of the other. If one of them was discovered in Antimone's room, he didn't want to make it easy for his mother to discover who she had been talking to by leaving his own number in the phone's contact list.

The plan had several flaws, not the least of which was how he would persuade the nurse to smuggle the mobile in. She seemed to be a decent person, and he hoped that he could convince her to help without coercing her. He wasn't sure how far he was prepared to go if she chose not to assist, but he decided to worry about that if and when the time came. In the meantime, his biggest concern was locating her and putting forward his proposition.

This was his third consecutive evening spent in the coffee shop. He only knew the nurse's first name, Rose, and he had no idea at what time she started or finished work. He could have asked at reception, but there was a good chance he would be recognised. It would be doubly suspicious if he asked about the working patterns of a woman whose surname he couldn't supply. He resolved to take that risk if he struck out for the third night in succession.

Jason took a sip of his coffee, his second of the evening. The brown liquid was cold, and he gave a shiver of distaste before putting the cardboard cup down. His eyes followed a tall, balding man heading outside. The man paused to chat to somebody entering the building carrying an open umbrella. As the person retracted the umbrella, Jason recognised the outline of the nurse. Finally.

In his haste to get up, Jason knocked over the cup, spilling coffee across the surface. He snatched a paper napkin from the holder in the centre of the table and dropped it on the expanding puddle. It quickly absorbed the liquid, turning a pale brown colour. Cursing his clumsiness, he trotted towards the door and burst into the foyer. The woman was still chatting to the man, but a couple of seconds later the man waved his hand and pushed through the revolving door. The woman shook her umbrella and glanced up as Jason approached.

"Oh, hi Rose," Jason said, trying to sound nonchalant.

"I've got to start work in a few minutes," Rose said, her face a mask of alarm. "I haven't got time to talk."

"Maybe we could have a chat when you finish your shift or maybe another day." He hadn't considered the practicality of his suggestion before the words came out.

"I don't think that's a good idea." Rose tried to edge past him.

"I know Antimone's alive."

Rose's head jerked upwards as her eyes fixed on Jason's. "You didn't tell your mother, did you?" she asked, a tremble in her voice.

Jason hesitated before replying. "Um, not yet. Could you just spare a minute for a quick chat?" he asked, gesturing towards the coffee shop.

Rose glanced at her watch and seemed to make a mental calculation. "Okay, but I haven't got long. My shift starts soon."

Jason re-entered the shop and took a seat at a table close to the door. Rose sat down opposite. "What's this about?"

"I know she survived. She's a friend of mine, and I wondered if you could do me a favour."

Rose placed her hands on the table. "I don't know. What sort of favour?"

Jason pulled one of the phones from his pocket and positioned it in front of him. "I was hoping you might be able to give her this. I've programmed my number into it."

Rose's face paled. "You've got to be joking. I'd be fired in the blink of an eye if they caught me taking a phone in. In any case, it wouldn't work."

"What do you mean? Why not?" Jason leant forwards.

"The basement is shielded from electromagnetic radiation," she replied. "Mobiles just don't work down there. Senior management have specially modified ones, but they're custom-built."

"There must be phones there. How do the medical staff talk to other people in the company?"

"They have land lines, but they're carefully controlled and monitored, apart from which they can only call other numbers in the building. All outside calls are blocked."

Jason sat back. "So, there's no way I can speak to her?"

"Not a chance. Didn't you see the guard sitting by her room?"

"So, what's that all about?"

"Keep her in and everybody else out," said the nurse. "Look, I can't help you. In any case, I'll probably get fired if your mother even sees me after what happened on Saturday night."

"Yeah, sorry about that."

"It was my own fault. No good deed goes unpunished." Rose's lips twitched in a half-smile. She got up to leave.

"If I gave you a message, could you get it to her?"

A look of trepidation flashed across the nurse's face. "What sort of message?"

"I don't know." Jason's gaze alighted on the stack of napkins in the centre of the table. He grabbed one of them. "What if I wrote something on this?"

She sat down. "Um, that's not a good idea. I'm already on the brink of being fired."

"Look, what's the harm in passing her a bit of paper? I already know she's alive although my mother doesn't know that I know." He paused and met her gaze. "Yet."

Rose looked down at the floor. She held the position for a moment before raising her head. "Okay, but just the once. I'm planning to find a new job soon, anyway. It's just a lot easier to do that with a decent reference."

"Thanks, Rose. Do you have a pen on you?"

The nurse delved in her handbag, pulled out a cheap biro and handed it over.

Jason scribbled a few sentences on the napkin, then folded it into a triangular shape. "I really appreciate this," he said, giving her both items.

"Right, well I better get to work." She rose to her feet again.

"How will I get her answer?" asked Jason, also standing.

"It's a twelve-hour shift so I won't finish until six fifteen in the morning. I'll meet you tomorrow afternoon at five o'clock by the entrance to the main car park. I've got a red Ford Calypso."

"See you tomorrow, then." Jason sat down and watched Rose's back as she crossed to the door and joined the flow of people in the foyer.

For the first time in three days, he smiled.

45

Wednesday 12th January 2033

Rose strode down the corridor towards the nurse's station. She had slipped the napkin that Jason had given her beneath her bra, and now she glanced down to make sure it wasn't visible through her uniform. Nothing was discernible, but the paper felt uncomfortable against her skin. She still hadn't decided what to do about it. She was within a whisker of being fired. If she encountered Rosalind Baxter, there was no guarantee she would keep her job whatever she did. There was no way she could avoid the woman indefinitely, but she hoped that Doctor Perrin had made a good enough case to convince the CEO to retain her services.

One thing was for sure, she planned to look for different employment as soon as possible. Yes, the pay was far higher here than she could earn elsewhere, but the way they took those young women off the street and experimented on them made her extremely uneasy. Even if they were prostitutes and drug addicts with low life expectancy, it was still hard to justify what was done to them. She knew that sacrifices had to be made to find a cure, the loss of a few lives would save countless millions more and so on, but surely there were other ways. If Mrs Baxter did choose to sack her, maybe she could use her knowledge as leverage.

The question still remained. What to do about the note from Jason? One redeeming factor was that Mrs Baxter didn't know that her son had seen Antimone. The boy had said that he hadn't told his mother… yet. There was definitely an implied threat, but if she was honest with herself, she wouldn't even be contemplating the idea without some form of coercion. Would he carry through with it if she refused to do as he asked? Probably not, she thought, but what was the downside? The girl would more than likely want to write a reply. If it ended there, that wouldn't be too much of a problem, but Jason didn't seem like the type to give up. The safest thing to do was to keep the note to herself and tell him that she had abandoned the plan.

Her mind made up, she pushed through the door. A woman wearing a nurse's uniform sat at the solitary desk. She looked up at the new arrival, then glanced at her watch. "You're late."

"Sorry," said Rose. "A doctor wanted to speak to me."

The woman humphed. She was in her mid-fifties, grey hair tied back in a ponytail and carrying four or five stone of excess weight. "Oh, that's alright then. I don't mind working unpaid overtime just so you can chat up one of the doctors."

Rose knew better than to argue. "How are the patients?"

The woman gestured towards the screen before her. "It's all written down in the log." After a brief pause, she relented. "They're all okay apart from the sixteen-year-old girl. She's not in a good shape at all. They took biopsy samples a few days ago, and she's been in a lot of pain. I gave her oxycodone a couple of hours back, but she can barely move."

"Biopsy samples? That shouldn't be too bad. I don't understand."

The older woman pressed her lips together. "I think you should see for yourself. When I say they took biopsy samples, they took them from everywhere, and bone marrow too."

"Right. I'll pay her a visit."

The other nurse stood up, groaning from the exertion as she did so. "See you, then."

Rose watched as the woman waddled to the door. Her eyes slid across the row of wall-mounted monitors until they rested on the one displaying Antimone's room. She approached the screen and peered intently at the image. The girl lay on the bed with her eyes closed, her scalp totally devoid of hair. A regular pattern of dark brown patches dotted her skin, interspersed with larger white areas. It was unusual for her to be in bed at this time rather than in the wheelchair. "What have they done to you?" Rose muttered.

She settled herself in the chair behind the desk, the seat still warm from the previous occupant. She signed into the computer, selected the log and waved her hand in front of the monitor to scroll down the entries. She went straight to Antimone's data. The last recorded item was the prescription of the painkillers just over two hours ago. As her gaze ran down the list, she noted that the same drugs had been administered almost every four hours over the past three days. It was also apparent that she had eaten practically nothing over that time period.

Rose logged off and headed out into the corridor. She turned the corner and strode towards the man in the brown uniform sitting outside the door. He hurriedly returned the mobile device he had been playing with to a pocket inside his jacket.

Rose didn't recognise the man. The napkin seemed to press into her breast. She made a conscious effort not to glance down. "Hi, I'm Rose," she said.

"John," the man replied. "I assume you've just started your shift. I've got another two hours to go and then I'm off."

"Twelve more for me," she said, flashing a nervous smile. She held her identity card to the reader and pushed the door open. The first thing to affect her senses was the smell of urine.

"Hi Antimone, it's Rose. How are you?"

A groan was the only response.

Rose approached the bed. She took a sharp intake of breath as her eyes took in the prostrate girl.

Antimone lay on her back, the white sheet pushed down to her waist. Small brown plasters were spaced in an even grid pattern across her exposed skin, one every two or three inches. The grid extended to her face and scalp. One or two had fallen off, leaving small circular scabs surrounded by an area of pink inflammation. A line of larger, evenly spaced, white dressings held down with surgical tape ran up both arms. The one on her left wrist hung loose, exposing an angry looking, dark-red disc at its centre.

The girl lying before her was a shadow of the feisty teenager Rose knew from before. Beneath each eye was a purple-coloured, half-crescent hollow. Her complexion was pale, the skin a pasty colour. Rose was staggered by the decline in her appearance.

"Um, Antimone, can you look at me?"

The girl opened her right eye and stared blearily at the nurse. "How's my son?" she mumbled.

"Oh… he's fine. When was the last time he was here?"

"Dunno. Two, three days ago. Before they did this to me. I've not been well enough to look after him."

"Look, I'm really sorry. I'll see if we can get him brought down here so you can at least see him. I'll give you a hand with him. Why don't we get you to the bathroom and get you cleaned up first?"

"Can't move," Antimone whispered, closing the open eye.

"I'll give you a hand. I think you've had a bit of an accident, and we need to sort you out." She withdrew the sheet and winced at the scabs covering her legs where the plasters had fallen off. The smell of urine was almost overpowering.

With excruciating slowness, Rose manoeuvred the girl off the bed. On several occasions, Antimone cried out in pain as pressure was applied to one of the sample sites. Finally, she was seated in the wheelchair.

Rose propelled the chair forward into the cramped bathroom. She found it telling that Antimone didn't complain about being pushed. "Why don't you brush your teeth while I sort out the bed? When I've done that, I'll come back and help you wash." She grabbed the toothbrush from beside the sink, applied some toothpaste and handed it over.

While Antimone brushed, Rose returned to the main part of the room and stripped off the sheets. The dried yellow stains indicated that it had happened several hours ago. "Couldn't be bothered to get off your fat arse, you lazy cow," she muttered under her breath. Anger seethed through her. She knew this girl was important in finding a cure, but what they had done to her amounted to torture. If she was undecided about what to do before, what she had seen in this room had made up her mind. The least she could do was hand over the note. She needed to be careful, though. Cameras recorded everything, but they didn't extend to the bathroom.

Rose wiped down the plastic under sheet and remade the bed. She glanced surreptitiously at the camera, then headed back to rejoin Antimone. The girl sat in the wheelchair staring blankly into the mirror, still holding the toothbrush. Rose gently took it out of her hand. She turned on the taps and crouched down so her eyes were at the same level as Antimone's.

"Antimone, I need you to listen to me."

Antimone's gaze rose listlessly to meet the nurse's.

"Before I tell you this, you have to understand that it's vital you don't discuss it with another soul. If anybody finds out, we'll both be in a lot of trouble."

"What are you talking about?" Antimone rasped.

Rose hesitated for a second. "I've got a note from Jason. He asked me to give it to you." She placed a hand beneath her uniform and withdrew the folded napkin.

Antimone unfolded the paper with quivering hands.

GLAD YOU'RE ALIVE. ARE YOU OK? LOVE JASON

She raised her eyes. "He knows I'm alive?"

"Yes. He was down here three days ago, and he saw you as they took you to the operating theatre."

The girl became animated for the first time since the nurse had arrived. "Can you get a message back to him?"

"Yes. Write it on here." Rose took a pen from her front pocket and handed it to Antimone.

Antimone clutched the pen in her right hand, pondered for a moment, then wrote below Jason's words with slow, deliberate strokes. When she had finished, she folded the napkin and passed it back.

"Do you mind if I read it?"

Antimone shook her head. "Go ahead."

Rose unfolded the paper and stared at the message.

YOU HAVE TO GET US OUT OF HERE. ANTIMONE.

46

Thursday 13th January 2033

Karen Atkins shifted her chair sideways to allow the skinny technician to sit beside her. They said that it was a sign of getting old when policemen started to look young, but this man looked like he should still be in school. He was not technically a policeman but a civilian who worked as an analyst for the police. He had a pallid complexion and several large, angry looking spots across his forehead. His black hair was greasy and parted to the side. He wore jeans and a faded T-shirt bearing the slogan 'Even duct tape can't fix stupid, but it can muffle the sound.'

Despite his appearance and the inappropriate T-shirt, he was good at his job. That entailed poring over video footage and analysing it to obtain nuggets of useful information.

"May I?" he asked, sliding his chair in front of the monitor. He tapped on a keyboard that seemed to float in mid-air and brought up a list of files. He selected the first, set the time bar to a point just over halfway through and hit the play icon. "Right, this is footage from the drone. The quality's not great, but you can see our man entering the post office compound here. Now, if we run the footage backwards, we see him talk to this man walking his dog. He's an elderly local, and we got one of the uniforms to have a chat with him. According to the officer, the old geezer wasn't quite all there, but he was adamant that the person he talked to was a boy of fifteen or sixteen."

"That's strange. Go on."

"Let's go back further. We see him walking along the road, and here he is emerging from the train station. Look at the time stamp. Nine minutes past one in the afternoon. The drone hasn't got an angle onto the platforms so it can't tell us which train he arrived on." The man paused.

"So that's it then?"

"No, not at all." The technician smiled, displaying his bad teeth. "There was one working camera near the entrance. Unfortunately, it's facing outwards so all we can see is his back." He opened a second file and froze the picture showing a figure dressed in a dark blue winter jacket exiting from the station. Once again, he hesitated.

"I'm guessing there's more," Kat said, sighing in exasperation.

"Yes, there is. Two trains arrived at around this time. One was from Leicester and the other from Saint Pancras. We managed to pick him up on the cameras at Saint Pancras."

"So, if he came from London, he could have started his journey just about anywhere, then?" Kat asked.

The man seemed to deflate. "Yeah, sorry. We went through the footage from Saint Pancras, and we spotted our suspect getting on the train, but it would take too long to work out where he came from." He selected another file, and the monitor displayed a grainy picture of what appeared to be a teenage boy wearing a blue jacket, his head angled downwards.

Kat leant forwards in her chair. "Is this the best you can get?"

"I haven't finished yet. So, we saw him arrive, but we also know he returned to Bedford train station when he left."

The technician opened the next file. The view changed back to an aerial shot. "Here we see him walk along the road and enter the station at…" He paused the video and pointed at the time stamp in the top right corner. "Three twenty-one."

"And this time, you should get a clear look at his face as he enters the station," Kat said excitedly.

The man grinned. "Exactly." He selected the final file in the list.

"At last," Kat muttered under her breath,

"And there we have him." The monitor displayed a figure wearing jeans and a dark blue winter jacket. This time, the face was clearly visible.

"I don't believe it," Kat said, sitting back.

A confused expression worked its way across the technician's face. "I take it you recognise him, then? Not who you expected?"

"I didn't know who to expect, but yes, I do recognise him. That's Jason Baxter, Rosalind Baxter's son, you know, the head of Ilithyia Biotechnology. But what the hell is he doing helping Daniel Floyd?"

***

Kat drummed her fingers on the desktop. "Yes, I'll hold." Before her lay several printed sheets relating to the investigation into Antimone Lessing's rape. Whilst all the records were computerised, she still liked to feel them in her hands and scribble notes on them. Her eyes roamed over the page. Jason Baxter and Daniel Floyd working together? She would never have guessed it in a million years, but the evidence was on the screen. Jason Baxter had broken into the old sorting office and had left at the same time as Floyd. She had asked the technician to go over the footage of the pair leaving the building one more time. The two men had clearly shared a conversation before going their separate ways, but it was impossible to detect facial expressions or read body language from the drone's vantage point. How did they even know each other? There was a link between Rosalind Baxter and Daniel Floyd, but how did Jason come into it?

Several witnesses had seen Floyd at Rosalind Baxter's house, and he had been sent on his way by the security men before later returning. But what had made him return? Was he meeting with Jason? Was Jason somehow involved in the rape? One thing was for sure, though—she intended to ask the boy.

A click on the line preceded the imperious voice of Rosalind Baxter. "Hello, Ms Atkins. What can I do for you?"

Now that it came to it, Kat hadn't really thought through what she was going to say. "Um, thanks for talking to me, Mrs Baxter. I'm calling about the Antimone Lessing case."

"Yes, poor girl. Have you found Floyd yet?"

"Actually, that's why I called. Floyd's still on the run, but I came across some surprising surveillance video, and I was wondering if you might be able to shed some light on it."

"Okay," Rosalind said.

"Well I—um, I don't really know how to put this. We discovered footage of Jason meeting with Daniel Floyd."

The line went silent.

"Mrs Baxter, are you still there?"

More silence then a more subdued voice. "Yes, I'm here. When was this?"

"Last Saturday afternoon in Bedford. Do you have any idea why they might talk to each other?"

"No. As you know I have some… ah… previous history with Mr Floyd, but I wasn't aware that my son had any interaction with him."

"Where is your son at the moment, Mrs Baxter?"

"Well, he's at school. They went back this week after the holidays."

"Okay. I'd like to have a chat and ask him why he met with Floyd. Your son's still under seventeen, isn't he? That means he needs to have a guardian present while we question him."

"You're not arresting him, are you?"

"No. I just want to have a talk with him for the time being."

The threat that it might turn into something more hung between them.

"Right," Rosalind said. "I'm really busy today."

"It doesn't have to be you."

"No, I want to sit in on this. Could you come here?"

"I assume here means Ilithyia," Kat said. "I could manage that."

"I can leave a message and get him to come to the hospital after he finishes school, say around five thirty or six o'clock."

"Okay, let's make it six. I'll see you later. Goodbye, Mrs Baxter."

There was a click on the line, and Kat replaced the handset in its cradle.

"This should be interesting," she muttered to herself.

***

No sooner had she ended the call than Rosalind Baxter placed another one. A voice responded before she even heard the ring tone.

"Hello, Mrs Baxter. What can I do for you?" The unctuous tones of Julian Stefano.

"Julian, I need the lawyers here in my office at six o'clock. No, make that five thirty. I want to have a chat with them first."

"May I ask what this is about, Mrs Baxter?"

"No, you may not. I pay you to do what I ask, not ask what I do."

"Um, sorry Mrs Baxter, I wasn't prying, I just wanted to know which particular lawyers you need."

"Right, Julian. The ones you contact before you talk to the police. Is that clear enough?"

"Yes, perfectly, Mrs Baxter. I'll sort that out. Is there anything else?"

Rosalind ended the call without speaking again. She stared out of the window at the glowering winter sky, but her mind was elsewhere. What the hell had the ungrateful imbecile done now? How did he even know Floyd? It must have been a coincidence, or the police had made a mistake, but the boy hadn't mentioned it to her. Surely, he would have told her about an accidental meeting, but maybe not. Over the last week or so, the distance between them seemed to have grown greater. She knew that she didn't spend enough time at home, but Jason was more than capable of looking after himself. After all, he was practically an adult now.

She wondered if it had anything to do with the girl. Maybe he still resented her for telling him to forget her, but if what the policewoman had said was correct, Jason had rendezvoused with Floyd before the night at the restaurant. Try as she might, she couldn't see any link that would lead Jason to deliberately seek out Floyd. The only way to find out was by speaking to her son, and preferably in advance of the police arriving. She retrieved her mobile from her handbag and signed in by holding the inbuilt camera up to her eye. She dictated a message and tapped the send button.

That left one last thing to do. She once again grabbed hold of the desk phone and spoke into the handset. This time, there were three repetitions of the ring tone before somebody answered.

"Hello, Grolby here."

"Anders, I've got another little job for you. I need you to get a man to follow my son, Jason."

"Your son, Mrs Baxter? Why do you want him followed? Are you worried about somebody attempting a kidnapping?"

"No, it's nothing like that Anders. I just had a call from the police saying that Jason met Floyd last Saturday."

"Floyd? I don't understand. Why would your son meet with him?"

"I don't understand either, which is why I want you to put a man on following him. He's at school at the moment. I don't want Jason to know he's being followed, though."

"Okay, I'll get right on it. I'll let you know if my man sees anything unusual."

"Thanks, Anders."

47

Thursday 13th January 2033

Jason leant against the stone gatepost outside the imposing school gates, deep in thought. All his friends had left for the day, and he had delayed his own departure with meaningless tasks that could have waited until the following day. He retrieved the phone from his pocket and read the message again. Just three words:

'Call me. Mum.'

Had she found out that he had tried to contact Antimone? Did the brusque request indicate she was angry about something? There was only one way to find out, and that was by calling her. His heart hammered in his chest as he spoke her name into the handset. He felt out of breath, inhaling in gulps as though he had been running hard.

A ring tone. Another. A click, then his mother's voice. "Jason?"

"Yes, Mum. You said to call you."

A pause at the other end. The cold, quiet voice. "The police called me this afternoon."

Jason's heart rate increased. "The police?"

"Yes, the police. They wanted to know why you went to see Daniel Floyd."

A roaring sound in his ears. He opened his mouth, but no words came out.

"I take it by your silence that you know what I'm talking about. I'd like to know as well."

"I… uh—"

"I said I want to know what you were doing meeting Daniel Floyd," she screamed.

Jason held the phone away from his ear. "It's a long story," he muttered.

"Well, I want you in my office at five thirty to explain it. Is that clear? There's a policewoman coming to talk to you at six. If they somehow manage to get hold of you before then, you say precisely nothing until one of my lawyers is present. Got it? After everything I've done for you, this is the reward I get?"

"Okay. I'll be at your office by five-thirty," Jason said. He hesitated, then spoke again, "I'm sorry, Mum," but the line was already dead.

He returned the mobile to his pocket and blew out his cheeks. Somehow the police knew he had met Floyd. Did they know he had warned him about the raid? Did that mean they had captured Floyd? But if that was the case, what had Floyd told them? Jason cast his mind back. He had informed the man that somebody else was responsible for making Antimone pregnant. It wouldn't take a huge leap of logic to deduce the true identity of the child's father.

At least he had time to rendezvous with the nurse and get the message from Antimone before he had to meet his mother.

48

Thursday 13th January 2033

Jason glanced at his watch. Five past five. The nurse had said she would be there at five, but no red cars had passed by in the last few minutes. He had even used the Internet to look up details of the type of car she drove to make sure he would recognise it. He couldn't afford to wait too much longer or he would be late for the meeting with his mother. The icy wind gnawed at the exposed skin of his face and pawed at his hair. He shuffled anxiously from one foot to the other.

A small red vehicle turned off the main road and merged into the steady stream of traffic heading to his mother's company. As the car drew closer, he identified the model as the one he was waiting for. It slowed as it came alongside, and the window lowered. With a sigh of relief, he recognised Rose's anxious face. The driver behind tooted his horn.

"I'll see you in D1," she called, then accelerated to close the gap to the car in front.

For a moment Jason didn't understand what she meant. Was she referring to a section of the hospital? After a moment's thought, it came to him. She was talking about the car park, of course. Cursing his stupidity, he studied the direction sign and jogged towards the area she had identified. A couple of minutes later, he spotted the entrance to car park D. Four blue signs with white text towered above the rows of parked cars, labelled from D1 to D4. D1 was at the near end, and his eyes ran down the lines, looking for the red car. The blip of an alarm being armed drew his attention. He caught sight of Rose as she strode along the footpath to the building entrance. Jason hurried to catch up with her.

"Did you give her the message?" he asked.

She stopped and turned to face him. "Yes, I gave it to her as agreed."

"Was there a reply?"

The nurse swivelled her head, inspecting the surrounding area for anybody showing an undue interest. Nobody seemed to be paying them any attention. She delved a hand into her coat pocket and pulled out a folded piece of white paper. Jason recognised the shape of a napkin, like the one he had written on the previous night.

"Before I give you this," Rose said, "you have to promise me that you're not going to involve me anymore. This is it. You're on your own from now on. I've got to think about myself too. If they catch me, I'll be without a job, and I won't be able to get a reference."

Jason nodded. "Okay. Can I see the note please?"

Rose handed the napkin over. Jason unfolded it and read Antimone's message scrawled beneath his own.

He took a sharp intake of breath. "You have to get us out of here?" His eyes locked onto the nurse's. "How is she? Is she alright?"

Rose grimaced. "She's in a bit of pain at the moment. She's recovering from some tests." She resumed her progress towards the entrance. "That's all I'm going to say."

Jason placed a hand on her shoulder.

Rose whirled around angrily. "This is exactly what I knew would happen. I should have just thrown the damn thing away. Now you need to leave me alone."

Jason raised his hands apologetically. "I'm sorry, but how am I going to get her out of there without help?"

"That's your problem. I suggest you start by talking to your mother. She's the one who's in charge."

"I don't think she's going to change her mind," Jason mumbled.

Rose turned away. "I can't help you anymore. Sorry."

"Thanks anyway," Jason called to her departing back. He watched as she pushed through the rotating doors and entered the glass and steel building beneath the logo of a new-born child. He pulled back his sleeve and glanced at his watch. Five thirteen. Just over fifteen minutes until the scheduled meeting with his mother and three-quarters of an hour before he had to explain himself to the police.

He took a step towards the entrance, then halted. He turned a full circle, deep in thought. "What the hell am I going to do?" he muttered to himself. His hand slipped into his pocket and emerged holding the phone. Almost subconsciously he unlocked the screen and scrolled through the list of contacts until he reached the names beginning with F.

For a long time, he stared at the display. Once, then twice, his finger moved to the connect button and hesitated.

"Ah, damn it," he said as he finally placed the call.

49

Thursday 13th January 2033

Jason stared down at the wooden surface of the table. On the opposite side sat his mother, a glower on her face. They occupied one of the meeting rooms on the executive floor of Ilithyia Biotechnology. The lawyers waited next door.

"What the hell were you thinking about?" Rosalind spat. "I want to hear it all. Why you visited Floyd, how you knew where to go, what happened when you got there."

"Well, I woke up that morning, the Saturday, and you'd already left for work. I was just sorting out my breakfast when my mobile rang. I didn't recognise the caller, but I answered anyway. It was Floyd."

"How did he get your number?"

"I'm not sure. He never told me."

"Go on then."

"Okay, so he starts by asking if I know who it is. I say no, and then he tells me, you know, that it's him. Floyd. I'm about to hang up when he says he has some information I might be interested in, but it's going to cost me."

"What information?"

"He wasn't specific, but he said it was about Antimone."

"Antimone? What could he possibly know about her?"

"Well, he wouldn't say on the phone. He said if I wanted to hear what he had to say, I had to bring him supplies. Food and stuff."

"Why couldn't he just get it himself?"

"He was in hiding," Jason said. "He didn't want to go out in case somebody recognised him."

"So, what happened next?"

"He tells me where to go, the old sorting office in Bedford. He says to go inside and he'll find me. He warns me not to tell the police, or he'll break into the house and hurt us."

"Hurt us?" Rosalind snorted. "What the hell does that mean?"

"He mentioned arson or something like that. Anyway, I didn't call the police. I caught a train to Bedford and bought the stuff he asked for."

"Right. And then what?"

"I found the building. It's surrounded by a fence, so I had to climb over it. I managed to get one of the doors open. There was no sign of Floyd on the ground floor, so I went up to the first floor. I go into one of the offices, and he jumps out, holds a knife to my throat. He makes me sit down while he goes through the supplies. When he's checked them, he says he's ready to give me the information."

"Go on then, spit it out," Rosalind said. "What's so amazing that it's worth risking your life for?"

"He says he knows that Antimone is alive."

"What?" Rosalind leant forwards sharply. "How the hell did he know that?"

"He refused to say. All he would say was that she survived the birth."

"Did he know where she was being held?"

"Like I said, if he did know, he didn't tell me," Jason said.

"So, it's just pure coincidence that you saw her later that night when that stupid moron brought you down to the basement?"

"Yeah, that's right. I didn't believe him. I thought he was winding me up."

"What happened next?"

"The police arrived. I thought he was going to kill me, but I managed to convince him that I hadn't called them. Anyway, he led me out, and we escaped just before they searched the building."

"And then you caught the train back home?"

"Yeah, from Bedford back to London Saint Pancras, on the underground to Liverpool Street and from there up to Northstowe."

"And have you heard from him since?"

"No," Jason replied.

"Have you got your phone on you?"

"Um, yes." Jason withdrew it from his pocket.

"Unlock it and give it to me." Rosalind stuck out a hand.

Jason held the camera up to his eye, then handed over the pebble-shaped block. His mother reached across the table to grab it. Her fingers danced in front of the screen. Her brow furrowed in concentration.

Finally, she looked up. "There's no record of an incoming call on that Sunday."

The accusation lay heavy in the air between them.

"He told me to delete the call record. He watched while I did it."

"Okay, that's convenient." Rosalind shook her head. "We aren't finished discussing this yet, but we need to get the story straight for the police. You tell them everything you've just told me, but emphasise that you didn't believe what Floyd said about Antimone being alive. I'm going to keep the phone. If they ask for it, just say you haven't got it. It's at home or something."

"But it's got all my contacts on it," Jason protested.

"That's the least of your worries right now. In any case, you won't be needing your contacts if you end up in jail. I'm going to have a chat with the lawyers now. Don't answer any questions unless they indicate that you can. I'll get one of them to nod if it's okay. When you answer, just state the bare minimum. Don't elaborate. If you're unsure about something, it's fine to say you don't know. Got that?"

Jason nodded in acquiescence and watched his mother stride across the room, leaving him sitting by himself.

"What the hell have I started?" he muttered.

50

Thursday 13th January 2033

Rosalind Baxter stared out at the deepening twilight gloom and scratched an earlobe.

"So, he's been talking to that damned nurse again?" she asked, turning to face Anders Grolby.

"That's what my man says, and I think the evidence is pretty conclusive." He waved a hand at the snapshots arrayed across Rosalind's desk.

"What's that in this shot?" She pointed to a photograph showing Rose handing a white object to Jason.

"It looks like she's passing over a note," Grolby said, shrugging.

"I don't suppose we can tell what's written on it, can we?"

"Not a chance. It might have been possible with a state-of-the-art camera and a telephoto lens, but not with the equipment my man's using. Anyway, that stuff would be far too big to carry around on a job, most of the time."

"Damn. I told Nigel to fire her. The bloody woman's a total liability. There's only one subject those two could be discussing, and that's the girl. You're going to have to deal with her, Anders."

"Are you sure, Mrs Baxter? If too many employees have accidents, the police might start to get suspicious."

"I know it's a risk, but the stupid cow is jeopardising everything, especially now that we're so close to developing a cure. Make it look like a suicide."

"Okay. What do you want me to do about your son?"

"That's a trickier one. Keep your man on him. We need to make sure he's not going anywhere near the girl—or Floyd, for that matter. I can't believe the little sod actually met with Floyd."

Rosalind had briefed Grolby on how Jason had paid a visit to Floyd at the old sorting office in Bedford, and how the police had questioned him half an hour earlier. The policewoman, Karen Atkins, had clearly been unhappy to see the lawyers present during the interview. Rosalind had asked the woman whether her son was under arrest, and when it became clear that he was not, she had emphasised she was only allowing the interview to take place as a courtesy. A smile twitched at her lips as she recalled the look of indignation on the woman's face when she had been informed that the interview was over.

"I want you to go through Jason's phone records," Rosalind said. "He told me that Floyd phoned him on the morning he went to Bedford, but there was no indication of an incoming call on his mobile. Apparently, Floyd made sure the record was deleted. Still, something doesn't ring true. For example, how did Floyd get hold of Jason's number? Check the outgoing calls as well."

"I'll look into it, Mrs Baxter. Is there anything else?"

"Yes," Rosalind said, thoughtfully. "How come Floyd knew that the girl survived? You don't think we have a leak, do you?"

Grolby ran his hand over the blond-grey stubble of his hair. "I don't know how he found out, but I'll be sure to ask him if I ever get my hands on him. If you can let me know who had access to that information, I can look more closely at their communications."

"I'll get a list to you. There are a couple of other things I need you to do too."

"Yes, Mrs Baxter."

"I think we should double the security on the girl's room. My son's still sniffing around, and Floyd knows that she survived the birth. I just want to make sure nothing untoward happens. That girl's worth billions. I'm sure we can afford the cost of another guard to safeguard our investment."

"I'll sort that out. And the other thing, Mrs Baxter?"

"Yes. I want you to find Floyd again and this time, no tip-offs to the police. He knows too much. When you find him, I want you to deal with him yourself."

"That would be my pleasure," Grolby said, smiling coldly.

51

Friday 14th January 2033

Antimone ate her breakfast without enthusiasm. The nurse had told her it was morning, but there was no visual indication it was true. For all she knew, it could have been the middle of the night. Despite feeling stronger, she had slept little, spending several restless hours twisting and turning, trying to get comfortable. A thin layer of stubble now covered her scalp. The sites where the biopsy samples had been taken were beginning to heal, but they were incredibly itchy, and it took all her willpower to resist scratching at the scabs.

She dropped her spoon into the empty cereal bowl. It ricocheted off the side with a metallic clang and bounced onto the floor. She looked over the edge of the bed and saw it just beneath the metal frame, a few inches away. For a moment, she debated whether to make the effort to pick it up. She could almost hear her mother's voice telling her not to be lazy, to clean up after herself, but after everything they had done to her, she was in no mood to cooperate. They were holding her prisoner, keeping her locked up against her will with no access to the outside world. Despite the vital nature of the work, it didn't give them the right to treat her like a lab rat, performing tests and experiments without her permission. And still the nagging doubt persisted. What they would do when they had the answers?

She wondered briefly whether Jason had received her note. Even if he had, what could he do? He could hardly come down here and demand that she be released. She had to assume the worst. No help was coming. She was on her own. With that thought, a weight seemed to lift off her shoulders. She needed to take action, to fight back. She didn't want to hurt anybody, but after the latest experiment and their callous indifference to her welfare, she was prepared to compromise on that objective.

The big question was how? A guard sat outside the room, and her every movement was monitored by the camera in the corner of the ceiling. The bathroom, however, had no surveillance measures, at least that's what Rose had told her. How could she use that to her advantage? If she could lure the nurse inside and disable her, she could take the key card and unlock the door into the corridor. She would still need to find a way past the guard and somehow get out of the basement.

Her thoughts came crashing down with the realisation that even if she did escape, her son, Paul, would still be held captive. She had no idea where they were keeping him, but she assumed it was in some other part of the building. A vision of Paul as an adult, locked up in a room like this, flashed through her brain. She couldn't allow that to happen, but even if she escaped from this room, the odds of finding him and freeing him were remote. Only one option remained. Once she was out of here, she would have to rely on the police to locate and release him.

If the attempt went wrong, they would undoubtedly use her son to punish her. That was a risk she would have to take. She couldn't afford to wait any longer. The first problem was how to incapacitate the nurse.

Antimone picked up the tray. It wasn't heavy enough to do any damage. She would have to find something else. Her eyes swept the room. Nothing obvious came to mind. She manoeuvred her legs over the side of the bed, eased herself into the wheelchair and propelled herself to the bathroom. Once inside, she closed the door behind her. Her gaze immediately settled on the shower chair, a white plastic construction with aluminium legs. She reached out an arm and pulled the device towards her. The legs were screwed on, and she tried to twist one. At first, it didn't move, but as she applied more pressure, the metallic tube turned with a screech. She detached it and swung it experimentally through the air: a little light, but adequate for the job.

Next, her mind turned to the guard. From the brief glimpses she had obtained when the nurse entered, he sat facing away from the door. The door opened into the room, so the chances were he would see her before she had the opportunity to hit him with the chair leg. She was confident that she could outpace him over a short distance but probably not for long enough to discover a way out. She needed a way to slow him down. Her first thought was the cutlery they provided with her food. A knife or a fork stabbed into the leg would more than likely have the desired effect. The main issue was that the nurse invariably took an inventory of the eating utensils after each meal and ensured that all were accounted for.

Her eyes slid across to the mirror above the sink. If she broke it, she could use one of the shards as a weapon. She would need to make a handle by wrapping the glass in some material. Toilet paper would do the trick if she used enough.

With a plan in place, the only remaining question was when to implement it. The nurse would arrive shortly to collect the breakfast tray. Antimone was glad that it was the older woman and not Rose. She would have felt bad about hurting Rose, but this nurse was both bad-tempered and insensitive, and she felt no such qualms about her.

"No time like the present," Antimone muttered. She made sure the door was firmly closed, then swung the metal tube at the mirror. A star-shaped depression formed at the point of impact, and a solitary crack ran from top to bottom, but no fragments split away. She drew back her arm and smashed the chair leg into the glass with more force. This time, several shards fell loose, some landing on the floor, others in the sink. She selected a jagged piece approximately six inches long from where it lay on the white tiles and carefully picked it up. Resting it on her lap, she propelled the wheelchair forwards, the wheels crunching as they rolled over the slivers of broken mirror.

She grabbed the end of the roll and kept pulling until she had detached the entire length. Next, she held the tip of the dagger-shaped piece of glass between two fingers of her left hand and wrapped the tissue paper around it with the right. Within a minute, she had transformed the fragment of mirror into a wicked-looking blade with a white handle. Antimone picked up the weapon and slashed it through the air experimentally. She opened the bathroom door a crack and waited for the nurse to return.

***

Fifteen minutes later, the electronic lock beeped. Antimone moved the wheelchair back so the door could open just over halfway before hitting the wheels. In her hand, she grasped the metal tube. The makeshift knife lay down the side of her seat.

"I'm in here," she called. "Um, I've had a bit of an accident." Her heart pounded in her chest, and her breath came in short gasps.

"What's that?" the nurse asked, moving closer.

Antimone said nothing, but raised the rod above her head. The door moved, scraping against the fragments of glass that lay scattered across the floor.

"What the hell's going on here?" The nurse pushed the door open, her gaze focused downwards. The door bumped into the rubber tyre.

A head appeared in Antimone's line of sight. "What—"

The question went unfinished as the metal tube swished through the air and smacked into the woman's skull with a dull thud. Her eyes rolled up as she toppled backwards like a felled tree. She remained unmoving, her skirt hitched up exposing her white underwear.

Antimone scooted forwards, bending down to pull one of the nurse's legs away before shutting the bathroom door. She was relieved to observe that the woman was still breathing, her chest rising and falling in slow, steady movements. She rummaged in the left pocket of the woman's uniform. Empty. She tried the right. Her fingers grasped the key card and slipped it free.

Antimone reversed and pulled the door back. The nurse's prostrate form would be visible to the camera if anybody was watching, but she didn't have the strength to drag the woman out of the way. She would just have to hope that nobody was paying close attention to the image. She edged past the woman's legs and re-entered the main part of the room, dragging the door closed behind her.

Forcing herself not to glance up at the camera, Antimone approached the door leading out. She placed the card against the reader, grabbed the handle and eased it towards her. A crack opened onto the corridor beyond. She reached down the side of the wheelchair and closed her fingers around the improvised dagger.

"All done then?" a male voice asked as the door swung open.

Antimone surged forwards and plunged the mirror fragment into the seated man's leg. The guard screamed and clutched at the shard protruding from his thigh. Antimone accelerated away. From behind came a groan of agony followed by the tinkle of falling glass. A second or two later the crackle of a radio and a man's urgent voice echoed down the corridor, the words unintelligible as they rolled into each other.

Antimone rounded the corner and spotted the elevator doors ten metres ahead. Powerful strokes sent her racing forwards before she slammed her hands down on the wheels to bring the wheelchair to a juddering halt. The heat from the friction stung her palms, but she forced the pain out of her mind. She stabbed a finger at the call button, and the doors slid apart.

The sound of multiple running feet bore down on her. Antimone jerked forwards. The footsteps were louder, closer. A shout. "She's in the lift."

A bright red light emanated from a control panel on the wall. "Where are the buttons?" Antimone smacked her hand against the metal. "Come on, damn you. Move."

The floor vibrated. Antimone whirled around. A green coated doctor stood beside her clutching an injection gun. Several more people crowded in behind him. He took a step forward and stretched towards her. She tried to bat his hand away, but he avoided the attempt with ease. A short hiss, a sting on the side of her neck.

"No," she said. "I can't go back to…"

52

Friday 14th January 2033

Jason's mother had departed half an hour earlier. True to her word, over the course of the previous evening, she had grilled him once again. She had made him promise that he would report any attempt by Floyd to make contact. That was one promise he was about to break less than twelve hours later.

Jason turned on the computer and started up the web browser. He navigated to the YouTube website and entered the text 'Deathly Daze' in the search window. He selected the topmost result, the video for a song of the same name. Within seconds, a thrashing beat emanated from the speakers. He muted the sound and scrolled down to the comments.

"I can't believe people listen to this shit," he muttered.

He reached out a finger and flicked the screen up several times before stopping.

"Here we go," he said to himself. "Running Man 1234."

Beneath the username, a string of nine digits preceded the words, 'Just because you're paranoid it doesn't mean they're not out to get you.' More digits followed the note.

Jason smiled. The message didn't seem to relate to the content in any way, but judging by most of the other comments, that wasn't unusual. He grabbed a pen from the desk and wrote down the two sets of numbers that surrounded the comment. Next, he created a new username and left his own message in reply. 'Keep wearing the tin hat. 1523129132220.'

When he had talked to Floyd by phone the previous day, they had settled upon this method to exchange information. The last three numbers of the first sequence in the original message were the identity of a left luggage box at Northstowe railway station. The first six provided the unlock code in reverse order. The second set of digits also in reverse order was the number to Floyd's new mobile. Floyd had not been best pleased when he had been forced to dispose of his old phone, knowing that the police would be able to backtrack the call made by Jason. Jason had mentioned that he already possessed a pair of new unregistered phones. His reply provided Floyd with the number of one of those phones, once again with the digits reversed. Floyd had instructed him to make contact only in case of emergency.

He glanced at his watch. Seven thirty in the morning. Plenty of time to get to the station before school started. He didn't know what was in the locker, but it had to be related to the deal he had struck with Floyd. At first, the man had been incredulous when Jason informed him that Antimone was still alive. After Jason had eventually convinced him that he was telling the truth, he had agreed to help Jason get Antimone out of the hospital if Jason did a favour in return. The locker contents were part of the price. Floyd had described in general terms what he intended to do and had told him that detailed instructions would be provided when he picked up the package. He had reassured Jason that nobody would get hurt as a result of his actions.

Jason consumed a hasty breakfast and hurried out of the house. He didn't notice the man watching from the silver vehicle parked at the side of the road.

***

Jason entered the bustling station. He couldn't help but gaze up as he did every time he came here. The domed, latticed ceiling made the building look like the interior of a Zeppelin. A row of spotlights ran down the centre of the roof, lending it an otherworldly appearance. Northstowe station was a highlight of the new town and was highly regarded by architects the world over.

Jason forced his eyes down. People streamed through the entrance, most of them heading to the platform for the Cambridge train. The buzz of the crowds echoed around the vast interior. Several passengers bumped into him as he read the signs, trying to identify where to go. After a few seconds of searching, he eventually spotted a wall covered in a grid pattern of metal doors of varying sizes. He retrieved the piece of paper from his coat. The lockers were ordered numerically, and it didn't take Jason long to locate the one he required. It was at waist level and big enough to accommodate a small suitcase. Once again, he consulted his notes and tapped out the remaining six digits on the small keypad.

The door beeped, and a red light illuminated. Jason frowned and studied the string of numbers. He cursed as he realised that he had forgotten to reverse the digits. He tried again. This time, a green light showed. The door swung open to reveal a padded, brown envelope propped up against the side. He grabbed the package and thrust it into his rucksack. This was not the time or the place to inspect the contents. He hurried across the busy concourse and exited into the frigid January air. After the noise and activity of the station, it seemed oddly quiet outside.

Hitching the rucksack higher on his back, Jason set off along the pavement in the direction of his school. A man in a black overcoat hurried after him.

53

Friday 14th January 2033

Rose Griffin yawned and stretched out her arms. She hated the dark, dreary days of winter. She had always promised herself that one day she would move to warmer climes. Maybe that time was now. She had handed in her notice at the end of her shift at six o'clock that morning. In a month's time, she would be free of Ilithyia Biotechnology and ready to start a new life. Maybe they'd even let her leave earlier. It seemed that Rosalind Baxter would be all too glad to see the back of her.

Australia sounded attractive. She had overheard some of the other nurses talking about it. There was a shortage of trained medical staff, and the climate was vastly superior to that of grey, old England. She resolved to give the month's notice on the small flat she rented in a two-storey block on the outskirts of Northstowe. Over a third of her monthly earnings went towards the rent. That was another thing about Australia—the cost of living was apparently far lower.

She peered blearily at the bedside clock. Just after eleven o'clock. No wonder she felt tired. Normally after a night shift she wouldn't wake until at least two o'clock in the afternoon. Something rustled in the corner. She hadn't forgotten to close the window, had she? The climate control maintained a steady temperature, but she liked to let some fresh air into the room for a minute or two before turning in. She wouldn't be able to sleep if the curtains were flapping in the breeze.

With a groan and eyes still half closed, she flung back the covers and slipped her feet into a pair of fluffy slippers. She inhaled through her nose. A musty tang tickled the edge of her senses. She sniffed again, trying to identify the incongruous scent. It reminded her of tomcat urine, but just the faintest trace. She wondered whether it was just the remnants of a dream playing with her sense of smell. Frowning, she glanced at the curtains. Not the slightest ripple of movement.

A figure burst from the other side of the bed. Before she had time to react, a hand clamped over her mouth. She tried to scream, but the strong fingers blocked her airflow. A hiss. A cold sensation running rapidly down from her neck. Dizziness clouding her mind. The man's voice.

"You're not going to call for help, are you?"

Rose shook her head. Terror enveloped her, but it was as if somebody else had occupied her body.

"You're going to get dressed now." The tone was calm, persuasive.

She switched on the light, closing her eyes briefly against the sudden brightness. As they adjusted, her gaze settled on the man who had by now moved to block the door. He seemed familiar, but her addled mind struggled to place him. A burst of clarity. Grolby, the Head of Security at Ilithyia.

"Hurry up, we're going out," he said, maintaining the same resonant timbre.

She stretched out robotically, grabbed the blue uniform she had discarded on the chest of drawers earlier that morning and pulled it on over her T-shirt.

"Put some shoes on," the man said.

Rose slipped her feet into the flat-soled black shoes she wore for work.

"Before we go out, you're going to tell me what you gave the boy when you met in the car park."

"A note."

"Who was the note from?"

"The girl in the basement."

"What did it say?"

A look of anguish crossed Rose's face. "I can't remember the exact words."

"Don't worry about that," the man said soothingly. "Just give me the general gist of it."

"She asked him to get her out."

"Good. Did you tell anybody else?"

"No."

"Right, here's what you're going to do." He spoke to her in a low voice, explaining what he wanted and emphasising several points. Rose's breathing came ragged and harsh until he told her to breathe more slowly. Outwardly she appeared to be calm, but a vein throbbed rapidly at her temple.

"Do you understand all that?" he asked.

Rose nodded, her eyes darting frantically around the room.

"Okay, I want you to go now. You're going to follow my instructions, aren't you?"

"Yes," she said, a quaver in her voice.

She descended the stairs and undid the lock. Grolby looked on from the top step. She pulled the door open and stepped out without closing it behind her. She began walking, wearing no coat, only her thin nurse's uniform.

By the time she arrived at the railway station, her skin was turning blue from the cold. She was shivering uncontrollably, and several passengers threw her worried glances. One man asked whether she was alright, but Rose ignored him. She held her phone to the reader as she proceeded through the gates and onto the platform. She walked until she reached the end of the concrete strip, then turned and advanced until her feet straddled the yellow line a metre from the edge.

A high-pitched screeching sound preceded the rattle of an approaching train. Rose took a step forwards, her whole body trembling. The twin lights of the locomotive rounded the bend. Rose's head shook rapidly from side to side. The driver was now clearly visible through the windshield.

A second or two before it reached her, Rose stepped directly into the path of the incoming train.

54

Friday 14th January 2033

Karen Atkins glanced up as the technician entered her office. It was the same guy who had captured Jason Baxter on the station camera. "I take it you've got something," she said.

The man smiled. "Well, um, not much really. The first problem was how to get hold of Jason Baxter's number. Luckily he had registered his mobile so that wasn't too hard."

Kat tapped her fingers on the desk. "Okay. You wouldn't be here if you didn't have something to tell me. I don't want to hear how clever you are, just give me the facts."

"Patience is a virtue," the man said. "So, I called in a favour and managed to get the phone company to release his records despite not having a warrant."

"If you've broken the law, keep it to yourself. Just cut to the chase."

"You told me he claimed to have received a call on the Saturday morning, the eighth of January, right?"

Kat nodded. "Go on."

"Well, the phone company have no record of that, so, in a nutshell, he was lying."

"That doesn't surprise me. There's something going on here that we don't know about. Did you check the rest of his phone records?"

"Yeah. There are some outgoing calls to numbers he's called several times before, but I'm pretty sure they must belong to his friends. He's also received a few incoming calls from his mother's office. I hear she's a real piece of work."

"You could say that," said Kat, grinning. "I guess you don't get to be head of a big company like that without a certain amount of attitude. So, nothing on the calls, then?"

"Well, there was one that may be of interest. A single call to a mobile he hasn't called before, unregistered of course, at seventeen sixteen yesterday afternoon. It's probably nothing."

"Hmm. That would have been just before our meeting. The other number was unregistered, you say? It might be worth putting a trace on it."

The technician grimaced. "I'd need a warrant for that, and given that we shouldn't have his call records in the first place, that's going to be difficult."

"Alright, let's leave it for now. We know the boy lied to us. We know he met with Floyd, but we don't know who told him to go there. The reason he gave for the meeting with Floyd is pure fiction. A girl surviving childbirth? He's got to be having a laugh. On top of all that, the drone pictures don't show him carrying any supplies. Basically, everything he told us is untrue.

"However, we do have him trespassing in the old post office. I think the time for playing games is over. I'm going to threaten to charge him with breaking and entering. We'll probably have to settle for a caution, but we might learn something while we're talking to him. I wouldn't mind seeing the look on that arrogant cow's face when we inform her that her precious son is facing charges."

"Sounds like a plan," the man said. "Anything else I can help you with?"

Kat frowned and remained silent for a second. "You know when the girl was raped at the Baxter house?"

"You mean the one in the wheelchair?"

"Yeah. Did we take DNA from everybody who was there?"

"I'd need to check. As I recall, we treated all the kids who were drugged as victims rather than suspects. Once a match was found with Floyd, we didn't bother to take any more samples."

"So, no DNA was taken from the Baxter boy?" asked Kat.

"I can't be sure, but I don't think so. I can check into it. Why? What are you thinking?"

"I'm thinking there's more to this than meets the eye. What if the pair of them were already in collusion at that stage?"

"Anything's possible, but Floyd only got out of prison a few weeks before the party, so I don't see what the relationship could be."

"It's just a hunch," said Kat. "Can you confirm we don't have the boy's DNA? Assuming that's the case, I'll see if we can't get a sample when he comes in."

"Good luck with that. I can't see his mother's lawyers agreeing to it without a fight."

55

Friday 14th January 2033

Jason glanced at his watch. Five thirty-four in the afternoon. He pushed open the outer door of his mother's office and was relieved to see that it was empty. He padded across the thick carpet and put his ear to the door leading to her inner sanctum. She might well be working, but no sounds came from within. He knocked tentatively and waited for a reply with bated breath. Silence. He gripped the handle and twisted, then stuck his head through the gap. The lights were off. Good. He eased his way into the room and flicked on the light switch. It didn't bear thinking about what would happen if his mother caught him here, but if she came back unexpectedly, it would look far worse if he was skulking about in the dark.

His heart raced as he approached her desk and studied the wiring that led from the desktop through a hole to the system box below. There were two wires. One was the mains cable and the other the data cable. He removed the rucksack from his back and retrieved the padded envelope. From inside, he pulled out a unit the size of a matchbox, encased in bubble wrap. He peeled off the protective covering and examined the object. On each of the two long sides of the black plastic box were connectors, one male and one female. The gold pins glinted in the glare of the bright ceiling light. The device gave off an unpleasant, oily, industrial odour.

He felt around inside the envelope again. His fingers closed around a single folded piece of paper. The same pungent scent rose as he unfolded the sheet. The instructions were already familiar, but he read them again anyway. It all seemed simple enough. He moved the chair and wriggled underneath. The processing unit was a matt-black slab of plastic with buttons on the front and an array of connection points at the back. He tracked the chunky cable that linked to the monitor and detached the connector. He pressed it into the mating half of the small black box and made sure that it was secure, then pushed the remaining connector into the system box. A small green light illuminated on the side of the unit.

The device sat between the monitor and the processing unit. It would take a well-trained eye to spot it was there. Jason once again contemplated the wisdom of his actions. From what he understood, the gadget intercepted all signals that went to or from the monitor. That included not only what was displayed but also the screen sensors and the iris recognition camera. Once the signals had been recorded, they could be played back to allow somebody to log in and use the machine remotely. It was designed to remain dormant during the day, simply monitoring and capturing data. At night, when the office was empty, the wireless link would be activated to retrieve the stored information and, if required, to take control.

In effect, Jason was giving Floyd full access to his mother's computer. During their phone conversation the previous day, Floyd had argued that this was necessary so that he could determine the scope of the systems being used to secure the girl. It only required his mother to log in once, and Floyd would have the same level of access. The man had been vague about his plan to release Antimone, stating only that he needed to explore the system first. Not for the first time, Jason wondered whether Floyd intended to hold up his side of the bargain. Only time would tell.

He worried that if his mother discovered what he had done, it would cause irreparable damage to their relationship. That was a gamble he was prepared to take. He could have gone to the police, but there was definitely no way back from there. Even if he did so, there was the risk that his mother would hide Antimone away before they conducted their search and deny that she had ever survived. After all, Jason had no proof other than what he had seen with his own eyes. If the rescue attempt failed, informing the police was always a backup.

Jason stuffed the envelope and the paper back into his rucksack and returned the chair to its original position. He surveyed the room to make sure he had left no trace of his presence and headed to the door. Turning off the light, he pulled it shut behind him and crossed the floor of the outer office. He emerged into the corridor just as his mother approached from the lift.

She strode towards him with a frown on her face. "Hello, Jason. What are you doing here?"

"I came to see you, but you weren't in your office."

"If you'd called me, we could've arranged a time to meet."

"Oh, it wasn't that important."

"So, what did you want to talk about?"

"Um, I just wanted to apologise again for going to see Floyd behind your back. I know it was stupid, and I could have been hurt."

"Yes," said Rosalind, pursing her lips. "Just remember he's a convicted murderer. I suppose there's no harm done, but if he contacts you again, please let me know. Anyway, I've got some important things to finish off. We can talk more later."

"No problem. I'll see you at home. You are coming home tonight, aren't you?"

"Yes, I should be back in an hour or two."

"Okay," Jason said, "I'll get myself a takeaway."

Rosalind took a pace towards her office, then turned back to face him. "Oh, by the way, what were you doing at the railway station?"

"The railway station?"

"Yes, somebody mentioned that they saw you there this morning. Not planning another trip to Bedford, I hope."

"Um, no. I was supposed to meet a girl there—at the station, not Bedford. We were going to walk to school together, but she didn't show. She got the day wrong."

"Oh, a girlfriend?"

"Maybe, it's too early to say."

"Good," said Rosalind. "I'm glad you're moving on."

56

Saturday 15th January 2033

The sound of a scraping chair brought Antimone to wakefulness. She opened one eye, then closed it again immediately, groaning at the bright light that seared her retina. Her head pounded with a pain that threatened to turn her brain to mush. She attempted to lift a hand to scratch her scalp, but something prevented it from moving. She tried again, but found she could only shift it a centimetre or two. Her eyes angled downwards. She immediately spotted the reason for her inability to move. A white plastic strap was wrapped around each wrist and attached to the bed frame. Antimone struggled for a moment before realising the futility of her actions.

"There's no point trying to get out of those." A woman's voice came from behind and to her left. "They're designed to hold far stronger than you."

Antimone craned her neck and gained an obstructed view of a nurse in a blue uniform through the bars of the headboard. The woman looked up from what appeared to be an electronic book reader.

"You caused quite a stir last night, young lady, going all superhero like that. You should have seen the shiner on that nurse, Emma what's her name—oh, I suppose you did. As far as I'm concerned, the silly cow got what was coming to her. She's a right lazy slacker, that one. Probably won't see her again for several weeks now, going off on sick leave and all that. Anyway—"

"How's the guard?" Antimone said, realising that she wouldn't get a word in edgeways without interrupting.

"Oh, a lot of blood, but no serious damage. He'll be off work for a week or two as well I should imagine."

"Good. Not that he'll be off work, but that there was no serious damage," she added hurriedly.

"I'm impressed by your ingenuity, young lady, but don't think about trying anything like that on with me." The woman's tone hardened. "There's a guard outside the door and another one patrolling the corridor. There's also another nurse in the monitor room keeping an eye on things. I only have to raise my voice and another half dozen guards will be down here in a flash. You never had a chance, you know. You can't make the lift move unless it scans your iris and finds you on the system."

"What's your name?" Antimone asked, knowing that the woman needed little encouragement to talk.

"You can call me Evie," the woman replied. "I'm going to be here for the next seven or eight hours. Plenty of overtime. I'll be able to afford a really good holiday this summer, I might even be tempted to go skiing if there was anywhere with snow in Europe anymore. I hear America's still okay, but it's a long way to go."

"I need to go to the loo."

"Right," Evie said. She rose to her feet and ambled across the room.

Now that Antimone could see her properly, she deduced that the woman was in her late thirties or early forties. Her brown hair was cut short and framed a face that looked like a five-year-old had assembled it. All the angles were wrong and everything was slightly out of proportion.

The nurse banged on the door with the flat of her hand. "Hey, Tony, open up. She needs to go to the toilet."

The lock beeped. A man's face peered through the glass window before he swung the door open and entered the room. His right hand rested on a half-metre long black stick tied to his belt. He wore a neatly pressed brown uniform and stood with his legs slightly apart, his eyes focused on the girl.

Evie loosened the straps on Antimone's wrists and helped her into the wheelchair. She escorted her to the small bathroom but made no attempt to leave.

"Can I have some privacy, please?" Antimone asked.

"Sorry, my dear. My instructions are to keep an eye on you at all times. After that stunt you pulled yesterday, they're not taking any chances."

Antimone shrugged and manoeuvred herself onto the toilet seat.

"It must be hard not being able to use your legs. I heard they've got this new treatment that can cure a fractured spine. People stuck in a wheelchair like yourself were walking around like a normal human being after a couple of weeks."

"I am a normal human being," Antimone said, frowning. "Now if you insist on watching, could I at least pee in silence?"

The nurse folded her arms. "I'm only making conversation,"

When Antimone had finished, she rinsed her face at the sink, then brushed her teeth.

"Back to bed for you, young lady," Evie said.

"Can't I stay in the wheelchair?"

"Dr Perrin said you were to be restrained all day. If you cooperate and behave, then they might let you sit in the chair, so you better start being nice to me."

Antimone groaned. "Can I see my son then?"

"The same applies. Not today. You need to earn the time."

"So, you're just going to leave me tied down all day with nothing to do?"

"You should have thought of that before hurting those people."

"Do you think it's right to hold me prisoner down here?" Antimone asked, scratching at one of the remaining scabs on her arm.

"I'm not paid to think about that sort of stuff. My only responsibility is to keep an eye on you. Now, back to the bed."

Once Antimone's wrists had been secured, the guard left the room and closed the door behind him. A deep despair descended upon her. Everything had gone so well at first, but the plan had been fatally flawed. Now her captors were prepared, and her chances of escape were even lower.

One thing was for sure, cure or no cure, if she got another chance, she would make it count.

57

Saturday 15th January 2033

"Don't answer that." The lawyer leant forwards. "Mrs Atkins—"

"It's Ms Atkins, actually," Kat interrupted. "Look, we've got the boy entering the compound and breaking into the building. On top of that, he's clearly seen leaving with a known felon."

"What you've got is a fuzzy picture taken from several hundred feet up of somebody who seems to be wearing similar clothes to my client." The man sat back in his chair with a smug grin. "And if associating with a felon was a crime, my profession would vanish overnight."

"One can only hope," Kat retorted.

"So, at best you have circumstantial evidence in a case that's not even slightly in the public interest. You're not seriously telling me that you intend to prosecute, are you?"

"We haven't yet decided. If Jason were to cooperate and tell us how Mr Floyd got in contact with him, we might be prepared to be lenient."

The lawyer drummed his fingers on the table. "My client has already told you that he received a call on his mobile from Mr Floyd."

"We both know that's not true."

"And how would you know that, *Mrs* Atkins? I don't recall seeing an order to check my client's phone records. I hope you're not playing fast and loose with the law. It sounds like you might have need of my services yourself. I'd be happy to do a special deal."

Kat snorted. "If you were the last lawyer in the world, I'd still choose somebody else."

"Are we finished yet?" Rosalind asked. "Much as I enjoy listening to this banter, I've got a lot of work to do. My lawyer also charges by the minute, so that little exchange has probably cost me several hundred pounds."

"Well," Kat said, "if you're not going to provide any more information, Jason, I have no option but to put this case forward for prosecution."

A worried frown creased Jason's forehead. "What does that mean?"

"Let me deal with this," the lawyer said. "There's absolutely no chance that this would be taken to court. However, to save my client several months of stress, we might be prepared to accept a youth caution."

"Is that like a conviction?" Jason asked.

"No." The man turned sideways to address Jason. "You would have to admit the offence. It would be recorded on the Police National Computer, but it's not a conviction or a criminal record or anything like that."

"So, what would it mean, then?"

"Like I said, there would be a record. It might make it harder in the future to get a job working with children, for example, but at your age, I don't think it would have much impact."

"Would this remain confidential?" Rosalind asked. "I wouldn't want some hack digging this up and plastering it all over the Internet."

"Under the age of eighteen there are clear anonymity regulations," the lawyer said. "Even so, once it's out on the Internet it's very difficult to stop. My recommendation would be to let the police attempt to prosecute if they think they have a case. I strongly suspect it'll be too much bother and they'll just drop it."

"Just remember one thing," Kat said. "The crime that Daniel Floyd committed was particularly nasty. A young girl died as a result of it. I'm prepared to push very hard to go after anybody who's preventing us from catching this criminal."

"That sounds like a threat," the lawyer said. "I don't think we'll consider a caution after all."

"Take it how you like. I'm just stating my personal viewpoint."

The man rose to his feet. "I think we're done here."

"But—" Jason began.

"Don't worry about it," the lawyer interrupted. "Your mother pays my extortionate fees for my advice. I really think you should take it."

Jason took a sip of water. His hand trembled slightly as he lowered the plastic cup to the table.

"Actually, there is one other matter," Kat said, still sitting down.

The lawyer remained standing. "No, I think we've finished."

"I'd like to take a cheek swab."

"That's a new one on me." The lawyer grinned. "You need DNA to prosecute a trespass case? I thought you said your precious drone was all the evidence you needed."

"This isn't directly related to the breaking and entering. I was going over the case file for the incident at the birthday party and realised we didn't have any DNA on record from the people who were drugged. Would you mind giving me a sample, Jason? It's a simple procedure. Just a swab of the inside of your cheek."

"Well, if you were to drop all charges," the lawyer said, "we might—"

Rosalind rose from her chair. "No. I've heard enough. You can prosecute my son if you wish, but we'll fight you every step of the way. I've wasted enough time already this morning, and I have urgent business to attend to."

The lawyer looked gobsmacked. "Well if you're sure, Mrs Baxter."

"Come on, Jason, we're leaving," Rosalind said, heading for the door.

Kat leant back in her seat while the other three people traipsed out of the room. When they had gone, she withdrew a clear bag from her pocket and used it to pick up the plastic cup that Jason had taken a drink from. She poured the inch of water that remained in the bottom into one of the other cups, then sealed the bag.

Kat considered Rosalind Baxter's reaction. *Now I'm really curious.*

58

Sunday 16th January 2033

A rhythmic chirping sound emanated from the corner of the room. At first, Jason couldn't identify the source of the noise. It seemed to come from the small blue rucksack. He unzipped the bag. The tone immediately became louder. He stuck his hand inside and closed his fingers around the smooth pebble shape of one of the phones he had bought to give to Antimone. The unit vibrated as he pulled it out and studied the display. An incoming call. He didn't recognise the number. He swept his hand from left to right in front of the screen and held it to his ear.

"Hello."

"Are you alone?" a male voice asked.

"Um, yes. Who is this?"

"Who the hell do you think, Sherlock? Given this number to a lot of people, have you?"

"Floyd," Jason said. "I thought we weren't going to call each other unless it was an emergency of some sort. What's happened?"

"Several things actually, but nothing to worry about immediately. The first thing is that somebody is watching you."

"Watching me?"

"That's what I said. Your mother's Head of Security has got a man tailing you. He's probably waiting outside right now—but don't look out of the window. They don't know we're onto them, so let's keep it that way."

Jason desperately wanted to draw back the curtains and attempt to locate the watcher, but he resisted the temptation. "How do you know that?"

"You're being particularly dense this morning. Didn't you get much sleep or something? Thanks to you, I've got access to your mother's computer. Several long-range shots of you were attached to emails. There are some of you talking to a woman. There's a close up of her handing something white over to you. Ring any bells?"

"That would be Rose. She passed a note to Antimone for me and then gave me her reply."

"Right, well they know she gave you something."

"Oh God. She was really worried about them finding out. I hope she's okay and hasn't been fired or anything."

"Hmm, I think I saw an email saying she'd resigned. Anyway, there were some more pictures of you entering what looks like a station."

"That would be when I retrieved the bug from the locker. Did they see me take the envelope?"

"No. The photos only show you going in."

"That explains how my mother knew I was there."

"What did you tell her?"

"I said I was meeting a girl, and we were going to walk to school together, but the girl got the days mixed up."

"There's hope for you yet," Floyd said.

"So, should I try to shake him next time I go out?"

"No, don't be stupid. Like I just told you, we don't want them knowing we're onto them. Just behave naturally. Anyway, the other thing I wanted to ask was whether you really want to go through with this."

"Why wouldn't I?"

"Once we start, there's no going back. You won't be able to return home. You'll be on the run like me, maybe from the police but also from your mother's people. From what I can tell, some of them are extremely dangerous. For instance, I was doing some research on the Head of Security, Anders Grolby. He was accused of killing civilians in Iraq before he worked for Ilithyia. From what I can tell, he only got off due to lack of witnesses."

"I'm more frightened of what my mother will do."

"So, you're ready to go up against her then?"

Jason remained silent for a moment. "Yes, I think so if it means Antimone will be safe."

"So why don't you just go to the police now and save us the bother?"

Jason sighed. "If my mother were to get wind of it, she would squirrel Antimone away somewhere they wouldn't find her and deny she ever survived. I can only talk to them when Antimone is out of there."

"On another subject, you weren't totally truthful when we last met, were you? You told me I wasn't the father of the child. You omitted to mention who the real father is."

"I was going to tell you, but the police arrived. I take it you know it was me. Anyway, I was drugged."

"Who drugged you?"

"I'm almost certain it was Dr Perrin's son, Max."

"Yeah, that stands to reason, judging by the emails I've read. Obviously, your mother has the same information, and I'm fairly sure she would be happy to use it if you pissed her off enough by doing something like, I don't know, stealing the one thing that she's counting on to make billions for her company. You can do what you like when the girl's free, but you might end up facing some tough questions from the police. On the bright side, at least I'll be in the clear."

"Nobody's going to get hurt when we do this, are they?" Jason asked.

"Probably not, but you never know. She's heavily guarded, so we're going to have to do something fairly radical to get her out. It's going to be mostly down to you. If I show my face, I'll be arrested straight away."

"I'm ready."

"They can't suspect anything beforehand. You have to act totally normally. I'll pick you up after school tomorrow. That's when we'll do it, but we have to shake your watcher. Here's what's going to happen."

Floyd explained the plan to Jason.

When he had finished, Jason hesitated before speaking again. "Jesus. Are you sure that's going to work?"

"Who knows? I think it's the best chance we've got, but it's not without its risks."

"I don't know. It does sound horribly risky."

"Have you got a better idea?" Floyd said, the exasperation evident in his tone.

"No." Jason paused, then exhaled loudly. "Alright, I'll do it."

"Good. Take some spare clothes with you tomorrow, but you have to use the same bag as usual. You can't do anything out of the ordinary."

"My mother won't notice a thing. She's long gone by the time I leave for school."

"Yeah, but the guy who's tailing you might notice if you drag a suitcase behind you, though."

Despite the seriousness of the situation, Jason laughed. "Is that it then?"

It was Floyd's turn to hesitate. "There was one other thing I wanted to talk to you about, but it'll keep until tomorrow."

"Go on, tell me now."

"No, it can wait."

"So, tomorrow it is," Jason said.

"Yeah and remember to destroy the phone like I told you."

There was a click, and the line went silent. He glanced around the room at his belongings, attempting to imprint it all on his mind.

What the hell have I got myself into?

Part Three: Extermination

59

Monday 17th January 2033

It took all of Jason's willpower to resist turning around and trying to spot the man who was surely following him. The weather was dank and blustery. Jason pulled the slate grey hoodie over his head. Even with the blue winter jacket, the wind still found a way inside the layers of clothing. It was still dark as he strode along the pavement, eyes forward. The small rucksack was bulging at the seams with the clothes he had bundled in earlier that morning. He had left some of his textbooks out, figuring that he would be unlikely to need them again if everything went according to plan. He would tell the teachers that he had forgotten to bring them to school.

He had barely slept a wink the previous night. The same thought kept bouncing around his head. *Was he doing the right thing?* One thing was for certain. His mother would be apoplectic with rage when she discovered what he had done. She claimed she was seeking a cure that would save countless lives, but what was her motivation? He strongly suspected that it was primarily the value it would add to the company, but if it ensured that women survived childbirth, was he wrong to intervene? Antimone's survival had provided a huge clue, but did that mean they could justify forcibly detaining her? Clearly, she didn't want to be there, or she wouldn't have asked for help.

He had retained the napkin, keeping it in one of the outer pockets of the jacket. He pulled it out as he walked and re-read his own words, and below them Antimone's reply.

GLAD YOU'RE ALIVE. ARE YOU OK? LOVE JASON

YOU HAVE TO GET US OUT OF HERE. ANTIMONE.

He had ended his own note 'Love Jason', but she had simply written her name. Was there any significance in that? Was she still suspicious of him? Maybe his mother had revealed his role in her rape, and she was just using him as a means to escape. It was impossible to tell from those few words. She had probably been in a rush, and there was no way to glean her feelings from something as simple as the way she had signed the note.

The other curious feature was the word, 'us'. That implied that Antimone wanted Jason to get somebody else out as well, but who could that be? Perhaps they were holding other women down there, and Antimone had befriended one of them. If that was the case, he was going to have to disappoint her. The plan would only enable him to get Antimone out. Anybody else would have to wait until the police arrived.

He returned the napkin to the pocket and put his head down into the biting wind that drove the fallen leaves before it. This would probably be the last time he made this walk. What would life be like after the escape attempt? His continued attendance at Oakington Manor would be out of the question, so he would have to find somewhere else to study if he wanted to continue his education. He struggled to get his head around the thought that he would be unable to stay in his mother's huge house. Would they put him into foster care? He was sixteen and old enough to get married, but he probably wouldn't be allowed to live by himself, even if he could afford the rent, which he certainly couldn't without a job.

And what would his relationship with Antimone be like? The fact that he had raped her, even if it was under the influence of mind-altering drugs, would be a huge barrier between them. Once the police were involved, it was sure to come out. Would she believe that he had not been a willing participant? How would he be able to prove he had been drugged and that Max Perrin was responsible? Again, there were too many imponderables.

On the positive side, Floyd would no longer be accused of a crime he hadn't committed. Not for the first time, Jason wondered whether the man really was a murderer. He was coarse and unrefined, but that was probably the result of spending all that time in jail. Underneath it all, he seemed decent. He had upheld his side of the bargain—or at least it seemed that he would do so—when it would have been easier to go to the police and present Jason as the rapist. Should he trust the man? At this point, there was little alternative.

The competing thoughts swirled through Jason's head as he trudged his way along the pavement.

Fifty metres behind, on the other side of the road, a man wearing a dark overcoat followed the boy.

60

Monday 17th January 2033

Karen Atkins studied the report before her. She scrolled down the page, trying to penetrate the technical mumbo jumbo. She picked up the phone, read the name of the technician who had performed the analysis and said it aloud. After three iterations of the ring tone, a voice answered.

"Hello, analysis lab. Derek speaking."

"Hi, it's Kat. Can you come up here and explain this stuff you just sent me?"

The man replied affirmatively, and she replaced the handset in its cradle. She paced backwards and forwards, waiting for him to arrive. Less than a minute later, there was a tap at the door.

"Come in. Hi…" She had already forgotten his name. Her eyes strained to make out the text on his nametag as he pushed open the door. "Um… Derek. Thanks for coming up here."

"No problem," the man said. "What can I do for you?"

"This report. Can you talk me through it?"

"Sure. Terminal restriction fragment length polymorphism, or TRFLP, is a technique that exploits variations in homologous DNA sequences to detect similarities between the genetic makeups of individuals."

"In English, please."

"Oh…" Derek said. "Well, basically we run a test on bits of DNA—you know what that is right?—to see if somebody, a man, is a child's father."

Kat rolled her eyes. "I know what DNA is. So, you tested the sample obtained from Antimone Lessing's child and compared it to Jason Baxter's DNA? Is that right?"

"That's about the size of it."

"And it came back as a match. I thought we'd already identified Daniel Floyd as the father."

"Yes, we did."

"So how can both of them be the father?"

"Well, obviously they can't. The test looks for matching sequences of DNA. As you know, those sequences are passed from parent to child. That's how the technique works. However, that's also one of its weaknesses. There are bound to be genetic similarities between the father of a child and its grandfather. When the rape was reported, they took blood from the girl because they didn't want to risk damage to the foetus. The test they did has limited accuracy because they didn't analyse the baby's blood directly. Now we have blood taken from the child rather than its mother, we can be much more certain of the father's identity."

"So basically, what you're saying is that Jason Baxter is Paul Lessing's father, not Daniel Floyd?"

"Yes, that would be the obvious conclusion. Jason Baxter's DNA is a better match than Floyd's. It seems we've been looking for the wrong man."

"And Daniel Floyd is Jason Baxter's father, right?"

"Correct."

"Hmm. It does explain a lot," Kat said, "but it also raises quite a few questions. I checked Jason's birth certificate. It says his father was an anonymous donor. His mother was apparently undergoing fertility treatment at Ilithyia. According to her death certificate, she died in childbirth from a pulmonary embolism."

"So, Daniel Floyd got this woman pregnant. He was married at the time, wasn't he?"

"Yes. Floyd's wife disappeared eight months or so before Jason was born. If Floyd was carrying on with this woman, maybe that was his motive for killing the wife. I suspect that Rosalind Baxter already knows that her son is the rapist. They were out of the door faster than a rat up a drain pipe when I requested a DNA sample from the boy."

The technician seemed embarrassed and hesitated for a second before he spoke. "Um, I notice the form you filled in didn't have a proper case number. I'm guessing there's also no parental permission, so all of this is unofficial."

"Yeah, bloody politicians love putting roadblocks in our way, preventing us from doing our jobs properly, but they still expect us to get results. I'm going to drag him in again, and this time it's all going to be above board."

"How are you going to get the mother's permission?"

"I'll hold him for a day. If he doesn't talk, or the Baxter woman refuses to give her assent, I'll go and ask a judge. Given the serious nature of the offence, I'm sure it'll get signed off. Can we do a more detailed analysis of the baby's and Floyd's DNA and prove that Floyd isn't the father?"

"Yeah," the man said, "but it'll take a week or so. I'll get the paperwork raised for the full test today."

"Right. I'm going to be waiting for him when he comes home from school. Arresting her son for suspected rape should wipe the smugness off that arrogant cow's face."

61

Monday 17th January 2033

The man wiped the condensation from the window and watched the stream of expensive vehicles entering the school driveway. Despite the heater being on full blast, his feet were still freezing. He placed the sports car magazine on the passenger seat and leant forwards. He examined the screen of his mobile phone and checked the position of the little green dot. For the time being, it remained somewhere inside the building. The first pupils emerged through the tall, black, wrought-iron gates and walked along the pavement. He planned to stay in the relative warmth of the vehicle for as long as possible.

Since leaving the army five years ago, he had drifted from job to job, working as a security guard and, for a brief spell, as a private investigator. Two years after entering civilian life he had been drinking with a group of friends in his local pub when he had run into an old acquaintance from his army days. The acquaintance worked at Ilithyia and had agreed to put in a good word for him with the Head of Security. After a short interview, Anders Grolby had offered him the job. Over the past two years, he had performed many tasks, not all of them strictly legal, but this had to be one of the strangest. Under normal circumstances, he would have considered spying on the owner's son as a seriously career limiting move, but his superior had assured him that he was following Rosalind Baxter's instructions.

The boy seemed to lead a very average life, and there had been few moments of interest. Most of the time was spent like this, waiting for him to either come out of his house or the school. There had been the incident in the car park when the woman had given the boy a note. Grolby had praised him for capturing the scene on film but had been less pleased when he had lost the subject for a minute or two at Northstowe train station. To make sure it didn't happen again, his boss had provided him with a micro transmitter, a small circular disc, no larger than the head of a nail. The small device was coated with an adhesive designed to bond to almost any surface. The previous day, the man had bumped into the boy on his way to school and had slipped the gadget into a pocket of the boy's winter jacket. The device's batteries held enough charge to track its location to within a few metres for the next ten days.

As he monitored the mobile phone's screen, the green dot moved. Finally, some action, even if it was just tracking a teenager on his way home from school. He set the Baxter house as the vehicle's destination so that when he arrived there after following on foot, the car would be ready and waiting, a refuge from the frigid winter afternoon. The map showed that his target was now less than fifty metres away. He returned the phone to his pocket and once more cleared the side window of condensation. The man recognised the blue jacket first. The boy emerged through the gates, the hoodie pulled over his head as it had been that morning. Unlike most of the other kids, he began the short journey home alone.

The man watched the boy in the rear-view mirror and waited. He didn't need to get too close because the tracker would tell him the target's location even if he lost direct sight of him. Opening the car door into the biting wind, he pulled the collar of his coat tight around his neck. He instructed the navigation system to follow the directions he had entered a minute earlier and slammed the door. The vehicle indicated and moved out. Ahead of him the boy turned left and passed around the corner out of view. The man increased his pace and hurried to catch up. He took the same turning as the boy down Huntingdon Lane and maintained the separation between them.

At the junction, the boy waited for a gap in the traffic and jogged across to the centre of the road where there was a narrow section of pavement. He stared to his left, studying the stream of vehicles, looking for the moment to complete the crossing. The man slowed down. He didn't want to end up standing next to the boy on the small paved area between the two busy lanes.

A car braked and indicated right. The boy darted across the remaining carriageway, then continued his brisk walk in the direction of home. The man speeded up again and followed the same route as far as the central section. The line of cars was continuous as commuters made their journeys home. The boy took a right down the next road, heading towards the railway station. The man wanted to get closer in case the subject went into the concourse again, but the traffic was too heavy to navigate.

"Come on, come on," he muttered under his breath. Eventually, a driver took pity on him, slowed and gestured for him to cross. The man gave a grateful wave and broke into a jog as he trailed his target. With a sigh of relief, he quickly spotted the blue coat and hoodie amongst the commuters streaming out of the station. The boy continued along the pavement, making no attempt to enter the glass and steel building.

At the T-junction, he headed left in the opposite direction to the majority of the traffic. The man relaxed slightly and kept the same pace as his quarry. The house was just over a half mile away down this road. As the boy progressed towards his destination, the properties increased in size. After three hundred metres, the buildings on the right gave way to open fields. The man gazed at the flat, featureless landscape, broken only by the occasional tree.

By now, most of the houses on the left would be classed as mansions. Closed gates and high fences screened the vast majority of them from the pavement. Not for the first time, the man wondered what people did for a living to afford to live here. Up ahead, the man spotted his white car parked at the kerb facing towards him, close to the entrance of the boy's house. Just beyond the gates was a stationary blue van.

As the boy bent down to type the access code into the electronic control box, the rear doors of the van burst open. Two men and a woman, all wearing dark uniforms, surged out. The boy whipped around in shock. The two men each took hold of an arm, and the woman pulled back his hoodie. She examined his face and seemed taken aback. She spoke a few words. He shrugged in response. The men released his arms, and he returned to the task of entering the gate's entry code.

The security man ripped off the glove to his right hand and rummaged in his jacket for the mobile phone. He inspected the map screen and confirmed that the green dot was located in front of the Baxter residence. He switched to the camera function and zoomed in to focus on the subject.

For several seconds he stared at the image before him.

The boy appeared to be approximately sixteen years of age and the same height and weight, but he was definitely not Jason Baxter.

62

Monday 17th January 2033

Jason slid into the car seat, dropped the rucksack at his feet and loosened the scarf that obscured half his face. "Bloody hell, it's cold," he said, turning to face Daniel Floyd.

"Mm," Floyd replied.

"Hey, a manual," Jason said glancing around the interior of the vehicle. "It's a long time since I've been in one of these. What, so you have to turn the wheel and press the pedals yourself? Isn't that a bit dangerous?"

"Not as dangerous as what we're about to attempt. We might need to get away quickly, so I don't want to be travelling in a car that'll obey the speed limits and stop at every red light."

Jason's face became serious. "Are you sure this is going to work?"

"No. There are loads of things that could go wrong, but I think it's the best chance we have. If you don't want to go through with it, now's the time to say. Once we start, there's no going back."

"I've given it a lot of thought, and I've made up my mind. I can't let Antimone remain a captive. We have to get her out."

"Good." Floyd turned the key in the ignition. "I'd hate to think I wasted all that money. I called in a huge number of favours to get hold of the stuff."

"Where is the gear then?"

Floyd jerked a thumb backwards over his shoulder, indicating a green canvas bag on the back seat.

"Can I see them?" Jason asked.

"Let's wait until we get there. I'll take you through what to do when we're parked up. I want you to change into the clothes I've brought. They're in the other bag."

"You didn't mention that before. Why do I need to change?"

Floyd indicated and pulled out into the light traffic. "Think about it. If you just wander in through the main entrance dressed like that, somebody will probably recognise you. You are the boss's son, after all. However, if you're wearing the same gear as one of the doctors and a surgical mask too, the chances of you being recognised are much less."

"Good idea. Just make sure you don't crash this heap of junk while I've not got my seat belt on."

Floyd glanced across at Jason. "It's not a heap of junk. I bought it six months before… well, before they arrested me. It hasn't been used for over fifteen years, but it still started first time. That's German engineering for you. None of this cheap Brazilian rubbish that people are buying today."

"I'll take your word for it," Jason said, pulling the green designer sweater off over his head. "By the way, that suggestion of yours about swapping clothes with somebody else was a good one. I had to agree to let Brad keep the hoodie, though. He said he'd wait at the house for a couple of hours. I just hope my mum doesn't come home and find him there. He's probably already drinking her expensive wine. I assume it worked. Did you spot the watcher?"

"Yeah, he was driving a small white car. I didn't recognise the make. He sent the car ahead and followed on foot."

"I think I've seen it outside on the road a few times. I thought it belonged to the neighbours." Jason slipped into the pale green shirt and did up the buttons. "I'm going to stand out if I walk across the car park just wearing this thin top. I'll freeze my nuts off."

"Good point. Put the jacket on over the top. When you get in through the main entrance, put the surgical mask on and take the coat off. If anybody's watching, it'll look like you just nipped out for a spot of fresh air."

Jason took off his school trousers and wriggled into the green ones provided by Floyd. "They're a bit big," he said.

"I don't think anybody's going to stop you for wearing the wrong size trousers, do you?"

"Did you bring any shoes? I've only got my black school shoes."

"Jesus, it's not a bloody fashion show. Nobody's going to notice if your shoes don't go with the rest of your gear."

"Fine." Jason tied his shoelaces. "Do I look convincing?"

Floyd's eyes darted across, then back to the road. "Just like the genuine article, although I'm not sure I'd want you operating on me."

Jason refastened the seat belt. "What should I do with my school clothes?"

"Just throw them in the back."

Jason exhaled loudly as Floyd indicated left at the Ilithyia Biotechnology sign. "So, take me through the plan again."

Floyd went through the details as he navigated towards the car park. He manoeuvred the vehicle into a parking spot and applied the handbrake. He turned sideways to face Jason. "This is your last chance to pull out."

"No, I'm doing this. Show me how these things work."

Floyd stretched over into the back seat and grabbed the canvas bag. He pulled apart the handles and gingerly reached inside. "You have to treat these babies with a lot of respect." He explained how the devices worked and handed the bag to Jason. Reaching behind the seat, he dragged out a portable computer. He pressed the power button and waited while the machine booted. Within seconds the display showed a login screen. "Good. Your mother's not logged in at the moment. Have you got everything you need?"

Jason nodded.

Floyd leant across, opened the glove box and pulled out a mobile phone. "Call me when you're inside. There's only one number programmed in, so you just need to press the green dial button. You'll probably have to hang up while you're getting the girl, but give me a call me when you're at the lift and ready to leave. I'll be waiting just outside with the car. Remember, put the surgical mask on as soon as you're through the main entrance. We don't want anyone recognising you. And try to look like you belong."

"Okay. Wish me luck." Jason pushed open the door. He stooped and leant inside. "By the way, what was it you wanted to talk to me about?"

"It's nothing to worry about. I'll tell you afterwards."

Jason shrugged. He slammed the door, turned towards the giant logo of the foetus and began walking.

63

Monday 17th January 2033

Pale streaks of light fought through the angry-looking clouds at the horizon. Jason tightened the collar of the jacket around his neck. The icy wind cut through the thin material of his trousers, plucking at the seams like a witch's finger. His heart hammered in his chest as he strolled self-consciously towards the entrance. He kept his head down and avoided eye contact with the handful of people passing in the opposite direction.

A downward blast of warm air greeted him as he pushed through the rotating doors. He moved to a wall at the side of the main thoroughfare and shrugged his way out of the winter coat. He pulled the surgical mask up and over his mouth and nose. His eyes darted around the tiled entrance area, but nobody seemed to be paying him any attention. His finger trembled as he stabbed the green connect icon on the phone.

A voice responded before he heard the ring tone. "Yes."

"I'm inside and heading to the security door."

"Okay. I'm ready. Tell me when you're ten paces away."

Jason headed towards the double set of doors, holding the coat under his arm. Ahead of him, a man wearing a dark business suit waved a card at the reader and pushed his way through. He glanced back at Jason and held the door open. Jason showed him the mobile and shook his head. The man shrugged and continued on his way.

"I'm there," Jason said. He could have followed the man, but he wanted proof that Floyd could control the security system remotely. Two seconds later there was a barely audible click, and the light on the box changed colour from red to green.

"I'm through," he said. The corridor seemed quiet after the bustle of the reception area. "I'm on my way to the lift."

"Just wait a sec. I'll call the lift and let you know when it's about to arrive. Make sure you have the car to yourself." Several seconds of silence passed. "Right, it's on its way."

A ting announced the lift's arrival, and the doors slid apart. To Jason's relief, nobody was inside. "Right, I'm in."

"Okay, I'm enabling the lift panel. I'm not sure what you're going to see, but you want the basement level."

"Nothing's happening yet," Jason said. "Hang on, the panel's lit up, and there's a B on it."

"Go for it," Floyd said. "You better get your respirator on. Don't press the button until you're ready."

Jason pulled the cloth mask down around his neck. "I'm putting it on now. It's not going to be easy to speak to you with this thing on. I'll call when I need the lift again." Reaching into the canvas bag, he retrieved a device containing a face-sized clear panel with a stubby black cylinder protruding from the front. He slipped it over his head, the rubber moulding to the contours of his face. He put the phone in the breast pocket of his shirt and placed his hand inside the bag for a second time. This time, he withdrew a six-inch long, blue, cylindrical object. White Cyrillic writing curved around the circumference. A silver-coloured lever ran down the side and connected to a hinge on the top. A metal ring linked to a pin inserted through the mechanism. Jason depressed the lever, put his forefinger through the ring and pulled out the pin.

He took a deep breath and pressed the icon on the lift's control panel. The doors started to slide shut, but before they met, a green-booted foot appeared in the gap. The doors separated. A male doctor dressed in similar attire to Jason stepped inside.

64

Monday 17th January 2033

Karen Atkins slammed the van door and stared at the illuminated building. "Let's see what you have to say this time," she said.

The man to her left turned to face her. "What did you say?"

"Oh, nothing. I'm just looking forward to Rosalind Baxter trying to talk her way out of this one."

Kat had managed to convince her superior to assign a couple of uniforms to assist her in arresting the boy. Her boss had not been pleased when he discovered how she had come across the evidence but had relented when she outlined the details of the case. He had even agreed to contact a judge who owed him a favour. Kat now held the authorisation to request a DNA sample whether the boy's mother assented or not.

It had come as a surprise when they had apprehended the wrong boy at the Baxter house. He had told them that Jason had asked him to swap jackets and wait in the house for a while before leaving. He claimed to have no knowledge of Jason's whereabouts or the reason for the bizarre arrangement. Judging by his confusion, he was as much in the dark about what was going on as Kat.

"Right, let's do this," Kat said, as a short beep signalled that the second man had locked the van. She strode towards the entrance to Ilithyia Biotechnology, the two policemen following three paces behind.

At the reception desk, the woman asked them what their visit was about. It was with some satisfaction that Kat announced they wished to discuss a serious police matter with the CEO. The woman placed the call, her eyes never leaving the three police officers. "If you'd like to wait here for a minute, somebody will be down to get you."

Kat paced backwards and forwards, sensing the receptionist's gaze flicking across to her at frequent intervals. She glanced at her watch and was about to approach the reception desk a second time when a small, narrow-faced man sidled up to her.

"Hello, I'm Julian Stefano," the man said, extending a hand. "I'm Mrs Baxter's personal assistant. Mrs Baxter is very busy. How can I help you?"

Kat grasped the man's sweaty palm and gave a perfunctory shake. "I don't think you recognise the seriousness of the situation. We're here to arrest her son."

Stefano did his best to hide the shock on his face. "I don't understand. Mrs Baxter's son?"

"That's what I just said. Now if you don't want to be arrested yourself for obstructing a police investigation, I suggest you either tell me where Jason Baxter is or take me to see his mother."

"Um… I have no idea where he is. Can you just wait a moment while I talk to Mrs Baxter?"

"I'm rapidly losing patience here. You better make it quick."

Stefano backed away, took out his phone and spoke into the handset in hushed tones. His eyes darted across to Kat several times during the conversation. He replaced the mobile in his breast pocket and retraced his steps. "Mrs Baxter will see you in the conference room. If you'd like to follow me."

He led the group through a door labelled 'Staff Only' and up a flight of stairs. He ushered them into an empty meeting room and hurried away. Three minutes later, Rosalind Baxter strode into the room, making no attempt to shake hands. She glared at the three police officers. "What's this all about? I thought we'd been over everything on Saturday."

"Mrs Baxter, we have a warrant for your son's arrest," Kat said.

"Not the trespassing thing again? My lawyers have assured me that there's zero chance of that ever going to court."

"No. This is about the rape of Antimone Lessing. Ironically, I believe the girl died at this very facility."

"What's that got to do with my son?"

"We've been re-examining the evidence and have concluded that your son was responsible. But I'm sure you already knew that. I also have a judge's order for a DNA sample."

"I don't know what you're talking about. You've been conducting a manhunt for Daniel Floyd for months."

"It appears we were mistaken," Kat said. "It seems that Daniel Floyd is your son's biological father. Would you care to explain?"

The blood drained from Rosalind's face. "That… that's confidential information."

"We can go into all that later. In the meantime, I want to know Jason's whereabouts."

"I have no idea. I assume he's at home."

"Apparently not. One of his school friends turned up wearing his clothes."

"Wearing his clothes? What do you mean?"

"We waited for your son to return—"

The ring tone from Rosalind's mobile interrupted Kat's words. Rosalind glanced at the display, then clicked the cancel button. "You were saying."

Kat grimaced, but before she could repeat her statement, the phone rang again.

"Excuse me," Rosalind said, "I need to take this." She left the meeting room and stood in the corridor. Her voice carried through the open door. "I'm very busy, Anders. I've got the police here asking about Jason … He what? … Another boy? … Well, where is he? … In that case, I suggest you find him as soon as possible."

Rosalind Baxter returned and faced the three seated police officers.

"I'm sorry, I have to go now. My assistant will show you out. I don't know where my son is. Please let me know when you locate him."

65

Monday 17th January 2033

Jason turned his back to the doctor, but he could sense the man's eyes boring into his back. Prickles of perspiration formed on his forehead. The harsh sound of his breathing rushed in his ears. He heard the doors come together, and the floor sank away beneath him.

"You must be new here. I'm not sure we've met. I'm John Edwards."

Jason remained silent.

"I hope you don't mind me asking, but why do you have a full facemask on?"

Pressure pushed up through Jason's legs, and a ding signalled that the lift had reached the basement. An elongated swish accompanied the opening of the doors. The doctor stepped out, but when Jason risked a glance, the man was waiting for him. A bead of sweat rolled down Jason's temple and onto his cheek. He took a deep breath, turned to face the doctor and followed him into the corridor.

The man was studying Jason intently. His gaze settled on the blue canister in Jason's hand, then flicked down to the black lace-up shoes. Finally, he raised his eyes and focused on Jason's chest. "Why aren't you wearing ID? Are you authorised to be down here?"

Jason still didn't answer. Instead, he dropped the coat, tossed the cylinder a few feet away and strode after it.

"Hey", said the man. "Come—"

The object made a hissing sound, but there was no visible effect. For a moment, Jason worried that the gas grenade was not functioning correctly, but when he glanced behind him, the doctor was leaning against the wall with both hands, his head hanging down. Three seconds later, he had slumped to the ground, unconscious.

Jason rummaged in the canvas bag and withdrew a second blue cylinder. Holding the lever down, he yanked out the pin. He raced down the featureless white passageway and skidded to a halt where it angled to the right. Assuming Antimone hadn't been moved, they were detaining her in the room two doors down. However, when he had last seen her, a guard occupied a chair outside the doorway.

Jason edged his head around the corner. The guard was there, but rather than sitting in the chair, he was on his hands and knees. As Jason watched, the man coughed once, and his arms slid outwards. His head hit the floor with an audible thump. The sound of running feet echoed along the corridor from his right. Jason lobbed the second grenade ahead of him in the direction of the approaching footsteps. It bounced a couple of times, rolled and came to rest. A man wearing a brown uniform and holding a long black baton in his hand staggered forwards and collapsed.

Jason sprinted to the door the man had been guarding and peered through the small glass window. A woman in a blue nurse's uniform stood on the other side, staring at him in confusion. She partially obscured another figure lying on the bed. He pushed the door, but it refused to open. *Locked.* His eyes flashed over the smooth white surface. *No sign of a keyhole.* His gaze settled on a small box, a red light at its centre, mounted on the wall. *An electronic lock.* He strode to the prostrate guard and rolled the man onto his back. With trembling hands, he rummaged through the uniform pockets until his fingers closed around a credit-card sized piece of thin plastic.

Jason waved the card in front of the box. The light changed from red to green. He shoved, and the door opened inwards.

The nurse took a step backwards. "What are you—" She clutched at her throat and sank to one knee. Seconds later she toppled sideways.

Jason stood over the figure on the bed and stared down. For a moment he thought he had the wrong room. The pallid-faced girl with the layer of stubble on her scalp and the scabs covering her face looked nothing like the vivacious athlete he had known before. "What the hell have they done to you?"

Confusion washed over Antimone's face. "Ja—" she began. Her eyes rolled up in her head as she sagged backwards.

"Let's get you out of here," he said to the now unconscious girl.

Jason yanked off the white sheet covering his friend. She wore a thin blue patient gown. Now he could see that the scabs extended along both arms and legs, several of them still partially covered by plasters and dressings that were hanging half off. He placed his arms beneath her before realising that a pair of white straps bound her feet to the bed frame. Fumbling at the buckles, he released her legs then lifted her. He deposited her in the wheelchair and wrapped the sheet around her, tucking it in down the sides. Her head lolled to one side as he manoeuvred the chair to the door.

Jason pulled the door handle, but it didn't budge. He glanced at the small box to the side of the doorframe and spotted the red light shining at its centre. *The damned thing was locked again. Where had he put the card?* He tried first one pocket, then the other and sighed with relief as he grasped the thin plastic. He stuck his head into the corridor and surveyed left and right. Other than the two unconscious men, it was empty.

Jason grabbed the wheelchair handles and reversed out. At any second, he expected the blare of an alarm, but all he could hear was the rasping of his own breath. He swivelled the chair and propelled it forwards, only slowing to turn the corner. Sprinting past the unconscious doctor, he reached the lift and jabbed at the call button. The doors slid apart immediately. Retrieving the coat from where he had dumped it, he dropped it on Antimone's lap, then pushed her inside and snatched the mobile from his breast pocket. His finger prodded the green connect icon. He held the device to his ear and waited for an answer. Silence. In a mounting panic, he stared at the phone's screen. No signal.

"No, no, no," he said. "Not now."

He stepped outside the elevator. Still no signal. "Oh, crap."

"Hang on," he said aloud. He withdrew the key card from his pocket and waved it in front of the control panel. No effect. The only sign of activity was a bright red light emanating from the centre of the blank console. Finally, it dawned on him. "Damn. An iris scanner."

In despair, Jason returned the card to his pocket. *Come on, think.*

He exited the lift again and stared first one way, then the other down the corridor. His eyes settled on the comatose form of the doctor. *Of course!*

He rolled the man onto his back and grabbed him under the arms. Gasping from the effort, he dragged the man inside the elevator, surprised at how much he weighed. He hauled the man to a half standing position and heaved him towards the reader. When the man was in roughly the right spot, Jason held him around the chest with one arm and prised open an eyelid with the fingers of the other. No reaction.

Maybe it was keyed to one eye only. He adjusted his stance and swapped to the other eye. After what seemed like an age, the red light turned off, and a green G took its place. His finger prodded the letter. The panel now displayed an up arrow.

"At last," Jason said, lowering the unconscious doctor to the floor. The doors slid shut with a swish, and the lift surged upwards.

66

Monday 17th January 2033

The lift doors slid apart. Jason expected a crowd of security guards to be waiting for him, but the corridor was empty. He removed the mask from his face and stuffed it into the bag. Next, he grabbed his phone and inspected the display. It was once again indicating a strong signal. He stabbed a finger at the green call button.

"Have you got her?" the voice at the other end asked without any preamble.

"Yeah. She's unconscious and in a wheelchair, but I think she's okay. I've got a key card, so I won't need you to do your thing. Where are you?"

"I'll bring the car as close to the entrance as I can get," Floyd said. "Let's get the hell out of here."

"See you in a sec." Jason pulled the doctor's card from his pocket and ran towards the security door. In his haste, Antimone's legs bumped into the sealed door. She gave a low moan, but her eyes remained closed. Jason waved the card at the small plastic box. The red light changed to green. Reaching forwards, he shoved the door open. A man wearing a pale blue shirt, yellow tie and black trousers stood on the other side, an access card in his hand. The man held the door for Jason as he propelled the wheelchair into the reception area. The man turned to stare as Jason hurried across the busy floor space.

Jason kept his eyes forward, but was aware of the glances he was receiving. He forced himself to slow down and tried to act as if he was simply taking a patient out for a breath of fresh air.

He was ten paces from the revolving door when a shout came from behind. "Hey you! Stop!"

Jason gave up all pretence of normality and sprinted the remaining distance. The front of the chair brushed against the leg of a woman who was chatting to a colleague to one side of the exit. She whirled around angrily. "Watch out, will you?"

Now all eyes were on him. Most people shrank back, but one man dressed in a thick, green, winter coat took a step forwards. The man reached out an arm, but Jason swatted it away and barrelled into the rotating chamber. He risked a glance behind him and was relieved to see that nobody had attempted to follow him inside the semi-circular compartment. It seemed like a lifetime before the gap opened onto the frigid January evening.

Jason snatched another hasty peek over his shoulder. A security guard had reached the glass panel and was pushing against it to make it turn faster. His actions had the opposite to the desired effect. The door juddered to a halt and stopped rotating altogether. The man glared at Jason and shouted something that was whisked away in the cold breeze. He removed his hands from the pane of glass, and the door lurched into movement again.

Jason surged ahead. He tipped the wheelchair back so that the small front wheels were in the air. The coat slipped off Antimone's lap and dropped to the ground, but he didn't try to retrieve it. A man and a woman who were heading to the building stopped to stare at the scene of a doctor propelling a patient at high speed towards the car park.

Another shout from behind. "Stop! Come back!"

Jason accelerated along the wide stretch of paving and spotted the blue vehicle parked at the side of the roundabout that led to the car parks and back to the main road. Floyd stood beside his car, hopping nervously from one foot to the other. Seeing Jason approach, he pulled the rear door open.

"Come on, hurry," Floyd shouted.

"I'm going as fast as I can." Jason skidded to a halt, one wheel of the chair bumping into the rear quarter of Floyd's car.

"Hey, watch that," Floyd said as he bent down and placed his hands below the unconscious girl's arms. "Give me a hand here."

"Piece of old crap," Jason muttered. He grabbed Antimone's legs and lifted. Floyd clambered across the back seat, dragging the girl with him. As soon as her legs were inside the vehicle, Jason slammed the door. He whirled to see the security guard advancing towards him, swishing his baton menacingly. The man jumped forwards and swung with all his power. Jason swayed backwards, the tip missing his chin by inches. Spotting that the man was off balance, Jason sought to nullify the weapon by enveloping him in a bear hug.

The man bucked and thrashed in an attempt to break free. Jason felt his grip weakening, and the guard released an arm. The man's elbow smashed into the side of Jason's head. Jason's vision turned grey as he staggered backwards. The man followed up with a vicious swing of the baton that caught Jason on the upper part of his arm. He fell to the ground and covered his head with his remaining good arm in anticipation of the blow that would end it.

A yell of rage erupted from a few feet away. Jason looked up to see Floyd flying through the air and crashing into the guard. The pair hit the pavement in a tumble of limbs. The baton bounced away. Jason sprang to his feet to retrieve it. He snatched it up and turned to face the two struggling men.

Floyd sat astride the guard, one hand pinning the other's throat. He drew his fist back and slammed it into the man's face.

"Leave..."

Another blow.

"... him..."

The crunch of knuckles against the soft cartilage of the nose.

"... alone."

Floyd cocked his fist again, but it was clear that his opponent had no fight left in him. Blood bubbled from his shattered nose and splattered the brown shirt of his uniform.

More shouts from the direction of the building.

Jason stared at the three men dressed in brown uniforms, sprinting towards them, batons drawn. "Come on. Leave him. We need to go."

Floyd clambered to his feet and faced the approaching guards. For a moment Jason thought Floyd would attack them too, but instead, he kicked the prostrate man in the ribs and headed back to the car.

"Does that collapse?" Floyd asked, gesturing to the wheelchair, his breath coming in huge gulps.

"I think so." Jason ran his eyes over the mechanism. "Here." He slid a lever across, and the chair concertinaed to half its original size.

"Toss it in," Floyd said, hurrying around the back of the vehicle and opening the boot. He slammed it closed and rushed to the driver's door.

Jason yanked the passenger door open and threw himself in beside Floyd. The engine roared into life, and the wheels scrabbled for purchase as Floyd released the clutch. The first of the guards made a grab for the rear door handle, but he was a second too late. The tyres screeched as the car surged forwards out of his reach.

Jason turned in his seat to see one of the men talking urgently into a phone and the other two tending to their injured colleague. He turned back to Floyd, a grin on his face. "That was close, but we did it."

"Yeah. I haven't had that much fun in ages, but it isn't over yet. We've still got to get to somewhere safe."

With that, Floyd gunned the two-litre diesel engine and raced towards the main road.

67

Monday 17th January 2033

Rosalind Baxter held the phone to her ear. She spoke with a cold fury. "So, you're saying that the boy single-handedly waltzed into a high-security area, unlocked God knows how many supposedly secure doors and then casually made his way out with a girl who is worth billions of pounds to this company? What the hell do I pay you for, Anders?"

The voice on the other end began an explanation, but Rosalind cut him off. "I don't care about that now. Get the girl and my son back. Use whatever force you deem necessary. If you get the chance to get rid of Floyd that would go some way towards compensating for this cock-up. Oh, and one other thing. I want two armed men guarding her child, twenty-four hours a day. Do you think you can achieve that without messing it up?"

Grolby once again launched into a protracted apology, only to be cut off a second time. "Look, I don't want to hear it. Get the bloody girl back, and we'll talk then. You better have a good explanation for how they got past your systems."

Rosalind placed the phone on its cradle and rose to her feet. Grolby had grown complacent. For the first time, she contemplated the idea of removing him from his post. The problem was the man knew too much. Retirement would have to be of the permanent kind. She resolved to put out feelers, although such a matter would have to be handled delicately.

The situation with the girl was bad, but it could have been much worse. Luckily, the police had departed ten minutes before the boy—she no longer thought of him as her son—had performed his audacious rescue. It was clear that he had received help from somebody, and there was only one person she could think of who that might be: Floyd.

One thing in her favour was that they now had enough information to develop a cure without the girl. They had retrieved all the samples they required and understood to a large extent how she had survived. Yes, there was still work to do, but Perrin had assured her that the first trials were imminent. He even believed that the treatment would be effective on women who were already pregnant. They could trial it on patients who had given their permission without resorting to unwilling guinea pigs. At least two were due to give birth in the next two to three weeks.

Rosalind strode along the corridor and descended the stairs. Instead of heading to the reception area, she approached the lift that led to the basement. A security guard stood outside the sealed doors.

"Hello, Mrs Baxter," he said. "They're just confirming whether it's safe."

"Is Dr Perrin down there?"

"I believe so."

"In that case, I'm going down to see him. If it's not safe yet, get me the gear I need."

"I'll just check in," the man said, glancing nervously at Rosalind. He turned away and conducted a hurried conversation using a walkie-talkie. "They think it's cleared," he said after a moment, "but somebody will meet you with a mask when you get down."

The man stepped aside to allow Rosalind to enter the elevator. Seconds later she emerged into the white corridor. A guard wearing a gas mask held a spare one in his hand. "You'd probably be okay anyway," he said. "Most of the gas has dispersed, but it's best if you put this on just as a precaution."

Rosalind slipped the mask over her head. "Where's Dr Perrin?"

"He's in the emergency ward," the man replied, his voice coming through muffled.

Rosalind strode along the passageway, her breath sounding loud in her ears. She turned the corner and pushed through the swing doors into a room containing four beds, three of them occupied. Nigel Perrin leant over a patient and peered through the faceplate of his mask. He raised the heavily pregnant woman's eyelid and shone a torch in her eye, then directed the beam away. He repeated the process three more times. He turned to a nurse who stood beside him wearing the same gear and spoke a few words to her.

When he had finished, he glanced up and spotted Rosalind. "I hear Jason was behind this."

Rosalind strained to hear his muffled voice. "Yeah. We need to talk. Now."

"Pardon," Perrin said, turning his head sideways. "I didn't catch that."

In frustration, Rosalind tore off her mask and dropped it on the floor. She inhaled deeply, then exhaled. "See, no problem. I said we need to talk."

Perrin removed his own mask and cautiously sniffed the air.

"You're not going to smell anything," Rosalind said in exasperation. "The gas was colourless and odourless. Some Russian grenade they apparently use for special operations. God knows where they got it from."

"So, she's gone, but we probably don't really need her anymore. Have you heard anything from Grolby?"

"I spoke to him a few minutes ago. He's got his men looking for the car, but nothing yet."

"So, what did you want to discuss?"

Rosalind beckoned him to the corner, out of earshot of the other people in the room. "We've still got her son, but they might decide to go straight to the police. If that happens, they'll be here fairly soon, I would imagine."

Perrin frowned. "So, what do you want to do?"

"Well, we can't risk them finding these women, can we? They'd find out about the test subjects and that we kidnapped them. I think we'd both end up spending a long time behind bars."

Perrin's face paled. "What do you propose?"

Rosalind fixed him with a hard stare. "I suggest we transfer some of the patients from upstairs down to the basement."

Perrin pulled the pen from his front pocket and began clicking the tip in and out. "Their families know they're here. We can't just bring them down and do what we like to them."

"No, you misunderstand. I mean transfer them down here and treat them the same as we have been doing."

"How's that going to help?"

"Well, we'll have to move the existing patients out first."

Perrin hesitated for a few seconds before speaking. "When you say move them out…" A look of horror spread across his face as realisation dawned. "You mean kill them?"

"Exactly. They're going to die anyway. If the police raid the place, we're both looking at a long prison sentence. This way, there's no evidence."

Perrin stared at his feet. He returned the pen to his pocket. His rate of breathing accelerated. A muscle began twitching on his cheek. Slowly, he raised his eyes. "So, you propose to euthanise them and cremate the bodies, even though some are heavily pregnant?"

"Well we can't afford for the police to find them, can we? This is the only answer. Now that we're close to a cure, we don't need to perform illegal experiments anymore. We can easily obtain patients' approval to trial the new drug. They're not exactly going to say no when the alternative is certain death."

"But you just want to murder these women?" Perrin whispered.

"How many women have we already murdered over the years? Forty? Fifty?"

"We didn't murder them, well not directly."

"Oh, come on Nigel. What's the difference? If we hadn't made them pregnant, they wouldn't have died."

"It's not the same thing."

"Why? To all intents and purposes, we killed them. Why is this any different?"

"At least they had a chance. This is just plain murder."

Rosalind scoffed. "Had a chance? All the women we abducted and what percentage survived? Precisely zero. By making them pregnant we were effectively killing them even though it took nine months to play out. Now, do you want to spend the rest of your life in prison, or are you going to do what's necessary?"

Perrin placed his hands on his head. "I don't know," he muttered.

"Pull yourself together, Nigel. It's them or us. We need to move quickly. The police could be here any minute."

Perrin lowered his arms, an expression of resignation on his face. "Okay, I'll do it, but we have to get everybody out of here. We also need people we can trust to get them to the incinerator. There may only be four or five women down here at the moment, but somebody might raise the alarm with that many dead bodies all at the same time."

A thin smile brushed across Rosalind's lips. "I knew you'd see reason in the end. It's regrettable, but it's got to be done. We couldn't continue this vital work from behind bars." She turned to leave, then hesitated.

"Remember that what's at stake is the survival of the human race."

***

When Rosalind had left, Nigel Perrin glanced around the room to make sure nobody was watching him and picked up the telephone handset. He spoke a number and waited for the ring tone. A voice answered after two rings.

"Max, it's your father. I want you to pack an overnight bag and come here to Ilithyia. Just pack a change of clothes and pyjamas or something. Bring your toothbrush and any toiletries you might need. Can you pack a bag for me too? Nothing too big, though."

"... Look, I haven't got time to answer your questions now, but you have to understand that this is very important."

"... No. It's nothing to worry about. I'll explain it all when you get here. Will you please just do as I ask? Give me a call on my mobile when you arrive."

Perrin replaced the handset and once more checked that nobody was paying any attention to him.

68

Monday 17th January 2033

The flat, featureless landscape flashed past the car window as they drove along the dual carriageway. The last tendrils of sunlight tinged the clouds at the horizon with an orange hue. After the initial rush of adrenaline, Jason's euphoria was wearing off. His eyes felt heavy-lidded as exhaustion crept up on him.

"How is she?" Floyd asked.

The words jolted Jason back to wakefulness. He loosened the seatbelt and twisted his neck to inspect the girl lying across the back seat. "She's still unconscious by the looks of it. Will she be alright?"

"She'll wake up with a headache, but there shouldn't be any lasting ill-effects—or at least that's what the guy told me."

"So where did you get those gas grenades from?"

Floyd glanced sideways. "When you've spent as long as I have in prison, you're going to make some contacts. He was just somebody who owed me a favour. I didn't ask where he got them, and he didn't tell me. Judging by the writing on them, I'd guess they were liberated from some Russian military armoury."

"Well, they were certainly effective." Jason lapsed into silence and stared sightlessly at the tarmac, lost in his own thoughts. By now his mother would know that he was responsible for freeing Antimone. He wondered what she was doing at that moment. No doubt she would be incandescent with rage. Before the rescue, he had been undecided about whether it was the right thing to do. His mother had presented a persuasive argument for studying the reasons behind Antimone's survival, but having seen the effects of the tests, he felt vindicated in his actions. Now he had crossed a line from which there was no coming back.

As he allowed his mind to wander, the memory of an earlier conversation rose to the surface. "You were going to tell me something. Before all this. What was it?"

Floyd said nothing.

At first, Jason thought he hadn't heard the question. He was about to repeat himself when Floyd indicated left, and the car slowed down. "Why are we stopping?"

Floyd pulled onto the hard shoulder, turned off the ignition and reached forwards to turn on the hazard lights. The whoosh of passing traffic seemed to intensity in the absence of the engine noise. He turned sideways in his seat to face Jason. "What did your mother tell you about your father?"

"He died. Of cancer."

"That's not true, Jason. She lied to you."

The car shook as a huge articulated lorry thundered past.

"Lied to me?" Jason said. "How do you know that?"

"Don't forget I've had access to her emails for the past few days. They tested your blood, didn't they?"

"Yeah, that was after they realised that it was me who… well, you know."

"You're right. They were checking whether there was something in your genetic makeup to explain how Antimone survived. But haven't you asked yourself why the police think I was the rapist?"

"Yeah, I thought it was a bit strange," Jason said. "My mother said it was because they were incompetent."

"Not that incompetent," Floyd said, letting the words hang.

"What are you saying? That you're my father?"

"Yes."

Jason gaped in shock. "My father? How did that happen?"

"You knew that my wife used to work for your mother, right? She was a researcher at Ilithyia. She was conducting research into infertility treatments before she died. This was all before the virus first broke out. She persuaded me to donate a sperm sample shortly after she joined the company, so I can only assume that somehow it was used to impregnate your biological mother."

"She told me my biological mother was a patient, and that she died in childbirth," Jason said. "A blood clot in the lungs or something. She never mentioned that she was responsible for making my real mother pregnant in the first place."

"It came as a shock to me too," Floyd said. "But think about it. If your mother was being given infertility treatments, it's entirely possible they would have used donated sperm, although I have to admit that I didn't realise that's how they were going to use mine. I thought it was just for experimental purposes."

"That explains why the police thought you were the rapist," Jason said. "We obviously share a lot of our DNA."

"Exactly."

"So, you're my Dad?"

"Yeah."

"And you've known for a day or two?"

"I wanted to tell you sooner, but you needed to be focused for this. That's why I waited until now."

Jason stared straight ahead and blew out his cheeks. The rhythmic tick-tock of the hazard lights was like a metronome accompanying his thoughts. After a few seconds, he turned and smiled shyly.

"Hi, Dad. It's good to finally meet you."

Floyd's relief was palpable. He grabbed Jason around the shoulders and pulled him in. "I'm proud to have you as my son."

Their hug was interrupted by a cough from the rear seat.

***

Jason shifted sideways and stared behind him.

Antimone's eyelids fluttered open. "Where am I?"

"We got you out of there," Jason said. "You're in a car."

Antimone scanned the interior of the vehicle and raised herself to a sitting position. "Jason?"

"That's right."

Antimone's fingers rasped as they scratched the stubble on her scalp. "I... I don't remember."

"I had to knock everybody out, including you, otherwise we'd never have made it. Mr Floyd managed to get hold of some gas grenades and—"

The cogs in Antimone's addled brain crunched into gear. She shrank backwards. "Wait. Did you say Floyd?"

Floyd turned around in his seat. "Hello, Antimone."

Panic flooded her voice. "What's he doing here? He's the—"

"It's alright, Antimone," Jason said. "He's not the rapist. The police got it wrong."

Antimone shook her head rapidly from side to side. "No, no, no. He's a murderer. He made me pregnant."

Floyd frowned. "Actually, neither of those statements is true."

Antimone pushed herself sideways along the seat and shoved the door open. The blare of an air horn stopped her in her tracks as a three-section articulated lorry swept past, rocking the car in its wake.

"Antimone, stop," Jason shouted. "I can explain."

She stared into his eyes, her hand still on the door handle. A second or two later, her head jerked to the left. "Where's Paul?"

"Paul?" Jason and Floyd asked in unison.

"Yes, Paul, my son. Where is he?"

Jason hesitated before replying. "Um, Antimone, I'm really sorry, but he died two weeks ago, the day after he was born."

Her initial look of terror morphed into one of anger as she processed his words. "I saw him only yesterday. Why would you lie about something like that?"

It was Jason's turn to be confused. "But he died of a bacterial infection, didn't he? That's what my mother told me."

A hush fell, as if all the air had been sucked out of the interior of the vehicle.

Floyd broke the silence. "She's right, Jason. I saw some of your mother's emails about a baby. Now I think about it, they may have mentioned the name, Paul. That would explain a lot. She must have lied to you about that too."

"So, he's still alive? That means I'm a father."

"What the hell is going on here?" Antimone yelled. "What are you talking about?"

"It's a long story, Antimone. Mr Floyd—um, Daniel—didn't rape you. I'm Paul's father."

Antimone dragged herself across the seat and yanked at the handle on the passenger side. She flung the door open and toppled onto the verge. Jason opened his own door. The roar of the passing traffic was suddenly much louder outside the confines of the car.

Antimone clawed at the muddy grass as she dragged herself forwards. "Get away from me, you bastard," she shrieked.

"It's not what you think. I was drugged. We both were."

"Leave me alone."

"I—we—were set up. Just let me explain."

Antimone said something, but it was swept away in the roar of a passing lorry. Even though she was breathing hard, she now remained stationary.

Jason crouched down beside her. "It was Max. He put a date-rape drug in the drink at the party. It made us all extremely suggestible. Look, can we discuss this in the car?"

"Leave me alone."

"Antimone, I swear I was drugged. Why would I go to all the trouble of getting you out of there if I wanted to hurt you? I only discovered I was the father a few days ago when they did a blood test."

Antimone rested her head on her arms and sobbed.

"Antimone, can I help you back in?"

She raised her head and nodded silently.

"Can you give me a hand here?" Jason called to Floyd, who stood a few paces away, looking on anxiously. Between them, they lifted her and eased her through the open door. Jason knelt, facing Antimone over the back of his seat.

Mud streaked her face and the front of the patient gown. Her limbs trembled as she studied the two men with tear-filled eyes. Several seconds of silence passed before she spoke. "So, tell me what happened."

Jason shot a sideways glance at Floyd, then spoke. "Like I said, Max slipped something into the fruit punch. It was some sort of hypnotic drug. He told us to go to the ground floor bedroom. Then he raped you."

Antimone wrapped her arms around herself and shivered violently. "But you said you were the father."

"Yeah, he used protection. When he'd finished, he ordered me to… well, you know."

As she processed Jason's words, it all seemed horribly plausible. "Christ, is there anybody who hasn't had sex with me?"

"Well, me for a start," Floyd said. "I just had the misfortune to be in the wrong place at the wrong time. I saw you both come out of the bedroom. Neither of you looked in the least bit distressed. I thought you were just, um… getting to know each other a little better."

"What *were* you doing there?" Jason asked.

"I didn't murder my wife all those years ago. Eileen called me from work on the day she disappeared. She sounded upset and said she was coming home, but she wouldn't tell me what it was about. She never arrived. When the police questioned the Ilithyia people afterwards, they said she hadn't turned up at all that day. They found a record of the outgoing call, but your mother explained it away by saying that somebody phoned me to ask if I knew where my wife was."

"That still doesn't explain what you were doing at the house."

"I think your mother was involved somehow, Jason. The police never discovered anything at Ilithyia's offices. I was hoping to find some evidence at your house, maybe a diary with an entry like *'Murdered a member of staff today and framed her husband.'*"

"What? After all that time?"

"Well, I'd exhausted every other avenue so…"

"How do you know it was my mother?"

"Well, I don't know for sure. I suppose it could have been somebody else at Ilithyia. In any case, whoever it was must have planted Eileen's blood in the boot of my car. You can't imagine what it's like serving a sentence for the murder of your wife when you know some other bastard was responsible and got away with it. All these years later, I still find it hard to talk about."

"What about when you threatened me at the seaside?" Antimone asked.

"Yeah, sorry about that. Not my finest moment, I know. Look, I thought the pair of you had set me up. Remember, this is the second time I've been framed for a serious crime. My head was all over the place. I followed you from Northstowe. Then I saw you messing around and having fun while I was still a wanted man, hiding from the police. It all just got to me. All I can do is apologise."

"Well you scared the shit out of me," Antimone said, folding her arms. "You must be really proud of yourself."

"Like I said, I'm sorry. I did help to get you out of there, though."

"Yeah, thanks. Anyway, the bottom line is that woman still has my child. How are we going to get him back?"

"We could go to the police," Jason said.

"That's a big risk," Floyd said. "I suspect your mother's not going to just give him up. But if that's what you want to do."

"So, what do *you* propose?" Antimone asked.

"We have access to her computer. I suggest we try to find out what she's planning before we make our own plans. We might even discover where she's keeping the boy."

"*The boy,* as you call him," Antimone said, "has a name. It's Paul. Before we do anything, I want to call my parents and let them know I'm alive."

"I think you should wait until we know what Jason's mother is up to before doing that," Floyd said. "Telling them would be like talking to the police."

"Hmm. So where is this equipment then?"

"It's back at my squat in Huntingdon. We've hacked into her computer and can read anything that's stored on it, like emails and so on."

Antimone fastened her seat belt. "So, what are we waiting for? Let's find out what that evil witch is up to."

69

Monday 17th January 2033

Jason, Antimone and Floyd sat around the tablet computer. The display showed a list of emails on the left side of the screen. The information was split into three columns: one for the title, another for the sender and the last for the time received. As they watched, the cursor moved to one titled 'Tim Belton reference request'. The sender was somebody named John James. The bold font indicated that the email had not yet been read. A second later, all the items in the list shuffled up one position.

"She just deleted it without reading it," Jason said.

"Who needs a reference anyway?" Floyd said. "You should try spending sixteen years in prison for murder. Then see how easy it is to get a job."

"When's she going to go home?" Antimone asked. Jason had lent her a chunky pale blue jumper which she wore over the thin hospital gown. On her feet was a borrowed pair of thick woollen socks. "How are we going to find out what she's planning if all we can do is watch her deleting emails without even reading them?"

"Patience," Floyd said. "She's got to stop at some point."

The three people fell silent as another five emails disappeared from the list without being opened.

The tablet rested atop an overturned plastic crate. An extension cable snaked away from a plug block into the adjacent room. The computer's power supply and a small fan heater occupied two of the four sockets. Antimone was in the wheelchair while Jason and Floyd leant against the pock-marked wall, sitting on the bare floorboards. A battery-driven camping lantern provided the illumination from its position on the floor in the centre of the room. At the side of the stark room was a sleeping bag resting on top of an airbed. A heavy brown blanket lay beside the opposite wall.

"So, have you found anything out about your wife?" Jason asked.

Floyd's eyes remained fixed on the screen. "I searched all over the network. There are files relating to other things at about the time my wife disappeared, but nothing directly relevant. There was one password-protected file on your mother's hard drive. It looked like it was last modified at around that time, but I wasn't able to open it."

"Sorry," Jason said, "I don't think I can help. You're talking, what, sixteen or seventeen years ago? I've no idea what my mother was into in those days. It could be pretty much anything. There are websites that list the most popular passwords, but I can't see my mother picking something that obvious."

"So, no suggestions?" Floyd asked, diverting his gaze from the tablet display to search Jason's face.

"What about her initials and her birthday or something?"

"It's worth a try. What's her—"

Floyd paused as a sudden movement on the screen caught his eye. The picture changed from that of an email program to what appeared to be a shiny, black surface. A hand entered the shot. The image jerked while the hidden person adjusted the camera angle. As the fingers moved out of the way, the picture stabilised, and Rosalind Baxter's face gained focus. A click came from the small speakers on the computer.

"Can they hear what I'm saying, Anders?" Rosalind asked a person who was standing out of the camera's line of vision.

Her eyes darted left and right then settled on a point at the centre of the screen. "Hello Jason, Antimone and Daniel. I assume you can all hear me. My Chief of Security, Mr Grolby, assures me that your little bug is picking up my voice and everything on the display. A very clever ploy, but I have to admit I'm disappointed in you, Jason. I'm assuming you're the one who put it in place. Don't bother answering by the way. I can't hear you.

"So, you managed to free your friend. First of all, I'm sure I don't need to remind you that she signed a contract when we agreed to treat her. She's now in breach of that contract, and I'll be seeking legal redress for the cost of her treatment."

"I don't believe this," Antimone said. "She's making out that I'm the one in the wrong."

Floyd waved a hand to shush Antimone.

"… generous offer to waive any legal action if she returns to the hospital immediately," Rosalind continued. "We're very close to a cure. The future of the human race depends on our ability to continue studying you, Antimone. You don't want to be responsible for the deaths of countless women who'll die in childbirth just because you couldn't handle a little discomfort, do you?

"I take it my son—my adopted son, that is—has told you that he is the father of your child, Antimone? Well, if he hasn't, welcome to the family."

A fleeting smile crossed her lips. She reached out her arms to somebody off-screen and accepted a small bundle, wrapped in a white blanket. "I guess I'm a grandmother now," Rosalind said, turning the bundle around to show the baby's face to the camera. She bounced the child gently up and down a couple of times. The baby opened one eye and yawned then settled back into a peaceful repose.

"Paul," Antimone said in a strangled voice.

"Don't worry, we're taking good care of him—for now," Rosalind said. Her arms extended to hand the child back. Her gaze focused back on the screen. "He's missing his mother, Antimone. So, here's what I'd like to propose.

"You—that's all of you by the way—come here to Ilithyia by nine o'clock tomorrow morning. Antimone, you'll be reunited with your son. You can call your parents and they can visit whenever they want. We'll continue to study you until we've developed a cure. We won't do any procedures without explaining them fully and obtaining your permission first, although I think we've already got all the data we need. When we start the first patient trials in a week or two, you'll be free to go home.

"I've decided to be generous and forgive your foolish actions, Jason. I was wrong to ask you to forget about your friend. I'm sure you'd much rather be at home than in some squalid hideout.

"Mr Floyd—Daniel—I'd be happy to show you the records we have available from the time of your wife's disappearance. I know you think my company had something to do with her death, but I can assure you that isn't the case. The police investigated very thoroughly sixteen years ago, and I'd be glad to let you see everything I showed them at the time.

"There is just one condition. If the police are involved, the whole deal's off. They'll only complicate matters. I'm sure we can sort this out like adults. If you want to discuss anything, Jason has my mobile number. If I don't hear anything, I expect to see you all tomorrow morning."

Rosalind gave a slight nod of the head. The screen flickered once then turned black.

70

Monday 17th January 2033

Jason pulled the phone out of his pocket and turned on the screen. "It's still before seven. We've got more than twelve hours to make a decision, but I think we should just call the police." He placed the device on the floor beside him.

"I don't trust her," Floyd said. "It's all just a bit too easy. I mean, she could have let me see the files months ago. She's hardly going to show me anything incriminating, is she? And if she's so relaxed about allowing you to see your parents, Antimone, why didn't she let you see them in the first place?"

"I don't know," Antimone said. "She's still got my son. I don't want to do anything that puts him at risk. I vote for doing as she says."

"It all just seems too good to be true," Jason said. "I walk into her company, gas her security guards, and she's just going to brush it all under the carpet and take me back. I'm sorry, but I don't buy it."

"Maybe we can set up a message that goes to the police automatically if we don't stop it so that they know where we are if anything happens," Antimone said.

"Hmm, maybe," Floyd said. "The question is whether they would believe us, especially if we're not there in person to argue the case."

"Whatever we decide, I think we should all do it together," Jason said.

"I'm just nipping to the loo," Antimone said.

"Do you need a hand or anything?" Jason asked. He blushed as he realised the stupidity of his question.

"I think I can manage," Antimone said, a thin smile brushing her lips. "I have been doing this for four years, you know."

Jason turned back to the tablet. Floyd had closed the remote display application and was now staring at a password box. "You suggested your mother might have used her birthday or initials."

"You don't know how many characters then?"

"No, it could be any number," Floyd said.

"Well her birthday is the eighteenth of April, and she was forty-five two years ago so that makes her year of birth… um… nineteen eighty-six, I think. Her middle name is Susan."

Floyd typed in '180486rsb' and pressed the enter key. An 'Incorrect password' message appeared, and the password entry box cleared.

Floyd quickly tried several combinations, reversing the date, reversing her initials, swapping the order of the initials and the digits. "This is hopeless," he said.

"I've got another idea," Jason said. "I know my mother sometimes swaps letters for similar looking numbers and vice versa. Try changing the S for a five and the zero for an O, maybe even an L for the one."

Floyd rapidly entered several permutations of Rosalind Baxter's initials and birthday. "No, that's no good either." He leant back against the wall and sighed. "After a day like today, I could do with a stiff drink."

Jason frowned, then jerked forwards. "What did you just say?"

"I said I could do with a stiff drink. Why? Do you have one stashed away somewhere?"

"My mother's always going on about a particular make and vintage of red wine. It costs something like a quarter of a million pounds a bottle. Even the newer vintages cost several hundred quid."

"You'll have to narrow the field a bit for me," Floyd said. "Can you remember what it's called?"

"Chateau something or other," Jason said. "I remember it sounds like a woman's name."

Floyd opened a browser window and typed in 'Chateau expensive wine'. He scrolled down the list of results. "Lafite? Rothschild? They don't sound like women's names."

Jason shook his head. "No, that's not it."

"Mouton? Margaux?"

"That's it," Jason said. "Margaux. Try Chateau Margaux expensive wine."

"It says here that one of the most expensive vintages is seventeen eighty-seven. Apparently forty-five years ago, some bloke who owned a bottle took it with him to a restaurant. He didn't open it or anything, but a waiter knocked it off the table. His insurance company paid out about a quarter of a million dollars for it."

"That's the one," Jason said excitedly. "I remember my mother telling me the story. Try Chateau Margaux seventeen eighty-seven."

Floyd transferred back to the password screen and entered the letters. "No," he said. "That didn't work."

"Try capital letters and swap the words around."

Floyd tried several alternatives, his mood deflating with every failed attempt.

"Remove the Chateau part. So just Margaux followed by the date."

Floyd typed in Jason's suggestion and shook his head.

"Leave a space between Margaux and the numbers."

The password box disappeared. A list of files took its place.

"Bingo!" Floyd said. "Good guess. Let's see what's in here then." He opened the first file and scrolled down what appeared to be a report. "Just some test results by the looks of it."

He selected the next file. The scrollbar indicated he was about halfway through the contents when he stopped. "Hang on, what's this?"

He read the words on the screen, then moved the document down a page. "What's your birthday, Jason?"

"Tenth of April."

"What year?"

"Twenty sixteen."

"My God," Floyd said, his mouth dropping open in shock. In a frenzy, he opened several of the other documents and quickly scanned the contents while Jason looked over his shoulder. "This is staggering. It's far worse than I thought. We've got no choice but to go to the police now."

Jason's face was pale. He clasped his arms across his chest and shivered. "I can't believe she would do something like that."

"The evidence is here in black and white. When Antimone comes back, we'll all go to the police station and show them these documents."

"I just can't believe it."

"She's always been a bitch, but I never thought she was capable of anything like this."

"I thought I knew her. All this time—"

"I know it's a lot to take in. At least now we know the truth, even though it may be hard to swallow."

"It's just…" Jason's voice tailed away.

Both men sat in silence. Floyd continued to scroll through the documents. He closed the last one and glanced up from the screen. "Where the hell has that girl got to? I guess things take longer in a wheelchair, but even so."

"I'll go and check on her."

"Do you want to borrow the light?"

"No, it's alright. I think there's a torch on the phone." Jason felt in his pockets and realised the phone wasn't there. He cast his mind back and remembered putting it on the floor shortly after his mother disconnected the computer. It was no longer where he had left it. "Did you pick up the phone?"

"No."

"Shit. We might have a problem. The phone's gone, and I think Antimone took it." Jason rushed into the hallway, calling her name. No response. He opened the front door and stared both ways along the quiet street. Seconds later, he sensed Floyd's presence behind him.

"How much money did you put in it? Enough to get a taxi?" Jason asked.

"I think it was about a hundred quid. That's probably just about enough to get to Ilithyia."

"Well she's left, and there's only one place she could be going."

71

Monday 17th January 2033

"So, you still don't know where they are?"

Grolby stared at a spot on the carpet. "My men are still looking, but as of this moment, no."

"Well, it's just not good enough," Rosalind said. "Floyd has been one step ahead of us the whole time. When this is all over, I'm going to need a full review of your security protocols."

"If I may say so, Mrs Baxter, our security against external attack was not at fault. The hardest thing to guard against is a breach from inside the company. By fitting the device to your computer, your son effectively gave Floyd the same access to our systems that you have."

"I never thought the boy would do anything like this, but even so, you're supposed to run a daily sweep for bugs. How did you miss it?"

"Well, Mrs Baxter, it uses a technology where it remains inactive for most of the time. It only starts to transmit when enabled remotely. When we did our sweep, it must have been in its dormant state. In this case, the best method of security would have been to prevent access in the first place."

Rosalind Baxter's eyes bored into Grolby's face. "So, you're saying it's my fault for allowing my son to get into my office?"

Grolby swallowed, but he raised his gaze and met hers. "Well… um… I'd strongly suggest that you keep your office door locked when you're not there. Rest assured that we'll perform a check on all other machines in the company just to make sure that no others have been compromised."

"I'd expect nothing less. So, do you know what data Floyd had access to?"

"Well he was logged on as you, so we've run a scan to see what files were accessed by your account from this machine when we know you weren't in this office. Clearly, he got into the security systems, which is how he managed to get your son into the basement."

"Yes. If that stupid cow hadn't brought him down there in the first place, none of this would've happened."

"Well, she's not going to be a problem in the future."

"It was a little public, though, wasn't it, Anders? Couldn't you have done something—I don't know—less dramatic? It'll only draw more attention from the police."

Grolby's jaw muscles twitched. "I try to vary my methods. The police are very good at picking up patterns. I remember warning you at the time that too many accidents in too short a space of time might make them suspicious. You told me to make it look a suicide, which is what I did."

"But you're the expert. It's not my job to do your thinking for you. Anyway, what else did Floyd get access to?"

"The majority of the folders he looked at were pretty old, dating from the time his wife worked here."

"That stands to reason. He's obviously obsessed with proving his innocence. There's nothing on the network for him to find. That was one of the first clean-up jobs you did as I recall. Was there anything else?"

"He could see all your emails."

Rosalind gave a short laugh. "Ninety percent of it's spam, anyway, and the rest is day-to-day drudgery. The only thing that might be awkward is the stuff about the girl and her child, but none of the emails mentioned either of them by name. Jason already knew most of it already. So, it doesn't look as though he found anything incriminating?"

Grolby hesitated before replying. "Well, there was one file that he transferred from your hard drive."

Rosalind frowned. "He transferred a file?"

"Yeah. He attached it to an email and then sent it to a disposable email address. Afterwards, he deleted the message from your email client, but it still shows up on the servers."

Rosalind's frown deepened. "What was the name of the file?"

Grolby consulted his mobile phone and read off the filename.

"The file's password protected, though," Rosalind said. "That should stop them seeing the contents, shouldn't it?"

Grolby returned the phone to his pocket. "That depends. If we're talking about a fifteen-year-old file then security standards have moved on a long way. Given enough processing power, it might be possible to crack the password."

Rosalind stared out of the window for a second or two, then turned back to her Head of Security, her face paler than before. "That file contains information that would be disastrous if it fell into the wrong hands. We've got to get it back."

"May I ask why you kept such sensitive information?"

"No, you may not," Rosalind snapped. "I want you to delete all records of that email from the server. I also want you to make sure it's gone from my computer."

"If you'll allow me," Grolby said, coming round the desk. "Would you mind logging in again?"

Rosalind swiped a hand in front of the screen and stared into the red eye of the scanner. When the welcome message was displayed, she stepped back to give Grolby access to the machine. She identified the location of the file and watched over his shoulder while he typed a sequence of commands.

"That's it. It's permanently deleted from this computer. It'll take a little longer to purge all record of it from the server. I'll do that from my office."

"No, I want you to do it now."

Grolby shrugged. "Okay, but I'll need to log on." He entered another set of commands and focused his gaze on the iris scanner. Next, he navigated his way through several layers of menu, muttering to himself as he did so. Finally, he swept his hand across the screen and turned back to Rosalind. "That's done too."

"All evidence of that file must be destroyed," she said. "If Floyd's got it, make sure you get hold of his computer and find out if he's saved copies anywhere else."

"You sound worried. Does it contain something I should know about?"

"Just remember who's in charge here. If what's in that file comes out and I go down for it, you're going down with me."

Grolby folded his arms. "The converse is also true."

The blood drained from Rosalind's face and gathered in two pink spots, one on either cheek. Her hands formed into fists, and her body trembled with rage. Grolby took a step backwards. The woman before him might be nearly a foot shorter in height, but the energy coiled inside her lent her the appearance of a dangerous wild animal.

Rosalind opened her mouth to speak, then closed it again. She took a deep breath, held it, then exhaled. "Yes… well. It seems our fates are intertwined. If you do your job properly, it won't come to that."

The colour slowly returned to her face. "Now I need you to do something down in the basement."

72

Monday 17th January 2033

Jason held Floyd's phone in his hand. It was an identical model to the one that Floyd had given him earlier and that Antimone was now using to pay for a taxi.

"I'm calling the police," Jason said.

"Is it still nine, nine, nine?" Floyd asked, taking his eyes momentarily off the road and glancing sideways.

"Are you serious? What else would it be?"

"You've got to remember I've been out of circulation for sixteen years. There wouldn't be much point dialling nine, nine, nine from inside, even if you had access to a phone. I just wondered if they'd changed it to the American nine, one, one or some such nonsense."

Jason shook his head and tapped out the digits.

"Hello, emergency services. Which service do you require, fire, police or ambulance?"

"Police," Jason said.

"What is the nature of the emergency?" a woman's voice said.

Jason hadn't thought through what he was going to say. "Um… you've got to get the police to Ilithyia Biotechnology in Northstowe. My friend is going there. I think they're going to kill her and her baby."

"What's your name?"

"Jason Baxter. My mother runs Ilithyia."

"And your friend's name?"

"Antimone Lessing."

"How old is your friend?"

"Look, it doesn't matter. She's taking a taxi there now, and she's in serious danger."

"Okay. You said she had a baby. I assume that's somebody else's baby."

"No, it's her baby."

"So, you're saying she had a baby, and she's still alive."

"That's right."

"And your mother is the head of Ilithyia Biotechnology? What's her name?"

"Rosalind Baxter. Why are you asking me this?"

"You realise that making hoax calls is a serious offence for which you can be prosecuted, right?"

"For Christ's sake, this isn't a hoax call. My name is Jason Baxter, my mother is Rosalind Baxter. Actually, she's my foster mother. I think she's going to kill my friend."

Jason noticed that Floyd was gesticulating towards him. "Just a sec."

"Hang up," Floyd mouthed.

"What?" Jason said, frowning in confusion.

"Hang up," Floyd repeated, this time out loud.

"I'll call you back." Jason ended the call. "Why did you want me to hang up?"

"You should listen to yourself," Floyd said. "You tell them that your friend and her baby are in danger from your mother. No woman has survived childbirth for what, sixteen years, and yet your friend has a baby? I don't think I'd believe you."

"So, what do you suggest?"

"I think we need to take a different approach. They're never going to accept that Antimone is alive. If they bother to check the records, they'll find out that she reportedly died in childbirth two weeks ago. But they're still after me."

"How does that help?"

"Tell them that I'm at Ilithyia."

"If they didn't believe me the first time, what makes you think they'd buy that?"

"You've got a point. What if you mention the name of the policewoman who's after me? Can you remember her name?"

Jason racked his brains. "I've got it: Karen Atkins."

"I take it you don't know her number."

"No. I can call nine, nine, nine again and tell them I've got information for Karen Atkins on your whereabouts."

"It's worth a shot. Just try to remain calm and think about what you're saying."

Jason inhaled deeply and dialled again. This time, a man's voice answered, and he requested the police.

Before he could explain the situation, the responder said, "I've got a record of a call from this phone three minutes ago. It's been classified as a hoax. You do realise it's a criminal offence to waste the emergency services' time."

"This isn't a hoax. My name's Jason Baxter. I'm with a man named Daniel Floyd who's wanted by the police. We're on our way to Ilithyia Biotechnology in Northstowe."

"Daniel Floyd, you say?" asked the man, the suspicion evident in the tone of his voice. The sound of keys being tapped came down the line. "I'm showing an active arrest warrant for a man of that name. Why are you going to Ilithyia?"

"To confront my mother. Look, if you don't believe me, call Karen Atkins. She knows all about Mr Floyd. We're going to be there in…" He glanced across to the driver.

Floyd held up the fingers of both hands.

"… about ten minutes," Jason continued.

"I need to make some calls," said the man. "Will you be contactable on this number?"

"Yes, but we're not waiting outside. When we get there we're going in, so you better be quick."

"I strongly urge you to wait for the police to arrive. I'll try to contact Ms Atkins. Somebody will call you back shortly."

Jason stabbed the disconnect button. He turned to Floyd. "Do you think they believed me?"

73

Monday 17th January 2033

Grolby entered the lift behind Rosalind. "What's this job?"

"I want you to move some things from the basement to the incinerator."

"What things and why do you need me to help?"

"You'll find out soon enough. I need somebody who I know won't blab."

"Okay, that sort of work. What about your assistant? Why can't he do it?"

"Stefano? I let him go home. Anyway, he doesn't know what's going on."

"I wouldn't be so sure," Grolby said, then lapsed into silence.

The lift doors slid apart. Rosalind strode down the corridor, the security chief trailing a couple of paces behind. She barged through the swing doors at the entry to the emergency ward and stopped to survey the three occupied beds. Grolby almost bumped into her.

A nurse sat at a desk to the side of the room. "Hello, Mrs Baxter. What can I do for you?"

"How are the patients?" Rosalind asked.

"At the moment they're all sedated. Dr Perrin was going to perform some tests."

"I see. Where is Dr Perrin?"

"He's in his office, I think."

Rosalind spun on her heel and retraced their route.

"Is there a problem?" Grolby asked, but Rosalind didn't reply.

She passed the lift and continued to the door labelled 'Chief Scientist'. She shoved it open without knocking. Nigel Perrin sat behind his desk, his head in his hands. Resting on the desk in front of him was an injection gun. He looked up at the sudden intrusion.

"I couldn't do it," he said in a monotone.

"For Christ's sake," Rosalind said. "I don't get it. You're happy to experiment on women we've dragged off the street, make them pregnant and watch them die when they give birth, but you haven't got the balls to do what needs to be done now?"

"Rosalind, be careful what you say," Perrin said, nodding at Grolby who stood awkwardly behind Rosalind.

"He's in this as deep as we are," she snapped, "as he reminded me a few minutes ago. So, you're just going to sit here feeling sorry for yourself?"

"The injection gun's loaded if you want to do it. I can't do this anymore."

"Can't do what anymore?"

"I'll help you develop the cure, but then I'm leaving. You won't need me after that. You'll have what you want. If you'd like to buy my shares at the current market price, you can have them. I've just had enough of all this."

"Jesus, Nigel. After all the years of effort and sacrifice, now of all times you want to quit?"

Perrin glared at Rosalind. "My mind's made up. I'll help you this one last time, and then that's it. No more."

"We've worked together for twenty years and finally, when we have the prize in our sights, you just want to walk away? If you see this through, we'll both be billionaires."

"Multi-millionaire or billionaire, what's the difference? I'm not like you. I want to spend time with my son. I want to be able to look him in the eye without feeling ashamed."

"Come on, Nigel. Pull yourself together."

"Sorry, Rosalind. I'm not going to change my mind."

The silence built between them. Finally, Rosalind sighed in resignation. "Okay, I see I'm not going to be able to convince you to stay. If that's your final decision, I accept the offer to buy your shares, as long as you agree to remain until the cure's developed. It'll take one or two days to raise the finance, but no more than a week. I hope you know what you're giving up."

"I'm going away for a few days with Max. It'll take that long to synthesize the latest treatment, anyway. I just need some time off from this place."

Rosalind looked thoughtful. "You *are* going to come back, aren't you? I can't do this alone, at least not at this critical juncture."

"Of course," Perrin said, nodding eagerly, "but I'm not going to inject those women. I couldn't live with myself if I did that."

"Okay, it's a deal. I'll clean up this situation. You spend a few days away, let's say no more than six. When you get back, we transfer the shares. That should give me enough time to get the money together. You stay on until we have a proven drug for the Orestes virus. How does that sound?"

"Good, good. It's a real weight off my mind."

"So, this is already loaded, is it?" she asked, reaching for the injection gun.

"Yes, everything's set up. Just press the trigger."

"Right. Come on, Anders, we've got some work to do."

Rosalind left the room clutching the medical instrument in her hand, Grolby trailing a few paces behind her.

They had reached as far as the lift doors when Grolby called from behind, "Mrs Baxter, can I have a word?"

Rosalind halted and spun around to face her Head of Security. "Yes, what is it?"

"Well… I've worked for you for many years. I've taken a lot of risks on your behalf and performed a large number of criminal activities. I want some of Dr Perrin's shares."

"You mean buy, right Anders?"

"The thing is, I don't have much spare cash at the moment. I want you to give me some—for free."

"Let's get this straight, Anders. You expect me to buy his shares, then just hand them over to you?"

Grolby lowered his eyes to the floor. He swallowed, then met Rosalind's gaze. "Yes. If what you say is true, and you do have a cure, the shares are going to increase massively in value. After what I've done for you, it's only fair that I benefit from that."

"You already have share options, Anders. You'll benefit like everybody else who works here."

"Yeah, but a few thousand shares isn't going to change my life. I'm sure you can afford to let me have more than that. Two hundred thousand more, for example."

Rosalind barked a short laugh. "You want me to buy two hundred thousand shares and just give them to you for nothing?"

Grolby frowned. "Didn't you just say that our fates were intertwined? If I understand correctly what you're planning, I'm about to become an accomplice to murder."

"Jesus, Anders, you're responsible for far more than five deaths, so don't play all innocent with me."

"All under your instruction, though, Mrs Baxter. I was only following orders."

Rosalind's eyes narrowed. "As you well know, that's no defence. I'll think about it."

A hard expression passed across Grolby's face. "Two hundred thousand shares, Mrs Baxter. I want your agreement now, or you're on your own."

Rosalind stared at him for a few seconds. "Okay, Mr Grolby, you have a deal."

74

Monday 17th January 2033

Antimone pushed the door open. The autonomous taxi was stopped at the side of the entrance road, two hundred metres short of the Ilithyia building. That was as far as the credit on the phone would take her. The wheelchair was on the rear seat, and there was no way she could get it out by herself. She had suffered the same problem in reverse when she had left Floyd's hideout. Luckily, a passing resident who was out walking his dog had been kind enough to help her by collapsing the chair and stowing it in the back of the car.

She felt bad about leaving Jason and Floyd at the house. It was hard for her to trust them. For so long she had believed that Floyd was the rapist, but now it seemed he was totally innocent. It was weird to think that he was Paul's grandfather. As for Jason, she struggled to put her feelings into context. Had he really been unaware he was raping her? He was obviously racked with guilt and on balance, she believed his story. It was all too conceivable that Max Perrin was behind everything, and all because she had accidentally tripped him during athletics training. She shivered at the thought of him undressing her and pawing at her naked body.

As she imagined the sequence of events and Max's calculated act of revenge, a feeling of rage enveloped her. But for a fluke, what he had done would have resulted in her death. Her breathing came hard and fast as she envisioned herself plunging a knife into his chest. The only good thing to come out of all this was Paul. At the thought of her son, her sense of anger morphed into one of concern. That, after all, was the main reason she was here.

Rosalind Baxter had offered to reunite them and allow her parents to visit whenever they wanted. Antimone still didn't trust the Ilithyia staff, but once news of her survival was out, they would have no option but to honour their side of the deal. She felt a moral obligation to assist in any way she could to develop a cure. As Mrs Baxter had put it, surely a little discomfort was worth it to save the lives of countless women who would otherwise die in childbirth.

On the journey to Ilithyia, Antimone had tried to call her parents, but paying for the taxi had used up every last penny of credit on the phone. Floyd and Jason were sure to contact the police when they discovered she was missing, so even if the people at Ilithyia wanted to keep her presence a secret, that would no longer be possible. She had considered waiting for the following morning before going to Ilithyia, but the way Jason and Floyd had been talking, it seemed they were more likely to go to the police. There were clearly long-standing issues between Rosalind and both of the men. By coming alone, she hoped to take the tension out of the situation.

The problem, for now, was how to get the wheelchair from the boot. The headlights of a car approached from the opposite direction. Antimone waved to catch the driver's attention. The car slowed but then carried on past without stopping. For a moment she contemplated lowering herself to the ground and lying in the road. Cars would have to stop then, but what if they didn't? It would be ironic to be the first woman to survive childbirth in a generation and then die because either a human or computer driver didn't see her.

The glare of headlights approaching from behind lit up her vehicle. Once again, she waved her arms. The car drew up alongside, and the window wound down.

"Is there a problem? Are you alright?" the middle-aged male driver asked.

"My wheelchair's in the back, and I can't reach it. Could you do me a favour and help me get it out?"

The window closed, and the car continued forwards. Antimone was about to swear in frustration when she realised it had pulled in ahead, its hazard lights flashing. The door opened. A short man wearing a dark-coloured winter coat and blue jeans walked back towards her.

"I assume you're going to Ilithyia," the man said. "Why didn't you go as far as the entrance?"

Antimone felt the man's eyes studying her as she held up the mobile. "Out of credit. I'm supposed to meet my Dad inside, but there's no money left on the phone to call him."

"Hmm," the man said. He opened the rear door and retrieved the wheelchair.

"Just pull the two halves apart," Antimone said. The man did as instructed, and the chair locked into shape. He wheeled it beside the door. "Do you need help getting into it?" he asked.

"No, I can manage, thanks. Could you just hold it still while I move myself across?"

Antimone manoeuvred herself from the seat into the wheelchair.

"It's a bit cold to be out without a coat," the man said.

"I'll be alright," Antimone replied, shivering as the freezing night air cut through the oversized blue jumper. "It's not far." She noticed the man staring at the muddy stains on the hospital gown and pulled the hem down. "Thanks for your help." She propelled the wheelchair forwards without waiting for a reply. Behind her, she heard the man shutting the door of the taxi. A moment later the man's car overtook her and then indicated right to turn into one of the car parks.

Antimone accelerated the chair, grateful for the exercise. No other vehicles passed her. She glanced behind and noticed that the taxi had departed. She received strange looks from a man and a woman walking in the opposite direction but reached the main entrance without further event. A curtain of warm air engulfed her as she negotiated her way through the rotating door.

The brightly lit area was relatively quiet. She approached the reception desk and waited for the receptionist to complete her conversation with a telephone caller.

"How can I help you?" the woman asked, peering down at Antimone from her raised seat with a bright smile.

"My name's Antimone Lessing. I'm a patient here. Could you call my doctors and let them know I'm back?"

"Lessing, you say. How do you spell that?"

Antimone spelled out her surname and waited while the woman tapped the information into her computer.

"I'm sorry, but I'm not showing any patient by that name unless you died two weeks ago." The woman gave a nervous laugh, then stared intently at the screen. "Oh, that's strange. Did you say your first name was Antimone?"

Antimone nodded. "That's me."

"They must have made an error entering the data. I do have a patient here with your name, but it says here that she died on the third of January and well… um… you're obviously not dead."

"No, I'm very much alive. Is there somebody you could call?"

"It also says your son… oh, never mind. That must be another mistake. It has Dr Perrin down as your main physician. I'll just see if he's available." The woman tapped the computer screen.

A second or two later she spoke again. "Yes, Dr Perrin. I've got an Antimone Lessing here for you. I think there's a mistake on the system. It says she's deceased but…"

"… Yes, she's here with me right now."

"… Okay, I'll ask her to wait."

The receptionist's smile had faded to be replaced by a slight frown. "Somebody will be here to fetch you in a moment if you'd just like to wait by the chairs over there."

Antimone felt the woman's eyes boring into her back as she wheeled herself to the waiting area.

75

Monday 17th January 2033

Rosalind held the injection gun to the third patient's neck and pressed the trigger. A brief hiss signalled the end of the woman's life as the lethal drugs travelled along her veins towards the muscles of her heart and lungs where they interrupted the signals from her brain. Within seconds her breathing had stopped, followed a short while later by her heartbeat.

"There are two more in the single rooms," Rosalind said. "I want you to take these three up to the incinerator while I deal with the other two."

"I don't know how to work it," Grolby said.

"Never mind. I'll be done by the time you've got them up there. I'll show you what to do, or I'll do it myself."

Rosalind positioned the sheet over the woman's face. "You need to hurry. The police could be here at any minute." She bustled through the swing doors and headed down the corridor. Five minutes earlier she had instructed all the staff in the basement level to return to the main part of the hospital, so she knew she had the place to herself. She had also been to the control room and turned off all the cameras.

She held her identity card up to the electronic lock and entered the small room. A heavily pregnant woman lay unconscious on the bed. Without hesitation, Rosalind transferred the instrument to the woman's neck and squeezed the trigger. She loosened the sheet and covered the patient's head without checking for a pulse. She hurried on to the adjacent room. There she repeated the process.

Releasing the brakes on the hospital trolley, she pushed it to the door with its lifeless cargo. She swiped her card against the reader, pulled the door open and using one foot to keep it ajar, dragged the trolley towards her. Her hand caught the door frame, and she cursed, holding it to her mouth. She glanced at her watch. This was taking too long.

Returning to the task, she backed into the corridor and swung the trolley around. She propelled it to the lift at a half-run. She jabbed at the call button and waited impatiently for the doors to slide apart. When they did, Grolby emerged pushing an empty trolley.

"How many have you done?" she snapped.

"Two, so far. I left them in the incinerator room like you told me. I assume you didn't want me to leave the trolleys in there."

"That's fine. Get the last one from the emergency ward, then come back and bring up the one from room 202. I'll make a start on the ones that are already there."

Rosalind entered the elevator. She faced the scanner and selected the ground floor. A bead of sweat trickled down her temple. She flicked it off with her forefinger, then wiped it on the bed-sheet. The lift surged upwards, announcing its arrival with a ting. The doors parted. She hurried past several locked rooms. At this time of day, the facility was largely deserted except for the handful of staff that cared for the residential patients. She passed nobody else before reaching a door that bore a flame icon. She held her identity card to the reader, depressed the handle and dragged the trolley in behind her. A wave of heat hit her as she reversed into the room. A large yellow-coloured metal cabinet filled most of the floor space. Emerging from the top of the box was a circular pipe that led up into the ceiling. On the front were an open sliding door and a control panel containing a number of differently coloured lights and buttons. A small glass window occupied one side wall. Two human-sized bundles lay alongside the right side of the cabinet, each draped with a white sheet.

Without pausing, Rosalind shoved the trolley into the enclosure. The wheels rattled as they crossed the tracks for the runners onto a metal grid. The dead woman's left arm slipped from beneath the sheet, hanging loosely down the side. Ducking her head to prevent it from hitting the low ceiling, Rosalind followed and applied the brakes. She heaved the body onto the grid. Stepping over an outstretched leg, she released the brake and pushed the trolley out ahead of her.

She turned her attention to the two sheet-wrapped bodies. She grabbed a foot in each hand and strained backwards. The corpse was halfway into the combustion chamber when the door to the room opened. With a sigh of relief, she recognised the broad shoulders of Anders Grolby backing in.

"Give me a hand here, Anders," she said.

"What do you want me to do?"

"Take the arms. Help me get her in here."

Grolby parked the trolley beside the wall, then strode across and seized the corpse's arms. The work was much easier with two people, and soon they had deposited the second body alongside the first.

"How many can you put in here?" Grolby asked.

"It should deal with three easily enough. Let's do the one on your trolley, and then you can take it back down."

"Wouldn't this have been a simpler way to dispose of some of our problems, Mrs Baxter?"

"What makes you think it hasn't? Anyway, it's not always feasible. That's one of the reasons I need your special talents. That reminds me. You need to delete all record of our entry into this room from the servers."

Grolby shrugged. "Whatever you say."

He picked up the corpse and lifted it over his shoulder. He stooped at the entrance and heaved it on top of the other two. "I'll go and get the last one."

Rosalind grasped the lever on the sliding door and hauled it towards her. The metal panel slid sideways and sealed with a loud clank. The green button on the control panel illuminated. She depressed it for a moment, then released it. The green light went out, and a red one came on in its place. A roaring, whooshing sound filled the room. The wall glowed orange where the light from the flames penetrated the small window. The temperature in the room rose by several degrees, and Rosalind wiped her forearm across her forehead. Four minutes after she had pressed the button, the burners fell silent. A rhythmic ticking sound emanated from the combustion chamber as the super-heated metal slowly cooled.

Three minutes later, the outside door opened once more. Grolby backed in, pulling a trolley containing the final dead body.

"Well done, Anders," Rosalind said. "We need to wait for the red light to go out, and then we can load these last two. It needs a while until it's cool enough to open."

Several minutes passed as they waited in silence. Finally, the red lamp turned off. Rosalind took hold of the lever and shoved the door back. Despite the cooling-off period, a wave of heat flooded into the room.

"It's like working in hell," Grolby said.

"Yeah, better get used to it. Let's get these two in there. Then we can relax a bit."

Grolby put his arms beneath the body on the trolley and slung it over his shoulder. He took a couple of paces and heaved it into the metal box.

"I can manage this one," he said, bending down to pick up the last bundle. His foot straddled the tracks for the runners as he pitched it forwards.

"It needs to go further back," Rosalind said, glancing inside.

"You're the boss," Grolby replied, entering the chamber and grabbing the corpse by the arms. He hauled backwards until the dead woman was up against the rear wall.

"Is this far enough?"

"Absolutely."

Grolby's eyes widened in shock as the door panel slid along its runners. He took a pace forwards, but he was too slow. The sturdy mechanism slammed shut, trapping him inside.

The sound of fists banging on the thick metal walls of the combustion chamber sounded muted from the outside.

"I'm sorry, Anders, but you've become part of the problem," Rosalind said as she pressed the green button. "And this is the perfect solution."

At the same moment as she released the button, the main door to the room swung open.

76

Monday 17th January 2033

Nigel Perrin surveyed the small room. He opened his mouth to speak, but the roar of the furnace drowned him out. He beckoned to Rosalind Baxter and moved into the corridor. His voice sounded loud in his own ears in the relative silence.

"I wondered if you'd be in here," he said. "I thought Anders was going to help you with that."

"Oh, he did, but Mr Grolby doesn't work here anymore. He's been fired."

Perrin picked up on Rosalind's slight smirk. "Fired? What do you mean? Oh, Christ, you didn't…"

"He made the mistake of overvaluing his own worth. He tried to blackmail me. If there's one thing I won't tolerate in my employees, it's disloyalty. Let's just say that he's probably feeling the heat a bit at the moment. Anyway, I'm sure you didn't come looking for me just to have a chat. What's going on?"

"It's the girl," Perrin said. "She's waiting in reception."

Rosalind frowned. "The Lessing girl? She's here now?"

"That's what the receptionist told me. Apparently, she asked for me."

"What about Floyd and the boy?"

"No sign of them yet. I couldn't get hold of Grolby, but I asked one of his men to escort her to one of the private rooms. She's refusing to go with him until she's seen her son. I ordered the security man to stay with her. What do you want to do?"

Rosalind closed her eyes for a second and inhaled deeply. She reopened them, her steely gaze boring into Perrin. "We don't need her anymore, do we?"

"No. I think we've got all the data we need. You're not going to—"

"Leave this to me, Nigel. I want you to get an injection gun."

"You're going to put her down like those other women?"

"If you'd let me finish," Rosalind snapped. "I want you to load it with sedative, something quick acting but with a short-term effect. I want to find out from her what Floyd and the boy are up to. I take it you did as I asked and kept test results relating to the girl on your own computer and off the network."

Perrin nodded.

"Good. I want you to bring your machine back here."

"You're going to destroy it?"

"Yes. If the police do come, we're going to need all the bargaining chips we can get. The more information is in our heads and the less there is written down, the stronger our position will be."

"But if the tests aren't successful, it could set us back months."

"I have every faith in you, Nigel. You're going away for a week. When you get back, we'll conduct the trials, and everything will work as expected. After that, you can retire and do what you want for the rest of your life."

Perrin remained silent. A moment later, the blood drained from his face as realisation dawned. "Hang on. It's all very well destroying the samples and test results, but anybody else could just analyse the girl again. That means you *are* going to… Oh God…"

Rosalind rested a hand on Perrin's shoulder. "You're right. The girl is the key to the cure. I'm sorry, Nigel, but she's got to go. You won't have to do anything. I'll deal with it all myself."

"Christ, Rosalind. She's only sixteen years old, the same age as our sons."

"I haven't got a son."

"You know what I mean: your adopted son. You're just going to put her down like an animal?"

"Look, Nigel. This is the only solution. Bring me your computer and any remaining test samples. Go away for a week with Max. When you come back, everything will have been sorted out. You can forget the whole thing ever happened."

"I don't know, Rosalind."

Rosalind's tone hardened. "Nigel, you *are* going to do this. Now get me an injection gun loaded with a sedative. After that, bring your machine here. Got that?"

Perrin nodded silently. His gaze lingered on Rosalind for a few seconds, then he turned away and headed down the corridor.

"And could you hurry, please?" Rosalind called to his back.

77

Monday 17th January 2033

The unfamiliar ring tone made Jason jump. From the displayed number, he identified that the call originated from a mobile.

Jason stabbed a finger at the answer button. "Hello"

"This is Karen Atkins. To whom am I speaking?"

"It's Jason. Jason Baxter."

"Hello, Jason. I received a call from an emergency service operator telling me that you're with Daniel Floyd. Is that true?"

Movement from the driver's seat caught Jason's attention. Floyd was gesticulating at him and mouthing something. "Hang on a sec," he said into the phone. He placed his finger over the microphone hole and turned to Floyd. "What?"

"Put it on speaker," Floyd whispered.

Jason studied the display and tapped a button that displayed a loudspeaker icon. "Can you hear me?" he asked, holding the mobile in front of him.

"Yes, fine. So, are you with Daniel Floyd?"

"He's sitting beside me and can hear everything you're saying."

"Jason, Mr Floyd. The operator told me that you're on your way to Ilithyia. Why are you going there?"

"To smash my fist into that evil, murdering harpy's face," Floyd shouted.

"Who's face?" Kat asked. "Rosalind Baxter? Has something changed?"

"She didn't die after all," Jason said.

"I don't follow. Who didn't die?"

"Antimone Lessing," Jason replied.

Silence greeted his statement.

Jason plunged on. "I know it sounds impossible, but she gave birth and lived. My mother was holding her a prisoner at Ilithyia in an underground laboratory. They were studying her, trying to work out how she survived so they could develop a cure. We managed to break her out, but later on she sneaked away from us. We think she's on her way back there."

"Okay, slow down a bit," Kat said. "You're telling me that Antimone Lessing survived the birth of her child? So, both she and her baby are alive?"

"That's right."

"That's not what the records show. Can anybody else verify that?"

"Well, other than the people who work at Ilithyia, only us two," Jason replied.

"You said she sneaked away. Where were you when this happened?"

"We were at an abandoned property in Huntingdon. She said she was going to the loo. After a while, we went to check on her, but she'd gone. We think she used the credit on the phone to order a taxi. She's going to go back to Ilithyia for her son."

"That's not everything," Floyd said. "Rosalind Baxter murdered my wife. We were able to get a file off her computer. But that's not the worst of it. Wait until you hear the rest."

Floyd explained what they had learned from the encrypted files.

"Can you send me a copy?" Kat asked.

"Yeah, I think so," Floyd said. "Jason, get the tablet."

Jason leant into the back seat and grabbed the computer. He clicked the on button and waited for the machine to boot. "Okay. Give me your email address."

Kat reeled off a series of characters.

Jason read the sequence back to her, and she confirmed it was correct. "I'll type the password in the body of the email. Sending it now." He studied the progress bar until it reached one hundred percent. "Right. It's gone."

"I'll make sure we get a team to Ilithyia immediately," Kat said. "I want you to wait for them to arrive. Where are you at the moment?"

Floyd shook his head silently.

"Can you hear me?" Kat asked.

Floyd drew a finger across his throat.

Jason pressed the disconnect button. "Do you think she believed us?"

"It doesn't really matter at this stage. The police are going to Ilithyia, and that's what we wanted. The file should convince them we're telling the truth."

The phone rang again.

"Don't answer," Floyd said.

The sound of the ring tone drowned out a ping from the tablet computer.

Had they heard the announcement and checked the screen, they would have seen an automated email stating that the previously transmitted message had been rejected because the attachment was too large.

78

Monday 17th January 2033

Rosalind glanced at her watch. *Where the hell was Perrin?* Her rising irritation dissipated when the door at the end of the corridor swung open. The white-coated doctor appeared, hurrying towards her. "Good. About time."

Perrin said nothing as he handed the injection gun over.

"Now fetch your computer and bring it back here. Then you can leave with your son."

Perrin turned and headed in the direction of the lift. Rosalind walked in the opposite direction and waved her security card at the reader before passing through the double doors that led to the reception area. Her eyes were immediately drawn to the girl sitting in the wheelchair and the guard standing a few paces away. Antimone's appearance wouldn't win any style awards. The thick woollen socks looked incongruous against the muddy hospital gown and the oversized blue jumper. The slack expression on her face sharpened at Rosalind's arrival.

"Where's my son?" Antimone asked without preamble.

A slight frown creased Rosalind's forehead. "We've been over this many times before, Antimone. We both know you don't have a son."

Antimone's mouth gaped in shock. "What? You agreed that I'd be able to see my son if I came back."

"It's very sad," Rosalind said, turning to the guard. "We've been treating her for months. She's obsessed with having a child, even though she knows that if she did, she'd die like all the others. I was worried this might happen."

"What the hell are you talking about?" Antimone shouted. "I gave birth to my son and survived. If you don't believe me, how do you think this happened?" She raised the heavy jumper, forced a finger through the thin material of the patient gown and ripped a gash above her abdomen. "How do you explain that then?"

The guard glanced at the livid scar and looked away. By now, several other people, including the receptionist, were watching from a distance.

"You're clearly very upset, Antimone," Rosalind said. "We've talked about this self-harm before. We both know that's one of the things we were treating you for. I see you've shaved off all your hair again. I thought we'd managed to beat this delusion, but I can see we were wrong. I'm afraid we're going to need to continue your treatment."

"Bring me my baby," Antimone screamed.

"The computer records did say she had a son," the receptionist said. She had left her desk and was standing two paces away. "Although—"

"Stay out of this," Rosalind snarled, turning to the woman in fury. "The records are wrong. Now can't you see I'm trying to help this poor girl?"

"I-I'm sorry."

"I'm going to have to sedate you," Rosalind said to Antimone, a thin smile playing on her lips. She held up the injection gun and took a pace forwards.

"No, no, no," shrieked Antimone, warding her off with both hands.

"Restrain her, please," Rosalind said addressing, the guard.

"Um... What do you–?"

"For Christ's sake, hold her down so I can give her a shot of sedative."

Antimone attempted to bat the man away. "Keep away from me, you bastard. She's got my son and..."

Rosalind darted forwards, held the nozzle against Antimone's neck and squeezed the trigger. A short hiss signalled that the device had fired. She sprang back out of range of Antimone's thrashing limbs.

"I want my baby," Antimone sobbed. Her arms slumped at her sides, and her head tilted backwards. "I want my..." Her voice tailed off into a whimper.

Rosalind stepped forwards and inspected Antimone's face. She raised an eyelid, then turned back to the small group of onlookers. "The show's over," she said. "I'm sorry you all had to witness that. She's a seriously disturbed young lady." She glared at the remaining two people who continued to stare at the unconscious girl. Eventually, they too moved away.

"Let's get her to a room," she said, turning to the guard. "Follow me."

She strode across the tiled floor towards the security doors.

79

Monday 17th January 2033

"So, what's the plan?" Jason asked as the vehicle drew to a halt at the turning circle by the entrance to Ilithyia Biotechnology.

"We have to find out whether Antimone came here," Floyd replied, opening the car door. "If she did, we need to make sure that she and her son—your son—are safe. The police will arrive at any second. After what that murdering harpy's done, I don't trust her further than I can chuck her."

"You're right," Jason said, shoving his door open. "We can't afford to wait for them."

Side by side, they strode in the direction of the brightly illuminated steel and glass building. Ten paces short of the entrance, a security guard emerged through the revolving door.

"Hey, is that your car?" the man said. "You can't leave it there."

"Piss off," Floyd growled, barging past him.

"It'll get towed," the man called to his back, but the pair were already entering the circular glass entryway. The man spoke urgently into his walkie-talkie, then followed Jason and Floyd inside.

Jason inhaled the familiar faint medical aroma, his eyes taking in the polished tile floor and the curving reception desk. It was almost as if he was seeing the interior of the building for the first time, so much had changed over the past few days. He hurried to keep up with Floyd, who was marching towards the alarmed-looking receptionist. The woman tracked the bearded man as he approached and, despite being separated by the chrome and plastic surface, she took an inadvertent step backwards.

"Um… can I–?"

"Did a girl in a wheelchair come in here a few minutes ago?" Floyd asked. "Sixteen years old and wearing a blue jumper."

The look of surprise was all the answer he required.

"How long ago?" he asked.

"Um, about ten minutes," the woman replied.

"Where did she go?"

"I'm not sure I'm allowed—"

"Get Rosalind Baxter here now," Floyd said.

The receptionist's frightened gaze flicked to the security guard who had drawn his black baton. "Who shall I say is asking for her?"

"You can tell her that Daniel Floyd and her adopted son are here."

"You're going to have to leave or I'm going to call the police," said the guard from behind Floyd, clasping the black cylinder with his left hand. Droplets of sweat beaded his forehead.

Floyd whirled to face him. "The police? Good, but they're already on their way."

"Mr Floyd, um… Daniel. Look," Jason said. Four more guards were running towards them, the double doors swinging in their wake. Each of them held a baton and appeared ready to wield it if necessary.

"These two are leaving," said the first security guard as the others drew alongside him.

"I'm not going anywhere until I see Baxter," Floyd growled.

"Throw them out," the man said, grabbing Floyd by the arm.

"Get off me," Floyd yelled, shaking the man's grip loose. The other men surged forwards. A baton swished through the air, striking Floyd on the shoulder. He stumbled under the blow. Several hands grabbed his arms and despite his frantic struggles to break free, dragged him towards the revolving door. Realising that Jason proved less of a threat, a solitary guard grasped his upper arm and propelled him in the same direction.

Halfway to the exit, a loud female voice rang out. "Stop!"

All eyes turned to Rosalind Baxter, who was standing by the security doors. "I will not tolerate this sort of behaviour in my facility. That man's a convicted murderer. We're going to restrain them until the police arrive. Bring them over here."

The intensity of Floyd's struggle increased. "You fricking bitch," he screamed, spittle flying from his lips. "You're the murderer." Despite the overwhelming odds, he managed to free an arm and swung it, connecting with a guard's ear. The man staggered backwards, but a flurry of blows rained down on Floyd from the man's colleagues.

The fight didn't last long. A blow to the right temple dropped Floyd to his knees. Blood immediately welled up from the wound, splattering the floor around the struggling men. Several more strokes landed on his back and shoulders. Seconds later, Floyd slumped to the ground, barely conscious.

Two of the guards grabbed an arm each and hauled Floyd to his feet. Jason found himself similarly restrained. It had all happened so quickly that it was over before he could decide how to react.

Rosalind walked forwards to meet the approaching group. She beckoned the spare guard towards her and whispered something to him. The man nodded, then hurried away to the revolving door.

She moved to stand in front of Jason. Fury blazed in her eyes. "You betrayed my trust. I raised you as my son, and you did this to me."

Jason met her stare. "I know everything. You murdered my mother and you—"

The slap snapped his head to the side. The backhanded blow that followed it caught him equally by surprise. Jason tasted blood in his mouth.

"I want these two restrained and gagged. This boy needs to learn some respect. Follow me."

80

Monday 17th January 2033

"Come on, Max," Nigel Perrin said. "We need to hurry."

"You keep me waiting about for more than an hour, and now, all of a sudden, we need to hurry," Max said petulantly. "Why the rush? I thought we were just going away for a few days."

"It's complicated," the boy's father replied as he exchanged the warm foyer for the frigid winter night.

The wheels of the small suitcase rumbled over the concrete paving slabs.

"Where are we going anyway?" Max asked, hurrying to keep up with his father. He still sported a black eye resulting from Jason's attack.

"I thought we might go to the coast," Perrin said, angling his head back to address his son.

"Why are we going during term time, though?"

"What do you mean? You've been off school for the last few days anyway, recovering. We don't spend enough time together. Work has been pretty intense recently. Now that there's a lull, I thought it would be a good time to get away."

The boy shrugged. "Whatever you say. You're the one who keeps telling me I need to take school more seriously."

The sound of sirens pierced the background hiss of traffic that drifted from the main road. Strobing blue lights cast a ghostly glow against the orange of the streetlamps.

"Shit," Perrin said, breaking into a run. The wail of the sirens grew louder.

"What's going on, Dad?" Max asked in consternation.

"That bloody woman's gone too far this time. She's out of control, and I'm not going to take a fall for her."

The wheels of the suitcase hit a crack between two paving stones and flipped it onto its back. Max stopped to right it. When he turned back, the first of three police cars blocked the way forwards, its bumper nudging up to the rear of the ancient silver vehicle with the broken passenger-side window. The siren tones from the different vehicles blended into a discordant wail until one by one they fell silent. At the same time, the intense blue flashing lights also turned off, leaving an imprint on Max's retina.

A mask of despair occupied Nigel Perrin's face. "No," he moaned. He hesitated for a moment, then came to a decision. "Quick, follow me."

"You're not in trouble with the police, are you Dad? I thought we were—"

"Just do as I say for once."

Max shook his head and grabbed the handle of the small suitcase. His father was running faster than he had ever seen him do before.

Perrin glanced behind. The gap between them had extended to ten metres. "For Christ's sake, leave that behind."

"But it's got all—"

"Just leave it!"

Max turned back to where a large group of policemen gathered beside the now silent police cars. He released the suitcase handle and broke into a sprint in the opposite direction. Despite the head start, he arrived at the revolving door at the entrance to the building a couple of paces ahead of his father. Both men barrelled into the same compartment. Max shoved against the glass. Sensing the pressure being applied against it, the mechanism braked and halted.

"Let it go," Perrin said, jerking his head around to check on the progress of the policemen. "You can't make it go any faster." One of the men was crouched by the abandoned suitcase, talking into a radio. The rest were jogging towards them and would be at the door in a matter of seconds.

With agonising slowness, the glass panels lurched back into movement. As soon as the gap was wide enough, Max slipped through into the stuffy warmth of the foyer. Perrin emerged and sprinted across the tiled floor, drawing several bemused glances from the small number of onlookers. He reached the sealed double doors and fumbled in his pocket for his identity card.

"Where are we going?" Max asked.

Perrin said nothing as the red light changed to green. The locking mechanism released. He barged through two steps ahead of his son. The doors swung back into position and locked with an audible click.

"Dad, I asked where we're going."

Perrin halted at a door labelled with a large flame logo. Panting for breath, he turned to face Max.

"God knows why, but I'm going to try to warn that madwoman."

81

Monday 17th January 2033

Rosalind Baxter glanced at the phone's display. That was the second time in a minute that reception had tried to get hold of her. It could mean only one thing. The police had arrived. There was still time. She had allowed the guards to go home early. Now that the fugitives were accounted for, their services were no longer required. Nobody knew where she was apart from Nigel Perrin, and he had departed ten minutes ago.

It wouldn't take long to dispose of the evidence, and then what? The police might have their suspicions, but they wouldn't be able to prove anything. There might be some awkward questions to answer, but she had no doubts that any prospect of criminal prosecutions would soon be swept under the carpet when she delivered a cure.

She placed the tablet computer on the metallic grid of the combustion chamber floor. She smiled at her good fortune. Not only had the email been blocked because the attachment was too large, but Floyd and Jason had been foolish enough to leave the machine in the car. The security guard had found it on the back seat after breaking the rear window.

Rosalind straightened up and looked down at the girl. She was still unconscious, facing the sliding door. Her head lolled to one side in the wheelchair. It was probably for the best. She would only struggle if she realised what was about to happen to her.

It would be a tight squeeze, but all three adults would fit in. She retraced her steps to the main part of the room. Floyd sat in one wheelchair, the right side of his face caked in blood from the gash in his temple. She had strapped his arms and legs to the frame of the chair with plastic ties. His eyes were closed, and his breathing sounded wet and shallow.

Beside him sat Jason, similarly restrained in a wheelchair. In contrast to his father, he was clearly conscious. His terrified eyes darted about the room as he struggled against his restraints. A cloth gag tied across his mouth prevented him from speaking.

"It's ironic that you should all be in wheelchairs," Rosalind said as she directed Jason's chair towards the heavy door of the furnace. He tried to speak through the gag as the wheels rattled across the thick metal grating. She positioned him to Antimone's left.

"You only have yourself to blame," she said. "If you'd done as I asked, you wouldn't be in this situation. I'm sorry it's come to this, but you know too much."

Jason attempted to talk again, but the gag turned his words into muffled grunts.

"You're trying to tell me that you told the police the whole story, right?" Rosalind said. "The thing is, that's *all* it is without proof, a story, and the evidence is lying there on the floor beside you."

She paused as if listening to him. "Oh, you sent an email to the police containing that encrypted file? Yes, I know. Unfortunately, it was too big and their server bounced it. Maybe you should've checked that they received it before storming in to rescue your helpless little cripple. After all that money I spent on your education, who'd have thought that you weren't even capable of sending a simple email? Still, I suppose it's partially down to your genetics. Anyway, much as I'm enjoying this little chat, I still have work to do."

Rosalind's footsteps echoed in the cramped metallic box as she strode across the gridded floor. She grabbed Floyd's wheelchair by the handles and swung it around so that it was facing the furnace. An electronic beep came from behind her.

Rosalind turned her head to the source of the noise and saw Nigel Perrin standing in the door frame beside his son.

82

Monday 17th January 2033

"Nigel, why are you here? I thought you'd left?"

Perrin entered the room, his gaze focused on the injured man in the wheelchair. "The police have arrived." His eyes rose to meet Rosalind's and then dropped once more to her captive. "What are you doing?"

"What does it look like, Nigel? I'm disposing of the evidence."

"Is he dead?"

"No, not yet."

"Jesus, Rosalind. You're going to incinerate him while he's still alive?"

"I'm right out of sedative shots, so unless you have something suitable in your pocket, yes, that's the plan. I'm sure it'll be very quick."

Perrin swallowed hard but remained silent. The focus of his attention wandered to the open incinerator chamber. He took two tentative steps forward, trying to pick out details from the dim interior. He squinted and angled his head forwards as he attempted to make sense of what he was seeing.

Gasping with shock, he stepped backwards. "The girl and—that's not your son, is it?"

"No, he's not my son," Rosalind said, a frown creasing her forehead. "He's somebody who lived in my house for sixteen years and then betrayed me."

"Christ, Rosalind, you're mad. You're going to kill your own son?"

"I just told you, he's not my son. You don't get it, do you? He knows everything. He and Floyd hacked into my computer and downloaded a file containing all the details going right back to the beginning. He tried to send it to the police. If he wasn't so incompetent, they would have all the proof they need to put both of us away for the rest of our lives. I'm not going to let that happen. This work is too important for anybody or anything to stop it."

Perrin reached into his pocket for a pen and began absent-mindedly clicking the tip in and out. "So, you plan to incinerate three more people to cover it up?"

"Oh, come on, Nigel. How many have we already incinerated today? And how many women died because you deliberately made them pregnant?"

"What's she saying, Dad?"

Perrin had forgotten that his son was standing beside him. "Look, Max, it's complicated. Sometimes you have to—"

"Actually, it's quite simple really," Rosalind interrupted. "Your father abducted women off the street and impregnated them so he could use them as guinea pigs for our tests. Why else do you think he had those drugs in his office that you then stole and put into the drink at the party?"

Max turned to face his father. "Is it true, Dad?"

Perrin hung his head, then looked up and met his son's stare. "Yes, it's true. The women we took were drug addicts and prostitutes. They had a very low life expectancy, anyway. At least this way, they were doing something useful with their lives. I know it's not right, but we were trying to save the human race. Somebody had to make the sacrifice, so why not choose those who valued their own lives so little?"

A wintry smile flashed across Rosalind's face. "While you two have your debate about the morals of the situation, I've got a job to finish here. That is unless you both want to spend a long time in jail. Don't forget that Jason knows what you did too, Max. He probably also told Antimone."

She turned away from the father and son and propelled the wheelchair towards the dark interior of the chamber. She positioned it in front of Jason's chair.

"Goodbye Jason," she said. His head rested on his chest so she couldn't see his face.

As she spun around to leave, a voice called out from behind her.

"Now!"

83

Monday 17th January 2033

The gag bit into the corners of Jason's mouth and obstructed his breathing. He inhaled loudly through his nose. His mother was talking to somebody. The sound of voices carried into the dimly lit chamber, but he couldn't make out the individual words. A droplet of sweat trickled down his chest as he struggled to free his hands. The tie-wraps were far stronger than the thin plastic suggested, and all he succeeded in doing was deepening the welts that already ran around both wrists.

Jason forced himself to relax. There had to be a way out of this. He glanced to his left. Antimone was still unconscious, her head lolling backwards, but unlike him, she wasn't bound. If only he could wake her, she might be able to release them.

He focused his attention on the gag. He contorted his face, trying to loosen it enough to get the knot out of his mouth. His frustration grew as the material resisted all his attempts. He slumped back in the chair and groaned in despair. Tendrils of panic teased away at the edges of his mind and threatened to overwhelm him. His mother apparently planned to burn them alive. Would she really go through with it? How much pain would he feel? How long would it last?

An idea occurred to him. He strained against the tie at his wrist and pushed his elbow forwards as far as it would go. At the same time, he angled his head downwards so that his chin was touching his shoulder. It felt as if the joint was about to dislocate as he tried to dislodge the gag, but he did manage to shift it down a millimetre or two. He attacked the task with renewed vigour. After a few more seconds, the damp material rolled down and hung loosely around his neck.

He turned to face the unconscious girl. "Antimone," he whispered.

No response.

"Antimone," this time a little louder. "Wake up."

A slight movement of her head. "Come on, for Christ's sake wake up."

Antimone's eyes fluttered. A dribble of saliva ran down from the corner of her mouth. She moaned as her head lolled to the side.

"Antimone, if you want to live you have to wake up."

A single cough. Heavy lids blinked open as she stared uncomprehendingly at her surroundings. "Where am I?" Her voice came out as a low rasp.

"Thank God. We haven't got long. We need to get out of here."

"Where are we? What's going on?"

"I don't want to frighten you, but my mother's got us in an incinerator. She's talking to somebody. If we don't do something, we're going to die. Is there any way you can loosen these tie-wraps?"

Antimone's frightened eyes darted around the interior of the chamber. "An incinerator?"

"Come on, the clock's ticking. My hands and feet are tied down so I can't move."

Shock tinged Antimone's words. "She's going to burn us alive?"

"Yes, unless we can free ourselves somehow."

Antimone moved her wheelchair forwards a short distance and peered down at the black plastic bands binding Jason's arms and legs to the chair. "I don't know. These are impossible to break without a cutter of some sort. You know, a knife or scissors." Her head jerked from left to right as she surveyed her surroundings. "I can't see anything in here that we could use."

Jason racked his brains, but his thoughts kept returning to the flames that could turn them to ash at any second. "Come on, Antimone. Think."

"I can't see anything in here that would do the job."

"She's talking to somebody outside. Maybe they can help us."

Antimone cocked her head to listen. "That sounds like Dr Perrin. He's in this as deep as she is. He was the main doctor who was investigating why I survived. We certainly can't trust him."

"So, we're dead then?"

Antimone's thoughts turned to her son. He would grow up without a mother—if they let him grow up at all. She couldn't allow that to happen. "If I can get her on the floor, it should even things up a bit."

"How are you going to do that?"

"I'm going to have to knock her over first."

"How do we know she's even going to come back in here?"

Antimone frowned. "We don't, but Floyd's not here. I assume he arrived with you."

"Yeah, she grabbed him at the same time as me, but what's that got to do with it? He was unconscious when I last saw him. He's certainly not going to be in any condition to help us."

"Whatever condition he's in, she's going to want to dispose of him just like us. He knows too much. So, somebody is going to have to come inside."

Jason struggled against the ties again. With mounting desperation, he tried to bounce the wheelchair forwards.

"Keep it down," Antimone hissed. "We don't want her being prepared."

"I can't believe she's really going to do this. Maybe she's just trying to scare us."

"She's certainly doing that. I'm not prepared to gamble that it's a bluff, though."

"You don't know her like I do. I've lived with her for sixteen years. She wouldn't do that to me."

Antimone's tone hardened. "Listen, Jason, there's something you've got to understand. That psychotic bitch out there—don't think of her as your mother—is going to kill us both unless we stop her. I've seen what she can do. She's more than capable of putting us down."

Jason swallowed hard. "Okay, so what's the plan?"

"I pretend I'm still unconscious. I need you to tell me when to move."

Jason did his best to hide the quaver in his voice. "I'll shout when it's time."

84

Monday 17th January 2033

The wheelchair surged ahead under Antimone's powerful strokes. The plan might have worked had her right wheel not clashed with the chair in which Daniel Floyd was restrained. As it was, the contact soaked up some of her forward momentum and threw her off course. Instead of striking Rosalind full on, the footrests caught her with a glancing blow. It was sufficient to knock the woman off her feet but not powerful enough to incapacitate her. The wheelchair slewed to the left and came to a halt, straddling the runners which guided the furnace door.

It took Antimone's eyes a moment to adjust to the bright illumination from the ceiling lights. The collision had winded her, and she struggled to recover her bearings. The wheel of her chair was jammed up against the wall of the incineration chamber. Nigel and Max Perrin stood side by side, staring in shock at the scene before them. Rosalind Baxter knelt on all fours, blood splattering the floor from a gash to her forehead.

Antimone tried frantically to release the trapped wheel, but the chair refused to budge. "Max, Dr Perrin, you've got to help us."

Father and son remained silent and motionless. Rosalind slowly rose to her feet and fixed Antimone with a hate-filled stare. Blood trickled from the wound to her head. She brushed a hand over her face, leaving a streak of crimson across her cheeks like an elaborate war-paint. Her voice shook with fury when she spoke. "You stupid little…"

Rosalind limped towards the immobile wheelchair and glared at Antimone. When she was a pace away, she halted, her face distorted in a grimace of rage. She lifted her leg, drew it back and stamped it into Antimone's knees.

Even though she felt no direct pain, Antimone cried out at the shock of the blow. The wheelchair lurched backwards a few inches. Rosalind moved closer and lashed out for a second time. The wheel broke free, and the chair rolled back a short distance before tipping on its side. Antimone used her arms to break her fall but found herself lying on the metal grating, her legs entangled in the wheelchair's struts.

Rosalind surveyed the three prisoners, her eyes picking them out one at a time. She inhaled deeply, then turned her back and hobbled to the sliding door. She grasped the handle and pulled it towards her. The door rattled as it ran along the runners and closed halfway. She took two paces to the right and reached for the handle again. The door slammed shut with a metallic clang.

She extended a finger to the green button. A beep from behind made her hesitate. She craned her neck and watched as Karen Atkins led a group of six men wearing dark coloured uniforms into the room.

"Mrs Baxter and Dr Perrin, you're both under arrest."

85

Monday 17th January 2033

Rosalind turned to face the group of policemen. "What are we under arrest for?"

"Where do I start?" Karen Atkins said. "Why don't we go back sixteen years or so?"

"You've got no proof."

"So, you know what I'm talking about? Good. Well, let me tell you what I know. Seventeen or eighteen years ago you started doing research on an artificial virus, creating its DNA from scratch. Somebody had the bright idea of mixing it with the flu virus to create a pathogen that would spread more easily. One of your researchers at the time, an Eileen Floyd—that's Daniel's wife—threatened to become a whistle-blower and stop what she regarded as dangerous research. To keep her quiet, you kidnapped her. Did I mention she was pregnant with Jason at the time?"

"So, you worked out who the boy's real mother was?"

"Yes, when we discovered that Daniel Floyd was Jason's biological father, it didn't take much effort to determine who his mother was."

"Well done," Rosalind said, clapping slowly. "It's only taken you sixteen years. And who says our police are slow on the uptake?"

"So, you framed her husband, Daniel, for her murder," Kat continued. "He didn't even know she was pregnant. You held onto her for eight months and used her as a test subject. She was the first victim of the Orestes virus. She didn't know you had infected her and nearly escaped. By the time you recaptured her, she had infected a number of other people. After that, it didn't take long for the virus to spread across the world. I still don't understand why you adopted Jason. I can only assume it was because you wanted to continue studying him."

For the first time since the police had arrived, Perrin spoke. "It was an accident. We never meant to release it. If that woman hadn't—"

"Shut up, Nigel," Rosalind snapped. "They've got nothing."

Kat ploughed on. "So, once that happened, hundreds of thousands of women died in childbirth, and the world desperately began looking for a cure. But you had a head start, didn't you? As the creators, you knew its exact genetic makeup and had already developed anti-virals for the laboratory-generated version. It was only a short step from there to developing the drug that propelled Ilithyia

Biotechnology to the forefront of medical science and turned you both into multi-millionaires."

Perrin fiddled with the collar of his shirt. "We were only trying to rectify our—"

"Pure supposition," Rosalind said, talking over him.

"But that's where it started to go wrong. The virus mutated, and the treatment became ineffective. Now you were in the same boat as all the other medical companies, desperately trying to come up with something that would actually work. It was the flu part of the virus that mutated. Ironically, that's what Eileen Floyd tried to warn you about in the first place. Fast forward sixteen years or so. The number of women who have died because of your actions is now in the millions, and your son gets Antimone Lessing pregnant while he's under the influence of some nasty drug that also originated from this facility. She doesn't know she's pregnant until it's too late for an abortion. By sheer coincidence, she ends up giving birth here and somehow survives. I understand her child survived too despite you writing a death certificate claiming that he died from a biological infection."

Rosalind folded her arms. "I had nothing to do with any death certificate. You won't find my name on it."

"So now you have the clue you need. You fake Antimone's death, making it look as if she died like all the other women. You study her in your basement laboratory, out of sight of any medical ethics committees. The only problem is that your son likes this girl and discovers you're holding her prisoner. He breaks her out, but then you grab her again. Luckily for us, he told me the whole thing. How did I do? Is that about right?"

"Very clever," Rosalind said. "A very good story, but with no proof whatsoever. Have you got any witnesses? Where's the evidence?"

"Oh, I'm sure if we dig deep enough, we'll find something. So where are you keeping them?"

"Who?"

"You know exactly who I mean, Mrs Baxter: Jason, Daniel Floyd, Antimone Lessing and her son, Paul."

"I have no idea."

"Well, that's strange because we have several eyewitnesses who saw you talking to the three adults no more than half an hour ago. What about you, Dr Perrin? You're heavily implicated in all this. What have you got to say for yourself?"

Perrin swallowed loudly. "Um… I don't know." He stared hard at the floor.

"The thing is, if one of you were to talk to me, we'd look very favourably on that. I can't guarantee you wouldn't serve any time, but your sentence would probably be much more lenient."

Perrin raised his head sharply and returned Kat's gaze. He turned briefly to Rosalind and back to Kat again. He licked his lips. "Um… if we had a cure, would that help to reduce the sentence too?"

"Yes, I'm sure a judge would show leniency for something like that," Kat said.

"Okay, I'll tell you everything. Sorry, Rosalind, but I can't live with this any longer."

"Don't say anything, Nigel," Rosalind growled. "They don't have any evidence."

"No, I've made my mind up."

Rosalind moved so quickly that it caught everybody else in the room by surprise. She lunged forwards and snatched up the pen poking from the front pocket of Perrin's jacket. She drew it back and jabbed the point into his eye. Perrin screamed and held both hands to the protruding cylinder, blood pouring through his fingers. But she wasn't finished yet. She formed her hand into a fist and slammed it into his face, driving the pen deep into his brain.

Nigel Perrin collapsed to the floor, his body convulsing. His son knelt over him. "Dad! Dad!" he yelled.

The policemen surged forwards, but Rosalind had already returned to her position by the control box.

"If anybody moves, I push this," she screamed. A silence fell over the room, broken only by Max Perrin's sobs. "I mean it. There are three people inside this incinerator. I'm the only one you're going to be making a deal with now."

One of the men took a step forward.

"I warned you," Rosalind said.

Then she pressed the green button.

86

Monday 17th January 2033

All eyes in the room focused on Rosalind. Even Max Perrin looked up from the prostrate body of his father.

"If I take my finger off this button, the furnace will start up. Once that happens, there's no stopping it until it completes its cycle."

"What do you want, Mrs Baxter?" Kat asked.

"Let me see. My arm's already starting to get a bit tired by the way. I want an amnesty for all previous crimes. My lawyers will have to check it over to make sure there are no loopholes. In return, I will complete the development of a cure for the Orestes virus, but I must be free to run my company how I see fit. I'm happy to make any deal conditional on the release of a treatment. Oh, and the people inside this furnace get to live."

"You're responsible for more deaths than any other person in living memory, and you just want us to sweep it all under the carpet? You're out of your mind."

"Well, I don't expect *you* to have the authority to make such a deal," Rosalind said, a thin smile lifting the corners of her mouth. "I'm guessing it'll have to go as high as the Prime Minister. Andrew Jacobs is a friend—well, maybe not a friend—but certainly an acquaintance of mine. I suggest you call him right away. I'm not sure how much longer my arm will hold up."

"I'll see what I can do," Kat said.

"You do that. Incidentally, I want all your colleagues to place their radios and mobile phones on the ground. I can't have you hatching some plot behind my back. I also want your phone on speaker so that I can hear what's being said. And don't mention where we are. Just so you know, if they try to cut off the power, this facility has a backup generator. If the lights so much as flicker, I'll release this button. Just tell them that I'll produce a cure if they agree to my terms. Otherwise, I'll destroy all the research and the girl too."

"You heard her." Kat turned to the six uniformed men. "Put your phones and radios on the floor."

"When you've done that, sit with your back to the wall over there," Rosalind said. She glanced down at Max, still crouched over his dead father. "You," she said, pointing at the nearest policeman. "I assume you're carrying handcuffs or something like that."

The man nodded.

"Right, I want you to restrain the boy. I don't trust him not to do something stupid."

Max stared up at her as he struggled to comprehend the meaning of her words. When they finally sank in, a look of hatred filled his face. "You murdering bitch," he screamed. He tried to stand up but slipped in his father's blood.

The policeman lunged forwards, enveloping Max in a bear hug.

"Help him," Kat snapped.

Two other men joined the struggle. Within seconds they had cuffed Max's hands behind his back. Still struggling against his captors, Max raised his head from the floor. Blood streaked one cheek. "I'll kill you for this," he yelled.

"Restrain his feet too," Rosalind said, "then put him against the wall with the rest of you."

The three men lifted the writhing boy and carried him to join their colleagues.

"I'll kill you," Max sobbed, mucus and tears mingling with the smears of blood.

87

Monday 17th January 2033

The beep from the electronic lock ratcheted up the tension that had enveloped the room. It had been ninety minutes since Kat had made the first of several phone calls. Standing apart from the seated policemen were two men wearing business suits but no tie, deep in discussion with each other. They were Rosalind's lawyers and had arrived half an hour earlier. They didn't seem happy about the situation and, at that exact point in time, were discussing the downside if Rosalind failed to deliver on her side of the bargain.

The door opened slowly. Two dark-suited men stood framed in the doorway. They held identical poses, right arm folded across the chest, right hand hidden inside the black jacket. Their eyes swept the room for any sign of imminent danger. When their inspection was complete, they stepped into the room leaving enough of a gap between them for Andrew Jacobs to walk through.

The Prime Minister glanced at the seated police officers. His eyes widened in shock as they focused on the dead body of Nigel Perrin. With a conscious effort, he directed his attention to Rosalind Baxter.

"About time, Andrew," she said. "I was beginning to think you weren't going to come."

"I'm a busy man, Mrs Baxter."

"So that's how it's going to be, is it? Well, Prime Minister, we seem to have a situation here. My terms are simple: an amnesty for any past crimes and freedom to run my company as I see fit. In return, I will provide you with a treatment for the Orestes virus."

"Yes, Mrs Baxter, my people told me about your proposal. I understand that you were responsible for creating the virus in the first place."

"It has been suggested that might be the case, but you're not going to get me to admit to anything unless you sign the amnesty. Just so you know, my arm is getting extremely tired."

"And you have three people trapped inside the incinerator chamber. I'm assuming that if you release that button, it turns on."

"That's right, Andrew, and if that happens, all our research and the only person to survive childbirth in fifteen years go up in flames."

"Your son's in there too, I hear."

A look of anger flitted across Rosalind's face. "He's not my son. I adopted him. Then he… well, never mind. Are you going to sign the documents, or are you going to consign those three people and thousands of women to a needless and painful death?"

"We don't negotiate with terrorists, Mrs Baxter."

"Is that a no then? I'll be sure to mention that you declined my offer when I go to trial. I'm sure that will play well with the electorate. Even your good looks won't get you out of that one."

Andrew Jacobs focused his gaze on Perrin's dead body. He sighed deeply and slowly raised his eyes to meet Rosalind's belligerent stare. He hesitated for a moment as he considered his options. Finally, he came to a decision. "On this occasion, I might be prepared to make an exception. However, any deal we make will be conditional on you delivering a working treatment."

"I've already offered that, Prime Minister."

"You will be placed under house arrest until such time as we have independent proof of the efficacy of any drugs your company produces. After that point, we can't allow you to remain as the CEO. You'll sell the company, and you'll donate ninety percent of the proceeds to childcare charities. That's my final offer."

"You want me to give away ninety percent of the company I've devoted the last twenty years of my life to?"

"I would've thought that was far preferable to spending the rest of your life in jail, Mrs Baxter, and I can assure you that prison wouldn't be a pleasant experience once the details of your exploits got out."

"And there would be a media ban on any news relating to Ilithyia's involvement in the creation of the Orestes virus?" Rosalind's gaze centred on the seated form of Max Perrin.

"Yes, although we don't have jurisdiction over the international press."

"If I agree, I think it would be in your interests to keep it out of the newsfeeds too. You and your party's ratings would certainly suffer if this deal ever became public knowledge."

"Yes, Mrs Baxter. Mutually assured destruction is the technical term, I believe."

Rosalind frowned and stared at the floor for a couple of seconds. Then she raised her head. "Alright, Andrew, I accept your terms. Get them written up and pass them by my lawyers. I'd like you and your men to remain here until everything's signed."

"Don't worry. I have no intention of leaving until this is resolved."

"Oh, and by the way, my finger is getting really fatigued. I'm sure you can see the need for expediency."

88

Seven months later

Rosalind Baxter reached forwards and held the stem of the wineglass between her fingers. The ruby coloured liquid clung to the edges as she swirled the contents and inhaled the earthy aroma. She tilted the glass back and allowed the liquid to brush against her lips. Room temperature, just as it should be. She sipped a small amount and rolled it around the inside of her mouth. With a sigh of satisfaction, she returned the glass to the place mat.

Rosalind picked up the bottle and inspected the label: Chateau Margaux, Premier Grand Cru Classe, 1975. Not the finest vintage but pretty damned good all the same and at over five hundred pounds a bottle, certainly not cheap. Not that money was an issue. Her bank account balance hovered somewhere between nine and ten digits now that the sale of Ilithyia had finally gone through. It wasn't as much as she had once dreamed of, but it was more than enough to last the rest of her life in considerable comfort. Even after donating ninety percent of the proceeds to charity, the remaining ten percent amounted to over eight hundred million pounds. If she drank a bottle of this vintage every day, it would still take over several thousand years to exhaust the funds she had amassed.

She hadn't seen Jason in months. He had collected his things accompanied by a social worker a couple of days after the incident in the incinerator room. She heard he was living with the Lessing family and that both he and Antimone were now attending a state school. Antimone's mother was looking after the child while the teenagers were at school. If Rosalind was honest with herself, she missed the company of another human being in the house, but she felt no remorse for her actions towards her adopted son. He had brought everything on himself when he chose the disabled girl in preference to the woman who had given him everything over the last sixteen years.

She leant back in the armchair and allowed the strains of Beethoven's violin concerto in D major to wash over her. Her enjoyment was disturbed by the banging of a door on the other side of the house. She rose to her feet and stared out through the darkness at the well-tended garden, faintly illuminated by the glow from the lights inside. A summer storm was due to build in strength that night, peaking at some point in the early hours of the morning. She closed the window and returned to her chair.

The door banged again. Rosalind gave a tut of exasperation. Another window must be open somewhere. She stood up once again and padded in her bare feet into the hall. The sound came from upstairs. Now that she thought about it, she remembered leaving the bedroom window ajar. She marched up the stairs and opened the door to check. Sure enough, the curtains were billowing in the stiff breeze. She strode across the room and pulled the latch shut without bothering to turn on the light.

Rosalind retraced her steps and sat once more. She grabbed the remote control and set the playback to the start of the second movement. The melancholy tone of the violins matched her mood exactly. She took a sip of the wine and closed her eyes, holding the glass in her hand. The notes seemed to resonate in her chest as they blended into one another. She swallowed another mouthful and started humming the melody.

"Hello, Mrs Baxter."

Rosalind jerked forwards, sloshing the remaining quarter of the contents on her cream-coloured trousers. "Jesus, Max, what the hell are you doing here? I thought you'd be in prison or youth detention."

Max smirked. "You say that after everything you've done. You're really quite something, aren't you? They can't prosecute me without the whole ugly story coming out, and that would jeopardise your little arrangement, wouldn't it? Anyway, I thought we needed to have a little chat."

Something cold ran down Rosalind's spine. "I'm calling the police." She placed the now empty glass on the mat and pushed off the chair.

"I don't think so. Sit down."

Rosalind found herself sitting down again. "What? I don't—"

"That drug I took from my Dad's office. I kept some. I thought it might come in useful again once I'd seen how effective it was."

"But—"

"Yes, Mrs Baxter, while you were upstairs, I poured some—rather a lot, in fact—into your wine. Ironic, isn't it, that you should fall victim to the same drug that you used to kidnap all those other women?"

Rosalind stared at the empty glass. Her head spun, and she experienced a strong sensation of watching herself from a distance. She tried to speak, but her mouth refused to work. A deepening panic built up inside. Try as she might, she was powerless to move. Whatever was coming next couldn't be good.

"You murdered my father in front of me. Now it's payback time."

"I… I…"

"No. Don't talk. I want you to listen. You rammed a pen into my father's eye. And then you shoved it all the way into his brain. That wasn't a very nice thing to do, was it?"

Rosalind lifted her eyes, trying to focus on his face.

Max reached into his pocket and pulled out a pen. "This is identical to the one you killed my father with." He clicked the end three times in quick succession. "My father used to buy them in bulk, that's how I know it's the same."

He took a step closer and handed the writing implement to Rosalind. "Here, take this."

She reached out and grasped it between her fingers.

"Make sure the tip is sticking out."

Rosalind's eyes seemed to move of their own volition. Her gaze pinpointed on the tiny circle of blue ink.

"Now I want you to listen carefully. You're going to push the pen into your right eye, and you're going to do it very slowly. You're only going to stop when I tell you to. Is that understood? By the way, you may scream if you want."

Rosalind's hand shook as she moved it closer to her face. "N-N-No"

"Yes, you're going to do this, Mrs Baxter, I want you to feel what my father felt before he died."

The tip quivered as it approached her eyeball.

"Do it!" Max yelled.

The point touched. Eyelashes fluttered up and down in a blur of movement.

"Do it!"

Rosalind pushed the tip through the surface of her eye. The tendons in her neck stretched tight. A howl of agony erupted from her mouth. When she had exhausted her breath, she drew in a deep, shuddering lungful of air and screamed again.

Max watched impassively as the pen penetrated millimetre by millimetre, every tiny movement followed by an ear-splitting shriek.

"That's far enough."

Rosalind's trembling fingers relaxed their grip a fraction.

"I could kill you right now, but I want you to suffer. You're going to wait until the music ends. When that happens, you're going to push it in as far as it will go. In the meantime, you're going to think about all the terrible things you've done in your life. Do you understand?"

Max raised his voice. "Do you understand?"

Blood, snot, and tears mingled together and dribbled down Rosalind's face. Her breathing came in short pants, each breath accompanied by a moan of torment. Her head moved in an almost imperceptible nod.

"Remember when the music ends, the pen has to go all the way in."

Her good eye focused on the panel showing the time remaining on the album.

When she forced her gaze upwards again, he was gone.

The End of Decimation: The Girl Who Survived

Book Two

TERMINATION: THE BOY WHO DIED

1

Friday 11th July 2036

Glasgow Olympic Stadium

The roar of the crowd reverberated through Antimone Lessing's chest.

"AN-TIM-OH-NEE! AN-TIM-OH-NEE!"

Her stomach flipped. Were they really chanting her name? As the poster girl for British athletics, this was the moment for which she and most of the people in the stadium had been waiting. The long hours of training, the soreness of tired shoulder muscles, the meticulously controlled diet; everything came down to the next few minutes and the final of the Olympic women's 1500-metres open wheelchair race. The weight of expectation hung heavy on her muscular shoulders.

Of the sixty-three entrants in the competition, only eight remained. Antimone had posted the fastest qualification time, but she knew that meant nothing. Half the field was capable of winning. All her major competitors conserved their energy in the heats and semi-final, hoping for some advantage when it mattered.

She glanced up at the giant screen. The camera panned across a packed stadium, the supporters grouped by nationality and waving brightly coloured flags. As she lowered her gaze, a different scene greeted her eyes. In reality, the crowd occupied barely a third of the vast bowl: the power of computer-generated imagery.

Almost every face wore a white cotton mask over the nose and mouth. The rest protected themselves with full plastic facemasks, complete with respirators and filters. More than three years after the cure, people were still reluctant to gather in groups without taking precautions. The general public remained paranoid about infectious diseases, aware that the deadly Orestes virus had swept across the globe and infected the entire population of the planet within days of the initial outbreak.

She let her eyes drift to the VIP section of the crowd. Somewhere up there, her three-year-old boy, Paul, and his father, Jason, were sitting. She'd never pick them out from down here, but she could imagine her son's excitement at the noise and colour of the occasion. Her thoughts turned to Jason. The situation with him was complicated and one she needed to resolve, but there would be plenty of time in the future to worry about the state of their relationship and where it was going.

A lull in the crowd noise drew Antimone's attention back to the present. Nearby, a muscle-bound athlete in the blue of Italy stepped up to the shot-put circle. The man crouched down, then exploded in a whirl of motion, heaving the black ball out beyond the twenty-five-metre line. A burst of raucous applause greeted his efforts. Antimone could almost hear her coach's stern voice inside her head, telling her to focus on the forthcoming race.

As she turned away from the field event, a shadow fell across her. A woman wearing a green, one-piece athletic outfit stood over her, blocking out the hazy afternoon sun. Emblazoned on the woman's chest was a black rectangle containing a white sickle embracing a six-sided star. She flashed a superficial smile and extended a hand. "Good luck." Her voice carried a slight Arabic accent.

The athlete from The Republic of North Africa: another of those with no disability. So far in the qualifying rounds, they had avoided each other. Today would be the first time they met in a race.

Antimone delayed just long enough to reveal her internal debate. When she finally accepted the handshake, her rival's palm felt surprisingly cool. "The same to you."

The woman turned away, revealing the competitor number on her back. Then she stopped and swivelled to face Antimone once again. "Do not judge me. You know nothing about me."

"I know you can walk." The words were out of Antimone's mouth before she had engaged her brain. Five years earlier, the Olympic Committee had abolished the T54 wheelchair events and opened up the competitions to all comers, irrespective of any disability. Their decision raised the profile of the sport but didn't prove universally popular, especially among the existing athletes.

The North African rocked backwards as if someone had slapped her. The smooth skin of her forehead creased in a scowl. "You call us Fake Olympians because we still have the use of our legs. But does it matter in a wheelchair race? Do I have any advantage over you? I think not."

"I didn't—"

The woman spoke over Antimone. "It is easy for you here in the West. Your scientists have developed a treatment for this terrible disease, but they do not share it with my people. Where I live, they do not care about women. They treat us like cattle, forcing us to have babies to increase the population. We must bear children knowing we will die when we give birth. If I was not competing in the Olympics, I too would be pregnant and facing death. This is my way of surviving. Only yesterday, my coach told me that if I do not win this afternoon, I will become a mother for my nation. You are very lucky. You had a child and survived."

Antimone's mouth opened, but no words came out. Had this woman somehow learned of her involvement in developing the cure? Her one-in-a-billion immunity to the effects of this organism? Only a handful of people, including her own family and the British Prime Minister, knew the truth. *No, she couldn't possibly know.*

"Well, have you nothing to say?" the North African athlete asked, staring down at her.

When Antimone finally forced her lips to move, all she could utter was, "I'm sorry."

The woman glared at her in silence for a second longer, then spun about and stalked back to her wheelchair. Antimone's eyes followed her opponent as she strapped herself into the machine. She flinched as a hand landed on her shoulder. She twisted around to see her coach, John Marshall.

His gaze tracked the green-suited competitor. "Has the delightful Aya Shaladi been trying to get inside your head?"

Antimone frowned at the man who had guided her preparations over the past three years. "What do you mean?"

"Let me take a guess: poor little me. If I don't win, they'll kill me… and probably a whole lot more if I'm right."

When Antimone didn't reply, he continued. "You should be honoured. She normally reserves her mind games for the competitor she considers the greatest threat. I should've warned you. She's renowned for it. If you're wondering, Miss Shaladi is in no danger of being conscripted into motherhood. Her father is a general in The Republic of North Africa's army. There's no way he would allow his little treasure to suffer the same indignities as the other women who get treated like breeding animals."

"Yes, but she—"

"What have we talked about? Visualise the race: the different stages from start to finish. Concentrate on your breathing. Conserve your energy. Don't go off too fast. This is your big chance, and you're the fastest qualifier in this final. When you hit the front, nobody comes past you. Is that clear?"

Antimone nodded.

"I asked if that's clear."

"Yes, Coach."

"Excellent. You've put in too much work to fail now because you allowed some smart-talking cow from the arse end of nowhere to mess with your head."

A bell rang. "That'll be the five-minute warning," Marshall said. "I won't wish you luck because you don't need it. You're going to smash this race."

"Yes, Coach," Antimone replied.

"Good. I'll see you after you cross the line in first place."

Her eyes followed the grey-haired, ex-army fitness instructor as he strode towards the stand. A fierce determination filled her chest. John Marshall had given up a comfortable job at the prestigious Oakington Manor private school to become her full-time trainer. She owed her presence at this final to his unwavering support and encouragement. He had placed his faith in her. *I won't let him down.*

She rotated her shoulders, trying to keep the muscles warm. Another ding of the bell drew her back to the race: three minutes to go. The other competitors were heading to the start. She tightened the strap on her helmet and flexed her fingers in the tight-fitting gloves. With a series of powerful shoves, she guided the wheelchair towards the painted number four next to the curving white line that signalled the starting point for the three-and-three-quarters lap contest.

Most of the other finalists were already in position. She inched forwards until the female official raised a hand. To her right was the green outfit of the North African. Antimone glared at the woman's back, annoyed with herself at being taken in by the mind games of her chief rival.

The announcer introduced the field. "In lane one, representing Great Britain, we have Natasha Jones from Cardiff. Natasha qualified as the fifth fastest competitor in this afternoon's final." A roar of approval echoed through the stadium.

Antimone tuned out the man's voice as he presented the French and Argentinian competitors. She closed her eyes and ran through the mental exercises her coach had drilled into her. The announcement of her own name dragged her back to reality.

"In lane four, from the town of Northstowe and also representing Great Britain, Antimone Lessing is the fastest qualifier in a time of three minutes, twenty point seven, just two-tenths of a second outside the world record."

Once again, a chant erupted from the crowd. "AN-TIM-OH-NEE! AN-TIM-OH-NEE!"

A ring of drones, each no larger than a tennis ball, settled into a tight formation around her head. They hovered in place, fixing her with the Cyclops eyes of their cameras. She raised a gloved hand in acknowledgement and fought back the irrational desire to swat away the tiny flying robots, buzzing like insects, inches from her face. She glanced up at the big screen. Should she wave towards the unpopulated parts of the stadium as well?

Before she could decide, the announcer moved onto the next competitor. "From Tripoli and representing The Republic of North Africa, in lane five we have Aya Shaladi. Aya qualified second fastest in a time of three minutes, twenty-one point one seconds."

The woman lifted her arm, but her look of cheerful confidence faded as several boos and catcalls mingled with the polite applause. Antimone stifled a grin of satisfaction. It seemed she was not alone in harbouring reservations about the relaxation of the entry requirements. The decision to allow athletes with no disability into the Olympic wheelchair events remained controversial as the Russian and Greek competitors—both of whom had full use of their legs—also discovered when they received the same reaction from the crowd.

Moments later, the announcer finished presenting the eighth finalist, an Ethiopian. A hush fell over the stadium as the race official raised the starting pistol.

"On your marks."

Antimone lowered her body and grasped the shiny hand ring. A sharp crack sent her surging into motion, her torso bobbing up and down as she accelerated to racing speed. The roar of the crowd drove her forwards, straining every sinew to emerge from the first bend clear of any bumping or barging.

As the curve ended, she tapped the compensator between strokes to straighten the wheelchair. Side-by-side, she and the North African athlete led the field. The green-suited competitor drifted to the left.

Conserve your energy. Don't go off too fast. With her coach's advice still resounding inside her head, Antimone slackened the push rate and allowed her main challenger to take the lead. The Welsh girl slipped into third, tracking the leading pair.

By the time they reached the finishing line after the first circuit, the group of three had broken away. The gap to fourth place now extended to at least five wheelchair lengths. Antimone settled into a steady rhythm, every ounce of concentration focused on maximising the output from each stroke.

At the end of the second lap, Antimone risked an upward glance at the large display screen. The distance from the leading three to the trailing pack had reached fifteen metres. Judging by the ache in her shoulders, it would be a fast time. The North African showed no signs of slackening the pace, and Antimone was consuming a lot of energy just to stay with her.

As they neared the finishing line for the last lap, Antimone's muscles burned from the build-up of lactic acid. The clang of the bell sent a fresh jolt of adrenalin surging into her bloodstream. She grimaced in pain, spurred on by the yells of encouragement from the crowd.

Despite the seething tension inside the stadium, a calmness settled over her. *This is what I've trained for. Just keep it together.* Ahead of her, the North African's technique was becoming more ragged. Antimone followed a wheel length behind, saving what little energy she had left for the sprint to the finishing line. At the start of the final bend, she allowed her wheelchair to swing wide. Agony flooded her body, but she forced her exhausted biceps to work harder. The Welsh girl tracked the manoeuvre, drawing alongside to her right. *Where the hell did she come from?*

***

The three leaders emerged into the home straight side-by-side. The audience rose to their feet, raising the sound level to a collective roar. But not everybody was watching the race. A lone camera drone drifted across the track just a few metres ahead of the leading pack, signalling the start of what was about to follow.

Moments later, the first bomb exploded.

Part One: Preparation

2

Thursday 12th June 2036

Infant Creche, Bani Waled, Republic of North Africa
Four weeks before the Olympic wheelchair final

"Sit still," the woman said in Arabic.

"No," the three-year-old boy replied, angling his head away.

She grabbed a tissue from the nearby box and tried to wipe the child's nose. He wriggled in her arms as she attempted to reach the twin trails of mucus dribbling down his face. She tightened her grip and pulled him closer. The boy's struggles intensified. He lashed out a foot and caught her in the stomach. Her hand immediately released his wrist, moving to the rounded bump protruding from her belly.

"Ibn kalb," she muttered under her breath. The words must have come out louder than she intended because the little girl, playing with the doll two metres away, glanced up sharply. She had just called the annoying brat the son of a dog. In truth, the identity of the boy's father was a mystery. Like all the children under her care, his mother had died in childbirth, probably moments after a multiple birth. The doctors would have given her fertility drugs to increase the number of eggs she released, then impregnated her with the sperm of a member of the ruling elite.

The woman gently rubbed the point of impact. In less than a month, she would suffer the same fate. She was already finding it hard to sleep at night. The rapidly expanding bulge in her stomach prevented her from getting comfortable. During the last inspection, the midwife had informed her she was expecting quadruplets. Not that she would ever get to see them. Within moments of severing the umbilical cord, the virus would transition to its active state. *I hope I'm no longer awake when that happens.*

The previous week, a cousin told her the Americans had developed a cure. Their women could give birth without fear of dying. It was typical of the infidel devils to keep such a discovery to themselves. No doubt it suited their purposes to reduce the number of true believers. It was her duty to help replenish her people's population, but that didn't make the burden any easier to bear. *Why do I have to die?*

Her eyes swept the room. The children played in groups of three or four. There were nineteen of them in total, twelve girls and seven boys. As well as releasing more eggs in the mother, the drugs raised the ratio of female to male foetuses. The rulers needed women to increase population numbers, but few, if any, would live past their teens.

The woman glanced at her watch. In half-an-hour, it would be time for the midday sleep. She was supposed to stay awake to supervise the children, but she would often try to grab a few minutes of rest herself. The combination of the energy-sapping heat and the steady, rhythmic whump of the ceiling fan were already making her feel sleepy. *Nobody will notice.* She closed her eyes and leant back in the wooden chair.

A tap on the knee jerked her out of her drowsiness. The boy with the snotty nose stood in front of her. He held one hand to his face. The other tugged at the black material of her robes. She swatted away his grubby fingers. He dropped the raised arm, revealing a trickle of blood originating from his left nostril and mingling with the trail of mucus.

Why can't he just leave me alone? With a groan, she reached once again for the box of tissues and tugged one free. When she returned her attention to the child, the red trail had developed into a stream. A reedy wail escaped from his lips. His open mouth revealed a rose-coloured stain on his tiny, white teeth. He balled his hands into fists and rubbed at his eyes.

The woman dragged him nearer and dabbed at the blood now gushing from his nose. Within seconds, crimson fluid saturated the tissue. She tossed it on the floor and grabbed another handful from the box.

The boy lowered his hands and grasped at his throat. His brown irises now sat amidst a labyrinth of burst veins where moments before there had been only white sclera. The boy's chest heaved as he tried to suck air into his oxygen-starved lungs. A wracking cough culminated in a spray of blood and mucus into the woman's face.

She wiped the glutinous mass away with her sleeve and levered herself upright. By the time she reached her feet, the child was convulsing on the floor. She lowered herself to one knee beside him, grunting with the effort. The boy writhed on the ground, his frantic movements creating red streaks across the discoloured white tiles.

What should she do? They hadn't trained her for anything like this. She placed a hand on his chest to still the jerking spasms that rippled through his body. With a final twitch, the child lay still. *Is he dead? That isn't possible.*

The sound of crying drew her attention away from the prostrate child. She raised her eyes to see three other children, each writhing in a pool of blood. The rest of the group backed up against the crude, childish paintings distributed along the roughly finished walls. As she watched, two more burst into a fit of coughing, hacking up gobbets of bloody phlegm.

The woman staggered to her feet, raising an arm to cover her face with her sleeve. Everywhere she looked, children were bleeding from their mouths, noses and ears. She took a step forwards as one of the closest victims stopped moving. *Is this some sort of chemical attack?* She turned in a full circle. Every single child in the room now either lay still or twitching in their bodily fluids. The mingled smells of blood and faeces assaulted her nostrils.

She stumbled to the mirror above the sink and studied her reflection: no nosebleed. The whites of the terrified eyes staring back at her remained clear. No blood emerged from her mouth or ears. *Why am I the only one not to be affected?*

When she turned around, every single child sprawled motionless on the floor. Those that faced her stared back with open, unseeing eyes.

The woman lumbered across the room as fast as her bulk would allow. When she reached the door, she fumbled with the lock and stumbled outside into the stifling midday heat.

"They're dead," she screamed. "The children are all dead."

3

Friday 13th June 2036

Northstowe Athletics Stadium

Four weeks before the Olympic wheelchair final

Antimone gave one last shove to propel herself across the finish line. She coasted to a halt, her breath rasping in her throat. Every muscle from her shoulders to her forearms burned from the build-up of lactic acid.

"Come on, don't forget the warm down," came a voice from behind her. The tracksuited figure of John Marshall jogged towards her, stopwatch in hand. "That was a fifty-five-second lap."

Her coach was old school. The sensors in her wheelchair rendered the archaic timepiece he used to measure her performance unnecessary, but the former soldier and PE teacher seemed to prefer the ancient mechanical technology.

A wry grin broke across his craggy features as he drew nearer. "Not bad… but still not fast enough to win a gold medal at the Olympics."

Antimone groaned. *What do I have to do to make him happy?* After a two-hour training session, it was actually a pretty good time. She considered voicing her thoughts. Instead, she bit her tongue and said, "Yes, Coach."

The sweat was already drying on her skin when her aching arms set the wheelchair into motion once again. As she coasted around the oval, her gaze wandered to a group practising high jump on the far side of the track. Somebody wearing a T-shirt and jeans was chatting to the athletes. A laugh carried across on the light breeze. The new arrival separated from the others and raised an arm in her direction. She squinted against the glare of the late afternoon sunshine, trying to identify the person. Through shaded eyes, she watched the figure head towards the finish line where her coach waited.

As she rounded the bend into the home straight, she recognised the outline of Jason Floyd. He waved once again. Antimone raised her hand long enough to return the gesture as she propelled the chair forwards. A stab of jealousy ran through her. Who had he been talking to? He found it so easy to mingle with other people whereas, for her, it was always a struggle. If only she knew what she wanted from their relationship. His good looks and effortless confidence made him popular with the fairer sex. There would be no shortage of interested girls if she ever cut him loose. Her heart sank at the thought. But could she really trust him after what had happened between them? Internally, she cursed her indecision.

She drifted to a standstill beside him.

"That looked fairly quick," he said, bending down to kiss her on the cheek.

"Yeah, but apparently not fast enough for the slave driver," she replied, rotating her shoulders to loosen the tension in her muscles. The pair turned together as John Marshall drew nearer.

"Good to see you," he said, shaking Jason's hand.

"You too, Coach," Jason replied.

"I haven't seen you down here for ages. Are you still throwing your javelin?"

"I've been to a few coaching sessions at the university, but there aren't really enough hours in the week with all the studying."

"That's a shame. You're a natural." Marshall shifted his attention back to Antimone. "That was a good workout. Are we okay for the same time tomorrow? You need to up the work rate. Another fortnight of intensive training followed by a competitive race, and I think you'll be ready. Then it's just a case of maintaining your fitness levels before the Olympics and not overdoing it."

Antimone groaned inwardly. The current workouts were painful enough as they were; the prospect of putting in more effort didn't appeal. Marshall must have spotted her expression because he grinned and said, "Remember, no pain, no gain. If you want a gold medal, you've got to work for it."

Antimone gave a grimace in return. "Yes, Coach, I'm well aware of that."

"I'll leave you two youngsters to it. See you tomorrow. 'Bye, Jason."

The pair waited until the grey-haired, former army fitness instructor was out of earshot.

"I wasn't expecting you back until later," Antimone said.

"I thought I'd catch you at the track and check out for myself how the training was going. Where's Paul?"

"Mum's looking after him at the moment."

Their son, Paul, was something of a miracle. Conceived while Jason and Antimone were both under the influence of a date-rape drug slipped into the fruit punch during a party, the three-year-old was the first child in a generation to have a living biological mother. Until he was born, every woman had died in childbirth, killed by the Orestes virus. The pathogen had infected the entire population of the planet, but only activated upon severing the umbilical cord. Antimone's unexpected survival had given the doctors the vital clue they needed to develop a cure. Pregnancy was no longer a death sentence, at least not for residents of those countries wealthy enough to pay for the treatment.

"What have you been up to?" Antimone asked.

"Oh, work, work and more work," Jason replied. "Just like you, they drive us hard." He was in the second year of a biochemistry degree at King's College in London. When it first became apparent the virus posed a serious risk to humanity's future, the British government had pumped huge sums into medical research, including grants to cover the full costs of relevant degrees. Jason was a beneficiary of this funding although now a treatment was in place, it wasn't clear for how much longer it would last.

"How long are you staying?"

"I've got lectures on Monday morning, so I'll need to leave on Sunday night."

Antimone tried to mask her disappointment. Despite her reservations about their long-term relationship, she found herself cheered by his company. Training for the Olympics was a solitary activity, and she would have enjoyed spending more time with her closest friend.

"Have you got the car?" Antimone asked.

"Yeah, your Mum sent the car to pick me up from the station and said I could borrow it to take you home."

"I just need to dump my stuff in the locker, then we can go."

Jason chewed his lip as he walked in silence alongside Antimone. When they reached the archway of the tunnel leading to the changing rooms, she stopped. "You're a bit quiet. Is something bothering you?"

Jason halted and turned towards her. He hesitated for a moment before speaking. "I wasn't going to mention it until later. I can't hide anything from you."

"Normally, I can't shut you up," she replied with a smile. "What's wrong?"

"I received an email."

"So what? Who was it from?"

"Her."

"You don't mean…?" A tremor ran through Antimone's body.

"When I got back to the house this afternoon, it was waiting in my inbox. From Rosalind Baxter, no less."

"What does that bitch want?"

"She wants to meet us."

Antimone blinked in confusion. "Let me get this straight. You're saying that evil witch wants to see you and me."

"Yes, and Paul as well."

"What on earth for?"

"Apparently, she'd like to discuss what happened—in person."

Antimone stared at Jason in disbelief, looking for some sign that he was joking. When none came and she eventually spoke, her voice started half an octave higher than usual. "I don't believe this. That woman murdered your biological mother, framed your father for her murder, killed millions of other women by releasing the virus and threatened to incinerate both of us unless she received a pardon from none other than the Prime Minister himself. And now she wants to *talk* about it?"

"I know. It's crazy, right?"

The blood pounded in Antimone's ears in time with her thudding heart. The breath rasped in her throat. For over three years, she had done her best to obliterate the memories from her mind. Now they all came crashing back.

Their eyes met until Jason could no longer meet the anger in her stare, and he looked away. When he spoke, his tone was subdued. "Don't worry, I'll delete it. I shouldn't have mentioned it."

“You weren’t seriously considering saying yes, were you?” Antimone asked, her voice trembling with fury.

“Of course not. I never want to see her again. I can’t even stand the sound of her name.” Within weeks of escaping from his adoptive mother’s hidden laboratory, he had changed his surname from Baxter back to Floyd to match that of his birth parents.

“Does she think that just because she raised you for sixteen years, it gives her any right to contact you? After everything she did?”

“I’ve no idea how her mind works.”

Antimone’s teeth ground together, trapping the inside of her cheek. The taste of blood filled her mouth. She spat on the ochre-coloured track.

“I’d rather spend an afternoon with the devil than with that murderous witch.”

4

Friday 20th June 2036

Oakington House, Northstowe

Three weeks before the Olympic wheelchair final

Rosalind Baxter flicked a wrist to dismiss the newsfeed hovering in front of her face. The overlay faded, restoring her vision to an unobstructed view of the room. She closed her left eye, then her right, comparing the images against each other. The latter was sharper and brighter, just as the specialists had promised.

Six months ago, they had installed the latest prosthetic technology to replace the glass sphere fitted after the initial catastrophic damage to her cornea. Her brain had taken a while to adapt to the electrical signals fed directly into the visual cortex, but she had to admit the synthetic organ performed far better than the biological original. It also contained additional features such as the ability to superimpose information on her vision.

She reached out for the glass of red wine resting atop the small wooden table and took a sip. The rich flavour of the dark berries rolled across her tongue. Chateau Margaux was the closest thing to perfection on earth. At over five hundred pounds a bottle there were certainly cheaper beverages, but if money was of no consideration—and it wasn't—little else came close.

As she leant forwards to replace the glass, her right arm trembled. She grabbed one hand with the other to still the trembling in her fingers. The symptoms had first surfaced three years earlier, shortly after the attack. Not that she had explained to the medical professionals what really happened that evening.

When the paramedics had arrived to discover the pen protruding from her right eye, she told them she had slipped on a wet floor. In truth, during the long minutes before the emergency services rolled up with sirens blaring, it took every inch of willpower to prevent herself from ramming the ballpoint home. The mind-altering drug coursing through her bloodstream at the time had removed all her free will, leaving her susceptible to the implantation of suggestions.

An icon flashed in the upper corner of her field of vision, drawing her back to the present. "Expand," she murmured, holding a finger to her earlobe. The action signalled to the implant that she was issuing it with a command.

Two circles, one red, the other green, slid to the centre of her view. Within each sat the outline of a white telephone handset. The text beneath stated *Number Unknown*.

The ability to suppress their identity suggested the caller was somebody important. Only a handful of individuals possessed the required privilege levels since it had become mandatory two years earlier for all phone users to display an identification. Her curiosity piqued, Rosalind flicked a finger to the right.

A man spoke. "Mrs Baxter?"

"Yes, who's calling?"

"Please hold for the Prime Minister." A click preceded a burst from a recent pop song.

Rosalind scowled and swiped to the left. "I'm not holding for anybody," she muttered, "least of all that arsehole."

Seconds later, the flashing icon reappeared. Once again, the message signalled an unidentified caller. Rosalind let out an exasperated huff and accepted the call with a flick of the wrist.

Before she could speak, Andrew Jacobs' sonorous voice came down the line. "Rosalind, how are you?"

"If you're using my first name, you must want something from me, Andrew. The last time we spoke in that incinerator room, you referred to me as Mrs Baxter."

"Yes… well." The Prime Minister's tone contained an atypical nervousness. "I heard you had an operation on your damaged eye."

"I take it you know what—or should I say who—caused the damage in the first place."

"I did hear a rumour."

"So, what can I do for you?" Rosalind asked, the coolness of her words suggesting whatever he wanted would be too much trouble.

"Straight down to business it is then. Our sources have reported a new strain of the virus coming out of Africa, North Africa to be exact."

"Why are you calling to tell me that? Why would I care what happens over there?"

"As the person who created the damned thing in the first place, I thought you would consider it a significant development."

"I still don't see how it affects me. As I recall, you forced me to sell my company and kept ninety per cent of the proceeds."

It was the Prime Minister's turn to express exasperation. "Which I'm sure you'll agree was better than the alternative of spending the rest of your life in prison. You wouldn't believe it, but I'm coming under considerable pressure to include you in the new year's honours list. If only people knew the truth."

"Just remember that your fate is intertwined with mine, Andrew. If the facts do come out, I can't see the electorate having much sympathy with the man who brokered the deal."

"I had no choice. If I had refused, thousands more women would have died, maybe the whole of the human race."

"Well, we both have to live with our decisions. Anyway, I'm still not sure what you want from me."

"I need you to reassemble a team to study this new strain. If we—"

"Let me stop you right there, Andrew. I have no interest in helping you. Why don't you contact the new owners of Ilithyia Biotechnology and ask them?"

"Ever since we cut back on the grants, they've been taking money from the Americans. There are rumours that one of the big international pharmaceutical companies is about to buy them. We might be able to delay the sale, but—"

Rosalind interrupted again. "None of that is my problem, Andrew. I have to say I think it was very short-sighted of you to reduce research funding when nobody has produced a cure."

Jacobs hesitated as he tried to make sense of her words. "I don't understand."

"Do I have to spell it out? I formulated a treatment, not a cure. The pathogen still exists in the bodies of every person on the planet. The drugs I developed address the symptoms and prevent the virus from activating its destructive phase. They most certainly do not destroy it. Until we eradicate this organism, the population will always be at risk of further mutations."

"All the more reason why you should come back to work."

Rosalind sighed. "I already told you. I'm not interested."

"And there's nothing I can do to make you change your mind?"

"No." The silence extended between them until Rosalind spoke again. "Now you mention it, there may be something that would persuade me to help you."

"And what's that?" Jacobs sounded wary at the sudden about-turn.

"Somehow, I don't think you're going to like my proposal, but my terms are non-negotiable."

"If it's about the monetary side, I'm sure we can come to an arrangement."

"It's not, but that would be a secondary precondition before I could work for you."

"If money isn't the deciding factor, what else do you want?"

Rosalind paused for a second before replying. "Have Max Perrin killed, and I'll do what you ask."

The line went quiet. When the Prime Minister spoke again, his voice came out as a whisper. "You know I can't do that."

"That's my price."

"You expect me to order the killing of a twenty-year-old boy? You can't be serious."

"Oh, come on, Andrew. I'm sure you have people who specialise in that sort of thing. In fact, I used to employ a man with the right skills myself before I fired him—in the literal sense. And of course, just to clarify, that was before you signed the pardon agreement for all previous crimes."

"Look, I know the Perrin boy blinded you in one eye, but you did murder his father right in front of him. Remember, I was there when it happened."

"He wasn't trying to blind me," Rosalind screeched. "He was trying to kill me." The terror of the moment came rushing back as she recalled the memory.

She swallowed hard before continuing. "First, he spiked my drink with a drug that removed all my self-control. He forced me to push the tip of the pen into my eye while he watched. Then, just before he left, he told me to ram it all the way in when the track ended.

"It was only his ignorance of classical music that saved me. I'm sure he had no idea that Beethoven's violin concerto in D major lasts for three-quarters of an hour. By the end, I had recovered just enough willpower to resist, but it was a close-run thing. The drug didn't dull the pain in the slightest. He wanted me to suffer. During all that time, I was fully aware and in excruciating agony."

Silence extended between them. Eventually, Andrew Jacobs spoke. "I'm sure it was awful, but I can't just order the execution of a British citizen. Rosalind, I must urge you to reconsider."

"In that case, I have nothing more to say to you," Rosalind Baxter answered, swiping left to end the call.

5

Sunday 22nd June 2036

Tripoli Military Headquarters, Republic of North Africa
Three weeks before the Olympic wheelchair final

Mullah Awad sat in silence, reading the printed report. The strands of his heavy beard coiled together, hiding the lower part of his face.

The scientist in the doctor's coat, Dr Naeem Kubar, licked his lips nervously as he stood before the black-robed cleric. Sitting beside the religious leader, Professor Muhammad Halfon, the director of the hospital, appeared equally uncomfortable. He fiddled with the hem of his white robes. The room was silent apart from the once per second squeal of protest as the ceiling fan laboured against the worn bearings on its perpetual cycle of rotation.

While he waited, the standing man allowed his gaze to wander. Outside the self-adjusting, tinted windows, construction cranes rose from the rubble like crooked nails. More than two decades of civil war had exacted a heavy toll on the city's buildings, many of which still exhibited gaping wounds three years after the conflict had ended.

Dr Kubar had mixed feelings about the current situation in his newly formed country. He welcomed the end of the fighting but was less enamoured by the religious fanatics who had seized control and ruled by fear and intimidation. At least the new rulers were realistic enough to understand that they required the services of doctors and scientists, especially since the Western governments still refused to supply the drugs the population so desperately needed to survive.

Many of his colleagues had fled during the war. Only the truly dedicated and those with family ties remained. The scientist had chosen not to leave, hoping that one day he would be reunited with his only daughter, who had disappeared five years earlier during a visit to the local shops. From what little information he had been able to gather, it seemed she accidentally strayed into a fierce battle between the opposing forces vying for control of this vital shipping port. Hope for her survival was waning, but he couldn't abandon the city without discovering her fate.

The cleric pushed the paper sheets away and looked up. "So, Doctor Kubar, you believe this is a new strain?"

"Yes, sir." The medic stared at the upside-down report, unable to meet the dark eyes of his interrogator, glaring at him from above the bushy facial hair like a predator studying its prey.

"I've read your words, but I want to hear your reasoning."

The scientist paused for a second as he tried to decide at what level to pitch his explanation.

"I'm waiting," said the religious man, tapping his fingers on the table.

"Of course, sir."

"And stop calling me sir. You may address me as Mullah."

Kubar took a moment to gather his thoughts. "Yes, Mullah. The symptoms in the victims match those in women who have given birth. Basically, the virus seems to have activated and destroyed all the vital organs. We are yet to perform a molecular-level analysis of the pathogen, but all the signs are that this is a mutation of the original strain."

"Why do you think it attacked these children?"

"I can't be sure of that, Mullah, but the research I have read from abroad suggests the disease is closely related to the influenza virus. The infected population is so large that mutations are inevitable. I believe this is what happened."

"What more do we know?"

"We placed the woman who was supervising the infants in isolation. She seemed unaffected, but since then she has given birth, dying shortly afterwards. Perhaps surprisingly, her four babies are fit and well, and have shown no symptoms to date."

"Is there any information on the affected age range?"

"All those who died in the original event were under five. There is currently no indication of an upper limit."

Professor Halfon cleared his throat. "If I may interrupt, Mullah. We have performed some additional tests and have established that those who have reached puberty seem unaffected. We have also proven that the Western drugs for pregnant women are ineffective in preventing the symptoms in children."

Kubar stared in surprise at his supervisor. "You didn't tell me this. How did you perform the tests? If you know who it affects, that must mean—"

"Be quiet," the mullah shouted. He waited a beat before continuing in a low, menacing voice. "I am the one asking the questions. You will restrict yourself to providing the answers or suffer the consequences."

The doctor took an involuntary half-step backwards.

When the cleric spoke again, his words carried a more conciliatory tone. "What can we do about it?"

Kubar hesitated before answering. "There's very little, really. I recommend keeping all infants in isolation. We don't possess the equipment or the expertise to develop a cure."

"We are working on obtaining the machines. They will be here soon."

"It won't make any difference," the scientist said. "Without the experts to operate them and interpret the results, they are useless."

Halfon shot an angry look at his subordinate. "Your attitude leaves a lot to be desired, Doctor. If you can't help us, we will find people who can."

The doctor's face flushed. "The Western countries have studied this disease for well over a decade. In that time, they have thrown millions—in fact billions—of dollars into medical research. All their best minds have worked on developing a treatment. Three years ago, they discovered a solution. It's not a cure, but it does prevent the virus from activating. And now a new variant of the contagion has appeared. What makes you think we can solve this problem when so many before have failed?"

The director thrust his chair back and leapt to his feet. "How dare you question our capabilities? I'm—"

"Enough!" The commanding voice of the mullah cut through the room like a knife. "If you would be so good as to leave us alone, Doctor." He gestured towards the exit.

The red-faced scientist glared at his supervisor, then stomped across the floor.

***

The mullah and the professor waited for the door to close.

"I must apologise for the behaviour of my staff, Mullah," the director said, returning to his seat.

"I like a bit of spirit," the cleric replied. "Don't go too hard on him. His report impressed me. I have learned that scientists resent being kept in the dark. He seems very competent, and we can ill afford to lose any more of the bright minds available to us."

"Even so…"

"Now, back to the matter in hand; the West will still not supply our country with this drug, Lucinase, so I want you to produce our own version."

"But…"

"You will also develop drugs to treat the new strain of the virus."

"Ah, Mullah, just the first of those will be very difficult. If I may ask, why can we not simply keep the children isolated from pregnant women?"

The mullah scowled at Halfon. "Do you expect our men to perform childcare? To cook and clean? To change nappies? This is women's work, but many have died giving birth. As we continue to grow our population, there are insufficient females for these tasks. I expect everybody in this country to do their duty, including those who are pregnant. They must contribute by caring for the infants, but until we develop a solution for the new strain, this is not possible. That is why I have commanded you to develop drugs to protect the children."

"I will do my best, Mullah."

"And I expect nothing less. It is unfortunate, but what Dr Kubar said is accurate. The machines are due to arrive in the next few days. We have been forced to deal with some unscrupulous individuals and have paid considerably more than the market value, but the equipment will not be a problem. What is more of an issue is the staff to operate them."

"I will put my top people on this project right away."

"Yes. Ensure the man who just walked out of the door is one of them. However, as the doctor said, your workers do not possess the necessary expertise."

The professor rubbed his chin. "I… I'm not sure what I can do about that."

"No, this is something which requires a different skill set. What if we could recruit the people you need?"

"How? Believe me, I have tried. The scientists with the required knowledge are only available in Europe and America, and they will not come here, no matter how much we pay them. It will take years to train our own citizens to the appropriate level."

"I am not talking about training although that is something we should do for our long term survival. No, the solution is far simpler. If the people with the skills we need won't work here voluntarily, then we must force them to come. Let me ask you this; if there was one person you could select for your team, who would it be?"

The director stared out of the window towards the signs of rebuilding amongst the ruins of the city. His gaze lingered for a few seconds before returning to the cleric. "There are many scientists in the world who could help us develop a cure, but if I had to choose one… it would be somebody who helped to develop Lucinase at Ilithyia Biotechnology."

"My thoughts exactly. What if I could offer you the former head of the company?"

"The woman?"

"Yes, Rosalind Baxter. I know we would all prefer a man, but her partner, Dr Perrin, died."

"Thank you, Mullah. That would help us greatly."

"And to make things better, what if I were to throw in the female who survived childbirth without taking any drugs?"

6

Sunday 22nd June 2036

The Beeches Play Area, Northstowe

Three weeks before the Olympic wheelchair final

Jason sat on the park bench and watched as Paul scrabbled over the climbing frame.

"Be careful," Antimone called.

The boisterous three-year-old ignored his mother's instructions and clambered higher. "Look at me, Daddy," he yelled excitedly.

"Very good," Jason replied.

"Come and push me on the swing," his son demanded.

Jason sighed. The opportunities for conversation were few and far between when Paul was awake. "I'll be there in a second. I just want to talk to Mummy."

Antimone stretched out a hand and took Jason's in hers. "He misses you during the week."

"Yeah, sorry to leave you with our little bundle of energy."

"Oh, don't worry about that. My parents look after him for most of the day. They love having him around. It's a good job too what with how much time I spend training."

"Did we do the right thing, keeping out of the spotlight? We can't even celebrate his birthday on the correct date."

Antimone turned and studied Jason's face. "God, yes. I get enough press attention as it is. I don't think I could take any more."

Jason laughed. "Darling of the athletics track *and* the first person in a generation to live after giving birth; your head would become so big it'd explode."

Antimone punched him playfully on the arm. "Seriously though, the media are swarming around that woman, Anna Mayfield, like flies. Barely a day goes by when there's not some new article about her and her daughter."

"I'm sure she's doing very well out of it."

"If they knew about us, we wouldn't be able to do anything like this. There'd be paparazzi hiding in the bushes and drones buzzing about, trying to capture an intimate moment."

Jason nestled closer. "Talking of intimate moments, didn't you say your parents were going out this afternoon?"

"Yes, and Paul will need his nap."

"Are you proposing to seduce me?" Jason asked, smiling.

"Perhaps," Antimone replied.

"I really miss you when I'm away at university." Slowly, Jason's smile faded. "I keep worrying that I'm going to blurt out some detail about what really happened. Sometimes, I wake up at night convinced I've let something slip, and they're coming to arrest me."

"Yeah, they certainly laid it on heavy afterwards, didn't they?"

"God knows what would happen if the full story got out. The government would fall for a start. My adoptive mother would become the most hated woman in the world."

Antimone grinned. "So, not all bad then."

"I read an article on one of those current affairs websites campaigning for her to be included in the new year's honours list."

"If only they knew the truth."

"I'm surprised Max Perrin hasn't talked to the press."

"Yeah, I wouldn't put it past him. To think our involvement in all of it started because of a stupid accident at the athletics track," Antimone said.

"That guy's definitely got a screw loose," Jason agreed. "I saw the look in his eyes after his father died. It's amazing he hasn't blabbed to somebody."

"Perhaps he did, and they've locked him up. Talking of fathers, what's yours up to?"

"He finally received the money for wrongful imprisonment. He was thinking about returning to university. I know it's a long time ago, but he has a degree from Cambridge. He told me he was planning to visit us one weekend, so you can ask him yourself."

"We certainly owe him. Without his help, I'd probably still be a prisoner in that basement lab."

The conversation lapsed into silence as they both remembered how close they had come to dying.

Jason patted Antimone on the knee. "I'm fed up with discussing the past. What about the future?"

Antimone stared straight ahead.

"Is something wrong?"

She turned to face him. "No, it's just… we're still very young. We've both got a lot on our plates at the moment. You have to finish your degree; I have to win gold at the Olympics."

Jason let out a snort of laughter. "No pressure there then."

Antimone's serious expression dissipated his attempt at humour. "I don't want you to feel you have to stay with me because…"

Jason leant in and cupped the back of her head in his hand. They kissed for several seconds. When they separated, his eyes studied every detail of her face. "I'm with you because I want to be."

The sudden appearance of an unhappy Paul broke the mood. "You said you would push me."

"Come on then, buddy," Jason replied. "Let's go to the swings."

"I want Mummy to do it."

Jason flashed a glance at Antimone. "I'm afraid she can't."

"Why not?"

"Well, it's hard for Mummy to push you when she's in a wheelchair."

"Why is she in a wheelchair?"

"Because she can't walk."

"Why can't she walk?"

"Mummy had an accident when she was younger," Antimone interjected.

"What happened?"

"A car hit me."

"Did it hurt?"

Antimone's grip tightened on the arm of her chair. "It was all very quick. I didn't see it coming, which is why you always have to check carefully before crossing the road."

"Yes, but did it hurt?"

"At first, I suppose, but then I fell asleep. Some people came and took me to a hospital. They gave me a wheelchair so I could move about."

The three-year-old's face scrunched up as he processed her response. "Couldn't the people fix you?"

"No," Antimone said. "Unfortunately not."

"I heard Grandma say they could make you better."

His parents' eyes met. Jason held Antimone's gaze for a second, then refocused his attention on his son. "Maybe one day, buddy."

"Come on, I'll try to push you," Antimone said, changing the subject. "Just as long as you don't want to go too high."

Paul scampered on ahead. Antimone followed a short distance behind, Jason's hand resting on her shoulder.

When they reached the swings, Paul was already seated and bouncing up and down in anticipation. Antimone moved to the side and pushed him gently in the back.

"Higher, higher," he yelled, forgetting all about her previously stated conditions.

"You better take over," Antimone said, backing out of the way and turning to Jason.

Soon, Paul was arcing through the air, propelled by his father and squealing in delight.

None of the young family noticed the man in the parked car taking photographs with the telephoto lens.

7

Tuesday 24th June 2036

Oakington House, Northstowe

17 days before the Olympic wheelchair final

Rosalind Baxter glanced blearily at her watch and then at the empty wine bottle resting atop the small wooden table beside her chair. Three-thirty in the afternoon. Already the first faint tendrils of a headache teased at the base of her skull. She leant back and allowed her eyelids to close.

The glow of the icon panel persisted in the upper corner of her right eye. She would have to mention that to her specialist. Surely, they could program the damned thing, so it turned off when her eyes were closed.

She was most of the way to dropping off when the trill of the doorbell shocked her back to full wakefulness. *Who the hell is that?* Nobody visited her other than delivery people and the occasional parcel drone, and she had ordered nothing recently.

She pushed herself out of the confines of the armchair and padded towards the front door in bare feet. The bell rang a second time.

"All right, all right, I'm coming."

She prodded the video control unit and stared blearily at the image. With a groan of annoyance, she pressed the green button and turned away without waiting to greet her visitor. Behind her, two dark-suited men slipped into the hallway, each with his right hand gripping an object beneath the cover of his jacket. They surveyed each of the rooms leading off the hall before returning to the open doorway.

"Clear, sir," one of them murmured before taking a pace to the side to allow Andrew Jacobs to enter.

"Thanks, gentlemen," the British Prime Minister replied. "Could you give us some privacy, please?"

A third man followed the leader of the country inside and took up a position at the foot of the staircase. His two colleagues stood back to back in the hallway. Jacobs trailed Rosalind into the lounge, shutting the glass-panelled door behind him. When he turned around, she had already returned to her armchair.

The Prime Minister's gaze settled on the empty wine bottle. "A little early to be sinking the booze, isn't it, Rosalind?"

"What are you doing here, Andrew? I gave you my answer over the phone, so what is there to talk about?"

"Thanks for the offer of a drink, but I'm fine."

Rosalind rolled her eyes. "You invited yourself here, so don't expect me to play the part of the gracious hostess."

Jacobs strolled to another armchair and dragged it closer until it was two metres from Rosalind's.

"Don't mind me," she said. "Just make yourself at home and organise the furniture how you like."

The Prime Minister sat and leant forwards. His hands rested on his knees. "We need to talk."

"I have nothing to say to you unless you've reconsidered your response to my terms."

"I've got people looking for Max Perrin, but he isn't living with his mother, and nobody has seen him for weeks."

"NMFP," Rosalind replied.

"I'm sorry."

"Not my—"

"Ah, yes, I get it," Jacobs interrupted. "It's not your effing problem. So, if we were to find him and come to some arrangement…"

"If by *come to some arrangement*"—Rosalind made air quotes as she spoke—"you mean ending his miserable life, then I'm all ears. But I'll need proof."

Jacobs flashed a glance towards the closed door. "This is all a bit medieval, isn't it? What do you want me to do? Bring his head on a plate?"

"That would do the trick."

"What you're asking for goes against everything I believe in."

"And yet here you are. That must mean you haven't discounted the idea."

"Look," Jacobs said, "the future of the world is at stake. If we don't get ahead of the curve on this thing, millions of children could die. Doesn't that bother you at all?"

Rosalind stared at the Prime Minister before replying. "Do you know what? Not really. I've told you I'll work on this problem if you agree to my terms."

"For God's sake, your own grandson could be affected."

"I haven't got a grandson," Rosalind snapped.

"Then why did you write an email to your son asking to meet him, his girlfriend and the child?"

"I don't believe this. You've been spying on me and reading my private messages."

An amused expression flickered over the Prime Minister's face. "You act all affronted at our surveillance activities, but you expect me to approve the execution of a twenty-year-old boy? Why won't you answer the question?"

Rosalind closed her eyes for a few seconds. When she reopened them, Jacobs' unwavering gaze remained fixed on her.

"If you must know, I just wanted to find out what he was doing. I raised him for sixteen years. It's not really that difficult to imagine I might want to keep in touch."

"As I recall, you threatened to incinerate him and the girl. That's probably not the basis for a meaningful relationship."

"I wouldn't have done it. You had me backed into a corner. Anyway, you're changing the subject. I thought you were here to discuss my proposal."

Jacobs folded his arms. "Let's say we agreed to your demands. When could you begin?"

"Have you got a sample of this new strain of the virus?"

"Not yet, but we're working on getting hold of one."

"There's not much point in me starting without it, is there? And another thing. I'll need some live test subjects."

"Jesus, Rosalind, you can't be serious."

"That's the trouble with you, Andrew. You're far too squeamish. Surely, it's all about the greater good. How can I develop a cure if I don't have any guinea pigs to trial it on? It's not like we would perform any tests before we were confident it would work."

"You really are unbelievable. What am I supposed to do? Kidnap children off the street?"

"Again, NMFP."

"You're a monster. How the hell do you sleep at night?"

"As it happens, not very well," Rosalind replied, "mostly due to the repeating nightmare about poking my own eye out. By the way, I'll also need written immunity from any future criminal charges arising from my work and a salary of fifty million pounds a year. And before you complain about the money, some footballers earn much more than that for kicking around a bag of wind."

The first hint of anger brought a flush to the Prime Minister's face.

"While we're at it," Rosalind continued, "you better have another big wad of cash to pay for the team and the equipment I'll require to support me. I reckon seven hundred million will do for starters. All the staff will want a sizeable bonus when we deliver as well. Maybe you should budget for double that figure."

Jacobs rose to his feet. "I can let myself out, Mrs Baxter."

"It's been a pleasure as ever, Prime Minister," she called after him.

8

Wednesday 25th June 2036

Republic of North Africa Military Headquarters, Tripoli
16 days before the Olympics wheelchair final

General Hamza Shaladi lowered himself into the chair. He would have preferred to stand, but the leader of his country had offered him a seat, so he felt obliged to accept. He was aware that his seated position emphasised the extra kilograms of fat, which seemed to have developed an affinity for his midriff.

"I need you to perform a mission for me," Mullah Awad said.

"I would be delighted to serve you however you see fit," the general replied, unconsciously sucking in his stomach.

"This particular operation is of a very sensitive nature and will take place on foreign soil. Under no circumstances must you discuss the details with anybody outside those explicitly authorised by me."

Shaladi raised his eyebrows in surprise. Over the last couple of years, his government had taken significant efforts to integrate with the international community. If the reports in the news media were to be believed, sanctions would soon be lifting. From the little he had heard so far, this possessed all the hallmarks of something from the old days.

The mullah studied the man sitting opposite him. "I know this is an unusual request. Many other nations have tried to shape and control this country, but now it is time for The Republic of North Africa to stand alone and set its own course. The Russians, the Chinese and the Americans have all flooded this region with weapons as they interfered in our affairs. This is one reason we suffered the long years of civil war. But no more. From this point onwards, our nation will become a major force on this continent and beyond."

Despite his doubts, Shaladi replied, "Of course, Mullah. You have my full commitment."

The mullah steepled his fingers. "Good, good. I knew you were a man I could trust. Failure would have a devastating effect on our relationship with the rest of the world. The success of this mission will directly impact the future of this land we have struggled so hard to bring back under control."

And it had been a struggle. Ironically, the support of the world's superpowers had been the major factor in prolonging the conflict. The supply of arms and covert intelligence to the various competing warlords meant no one faction gained an upper hand. In the end, it was the involvement of the Iranians that made the difference. After years of manipulation and subterfuge in the Middle East, they turned their attention to North Africa and found sufficient common ground for two of the main rival groups to unite.

This shift in the balance of power was enough to bring the conflict to a resolution. The major world powers, whose coffers had become depleted funding the opposing parties, uttered a huge, if temporary, sigh of relief. The price of peace was the birth of a new state. Even though the religious fundamentalists running the country made them all uneasy, none of them was inclined to intervene any further.

"Of course, all they are really interested in is making money," the mullah continued. "While worldwide fossil fuel usage is reducing, the decline in output from the Middle East means that demand is still strong. One benefit of the years of fighting on our soil is that the oil stayed in the ground and remains easily accessible. The international community are all too keen to make profits as we use the proceeds from petroleum sales to rebuild the infrastructure of this country."

"Yes, sir," Shaladi agreed, unsure where the conversation was leading.

"I have been studying your military record," the mullah said, "and it is impressive."

In truth, the general was lucky to have picked the winning side. After cutting his teeth as a young officer in the final days of Gaddafi's rule, he allied himself with a faction commanded by a former army brigadier. His tactical skill and cool head under enemy fire led to several promotions, culminating with the appointment to his current rank in the newly formed Republic of North Africa's armed forces.

"I need your skills to resolve a grave problem facing our country," the mullah continued. "This disease, which has swept the world, now offers an even greater threat."

The general nodded. He had heard rumours about a new strain of the virus, but he couldn't see how that affected him directly. The first tendrils of fear coiled in his stomach. Was his daughter, Aya, at risk? She was the sole surviving member of his family. The girl's mother had passed away years ago, giving birth to a second child who also died despite the best efforts of the midwife.

"What is the nature of this threat?" Shaladi asked, pushing the anxiety to the back of his mind. "How may I be of assistance?"

"We must grow our population, or our new country will wither and die," the mullah replied. "But now this disease has mutated and is killing our children."

The general grasped one hand in the other. "I know nothing of medical matters, Mullah," he said.

The religious leader gave a tut of irritation. "That is obvious. I have tasked our doctors with increasing the number of our citizens. This is no concern of yours."

It was hard to be unaware of what the growth in numbers entailed. The new leaders treated women like cattle, forcing them to become pregnant after pumping them full of fertility drugs. The Republic of North Africa remained on the United Nations sanctions list, and that meant no access to the newly developed Western treatments that would enable the unfortunate mothers to survive childbirth.

While the general had taken steps to protect his only child from this fate, his options were severely limited. He had considered smuggling her out of the country, but that would emphatically end his career and put a huge target on both their backs.

"The mission requires the support of your daughter," the mullah said.

In that one sentence, the general's greatest fear rose to the surface. "She has no military training," he replied automatically. "She is an athlete."

"I am well aware of that. Her role will be small, but nevertheless vital to our success. I have little time to follow athletics, but I believe she has become something of a national celebrity."

Despite having no disability, Aya had discovered a talent for wheelchair racing. Keen to improve the image of their country on the international stage, the state's rulers had approved her entry into the Olympics. She achieved the qualifying time with ease. After many years of war, The Republic of North Africa needed a hero to raise the spirits of the population. The newly created nation's hopes rested on the abilities of his only daughter.

The general swallowed hard. "Will she be in any danger?"

The mullah offered a thin smile, his lips barely visible through the dense beard. "No more so than anybody else on the team."

"Does the operation require the use of weapons?"

"That depends upon how the mission proceeds, but if all goes well, then probably no."

"Where and when will it take place?"

"You ask a lot of questions. Maybe I should brief you in full now."

"That would be useful, Mullah."

The religious leader outlined the plan.

When he had finished, the general stared at him in disbelief. "Why do we need to involve my daughter? Surely we could accomplish the same goals in a different way."

The mullah's stare hardened. "This is not for debate. If you would rather she didn't help our cause directly, she can always provide indirect support by bearing children to restore our population."

Shaladi opened his mouth to reply, but the mullah spoke again. "You must think you are very clever."

The general blinked in confusion.

The mullah continued. "Did you really believe we were unaware of the operation performed on your daughter when she was thirteen years old, General?

We know all her eggs were removed and frozen. Just because she cannot conceive naturally, it does not mean the doctors cannot implant embryos."

The soldier's shoulders sagged. A lifetime of military experience had taught him to recognise tactical situations in which the overwhelming strength of the enemy made surrender the only viable option.

He rose to his feet and saluted. "My daughter and I would be happy to perform this mission on behalf of our country, Mullah."

9

Monday 7th July 2036

Oakington House, Northstowe
4 days before the Olympics wheelchair final

The article scrolled down automatically as Rosalind Baxter read the penultimate paragraph on the page. She had to admit this was one feature of her prosthetic eye the scientists had implemented well. It took some getting used to, but the auto-scrolling function was a definite plus point.

The latest annual report from Ilithyia Biotechnology made for interesting reading. The new management team had sought to grow the company through acquisition, but their due diligence was sadly lacking. Now, it seemed, they were paying the price for their unwise investment decisions. No wonder they were seeking external funding. If she had been at the helm, she would never have allowed the corporate finances to get into this state.

She found her mind wandering back to the Prime Minister's proposition. After three years out of the game, it would be good to rejoin the world of medical research. Maybe her terms were a little ambitious. The challenge of beating the virus for the third time held some appeal.

The principal sticking point seemed to be her demand to assassinate the Perrin boy. There had been no recent communication from the Prime Minister or his people. Perhaps she should attempt to locate a private contractor willing to undertake the task. In some ways, she regretted losing the services of her former head of security, Anders Grolby. He would have dealt with the problem with the minimum of fuss. Such a shame she had been forced to terminate his employment—and his life.

The main issue with this approach was knowing where to start. It wasn't as if one could just search the Internet for contract hitmen. After the attack, she had considered using the services of a private security consultant to provide protection. Perhaps she should revisit that idea. Even if the person was unwilling to perform the task personally, they would probably have the contacts to complete the job.

The shrill ring of the doorbell jolted her from her thoughts. She received so few visitors. Had Andrew Jacobs decided to pay her another visit? If it was him, she would drop the assassination request but instead demand the damehood he had mentioned during his last house call. It would be nice to have a day out and meet the King.

She pushed herself upright and headed towards the hallway. The video display showed a pair of men wearing dark uniforms. A third, suited figure stood behind, his body angled away from the camera. She smiled inwardly and pressed the green entry button, already mulling over in her head how she would pitch her new proposal.

As soon as the lock released, the two uniformed men stepped inside. They positioned themselves, one on either side of Rosalind. The last member of the group strolled after them in a more casual fashion and surveyed the expansive hall. He gestured with an eyebrow towards the open door. The man to his left hurriedly grabbed the handle and shoved it closed before returning to his initial position.

"This is a very nice place, Mrs Baxter," the newcomer said, his voice tinged with a slight foreign accent.

"Is the Prime Minister too busy to visit me himself these days? You can inform him that I'll only deal with him face to face and not through one of his minions."

"What is minions?" the man asked in confusion. "I do not know this word."

"Oh, for heaven's sake. Tell Andrew Jacobs I want to see him in person."

"Who is Andrew…? Ah, I understand. I think you are confusing me with somebody else. I do not work for your government."

"Then who are you?" Rosalind asked, folding her arms.

"My name is General Hamza Shaladi." He didn't introduce the other two.

Now that she had time to study the group of three up close, they all had a Mediterranean tint to their skin. "What do you want?"

"I thought we could have a little talk."

"What the hell is this about?"

"No pointless chitchat. I like that. My government has need of your specific skill set."

Rosalind scowled in annoyance. "Will you please stop talking in riddles? Why are you here?"

The general picked at some lint on his sleeve. "I represent The Republic of North Africa. My country has something of a medical emergency, and I believe you have a great deal of expertise in this particular subject area. We would like you to come and work for us."

"I have no interest in working for you or your country. I want you to leave immediately."

"Mrs Baxter, it seems you do not understand the seriousness of the situation. Did you not lead the team which developed a treatment for the Orestes virus?"

"Yes, twice in fact." Despite the unwanted intrusion and her increasing irritation, a hint of pride touched Rosalind's voice.

"And now there is another strain, which is killing the children."

"What concern of that is mine?"

The general seemed genuinely perplexed. "You do not care about saving the lives of children?"

Twin spots of red surfaced on Rosalind's cheeks as irritability turned to anger. "I've heard enough, and I have no interest in helping you. Now, get out of my house."

A hardness appeared in the general's eyes. "I wish to make one thing perfectly clear, Mrs Baxter. You will come with us, either of your own accord or by force. Which is it to be?"

"What are you saying? You're going to kidnap me?"

"I would prefer for you to join me willingly, but I cannot accept no for an answer. Of course, we will reward you for your efforts."

"I don't want your money. Do you seriously think you can abduct me from my home in broad daylight?"

The general's dark eyebrows narrowed. "Time is of the essence, Mrs Baxter. Now, you must come."

Rosalind's gaze tracked to the control panel beside the closed front door. If she could only reach the emergency button. The two uniformed men took a step closer as if reading her intentions. Her shoulders slumped in defeat. "Fine, but I want to take some things with me, like a change of clothes."

"We have everything you need," the general said.

"May at least put on some shoes?"

The man stared at her bare feet. He nodded silently at his two accomplices. They accompanied her towards the dark wood of the writing desk and the pair of low-heeled, white espadrilles lying beneath.

"Give me a bit of space, please," she said, bending down. The nearest guard took half a pace backwards. Rosalind seized the opportunity. Still in her bare feet, she burst upright like a sprinter from the blocks, making for the kitchen and the back door leading into the garden.

She had taken fewer than three paces when a muscular figure crashed into her thigh and tackled her to the ground.

"Leave me alone," she shrieked, scratching at his face with her nails.

Strong hands grasped her upper arm. The hiss of a hypodermic spray followed. Seconds later, her vision faded to black.

"Let's get her out of here," Shaladi said in his native Arabic.

The two men each draped one of Rosalind's arms over a shoulder and lifted her off the expensive carpet. They dragged her unconscious body back through the way they had entered.

The general paused at the open doorway, checking that none of the neighbours was paying any attention. Satisfied nobody had seen anything, he pulled the door shut behind him and followed the others to the waiting van.

10

Tuesday 8th July 2036

Republic of North Africa Embassy, London
3 days before the Olympic wheelchair final

Aya Shaladi pushed through the heavy wooden door into the oak-panelled room.

Her father stood with his back to her, staring out of the window. At the sound of her arrival, he spun around and strode towards her with a broad smile. "As-salam alaykom," he said.

Aya hugged him and returned the greeting. "What are you doing here in London, father?" she asked, still speaking in their native tongue. "I did not think you would be arriving in the UK for another day or two."

"Do I need an excuse to visit my daughter?"

"Of course not. I am always delighted to see you."

"How is the training going?"

"Very well. I achieved the fastest time of my career during practice last week. My coach is confident I will bring home a gold medal."

The general surveyed his only child. She dressed like the locals in jeans and a long-sleeved shirt. Her only deference to the dress code of her native country was the colourful headscarf covering her hair. He knew some of the more hard-line members of the ruling party objected to women who failed to follow the traditional customs. If the leaders wanted to be taken seriously on the international stage, they would have to change their views. After all, they could hardly expect his daughter to race in a burka.

Despite his own Muslim faith, he had no great love for the religious fanatics who now ruled his country. The enforcement of strict Sharia law turned his stomach at times, but he hid his misgivings and followed orders. Not for the first time, he fantasised about living here in the West, not that his government would ever willingly let him leave. In some ways, he was trapped by the success of his army career.

"Excellent, my dear. Um… there is something I need to discuss with you. It concerns the Olympics."

Aya's face tightened into a scowl. "Those bearded fools aren't going to stop me competing, are they?"

The general glanced uneasily at his daughter. "No, it's nothing like that. Our leader has entrusted me with a very important mission. I will require your help to complete it."

"I don't understand. You've never asked me before. I mean, they don't even allow women in the army."

"I know. Nevertheless, your support is vital to our success."

"What do you need me for?"

The general explained the kidnapping of Rosalind Baxter and the plan for the Olympic final. The more he told her, the darker her expression became.

"Where are they keeping this doctor?"

"They are transporting her north to meet up with us later."

"Why can't you just snatch the others in the same way?"

"The rest of the world cannot suspect our country. That is why it must appear that we have been taken as well."

"But this is my one chance to win a gold medal. How could you do this to me?"

"I'm sorry, Aya. It was not my decision. The blasts will be timed to occur after the end of the race. You can still take away a winner's medallion."

"No, I can't. You only receive those at the ceremony that happens hours afterwards."

"But you can pick it up later."

"If they give out medals at all after something like this."

"I'm sorry, Aya. There's nothing I can do about it."

"It's all the fault of those idiots who seized our country."

The general glanced nervously at the door. "Keep your voice down. This place is probably bugged."

"What are they going to do?" Aya asked with a sneer. "They can't put me to work making children like they do with the other women."

"They know about the eggs."

She glowered at her father. "Why did you tell them?"

"I didn't. They must have found out via other means. Anyway, the mullah informed me they could still implant embryos."

The self-assurance vanished from her expression. "Would they really do that?"

"Anything is possible, but if we do our job properly, they won't need to."

Aya lowered her voice. "I'm fed up with the people who rule our country and what they force the women to go through. They treat us worse than cattle. Can't we defect? If we went to the British Government and told them everything, surely they would allow us to stay."

The general paled. "Do not ever say such things. If they hear you, we are dead. They would never let us live after such a betrayal. We would spend the rest of our lives looking over our shoulders."

Aya huffed in exasperation. "It just makes me so angry. Do they really think this woman will develop a cure?"

"She has done it before," the general replied. "Even if she does not come up with a solution to the new problem, she can teach our scientists how to make the medicine so our mothers need not die when giving birth."

"What will happen to the people we kidnap?"

The general stared at his daughter in silence. When he spoke, it was in a subdued tone. "They can never be allowed to leave."

11

Wednesday 9th July 2036

Shipping Container, M1 Motorway near Sheffield, UK
2 days before the Olympic wheelchair final

The jolting movement gradually abated. The hiss of the air brakes penetrated the interior of the shipping container. A few seconds later, the incessant rumble of the diesel engine faded into silence.

Rosalind pushed herself upright on the mattress. The only illumination came from the narrow wedge of light infiltrating the top of the rear doors. For a moment, she considered hammering her fists against the metal sides. When she had last done that, they bound her hands and feet with thin nylon rope and gagged her. The friction burns on her wrists bore witness to how tightly they had tied the knots. The skin was still raw two days later. Perhaps that wasn't such a good idea after all.

She waited to see what would happen next. The sound of male voices speaking in a foreign language originated from somewhere down the side. She gazed towards the pile of pallets, positioned to block the interior of her prison from the gaze of outside observers. A series of metallic clanks rattled through the container. Moments later, she shielded her eyes at the sudden increase in brightness.

A slight vibration through the floor signalled that one of her captors had climbed up. The man uttered a low curse as he edged his way past the obstacles. After a few seconds, the silhouette of a man's head appeared in the bright band of sunlight streaming through the open doors. Rosalind blinked as the beam of a powerful torch swept over her.

"Everything is good, yes?" he said in heavily accented English.

"If you call being kidnapped and locked up in the back of a lorry good."

"This cannot be avoided. Here, I bring you food and drink."

The man tossed a plastic bottle of water and a cellophane-wrapped baguette onto the mattress. Rosalind grabbed them and positioned them by the side where she could find them easily when darkness returned.

"I need to pee," she said.

The man gestured towards the chemical toilet wedged in the gap between the pallets and the metal wall. "You go there. It is easier when we are not moving, no? Make sure you put it back after. You do not want it to fall over." He let out a deep, guttural laugh.

"How much longer are you going to coop me up in here?"

"What is coop?"

"Keep in a prison, like a chicken."

"First, we travel to Grainger Mooth."

"Where?"

"Grainger Mooth. It is big port."

"Oh, you mean Grangemouth. What happens after that?"

"We load this container on a ship and sail to my country. There you work to make a cure. Then we let you go."

Rosalind believed all of it except for the part about releasing her. Unless she escaped, she would probably end up spending the rest of her life in captivity. Once they reached Africa, the task would be that much harder.

"We charge the battery for one hour," the man said, "then we leave."

This vehicle had an electric motor to supplement the diesel engine. In recent years, it had become common for truck stops to include an area containing charging stations. In all likelihood, they were on a motorway or at least a major road. If she got out, she could ask another driver for help.

"Can't you leave the doors open? I just want to see some light."

"No, this is not possible. I do not think you are afraid of the dark." He laughed once more. "If you make any sound, I will use the ropes again. And this time, I will tie the knots tightly."

"I won't do anything. Please. Just a small gap."

"No," the man said. "One hour." He edged back through the narrow aisle. Moments later there was a metallic clank, and the interior plunged once more into darkness.

Oh, well. It had been worth a try.

Rosalind extended her arms ahead of her and crept towards the stack of pallets. Once there, she held out her left arm and shuffled sideways until her fingers touched the cold metal side. She reached into the gap and pulled out the portable toilet. She hadn't been lying about needing to relieve herself.

When she had finished and restored everything to its rightful place, she followed the route her captor had taken until she encountered the rear doors. There was insufficient room at the back of the container to explore further.

How the hell was she going to get out of here?

She retraced her steps and lowered herself to the mattress. The material was slightly damp and carried a faint smell of mildew. She dreaded to think where they had obtained it from, but it was more comfortable than lying on the cold, metal floor.

As she crawled towards the refreshments they had left for her, the first glimmer of an idea formed in her head. She felt around in the dark and grabbed the water bottle. After taking a long swig, she started on the baguette. It contained some type of meat, maybe beef, and a leaf of limp lettuce.

It might just work. If she failed, they would tie her up, but the longer she delayed her attempt, the fewer chances she would have. She staggered upright and approached the stack of pallets. Her fingers explored the crates and detected wooden strips running horizontally between the layers. She kicked off the cheap shoes they had bought for her to replace the ones she had left in the house and set about scaling the pile. The sharp edges cut into her feet as she rose higher. When she reached the top, the gap to the ceiling was less than half a metre.

She inched forwards. If she stretched out, she could just about reach the rear door of the container. This was it. She went over the plan one last time in her head. Taking a deep intake of breath, she pounded her fist against the metal and yelled at the top of her voice. "Help! I've been kidnapped. Get me out of here."

She continued to hammer and scream until she heard the familiar clank that signalled the door was about to open. As daylight streamed inside, she shuffled backwards.

A man's voice cursed in Arabic. From her vantage point, she sensed a slight movement as he clambered up into the container. She waited until he had moved down the side. The beam from his torch played over the mattress and inspected the corners ahead of him. He swore again as his search came up empty.

Rosalind scrambled forwards and lowered herself down. In her haste, she slipped and only just caught herself. The sudden movement drew the man's attention. She dropped to the narrow lip behind the pallets, shielding her eyes against the bright glare of the sun. A quick survey of her surroundings told her they were in a large parking area for commercial vehicles. They had parked the truck well away from any others. The closest was at least fifty metres distant, but the cab seemed to be empty.

Rosalind made the short drop to the road surface and sprinted towards the vehicle in her bare feet. "Help!" she shouted, waving her arms above her head.

A man's yell came from behind. A hand landed on her shoulder, dragging her back. She lashed out at her assailant with an elbow and connected with something soft. Shaking loose from his grip, she tried to scramble away.

She didn't see the fist coming as it slammed into her face. Once more her world was reduced to darkness.

12

Wednesday 9th July 2036

10 Downing Street, London

2 days before the Olympic wheelchair final

Andrew Jacobs entered the plushly-furnished cabinet room. The two people he was due to meet were already present, and both rose to their feet.

"Good morning, Prime Minister," the shorter and slimmer of the pair said. Iris Stanley wore an expensive designer jacket and matching skirt. In a world where the correction of sight defects had become routine simply by the administration of specialised drugs, the wire-framed glasses signalled her distrust of medical technology. Despite the archaic eyewear, her piercing blue eyes missed little, a characteristic that served her well in her role as the head of Britain's MI5 internal security service.

"Good to see you, Iris," Jacobs replied.

The second person fastened the middle button of his jacket as he stood and extended a meaty hand. His dark hair was thinning, and his stomach strained against the thread holding the fastening in place. When he spoke, his voice carried a cultivated public-school accent. "It's been a while, Andrew."

The two men were long-standing friends from their days at Oxford University. They had progressed in their careers at similar rates, both reaching the pinnacle of their professions at around the same time, twelve years earlier. Charles Moreland headed up MI6, the outward-facing secret intelligence service.

"Thanks for coming in, Charles," Jacobs said.

The Prime Minister sat at the head of the long oak table. His visitors took their places, one on either side of him. "Let's get down to business."

"It must be serious if you have both the internal and external arms of the security services in attendance," Moreland said, "especially since we were specifically told not to bring any aides."

Jacobs leant back in his chair. "You might say that. I'm sure you've both been briefed on the news coming out of North Africa about a new strain of the virus."

"Yes," the head of MI6 replied. "We have an informant high in the Reponan medical establishment. I guess that's the source you're alluding to." The term Repona had become commonplace when referring to the newly formed Republic of North Africa.

Jacobs nodded. "Right."

"They're in a bit of a panic. They've lost a lot of children to this new variant. I heard only this morning that one of our operatives has smuggled out a blood sample from an infected child. It's on its way over here as we speak."

"That's good news. I was going to ask about the progress on that front. Well done."

"There've been no reports of any outbreaks here," Stanley said, "at least none that I've been told about."

The Prime Minister tapped his fingers on the polished surface of the table. "Luckily, we've had no confirmed cases, but I suspect it's only a matter of time. All incoming flights from the region have been cancelled, not that there were many to start with given the sanctions. The problem is that people travelling overland or via countries not affected by the flight embargo might be carriers. We're coming to the height of the tourist season, and the timing of the Olympics up in Glasgow at the moment couldn't be worse."

"You could always cancel the games," the head of MI5 said.

"No," Jacobs replied. "That's not really an option, not when they're halfway through. Pretty much all the athletes are already over here."

"What about running the remaining events behind closed doors?"

"It's difficult enough to fill the stadia as it is. So far, we've only sold about a fifth of the tickets. The rest of the world will be watching. We want to portray a good impression. I'm not keen to follow your suggestion unless I absolutely have to."

"Changing the subject, what about offering the North Africans medical assistance?" Moreland asked.

"They've been keeping this outbreak to themselves. If we were to offer help, we'd be letting them know we have a highly placed source inside their country."

"Good point."

"The way they deliberately impregnate their women doesn't sit well with me either. Anyway, that's not the reason I've called you here this morning. I want us to get ahead of this new strain. That means starting our research efforts as soon as possible."

Stanley's brows knitted in a frown. "I don't understand. How does that affect Charles and me?"

"Who would you suggest to head up the team?"

"The woman who came up with the cure last time, I suppose," Moreland replied. "In fact, make that the previous two times."

"My thoughts exactly: Rosalind Baxter."

"I thought she had retired," Stanley said, "although I've heard rumours there might be more to her retirement than meets the eye. Despite her contribution to medical science, it seems there's a reluctance to offer her anything in the new year honours list. There must be a good reason."

"Very perceptive," Jacobs replied. "What I'm about to tell you mustn't leave this room."

When he had finished telling the story, both members of his audience sat in dumbfounded silence.

"There was nothing else I could do," the Prime Minister said. "If I had refused her terms, she would have incinerated everything, including all details of the cure, her adopted son and the girl. Without the drug she had developed, the human race was doomed."

Stanley's blue eyes locked onto Jacobs. "So, the woman who is being hailed as the saviour of mankind was in fact the instigator of the whole thing. The most prolific mass murderer in history is free to live her life in luxury, and there's nothing we can do about it."

"Not without bringing down the government and leaving us open to claims from every other country in the world. We'd become pariahs. The compensation costs alone would cripple us for years to come, never mind the sanctions we would face from the international community."

Moreland retrieved a handkerchief from his pocket and dabbed at the bead of sweat rolling down his temple. "Bloody hell. I can't believe this. Who else knows about it?"

"Only the seven or eight people who were there and a handful of civil servants who prepared the paperwork."

"Is that the reason you've called us here today?" Stanley asked. "Are you planning to reduce the number of potential witnesses?"

"What?" Jacobs replied in confusion. "You don't think I want you to..."

"We've done far worse in the past in the interests of national security."

"No. It's not that. At least, not directly."

"You better explain then," the head of MI5 said, folding her arms.

"As we discussed a second ago, of all the medical researchers at our disposal, Rosalind Baxter is our best bet to get ahead of this latest outbreak."

"Christ, Andrew," Charles Moreland interjected. "You can't seriously be telling us you trust the woman who caused all this mess in the first place to develop a cure."

"She is uniquely qualified, I suppose," Stanley added.

"You're right," Jacobs said. "She's the one person who knows the most about this virus. But unfortunately, she's set several conditions before she'll return to work."

The head of MI5 grimaced. "Oh, this keeps getting better and better. What does the woman want?"

The Prime Minister tugged at his collar. "You know I mentioned how she murdered her partner and co-founder of the company by stabbing him in the eye. Well, six months later, the victim's son, who incidentally witnessed it all, returned the compliment. He sneaked into her house, laced her drink with a drug that made her extremely suggestible, then forced her to do the same thing to herself."

Moreland paled. "You mean she poked her own eye out."

"Yes. He ordered her to wait for a while so she could experience the same agonising pain suffered by his father, then shove it all the way into her brain. Luckily for her, she recovered enough self-control to resist. The story never made it into the press. She told the doctors it was an accident, and she slipped on a wet floor."

Stanley raised an eyebrow. "It sounds to me like she got what was coming. I can guess where all this is heading; she wants revenge on the son."

"Correct," Jacobs replied.

"You're saying she won't work on developing a treatment for this new strain unless we kill the boy. How old is he?"

The Prime Minister exhaled a weary sigh. "He's twenty. There doesn't seem to be any way out of it. I tried to talk her round. I even paid the woman a visit. Now, she isn't answering my calls. She was adamant she wouldn't start work unless I met her conditions, one of which was the execution of her former partner's son."

"There were others?"

"Yes, but I can deal with those without your help."

"Let me get this straight," Moreland said. "You've called this meeting because you want us to assassinate this individual."

Jacobs nodded.

"I guess that would reduce the list of people with the knowledge to destroy this country," Stanley chipped in, drily.

Nobody spoke. After several seconds, the Prime Minister broke the silence. "There's another complication; the boy has disappeared. I've had my team and the police looking for him, but he seems to have vanished without a trace."

"And you want us to find him," Moreland said.

"Then dispose of him," Stanley interjected.

Jacobs lowered his head. When he raised his eyes, they carried a haunted look. "God help me, but yes. There is one last thing. She wants proof of his death."

The ticking of the large carriage clock sitting on the mantelpiece seemed to fill the room.

Finally, Stanley stood, then straightened her skirt. "Well, we should start by finding him. Once we've done that, we can decide how to proceed. We'll focus our search on this country, and your guys will look elsewhere, right Charles?"

The head of MI6 also rose to his feet. "I'll let you know what we turn up."

The Prime Minister stared first at one and then the other of the two secret service heads. "I'm sorry to have to make this request. But what else can I do?"

Part Two: Expatriation

13

Friday 11th July 2036

Glasgow Olympic Stadium

The Olympic wheelchair final

Antimone Lessing rounded the last bend, sandwiched between the other two race leaders. The gap from the leading group to the rest of the field extended to greater than twenty-five metres. With only the length of the home straight remaining, it seemed certain all three would end up on the podium; the only question was in what order. The roar of the crowd reverberated around the bowl of the stadium as they willed the finalists onwards.

A chant built up from the supporters behind the finishing line.

"AN-TIM-OH-NEE! AN-TIM-OH-NEE!"

The pain burned in Antimone's shoulders as she channelled her last reserves of strength into forcing the wheelchair forwards. Her front wheel eased half a metre ahead of the North African in the green one-piece. The Welsh girl trailed a few centimetres behind in third place. The three leaders matched each other push for push.

***

A quarter of the way down the straight, the first bomb exploded. The blast instantly vaporised the server room, cutting off all communications with the outside world. The second detonation a moment later took out the substation supplying electricity to the stadium and the surrounding area.

Other than the dull thud of the explosions, the targeted devastation did not immediately impact the spectators or contestants. It only became obvious something was wrong when the four huge display screens mounted above the stands flickered and died. The lighting beneath the roof dimmed at the same time. Unnoticed by the competitors, the cluster of tiny camera drones drifted across the track and settled gently onto the grass at the centre of the oval.

When the leaders were still forty metres short of the finish, the first of several bombs inside the stadium detonated. The explosion in an unpopulated seating area created a billowing cloud of smoke. The cheers of the crowd turned to stunned silence, then screams.

***

Antimone propelled herself forwards, aware that something unusual was happening behind her, but still intent on reaching the finishing line ahead of her two rivals. The next blast was far closer, throwing her sideways as if a giant hand had swept her off the track. Her wheelchair careened across the lanes and smashed into a prone marshal who had been knocked off his feet by the wall of turbulent air. The collision sent her into a tumble. Antimone stuck out an arm to cushion the impact. She landed on her shoulder and skidded to a halt, lying on her side and still strapped into her chair. She remained motionless for a moment as the scent of fresh grass mingled with the acrid stench of the explosion and filled her lungs.

Debris from the blast rained down all around her. A razor-sharp fragment of metal thumped into the ground less than a metre to her right. The dense, swirling clouds of smoke thickened.

Fear surged though her veins. She stuck out an arm and righted the wheelchair with a single shove. The jarring impact had disorientated her. She tried to align her sense of direction, but her gaze couldn't penetrate the choking fumes. *Oh God! My family.*

The percussive thud of another explosion sent a shockwave rolling over her from the left. A man sprinted past, his face etched in panic before he disappeared into the gloom. Shrieks of terror originated from behind. *That must be coming from the main stand.*

She spun in a tight circle and propelled herself in the direction of the cries. She had covered only a few metres when a figure dressed in green staggered through the smoke: the North African athlete.

"We must get out of here," Aya Shaladi said.

"I've got to find my family."

"They are in the VIP area, yes?"

Antimone continued to advance towards the screams, her fellow competitor jogging alongside. The drifting smoke showed no signs of clearing.

The woman placed a hand on her shoulder. "My father—he is there as well. He is a powerful man in my country. He told me that the security team has prepared a safe place for important guests in case there is any trouble. I know where they are going. I promise your family will be there. Now we have to leave. There may be more bombs."

Antimone stopped pushing and stared at the figure with the broad shoulders, wreathed in smoke. "You're sure that's where they'll go?"

"Yes. It is this way." The African athlete pointed.

Antimone hesitated, caught in an agony of indecision. There were important people here, including world leaders, and the authorities would have a plan to escort them somewhere secure in the event of a terrorist incident. This certainly qualified as such. Everything the woman said sounded plausible. She fought down the terror worming its way through her stomach and up her throat. "Okay then."

"Good. Follow me."

The North African set off at a jog, glancing back every few paces to ensure Antimone was trailing behind. She led them through the drifting smoke to the wide archway that provided the chief entry point into the stadium. Scorch marks on the walls and a patch of exposed brickwork signalled where one device had detonated.

"Down here." The woman's voice was barely audible above the screeching of the alarms. The air was clearer inside, but the corridor lay in a gloomy twilight, illuminated only by the emergency lighting. A pair of men in yellow jackets rushed past in the opposite direction, heading towards the mayhem.

The two athletes pushed through a set of swing doors. The logo of a green running man marked a fire exit to the right.

"Shouldn't we follow the sign?" Antimone asked. Her teeth chattered as the sweat from the race chilled her skin in the air-conditioned interior.

"No," the woman called over her shoulder without stopping. "This way." She trotted along the corridor to another door and held it open. As Antimone brushed past, the North African said, "You know I would have won, yes?"

Despite the desperate situation, a glimmer of a smile crossed Antimone's lips. "Yeah, right. That gold medal was mine."

"I think not. Next time I will show you who is the fastest."

Antimone shook her head in disbelief. They progressed through a further set of doors without speaking.

"Here," the woman said, pointing. She barged through the wide emergency exit and into the afternoon sunshine. Faint wisps of smoke rose from the top of the stadium into the hazy, blue sky. A solitary black van waited on the tarmac. The rear doors were open, but Antimone couldn't see into the gloomy interior.

A man with tightly cropped black hair and wearing a grey suit separated from the other two men to whom he had been talking. Both wore dark uniforms. He rushed forwards and embraced the African athlete.

"Alhamdulillaah, Aya."

"In this country they say thank God, father."

The man smiled fondly. "Of course, my dear. I'm just grateful you are unhurt."

His daughter's face remained set in a scowl. "You said they would allow the event to finish."

Antimone stared at the pair in confusion. There were only a handful of people in this area and certainly far too few to account for all the VIPs who must have been in attendance. Where was her family? Why were they talking about the race?

"Is my son here?" she asked, her voice quivering with tension.

The man released the African athlete and turned his attention to Antimone. "Hello, Miss Lessing. Please forgive my bad manners. I am General Hamza Shaladi, and of course, you already know my daughter, Aya. Your son is safe inside the van with your… friend."

Antimone wheeled herself forwards and peered into the gloomy interior. Sitting on a seat bolted to the floor, hugging the tiny figure of her three-year-old boy, was Jason. Another man, wearing the same black uniform as the other two, stood beside them. As her eyesight adjusted to the sudden reduction in brightness, she realised the man standing over her son and Jason was holding what appeared to be a pistol.

She sighed with relief. They were safe. The sensation lasted only a few seconds as Jason turned, and his gaze locked onto her. His dull, wide-eyed expression sent a shiver of apprehension through her body.

14

Friday 11th July 2036

Outside Glasgow Olympic Stadium
10 minutes after the start of the attack

Antimone whirled back to face the general. "What's going on here? Where is everybody else? Why did your daughter say something about finishing the race?"

The man paused before replying. "Every day in my country, women die giving birth, and yet your government will not provide us with the drugs to keep them alive. Now, a new form of this terrible disease is killing the children. We need your help to develop a cure."

Antimone stared at him, shocked into silence.

The general continued. "We know that you survived childbirth before they developed a treatment. Your boy is the first to have a mother who lived past the birth without the aid of any medicine. This man is the father of the child."

"You've got it all wrong. Anna Mayfield and her daughter came before us."

Shaladi let out a low laugh. "There is no point in lying. We already know the truth. Now, we must leave before the police get here."

"You don't seriously think I'm going anywhere with you, do you?"

A man in a black uniform stepped alongside the general. In his hand, he held a pistol. The barrel pointed at Antimone's chest.

"On the contrary. Let me be absolutely clear. All three of you are coming with us. I will show you how serious I am." He beckoned the second uniformed guard forward. "Give me your weapon."

The man handed over the firearm, handle first.

"Thank you." The general raised the gun and pointed it at the guard's head. Before the unsuspecting victim could even register surprise, the pistol emitted a loud bang.

Antimone gasped in shock and averted her gaze from the body and the rapidly expanding pool of blood surrounding it.

"Make sure he is not carrying any details of our plan," the general said to the dead man's colleague. "We do not want to give them any easy clues. When you have done that, leave him there." He turned back to Antimone. "This man died because he did not follow orders. I instructed him to delay the detonations until after the race had finished. His actions put the lives of both you and my daughter in danger. I hope you no longer have any doubts about the seriousness of my intentions. Now, get in the van with your son and friend."

Antimone raised her eyes, taking great care to avoid looking at the dead body. Her voice came out in a hoarse whisper. "Unlike your daughter, I can't walk."

The general flicked his weapon at the remaining guard and barked a command in Arabic. The man returned his gun to a holster below his jacket and hurried to Antimone's side.

Aya Shaladi stepped to the opposite wheel. Her face was pale. "Do you need help with the straps?"

"No," Antimone snapped. Her hand moved to the bindings holding her to the wheelchair. She fumbled at the mechanism with trembling fingers but couldn't loosen them.

"Here," Aya said. "Let me." She knelt and released Antimone. "I am sorry for this."

Aya and the guard lifted Antimone out of the chair. They carried her to the back of the van and sat her on the rear shelf.

Shaladi called to the second man, who retrieved a package wrapped in clear plastic from the front seat of the vehicle. The general removed a tracksuit in the same shade of green worn by the North African athlete from the packaging. "You must be getting cold. Put this on. We do not want you to get ill."

"You," he said, pointing at Jason. "Help her to dress, then lift her up."

Jason tried to rise, but Paul buried his face in his father's chest. "I've just got to give your mum a hand." He peeled the boy away and patted the seat beside him. The frightened child sat, hunching his shoulders, his feet not quite reaching the floor.

Jason bent over under the watchful gaze of the armed man. He slipped the ends of the tracksuit bottoms over Antimone's legs and helped her pull them up over her athletic outfit. He placed his hands under her armpits and hauled her up. Once inside the van, he dragged her back towards the seat.

"No, there is a folding wheelchair," the general said, pointing with the gun. "Use that." Jason lowered Antimone to the cold, metal floor.

"Are you all right?" she whispered.

"No talking," Shaladi barked. "We must leave now."

Jason unfolded the mechanism, lifted her once more and placed her into the canvas seat. The chair had handles at the back and lacked hand rims, requiring somebody else to propel the occupant.

"Turn it sideways and apply the foot brake," the general commanded, "then sit down."

"There aren't any seatbelts," Jason said.

"Do not worry," Shaladi replied. "In our country, we must drive carefully because we do not have computers to control our cars." He turned to his daughter and muttered something in Arabic.

She glared at him for a moment, then clambered inside. As she reached the seat, she turned back. "What about her racing wheelchair?"

"Leave it. Neither of you will be in a race for a long time."

She sat on the opposite side to Jason, her face screwed up in anger. The guard took up position between them. Moments later, the rear doors slammed shut, plunging the interior into darkness.

"Don't worry, Paul," Antimone said. "Mummy's here. Just hold on to Daddy."

The clunk of more closing doors reverberated from the front of the vehicle.

"How do you think you're going to get away with this?" Antimone asked.

At first, nobody responded. Then Aya spoke. "You believe we want to do this? The leaders of our country gave us orders. If we do not follow them, they kill us. We have no choice. We do what they ask, or we die."

"Where are you taking us?"

"We are bringing you to The Republic of North Africa. There we will try to discover how you survived."

Antimone swallowed hard as she digested the answer. She had heard of the country but would struggle to point it out on a map. "I already told you, they gave me the drugs like everybody else."

"That is the story, but it is not the truth. We both know this. What I do not understand is why everyone lies, but we will find out."

Before Antimone could respond, the van set off. After the initial lurch, the movement settled into a swaying motion as they navigated the streets around the stadium. Several times over the first few minutes, the sound of blaring sirens rose, then fell away behind them. Antimone prayed somebody would stop their vehicle, but the whine of the motor and the soft rumble of the tyres became louder as the speed increased.

"Who told you about us?" Antimone asked the darkness.

When there was no reply, she repeated the question. Silence greeted her words. She chewed her bottom lip. Maybe she would get some answers when the first part of their journey ended.

15

Friday 11th July 2036

10 Downing Street, London

45 minutes after the start of the attack

The room buzzed with activity as members of the cabinet discussed the situation with their aides and a small army of civil servants. Andrew Jacobs ran his hands through his hair. "Can anybody tell me what's going on?"

His chief of staff, David Wagner, broke off the conversation he was having with a colleague. "Yes, Prime Minister. We know there were five bombs inside the stadium proper and one each in the server room and the electricity substation."

"Casualties?"

"We're still trying to get all the details, but there were three fatalities, including a suspected heart attack. There have also been several injuries from flying debris, but none of the surviving victims are in a serious condition. We haven't accounted for everybody yet, but the authorities on site have informed me they don't expect the number to rise significantly."

"I suppose it could've been worse."

"Definitely, Prime Minister. From the reports on the ground, it seems the bombs were placed to create maximum confusion. If they'd been inside the main stand, we'd be looking at hundreds or even thousands of fatalities. First impressions suggest the perpetrators were going for effect rather than death and destruction."

Jacobs' face clouded in puzzlement. "That doesn't make sense. Didn't you mention they targeted the server room and the electrical substation? If the goal was to send a message, why take out the means for recording the scene?"

"The teams on site are looking at all angles, but it's too soon to attribute motive at this stage."

"Were any of the athletes injured?"

"A few cuts and bruises, Prime Minister. The race leaders were close to a blast. One of our girls and a North African athlete are still unaccounted for. It's possible they just got lost in the confusion. We're trying to track them down. I'll let you know as soon as we hear anything."

"Has anybody claimed responsibility yet?"

"So far, only the usual suspects. Most of them are small groups of lunatics without the resources to pull off something like this. From what I've heard, there haven't been any credible claims."

"What a bloody mess. Keep me informed of any progress in the investigation."

"Of course, Prime Minister."

Wagner turned away and immediately lifted a phone to his ear. The clamour of raised voices filled the high-ceilinged room. Andrew Jacobs studied the occupants as they scurried about. Instead of the usual smart attire more often seen at the centre of government, many wore casual clothes. Most displayed harried expressions as they talked into handsets or conversed with colleagues. The atmosphere was stuffy and carried a hint of body odour.

His gaze settled on a large display, which somebody had wheeled into the corner. The main part of the screen showed jerky images from inside the stadium. Three separate inset boxes displayed a variety of newsfeeds, including one from the BBC. In all of them, sombre commentators addressed the camera. The sound was either off or turned down low.

Jacobs focused on the scene from the site of the explosions. A faint, smoky haze still hung in the air. A group of paramedics in hi-vis jackets knelt beside a figure lying on the ground. The lanyard around the victim's neck identified him as a race official. His foot twitched as the man tending to him injected a colourless liquid into his arm. Everywhere, people milled about or congregated in small groups. Debris lay scattered across the track.

A slight touch on the shoulder drew Jacobs back to his surroundings. One of his personal assistants, an attractive woman in her mid-twenties, stood beside him.

"Sorry to disturb you, sir, but I have a call from the ambassador of The Republic of North Africa."

Jacobs knew the diplomat had taken up the role less than two months earlier following the thawing in relations between their respective countries, but they had never met in person. The Prime Minister scowled in irritation. "Sorry, Sally. I haven't got time for this right now."

"He's asking about their missing athlete. He claims they found a wheelchair outside the stadium alongside the dead body of one of their security team. The athlete's father is a general in their military and has also apparently disappeared."

"He seems to be better informed than I am," Jacobs snapped. "I'll take it in my office. And make sure David knows what you just told me." He whirled around and strode across the room. When he reached his well-appointed workspace, he closed the door behind him and settled himself at the polished mahogany desk. He took a deep breath and picked up the old-fashioned-looking telephone handset. Despite the antique appearance, the equipment contained state-of-the-art technology for encrypting and decrypting voice calls.

He stabbed a button on the base. "Put me through."

"Right away, sir."

A click followed moments later.

"Good afternoon, Ambassador," Jacobs said. "What can I do for you?"

"Good afternoon to you also, Prime Minister." The man spoke in a mellow baritone with barely any accent. "May I start by offering you my condolences on this terrible attack at the Olympics."

"Thank you, Ambassador. I believe you may have news concerning the atrocity."

"This is true. My security people are telling me they discovered the body of a colleague outside the stadium. He had been shot in the head."

"Ah... I'm afraid I can't provide you with any further information, Ambassador. We have several teams on site, and I assure you they are giving this crime their highest priority."

"I'm sure they are, Prime Minister. More importantly for my country, our top Olympic athlete, Aya Shaladi, and her father, General Hamza Shaladi, are also both missing."

"Yes, I heard they discovered her wheelchair beside the dead body."

"It seems you may have been misinformed, Prime Minister. The wheelchair does not belong to our athlete, but to yours."

"I'm sorry. What do you mean?"

The ambassador paused before replying. "I don't want to give you any more bad news at this difficult time, but I believe the chair belongs to the British competitor, Miss Lessing."

"Are you suggesting that whoever took your people also kidnapped our girl?"

"It is not for me to say. I do not wish to draw conclusions at this early stage, but that is how it appears."

"Thank you for bringing this to my notice, Ambassador. I'll ensure our security services act upon this information right away."

"May I ask, Prime Minister, how an attack like this could be allowed to happen? Surely it is your duty to protect the audience at such events, especially given the number of VIPs in attendance."

"You have my sincerest apologies, Ambassador. Rest assured we will put every effort into tracking the perpetrators down and bringing them to justice."

"It is just a shame you did not apply the same rigour to protecting our athletes and their families."

"Like I said, I can only apologise and promise you we'll do everything in our power to recover your countrymen."

"Thank you, Prime Minister. I will be in touch if I learn anything more. I would be grateful if you could keep me informed of any progress in your own investigation. Good day."

The line clicked before Jacobs could respond. He replaced the phone and blew out his cheeks. Then he rose and marched back to the conference room. His eyes scanned the crowd of people and settled on his chief of staff. The man was still talking on a mobile.

"David, a moment of your time."

Wagner uttered a few words into the handset and pressed a button to end the call. "Yes, Prime Minister."

"I've just held an uncomfortable conversation with the Reponan ambassador. He informed me that not only has someone in their security team been murdered, but also one of their athletes and her father, a general in their military, are unaccounted for."

"Sally told me a few minutes ago. I was just speaking to the senior police officer on site."

"Good. Perhaps you could call him back and make him aware that a British athlete is missing as well: Antimone Lessing."

"How does the ambassador know that?"

"Because, David, her wheelchair was discovered alongside the dead body. What I want to understand is why I'm hearing this information from the Reponans and not from our own people."

Wagner's cheeks flushed. "I'll get on it right away."

"And while you're at it, please track down the rest of Miss Lessing's family and check on their status."

"Of course, Prime Minister. May I ask why?"

A haunted look appeared on Jacobs' face. He stared his chief aide in the eye.

"I have a horrible feeling you may discover they're also missing."

16

Friday 11th July 2036

Grangemouth Docks

80 minutes after the start of the attack

After what seemed like hours but was probably less than one, the van stopped moving. The sound of doors opening came from the front of the vehicle. Moments later, the rear door swung back, flooding the interior with bright afternoon sunlight.

Antimone squinted against the glare. The figure of General Shaladi stood silhouetted before her. As her eyes accustomed to the brightness, she identified the outline of rows of shipping containers against the background of a fenced-off compound.

"I want everybody out," he said.

Aya Shaladi and the guard rose to their feet. Paul wriggled out of his father's grasp and rushed to Antimone. He flung himself on top of her and wrapped his arms around her neck. She embraced him in a tight hug and whispered soothing words in his ear.

"You." The general pointed at Jason. "Hold the boy."

Jason stood slowly and moved towards the wheelchair. As he reached out for his son, Paul clung to his mother and buried his head in her chest.

"Come on, Paul," Antimone said. "You need to go with your daddy."

Jason lifted the frightened child from his mother's lap despite the squeals of protest. "It's okay. They're just getting Mummy out," he murmured. The boy struggled for a moment before grasping his father in a tight hug.

The North African athlete and the guard lifted Antimone out of her wheelchair and lowered her to the lip at the back of the van. She sat, watching them as they passed the crude contraption down to the waiting general. Then they both jumped the short distance to the tarmac, raised her with a shoulder under each arm and repositioned her on the canvas seat.

Jason clambered down, his son still clinging to him like a limpet.

"This way," Shaladi said, striding ahead. Jason followed behind. Aya grabbed the wheelchair handles as the guard brought up the rear.

"Couldn't you have found something better, so I could at least push myself?" Antimone asked. If there was one aspect of her condition she hated more than anything else, it was when people tried to help by pushing her. She told anybody who would listen it was like being poked in the back or having somebody fiddle with your hair. On this occasion, the lack of hand grips left no alternative.

The North African athlete steered her forwards in silence.

Biting down on her irritation, Antimone took the opportunity to study her surroundings. A high metal fence enclosed the tarmacked area. Behind the barrier, several tall masts rose into the sky, draped in webs of rigging. A variety of different sized shipping containers in a range of pastel shades filled the compound. No other vehicles were visible. The sea air assaulted her senses, clogging her nostrils with the sulphurous scent of decaying seaweed.

They rounded a corner and Antimone's hopes lifted briefly at the sight of two men wearing dark-blue overalls and lounging against a large, lime-coloured unit. She opened her mouth to shout for help, but the way the pair snapped to attention at the general's arrival dashed her brief bout of optimism. They were clearly part of the team. A short conversation took place in Arabic. One of them hauled down a lever, allowing the huge doors to swing open.

"Everybody inside," the general said, pointing.

Jason stood stationary and peered into the gloomy interior. A rectangle of material occupied the furthest corner. On top lay a long, thin object. A rounded cube shape nestled on the opposite side. "You don't seriously expect us to go in there, do you?"

Shaladi withdrew the pistol from his jacket and pointed the barrel at Jason's chest. "That is exactly what I expect, and what you will do."

A muffled sound came from inside. The object moved slightly. With a jolt of recognition, Jason identified the shape as a person, tied up and lying on a mattress.

"Who the hell is that?"

Shaladi grinned. "I think it is somebody you know well. Now move or I start shooting."

Paul whimpered in fright as his father shuffled forwards.

"How long are you planning to keep us in here?" Antimone asked.

"A few hours. When we set sail, you may have more freedom if you behave."

"What about food and drink?"

The general held a brief discussion with one of his associates. The man picked up a plastic bag and emptied the contents onto the tarmac. He tossed two water bottles and a pack of sandwiches inside. They landed on the mattress, narrowly missing the bound figure.

"We'll need a toilet."

Shaladi gestured towards the cube shape. "Use that."

His daughter pushed the wheelchair forwards three paces and released the handles.

"Do not bother calling for help," the general said. "My men will be outside. If they hear any noise, they will tie you up and gag you like her. They start loading the containers on the ship in two hours. When that happens, I suggest you sit on the floor." He gestured to the man standing beside him.

The huge door started to move.

"Wait!" Antimone called. "My son is afraid of the dark. Can we at least have a torch?"

Shaladi talked briefly to his nearest subordinate. The man withdrew a cylindrical object from a pocket in his overalls and handed it over. The general threw it towards Antimone. She caught it and tested the switch, sending a beam of light carving through the gloom. "I am not a monster. I suggest you use it only when necessary. The battery will not last for ever."

The door moved again and slammed shut with a metallic clang, plunging the interior into inky blackness. Paul clung more tightly to his father. The tang of the chemicals from the toilet hung in the air, overpowering the smell of the sea. The stench of urine overlaid the mix.

"What do we do now?" Antimone asked, clicking on the torch and directing the beam towards Jason and their son.

Jason shielded his eyes. "Let's find out who else is in here with us for a start. If you hold Paul, I'll take a look." He carried the child to Antimone and lowered the boy into his mother's arms. "You cuddle Mummy," he said.

The three-year-old clambered onto her lap and buried his face in the gap between her shoulder and neck. In the meantime, Jason directed the beam towards the bound figure and inched forwards. As he drew nearer, the overpowering stink of urine became stronger, now mingling with a damp, musty smell from the mattress. Ropes secured the person's hands and feet, and a cloth tied behind the head obscured the captive's mouth.

"Who is it?" Antimone whispered.

A pair of eyes blinked in the circle of brightness.

Jason took a step back as recognition dawned. "You!"

17

Friday 11th July 2036

Grangemouth Docks

85 minutes after the start of the attack

Rosalind Baxter blinked in the bright light filtering into the container from outside. After her abortive attempt to escape several hours earlier, the men had left her tied up. She tried to move her head to identify the newcomers, but her bonds restricted her ability to shift position. Judging by the voices, there were at least three of them, including a young child. She struggled to pick up the exchange taking place between her captors and the new prisoners. The echoes from the metallic walls and the harsh sound of her breathing made it hard to make out the words.

The door clanged shut, once more plunging the interior into darkness. A cone of light probed the corners and settled on her face. She screwed her eyes closed and let out a groan of protest. One of the group broke away from the others and approached. The dazzling point of brightness bounced about as the figure drew nearer.

"Who is it?" came a female voice from the far side.

A sharp intake of breath. "You!"

Rosalind attempted to identify the speaker. Clearly, the person recognised her. The beam moved down her body.

"It's my mother," said the man standing over her. A stunned silence greeted his statement.

Rosalind's mind raced. The other two had to be the wheelchair girl and their child. Her heart sank. She tried to speak through the gag, but the only sound to emerge was a muffled croak.

Jason knelt on the mattress. His fingers worked on the knot behind her head. After a few seconds, the ends parted, and she spat the damp material from her mouth.

"Thanks," Rosalind rasped.

"What the hell are you doing here?" Jason asked.

"I could ask you the same thing. Obviously, I'm not here because I want to be. Those bastards kidnapped me from my home and kept me in this container. It must have been two or three days ago they took me. I assume we're at the docks. Could you untie my hands and feet too?"

"Leave her as she is for the moment," came Antimone's voice from behind Jason.

"It seems we're all in the same boat," Rosalind said, "quite literally, if we don't get out of here soon."

"And how do you propose we escape?" Antimone asked.

"I'm not sure, but whatever we do, it would be a lot easier without being trussed up like this. How did they capture you?"

"They set off bombs at the Olympic wheelchair final and grabbed us in the confusion."

"They must want you really badly to go to all that trouble," Rosalind said.

"Somehow they discovered I survived childbirth. From what they've told us, this is all about finding a cure for the virus you created."

Rosalind huffed. "I didn't create it. It evolved."

"Yeah, but it *evolved* from work at your company where you were performing recklessly dangerous research. Let alone the fact you infected Jason's biological mother, held her captive until she died and framed his father for her murder."

"She released the virus, not me. Anyway, that's all ancient history. We need to find a way out of here. Are you going to untie me?"

Antimone's voice increased in volume. "Give me one good reason why we should lift a finger to help you. The last time we met, you put us inside a medical incinerator and threatened to press the button if they didn't agree to your demands."

"I would never have done it, but I had to make them believe I would."

"What about the murder of Nigel Perrin? You killed your own partner."

"He lacked the bottle to stand up to them. He crumbled at the first threat. If he had just kept his mouth shut, he'd still be alive."

"And what about me? Did you ever plan to let me go?"

In the reflection of the torchlight, Rosalind looked away.

"I thought not. As far as I'm concerned, you can stay there and rot."

Jason shuffled sideways. "We need all the help we can get at the moment." He picked at the knots until the blue nylon cord binding his adoptive mother's wrists loosened its grip.

"Thanks," Rosalind said, flexing her fingers to restore the circulation. "Can you sort out my feet? I still can't feel anything in my hands."

Antimone huffed in disgust as Jason focused his attention on the rope around her legs.

Moments later, Rosalind sighed with relief, rubbing at the chafed skin on her ankles.

Antimone glared at Jason in the torchlight. "I don't understand why you'd want to help the woman who murdered your biological mother and damned nearly killed us as well."

"And I have no idea what he sees in you either," Rosalind snapped.

Despite being too young to follow the argument, Paul sensed the animosity between the three adults and let out a low wail. Antimone patted his back and drew him closer.

"Let's all try to stay calm. What are we dealing with?" Jason asked.

"The guy in charge—General something-or-other—told me I would be working for them to develop a new treatment," Rosalind replied, "so they must be aware I led the team."

"How much have our abductors found out about what really happened?"

"Anybody who has seen the news or can use a computer could learn about her work," Antimone said, "but they also know I was the first to survive childbirth, and that certainly isn't public knowledge."

"Why *did* you keep that quiet?" Rosalind asked.

"We didn't want all the media attention. Our lives wouldn't have been our own. And, of course, lunatics like this lot would have tried to kidnap us—oh, wait a minute, they just did."

"Well, I'd recommend we don't mention that part," Jason said. "Let's not tell them anything they don't already know. Now, has anybody got any ideas about how to get out of here?"

"We could rush them when they open the door," Antimone replied. A strong sense of déjà vu settled over her as she recalled the last occasion she had been trapped in a metal room. Back then, Rosalind Baxter had been the one making the threats.

"They'll be expecting us to try something," Jason said, "and they're armed. I think we should bide our time and attempt to catch them unawares."

Rosalind folded her arms across her chest and shivered. "Once we get to wherever they plan on taking us—North Africa from what I remember them saying—escape will be that much harder. We should take our chances now."

"Surely it's been long enough since they kidnapped us for the authorities to work out we're missing. They're bound to conduct a search."

"The more time goes by, the more difficult it will be to track us down," Antimone said. "If they haven't already located us, I wouldn't hold out much hope for a rescue. It pains me to agree with that psycho, but I think she's right. We can't rely on anybody else for help."

Jason turned away and directed the torch beam at the walls. "I'm going to see if I can find another way out."

"You're wasting your time," Rosalind said. "There's one door, and it can only be opened from the outside."

Jason ignored her statement and shuffled down the long side, running his hand over the cold metal. Antimone tracked the bobbing light as he completed a circuit. He returned to his starting point in silence.

"Well?" Rosalind asked.

Jason's eyes glinted in the torchlight. "Like you said, there's no way out and nothing we can use as an improvised weapon. We can't do anything that puts Paul at risk."

"So, what do you suggest?"

"Unfortunately, I reckon we have only one option. We wait to see what happens next."

18

Friday 11th July 2036

10 Downing Street, London

2 hours after the start of the attack

Iris Stanley and Charles Moreland, the heads of MI5 and MI6 respectively, sat opposite Andrew Jacobs. David Wagner, his chief of staff, occupied a chair to the side of his desk.

"What can you tell me?" the Prime Minister asked.

Stanley readjusted her glasses. "I assume we're talking about the bombing and not the…" She cast a glance towards Wagner. "… matter we discussed a few days ago. Although it's possible they might be related."

"Yes. What have you learned?"

"We know the explosives were installed in micro drones, disguised to look like the flying cameras used by the media. During the race, there were hundreds of the genuine item hovering around the stadium. They're programmed to land in a pre-defined spot if they lose contact with the controller or develop a fault. That's why nobody paid any attention to the fakes when they landed. Five of them exploded. We've recovered a small amount of debris, but so far there's not enough to determine a manufacturer or point of origin."

"Have you come up with a motive?"

The head of MI5 narrowed her eyes. "If one of those bombs had detonated above the crowd, hundreds would've died. They all went off in relatively unpopulated areas of the stadium. From that, we can infer the intention was not to cause damage or devastation. The payload also seemed designed to create a lot of smoke. Our best guess at the moment is that it was all a distraction."

"Just so they could abduct people?" Jacobs asked. "I spoke to the Reponan ambassador a few hours ago, so I know about their athlete and the general. I take it the Lessing girl is still unaccounted for."

"Yes. They're all missing. Her boyfriend and their child, who were both at the stadium, have also disappeared. Mr Wagner requested that we look into the Baxter woman. It seems she hasn't been home for several days. It's all looking like far too much of a coincidence. Five of the people involved in the events surrounding the development of the cure for the virus seem to have vanished off the face of the earth."

"I take it you haven't found Max Perrin either?"

"He crossed the Channel to Calais as a foot passenger three months ago," Moreland said. "Since that time, there've been no sightings."

"So, he's probably still in France?"

"Not necessarily. From there, he could travel pretty much wherever he wanted in mainland Europe without having to show identification. On top of that, many of their borders are porous. He could be anywhere in the world by now."

"We've tried to trace his phone," Stanley said. "The number was last used over a year ago."

"What about his mother?"

"We talked to her," Stanley replied, "but she hasn't heard a thing from him in over two years. From what I understand, there was a bit of a falling out between the pair of them."

"Any idea what that was about?"

"She wasn't exactly talkative, but it appears they had an argument about her husband's will. From what we've determined, it seems the boy received nothing. Apparently, she told him he wouldn't get a penny until he demonstrated he would use the money responsibly."

"Sounds fair enough to me." The Prime Minister rested his elbows on the polished mahogany and leant forwards. "Back to the missing people. If, as looks increasingly likely, somebody abducted them, can't we track vehicles leaving the stadium?"

"In theory, yes," the female head of MI5 replied. "What makes it a lot harder is that they took out the local electricity substation. That loss of power disabled most of the cameras in the surrounding area. As you might expect, most of the crowd were keen to get away as quickly as possible in case there were more blasts. We're processing the satellite imagery, but tracing the movements of everybody who was present will take a long time."

"So," Jacobs said, "a whole load of people associated with curing the virus have disappeared. The big question is how it ties into the Reponans. Assuming one group is behind everything, why grab the general and their athlete too?"

"All I can say at this stage, Prime Minister, is that we're still looking for answers," Stanley replied.

"What about your guys, Charles? Have they turned up anything that might indicate who's responsible?"

"Sorry, Andrew," Moreland said. "As I'm sure you're aware with any terrorist event of this magnitude, there are always groups claiming responsibility. We have to investigate all claims. So far, it seems none of them possess the capability to pull off an operation on this scale. As you would expect, several countries are revelling in our misfortune, but that doesn't necessarily make them suspects."

"Why do *you* think they were taken?"

"Given the mix of abductees, if I had to guess, I'd say somebody was trying to develop a treatment of their own," Moreland replied.

"Agreed," Stanley added. "It's the only logical conclusion."

"Well, if that's the case," Jacobs said, "we should direct our attention towards countries who don't have access to the drugs."

The head of MI6 tugged at his earlobe. "If it wasn't for the abduction of their people and the murder of their man, The Republic of North Africa would be a prime suspect. What if that was just a ploy to make us think they were the victims in all this?"

The idea bounced around the room in silence as the four people tested the suggestion in their heads.

Finally, the Prime Minister stood. "It's the most likely explanation I've heard today. I suggest you focus your attention on that angle to start with. Thanks for your time."

The two secret service leaders and his chief of staff also rose to their feet.

"I'll get on it straight away," Moreland said.

"Likewise," Stanley murmured.

19

Saturday 12th July 2036

North Sea, thirty miles off Newcastle
14 hours after the start of the attack

Jason sat with his arms wrapped around the chemical toilet. The other three lay on the stinking mattress, although the dark interior of their prison meant he couldn't see them. The gentle pitch and roll of the ship sent another wave of nausea sweeping through his body. His mouth filled with saliva, and he spat into the plastic bowl. The muscles in his abdomen ached from the repeated attempts to throw up, but he had long since evacuated the contents of his stomach.

A dull rumble reverberated through the metal floor. The sound had started in the early hours of the morning, shortly after loading finished. The only notice they had received of the impending activity was the clunk of the electromagnets as they landed on the metallic roof. At the first sounds, Jason turned on the torch, expecting somebody to open the door and explain what was happening.

Instead, the box in which they were imprisoned lurched upwards and swayed as a crane transferred them from the storage area and onto the cargo ship. The sudden movement caught them all unawares. Antimone's wheelchair careened from one side of the container to the other. It was only by sheer chance that she passed close enough to Jason to allow him to lunge forwards and prevent her from smashing into the wall. Fortunately, Paul was asleep on the mattress and remained unconscious until the jarring impact on the ship's deck plates woke him.

With nowhere comfortable to sit, the group were forced to share the filthy bedding. Jason had gagged at the stench of mildew and worse, but gradually, his senses adapted and filtered the foul smells from his consciousness. Three hours of restless sleep followed until the rolling motion of the waves induced the first bout of vomiting. He had spent the time since then clutching the plastic sides of the toilet.

The muffled sound of male voices distracted Jason from his misery. A metallic clang echoed through the container. Moments later, the huge door cracked open, allowing the light from an overcast sky to flood the interior, accompanied by a chill sea breeze. He glanced at the thin band of smart plastic wrapped around his wrist: seven-thirty.

Two men in blue overalls stood silhouetted in the opening. One carried a pistol, the other held a cloth rucksack. They stepped inside. The man holding the pack dropped it with a dull thud.

"Good morning," the armed man said, his voice carrying a strong Mediterranean accent. He studied Jason's position on the floor. "I hope you are not too sick." His colleague laughed. The first man frowned, then continued. "I bring you food and drink. We leave the door open for a few hours. Do not try to escape. We are a long way from land. It is too far to swim. Also, the water is cold. If you fall overboard, we cannot stop for ten miles, and you will drown."

"Where are we?" Jason asked.

"You do not need to know."

"How much longer is this journey going to take?"

"A few days."

"Can we have some more blankets? It's chilly in here."

The man pondered the question for a moment before replying. "I will ask the general. Now, you may move about outside, but do not leave this deck. If we tell you to get inside, you do this immediately. If not, you will be punished."

"What about a change of clothes? If we're going to be here for a while, we'll need something clean to wear."

"Maybe I will send my friend to the shops, yes? But it is a long swim." His colleague mimed the action of swimming.

"Is there somewhere we can wash?"

The armed man scowled. "You ask too many questions. Remember what I said."

"Right," Jason muttered.

"What's going on?" came a voice from behind him.

Jason turned to see Antimone sitting up on the mattress. "These two…" He gestured towards where the men had been standing, but they had already left. "Anyway, they said we could go out on deck. They brought some food and water."

"Can you help me into the wheelchair?"

Jason stood but quickly crouched again as a wave of dizziness swept over him. He rose again, more slowly this time, and staggered the short distance on unsteady legs. After unfolding the mechanism, he bent down, lifted Antimone and placed her on the canvas seat.

"Thanks," she murmured. "You're looking a bit pale."

"Just a bout of sea sickness. I spent half the night hugging the toilet. Did you sleep okay?"

"As well as could be expected in the circumstances."

"Should we get Paul up?"

"No," Antimone replied. "Let him rest. Did they say where we were?"

"They wouldn't tell me, but I guess we're somewhere in the North Sea."

A groan came from the mattress. Rosalind stared at the young couple with bleary eyes. Even in the dim light penetrating to the rear of the container, Jason could clearly pick out the red and purple tinge of the chafed skin around her wrists. Sensing the direction of his gaze, she rubbed self-consciously at the damaged area.

"Did I just hear you say we're allowed outside?" she asked.

"Yeah, there's also food in the bag," Jason replied.

"I'm not feeling particularly hungry."

"Join the club."

Rosalind forced herself upright and hobbled towards the open door. When she reached the opening, she stopped and gazed upwards. Jason grabbed the wheelchair handles and propelled Antimone forwards. As he drew alongside his mother, he also halted, staring in awe at the scene greeting his eyes.

Four huge sails rose to a height of fifty metres above the deck, the aerofoil shapes all angled in the same direction. The base of the masts rotated in synchrony, continuously adjusting their angle in relation to the ship to gain maximum advantage from the light wind. Two rows of containers, all the same size as the one they had spent the night in, extended along the length of the vessel.

"Wow," Jason murmured.

A child's cry came from inside the container. "You better get him," Antimone said.

Jason released the handles and turned to see Paul rubbing the sleep from his eyes. The three-year-old spotted the approach of his father and held out his arms. "Daddy."

As Jason crouched down to pick up his son, a scream rose from behind him. He whirled around. Antimone's wheelchair was moving forwards down the slope as the hull heeled over in a gust of wind. Antimone screamed again.

"Grab her," Jason yelled. Rosalind stood rooted to the spot. He abandoned Paul and sprinted after the accelerating chair. The gap was closing, but he would never make it in time. Antimone reached down in a vain attempt to slow the wheels. The black rubber slipped through her hand, stinging her palms. Ten metres to the edge and the plunge to the ocean below.

"No!" Jason howled.

Antimone heaved her body sideways. The wheelchair balanced on one wheel for a moment, then toppled over. She hit the metal plating with a resounding crash but continued to slide forwards.

Human and machine skidded across the damp deck towards the drop.

20

Saturday 12th July 2036

North Sea, thirty miles off Newcastle
14 hours after the start of the attack

The wheelchair tyre slammed into the raised rim at the edge of the deck, coming to an abrupt halt. Antimone's body continued its forward momentum. She slithered to a stop with her legs dangling over the side.

Jason raced up to her and dropped to all fours. He reached out an arm and hauled her back towards him. Both lay on the metal plating, inhaling the sea air through heaving lungs.

"I'm sorry," Jason murmured between breaths.

"Don't worry. It was an accident." Antimone's gaze lifted and focused on the approaching figure of Rosalind Baxter.

"I didn't really see what happened," Jason said. "I was looking after Paul when I heard you scream. It was my fault; I forgot to apply the brake."

Antimone jabbed a finger in Rosalind's direction. "She was standing right next to me. She could have grabbed the handles."

"Are you all right?"

Jason and Antimone raised their heads simultaneously. Rosalind stepped closer, her arms wrapped across her chest.

"Yes, but no thanks to you," Antimone replied.

Rosalind's brows drew together in a scowl. "It all happened so quickly."

"You didn't try to help."

"I can't run. I hurt my knee trying to escape. There was nothing I could do."

"But you wouldn't have shed a tear if I'd fallen in the ocean and drowned?"

"I never said that."

"You probably think I hate you," Antimone said, "but I don't; I pity you. You're so wrapped up in yourself, you don't care about anybody else. Your life must be so shallow. Yes, you may have loads of money, but does it make you happy? Was it worth it? Don't you feel any regret for what you did?"

Rosalind's face drained of colour apart from the two vivid, red blotches in the centre of her cheeks. "My only regret is letting you live after we worked out why you survived. You think you're special because you have this disability and race around a track in a wheelchair. What a pathetic waste of time. It's a shame the car that fractured your spine didn't finish the job."

"Well, at least we all know your true thoughts now. I told you we should have left her tied up. This psycho won't lift a finger to help either of us. Her only interest is saving her own skin."

The two women glared at each other. Jason's gaze alternated between the pair.

"Are you going to put me back in that death-trap," Antimone snapped, "or do I have to drag myself across the deck?"

"Oh, right. Sorry." Jason righted the wheelchair, taking great care to apply the brake and test its operation before returning his attention to Antimone. He knelt, placed his arms beneath her body and deposited her on the canvas seat.

"Thanks," she muttered, her eyes avoiding his mother.

Jason released the braking mechanism with his foot and pushed the wheelchair back towards their container. Antimone called out Paul's name. The brightness of the morning made it difficult to see inside the metal box, but as they drew nearer, it became clear the interior was deserted.

"Paul, are you there?" Antimone yelled. The only response was the ever-present rumble of the engines and the clink of the rigging. "Oh God, where is he? Please find him."

Jason locked the wheelchair brake in position and jogged along the length of the ship, calling their son's name.

A wave of icy terror wormed through Antimone's stomach. "Let him be okay," she whispered, repeating the words in a mantra. The faint sound of Jason's voice carried towards her on the wind. A deep sense of guilt settled over her. If she hadn't started the slanging match with the Baxter woman, they might have arrived back before Paul wandered off.

Antimone leant forwards in the chair, straining her eyes to pick out any sign of her missing son among the forest of containers piled across the deck.

"Have you lost something?" a voice asked from behind her. Antimone twisted her head. She drew a sharp intake of breath.

Rosalind stood five metres away, grasping Paul's tiny hand in her own. She offered a look of barely concealed hostility. "You really should take better care of your child. A ship can be a dangerous place, especially for small children."

"Come here, Paul," Antimone said in a strangled voice, holding out her arms.

Her son flashed a cheeky grin and shook his head.

"Let go and walk over to me," she said, forcing her tone to remain light-hearted. The muscles in her forearm contracted as she clasped the armrest to prevent her fingers from shaking.

Paul sensed the unease in his mother. He glanced up at the woman. She continued to stare straight ahead. He tried to tug his hand free, but her grip tightened.

Rosalind concentrated her gaze on Antimone's face. "You can thank me if you want."

"Thanks," Antimone said, her voice barely more than a whisper.

"I'm sorry, I didn't quite get that."

Antimone spoke louder. “I said thank you. Now, please let my son go.”

“You’re welcome.”

Rosalind released Paul’s hand, then wiped her palm on her trousers. He rushed to his mother. “Mummy,” he said, clambering onto her lap.

Antimone enveloped Paul in a tight hug. She closed her eyes and inhaled the smell of his hair. After a while, he squirmed, trying to free himself from his mother’s embrace.

“Thank God,” said a breathless Jason as he jogged into view around the corner of the container. He swept his son up in his arms and planted a kiss on his cheek. “What happened?”

Nobody spoke until Rosalind broke the silence. “I discovered my grandson wandering about by himself, so I thought I better return him to his parents.”

Jason’s stare switched from one woman to the other as he struggled to navigate through the undercurrent of tension. “Um… right. Thanks.”

“I’m going to stretch my legs now.”

When she had moved out of sight, Jason placed Paul on the ground and rested a hand on Antimone’s shoulder. She flinched at his touch.

“What was that all about?” he asked.

“I’ll tell you later,” she replied in a subdued voice. “Shall we see what they’ve left us to eat?”

“I can’t say I’m feeling particularly hungry,” Jason said, “but we do need to get some food inside Paul.” He crouched to talk to his son. “Why don’t you sit on Mummy’s knee while I push you along?”

Paul needed no second invitation.

Unseen by the family of three, a figure on the bridge studied them through powerful binoculars as they covered the short distance back to the container.

21

Saturday 12th July 2036

North Sea, thirty-two miles off Newcastle
15 hours after the start of the attack

Jason picked the filling from the sandwich, removed the crust and handed a slice of buttered bread to his son. "Do you want this?" He lifted the sliver of meat between his fingers and offered it to Antimone.

"What?" she said. "Sorry, I was miles away."

"I asked if you wanted to eat this, although I'm not sure I could name the animal which it came from."

Antimone grimaced. "No, thanks."

Jason strolled to the entrance of the container and tossed the brown triangle outside. He turned back to her. "How about the crust?" When she declined, he popped the fragments in his mouth. As he ate, Antimone stared at the wall.

"Are you going to tell me what happened?" he asked.

"She threatened our son."

Jason frowned in confusion. "I thought she was the one who found him."

The scowl on Antimone's face deepened. "She did, but she wouldn't let go of his hand until I thanked her."

"Okay."

"She said that a ship can be a dangerous place for children."

"Well, she's right."

"She used it as a threat," Antimone yelled. She took a shaky breath and held it for a moment. When she spoke again, her voice trembled with tension. "Don't you see. She hates me. Three years ago, I stood up to her and won."

"I think you mean *we* stood up to her."

"Yes, of course. I wasn't having a go at you. She could've stopped my wheelchair from running away, but she didn't. She just watched. If we need her help to escape, we're in big trouble. And I don't trust her around Paul. She might try to use him to get back at me."

"I'm sure even somebody like her wouldn't deliberately hurt a child."

Antimone lowered her head and let out a sob. "I want to go home. I haven't got the strength for this."

Jason reached out and ran a finger down her cheek. "You're the strongest person I know. We'll come up with something. I won't allow anything to happen to you or Paul."

"You might not be able to protect us this time."

Jason leant forwards and kissed Antimone gently on the lips. She placed a hand behind his head and drew him closer.

A voice from the corner brought an abrupt end to the moment of intimacy. "I've finished my sammich. My hands are dirty."

Jason flashed a wry grin at Antimone. "We'll have to finish that another time." He pulled a handkerchief from his pocket. "Come here then, buddy. Let's get you cleaned up." Paul scrambled to his feet and approached his father with both arms extended, palms facing outwards.

Jason wiped the grease off his son's fingers. "Are you still hungry?"

Paul nodded.

Jason rummaged in the plastic bag. "There's an apple in here. Do you want that?"

"I don't like the skin."

"We don't have a knife. If I bite off the outside, will you eat the middle?"

Paul gave the question a moment's thought, then said, "Yes."

Jason worked his way around the circumference, removing the outer layer with his teeth. When he had finished, he handed what remained to Paul, who accepted it with both hands. For the next few minutes, he munched down to the core under the amused gaze of his parents.

After another wiping session, Jason suggested they go for a walk on deck. Paul asked whether he could ride on the wheelchair and scrambled onto his mother's lap when she agreed. Jason removed the brake and pushed the chair across the metallic floor of the container.

As they emerged from the shadowy interior, General Shaladi stepped into view, beaming at them. "Good morning." He ruffled Paul's hair. "How are you, young man?"

"Please don't touch my son," Antimone said, pushing the general's hand away.

The cheery look vanished abruptly from the man's face and his eyes narrowed. "That is not very friendly."

Antimone glowered at the general. "You kidnap my family, hold us prisoner in a metal box, and then you want us to be friends? You've got some funny ideas about what friendship means."

Shaladi shrugged. "These are my orders. I must do what my superiors ask. I do not wish to make your confinement any more unpleasant than necessary. Now, my men told me you nearly fell into the sea."

Antimone and Jason stared back in silence.

"A ship can be a dangerous place," Shaladi continued.

"Have you been talking to Mrs Baxter?" Antimone asked, her voice shaking with fury. "That's exactly what she said. Are you threatening us as well?"

The general raised both hands. "I have not talked to her today, and I am not making threats. I am only warning you of the dangers. We do not want to go to all the trouble of capturing you and then watch you fall over the side."

"But you have been spying on us?" Antimone said.

"Yes," Shaladi replied. "My men have been observing you. That is their job."

"It's a shame they didn't intervene and help me."

"You are right. In future, they will stay closer."

"I'd feel a whole lot safer if I had proper control over this wheelchair," Antimone said.

"I will see if it is possible to find something more suitable when we reach our destination, but for now, regretfully, I cannot do anything. However, I can improve your accommodation."

"What does that mean? Are you going to move us to a bigger metal box?" Jason asked, his voice dripping with sarcasm.

"No. I have talked to the captain, and he says he has some empty crew cabins. They are small—much smaller than the container—but more comfortable, I think. You would have a proper bed and a mattress each. Oh, and windows but unfortunately, there is no toilet inside the room. That is in the corridor. Also, my men can watch over you more easily."

"Do we have to share with Mrs Baxter?" Antimone asked.

The general's eyes crinkled in amusement. "You really dislike this woman, do you not? But no, that will not be necessary."

"In that case, we would like to accept your offer," Antimone said.

"Good. Please follow me."

The general led the way along the deck. Jason pushed the wheelchair, Paul bouncing with excitement on his mother's lap. As they walked, the low sun reflected from an object on the top floor of the rounded structure rising from the prow of the ship.

Jason shielded his eyes with his hand and stared upwards. The figure at the window continued to study them for a moment, then lowered the binoculars and turned away.

22

Sunday 13th July 2036

10 Downing Street, London

2 days after the attack at the Olympics

Andrew Jacobs moved behind the large mahogany desk and sank into the leather chair. "Please sit," he said, shrugging off his jacket and loosening his tie. "Sorry to have kept you waiting."

The two secret service heads who had risen as the Prime Minister entered his office followed his lead and took their seats.

"No problem," Iris Stanley replied, polishing her glasses. Charles Moreland clasped his hands in front of his stomach.

"David Wagner tells me you've made some progress in the search for our missing people," Jacobs continued. "I could do with some good news."

"It's been a mammoth job," Stanley, the head of MI5 said. "We've been working around the clock on this. As you can imagine, tracking the movements of over thirty thousand individuals was quite a task. Your suggestion to concentrate on the Reponan angle made it significantly easier.

"Once we assumed this was a kidnapping with an ultimate destination of North Africa, it narrowed down the search somewhat. The first question to answer was how the kidnappers proposed to transfer the targets over that distance. Security at our airports is so tight, they couldn't have smuggled them through that way. The only other method was to transport them by sea.

"Luckily, the skies were clear on the afternoon of the wheelchair final, so we had good satellite coverage. The resolution isn't sufficient to identify a person, but we can track traffic movements. When we searched for vehicles travelling from the stadium to a port, we came up with a handful of potential leads. After further investigation, we narrowed the results down to just one; a black van began its journey shortly after the blasts from the spot where we discovered the dead man. It led us to Grangemouth. Other than a couple of small yachts, a single vessel, a container ship, set out on the night following the attack.

"That makes sense," Jacobs said. "Grangemouth is less than an hour from Glasgow, isn't it?"

"That's right. It's a forty- or fifty-minute journey by road."

"What do we know about their destination?" the Prime Minister asked.

"The vessel is registered in Tunisia and, according to records, is heading for the port of Tunis," Moreland replied.

Jacobs leant forwards in his chair. "That fits in with your theory. Where are they now?"

"The satellite puts them roughly one hundred and fifty miles north of Spain," Stanley replied. "They're currently making way at about thirty-five knots using a combination of engines and sails. They must be working the turbines hard to achieve that speed, even with wind assistance. It's costing them a lot given the current price of fuel, so it seems they want to reach their destination in a hurry. That said, the Reponans possess some of the largest remaining oil reserves in the world, so if they are behind this, they can afford it."

"How long until they arrive?"

"If they maintain their present speed, another two or three days."

"And you say they're heading for Tunis. How far is it from there to The Republic of North Africa?"

"The two countries adjoin each other. Tunis is about two hundred and fifty miles north west of Repona. If they travel by road, it'll take them around ten hours to reach the border. We don't yet know what they plan to do with the abductees after that."

"Do we have any warships in the region?" the Prime Minister asked.

"They'll have to pass through the Straits of Gibraltar to get to North Africa. We've got a cruiser and a pair of fast patrol boats that could intercept them."

"How can we be sure our people haven't already disembarked?"

"We can't be absolutely certain," Moreland replied, "but the satellites have shown no other vessels coming close enough to offload passengers. If the analysis is correct—and I believe it is—there's a good chance they're still aboard."

"Great work," Jacobs said. "I take it you haven't mentioned to your teams any of the… ah… more sensitive details of this case?"

The two secret service leaders on the opposite side of the desk exchanged a glance. Stanley broke the silence. "Well, Prime Minister, we employ a lot of very bright individuals. Obviously, in circumstances like these, one of the initial steps is to identify the motives of the perpetrators. It's common knowledge the girl has a child, even if very few are aware she was the first to survive. It's also no secret that the Reponans are suffering under the restrictions of the trade embargo. You don't need to be a genius to work out it has something to do with this damned virus."

"But you haven't informed them of the Baxter woman's involvement?"

Stanley pinched the bridge of her nose. "You tasked us with tracking her down, so quite a few of the team know she's missing."

"For heaven's sake, make sure they don't learn about the part she played in the initial outbreak."

"Of course not, Prime Minister," Stanley replied.

"So, what are you proposing to do, Andrew?" Moreland asked.

Jacobs placed his elbows on the desk and clasped his hands together. "Step one is to summon the Reponan ambassador for a little chat. He certainly has some explaining to do. It all rather depends on his reaction. Let's see what he has to say. If he chooses not to cooperate, we'll intercept the ship and take them back by force. As for what we do after that, I don't really want to consider military action against the North Africans after the long civil war, but they need to be taught a lesson. Do we have any assets in the country?"

Moreland's eyes narrowed. "This information mustn't go any further, Andrew, but we've infiltrated the mid-levels of their government. Unfortunately, our feelers don't reach to the top. If they did, we'd probably have received prior notice of their intentions."

"The public will want to know who was responsible for the attack," Stanley said, adjusting the frame of her glasses. "The press will demand we punish the perpetrators. Given the high-profile nature of the abduction, it's likely many of the details will come out however much you may try to hush them up."

Andrew Jacobs rose to his feet. "We can worry about the news media later. Let's focus on getting our people back first."

23

Sunday 13th July 2036

Bay of Biscay, twenty miles west of Spain
2 days after the attack at the Olympics

Jason leant over the edge of the top bunk and looked down at Antimone. "This is an improvement on sharing a stinking mattress between the four of us."

Antimone glanced sideways at Paul and adjusted the sheet covering his small body. After the initial excitement of their new accommodation, he had crashed out and now lay asleep beside her on the narrow bed. "Keep your voice down. We don't want to wake him. Anyway, why are you so cheerful? We're still prisoners."

"We'll get out of this. I have a good feeling."

"Hmm. I'm not so sure. How do you propose we escape?"

"Ah, well, that's the problem isn't it? We have a guard in the corridor, and here we are, stuck in the middle of the sea with no land for miles."

"What about the lifeboats?"

Jason rubbed the two-day stubble on his cheek. "I've no idea how we'd go about launching one. Anyway, we might be swapping the frying pan for the fire. The ocean is a big place. We could be adrift for days. And that's always assuming we can lower one to the water without being detected."

"Surely they have emergency radios?"

"Good point. Even if we can't launch a lifeboat, we should be able to use its radio to call for help."

Antimone lifted her upper body with her elbows. "It's not the worst idea I've heard today. How would we get onboard one?"

"They must have them, but I don't remember seeing any."

"Me neither."

Jason swung his legs over the side and lowered himself to the floor. The thrumming of the deck plates seemed more pronounced in this part of the vessel. He moved to the porthole and peered through the circular window. The midday sun sparkled on the waves like thousands of diamonds.

"What can you see?" Antimone asked.

Jason shifted his head to gain a better view, squinting against the brightness. "Nothing that looks like a lifeboat."

"They must have at least one out there somewhere."

He shielded his eyes. "Hang on, there are a couple of cylinders close to the side. There's writing on them, but they're too far away to make out what it says."

"Those are probably what you're looking for. I expect you need to pull a cord or something to inflate them."

Jason turned back. "That's why they weren't overly bothered about us wandering around on deck. We wouldn't have been able to access the radio without inflating one, and no doubt they would have spotted that."

"Why does it have to be the lifeboat radio?" Antimone asked. "The main ship's radio would do just as well."

"That may be harder to reach. I can't imagine they'd be careless enough to let us walk up and start talking."

"It wouldn't hurt to find out where it is though."

Jason stared at the door. "It'll be on the bridge. That's above us. Why don't I try to get up there now?"

"There's a man in the corridor for starters."

"I'll say I need to go to the toilet. While I'm in there, you create a distraction, and I'll sneak upstairs."

"How am I going to do that?"

"You call out. When he comes in, you tell him you fell off the bunk."

Antimone glanced at the sleeping three-year-old lying beside her. "I don't want to wake Paul."

"If we don't get out of here, there will be far more to worry about than our child losing sleep."

"I suppose you're right. Can you help me down?"

Jason lifted Antimone off the thin mattress and lowered her to the metal floor. "Give it a minute or two then start banging on the door. When I hear you, I'll slip out and make my way upstairs. Try to keep the guard busy for as long as possible."

"Fine. Let's do this."

Jason pulled down on the handle and stuck his head into the corridor. A man wearing a black uniform sat on a chair, his chin resting on his chest. He jerked upright at the unexpected intrusion.

"I need to go to the toilet," Jason said.

The man gestured impatiently towards a sign two doors down from his position. "There."

Jason stepped outside the cabin and hugged the wall to get past the seated guard. As he pushed inside the small room, the overpowering floral scent of an air freshener assaulted his nostrils. In some ways it was worse than the smell it was trying to hide. He stood with his back to the metal door. The seconds extended into a minute. Breathing through his mouth, he waited impatiently for his cue. After what seemed like a lifetime, the sound of banging accompanied by the shouts of a raised female voice echoed down the corridor.

Jason pulled the handle and stuck his head in the gap between door and frame. Unseen by the guard, he watched as the man hauled himself to his feet and ambled towards the commotion. He experienced a stab of guilt at the noise of his son's crying.

Jason slipped out and jogged to the door marked with a staircase sign. He pushed through and climbed the steps, placing each foot carefully to avoid making any sound. After two flights, he arrived at a spot, which matched his starting point in every detail. Feeling like a character in an Escher print, he encountered another identical floor before reaching the top.

Here, the door contained a rectangular window. Jason crept forwards and peered through the glass. The bridge afforded a two-seventy degree view out over the sea, covering the bow and both sides of the vessel. Multiple computer screens sat atop cabinets arrayed in a semicircle around a black leather chair. Switches and indicators filled every available surface.

A man with wiry grey hair and wearing a short-sleeved white shirt occupied the captain's seat. A second figure, dressed in a brightly coloured T-shirt and khaki chino shorts, stood to his left, a pair of binoculars hanging from a strap around his neck. The close-cropped blond hair protruding from beneath the baseball cap suggested somebody much younger than his companion.

Jason's eyes scanned the console as he attempted to identify the radio among the array of instruments. He wasn't sure what he was looking for, but he assumed there had to be a microphone. Finally, he spotted what looked like an old-fashioned telephone handset attached to the front of one cabinet.

A sudden movement at the periphery of his vision drew Jason's attention. The white-shirted man leant forwards and extended a finger to press the screen mounted to the armrest. He peered closer and touched the glass a second time. He turned to his companion and said something, gesturing at the display.

The younger of the two men approached his colleague. As he did so, his gaze lifted and settled on the face peering through the window.

A shock of recognition flashed between the pair. For a moment, Jason's jaw hung open in surprise.

"Max Perrin," he muttered.

24

Sunday 13th July 2036

Bay of Biscay, twenty miles west of Spain
2 days after the attack at the Olympics

Jason remained rooted to the spot. The man in the white shirt leapt from the chair and grabbed the telephone handset. He jabbered into the mouthpiece in Arabic, casting frequent glances in Jason's direction. Moments later, the sound of pounding feet echoed up the staircase.

The sudden noise shook Jason from his inertia. Only two routes lay open to him: either through into the bridge or back down the stairs. Before he could decide, a pair of men in black uniforms, each holding a pistol, rounded the final bend and clattered up the last few steps. Jason raised his hands in surrender.

"What are you doing here?" one of the armed newcomers demanded, pressing the gun against his chest. "You know you must stay in your room."

"I… got lost," Jason replied. "I was going to the toilet and—"

"You are lying," the same man interrupted. He turned to his colleague and muttered a few words. The second guard stepped around Jason and pushed open the door into the bridge. There, he held a brief conversation with the ship's officer. Max Perrin stood to one side, his gaze locked on Jason.

"What's he doing here?" Jason asked, pointing at his former classmate. He found it impossible to read Max's expression.

"You, be quiet," the guard replied, jabbing him with the gun barrel.

The seconds ticked by, and still, nobody moved. Finally, the sound of more footsteps rose from below. The pair of armed men stiffened as the out of breath figure of General Shaladi came into view. A yellow, short-sleeved shirt and beige chinos had replaced the military uniform. He barked questions at the guards in Arabic. Their replies comprised monosyllabic responses.

"What is going on?" he said, turning his attention to Jason and glowering at him.

"I was just telling your men I got lost."

The general stared at him in silence for several seconds before responding. "Do you think we are stupid?"

"No, I—"

"Do not insult me further by lying. Because of your actions, you will all go back in the box."

"I'm sorry, it was a mistake."

"Yes, it was. But now you must pay the price."

Max stepped forwards and coughed. "Um... excuse me, sir, but there's something you need to see."

"I thought I instructed you to stay out of sight," the general snapped.

"How could I—?"

Shaladi cut him off with a sharply raised hand. "What is it then?"

Max took a deep breath before continuing. "The captain told me the radar shows what could be another vessel approaching rapidly from the south. The return keeps fading and reappearing, almost like the signal a whale might give—except whales don't travel at forty knots. Whatever he's picking up, it's currently about sixty nautical miles away. He thinks it may be a warship."

"Is this true?" Shaladi asked, turning to the older man. A brief conversation conducted in Arabic followed.

"Take them all and lock them in the container," the general instructed the guards. "You go too." He pointed towards Max.

"You don't seriously plan to keep me locked up with them, do you?" Max replied. "I've delivered everything I promised."

"Do not tempt me. You must stay in your cabin. My men will accompany you."

"So, it was you who sold us out," Jason said, glowering at Max.

A malicious grin spread across the face of Jason's former classmate. "I warned you not to mess with me. Now look what's happened."

"Are you saying I started this? You slipped a mind-altering drug into our drinks and raped a girl. Then, just for good measure, you forced me to rape her as well. She came within a hair's breadth of dying because of your actions, and you tell me it's my fault. You've got to be mad."

"She shouldn't have tripped me."

"It was an accident," Jason yelled. "Why would she deliberately trip you with her wheelchair? She could just as easily have injured herself."

"Wait," the general said. "You are talking about Miss Lessing?"

"Yes," Jason replied. "I bet he never told you any of his dirty little secrets, did he?"

"And the child? This is how it happened?"

"I'm the father," Jason said, "but I knew nothing about it. Antimone only became pregnant because he drugged us both with a nasty substance that removed our free will."

Shaladi glared at Max. "No, he did not tell me this."

"How much are you paying him?" Jason asked.

"I wouldn't have needed to do this if the authorities had given me what I was owed," Max shouted.

"What's that got to do with me?"

"That woman, your mother, killed my father right in front of the British Prime Minister, yet she doesn't get to spend even one day in prison. That's not to mention the millions of women across the world she…" His voice trailed off.

"What did she do?" Shaladi asked.

"Nothing," Max mumbled.

Shaladi studied Max's face, searching for answers. The boy refused to meet his gaze. After a moment, the general said, "We will continue this conversation later. Now, you go down the stairs."

Jason glared at Max for a second, then turned away. The barrel of a gun jabbed him in the back. He set off down the staircase, four pairs of feet clanking down the steps after him. When they reached the floor on which the other prisoners were being held, the armed man instructed Jason to pass through the door and followed behind. The other three members of the group continued down the stairwell.

The guard standing in the corridor sprang to attention. He brushed a droplet of sweat from his temple. His eyes flicked anxiously towards the exit. The two men conducted a brief conversation in Arabic.

"Get the woman and child," said the man with the gun, waving it at Jason.

Jason twisted the handle and entered their cabin. Antimone sat in the wheelchair. Paul clung to her, wrapping his arms around his mother's neck.

"What's going on?" she asked.

"They're moving us back to the container."

Antimone scowled. "Why?"

"They caught me outside the bridge. Guess who was there with the captain."

"I have no idea."

"Max Perrin."

Antimone's face clouded. "What the hell is he doing here?"

"It seems he sold the North Africans the information about you surviving childbirth. But there is some good news. They detected a ship heading towards us. They think it might be a warship."

"Coming to rescue us?"

"Who knows, but let's hope so."

"But that could put us in more danger. They aren't just going to let us go without a fight."

Jason shot a worried glance at Antimone. "Shit. I hadn't thought of that."

A rap on the door brought the brief conversation to an end. "We have to go," he said. "If it is one of our ships, let's pray this lot surrender." He released the brake and pushed the chair into the corridor. At the same time, his mother emerged from the cabin two doors down.

"What the hell is happening?" Rosalind asked. "Why are you moving us?"

Jason watched on in silence.

"I'm not going anywhere," she stated, jutting out her chin as she turned to the guard.

The man's hand whipped out, slapping her cheek. She staggered backwards a pace and raised a palm to the reddening skin.

"Move! Now!"

Wordlessly, she limped towards the exit sign.

When they reached the door leading into the stairwell, Jason stopped. "How do we get down there?"

"You carry her," the armed man replied, waving the gun at Jason. "I will take the wheelchair."

Paul still clung to his mother.

"I'm afraid you'll have to walk, buddy," Jason said, reaching out his arms to lift his son off Antimone's lap.

Paul uttered a squeak of denial and held on tighter.

"Come on. You need to let go."

The three-year-old reluctantly released his grip and allowed his father to pick him up. Jason deposited him on the floor, then scooped Antimone out of the wheelchair and staggered through the doorway. Paul grasped the handrail and negotiated the first step. He turned back, seeking his father's approval.

"Keep going," Jason said with a smile of encouragement.

Paul descended the next stair and once again stopped. The guard muttered something under his breath and barged past the boy's parents. He snatched the child up and, despite Paul's screams of protest, carried him under his arm down the stairs.

"Leave my son alone," Antimone yelled at the man's back.

Jason hurried down the stairwell. He apologised as Antimone's feet banged against the wall. Her body trembled with fury as they wound their way down to the next floor.

They emerged into bright afternoon sunshine. A sobbing Paul immediately rushed to his father and clung to his leg. Antimone looked daggers at the guard. The man ignored her and retraced his steps. He returned moments later carrying the folded wheelchair. He expanded the mechanism and stood back. "Come. You hurry."

Jason lowered Antimone into the chair. Paul once again clambered onto his mother's lap. The second guard followed Rosalind outside. She blinked in the brightness.

"This way," the first man said, striding ahead without a backward glance.

Jason raised a hand to shield his eyes from the sun and stared up at the huge expanse of white sails towering above them. His gaze tracked along the mast to its summit. A small black dot moved against the cloudless azure sky and drew his attention. Was it a bird? As he watched, the object dropped rapidly and hovered once again. The movements were far too jerky for it to be a living creature.

In a flash of inspiration, he realised what he was staring at. "It's a drone," he murmured.

Antimone heard and swivelled to survey the area at which he was pointing. "Where? I don't see anything."

"Just there."

A moment of silence passed as all the members of the group scanned the region of blue in the direction of his finger.

Antimone pointed in excitement. "Yes, now I see it."

Jason stood still, watching the tiny aircraft as it darted from one point to the next.

The guard poked him from behind. The action had no effect, so he smashed the gun into the base of Jason's skull.

Jason dropped to a knee, clutching the point of impact. Antimone slowly lowered her raised arm.

"Move now!" barked the armed man.

Jason rose groggily to his feet and cast one final glance towards the drone. Before he could pick it out, a shove in the back sent him staggering forwards. The other guard strode along the deck ahead of the group. Jason pushed the wheelchair after the man. When they reached the familiar yellow container, the armed guard pulled the lever and swung the door open.

A wave of warm air rolled out from the interior.

"It's too hot in there," Rosalind said.

Two guns pointed at her. "Get inside."

"We're no use to you if we die from heat exhaustion."

The man took a step forwards and placed the barrel of the weapon against her chest. "Do it."

The prisoners reluctantly entered the gloomy metal box. The sweltering, stale air rasped in their throats as they breathed it in. Within seconds, sweat broke out over their bodies.

"No noise or you will be punished," the armed man said as the square of brightness leading to the outside world reduced to a thin wedge.

25

Sunday 13th July 2036

10 Downing Street, London

2 days after the attack at the Olympics

"Thank you for coming in at such short notice," Andrew Jacobs said, studying the diplomat standing before him. A bushy moustache flecked with patches of white sat over his top lip. The man adjusted the knot of the striped blue and green tie, then tugged the sleeves of his dark, tailor-made suit.

"The urgency of your invitation suggested speed was of the essence," replied the Republic of North Africa ambassador with barely any foreign accent. His eyes roamed across the interior of the Prime Minister's office. He strolled to a bookcase and studied the spines of the books. "You have an interesting taste in reading, Mr Jacobs," he said, pulling one out.

"Yes. Would you like a drink? Tea or coffee?"

The man placed the book back on the shelf. "Tea would be fine, thanks."

Jacobs gestured towards a leather chair on the opposite side of the desk. "Please take a seat." He lifted the telephone handset and muttered a few words. He replaced the phone and drummed his fingers on the mahogany surface. Less than a minute later, a light tap came from the door.

"Come," Jacobs called.

An attractive woman in her early thirties entered, carrying a tray on which rested a teapot and two teacups. "Will there be anything else, sir?" she asked.

"No, thank you, Sarah," the Prime Minister responded. He turned to the North African. "Milk? Sugar?"

The ambassador watched on with an amused expression. "Neither," he replied. He waited in silence while Jacobs filled the cup. "You British are a strange people," he said. "You call me here for an urgent meeting, then spend time pouring tea. Shall we talk about the weather as well before we get down to business?"

Jacobs passed across the bone china teacup, his features tight with disapproval.

"What is this matter you wished to raise with me?" the diplomat asked.

Jacobs placed both hands on the edge of the desk, raised his head and stared the North African in the eye. "I want to discuss the terrorist atrocity at the Glasgow stadium and the abduction of several British citizens."

The ambassador pursed his lips, sipped the steaming liquid and replaced the cup in the saucer. "And what is the connection to my country?"

"We believe some of your nationals took part in the attack."

"This is a serious accusation. It is telling that you have no aides present to assist you."

Jacobs' eyes narrowed. "I thought we should keep the circle of people involved in this discussion as small as possible before it escalates out of control."

"Or you have something to hide."

"Let me be frank. There is strong evidence that your countrymen were responsible for the blasts at the Olympics, resulting in the deaths of three civilians. We also know that you kidnapped our people. They are currently being held prisoner on a containership off the coast of Portugal."

"Yes. My contacts in Tunisia have informed me that a warship of yours is harassing one of their vessels in international waters. Apparently, your ship has fired shots across the bow of the Tunisian vessel, forcing it to slow and lose valuable journey time."

"Your country has performed an act of terrorism, but I don't sense any remorse in your statements."

"Let me be blunt, Mr Prime Minister. The actions taken by my nation have been forced upon us. It is three years since you developed a treatment for this terrible virus, yet still you refuse to share it with my people. In that time, tens of thousands of our women have died. You complain about one attack in which three civilians lost their lives. This was an accident. We had no intention of causing any deaths. Many times that number die in my country every day because you will not supply us with the medicines we need."

Jacobs leant forwards. "The reason you do not receive the drugs you require is exactly because your state has performed or supported acts of terrorism in the past. That is why the international community has applied sanctions. But those were due to end soon. I don't understand why you would jeopardise the significant progress you have made in recent years by this foolish action."

The ambassador stared across the desk, the cup of tea long since forgotten. "You may regard our behaviour as foolish, but my government deems it necessary. It is probably not news to you, but a new strain of the virus has emerged. Now, it attacks both mothers and children. We cannot just sit back and allow our people to die."

"Neither can you conduct acts of terrorism and snatch the citizens of another country and expect there to be no consequences."

"My nation has suffered many *consequences* over the last two decades as the rest of the world squabbled for control of our resources. Most of my countrymen regard our petroleum reserves as a gift. I see them as a curse. Without the oilfields, we would be of no interest to anybody else. The irony is that we are only now recovering just as the value of oil diminishes."

"That still doesn't excuse your actions."

"We would prefer that we were not forced to act. Sadly, that is not so. Everything my government has done is to assist our people because others are unwilling to help us."

"In that case," Jacobs said, "you leave me little option but to instigate military action."

The ambassador chuckled. "Oh, I do not think that will happen."

The Prime Minister stared at the North African in confusion. "What on earth gives you that idea?"

"On the contrary, you will do everything in your power to provide assistance to my people." The ambassador's expression hardened. "We know how the virus originated. Your Mrs Baxter created it in a laboratory. Three years ago, you offered her a pardon, knowing she is personally to blame for the deaths of millions of women. You may think my country has a bad reputation on the international stage. Just imagine the impact such information would have on Britain's standing in the world: a British citizen responsible for creating the biggest killer the planet has ever seen and the Prime Minister complicit in covering up her involvement then allowing her to go free. I wonder how that would play in the media."

Jacobs blinked at the man sitting calmly on the other side of the desk.

"You've gone very quiet, Prime Minister. How do you say? Has a cat got your tongue?"

Jacobs shook off his inertia. "But that's ridiculous," he blustered. "I've never heard so much rubbish in my life."

"We both know it is true."

"This pathetic attempt at blackmail won't work. Nobody believes a word coming out of your country."

The ambassador flashed a wintry smile. "Let me tell you what will happen next. You will start by calling off your warship. If I hear anything in the news media about the occupants of the Tunisian vessel, I will release the information we have gathered about the origins of the pandemic to the world. Are we clear?

"Secondly, you will commence shipments of any existing treatments for the Orestes virus to the Republic of North Africa in the next week. Finally, I expect you to sign a commercially binding contract to share the results of any research into the new strain of this disease. Oh, and all sanctions against my country will cease immediately. I may have more demands in the future, but that is all for now."

Jacobs stood and glared angrily at the man sitting opposite. "Get out of my office right now."

The ambassador stood. "I recognise this has come as quite a shock to you, Mr Prime Minister. I will see myself out."

26

Sunday 13th July 2036

Atlantic Ocean, thirty miles west of Porto
2 days after the attack at the Olympics

The container door swung fully open. Despite the guards leaving a small gap for the past two hours, the interior had become a cauldron. A welcome gust of cooler air swept inside.

The outline of General Shaladi stepped forward, an apologetic look on his face. "I am sorry for your uncomfortable confinement. We needed to keep you out of sight while we resolved a few minor difficulties. Here, I have brought some water for you."

Antimone inhaled deeply. Every breath up to that point had felt as if she was inhaling molten syrup. She had discarded the green training top at the start of their most recent incarceration, but even so, sweat stained the fabric of her athletic vest. Her eyes took in the three other occupants. Jason and Rosalind rose wearily from their positions on the metal floor where they had moved to benefit from the meagre breeze entering from outside. Paul lay spread-eagled across the ancient mattress, his damp hair plastered against his scalp.

Antimone caught the bottle tossed towards her. Unable to move by herself, she offered it to Jason and pointed at her son. He took it from her and knelt beside the unconscious boy. A thin cry signalled his return to wakefulness. After a moment of disorientation, the three-year-old drank greedily from the plastic container.

Shaladi distributed more bottles. Despite the lukewarm temperature, nothing had ever tasted better to Antimone. She stopped drinking only when she could feel the water sloshing around inside her stomach. When everybody had satisfied their thirst, they emerged into the bright afternoon sunshine.

Antimone immediately scanned the horizon, searching for the vessel from which the drone had originated. Her gaze settled on a distant, grey smudge, hugging the boundary between sea and sky.

Shaladi followed the direction of her stare. "Please do not raise your hopes that help is coming. They are just leaving."

Ninety minutes earlier, the prisoners inside the container had detected a change in the note of the engine vibrations reverberating through the floor. An hour later, the pitch rose once more.

"Who are they?" Antimone asked.

"It is a British warship, but like I said, there will be no rescue."

"But they must have seen us."

"Yes, I think so."

"Our government wouldn't just abandon us."

Shaladi turned back to the group. "You have too much confidence in the rulers of your country. They have agreed to let us proceed."

Antimone reluctantly switched her gaze from the outline of the ship to the general. "You're lying. The British authorities would never willingly permit somebody to kidnap their citizens."

"Fine," Shaladi said. "If you do not believe me, keep watching. I promise you the warship will no longer follow us."

Antimone studied the distant grey shape in silence. She couldn't tell from this distance whether the gap between them was closing.

"Yes, it's moving away," Rosalind confirmed. Nobody questioned her conclusions.

"Why would they give up on us?" Jason asked.

"They know," Rosalind muttered in a dull voice. "It's the only explanation that makes sense."

"Very perceptive, Mrs Baxter," Shaladi replied. His expression turned cold. "I never thought I would meet the person responsible for the deaths of my wife and daughter. I should kill you now, but unfortunately my masters have ordered me to deliver you alive."

Rosalind's voice trembled with barely suppressed rage. "The Perrin boy told you, didn't he?"

Shaladi's piercing gaze homed in on her. "Not directly, but he provided enough clues for me to work it out. The vital piece of information was that the British Prime Minister saw you kill Perrin's father but agreed to let you go free. I asked myself why you would murder your partner of many years. I assume he was about to confess. Our scientists have suspected for some time that the virus was manmade. Young Perrin also mentioned millions of women dying. Mr Jacobs confirmed our suspicions."

"I'll kill the little bastard."

The general's expression darkened. "You will do no such thing. Perrin is working for me."

A vindictive glint appeared in Rosalind's eyes. "You do realise he was involved in making the girl pregnant?"

"I learned this two hours ago," the general replied.

"He raped her. There's a strong possibility his actions had something to do with her survival."

Shaladi studied her face, searching for signs of truth. He pointed at Jason. "He is the father of the child, though."

Rosalind pressed home her advantage. "Yes, but two people had sex with her. It's a potential factor in why she survived. Perrin might be the vital clue to finally developing a cure."

Antimone debated whether to chip in. She knew the scientists had ruled out the part played by Max in her pregnancy. Instead, she changed the subject. "What happens now?" she asked.

"We continue our journey to my country."

"And afterwards?"

"We shall see."

27

Monday 14th July 2036

10 Downing Street, London

3 days after the attack at the Olympics

The blue eyes of Iris Stanley peered through the lenses of her glasses and pinned Andrew Jacobs with her gaze. The Prime Minister seemed to be a diminished version of the man she had last seen just a day earlier. It was as if his body had shrunk in on itself.

"So, the North Africans have discovered Mrs Baxter's involvement in the creation of the virus?"

Jacobs nodded, placing a hand on either side of his face in a passable impression of Edvard Munch's painting, The Scream. "Yes, they know she released it and that I pardoned her of all crimes in exchange for the cure."

"That's not good," Charles Moreland said, loosening the middle button of his jacket. "That's not good at all."

"Have you discussed this with anybody else?" Stanley asked.

Jacobs' gaze snapped towards the MI5 head. "No, of course not. Who would I tell? How the hell am I going to persuade the cabinet to drop sanctions against the Reponans? They'll want to know why."

"Yes," Moreland said. "If Britain were to break rank, it'd also cause considerable consternation in governments across the world."

"Not to mention politicians on both sides of the House at home," Stanley added.

"How the hell did they find out?" the Prime Minister asked.

Stanley's eyes narrowed. "It seems highly unlikely Rosalind Baxter would have told them. That would be suicide. Similarly, the other two aren't stupid enough to say anything."

"Unless they were tortured or threatened," Moreland said. "I wouldn't put it past the North Africans. Remember, they've got a young child with them. That makes them very vulnerable to coercion."

"No, there must be more to it than that," Stanley replied. "How would the Reponans even know what questions to ask? I think somebody else told them."

"And I might have an idea who that could be."

Jacobs and Stanley both turned to stare at the head of MI6.

"The drone images clearly show the three missing British adults and the child," Moreland continued. "We also captured a shot of Shaladi, the Reponan

General. The video failed to pick up his daughter. We spent a lot of time trying to identify the other occupants of the vessel. Some of them are members of Shaladi's security team, but there is one other person of interest. The camera didn't get a clear image, so I've had my technical experts working on cleaning up the material." He opened the folder and passed a grainy black-and-white photograph to each of the others.

The picture showed a figure wearing a light-coloured short-sleeved shirt and knee-length shorts. A baseball cap obscured the upper part of his face.

Jacobs moved the glossy paper closer. "Is this the best you can do?"

"You should've seen it before they started. We won't glean much more given the quality of the raw images. The subject was standing in shade at a distance of at least half a mile from the lens. But I think there's enough of a match to determine the person's identity with a reasonable amount of certainty."

"Really? Who is it?"

Moreland settled back in his chair. "The facial recognition algorithm puts an eighty percent probability on our mystery man being none other than Max Perrin."

"Perrin?" the Prime Minister asked, his eyebrows lifting in surprise.

"That makes sense," Stanley said. "It would explain why we couldn't track him down. He knows all the history. From what you told us, the Baxter woman murdered his father. That would provide him with all the motive he needed to tell the Reponans."

"Yes, there's no love lost between him and the other two either," Jacobs said. "His actions resulted in her getting pregnant. What's he doing on the ship though?"

"Maybe they're paying him."

"Well, if it is who we think, I feel less bad about considering Mrs Baxter's demands to liquidate him. Where are they now?"

"They've passed through the Strait of Gibraltar and are north of Morocco as we speak," Moreland replied.

Jacobs switched his gaze from the head of MI6 to his counterpart in MI5 and back again. "What do I do next?"

A moment of silence followed the question. Finally, Stanley leant forwards and inhaled deeply. "It will all come out in the end, whatever you do. My recommendation would be to control the narrative by informing the world before they find out for themselves."

The Prime Minister turned pale, and his mouth opened like a stranded fish. "You mean confess to all of it."

Moreland nodded. "I agree with Iris. It'll be bad now, but a whole lot worse if you try to keep it quiet. In this case, honesty is the best policy."

"But…"

"Look, Andrew," Moreland said. "If you just go along with the Reponans' demands, you'll have to answer some impossible questions. People will want to know why you're stopping sanctions. I doubt you could push something like that through without considerable support from Parliament. And how are you going to obtain that unless you reveal some part of the truth? If you confess to the global press what really happened, the Reponans will no longer have a hold over you."

"But that would be the end of my career. Hell, the entire country will be ruined. We'll become outcasts among the international community. Half the world hates us already. We'd be providing all the evidence to convert the other half."

"I'm afraid there are no easy options," Stanley said. "Of course, you could just destroy all the evidence."

Jacobs looked up hopefully. "What do you mean?"

"I'm not suggesting this for one moment, but ships sink without trace all the time. Without any witnesses to what happened back then, it would be their word against ours."

The Prime Minister covered his face with his hands. "I need some time to think about this."

28

Tuesday 15th July 2036

The Mediterranean, thirty miles north of Tunis
4 days after the attack at the Olympics

The orange orb of the sun kissed the horizon. The corona blazed in a sky transitioning from blue to grey, sending a cascade of sparkles across the shimmering ocean. Jason shielded his eyes as he craned his neck to peer through the porthole at the distant low-lying land off the starboard side of the ship. The first twinkle of streetlights appeared, glittering like fireflies.

"We must be getting close," he said.

Antimone acknowledged his statement with a grunt. Their imprisonment seemed to have lasted forever. At least the general had spared them from the cauldron inside the metal container and allowed them to return to the cabin. Now boredom was the main enemy. Keeping a boisterous three-year-old entertained had sapped her energy. With few resources to hand, she and Jason had resorted to making up stories for their son. As she concluded Paul's latest request for a tale involving a monkey, a dog and a magic rabbit, she was ready to scream.

"And so they lived happily ever after."

"No, they didn't," Paul said. "The monkey had a baby and—"

"Why don't you come and look out of the window?" Jason asked, flashing a glance of sympathy at Antimone.

Paul bounded over to his father. Jason lifted the boy so he could peer through the circular glass frame and pointed. "Over there. Can you see the land?"

Paul nodded. "When are we going home, Daddy?"

"Well… it'll be a few days yet."

"Are the nasty men coming to live with us?"

"No, of course not."

"I want to go back to our house."

"I know, but we can't at the moment."

"Why?"

"Because we're stuck on a ship."

"But why?"

Jason glanced towards Antimone, searching for an answer. She shrugged in response. "This is all a big adventure, isn't it?" he said. "You hadn't been on a boat trip before this one, but you have now."

"I still want to go home."

"We will… soon."

"Put me down." The three-year-old wriggled in his father's grasp until Jason lowered him to the ground.

Paul clambered onto the bottom bunk. "I want another story," he announced.

Antimone groaned. "Why don't you try to sleep?"

"I'm not tired."

"It's after your bedtime. Maybe if you lie down and close your eyes, you'll start to feel sleepy."

The past few days had played havoc with Paul's sleeping patterns, not helped by the lack of exercise during their confinement in the tiny cabin.

Jason moved away from the porthole and approached his son. "Let's take your shoes off and get you under the sheets." Antimone watched as Paul placed his head on the lumpy pillow. At least the bed-linen was clean compared to the stinking mattress in the container.

Jason perched himself alongside Paul and gently stroked his hair. After several minutes, the three-year-old's breathing settled into a regular pattern. Taking care not to disturb the sleeping child, Jason rose gingerly and crept over to Antimone. There, he crouched beside her.

"How are you holding up?" he whispered.

Antimone took a deep breath, then exhaled slowly through her mouth. "I'm terrified about what'll happen to us."

"We'll find a way out of this."

Antimone studied Jason's features. "Nobody's coming to rescue us, are they?"

He hesitated before replying. He met her gaze for a moment, then looked away. "No, I don't suppose they are."

"When we saw that drone, I thought we'd finally be freed."

"Yeah. But then Max Perrin opened his big mouth and gave them the ammunition to blackmail our government. He obviously hadn't previously mentioned that Rosalind Baxter created the virus with his father. Why do you think that was?"

Antimone bit her bottom lip in concentration. "It's probably not something he wanted to broadcast. He realised he could earn some money by selling us out. The North Africans would already have known about Baxter's involvement in developing the drug, Lucinase. It's common knowledge, and that's why they grabbed her. But if he mentioned the part she played in the creation of the virus, he'd also be incriminating his own father. Whatever the reason, it's out in the open now."

"Still, if he hadn't said anything, we'd be on our way home instead of heading towards Africa."

Two days earlier, as the general had promised, the warship gradually fell back before disappearing over the horizon. Even when they passed through the Strait of Gibraltar, within ten miles of the British base located there, no military forces approached the ship.

"I can't believe he sold us out," Antimone said.

"There's something seriously wrong with that guy," Jason replied. "He still feels justified for everything he did because you tripped him. But I suppose he didn't exactly have a good role model for a parent."

"I could say the same about you, but you turned out okay."

"That's the weird thing. My mother—my adoptive mother—spent all her time working, but she never treated me badly. I find it hard to reconcile what we discovered about the crimes she committed with her behaviour towards me. She was always just my mum."

A grim expression settled on Antimone's features. "Don't forget, the murderous bitch threatened to kill us both. She told us she wouldn't have gone through with it, but I saw the look in her eyes. She practically admitted that she had no intention of letting me go. If there's an opportunity to escape, she's on her own. And if that bastard, Max Perrin, gets in the way, God help him."

29

Wednesday 16th July 2036

The port of Tunis

5 days after the attack at the Olympics

The clank of metal on the roof of the container dragged Antimone from the drowsy half-sleep in which she had been lingering for the past couple of hours.

"Something's happening," she said, reaching over the sleeping form of her son to shake Jason by the shoulder.

In the pitch dark, he groaned and propped himself up on an elbow. The four prisoners lay sideways across the ancient mattress. Rosalind Baxter occupied one end and the family of three, the other. Both groups were eager to avoid any contact. After much begging and cajoling, the general had permitted the occupants to take the sheets from the cabin with them. They were a poor fit, having been designed for the narrow bunk beds, but the thin covering was infinitely better than lying directly on the suspiciously stained bedding.

Even though it was night-time, the interior was still uncomfortably warm. Shaladi had promised that on this occasion their confinement would be a short one, lasting only as long as it took to unload the container. Once again, he had warned them against making any noise.

Suddenly, the floor tilted. Antimone squealed in fright at the unexpected lurch sideways. For a moment, she had the sensation of being on a giant swing until the motion smoothed out. Moments later, a loud thud reverberated through the interior. Paul stirred briefly, letting out a whimper of protest before his breathing settled back into a steady pattern.

"We must be down," Jason whispered.

"What's going on?" came a bleary voice from his right.

"As far as I can tell, we're on dry land," Jason replied. They were the first words he had spoken to his mother since the guards had returned them to the metal box.

"What time is it?"

Jason peered at the faintly glowing digits of the watch band on his wrist. "It's just after three in the morning."

"Wake me if anything else happens."

Jason sat fully upright, straining his ears to detect sounds of movement from outside.

"What is it?" Antimone asked.

"Nothing. I guess we wait until they come and get us."

"Let's hope they arrive before the sun comes up. I imagine it'll be like a furnace in here, especially with no ventilation."

Jason lay down again. A waft of something unpleasant permeated through the thin sheet. He turned sideways and reached out an arm, touching Antimone on the shoulder. She took his hand in hers and kissed it gently. Despite their dire circumstances, both drifted into an uneasy sleep.

A clang from outside woke all the adults simultaneously. The metal door swung open, and the bright beam of a torch swept over the occupants.

"I know it is the middle of the night, but everybody must come out now," called General Shaladi, clapping his hands.

With a groan, Jason levered himself off the mattress. A glance at his wrist told him another hour and a half had passed. He shuffled over to the collapsed wheelchair and reassembled it into working order. Paul lay in the same spot, asleep despite the disturbance taking place around him. Jason left his son where he was, bent over Antimone and lifted her in his arms. After depositing her in the chair, he returned to Paul and hoisted the three-year-old off the sheet. The sleeping child moaned without waking up. Placing him in his mother's lap, Jason wheeled the pair out into the Tunisian night.

The location reminded him of the shipping yard in Grangemouth. Huge, multi-coloured containers lay stacked across a fenced compound. One major difference was the chirping of cicadas, which provided a constant background noise. Jason inhaled the warm, dusty air. The odours of raw fish and jasmine competed for dominance as he filled his lungs.

The general paced impatiently beside his three men. His daughter, Aya, and a smug-looking Max Perrin stood apart, several yards away.

"You two and the child get into that car," Shaladi said, pointing to the nearest of two large, black vehicles with tinted, one-way windows. One guard pulled on the handle and swung the sliding door back. Inside, two rows of seats faced each other. A glass partition separated the passenger area from the driver.

The general beckoned Rosalind forwards. "You too."

"It's not autonomous then," Jason asked, gesturing at the man waiting patiently behind the steering wheel.

"Not everywhere in the world is quite as technologically advanced as your country," Shaladi replied. "Here, we still do things the old-fashioned way."

"I see you don't have a child seat either."

"And?" the general said.

Jason peeled Paul from his mother, eliciting another cry of protest, and fastened the seatbelt around his tiny body. He returned to Antimone and placed her next to their son by the furthest window.

Jason turned back to Shaladi. "What shall I do with the wheelchair?"

"Leave it. My men will take it with us."

Jason stepped further inside and settled into the one remaining space on the forward-facing row. Rosalind sat on the opposite side.

Shaladi spoke to the closest guard and pointed to the occupied car. As the man climbed into the vehicle, the general beckoned Max Perrin closer. A low conversation ensued, Perrin's face growing darker by the second.

Perrin took a pace backwards. "No, that wasn't the deal," he yelled.

Shaladi tilted his head towards the guard to his left. Seconds later, a pistol pointed at Perrin's chest.

Jason watched in fascination as his former classmate jabbed a finger at Shaladi.

"I'm not coming with you. I want the rest of the money paid into my account like you promised."

"Get in the car," the general growled.

"No."

Shaladi took the gun from his man and smashed the base of the grip into Perrin's face. Blood immediately welled from an inch-long gash in his cheek. Perrin dropped to one knee. The general muttered a command to his men. One of them jogged to the boot of the second vehicle, delved inside and withdrew a length of nylon rope.

He returned as Perrin pushed himself upright. The other guard yanked Perrin's hands behind his back while his colleague bound his wrists.

"I'll get you for this," Perrin yelled, the spittle flying from his mouth.

Shaladi took a pace forwards and slammed his fist into the defenceless man's stomach. He followed it up with a vicious punch to the side of the head. Perrin collapsed, the breath wheezing in his chest.

The general gestured towards the man with the rope. Moments later, Perrin found both his hands and feet trussed. Shaladi poked a booted foot into the abdomen of the prostrate figure. "I do not want to hear any noise during the journey. Am I clear?"

When there was no response, he swung his boot again, harder this time. "Is that clear?"

Perrin choked out a "Yes".

"Good. If there is shouting, you will suffer much pain, and then I will see to it that you are incapable of making further sounds."

The general gestured towards his men who lifted their new prisoner, one at each end, and slung him into the boot. He strolled to the first car and peered inside.

"I apologise for the unpleasantness. Mr Perrin will be joining us in Tripoli. Unfortunately, it is a long journey. I will see you when we arrive. Have a good trip."

The door slid shut with a metallic clunk.

As Jason turned forwards, he met his mother's gaze. A malevolent grin formed slowly on her face.

Part Three: Investigation

30

Wednesday 16th July 2036

Cabinet Room, 10 Downing Street, London

5 days after the attack at the Olympics

Andrew Jacobs rose to his feet and waited for the hubbub of conversation to die down.

"Good morning, everybody. Thank you for coming in."

"It must be important if we aren't allowed to bring any aides," said the Home Secretary, a smartly dressed man in his early forties. At most cabinet meetings, a circle of men and women sat at the periphery of the room, ready if required to assist the political leaders of their departments.

"I don't seem to have received an agenda," added the Chancellor of the Exchequer. She was a thin, black woman in her late fifties. Her fingers fiddled with the string of pearls around her neck.

Heads shook, and a variety of whispered exchanges took place.

"When you hear what I have to say," Jacobs said, "you'll understand why no aides are present and why we haven't published an agenda. I want to start by telling you all that I plan to resign."

A deathly hush settled over the room.

"What I'm about to tell you will be difficult for you to take in, and there will certainly be dark times ahead. It is just under two decades since the deadly Orestes virus first emerged. Until recently, no woman had survived childbirth for a very long time. Three years ago, I learned that this terrible disease did not evolve naturally; it escaped from a British laboratory."

Consternation erupted around the table. Voices rose as the members of the cabinet tried to make themselves heard. Andrew Jacobs watched on helplessly as the volume increased.

"Please," the Prime Minister shouted, raising his hands. "Let me finish what I have to say, and then I will answer your questions."

Gradually, the sound level reduced.

"Who was responsible?" called out the Secretary of State for Health. Anger blazed on the face of the grey-haired man sitting to Jacobs' left.

"The virus originated at Ilithyia Biotechnology, a company run at the time by Rosalind Baxter and Nigel Perrin. The events surrounding the release are not entirely clear, but from what I have learned subsequently, it was an accident. We can't be sure, but it seems there was no deliberate intent to infect the population.

That doesn't alter the fact that the company's actions were highly irresponsible in both failing to follow adequate safety precautions in the first place and not informing the authorities afterwards.

"Just over three years ago, by sheer chance, a woman survived childbirth at Ilithyia's facility in Northstowe. Her survival provided a vital clue in the development of a drug to treat this awful disease. In fact, the owners of the company believed this event was so significant they told the mother's family she and her child had died. They held her prisoner in a secret underground laboratory and studied her biological makeup. We only uncovered the facts sometime later when Mrs Baxter's adopted son, who was a friend of the kidnapped mother, alerted the authorities. As it turns out, he was also the father of the child, but that's another story.

"I found myself in an impossible situation. The same organisation responsible for creating the virus had developed a cure. In doing so, several of their employees committed a range of serious crimes, including kidnap and murder. Mrs Baxter threatened to destroy all their research and findings. She had also imprisoned three innocent people—the mother and father of the child and the child's grandfather—and planned to execute them unless I accepted her terms.

"The price for providing the treatment and sparing the captives was a full, legally binding pardon. As part of the deal, she agreed to complete development of the drug—the same Lucinase now routinely prescribed to all pregnant mothers—then sell the business and hand over ninety percent of the proceeds to childcare charities. By this stage, Nigel Perrin was already dead, murdered by Mrs Baxter in front of my eyes because he was about to cave in. They had been careful to ensure nobody else at the company knew any details about the drug's composition. I had no option but to accept the agreement."

Stunned silence greeted the Prime Minister's statement.

The Secretary of State for Health was the first to speak. "That bloody woman stood in this very room and briefed us on her company's progress. I remember thinking at the time she was arrogant and full of herself, but I never took her for a murderer."

"You were more than happy to continue funding her," the Chancellor of the Exchequer snapped in reply. "I recall trying to convince you to transfer the funds to international research efforts. If my memory serves, you were also one of those pushing for her to receive a damehood in the new year's honours list."

"Excuse me, Prime Minister," said a rake-thin man in his mid-fifties. Gregory Charlton had held the role of Defence Secretary for the past decade. "Clearly, you didn't see fit to inform us three years ago. So, what has changed now?"

Jacobs rubbed his eyes. An overwhelming tiredness settled over him. "The Republic of North Africa has discovered what happened."

Once again, the room broke out in an uproar. Several minutes passed before the sound reduced to a level where Jacobs could be heard.

"Somehow they found out that Mrs Baxter created the virus," he said, speaking above the babble of voices. "They're threatening to tell the rest of the world unless we agree to their demands. I might add that they have kidnapped at least four of our nationals, including Mrs Baxter, the child and the child's parents I mentioned earlier."

"Is this anything to do with the attack at the Olympics?" Charlton asked.

"Yes. Antimone Lessing was, in fact, the first to survive childbirth."

"The wheelchair girl?"

"We agreed to keep secret her natural immunity from the virus and her role in developing the cure. We thought it might make her a target. Despite our best efforts, it turns out we were right. We have determined the incident at the stadium was actually a kidnapping. They also snatched her child and her partner, the father of the boy, at the same time. They abducted Mrs Baxter separately."

"So, the taking of their own people was all a smokescreen? Sneaky bastards. I can hazard a guess, but what are their demands?"

"As you might expect, an end to sanctions, drugs for the virus and access to any future research. As you are probably aware, a new strain has recently emerged in North Africa. Now it's attacking their children. We think they took Mrs Baxter to develop their own treatment."

"This is outrageous. We can't just let them kidnap British citizens when they feel like it."

"I suppose you called us here because you plan to call their bluff," said the Secretary of State for Health. "Do we have any idea where they're holding our nationals?"

"Yes, I won't allow us to be blackmailed by a rogue state. At the moment, we believe they're transporting our people from Tunis to the Republic of North Africa by road," Jacobs replied. "We don't know their ultimate destination, but it's likely to be somewhere around Tripoli."

"The bigger question is what we tell the rest of the world," said the Chancellor of the Exchequer. "The reparations will bankrupt this country."

"But this crime was committed by a private company," the Secretary of State for Health replied. "They can't hold the government responsible."

"I'm not sure the international community will see it that way," Jacobs said in a resigned voice. "No doubt they'll argue that once we had a cure, we should have provided the drugs to anybody who needed them."

"Didn't we do that?"

"Well, yes, apart from the obvious exceptions, which is presumably why the Reponans took matters into their own hands. And Ilithyia Biotechnology still charged everybody. They made billions from the sales of Lucinase. The taxes more than funded our own purchase of the drug."

"Let's just hand her over to the International Court of Justice. We may not be able to prosecute her, but that won't stop anybody else having a go."

Jacobs sat and watched the discussions unfold around him. After several minutes of intense debate, the Defence Secretary stood and banged the table for attention.

"Excuse me, everybody. There's something I'd like to say to you all. Andrew Jacobs has led this country and this party for over a decade. At the start of this meeting, he announced his intention to resign. If everything he has told us is true—and I have no reason to doubt him—then he faced an impossible decision: allowing a murderer to go free or standing by as three innocent people died along with countless pregnant women. It's not a choice I'd have wanted to make myself.

"Now is a time for strong leadership. I recommend that we ask him to continue as Prime Minister, at least until this crisis is resolved."

Most heads around the room nodded together with voices of assent.

Jacobs rose once again, his gaze lingering on each person at the table in turn. His eyes took on a steely sheen. "I'm humbled by your support and will put all my efforts into addressing our problems. Thank you."

31

Wednesday 16th July 2036

Tripoli Infectious Diseases Hospital, Republic of North Africa
5 days after the attack at the Olympics

Jason leant forwards in his seat as the first of the black vehicles rolled past the raised barrier and through the entrance to the underground car park. Its twin followed a few feet behind.

"Does that mean we've arrived?" Antimone asked the guard sitting opposite.

The man ignored her question. He turned away and gazed through the tinted glass.

The car slowed to a stop at a second security point where two men, each carrying a locally manufactured variant of the ancient AK-47 automatic rifle, stepped forwards. The driver wound down the front window and held a brief conversation in Arabic. After a few seconds, the rear window also lowered. A wall of warm air rolled over the occupants as an armed guard peered inside, studying each of the passengers carefully. Satisfied by what he saw, he stood back and waved the vehicle on.

Several turns later, the engine fell silent. With a groan, the man behind the wheel eased himself out of his seat and strolled stiffly to the side of the car. He grabbed the handle and slid open the door. The pleasant coolness of the interior dissipated immediately to be replaced by an oppressive heat accompanied by the smell of exhaust fumes.

"Out! Now!"

They were the first words he had spoken over the entire journey. Antimone leant over to unstrap Paul. Her son's head lolled to the side. He opened one bleary eye, emitted a brief cry of protest, then closed his eyes again.

The guard got out, followed by Rosalind. Jason picked up the sleeping child and shuffled across the seat. He stepped out onto the concrete and winced at the harsh glare of the fluorescent lighting. The second car drew up alongside. The engine rattled to a halt. Moments later, a suited General Shaladi, his daughter and a pair of armed men emerged.

"Good, we are here," Shaladi announced. He muttered a few words in Arabic to the nearest guard, who moved to the rear of the first vehicle and returned carrying the folded wheelchair.

Paul continued to sleep, his head resting on his father's shoulder. Jason's gaze wandered over to the six adults. "Could someone look after my son while I get Antimone out?"

Nobody stepped forwards. The general gestured to one of his men.

"I'll hold him," Rosalind said before the man could move, holding out her arms.

Jason hesitated for a moment before handing over the sleeping child. A thread of drool landed on Rosalind's shirt as Paul's head lolled against her shoulder. Rosalind glanced down at the damp spot with a look of distaste.

Jason pretended he hadn't noticed and turned his attention to the folded wheelchair. A few seconds later, he clicked the frame into place.

"Is anybody going to get me out of here?" Antimone called from inside the car.

"I'm coming," Jason replied, pushing the chair around to the far side of the vehicle. He slid back the door and lifted her out, then deposited her into the seat.

"Thanks," she murmured.

For a moment, he contemplated making a run for it, but reality soon returned; he could hardly leave Paul behind. In any case, they wouldn't get ten paces before the guards intervened. In a minor act of defiance, he left the door open as he wheeled her towards the waiting group.

Antimone clenched her fists when she spotted who was holding her son. "Give him to me," she snapped.

"You're welcome," Rosalind replied, her face an expressionless mask, "but you could say please."

Antimone accepted the sleeping child. She opened her mouth to hurl an insult back when a commotion a few feet away drew her attention. Two guards dropped a bruised and battered Max Perrin onto the concrete beside them.

General Shaladi stepped up to the prostrate form and prodded a boot into his ribs. "Now, are you going to behave, or do I need to keep you restrained?"

Max muttered an inaudible response.

The general jabbed him again with his toecap. "I'm sorry, I didn't quite hear that."

"I said yes," Max replied in a louder voice.

"Excellent. In that case, we can untie you." Shaladi flicked a finger towards the bound figure and watched while his men unravelled the knots.

Max rose shakily to his feet, wincing as he rubbed his wrists.

"From now on you will do exactly as I say. Understood?"

Max nodded.

The general glowered at him for a second longer, then turned back to the rest of the group. "Right. Let's get you inside. Follow me." He led them towards a set of swing doors labelled with Arabic script. "Wait here," he commanded.

Moments later, two men in white hazmat suits emerged. One carried a clipboard while the other held an instrument that looked like a futuristic pistol in his hands.

"Roll up the sleeve on your left arm," Shaladi said.

Tired after the long journey, the prisoners did as instructed without complaint. The first figure moved from person to person, starting with the North Africans. As he approached each subject, he held the device against the exposed skin and pressed the trigger, generating a sharp click. A few seconds later, he peered at the small display on the top of the instrument and read out the reading, which his colleague noted down on the sheet of paper. The general confirmed each person's name as they passed around the group.

When it came to Jason's turn, the man pressed the object against his arm. A sharp sting accompanied the clicking sound. "What's this for?" he asked, wincing.

"We must check that you do not have the new virus," Shaladi said.

"And do I?"

"No," the general replied, moving on to Antimone. Paul was the last. He cried for a moment but soon returned to a state of drowsiness in the stifling heat.

Shaladi moved to the front and addressed the group. "You will be pleased to learn that you are all clear."

"What would have happened if we weren't?" Jason asked.

The general's brow lowered in annoyance. "We would be forced to keep you in isolation. Now, please follow these men."

The two white-suited figures pushed through the swing doors and led the way down a brightly lit corridor with no doorways on either side. The prisoners followed, trailed by Shaladi and the three guards. Both drivers stayed with their vehicles.

The air became cooler the further inside they progressed. At the same time, the acrid odour of disinfectant grew stronger. The passageway ended at a set of double doors, each with a small, inset, rectangular window.

Shaladi moved to the front and pressed a button mounted on the wall. A buzzing noise sounded from within. Several seconds passed before a face peered through the glass. Moments later, a clunk signalled the operation of the lock, and a thin man in a white doctor's coat stepped out. The most noticeable feature about him was his jet-black hair. Antimone wondered whether it was dyed or a wig.

"Welcome, welcome," he said, holding the door open. "Do come in."

The general entered, and the white-coated man followed the group, allowing the doors to swing closed behind him. Moments later, the lock shot home with a loud clunk.

Jason inhaled the scent of antiseptic and fresh paint. They stood inside a square area with doors set in each of the four sides. The walls and ceiling were painted white. A reception desk, currently unmanned, sat in the centre of the room.

The door on the left opened, and five armed men wearing dark uniforms emerged. They held their weapons ready but with the barrels pointing down, warily eyeing the newcomers. The man in the lab coat shuffled from foot to foot in excitement, studying each of the new arrivals in turn. His every movement was short and abrupt, like a robin pecking for worms. "Allow me to introduce myself. I am Professor Halfon, the director of this facility. You must be General Shaladi. And this is your lovely daughter, Aya, I assume. I am pleased to meet you."

Halfon pumped the general's hand and then Aya's.

The professor turned his attention to Rosalind. "Mrs Baxter, we have much to discuss."

Rosalind folded her arms and stared stony-faced at the director.

Next, he focused on Max. His genial mood lost some of its shine as he studied the bruised cheekbones and dried blood around the nose. "Mr Perrin, I once attended a lecture given by your father. I was sad to learn of his passing."

"His murderer is standing right there," Max replied with a grimace, pointing at Rosalind.

Halfon ignored the comment and spoke to Antimone. "Miss Lessing, if what I have heard is correct, you are a remarkable woman. I am fascinated to discover how you survived. And this must be your son, Paul."

Once again, a wall of silence met his greeting.

"And finally, the father of the child, Mr Baxter."

"Actually, it's Floyd," Jason replied.

The professor stared at him in confusion. "I do not understand."

"My name is Jason Floyd."

"But I—"

"I changed my surname back to my father's after…"

"Oh, I see," Halfon said. "Well, welcome, all. You must be tired and hungry after your journey. Please follow me, and we will find something for you to eat."

As he turned, Rosalind placed a hand on his shoulder. Halfon spun around.

"What's going on here?" she asked. "You kidnap us and transport us halfway across the world, then greet us like a long-lost uncle. You can't seriously expect us to help you?"

The genial expression vanished from the professor's face in an instant. "Let me be absolutely clear, Mrs Baxter. You will assist us with whatever we ask for, or your life will become very unpleasant. My sources tell me you were responsible for the terrible disease that is afflicting this planet. There are many people in this country who have lost loved ones and would dearly like to spend several minutes alone with you. But you are of no use to me dead. In here, you are safe, but out there… Well, let's just say, I don't think you would survive for long."

"You can't force me to work for you."

Halfon marched to the reception desk and picked up a black, cylindrical object. He returned and stood opposite the former head of Ilithyia Biotechnology. He glared back at her with narrowed eyes. "We will see."

He jabbed the end of the cylinder into her shoulder and pressed the button on the side. A sharp crack echoed through the room. Rosalind immediately dropped to the floor where she flopped about, writhing in agony. The rest of the group watched on in horrified silence.

"We may not be as advanced in treating diseases as you Westerners," Halfon said, raising his voice above the gasps of the prostrate woman, "but we have learned many ways to inflict pain." He barked a command in Arabic, and two of his men grabbed an arm each and dragged a semi-conscious Rosalind Baxter through the doorway at the back of the reception area.

The commotion woke Paul, who began to cry. Antimone tried to shush him, but that only made matters worse. Soon, he was bawling at full pitch.

General Shaladi winced at the high-pitched noise. "Well, if you have everything you need, Aya and I will be leaving."

Halfon gestured to the armed men standing behind him. The barrels of their automatic rifles lifted to point at the general and his daughter.

"I'm sorry," the professor said, "but I regret that won't be possible. I am under strict instructions to keep you here with the other prisoners. Now, please place any weapons you may be carrying on the ground."

Shaladi opened his mouth in shock, but no words emerged. After a few seconds, he regained his composure. "What are you talking about? I have always been loyal to this regime. Who gave these orders?"

"They came from Mullah Awad himself. The rest of the world believes that you were abducted at the Olympics. If you were to appear in public, they would know this to be a lie."

"I could stay out of sight. I have completed this mission exactly as ordered, at considerable risk to both myself and my daughter. And this is how I am rewarded? I demand to speak to the mullah."

"Unfortunately, he is otherwise engaged. I am sure he will find time to talk to you in the coming days, but for now you must put down your weapons."

"Or what? You will shoot me?"

Shaladi's soldiers looked to him for guidance. He gave a slight shake of the head.

Halfon sighed. "There has been enough unpleasantness already. Let me point out to you that they"—he gestured towards the British contingent—"are of great importance to the future of our country. You, on the other hand, have no such value. If you do not surrender immediately, I will order my men to open fire."

The general stared belligerently at the director for a moment, then slowly withdrew the pistol from his jacket and placed it on the ground. "All right, but do not think this ends here. I shall complain to the highest level of our government about my treatment." He uttered a brief command. Moments later, the members of his team placed their weapons on the floor.

Jason glanced sideways at Max Perrin. Their eyes met briefly. A smirk flashed across Perrin's face, then disappeared just as quickly.

Halfon nodded to the nearest guard, who scooped up the assortment of guns and knives and carried them through the door from which he had emerged moments earlier. The remaining men kept their weapons trained on the prisoners.

The professor waited for his man to return. "Given the circumstances, I think perhaps we should escort you to your accommodations directly. Please follow me."

He strode towards the doorway through which Rosalind had been dragged and down a featureless, white corridor. The smell of fresh paint and disinfectant became stronger. He stopped at a door with a reinforced glass window, presented a card to the wall-mounted reader and pressed a button on the keypad beneath. The electronically operated bolt slid back with a metallic clunk. Halfon ushered Shaladi and his daughter inside.

"Each room contains a bathroom. My men will return shortly with refreshments."

Shaladi turned and glared at the professor but said nothing. Seconds later, Halfon touched the control panel again, and the lock clicked into the closed position.

Halfon repeated the procedure at the next doorway. "Miss Lessing, Mr…" He hesitated.

"Floyd," Jason interjected.

"Yes, of course. The pair of you and your child in here, please."

Jason pushed the wheelchair holding Antimone and Paul inside. Three single beds extended from the wall with just enough gap between for a person to walk. A folded beige blanket and a white towel sat at the foot of each bed. The décor matched everything else in the facility, comprising white walls and ceiling. Judging by the odour of fresh paint, the decoration work had only recently finished.

"I'm getting a strong sense of déjà vu," Antimone muttered as the door slid shut, followed almost immediately by the thud of the lock.

32

Thursday 17th July 2036

Tripoli Infectious Diseases Hospital, Republic of North Africa
6 days after the attack at the Olympics

Rosalind Baxter opened her eyes and found herself lying fully clothed on top of the sheets of a single bed. Her feet rested on a folded blanket and a towel. For a moment, she tried to remember how she had arrived there.

As her brain ground into gear, the memories returned: the black cylinder, the jab to the shoulder and the sudden, all-consuming agony. She sat upright and gingerly probed the area of contact. She undid the topmost buttons of her shirt and pulled back the material to study the twin purple bruises on her left side, just below the clavicle.

With a wince of pain, she refastened her blouse and inspected her surroundings. She was in a room, approximately five metres square. Every surface was white, the uniformity broken only by a large clock with an analogue dial hanging on the wall. There were no windows other than a rectangular clear panel set in the closed door in the corner. On the opposite side was a second, partially open door. A single, unshielded bulb hung from the ceiling. On top of the small bedside cabinet to her left rested a plastic tray containing a covered plate and a glass of water.

As she sat gathering her wits, she noticed a green flashing light in her right eye at the periphery of her vision. After a moment's confusion when she thought the source originated from inside the room, she realised it was a status signal from her prosthetic implant.

She touched her ear and murmured, "Expand."

A message box appeared at the centre of her view. *Battery Low.*

"That's all I need."

The damned thing needs recharging. It wasn't something she had worried about before. She vaguely recalled the doctors telling her after the operation that her false eye contained a rechargeable cell. They had reassured her that the batteries would recharge overnight while she slept, as long as she kept the specially designed pillow containing the inductive charger plugged into the mains. She remembered asking what would happen if the battery ever went flat, but right now she couldn't recall the answer. No doubt she would find out soon enough.

She swung her legs onto the floor. Somebody had placed her shoes beside the bed. She slipped her feet inside and pushed herself upright. The sudden increase in pressure sent a stabbing pain through her knee. Her fall the previous night must have exacerbated the injury she sustained while trying to escape from the truck. Resting a hand on the mattress for support, she stumbled towards the open door into a narrow, tiled bathroom. The room adopted the ubiquitous white colour scheme of the facility, with a shower stall at one end, a toilet at the other and a sink in the middle.

She relieved herself, then splashed the lukewarm offering from the cold tap onto her face. The metal hoop beside the basin was empty. She navigated her way back, blinking to clear the water from her eyes. When she re-entered the main room, a figure was standing in the doorway to the outside corridor.

"Good morning, Mrs Baxter," Professor Halfon said. "I trust you slept well."

Rosalind grabbed the towel off the bed and dried herself. "No thanks to you. Don't you know it's bad manners to enter a lady's bedroom without knocking first."

The director acknowledged her statement with a tilt of the head. "I should point out there are cameras in every room within this facility. There is no such thing as privacy here. But I must apologise for the unpleasantness last night. I hope we can get over that and work together productively. Now, I see you have not eaten the food we brought you. Would you care to join me for breakfast to discuss my proposed itinerary?"

"You can talk about your itinerary all you want, but I still have no intention of working for you."

"At least allow me to show you around our facilities. Perhaps you will reconsider."

Despite her misgivings, Rosalind was eager to learn what the professor had in store for her. "Fine, I'll take a look, but before we start, I'd like to wash properly and change my clothes. I feel as if I've been wearing this stuff forever."

Halfon pointed at the bedside cabinet. "You will find something to wear in there together with basic toiletries. I will return in twenty minutes." The man turned away, allowing the door to close behind him.

Rosalind knelt and examined the items. She pulled out a clear plastic pouch containing soap, toothbrush and a small tube—toothpaste, she assumed. She deposited the pack on the bed. The folded clothes beneath comprised plain, white underwear and a cheap, blue dress. She inspected the room, trying to spot the cameras but couldn't identify anything beyond the smooth walls.

She removed her shirt, then wrapped the towel around herself before removing the remainder of her clothing. The linoleum felt cool on her feet as she padded into the bathroom. She brushed her teeth at the sink, then turned on the shower. A spluttering stream of lukewarm water emerged from the nozzle. She adjusted the controls, but the temperature remained the same. With a glance behind and keeping her back to the rest of the room, she stepped beneath the flow. The bar of soap barely produced a lather, but it still came as a relief to rinse away the grime of the last few days.

When she had finished, she dried herself. She returned to the bedroom with the towel fastened above her chest and slid the loose-fitting, blue dress over her head before allowing it to drop. She manoeuvred the bra into place beneath the coarse material and slipped into the panties.

There was no comb in the plastic pouch, so she ran her fingers through her damp hair. No sooner had she finished than a clunk emanated from the door and it swung open. Either the timing was a coincidence or they really were watching everything she did.

"Please follow me," Halfon said. "I will see that your clothes are washed and returned to you."

Rosalind followed him down a corridor. A series of equally spaced doors lined both walls, each inset with a glass panel. They emerged through a doorway at the end into an area containing four plastic tables, each with three chairs arranged per long side. Jason, the girl and their son sat at one table. General Shaladi, his daughter and their team took up another while Max Perrin occupied the third on his own. All the prisoners wore cheap Western clothes, dresses like her own for the women, and loose-fitting shirts and trousers for the men. A pair of armed guards watched over them.

The eyes of all the occupants tracked the new arrivals as they entered, but nobody offered a greeting. The professor gestured towards a steel cabinet on the opposite side of the room. On top sat plates containing an assortment of different foods, including a range of breads and fruits. A basket of plastic cutlery lay beside the food.

"Help yourself," Halfon said.

Rosalind grabbed a piece of fruit loaf, an apple and a banana. She followed him to the one vacant table and lowered herself into the chair on the opposite side.

Halfon placed his elbows on the table's surface and leant forwards. "When we have finished here, I will introduce you to our team and show you the equipment. We have spared no expense."

Rosalind uttered a non-committal grunt as she tucked into her meal.

"We have a Genesys four thousand gene sequencing machine."

"I hope you aren't trying to impress me. That technology is at least five years old." Secretly, she was surprised they had got hold of such sophisticated equipment. But she wasn't about to reveal her true thoughts.

The professor seemed taken aback at her apparent lack of enthusiasm. "The Americans won't sell us the latest machines, but it is still good enough, is it not?"

Rosalind shrugged her shoulders. "Those things need a lot of maintenance. I assume you've assembled a team of technicians to keep it running."

"Yes, of course," Halfon replied, but his thoughtful expression told a different story. He watched in silence as Rosalind consumed her meal. "Shall we go?" he asked as she placed the last piece of bread in her mouth.

"Is there no coffee?"

The professor tutted. He pushed back his chair, strolled to the steel cabinet and returned seconds later with a cup of steaming black liquid.

"What about milk?"

Halfon let out a huff of exasperation. "We only have goat's milk. I do not think you will like this."

"Don't worry. I'll drink it as it is."

The director drummed his fingers on the table as Rosalind sipped the hot beverage. "I've had better."

"You should be grateful. Most of my countrymen do not have the opportunity to consume such luxuries."

Rosalind grimaced as she put the half-full cup down. "Aren't they the lucky ones?" she muttered. "All right, show me what you've got." She rose slowly, wincing as she flexed her bruised knee.

Halfon led her to the doorway opposite the one through which they had entered, their progress tracked by every other eye in the room. He held a card to the reader. The lock released with a clunk, and he pushed through the door.

A large open space greeted them. Half a dozen large floor-standing machines occupied the periphery, each surrounded by workstations. Shelves holding an assortment of glassware and chemicals behind padlocked transparent doors split the room up into sections. Computers dotted the work surfaces. On the right, glass panels provided three sides of a square, enclosing an area at least twice the size of Rosalind's bedroom. Through the windows, Rosalind could see workbenches on which a variety of equipment rested. There was no way in or out other than through the door in the outside wall.

Between ten and fifteen scientists, not one female among them, congregated in small groups. All wore white lab coats and seemed focused on their work, barely glancing up at the visitors. Four armed guards patrolled the workspace.

"Doctor Kubar," Halfon called.

A scientist on the far side of the room rose from behind his computer screen and hurried to greet the professor. The man was short, standing only two inches taller than Rosalind.

"This is Rosalind Baxter," the director announced. "She is the former head of Ilithyia Biotechnology."

Kubar extended a hand. "Pleased to meet you." His palm was clammy as Rosalind accepted the shake.

"Doctor Kubar is one of our foremost scientists. Perhaps he could introduce you to the team and show you our equipment. Meanwhile, I have other matters to attend to. You will be interested to see the demonstration I have planned for you later this afternoon."

The doctor waited until his superior was out of earshot before speaking again. "We are very honoured to have you working with us on this project. However, I must admit I am surprised that somebody with your background would be prepared to come to The Republic of North Africa. This is my country, but there are many problems here, and it would not suit everybody."

Rosalind stared at the man. His words seemed genuine. She hesitated for a moment, unsure how to respond. Maybe this was some kind of test. She chose not to reveal her situation. "It was an offer I couldn't refuse," she said, maintaining a deadpan face.

"I see," Kubar said. "Unfortunately, we always must pay much money to get what we need." His tone brightened. "Let me show you our machines."

Rosalind scrunched her eyes closed, distracted by the flashing green light at the edge of her vision.

"Is something wrong?" Kubar asked.

Rosalind blinked twice. "It's nothing. Professor Halfon already mentioned the Genesys four thousand. What else have you got?"

The doctor guided her to the nearest machine. An overweight man in his early fifties was peering at the display. As they drew nearer, he pressed a button on the front panel. "Allow me to introduce my colleague, Dr Brandt," Kubar said.

The scientist turned to the new arrivals. His eyes widened in surprise. "Mrs Baxter?"

"So, you two already know each other?"

"Have we met?" Rosalind asked.

Brandt shook hands. "I have attended many conferences in Europe. I watched your presentation on viral mutation rates five years ago in Berlin: very interesting. Please call me Gerhard."

"Gerhard Brandt, that name rings a bell. I remember reading something in the press—"

Brandt's face flushed red. "Yes, that was some time ago. Unfortunately, the regulators decided my methods crossed ethical boundaries. I may have cut a few corners, but I still believe the risks were worth it. Anyway, you won't find such restrictions in place here. And thanks to the scientific authorities in Europe, my opportunities to work elsewhere are somewhat limited."

Rosalind recalled the scandal. Brandt had been caught performing unauthorised experiments on human subjects and had been struck off the medical register. It seemed he was here of his own volition. "What are you working on?"

"I'm developing an uncoating inhibitor using this Labtech molecular synthesiser. It holds promise, but initial patient trials have shown up some severe allergic reactions."

"I assume there was no reaction during animal tests?"

Brandt stared at Rosalind for a second before replying. "We went straight to human testing."

"I see." In the highly regulated medical industry of the West, that kind of approach would be unthinkable. Rosalind glanced towards Kubar and detected an almost imperceptible shake of the head.

"Thank you, Dr Brandt," Kubar said. "We will talk more later."

They strolled to the next machine, which was unattended. Kubar cleared his throat. "You will find that the methods used here are… somewhat different to what you are familiar with. I hope this will not stop you working with us."

Rosalind shrugged. "I don't really have much choice." Seeing his confusion, she decided to reveal her true situation. "They took me from my home. I didn't choose to come here."

The doctor stared at her in surprise. "I had no idea. I can only apologise."

"It's not your fault. You didn't abduct me."

Kubar lowered his voice. "If I may offer one piece of advice to you, make yourself useful and do not go up against my superiors. Those who oppose the regime have a tendency to disappear."

33

Thursday 17th July 2036

Tripoli Infectious Diseases Hospital, Republic of North Africa
6 days after the attack at the Olympics

Professor Halfon drummed his fingers on the top of the desk as he waited in his office. He stopped for a moment and wiped his hands on his trousers. It wasn't every day Mullah Awad himself chose to make a surprise visit.

The last time had been three years ago during the opening of this refurbished section of the hospital when the cleric turned up unannounced. That had been a stressful event, and today would likely be no different. The man was notoriously intolerant of any failings in his subordinates. At least on this occasion, the religious leader had provided an hour's notice.

A message box popped up on the screen; the mullah's entourage had just left the airport. Halfon jumped up and left to greet the ruler of his country. He reached the reception area to discover his head of security waiting with a team of five armed men.

"Why are they carrying guns?" Halfon yelled.

"I'm sorry, sir. I thought—"

"You didn't think. That's the problem. Why am I surrounded by incompetent morons? You should know the mullah's people are the only ones permitted to carry weapons of any type in his presence. Get them out of my sight immediately. And make sure the rest of your team does the same."

The chastened head of security barked out a command. His men rushed away and returned moments later unarmed.

Halfon's heart thudded in his chest after the close call. After several failed assassination attempts, Mullah Awad was rightly paranoid about his personal safety. The director dared not imagine what would have happened if the leader of the country had arrived to discover a weapon-carrying reception committee. "Now, where is the convoy?" he asked.

"The mullah's cars have passed through the entry gates and will be here shortly."

"Well, let's not keep him waiting."

Halfon placed his card against the reader and pushed the door open. He stepped into the uncomfortable heat of the underground car park. Moments later, the roar of an approaching engine echoed through the concrete space. A grey van screeched to a halt by the entrance. As soon as it stopped moving, eight heavily armed men surged through the rear doors and took up position, weapons at the ready.

A black sedan drove up at a far more sedate pace and braked gently to a stop. A second dark-coloured van followed, stopping behind the car. Another group of weapon-toting troops emerged from the rearmost vehicle to take up station.

Nothing happened for a few seconds until an armed man raised his wrist and spoke into a device that looked like a large wristwatch. The driver of the limousine got out and rushed to the passenger door. Moments later, Mullah Awad eased himself out of the plush, air-conditioned interior.

Halfon stepped forwards and bowed his head. "Welcome, Mullah. I am honoured that you have chosen to visit my humble facility."

The bearded man in the black robes flicked a hand in dismissal. "Enough with the trivialities. I want to know how the research is going."

"Our… ah… guests only arrived yesterday. Our new recruit started work this morning, familiarising herself with the equipment."

"Her first task is to provide the information we need to manufacture Lucinase."

Halfon frowned in surprise. "But I thought—"

"The British have not yet agreed to our demand to supply us with the drug. I do not want to depend on foreign sources in the future, so we must obtain the instructions to make it ourselves."

"I understand, Mullah."

"Make sure she gives us everything we need to start production. I hear you used excessive force to reprimand her."

Halfon cursed inwardly. *How did he find out about that?* "She resisted initially, but now she is cooperating fully with my people."

The mullah narrowed his eyes. "I did not take the risks to capture this woman so you could risk her life before she has completed her work."

"Of course not, Mullah. It will not happen again."

"It better not. Show her to me. I want to meet her."

"Please follow me."

Halfon led the group into the facility. Half the mullah's men walked ahead of him; the rest followed behind. They emerged into the laboratory area and followed the professor towards the workstation where Dr Kubar sat alongside Rosalind Baxter. All conversation stopped immediately as heads whipped around to identify the visitors. Halfon breathed a sigh of relief that the members of the security team guarding the room appeared to be unarmed.

The North African doctor jumped to his feet at the sight of the new arrivals. Rosalind was slower to react, rising slowly with a wince of pain.

"This is one of my senior researchers, Dr Kubar."

"Yes, yes. We have already met," the mullah replied. "So, this is Mrs Baxter."

Judging by the way the woman glanced sharply at the cleric, she must have recognised the mention of her name.

She extended a hand. "Hello, I'm Rosalind Baxter," she said. When the bearded man failed to reciprocate her gesture, she slowly lowered her raised arm.

Halfon turned to Kubar. "You may leave us now." The doctor needed no second invitation as he bowed briefly at the mullah and went to talk to one of the other scientists.

The cleric in the black robe spoke in Arabic again. He stared at a spot between the professor and his prisoner, avoiding eye contact with both.

"Our leader, Mullah Awad, welcomes you to our country," Halfon translated. "He trusts that you have all the equipment you require to develop a cure."

"Pleased to meet you," Rosalind replied. "Some of the machines are a little dated, but the main issue is people to operate them."

Halfon began to translate, but the mullah cut him off. "Just because I choose not to address her in English, it does not mean I cannot understand her words. Tell her she must work with what we have."

Halfon addressed Rosalind. "The mullah understands your concerns and will do everything in his power to provide you with the equipment and personnel to perform the required tasks."

The bearded leader turned to Halfon and glowered at him. "That is not what I said."

The professor bowed again. "I have found she responds better to politeness rather than threats."

"I have a question," Rosalind began. "Will your boss allow me to leave if I deliver a cure?"

The mullah let out a grunt of derision. "The only thing I will release her to is a prison cell, followed shortly afterwards by a long length of rope with a noose at the end. But tell her what you like."

Halfon nodded. "He will be happy to return you to your home if you can develop suitable drugs."

"Good. I appreciate knowing where I stand. I will do my best to do what you ask."

Halfon's lips twitched in a self-satisfied smirk. "Excellent." He turned to the mullah and switched back to Arabic. "If there is nothing else for Mrs Baxter, General Shaladi requested a conversation with you. As per your instructions, we are holding him here with his daughter and his men."

"We cannot allow him to leave. It is a shame because other than allowing the drone to approach the ship, he performed his mission almost without fault. Take me to him."

Halfon sent a guard ahead to inform the prisoner of his important visitor. He guided the mullah's entourage back the way they had come, leaving Rosalind in the laboratory. They entered the dining area just as the dishevelled general and his daughter emerged from their room.

Shaladi smoothed down his unruly hair and flashed a salute. "It is a pleasure to meet you again, sir."

"Congratulations on a well-executed operation," the mullah replied. "I regret having to confine you in this facility after your excellent work, but we must keep you here for a few days longer until matters settle down."

"Aya and I can stay out of sight at our home. Nobody would see us."

The mullah glared at the general. "That will not be possible. You will obey my orders."

Shaladi flushed. "I apologise."

The mullah's stern expression softened. "We cannot afford to take any chance that you could be seen. Once we have a cure, the rest of the world will beg us to give it to them. Maybe then we can allow you to leave."

The general's frame sagged in a subconscious sign of defeat. "Of course, I am happy to follow your instructions, Mullah."

The bearded cleric turned to Halfon. "That reminds me. We cannot permit any of the workers here to have outside contact for the same reason. We do not know who they might tell about what we are doing. If your work is successful, none of the foreigners can ever be allowed to leave. We do not want the rest of the world to steal our hard-earned secrets."

"Very good, Mullah."

"I expect to see results within three weeks."

"Three weeks?" Despite the exalted rank of his visitor, Halfon failed to hide the incredulity from his voice. "But that's—"

The mullah cut him off with a raised hand. "I have given you what you requested. Now, I trust you to make it happen. My staff will be in regular contact to monitor progress."

The mullah turned away and headed to the exit, surrounded by his men. As Professor Halfon followed behind, one thought hammered at the centre of his brain.

A cure within three weeks? That's totally impossible.

34

Thursday 17th July 2036

Tripoli Infectious Diseases Hospital, Republic of North Africa
21 days until the deadline

Rosalind stared at the computer screen. Dr Kubar was explaining the direction of his previous research, but her thoughts were elsewhere. She kept thinking over the conversation with the mullah. When she asked whether he would release her if she successfully delivered a cure, his immediate reaction had been in direct contrast to Halfon's translation. Was there any chance they would let her go?

The arrival of Professor Halfon dragged her back to the present.

"I hope you have everything you need," he said.

"There are some expensive machines here but—"

"Excellent," Halfon said, interrupting Rosalind. "I mentioned a demonstration earlier. We are ready to start if you would like to follow me."

Halfon led Rosalind and Kubar towards the window separating the central area from the rest of the laboratory. He tapped on the glass.

"Whatever it is you're about to show me," Rosalind said, "I doubt I'll be impressed."

Halfon ignored her statement. His gaze remained fixed on the empty chamber.

The door to the enclosed room swung open, and a man dressed in a white hazmat suit came in. He held the hand of a barefoot boy wearing shorts and a colourful T-shirt. The child, who couldn't have been more than five years old, looked around in bewilderment.

"Good," Halfon said. "Now observe carefully."

Rosalind dragged her gaze away from the pair who had entered the confined space and switched her attention to Professor Halfon. "What is this? What's going on?"

Halfon continued to stare straight ahead. "I told you to watch."

She ignored the constant distraction of the green icon blinking at the periphery of her vision and turned back to the enclosed room. The scientist in the white hazmat suit released the boy's hand. The child's disinterested eyes flitted across the observers regarding them through the glass. He jammed his thumb in his mouth and settled onto the floor. The man retraced his steps and pushed through the door. Moments later, he returned, this time accompanied by a woman wearing a black, full-length dress together with a matching headscarf.

The woman's pale features peered out from beneath the head covering, taking in the onlookers. She seemed as bewildered as the child as she shuffled forwards. Her right hand grasped the man's elbow for support. Her left rested on the bulge protruding from the dark material. Clearly, she was heavily pregnant.

The man gently prised her grip loose and retreated towards the sole exit. The woman took a step after him. She stopped as the door swung shut behind him with a metallic clunk. For a moment, she stood still, then she shuffled around to scrutinise her audience. Her gaze settled on the boy as she noticed him for the first time.

A low moan escaped from her mouth. She backed away until she butted up against the locked door. A tear ran down her cheek. She covered her face with her hands and sank down on her haunches. After a while, she used the sleeve of her dress to dry her tears and stared at the child in weary resignation.

The boy sensed her distress and clambered to his feet. He took a tentative step towards her. He asked her something, and she snapped a reply back at him. Wearing an expression of bewilderment, he retreated to the opposite side of the room.

Rosalind repeated her initial question. "What the hell is this?"

Halfon replied without looking at her. "She is eight months pregnant. Now, just keep watching."

The boy once again sat on the floor and put his thumb in his mouth. Every so often, he lifted his gaze towards the woman. She stared back at him in silence.

Rosalind became aware that all conversation in the laboratory had ceased. She glanced behind her. All the scientists and guards had stopped what they were doing. Every eye in the place stayed locked on the scene in front of her. She returned her focus to the child.

What was Halfon trying to prove?

The first trickle of blood appeared at the boy's right nostril. He ran his hand over his nose, smearing a crimson streak across his skin. He let out a choking cry. The trickle developed into a flood. Moments later, he was convulsing on the floor.

Rosalind could no longer watch. She turned away. To her left, Kubar stood with a troubled frown on his forehead. She twisted to her right, and her gaze locked onto Halfon. His lips parted slightly as he stared straight ahead.

"Why did you do that?" Rosalind asked. Her voice crackled with tension.

Halfon tore his gaze from the occupants of the enclosed room. "I wanted you to see first-hand what we are up against."

"You could have just told me."

"I believe actions speak louder than words. It surprises me that you are squeamish at the death of a single street urchin."

"It was totally unnecessary."

"That may be so, but I want to make one thing perfectly clear to you, Mrs Baxter. In three weeks, I shall repeat this experiment. On that occasion, the child in the room will be your grandson. Unless you wish to see him die, you must develop a treatment. I also expect you to provide us with the details to enable this country to manufacture Lucinase."

"I already told you I'd help you but three weeks? That's just not feasible. Anyway, he's not my grandson." She turned to Dr Kubar. "Tell him. You know as well as I do that he's asking for the impossible."

Halfon continued before the doctor could reply. "Then I will let you explain that to the boy's parents. I wish you luck." A cold expression settled on Halfon's face. "Now, are you ready to get to work?"

Rosalind studied the professor for a moment before replying. "I'll do what I can, but it's still a ridiculously tight deadline."

"In that case, I suggest you start right away. I will provide you with whatever you need if it is in my power to do so. As you have just witnessed, you will not be constrained by conventional medical ethics. If it costs a few lives to develop a cure, the sacrifice will be well worth it. You may use as many test subjects as you require."

"And if I do deliver, you'll release me like you promised?"

The professor shot her a haughty smile. "Of course. When the work is complete, we will discuss how to get you home. Now, I have other matters to attend to. Dr Kubar will assist you with anything you may need."

Rosalind stared at the departing director's back as he strode across the laboratory. When she returned her focus to the enclosed room, the pregnant woman was no longer present. The rasp of a zip carried through the glass as two men in white hazmat suits zipped up a small body bag and lifted it through the door on a stretcher.

35

Thursday 17th July 2036

Tripoli Infectious Diseases Hospital, Republic of North Africa
21 days until the deadline

Antimone stared across the table at her son. Jason was trying to persuade him to eat the mixture of tomato and couscous on the plate before him. They were the only prisoners in the dining area. A bored-looking armed guard stood silently on the other side of the room.

"I don't like this," Paul said. "I want chicken nuggets." His face was still blotchy from the tears of the last few hours.

The scientists had performed a battery of tests over the course of the morning, including the drawing of numerous blood samples. Despite vociferous protests, the men in white coats had poked and prodded all the members of the young family. Now, the mere sight of a needle was enough to send the three-year-old screaming and sobbing into his parents' arms.

Jason puffed out his cheeks and caught Antimone's eye. "Unfortunately, they don't have that here. You need to eat, or you'll never grow into a big, strong boy."

"But it tastes horrible."

"What about some bread?" Antimone asked. "You like that, right?"

Jason rose from his chair, walked over to the array of food and returned carrying a thin, circular loaf with a hole through the middle. He tore off a piece and handed it to Paul. "Here, what about this?"

The three-year-old studied the unfamiliar offering for a moment, then shook his head. "No."

"At least try a little." Jason lifted the bread to his son's mouth. "Come on. Open the gates and let the train in."

The food touched Paul's lips, but he stubbornly kept them sealed.

"Well, it's up to you, but don't complain if you're hungry later."

Antimone closed her eyes for a second. At home, it was her mother who performed most of the childcare duties. In some ways, Antimone's relationship with her son was more that of a big sister rather than a parent. When it came to feeding Paul, the boy's grandmother was the one who could persuade him to eat when others failed. Antimone wondered what her parents were doing at that moment. No doubt they would be worried sick.

Her reflections were cut short when a side door opened and a man wearing a white robe emerged pushing a trolley. He moved to the steel cabinet and began transferring the leftover food to the cart.

"Let's take the bread with us," Antimone said, her thoughts turning to their current situation. "I'll look after it."

"Good idea," Jason replied, placing the remaining segment of the loaf on her lap.

The man collected the plates from their table without a word or any sign of acknowledgement. He piled them on top of those he had already stacked and left the way he had come.

"Service with a smile," Jason said.

"What now?" Antimone asked.

"More tests, I suppose."

Paul yawned.

"It's time for your afternoon nap," Antimone said. "Why don't you have a lie down?" In the moments between the sessions with the scientists, the guards had allowed them free access to their room and the dining area.

"Not tired. I want Granny Helen." This was the name they had given Antimone's mother.

Jason picked him up. "Unfortunately, you can't see her at the moment."

"I want my toys."

"Why don't we do some colouring?" Half an hour earlier, a woman had brought a pad of paper and a variety of coloured pencils.

"No." Paul wriggled in his father's arms. "Put me down."

Jason shot a glance at Antimone. "I really think—"

His thought went unspoken as the door from the laboratory opened. Professor Halfon stepped into the room. An armed guard stood two paces behind the director.

Jason released his son. Sensing the sudden tension, the three-year-old clambered onto his mother's lap.

"I trust everything is good," the professor said.

Antimone scowled at him. "If you call treating us like lab rats—"

"Let me assure you," Halfon interrupted, "things could be a lot worse. You have suffered a small amount of discomfort. Many of my countrymen would kill to eat the food you are given. You should consider yourselves lucky."

"Have you finished taking samples?" Antimone asked.

"For now," the professor replied.

"Good. So, you can release us then?"

Halfon let out a humourless laugh. "Unfortunately, not. In three weeks, we will see whether we have what we need. In the meantime, you will remain our guests."

Jason let out a derisive chuckle. "Guests? You mean prisoners."

"If you prefer, perhaps we should move you all to the cells, but believe me, they are far less comfortable than here."

A shiver ran through Antimone's body. "Wait. What happens in three weeks?" she asked.

"We conduct the final tests. Your son will play a major part."

Antimone felt her scalp tighten, and the blood drained from her face. "What the hell do you mean?"

The professor hesitated a moment before replying. "Mrs Baxter will tell you later."

A surge of rage flooded Antimone's veins. "What does that murderer want with Paul?" she yelled.

"You keep her away from him," Jason growled.

The guard stepped forwards and jammed the barrel of his weapon into Jason's chest.

Halfon raised a calming hand. "You misunderstand, Mr Floyd. All I said was that your mother—Mrs Baxter—will explain my statement to you."

Jason stared hard at the professor. "That woman is not my mother, and I swear, if either of you hurts our son in any way, I'll kill you both."

Halfon's eyes narrowed. "You are in no position to make threats. Please remember that if you do not cooperate, life could become very uncomfortable for you. Now, I have much to attend to."

Halfon beckoned to the guard. The pair departed, but the atmosphere of trepidation they had created stayed in the room.

36

Thursday 17th July 2036

Tripoli Infectious Diseases Hospital, Republic of North Africa
21 days until the deadline

Rosalind Baxter glanced up at the dial of the wall clock. It was just after seven in the evening. All the other workers apart from Dr Kubar and a solitary guard had departed at least half an hour earlier. The armed man paced back and forth with a bored expression on his face.

The doctor, who had spent the past few hours talking her through the current state of their research, glanced at his watch. "It has been a long day. Perhaps we should stop and start again tomorrow, yes?"

Rosalind yawned. "It looks like we're the only ones left, and I must admit I could do with a rest." The flashing rate of the green warning indicator had increased, and her headache was getting worse.

"What do you think of our work?"

She turned and studied the scientist. "Do you want an honest answer?"

Kubar met her gaze. "If we are to be colleagues, honesty is best."

Rosalind hesitated before replying. "Well, you asked for it. The team is woefully inexperienced to understand the problem, let alone to produce an effective treatment within three weeks. The facilities are actually pretty decent. I can see you've spent a lot of money to pull together the right equipment. You have some promising ideas, but that's all they are. Unfortunately, there is no chance of meeting the goals set by Professor Halfon."

Kubar lowered his eyes. "Thank you for telling me your true thoughts. What can we do?"

Rosalind sighed. "Short of bringing in better qualified people, nothing. Even if you kidnap them like you kidnapped me, and they all agree to work for you, the timescales are simply unrealistic. Don't you realise the rest of the world has been trying and failing to solve a similar problem for the past two decades? And I'm talking about well-funded, well-trained teams, not a bunch of mavericks who've only come here because nobody else will employ them."

"So, you believe we will fail."

"Look, if you get really lucky, you might develop something to a level suitable for widespread use in five to ten years."

"Maybe we do not need to apply the same level of safety testing as in the West. But in any case, you had some luck, did you not? I understand the girl was in your hospital when she gave birth."

Rosalind folded her arms. "Yes, it was certainly a stroke of good fortune when she fell into our hands. Although on balance, I would have preferred it if we'd never met."

"You cannot mean that. Thousands of women—perhaps not in this country but elsewhere—survived because you studied her biology."

"You may be right. But in some ways, it felt like cheating. She handed us the answer on a plate. I'd rather have found a solution without her."

"I do not understand why you say this. It is not a game. But now you can tell us how to make Lucinase, the drug you developed at Ilithyia, no?"

"My colleague, Dr Perrin, was responsible for most of that, but I know enough to put you on the right path."

Kubar rubbed his hands together. "Good. This is progress for us."

"That's if I choose to give you the information. And it won't help the boy, will it?"

Kubar's upbeat tone turned more sombre. "No, I am sorry for this. It is not my decision. But you must tell me what you know, or they will punish both of us. We will start this tomorrow."

Several seconds of silence passed between the pair.

"So, why are you working here?" Rosalind asked. "You seem different to the others."

The doctor's eyes flicked towards the guard, who seemed disinterested in the conversation. He moved his head closer and spoke in a hushed voice. "I cannot leave. They watch me closely."

"But presumably you chose to stay during the fighting."

"My daughter: it is five years now. She went to the shops but did not return. I think somebody took her. Maybe she is still alive."

"That's a long time."

Kubar's shoulders sagged. "Yes, I know, but she is my only child. I cannot give up hope."

The germ of an idea formed in Rosalind's head. Was it worth the risk? What could be worse than her current predicament? "If you help us escape," she said in a whisper, "we could take you with us. I still have a lot of contacts. I'm sure I could find you work in Britain."

The colour drained from Kubar's face. He cast several surreptitious glances around the room. His accent became stronger as he replied in a hushed voice. "Like I say, they watch me. If I try to leave, they kill me no matter how important the research I do here."

"You don't have to decide now. Let me know when you make up your mind."

Kubar turned away and spoke louder. "Come with me. I will take you to eat."

Rosalind trailed behind as he led the way towards the dining area. He presented his card and stepped back to allow her to pass. They proceeded down the corridor to the next security door.

The doctor once again waved his badge at the reader. "I will leave you here."

Rosalind took a pace through the doorway, then turned around. "Think about what I said."

Kubar stared at her in silence as the door swung closed.

Two men guarded the room. Jason and the girl in the wheelchair were the only detainees present. They sat at a table but didn't seem to be eating. Their eyes tracked her as she limped across to the steel counter and loaded her tray up with food. The child was nowhere in sight.

Rosalind took a seat two tables away and glanced at the young couple. "Everything okay?"

Jason rose, strode towards her and sank into the chair opposite. Antimone manoeuvred herself beside him. Both glared at Rosalind with stony expressions.

Jason folded his arms and leant forwards. "What are you planning to do to our son?"

Rosalind's petulant gaze switched from one to the other. "I don't know what you're talking about. Where is he, anyway?"

"He's asleep in our room at the moment, but they—you—have something planned. That arsehole, Halfon, told us you would explain."

"I honestly have no idea what you mean."

"He said they would perform some big test in three weeks. What's that about?"

Damn! Why did Halfon wait for me to tell them? "All I can say is it's nothing to do with me," Rosalind replied.

Jason slammed a clenched fist down on the table. "What the hell is going on?"

The guards, who had been leaning against the wall on the other side of the room, both advanced a pace and raised their weapons.

Rosalind lifted her eyes to the ceiling and took in a deep breath. She would have to reveal what she knew. She lowered her head and met Jason's gaze. "All right, I'll tell you what they told me. But you won't like it."

"I swear, if I have to ask again..."

Rosalind's jaw muscles tensed. "You should already know I don't respond well to threats. And you need me on your side, now more than ever. You asked for it, so here it is. Professor Halfon gave me a first-hand demonstration of the effects of the mutated virus. He placed a pregnant woman and a young boy in the same room."

Antimone held her hands to her cheeks. "What happened?"

"What the hell do you think?" Rosalind snapped. "The child died."

Antimone let out a sob. "Why would they do that?"

Rosalind cleared her throat. *Here goes*. "Halfon told me he would repeat the experiment in three weeks—this time using your son as the subject."

The young couple stared back at her. The silence extended to several seconds.

"But why?" Jason croaked eventually.

"He expects me to develop a cure."

"But that's a ridiculously short—"

Rosalind cut in. "I said exactly the same thing."

"Why didn't Halfon tell us about this test himself?"

"I'm not sure, but if I had to guess, I imagine he's trying to apply pressure to make me cooperate."

Antimone leant forwards. Her face had taken on a similar shade to the white walls. "What are the chances of developing something in that timescale?"

Rosalind hesitated before replying. "I promise you I'll do my best."

"That's not what I asked. Just answer the question."

Rosalind looked away. After a moment, she turned back to meet the accusatory stares. She spoke in a hushed voice. "The probability of producing a drug to counteract the symptoms in that timeframe, with the facilities and staff they have here, is somewhere between zero and a very small number."

37

Friday 18th July 2036

Tripoli Infectious Diseases Hospital, Republic of North Africa
20 days until the deadline

"It's nice to be wearing my own things," Rosalind said as she followed Dr Kubar into the laboratory. Somebody had returned her clothes to her room the previous afternoon, washed and folded, although they had been unsuccessful in removing the stain from the knee where she had fallen during her escape attempt.

The doctor seemed distracted as he led the way. She glanced around her. Most of the other stations were already occupied. "Good morning," she said. Several heads swung in her direction, but nobody acknowledged her greeting. "Friendly lot, aren't they? Is something wrong?"

Kubar gave a non-committal grunt. He headed to an unoccupied desk. He dragged across a second chair from an adjacent workstation and sat, gesturing towards the spare seat. "This morning, I want you to tell me everything about the drug, Lucinase, you created at Ilithyia. Please explain how you discovered the formula and how you synthesise it."

Rosalind lowered herself beside him. "As with many serious problems, the solution was actually quite simple and was largely down to luck. The girl was pregnant and survived childbirth. Of course, we studied her carefully to understand the reasons behind her survival. It turns out she's a chimaera."

Kubar scribbled the information in a notebook, then continued his questions. "You say a chimaera?"

"Yes. Unknown to the girl's mother, it seems she was pregnant with twins, one male, the other, female. At an early stage of the pregnancy, the two foetuses fused together. The single remaining foetus contained cells from both."

"So, her body contains DNA from two separate individuals?"

"Correct. We took extensive biopsy samples. At first, I thought the technicians had mixed up two different patients. It turned out they hadn't. As you know, although males are carriers of the Orestes virus, they don't exhibit symptoms."

"Until now."

"Well, yes. That may be the case today, but it wasn't then. We realised that the reason she survived was because the male cells somehow prevented the organism from triggering its lytic phase."

"Fascinating," Kubar said.

"That was the vital clue we were missing. Effectively, Lucinase masks the pheromones emitted during childbirth. Provided the mother starts taking the drug at least a week before going into labour, the virus remains dormant when she gives birth."

"Did you discover anything special about the father or the child?"

"No. We performed extensive tests. I take it you know how she became pregnant?"

Kubar gave a slight nod of the head. "Yes, I heard from one of the other scientists. It is a shocking story."

"The Perrin boy raped her while she was under the influence of a mind-altering drug, but he wore protection. He instructed my adopted son, who he also drugged, to have sex with her, then told them both to forget what had happened. She didn't realise she was pregnant until it was too late to have an abortion. As far as we could tell, there was nothing significant or unusual about the child."

Kubar scribbled in the notebook, then looked up. "Even so, we have taken samples from all involved."

"That's sensible after going to so much trouble to kidnap them." Her lips twisted in a malicious smile. "And don't forget Perrin. I'd especially like to take a biopsy from his retina, preferably while he's still conscious."

"Why do you say this?"

Rosalind studied the North African doctor. *What should I tell him?* "This is artificial." She pointed to her right eye. "And Perrin caused it."

Kubar blinked in surprise. "I did not know. What happened?"

"It's a long story. Maybe another time."

Kubar hesitated a second before continuing with his questions. "Let us talk about the production of Lucinase."

Rosalind exhaled slowly, relieved to be on firmer ground. She explained the main steps in the manufacture of the drug. Kubar entered the details in his notebook as she spoke. When she next glanced up at the wall clock, over two hours had passed.

"I need caffeine," she said. "I don't suppose you could find me a coffee."

Kubar rose from his chair. "Wait here. I will return soon."

Rosalind watched him cross towards the door. As her gaze swept across the room, the eyes of all the other occupants seemed to focus on her. The hum of background conversation ceased. She glanced uneasily at the nearest guard. He glowered at her, his finger tapping the stock of his automatic rifle.

She sensed movement to her left and spun around. A man in a white lab coat approached her. His Mediterranean complexion identified him as a local. She put his age at somewhere between forty and fifty. He stopped a pace away.

"Can I help you?" Rosalind asked.

The man regarded her silently for a moment before speaking. "You did this."

"I'm sorry. I don't understand."

He uttered a low curse in Arabic. Then he lunged at her. Light glinted off the scalpel he wielded in his hand like a dagger. She barely registered the narrow blade as it sank into her biceps. The assailant drew back the weapon for another strike and rapidly stabbed twice more in the same place. She raised her forearm to block a blow aimed at her neck.

Rosalind was dimly aware of shouts from the other side of the room. Blood bloomed on the material of her blouse around the sites of the stab wounds, but as yet there was no pain. The man readied himself to fling his body at her again. Before he could move, a pair of armed guards wrestled him to the ground. The assailant continued to struggle until the butt of a rifle slammed into his skull. All the fight went out of him. He lay curled in the foetal position, sobbing and mumbling in Arabic.

Rosalind blinked in confusion. She rose to her feet and stared at the crimson stain expanding at the top of her sleeve. As the adrenaline dissipated from her bloodstream, the lacerations began to throb. The pain built to a crescendo of agony. She bent over, clutching the site of the injuries. Nobody moved to help her.

A barked command came from the far side of the room. She raised her head and spotted Dr Kubar approaching at a run. The crowd of onlookers parted to allow him through. In his hand, he carried a white plastic box marked with a green cross. He placed it on the ground and rummaged inside. He withdrew a pair of scissors.

Rosalind backed away.

"I must cut the cloth so I can treat the injury," Kubar said, panting from his recent exertion.

Rosalind uttered a groan.

The doctor moved slowly as the blades neared her arm. "Please stay still."

The thin material parted, exposing three closely spaced, centimetre-long slits in the skin. Blood seeped out of the wounds and dripped onto the floor.

Kubar once again poked around in the medical kit and grabbed a gauze pad. He ripped away the covering and slapped it over the wound. "You will need stitches," he said, "but this will stop the bleeding for now. Here, hold it in place."

"But why?" Rosalind stammered.

Her eyes strayed to the screen of a nearby workstation. A video played with the sound turned off. The pictures showed an angry crowd surging towards a closed, wrought-iron gate. Armed men stood behind the barrier, facing the mob. A stone flew through the air, landing harmlessly on the ground. A man held a burning Union Jack aloft before dropping it on the floor as fire consumed the thin material. The mass of bodies backed away, forming a circle around the flames. Arabic writing scrolled along the bottom of the picture.

The newsfeed swapped to another location with a similarly incited crowd. Moments later, the video shifted again to an almost identical scene. The montage of enraged crowds gave way to a different setting, this one immediately recognisable to Rosalind. With a gasp of shock, she identified the outline of her home in Northstowe. Tall flames leapt from the upstairs windows, licking at the roofline. The screen reverted to a young male news presenter.

She turned to Kubar. "What's going on?"

"Is it true?"

"Is what true?"

The doctor studied her for a moment before replying. "Your Prime Minister has announced to the world that you and your company were responsible for the creation of the virus. Many people are very angry. Crowds demonstrate at British embassies. In your country, they burned down your house."

The breath caught in Rosalind's throat. Her dark secret was out. "It was an accident. We never meant to…"

"So, it was your company that created this disease?"

The shock of the attack combined with the blinking green light in her right eye was giving her a piercing headache to add to the pain of her injuries. "It all happened a long time ago. A patient escaped from a quarantine area. She was carrying an experimental virus that mutated. It certainly wasn't deliberate. I have devoted my life since to developing a cure."

"But the pathogen originated from Ilithyia Biotechnology?"

"Isn't that what I just said?" Rosalind snapped.

Kubar remained silent as he wrapped a bandage around her upper arm.

The screen changed to a shot of Rosalind accepting an award at a medical conference. Moments later, a picture appeared of Antimone Lessing crossing the finishing line in a racing wheelchair, hands aloft in a victory salute.

"What are they saying about her?" she asked.

"They say she is the first to survive, not the other woman. There is also much anger that she hid her involvement from the world."

A shot of Antimone's parents being escorted by police into a waiting car filled the screen. An angry mob jostled the couple and their escorts.

"Everybody here has seen these pictures," Kubar said. "We must be careful nobody else attacks you."

Rosalind's eyes darted around the groups of scientists. A battery of stony glares greeted her gaze.

The doctor studied her with an unreadable expression. "Come with me, and I will see to your injuries properly."

38

Friday 18th July 2036

Tripoli Infectious Diseases Hospital, Republic of North Africa
20 days until the deadline

Dr Kubar knocked on the door of Professor Halfon's office. Should he reveal Rosalind Baxter's offer to his supervisor? She had made the proposal over twenty-four hours ago, so if they knew what she had said, his window of opportunity was diminishing rapidly. The news about her role in the origins of the virus had cemented his decision.

"Come in," came a voice from inside. Kubar turned the handle and stepped into the well-appointed room. The dark wood of the desk contrasted with the white walls. A large, framed photograph showed Halfon standing in front of his staff and welcoming Mullah Awad at the opening of the new research wing of the hospital.

Halfon sat in the leather-backed chair and pointed to the basic wooden seat opposite. He placed his elbows on the polished surface and leant forward. "I take it everything is going well. The woman is back at work, right?"

"That is correct, sir. Her wounds were superficial. Did you know about her involvement in creating—?"

"Of course."

"But, would it not have been advisable to inform me?"

Halfon steepled his fingers. "What difference would it have made?"

"She is responsible for the deaths of millions of women. The rest of the science team does not want to work with her. Many have lost loved ones to the disease she created."

"Surely her background also makes her best qualified to develop a cure."

"I suppose so."

"Before we discuss this further, there is another matter we must talk about. As you know, our leader visited yesterday. He is concerned about our research getting into the hands of the Westerners. Many of our workers come from the West and have friends or family there. We cannot risk them stealing our work."

"Yes. I—"

Halfon glowered at his subordinate. "Do not interrupt me until I finish speaking."

"Of course, sir."

"As I was saying, the mullah is worried about losing our intellectual property. We have taken many risks and spent much money to bring this team together. We must prevent anybody from stealing our findings. For that reason, from now on, all people working on this project will remain on site. We cannot permit them to communicate with the outside world. I want all portable devices confiscated. All forms of communication in this building will be carefully controlled and monitored. Nobody who works here can be allowed to leave."

"This will not be good for morale, sir."

"I am not stupid. I know it will be difficult. That brings me to another matter. I have decided to step back and allow you to lead the scientific activities."

Kubar's mind spun. The pieces fell into place immediately inside his head. He had worked with Halfon too long to be taken in by his machinations. The professor needed a fall guy in case they failed to attain their goal. No doubt, he would be more than happy to grab the glory if they succeeded. Unfortunately, there was no option but to accept.

"I would be honoured to take on this responsibility, sir."

"Excellent. You may tell your staff this confinement is a temporary measure if you wish."

Kubar swallowed hard. "Yes, of course, sir." The change would have little impact on him; he already spent most of his time on site, and he had no immediate family other than his missing daughter. The others, however, would not be happy. It was all very well paying them a good salary, but at some point, they would want the opportunity to spend the money. This would only add to their discontent about working with the woman who had created the virus.

"I will make the announcement tomorrow," Halfon said. "Do you have any questions about this?"

Kubar hesitated. He had been about to reveal Rosalind Baxter's offer of work in the West in exchange for helping her to escape. The more he considered it, the more convinced he became the conversation had gone unheard. Surely, Halfon would not have given him this new responsibility if he suspected him of plotting to abscond. Assuming that to be true, it would do no harm to have a backup plan in the likely event they failed to deliver a solution within the three-week deadline.

"Come on," Halfon said, "I am a busy man."

"Sorry, sir," Kubar replied. "I was just thinking about your instructions. You realise it will be very difficult to achieve a cure in three weeks?"

"I am aware this is a big challenge, but I have every faith in you, and so does Mullah Awad. Failure is not an option. Do not let us down."

"I will do what I can. May I ask a question? Where will the workers sleep if they are to remain on site?"

"Good point. Are there no spare rooms?"

"There are a few free ones, sir, but we're using at least five to hold the prisoners. There is much space on the next floor down, but it is in severe need of refurbishment. The facilities there are in a much poorer state of repair. We need to accommodate twenty or twenty-five people."

"They can share," Halfon said.

"We will still be short."

Halfon's eyes narrowed in thought. "In that case, move the prisoners to the lower level. That will free up another five rooms, no?"

Kubar did a quick calculation in his head. "If we put two scientists to a room and transfer the captives to the next floor, we should have sufficient space."

"Good. That is settled." Halfon drummed his fingers on the desktop. "Now, there are some other matters you wished to discuss with me?"

"Um… I just wondered if there was any news of my missing daughter. You remember I asked you about this a few weeks ago."

The professor huffed. "I am very busy, but when I get some time, I will chase them for a response. If that is all, I have much work to do. Please see yourself out."

Kubar rose from his seat. As he crossed to the door, he questioned whether he really wanted to receive the information he had requested. Until he heard otherwise, a sliver of hope remained that his daughter was still alive.

39

Saturday 19th July 2036

Prime Minister's Office, 10 Downing Street, London
19 days until the deadline

Andrew Jacobs sank into the high-backed leather chair. He pressed the intercom button. "Send them in, please."

His secretary gave a brief acknowledgement. Moments later, the secret service leaders entered his office.

"Take a seat," he said, waving a hand at the two chairs on the opposite side of the desk.

"Good afternoon, Prime Minister," Iris Stanley said. She removed her wire-framed glasses, pulled out the front of her blouse and polished the lenses. Despite the current crisis, the head of the British inward facing security agency seemed totally unfazed.

Charles Moreland took out a handkerchief and dabbed at the trail of perspiration at his temple. He lowered himself into the second visitor's chair. "How are things, Andrew?"

Jacobs drummed his fingers on the polished wood. "They could certainly be better. Pretty much every leader in the world has been on the phone demanding to know why we didn't inform them sooner of the true cause of the virus. Funnily enough, one of the few people who hasn't asked to speak to me is the head of the Reponan government. Ever since I made my statement, they've been noticeably silent."

The Prime Minister paused for a second and regarded each of the two secret service heads in turn. "Do you think I did the right thing when I revealed the source of this virus?"

Moreland nodded. "I don't see that you had any option. We couldn't carry on allowing the Reponans to dictate their demands to us. It's better the announcement came from you than from them."

"You were in an impossible position," Stanley added. "It was going to be bad whatever action you took."

"Thanks. I keep wondering if we handled things correctly. If I'd acted sooner, we could've rescued our people from that ship. I don't suppose we can do much about it now. Give me an update on the foreign situation, Charles."

The head of MI6 replaced the handkerchief in his pocket and fixed his gaze on the Prime Minister. "As you might expect, there's been a huge amount of anti-

British sentiment around the world. Crowds have been demonstrating outside almost all our embassies. We've been forced to shut down some of them. Demonstrators broke into the compound in Baghdad. Luckily, we had already evacuated the staff. The building is well fortified, so the only damage is some broken windows. We have marines on site. They used a sonic cannon to disperse the trespassers. I can assure you anybody who experiences that won't be keen on a second dose. Our guys are under instructions to open fire with conventional weapons if the protesters get inside."

"Let's hope it doesn't come to that. We don't need any more bad publicity. I take it all sensitive material has been taken care of?"

"Of course, Prime Minister. Most intelligence is quantum encrypted as soon as it's received, so there's little danger of it falling into the wrong hands from that route."

"What about the terrorist groups?"

"As you might imagine, we've seen signs of increased activity. The current threat level is at critical. I'm afraid for the foreseeable future, we can expect our people and assets, especially those on foreign soil, to be targets. Perhaps unsurprisingly, the Reponans still deny they had anything to do with the attack at the Olympics and for the kidnapping of our citizens. We released the drone footage showing the captives on the deck of the ship."

"Humph," Jacobs grunted. "I saw that. The cheeky bastards claimed it was a fake and put out their own shots, replacing Shaladi's face with mine. I assume nobody believes their denials."

"Opinion seems to be split along normal lines. Countries we traditionally count as allies have acknowledged their belief that the original pictures are genuine. The usual suspects have sided with the North Africans. There appears to be one thing they all agree on, however; everybody wants to extradite Rosalind Baxter and try her for her crimes."

"They're welcome to her as far as I'm concerned. Talking of that bloody woman, do you have any more information on the location of our people?"

"Even though our warship backed off," Moreland replied, "we continued to track the container vessel using satellite surveillance. They docked in Tunis as expected. From there, we tracked two vehicles as they travelled to Tripoli. It seems the group is being held at the Infectious Diseases Facility, but it's a huge site, so we don't know their exact whereabouts."

"Could we send in a team to retrieve them?" Jacobs asked.

"There's a large military presence in the city, and they're sure to be well guarded. The chances of a successful operation are very slim, in my opinion. If we knew exactly where they were being held, the odds would be far higher."

"So, we just let them keep our people?"

"We can't do much else for now, Prime Minister. I suggest we relocate at least one of our cruisers to the Mediterranean and put a rescue team onboard so that if an opportunity does arise, we're ready to go."

"That's a good idea, Charles. I'll talk to the admiralty and get them to do as you propose. Do you have any update on the new strain of virus?"

"There've been several outbreaks in The Republic of North Africa and a few cases in Tunisia, but for the moment, it hasn't expanded outside that region. Travel restrictions seem to be slowing the spread, but it's only a matter of time before it gets here."

"The infected blood sample arrived a few days ago," Stanley said. "We've got a team at Porton Down working on it. That said, if this strain is anything like the original, it'll take a lot of effort to develop a cure."

Jacobs rubbed his face with his hands. "I want our top people on this. There's no higher priority."

"Understood."

"What about the home front, Iris?" the Prime Minister asked.

"A very similar story to abroad," the head of MI5 replied. "There've been mass demonstrations in every major city. As you might expect, Northstowe has been particularly badly affected. A mob stormed the Ilithyia facility and caused a lot of damage. The company has filed for administration, not that I suspect there will be many takers in their current position. Rosalind Baxter's home was destroyed in an arson attack."

"So, not all bad news then," Jacobs said, remaining deadpan.

Stanley suppressed a smirk. "I suppose not." Almost immediately, she rearranged her features into a serious, thoughtful expression. "We also had to relocate the Lessings. Some online newsfeeds are suggesting their daughter should've revealed that she was the first to survive. A crowd gathered outside their house, and things got a little ugly."

"That girl doesn't owe anybody anything," Jacobs replied. "I'm surprised she agreed to keep quiet after what she went through. And now she and her family are caught up in this new mess."

"I understand your concerns," Stanley said, "but until we have more information about where they're being held, there's not much more we can do."

"I want you to put all your efforts into determining their location. If there's any chance of rescuing them, I'll take it. She doesn't deserve any of this."

40

Saturday 19th July 2036

Tripoli Infectious Diseases Hospital, Republic of North Africa
19 days until the deadline

Antimone sat in her wheelchair, enjoying a rare moment of peace while Paul took his afternoon nap. Jason lay on the adjacent bed with his eyes closed and his hands behind his head. This incarceration should have been an opportunity for the couple to spend precious time with their son, but they were finding it increasingly hard to provide the enthusiasm and energy required to keep him entertained.

For Antimone, the hardest part of being held in captivity was the lack of exercise. After the intensive training and the high of the Olympic final, the enforced inaction was sapping her spirits. She could sense her fitness draining away with each passing day, leaving her feeling weaker and diminished. At home, her mother took on most of the childcare duties, allowing Antimone to concentrate on her athletic career. The time spent with her son had been a rewarding distraction. Now, the monotony was driving her mad. Worse still, it made her feel like a bad parent.

A knock at the door drew Antimone from her morose thoughts. Jason sat up. *Not more tests.* Moments later, Dr Kubar entered. He held a green canvas sack in his hand.

"I hope I am not disturbing you," the doctor said. "I must talk to you both."

Antimone shrugged. "Don't let me stop you. There's not exactly a whole lot going on here."

"I know this is difficult for you. I will see if I can find some toys for your boy. Here are some books for you. I studied them when I was learning your language. They are not recent. We do not have access to modern western literature here."

Antimone picked one up and inspected the cover: Harry Potter and the Chamber of Secrets. The smell of the old paper reminded her of her childhood. She grunted her thanks. She had read the books several times as a child and seen all the films but didn't want to come across as ungrateful.

An uneasy silence developed. Eventually, Kubar drew a deep breath and spoke again. "I am afraid I have some bad news." Seeing Antimone's expression, he quickly pushed on. "It is nothing to do with our work, at least not directly.

Professor Halfon has decided that all the scientists must remain on site at all times."

"Are they prisoners as well, now?" Antimone asked.

"Ah… no. But they need to live here."

"So, you're saying they're not allowed to leave, but they aren't prisoners. I'll take your word for it. That's all very interesting, but why are you telling us?"

"We require this room."

Jason swung his legs off the bed. "So, you're moving us?"

Kubar glanced away for a second. "Yes. Unfortunately, your new accommodation is—how to say this?—not so good. Also, you must move your things now."

Antimone glared at him. "Can't you see our son is sleeping? If we move him, he'll wake up."

"I am sorry, but I have no choice. Place your things in here." He handed a bag to Jason.

Jason studied the doctor for a second, then muttered, "Whatever." He moved to the bedside cabinet and transferred the few items within to the green sack. Meanwhile, Kubar removed the blankets from the bed, put them in another bag, then proceeded to the bathroom. Moments later, he returned. "I think that is everything. Let us go."

Antimone reached across and placed a hand on her son's shoulder. "Paul, you need to wake up." The three-year-old gave a whimper of protest and jammed his thumb in his mouth. She gently shook him. "Come on, we have to leave."

Jason leant over, lifted the boy and deposited him in his mother's lap. Paul opened a bleary eye and cried.

Antimone tried to comfort him, but the crying continued. "Somebody will have to push me," she snapped. "I can't turn the wheels on this piece of crap by myself while I'm holding my son. That reminds me; General Shaladi promised to get me a better model."

"I will see if I can find something more suitable," Kubar replied.

Jason handed his bag to Kubar and guided the wheelchair down the corridor behind the doctor. At each set of locked doors, Kubar presented his key card. They turned a corner and came to a lift. To the right, a staircase sign hung over another sealed door.

Once again, the doctor applied his pass to the control box, and the two metal panels parted. Jason pushed Antimone's wheelchair into the cramped interior while Kubar peered at the Arabic writing beside the buttons. The doctor selected the second button from the bottom. The floor sank down before juddering to a halt moments later. It seemed they had dropped just a single level. By now, Paul's cries had diminished to sniffles of discontent as he jammed his head beneath his mother's chin.

The panels parted to reveal a grey concrete wall, partially coated with peeling, discoloured, white paint. The air was warmer and carried a faint, unpleasant, musty smell. Kubar pushed the wheelchair down another corridor and used his key card to pass through a set of swing doors. The odour of cigarette smoke immediately stung Antimone's nostrils.

To the left was a glass-fronted office occupied by three armed men. On the right was a large open area, lit by a flickering fluorescent strip light. Ten equispaced beds extended in a row along the far wall, the metal frames streaked with rust. Thin, cream-coloured curtains stained with speckles of something dark and unpleasant-looking surrounded each bed. The state of the décor matched what they had seen upon exiting the elevator. In the middle of the room sat a long wooden table with benches on either side.

Three men perched at the far end. All held lit cigarettes between their fingers. Antimone recognised them as members of Shaladi's team. They were playing cards and glanced up briefly at the new arrivals before resuming their game.

"What the hell is this?" Antimone asked, glaring at Kubar. "You're not telling me we have to sleep next to them, are you?"

"I apologise for the poor conditions, but there is no space. We stopped using this part of the hospital ten or fifteen years ago. Now we must put it to use again."

"Why are they smoking?" Jason asked. "It's a criminal offence back home."

Kubar tilted his head apologetically. "Standards are different in my country. Here it is common. I cannot stop them."

"You can't seriously expect us to live like this," Antimone said. "We have a three-year-old child."

Kubar's face hardened. "I know it is not perfect, but it is all I can offer unless you would prefer a prison cell. Believe me, that is much worse."

"I want to talk to the man who runs this place."

"It was Professor Halfon who instructed me to put you here. He will not change his mind. Perhaps you forget you are a prisoner."

"Don't worry," Antimone replied, sarcasm dripping from every word. "That's one thing I won't be forgetting in a hurry. So, who else will be sleeping in this… this hovel?"

"All the prisoners will stay here."

"What? Rosalind Baxter and Max Perrin too?"

"Yes, together with the general, his daughter and their men."

"Oh, fantastic. You're putting us next to a bunch of murderers and kidnappers. How do you know they won't try to hurt us in some way?"

"Do not worry. Somebody will always watch them carefully."

"What about toilets and washing?"

"There are bathrooms there." Kubar pointed at two adjacent doorways on the far side of the room. "You must ask the guards before you enter."

"And do they have facilities for disabled people?"

"Of course. Remember, this was once a hospital ward. Now, I have much to do."

"Don't forget you promised to find me a better wheelchair."

Kubar deposited the green sacks on the endmost bed, then headed towards the exit. Halfway there, he turned. "I will see what I can do."

Antimone waited until the doctor passed through the secured door. *Let's check out how bad it really is.* "I'm going to take a look at the bathroom," she announced. She lifted Paul and handed him to his father. Her son's fists made a half-hearted attempt to retain a grip on his mother's training top, but the material slipped through his fingers. Jason accepted his sleepy son, hugging him close to his chest.

"I'll be back in a minute," Antimone said.

She manoeuvred the wheelchair across the cracked tiles in a zig-zag, bending down awkwardly on each side to push one wheel at a time.

"Do you need any help?" Jason asked from behind her.

"I can manage," she snapped.

The three guards in the office ceased their conversation as she approached the twin doorways at the opposite end of the large room. The nearest man stood and strolled nonchalantly towards her. He raised his cigarette to his mouth, inhaled deeply, then blew the acrid smoke at the ceiling.

"I want to use the bathroom," Antimone said, pointing.

The guard stared at her stony-faced for a moment, then turned silently to rejoin his colleagues.

I guess that's a yes. She guided the wheelchair towards the door with the female symbol and shoved it open. The room contained a porcelain toilet with a cracked plastic seat accompanied by a rusty bar to assist disabled users, a washbasin without a plug and a showerhead over a slatted metal grid. A white chair with rust-streaked legs lay on its side beside the shower.

She twisted the lock. It rotated freely, but the mechanism stubbornly refused to engage. *Okay, so no privacy then.* Her eyes scanned the room, searching for hidden cameras, but she failed to spot anything suspicious among the mildew-stained walls and ceiling. Her skin crawled at the thought the men in the office might be watching her, but there was no option if she wanted to relieve herself.

She steered herself towards the toilet. As she drew nearer, a stomach-churning sewage smell rose from the dark recesses of the grate beneath the shower. Gagging from the stench, she leant forwards to peer into the porcelain bowl and was relieved to find clear water at the bottom despite the limescale stains. The bar lowered with a squeal of protest, and she used her powerful arms to shift herself across to the seat.

When she had finished, she shifted back to the wheelchair and moved to the sink. She turned the tap. For several seconds, nothing happened. Eventually, a meagre stream of rust-stained water spluttered from the spout. She rinsed her hands, drying them on her tracksuit bottoms.

She emerged through the door to discover Jason waiting for her, watched over by one of the armed guards. The breath hitched in her throat. "Where's Paul?"

"Don't worry. He's on the bed, asleep. So, how is it?"

"It's a shit hole," Antimone replied. "Literally."

41

Saturday 19th July 2036

Tripoli Infectious Diseases Hospital, Republic of North Africa
19 days until the deadline

"I'm sorry, my dear, but you must be patient," General Shaladi said, addressing his daughter in Arabic. "Hopefully, it won't be for long."

"It's totally unacceptable," Aya replied in the same language. "We did everything they asked, and they treat us like this. Do you even think they'll let us go when this is over?"

The general turned sideways on the bench and studied his only child for a moment, then looked away. "I don't know. Professor Halfon told me we can't be seen in public, at least not until they have a cure. From what I've overheard, the scientists are not optimistic about meeting the deadline."

"So, they may never release us. How do they expect us to live in these conditions?"

"Unfortunately, we can do nothing about it."

"This has ruined everything. Just a few days ago I was in an Olympics final with hopes of a gold medal. Now, it looks like I'll never race again."

The general stared angrily at his daughter. "There's more at stake than your precious wheelchair racing career. If we hadn't done what they asked, they would've killed us. Be thankful we're both still alive."

Aya folded her arms. "It's just not right. And he's creeping me out." She angled her head towards Max Perrin. "He keeps staring at me." Her father directed his gaze to observe the fair-haired Westerner.

It seemed the focus of their attention had not gone unnoticed. A few metres away, Max eased himself off his bed, strolled to the wooden table and sat opposite the pair. "Well, here we are, all together. If it wasn't certain before, there's little doubt now; you're both prisoners here as much as we are. I have to say, I'm not happy about the situation, but it makes me feel better to have you stuck in the same hole as the rest of us after you broke our little agreement."

Shaladi's men stopped playing their card game as they watched to see what would happen next. Rosalind Baxter had not yet returned from her day at the laboratory. Jason was taking a shower. Antimone, who had been helping Paul to draw a picture, glanced across from her position by the second bed from the left.

Shaladi glowered at the man sitting opposite. "You did not inform me of your involvement with the girl," he said, his voice low and menacing. "And I feel no need to honour agreements with people who lie to me, especially if they are rapists."

"I didn't lie. You never asked. Anyway, she was desperate to sleep with me."

"I find that hard to believe," the general replied. "But we can ask her if you want."

"Perhaps I could spend the night with your daughter. She looks like she could do with the attentions of a real man."

"I would not go to your bed if you were the last person alive," Aya said, her eyes blazing with fury.

Max let out a bark of humourless laughter. "Maybe I'll sneak in beside you tonight and cuddle up. I bet this is hard for you, Princess, isn't it? One minute you're the darling of the athletics track and a celebrity in this armpit of a country, the next you're just a lowly prisoner along with the rest of us."

"You will not speak to my daughter like this," Shaladi snarled. He rose and leant forwards across the table. His men also stood.

"And what are you going to do about it?" Max asked with a sneer, mirroring the general's stance.

Before Max could react, Shaladi shot out his left hand and grasped him around the collar. Shaladi's right fist slammed into the younger man's jaw. Two further blows followed in quick succession. Shaladi straightened his arm and tossed his victim backwards. Max toppled over the bench, sprawling on the floor with a thud. One of Shaladi's security team exchanged a comment with his colleague. All three laughed.

Shouts erupted from the glass office. Shaladi moved swiftly for a man of his size as he rounded the end of the table. Max scrabbled like a crab to escape his enraged attacker. He staggered to his feet and backed towards the approaching men.

"Did you see what he did to me?" he screamed at the nearest guard, pointing a shaking finger at Shaladi. The man's rifle butt smashed into Max's face. He crumpled to the floor and rolled half-conscious onto his side.

The aim of the guards' rifles transferred to Shaladi's chest. The general raised his hands slowly. A rapid-fire conversation in Arabic between Shaladi and the armed men followed. The man who had struck Max lowered his weapon and spoke into the device strapped to his wrist.

Seconds passed as both sides stared at each other in silence. The clunk of the lift doors and the sound of rapidly approaching footsteps drew all the eyes in the room. Professor Halfon marched through the doorway and surveyed the scene. He stormed up to the general, his features contorted in anger. Shaladi and Halfon exchanged several words in Arabic. The professor barked an instruction at the man with the wrist communicator. He lowered his mouth to the device and spoke in a hushed voice.

Max pushed himself to a sitting position and spat a bloody gobbet of saliva on the floor. "He hit me."

"Be quiet," Halfon bellowed. "Miss Lessing," he added in a calmer tone. "Please join us. You may leave your boy where he is."

Antimone murmured a few words to her son and manoeuvred herself awkwardly the few feet to the rest of the group. "What's going on?"

Halfon raised a finger to silence her. A guard crossed to the male bathroom and barged in without knocking. Moments later. Jason emerged with a towel around his waist. He stood beside Antimone, water dripping on the surrounding floor.

"Wait there," Halfon barked, "and no talking."

Jason shot Antimone a questioning look. She responded with a shrug of the shoulders.

The general glared at Max. The rasp of Max's breath in his throat was the only sound to break the silence. His fists clenched and unclenched periodically. One minute turned into two. Eventually, the muffled clunk of the lift doors parting reached their ears. Seconds later, Rosalind Baxter entered the room, accompanied by Dr Kubar. She stared at the others in confusion.

"Good. We are all here," Halfon said. "Let me start by apologising for the lower quality of your accommodation. Unfortunately, this is necessary due to lack of space."

His voice took on a frostier tone. "Now, I want to make this absolutely clear. I will not tolerate any insubordination. If you misbehave, we have prison cells, which are far more uncomfortable than this. Any further incidents like the one that happened here this evening will result in all of you being transferred there… or worse. Mr Perrin, you will sample the delights of a cell tonight."

"But I didn't do anything," Max said, the words distorted by his swollen mouth. "He hit me."

"Enough!" Halfon yelled. The guard raised his rifle butt again.

"Okay," Max muttered, shuffling backwards.

"The work we are doing here is extremely important. Having prisoners on site is a distraction I do not need. In future, you will do as you are told without question or complaint. Am I making myself clear?" Halfon stared belligerently at each of the captives. "Good. Food will be here shortly."

***

Professor Halfon beckoned to Dr Kubar, turned and moved out of earshot of the others. When the doctor joined him, he spoke to his subordinate in Arabic, his voice just above a whisper. "This incident has made me think. The Westerners are needed for the medical research and might be useful as hostages. Shaladi and his daughter may also still have their uses. The general's men, however, are simply a potential risk. While I escort Perrin to the cells, talk to our security people. I do not want them here any longer."

"So, you're freeing them?"

Halfon tutted. "Of course not."

"You wish to transfer them somewhere else?"

"In a manner of speaking. They know too much. If they are kept with other prisoners outside this facility, they will discuss what they have seen."

Kubar turned pale as he comprehended the professor's intentions. "You intend to have them killed?"

Halfon's eyes narrowed. It seemed his subordinate might not yet be ready for the additional burden of leadership after all. "That is not your concern. Never mind. I will arrange it myself. We will talk later." His gaze followed Kubar as he passed through the doorway leading to the elevator. When the doctor had disappeared from sight, Halfon returned to the group. He uttered a series of curt instructions to one guard and beckoned to another to join him.

"You will come with us now," he said to Max. "We will see how you like the facilities in our basement. This way."

Halfon turned and strode towards the same door through which Kubar had just passed. He didn't look back. Max limped behind, shoved forwards by the armed man. The professor used his key card to summon the lift.

"I can help you," Max said as he drew alongside.

Halfon whipped around and looked the injured prisoner up and down. "How could you possibly help me?"

A shrewd expression crept onto Max's face. He leant closer and spoke in a low voice. "I could spy on them for you, let you know if they're planning an escape."

"I have guards to watch them. What makes you think I need you?"

"They won't discuss their plans in front of your men, will they?"

"Yet you expect them to do so when you are present?" Halfon asked.

"I could still eavesdrop on them. It's worth a try, isn't it?"

"Even if they escaped this facility, they would never get out of this country."

"But it would be better to stop any attempt before it happens, wouldn't it?"

"Hmm." Halfon tapped his teeth with a fingernail.

Max studied the professor hopefully. "I saw the girl take a knife. I bet your guards didn't notice that."

Halfon lifted an eyebrow in surprise. "Which girl?"

"The one in the wheelchair," Max replied hurriedly.

"And what sort of knife?"

"Ah... just a normal cutlery knife."

Halfon's eyes bored into Max. "The kitchen workers are under strict instructions that the prisoners should not be given metal knives or forks. How did she get this item?"

Max swallowed hard and looked away. "Um... I don't know."

The professor maintained his glare. "Really?"

"Look, I'm sorry I lied," Max gabbled. "I'm not like them. I'll do whatever you ask."

Halfon allowed himself a moment of smugness. *The boy might have his uses after all.* "Oh, I believe you will. But what do you wish for in return?"

"I understand that you have no intention of releasing us. For the moment, all I'm after is preferential treatment. I really don't want to spend the night in the cells. In time, I could perform other tasks for you. Surely it would be useful to have a Westerner working for you. I'd be happy to act as a spy for your government if you were to pay me."

Halfon stood silently for a moment, his eyes narrowed in thought. "Very well. I like people who are motivated. Tonight, you may return to your old room. Tomorrow, we will bring you back here. You can tell them you enjoyed our hospitality in the basement. But I expect results. I want you to inform me immediately if they have any plans to escape. And if you lie to me again, you will be severely punished."

Max nodded enthusiastically. "You won't regret this. I'll let you know if I hear anything at all."

42

Sunday 20th July 2036

Tripoli Infectious Diseases Hospital, Republic of North Africa
18 days until the deadline

The clatter of crockery woke Jason. He eased an eye open and glanced to his right. Paul lay in the adjacent bed and Antimone one further over against the wall. Both were still asleep. A thin curtain divided their set of three beds from the rest, although the stained material provided no privacy from the gaze of the guards in the glass-fronted office. A man wearing a white jacket over dark robes was transferring food from a trolley to the end of the wooden table.

Jason's eyes felt gritty as he rubbed his cheeks. The fluorescent light had remained on all night, and the persistent buzzing and flickering had kept him awake. To make matters worse, in the early hours of the morning, a group of men had entered the room and dragged Shaladi's team from their beds. After a loud argument that lasted for several minutes, the guards and their prisoners departed, leaving General Shaladi and his daughter behind. The army officer continued to pace backwards and forwards until threats of violence from the armed watchers drove him back to his bed. Thankfully, Paul slept through it all.

Sheets rustled to his right. Antimone propped herself up on an elbow, her hair tousled. Judging by the dark crescents beneath her eyes, the disturbances during the night had affected her sleep as much as his.

"Do you need any help getting into your wheelchair?" Jason asked.

Antimone glanced to her left at their son. "Yeah, if you wouldn't mind," she replied.

Jason swung his legs onto the floor and hesitated for a moment before standing. They both still wore the clothes they had been wearing the previous day. Neither was comfortable stripping to their underwear in the shared accommodation, particularly under the watchful gaze of the guards. "That was some night. I barely slept a wink. What do you think happened to Shaladi's men?"

"Who knows?" Antimone replied. "Perhaps he'll tell us later."

"They will probably execute them," came a gruff voice from behind the curtain. "It is what I would do. I am surprised they did not also take me."

Antimone and Jason exchanged a glance. It seemed the general had been listening to their conversation.

"Um, right," Jason said. His eyes locked onto Antimone's. "Thanks." He laced his shoes and crept past the end of the bed in which his sleeping son lay. He lifted Antimone, then deposited her on the scuffed, black seat of the wheelchair. "Shall I push you?"

He half expected a sharp retort. Instead, she shrugged. "If you don't mind."

"Do you need anything?"

"Yeah. Can you get my toothbrush? It's in there."

Jason retrieved a toiletry bag and towel from the battered bedside cabinet and handed it to Antimone, then went back to grab his own. He pushed the wheelchair across the cracked tiles towards the twin doorways. One of the two guards on duty stepped out of the office, his weapon aimed casually at Jason's chest. A cigarette dangled from the corner of his mouth.

"We want to use the bathrooms," Jason said, pointing.

The guard nodded and returned to the smoke-filled room. Jason guided the wheelchair towards the entrance to the ladies.

Antimone twisted around. "I can take it from here." She leant to the side, alternating between each wheel, and steered herself in a zig-zag through the doorway.

When he emerged a few minutes later, the sound of running water continued from the adjacent room. General Shaladi and his daughter sat beside each other at one end of the table. The dishevelled form of Rosalind Baxter still lay in bed. She raised her head and studied him with bleary eyes. Paul showed no signs of stirring. Jason chose to let his son continue sleeping.

He replaced the sponge bag and towel in the bedside cabinet, then returned to the stack of food and loaded up his plate. He was about to lower himself onto the bench furthest from the Shaladis when the general spoke in a low voice.

"We must talk."

Jason turned, wondering whether the comment had been addressed to him.

Shaladi gestured towards the seat to his right. "Please sit."

Jason moved along and sat beside the general.

"You know they will never let us go," Shaladi said without turning his head. "Do not look at me and keep your voice low."

Jason popped a fig into his mouth but didn't reply.

"So, we must escape," the general continued. "I have men loyal to me if we get out of here. And I need your help for that."

"How will you contact your people?" Jason whispered.

"This is the first problem."

"And how do I know I can trust you? I mean, you're the reason we ended up in here. What's to stop you abandoning us once we're out?"

"I give you my word. We will take you as far as the border. After that, you are on your own."

"What do you want me to do?" Jason asked, turning to stare at the general.

"They must not see us talking."

"Right," Jason said, facing forwards. "Sorry."

"We have to combine forces. First, we need a plan."

"Don't you have any ideas?"

Shaladi gave a brief shake of the head. "No. Not yet."

"Okay. This offer of yours; who does it extend to?"

"I do not understand."

"If we do as you suggest, who comes with us?"

"Just you and the girl and of course, your son."

"What about Mrs Baxter?"

Shaladi's jaw clenched. A vein pulsed at his temple. "This woman is responsible for the deaths of my wife and millions of other women. Did she not also kill your real mother? She can stay here and rot."

Jason inhaled deeply and stretched his neck muscles. "Fair enough."

"And the Perrin boy, I will not work with him."

"You'll have no complaints from me on that front."

The sound of approaching footsteps came from the door leading to the lift. It opened to reveal the figure of Max Perrin, accompanied by a guard.

"Talk of the devil," Jason muttered.

As Perrin drew nearer, the vivid purple bruising around his left eye became apparent. The scent of body odour wafted over the table. He grinned as he studied the diners. "Are you glad to see me?"

"I thought you'd be spending more time in the cells," Jason said.

"I missed your sparkling company so much, I begged them to let me come back." He grabbed a plate, filled it with fruit and bread and plonked himself down beside Aya. She immediately shifted along the bench away from him.

"Aren't you pleased to see me, Princess?" he said, talking through a mouthful of food.

She glowered at him silently.

Max continued to eat as the others studiously ignored him. After a while, he placed his hands on the table. "So," he whispered, leaning forwards conspiratorially, "if you three are suddenly friends, you must be up to something. What are we doing to escape?"

Nobody replied.

"Come on," he tried again, "we should make a plan... unless you already have some ideas. Hey, there are only two guards over there. If we could get close enough, we should be able to overpower them and take their weapons. The lifts are just over there. What do you think?"

A wall of silence greeted his question.

"We need to create a distraction. Maybe one of us could go up to them and ask to borrow a cigarette. Or perhaps we could simulate a fight."

"That is a great idea," Shaladi growled. "Then I could hit you again."

"Look, we're all in the same boat. We'll never get out of here unless we work together. Think about it. Let's have another chat later and pool our ideas."

General Shaladi rose and marched towards the bathrooms. "I don't think so," he said over his shoulder. "I have better things to do."

43

Sunday 20th July 2036

Tripoli Infectious Diseases Hospital, Republic of North Africa
18 days until the deadline

Antimone lay facing Jason as they shared the narrow mattress. A loud snoring sound came from behind the curtain separating their group of three beds from the rest. Another day of stultifying boredom had passed.

Her right hand grasped Jason's left. Paul occupied the adjacent bed, his head barely visible where it poked out above the threadbare sheets. His chest rose and fell in a regular rhythm as he slept beside them. Despite somebody turning off the fluorescent strip lights, both adults were finding it hard to sleep. The only source of illumination was the glass-fronted office where the two guards smoked their ever-present cigarettes.

"I'm scared," Antimone whispered. "What are we going to do?"

Jason stared up at the ceiling. "What can we do?" he replied. "She said she would try her best to develop a cure."

"I don't trust her. Anyway, she also admitted the likelihood of developing anything in the time available was practically zero. Somehow, we have to find a way out of here."

"Do you think we should join forces with Shaladi? I mean, he's no better than her, but at least he's got people on the outside."

Antimone turned sideways. Her eyes glinted in the near darkness. "We need to come up with something. If he can help us to get out of here, we shouldn't turn him down. We can't just sit around and wait for that woman to save our son."

"What chance do we have? We're locked in a room with armed guards watching our every move, day and night. Even if we managed to escape from this building, we're in a hostile country."

Antimone raised herself on an elbow. "So, what are you suggesting? We should just give up and hope for a miracle?"

"That's not what I'm saying at all, but what other options do we have?"

She sank back onto the pillow. "Do you really think they'd go through with it? Threatening Paul won't make her work any faster, will it? That bitch doesn't care about our son. I don't know what I'd do if something happened to him."

Jason sighed. "For the moment, she's all we've got. She told us she'll do everything possible, and I believe her. They'll use whatever they can to put pressure on her. They killed a child just to prove a point. That shows how ruthless they are and how little they care about human life. We can't assume they won't follow up on their threat. Maybe we should do what Perrin suggested; try to overpower the guards and take their guns off them."

Antimone squeezed his hand. "It's too dangerous. We could be shot. Even if we did grab their guns, how would we get past the locks? They'd see us coming. Remember, there are cameras everywhere. Somebody would definitely notice, and they're all heavily armed."

"Do you have any better ideas?"

"No, not at the moment."

The pair lapsed into silence, each lost in their own thoughts. Suddenly, Jason twisted towards Antimone. "They keep us locked up in here day and night. There's nothing in this room to help us escape. But what if I got into the laboratory?"

"I don't follow," Antimone whispered.

"There must be computers in there. If I could get access to one, we might be able to send a message to somebody back home and tell them where we are."

"Who would you contact?"

"Anybody. Who cares? The first step is to find a way in there."

"Okay, but you've got the same problem as before. How are you going to sneak past the armed men and the locked doors?"

"I've worked in a lab. Perhaps they'd let me help my moth—I mean Mrs Baxter."

Antimone was thankful the darkness hid her expression of doubt. The last person she wanted to involve was the woman who three years ago had threatened both their lives. She hesitated before replying. "It may be worth a try."

"They have to agree to it first."

"They're bound to keep a close eye on you. You'll need to be careful. You don't want to end up in the cells like Perrin."

"At least it'll feel as if we're doing something rather than waiting for the axe to fall. Anyway, I'm going to get some sleep."

Jason rolled off the narrow mattress, bent over and kissed Antimone. "I love you," he said, returning to his own bed.

"You too," she replied.

Both adults lay on their single beds, wide awake and staring at the ceiling.

44

Monday 21st July 2036

Tripoli Infectious Diseases Hospital, Republic of North Africa
17 days until the deadline

The sound of clanking plates woke Rosalind Baxter. As her eyes blinked open, the vision in her right eye remained dark. Still half asleep, she raised her hand and rubbed at the eyelid. Eventually, realisation dawned. *Damn. The rechargeable battery has finally lost all its charge.*

She cursed under her breath. She had been putting off bringing it up with Dr Kubar in the hope the implant would keep working for a while longer. Now, she would have to ask him about finding a charger. If they wanted her to work at peak effectiveness, they would have to find a way to recharge the battery.

She swung her legs off the bed and winced as she placed her weight on her right knee. Maybe she should request the services of a physiotherapist at the same time. She limped to the bathroom and returned a few minutes later refreshed by the shower despite the gut-wrenching sewage smell emanating from the drain.

Jason ate alone at the wooden table. She walked straight to the food trolley without acknowledging him. She loaded her tray and sat at the opposite end.

Jason rose from where he was sitting and joined her. "Good morning to you, too," he said.

Rosalind looked up. "Eating by yourself today? Where's the love of your life?"

Jason scowled. "She's sorting out Paul. I offered to help, but she insisted on doing it by herself even though she can't—"

"You realise they could probably cure her now, don't you? From what I've heard, the operation is fairly routine these days. It sounds to me like she wants to stay in a wheelchair."

"She said she'd consider it when she stops racing. Anyway, it's her decision."

Rosalind made a non-committal grunt and continued to eat. Jason's eyes bored into her. Eventually, she raised her head and met his gaze. "Look, I told you I'll do what I can to develop a vaccine for your son, but the chances of producing anything in three weeks are infinitesimally small. Sorry to be so blunt, but you need to be prepared."

Jason leant forwards. "I want to help."

Rosalind lowered the fruit in her hand. "Really? How?"

"I'm in my second year at university, and I know my way around a laboratory. I could act as your assistant, like a lab technician or something."

"Well, thanks for your kind offer but—"

"Surely you could use somebody to assist with data entry and stuff. And I certainly have a vested interest."

Rosalind leant forwards and stared at Jason. "I really don't want someone I need to nursemaid."

"Come on. When I was growing up, you were always keen for me to join you in the business. Let me show you what I can do."

"That was before you betrayed my trust by siding with the girl."

Jason folded his arms. "Remember that you kidnapped her and told me she was dead. You forced me into a choice between the pair of you, and she'd done nothing wrong. If I hadn't intervened—"

"We'd all be living comfortably at home and not in this bloody prison," Rosalind interrupted.

"Look, let's not rake over old ground. We're all in this mess together. I genuinely want to help."

Rosalind eyed Jason with a calculating stare. In the past, she had hoped one day he would join her at Ilithyia Biotechnology. As a child, he had shown promise for a career in science and surprised her on several occasions with his intelligent questions. Both his biological parents had worked in the medical field, so perhaps it ran in his genes. She would need somebody to monitor the test results, and as he had explained, he didn't lack motivation. *Hell, why not?*

"Fine. I'll ask Dr Kubar if you can be my assistant. Now, will you please allow me to eat the rest of my meal in peace?"

Jason grinned as he rose from the table. "You won't regret this."

Rosalind continued to chew in silence. She had just emptied her plate when the doctor arrived. "It is good you are up early," he said, standing over her. "We have much work to do today."

"Give me a second to drink my coffee. Why don't you join me?"

"Um, okay," Kubar replied, taking the seat opposite.

"Actually, there were a couple of things I wanted to ask you."

"Go on."

"You know I have an artificial eye. It has a rechargeable battery, but now it's run out of juice. Can you find me a charger?"

Kubar leant forwards to study her implant. "I cannot tell. This is not something we have in my country."

"From my understanding, it uses inductive charging. They use the same technology for phones and electric toothbrushes. At home, I have one built into my pillow."

"I am certain I cannot obtain this here."

Rosalind gave an exasperated sigh. "I just told you they build the same thing into all sorts of everyday devices. Perhaps you could buy a wireless phone charger. I'm sure that would do the job."

"I will see if I can get this for you."

"Thank you. If you want me to work at my best, I need the use of both eyes." Rosalind drained the cup, wincing at the bitter taste, and replaced it on the table. "There was another thing. My son asked whether he could assist me."

"Your son?"

"Yes, Jason. He's studying Biochemistry at university. It would be useful to have somebody to enter data while we focus on the important stuff. And he also wants to save his boy."

"Okay," Kubar said. "If you think he can help, I will ask Professor Halfon."

"Good. And the other matter we talked about?"

Kubar threw a glance at the guards sitting in the glass-fronted office on the other side of the room. "I do not want to discuss that here. Now, if you are ready, shall we start work?"

Rosalind rose to her feet and followed him to the locked door. He waved his badge at the reader, and the lock clunked.

"If you don't mind me saying, it doesn't seem very high tech to open doors with a card," Rosalind said.

Kubar turned to her. "Oh, it is not just that. Somebody is watching all the time." He gestured towards a small black circle in the ceiling. "It will not operate unless an operator in the control room gives approval. It is like when you buy petrol."

"Petrol?"

"Ah, of course. I forget. All cars in the west use electricity now. Here, we still burn oil. When you pick up the handle, a person must approve before fuel flows."

"Yeah, I vaguely remember those disappearing a few years ago when everybody swapped to electric. So, you're saying you can't open the door without somebody operating the lock remotely."

"Yes, that is true for most," Kubar replied. "I heard a colleague say Professor Halfon does not need this. His card operates the locks immediately. He does not like to wait."

"Hmm. I get the impression he's not a patient man." Rosalind put down the empty cup. "Shall we go?"

45

Monday 21st July 2036

Tripoli Infectious Diseases Hospital, Republic of North Africa
17 days until the deadline

Dr Kubar lowered himself into the uncomfortable wooden chair.

Professor Halfon regarded him from the other side of the heavy wooden desk. "So, tell me, how is the research going?" he asked.

"She has given us much information about the manufacture of Lucinase. I have passed it on to the chemists."

Halfon grunted. "I know this already. I expect production to start in the next few weeks. What of the work on developing a cure for this new strain?"

"We have been reviewing the previous research from the team."

"*Your* team," Halfon interjected. "Go on."

"Yes, of course, my team. We have not yet discussed her ideas."

"I am sure I need not remind you that time is short."

"No, sir. I am well aware of the deadline. This is why I wanted to talk to you. I have some requests to help speed up our work. Did you know the Baxter woman has an artificial eye?"

Halfon let out a scoff. "Yes, this is the reason she hates another of our guests."

"She told me Max Perrin was involved, but she did not tell me what happened."

"He broke into her house and gave her a drug that removed her free will, the same one he used to rape the girl. Then he ordered her to push a pen into her own eye."

Kubar gasped. "Why did he do this?"

Halfon leant forwards. "She killed the boy's father in front of him using an identical pen she snatched from his pocket. Perrin senior was about to give the formula for Lucinase to the British authorities before she had negotiated an amnesty for their past crimes. You wouldn't think she was capable of such violence to look at her. Anyway, why do you bring this up?"

Kubar hesitated for a moment as he processed the professor's words. There was far more to the woman than he had ever imagined. Still, she had offered him a possible route of escape. After what he had heard, could he trust her? He took a deep breath before continuing. "Her implant contains a rechargeable battery, which is now empty. She needs a charger to replenish the charge and make it function again."

"She has another eye. Isn't that enough?"

"Perhaps, but she tells me she requires the use of both eyes if she is to work at peak efficiency."

Halfon studied his subordinate carefully. "And you are sure this is not a trick?"

"I don't think so, sir."

"Where would we get such a thing?"

"It is unlikely the manufacturer would sell us this item, and in addition, it would take too long to import. She has informed me that the technology is the same as that used to charge mobile phones. This we can buy at the local market."

Halfon nodded slowly. "All right, but I hold you personally responsible if there are any problems. Was there anything else?"

"Yes. She has also requested that we allow her adopted son to work with her."

"You surprise me. Did she not threaten to kill him along with the girl? At least that is what Mr Perrin told us."

"I was not aware of that, sir."

Halfon tapped the table with his fingernails. "Well, if she is asking for his help, it seems they must have put it behind them. Go on."

"He is studying Biochemistry at university. He has the skills to perform the role of a lab assistant. We can always use more staff."

Halfon glared at his subordinate. "You lead the science team. The decision is yours. He is your responsibility. Is that all?"

"Have you had the time to check up on—?"

"Enough!" The professor leant forwards with both palms on the desk. A deep scowl clouded his features. "I told you before, I am still waiting for a reply about your daughter. When I receive an answer, you will be the first to hear."

Kubar stood. "Thank you, sir. I will get back to work."

46

Thursday 24th July 2036

Tripoli Infectious Diseases Hospital, Republic of North Africa
14 days until the deadline

"There, that should do the business," Jason said, pointing to the device on the desk. This was his third day working with the science team. So far, he had helped one scientist to monitor an experiment, but the others seemed suspicious of the relationship between him and his adoptive mother and declined his offers of help.

"What?" Rosalind Baxter replied. She was deeply engrossed in an article from a virology journal.

"The charger for your eye."

Earlier that day, Dr Kubar had brought a couple of different charging devices. Jason had skimmed through the pidgin English of the manuals and connected the larger of the two. Operation of the units seemed simple enough.

Rosalind studied the black plastic slab lying on the surface of the desk with a wire trailing to the mains socket. "Are you sure this will work?"

"There's only one way to find out. I assume your implant uses the same frequencies to charge as mobile phones. If it works, I can look at ways of charging while you do other things."

"Let's give it a go. What shall I do?"

"We need to get the pad as close to your eye as possible. Rest the right side of your head on there."

Rosalind followed his instructions. "Like this?"

"Yeah. Is anything happening?"

She waited a moment before responding. "Nothing yet."

"It might take a minute or two."

Rosalind held the same position. "No, nothing's… hang on. I just saw a flicker, but it was very faint. I can't quite make out… There's some text. It says it's booting."

"Excellent," Jason said. "I was wondering whether you had become desensitised to the signals."

"What do you mean?"

"The human brain is always making and breaking connections. You remember the experiments they did in the nineteenth century when they got people to wear glasses fitted with special lenses which inverted the images reaching each eye. At first, the subjects couldn't see properly, but after a few days, they adapted and saw things correctly even though the light hitting their retinas was the opposite way to normal."

Rosalind grimaced. "Yes, Jason. I have read a thing or two about science in my time. Afterwards, when they took off the glasses at the end of the experiment, everything was upside down again for a while until the patients' eyesight automatically adjusted back."

Jason grinned sheepishly. "So, you already know the story. I was worried your brain might have forgotten how to process the signals."

"Well, the good news is that the startup messages are visible. And they're the right way up. It's about to reach a hundred percent. Yes! I can see again."

"So, everything looks all right?"

"There are various message boxes popping up. There's a warning that the charge is low. Hardly surprising, I suppose. Let me just clear that." She swept a hand in front of her face as if waving away an insect. "The next one is asking if I want to connect to a Wi-Fi network."

Jason grasped Rosalind's arm in excitement. "You never mentioned you could link to wireless networks." He lowered his voice to a whisper. "Maybe we could use your eye to contact somebody back home and ask for help."

"It never occurred to me until now. Let me check which ones are available." She held a finger to her earlobe and muttered a few words.

"Sorry, I didn't get that."

Rosalind released her ear. "I wasn't talking to you. It lets the implant know I'm giving it a command. I've no idea how it works. Anyway, there are two signals: TIDH one and TIDH two. Damn! Both are password protected."

Jason's shoulders sagged in disappointment. He was about to ask another question when he sensed a presence behind him. He whirled around as Professor Halfon strode towards them.

Rosalind hadn't detected the director's approach. "Perhaps we could—"

Jason dug his fingernails into Rosalind's arm.

"Ouch! Why did you—?"

"Hello, Professor," Jason said in a loud voice. Rosalind jerked upright.

"Did you not sleep properly last night, Mrs Baxter?" Halfon asked as he stared down suspiciously at the two prisoners. "I hope it is not because of your new accommodations."

"I don't know how you expect us to work at peak efficiency when you're detaining us in these appalling conditions," Rosalind replied, "but as it happens, I slept fine."

"We were charging her eye," Jason added.

"Ah yes, Doctor Kubar mentioned this to me. But how do you intend to perform research with your head on the table?"

"I won't," Rosalind said, her tone frosty. "We're just proving the charger works. Now that we know it does, we'll set up something more practical. Is there anything else we can help you with?"

"What progress are you making? Are you any closer to a cure?"

Rosalind stared at Halfon. "We've been here about a week. I'm not a miracle worker. I retired three years ago, so it'll take a while for me to catch up with the latest research papers."

"Just remember that in two weeks, your grandson will be the test subject. His life depends upon your efforts."

"I'm well aware of that," Rosalind snapped, "and as I've told you several times already, that's a ridiculously short amount of time to solve this problem."

"Be that as it may, the deadline remains the same. I am sure we will talk soon."

Halfon turned away and headed across the room.

"The damned thing's packed in again," Rosalind said.

Jason waited until the professor was out of earshot. "I take it you still believe the timescales are unrealistic."

"What do you think? Of course they are. I told you the chances of developing a cure in a three-week timeframe were almost non-existent, and we're already one-week in."

Jason stared at his mother. "In that case, we'd better start planning our escape. And the fact you can link your eye to Wi-Fi networks may help us. Now what we need is a password."

47

Friday 25th July 2036

Tripoli Infectious Diseases Hospital, Republic of North Africa
13 days until the deadline

Jason slipped the T-shirt over Paul's head as Dr Kubar entered the room. Antimone rearranged her son's fine hair. A few yards away, Rosalind Baxter sat at the dining table, a look of thunder on her face. The doctor's arrival came as a welcome relief to the tension in the room.

"Did you sleep well?" Kubar asked.

Rosalind fixed the doctor with an icy stare. She gestured towards the black slab of plastic on her bed. "They wouldn't fetch an extension lead for the charger, so I'm still blind in one eye."

"I apologise. Tonight will be different. I will speak to the guards. Are you ready to start work?"

"I'm good to go," Jason replied.

"Excellent. I have some ideas I want to discuss with you," Kubar said.

"Can't wait," Rosalind muttered.

Jason bent to kiss Antimone on the cheek. "I'm off to the lab now." He patted his son on the head. "See you later, buddy. Look after Mummy."

Antimone stared up at him listlessly. She wasn't coping well with the boredom of their confinement.

"I'm sorry," he said. He lowered his voice. "I'll try to get hold of the Wi-Fi password."

"Good luck," she murmured.

He shot her a guilty sideways glance as he walked away.

The threesome made their way to the lift where Kubar presented his access card. The doors opened, and they stepped inside. Jason watched as the doctor selected the centremost of five buttons. "What's on the bottom level?"

"It is the basement where the cells are. You do not want to go there."

"Is that where they're keeping Max Perrin?"

Kubar glanced at Jason but didn't reply.

"I was just curious," Jason said.

They emerged from the lift and followed the corridor through the dining area. The low hum of conversation quietened as Kubar led them past the tables where groups of scientists sat eating their breakfast. Several pairs of distrustful eyes tracked their progress. After passing through a final set of locked doors, they entered the laboratory.

Nobody acknowledged their arrival as they approached a pair of workstations.

"So, what was this idea of yours?" Rosalind asked.

"Oh, it is probably stupid," Kubar replied, "but we know the lytic phase of the virus is triggered by pheromones emitted by pregnant women. I wonder if we can stop these molecules binding to the receptors on the target cell's outer membrane. Without a trigger, the cell won't lyse."

"I was reading an article on the subject only yesterday. In principle, something like that might work."

"I think I understand what you're saying," Jason said. "If we block all the cell receptor sites with a compound that doesn't react with the virus, it would never receive the signal that makes it activate."

"Correct," Rosalind agreed. "The big problem is finding a substance that won't prevent normal operation of the cell causing it to die and that isn't toxic to the patient in some other way. It's an approach we spent a lot of time on at Ilithyia."

Kubar's eyes lit up with excitement. "Good. Tell me more about this work."

"Before we do any of that," Rosalind replied, "I'm going to charge my implant." She moved across to the desk she had been using the previous day, flicked on the mains switch and rested her head sideways on the charger pad.

"Mrs Baxter," the doctor said, "your grandson's life depends on this research. Can you not do this tonight?"

"Well, if the guards had brought the extension lead last night as I requested, I wouldn't need to do it now, would I?"

Kubar shot a glance at Jason.

"All right," Jason replied, "I can't really contribute much to the medical side. But I can probably improvise something that would enable you to work and charge your eye at the same time."

"How long would that take?" Kubar asked.

"Half an hour at most."

"Surely you can wait for thirty minutes, Mrs Baxter."

Rosalind raised her head. She alternated her gaze between Jason and the doctor. Finally, she let out a sigh of exasperation. "If this doesn't work, I'm going to lie here until my eye is fully charged."

"Good. What do you need, Mr Floyd?"

Jason reeled off a list of items. Kubar left to pass on the request.

Jason cleared his throat. He turned to his mother but didn't speak.

"Is something on your mind?" she asked.

"Ah… I was just wondering."

"Go on then. Spit it out."

Jason stared at the surface of the desk. "That email you sent: the one where you wanted to see us. What was that all about?"

Rosalind glared at him. "Why does that matter now?"

Jason raised his head slowly. "Three years ago, you trapped us in an incinerator and threatened to turn it on. Then a few weeks back, you proposed we meet up as if nothing unusual had happened. Isn't that a bit strange?"

Rosalind looked away. After a few seconds, she returned his gaze. "I don't know. I'd probably had too much to drink."

"Is that really it?"

Rosalind hesitated for a moment. "Okay, I'll admit I missed having another person in the house. I never had any close friends, at least not in recent history, and it was hard having nobody to talk to. All my life, I've struggled to achieve something, to prove I'm the best. Then, at last, it happened. It was like swimming underwater, being pulled along by a strong current. I surfaced only to find I was all alone, miles from land."

"So, you felt sorry for yourself?"

"No… well, maybe a little. If I'm being totally honest, I regret the way I behaved towards you. You might not believe it, but I'd become quite fond of you. I allowed my anger to get the better of me, and now… I wish things had turned out differently between us."

"Why did you bring Antimone and Paul into it? Why didn't you ask to see me alone?"

"I'm not sure. I guess I wanted to apologise to her as well."

Jason frowned. "Seriously? You never liked her, even before everything."

Rosalind stared at him for a moment. "If you really want to know, I thought you could do better."

"Is that why you made no attempt to stop her wheelchair when we were on the boat?"

"No, of course not. I told you I couldn't move properly because of my knee, and that's the truth."

"Anyway, we're an item now, Mum."

Rosalind blinked at the unexpected term of address. "Yes, I realise that."

"So, why ask to see all of us together?"

"I thought there was more chance of you coming if I invited the three of you."

Jason mulled over his mother's words. He still didn't fully trust her, but they bore the ring of truth. He stared at her for a moment before speaking. "Fine. If we ever get out of here, we'll come as a family and visit you—but only if you save Paul."

Rosalind ran her fingers through her hair. "I've already told you, the likelihood of developing a cure in the available time is miniscule. We have a far better chance of surviving by escaping from this hole—and at the moment, our only hope of doing that depends upon me connecting to the Wi-Fi and getting a message out."

"A day or two back, General Shaladi suggested we join forces. He has people on the outside who are still loyal to him. He wants us to work together."

"And you trust that bastard?"

"Not entirely, no, but he gave me his word that if we help him, he'll get us out of here."

"Who would he take with him?"

Best not to tell her what Shaladi had said. "You, Antimone, Paul and me. And of course, his daughter."

"So, not Perrin?"

"No."

"Good." Rosalind's eyes narrowed in thought. "Maybe Shaladi knows the Wi-Fi password. The other option is Kubar. I've told him I'll try to find him a job in Europe if he helps us escape. I reckon he'd do it except that he doesn't want to leave until he finds out what happened to his daughter. She went missing a few years ago, and he hasn't heard from her since."

"Does he know about the wireless function of your implant?"

"No, I haven't told him about that. I'm not sure I trust him enough yet."

"Surely he would have the Wi-Fi password."

"You'd think so," Rosalind agreed, "but I can't ask him without telling him what my eye can do."

"I suggest we keep it that way for the moment."

"Agreed. Here he comes now."

Kubar strolled towards them. "Here are the items you asked for, Mr Floyd."

"Thanks."

"Mrs Baxter, while Jason works on the charger, perhaps you can tell me more about your previous work."

Rosalind and the doctor moved to the adjacent workstation. Soon, they were deep in discussion. Kubar scribbled in a notebook, stopping occasionally to ask a question, as the former CEO of Ilithyia Biotechnology described the research her company had undertaken.

Jason laid out the parts. He picked up the baseball cap, tore off a length of duct tape and used it to attach the charging pad to the right side. It took several attempts to get the plastic slab to hang in the right position. When he was satisfied, he strengthened the join with more strips. He placed the contraption on his head and adjusted the strap at the back of the hat until it was a tight fit. The design wouldn't win any awards for style, but hopefully, it would perform its function.

He detached the mains cable and carried the assembly to where Rosalind and Kubar sat. "Are you ready to give it a try?"

Rosalind couldn't hide her dismay as she took in the arrangement. "You don't seriously expect me to wear that?"

"I know it doesn't look great, but it should mean you can work and charge your eye at the same time. If you put the charger under your pillow tonight as well, you probably won't need it tomorrow."

Rosalind reluctantly accepted the equipment. "If either of you two laughs, I'm taking it off immediately."

Jason stifled his amusement and helped her to tighten the strap. Next, he plugged in the power cable and flicked the switch. "Is anything happening?"

Rosalind stared straight ahead for a moment. "Yes, there was a flicker. It's booting."

Jason flashed a glance at Kubar. Somehow, they needed the wireless password. The doctor was their best chance, but would he help or turn them in?

48

Friday 25th July 2036

Tripoli Infectious Diseases Hospital, Republic of North Africa
13 days until the deadline

Jason glanced at his watch band: 19:05. A surge of guilt hit him. During his long day in the laboratory, Antimone had been looking after Paul by herself.

Dr Kubar rubbed the back of his neck. "So, you do not want to sleep with the charger beneath your pillow?" he asked.

Rosalind continued to stare at the screen. "No," she replied absentmindedly.

"But I thought you wanted to charge it fully."

She tore her gaze away from the computer display and turned to the doctor. "If I wear this ridiculous contraption again tomorrow—no offence, Jason—it should reach at least seventy percent."

"None taken," Jason said. "I told you it wouldn't win any fashion prizes."

"Hmm," Rosalind grunted. Her focus had already returned to the three-dimensional molecular model that spun as she waved her fingers in front of the monitor. She continued to study the image for a few seconds longer, then sat back. "It's worth a try," she said. "Do you have any way to make this?" she asked, directing her question at Kubar. "We should perform some cell culture trials when we've done a few more simulations."

"Doctor Brandt has used the molecular synthesiser a few times to manufacture various compounds."

"I don't think I'm his favourite person," Rosalind said. "Then again, none of them seem to like me."

"You can hardly blame them. Everybody has lost loved ones to this virus, and you created it. On top of this, they all hold you responsible for Professor Halfon's demand that they do not leave the building."

"But that's nothing to—"

"I know, but it does not stop them making you a—how do you say?—escape goat.

Jason stifled a snort of laughter. "I think you mean a scapegoat."

Kubar smiled apologetically. "Ah yes, please forgive my poor English."

Rosalind remained unamused. "Have you considered my offer?"

Kubar's smile dropped instantly. He glanced anxiously at the bored-looking guard, leaning with his back against the wall on the other side of the room. He lowered his voice to a whisper. "As I have told you before, I cannot leave until I know the fate of my daughter."

"And what are you doing about that?"

"I have asked Professor Halfon."

She raised an eyebrow.

Kubar stared at her for a moment. "He promised me he will check the database. I will ask him again."

"Well, here's your chance." Rosalind's gaze shifted to an approaching figure.

The doctor twisted in his seat, then hurriedly turned back.

"What is this?" Halfon asked, pointing at the screen.

"You're not one for small talk, are you?" Rosalind said, scowling at the director. "It's an idea we've been discussing this afternoon, but we're not ready to take it further yet."

Halfon's eyes narrowed before he spoke. "There is no shortage of test subjects. Please remember there is a tight deadline."

"We haven't forgotten that, but it's still at a preliminary stage. It'll be a few days before we contemplate any form of testing. We'll run it through a suite of simulations first. If you want me to work for you, we'll do things my way."

"Very well, but Mullah Awad is not a patient man. Now, is there anything you need for this to go quicker?"

"Not really," Rosalind replied. "A team of real experts would help, but nothing that you can provide right now."

"In that case, I will leave you to your research."

***

"Excuse me, sir," Kubar called as he jogged after Halfon.

The professor stopped and turned to his subordinate. "What is it?"

The doctor lowered his head in deference. "If I may speak in private for a moment," he said.

They moved a few paces away from Rosalind and Jason.

Halfon glared at Kubar. "If this is about your daughter again, I told you I would look into this matter. However, I am a very busy man. Your only concern right now is to find a cure for this disease. Unless we deliver a treatment, I cannot guarantee any of us will leave this building. Do you understand?"

Kubar bobbed his head in acquiescence. "Yes, of course."

"Good. If there are any *technical* matters for which you need my help, please do not hesitate to contact me. If there is nothing else, you should get back to work."

"Right away, sir."

"By the way, I assume that ridiculous contraption the infidel woman is wearing is for her eye."

"Yes. It is an improvised charger."

"Well, as long as it doesn't stop her working."

"On the contrary. Unless the battery is charged, she cannot see properly."

"If we ever solve the virus problem, perhaps we should study the technology inside her head. It might provide our people with something we can use ourselves."

"That is a good idea, sir."

"Right, I have much to do."

Halfon marched towards the exit without acknowledging the two Westerners.

After he had passed through the security door, Rosalind asked, "What did he say? I bet he hasn't done anything, has he?"

Kubar picked at a fingernail. "He told me he is looking into it."

"Just like he does every time you ask. You have to accept he can't be bothered."

Kubar's jaw took on a stubborn tilt. "I cannot leave until I discover my daughter's fate. As a mother yourself, you must understand this."

Rosalind locked eyes with Jason. Nobody spoke for a few seconds. Eventually, she broke the silence. "Don't you think we've done enough for tonight?"

Kubar glanced at his watch. "I have nowhere else to go, but I am feeling hungry."

"Let's call it a night then. We'll look at this with a fresh perspective tomorrow. I need a rest."

"I will take you back to your quarters," Kubar said, standing.

Rosalind removed the headset and placed it on the desk. "It's a relief to get that thing off."

"What's the charge level?" Jason asked.

Rosalind's features took on an absent expression as she studied the image being transmitted directly into her brain. "It's saying thirty-six percent. That should keep me going for at least a week."

"You're welcome," Jason said drily.

Rosalind scowled at him. "I already thanked you earlier. But if it makes you feel better, thanks again."

Kubar's gaze switched from one to the other. "Come. Let us find some food." He gestured towards the doorway.

Jason led the way, trailed by Rosalind and the North African doctor. They followed the corridor to the eating area. Once again, the conversation hushed as they entered.

"Murderer," a voice whispered.

Rosalind whipped around. Several of the seated scientists glared at her with hatred in their eyes.

"Just ignore them," Kubar muttered, lengthening his stride. They reached the next sealed door without further incident. Moments later, the group of three stepped into the elevator.

"That was uncomfortable," Jason said, glancing at Rosalind. She stared straight ahead without acknowledging his comment.

The doors slid apart. Kubar led them down the corridor and into the area holding the other prisoners. "Here we are," he announced brightly. "Enjoy your meal. I will see you tomorrow morning. I hope you dream of a solution to our problem."

Rosalind grimaced. She waited silently until the doctor was out of sight.

"I can't wait to get out of here," she said.

49

Friday 25th July 2036

Tripoli Infectious Diseases Hospital, Republic of North Africa
13 days until the deadline

When they arrived back at the communal area, Paul was sitting on Antimone's lap, his arms wrapped around his mother's neck. Jason lowered his upper body to envelope mother and son in a tight embrace. Meanwhile, Rosalind grabbed a plate and filled it with food from the dishes laid out on the trolley.

"What's your day been like?" Jason asked. "I see you've got a new wheelchair."

"Boring as hell," Antimone replied, "but this one is a vast improvement. At long last, I can steer myself around without having to lean down to those tiny wheels. I've been spending some time with Aya Shaladi too. She's not so bad when you get to know her."

"Really? I thought you hated her guts."

"She was telling me what it's like for women here. The men treat them as second-class citizens. It's like something out of the dark ages. If she'd refused to help her father in their mission, the authorities would've had both of them killed."

"That doesn't excuse what they did to us," Jason said, grimacing.

"Maybe not. She's been helping me keep Paul entertained as well. She was driving him around in my old wheelchair. He told me afterwards he wanted to be in a wheelchair when he grew up."

Jason stifled a laugh. "That's kids for you."

"He even asked me whether she could be his mummy too."

"Christ."

"Anyway, what about your day?" Antimone asked. "Are they getting any closer to developing something to keep Paul safe?"

"Well, all the other scientists seem to hate us, and Professor Halfon is itching to test every random compound we consider on a live subject before we've even simulated the effects, but apart from that, it's been great. Seriously though, I think we're making good progress."

"Enough to come up with a cure in the next two weeks?"

Jason lowered his voice. "Probably not. My mother keeps saying the timescales are impossible."

Antimone glanced around. Max sat alone at the far end of the adjacent table. Rosalind occupied a spot on the opposite side, maximising the distance between herself and the main target of her hatred. General Shaladi and his daughter were helping themselves to food.

"That just confirms what we suspected all along; we've got to escape," Antimone whispered. "Have you made any progress on a plan?"

"Not so far," Jason replied.

"Well, we better come up with something unless you fancy trying to overpower those three." She nodded towards the guards sitting in the smoke-filled office a few yards away. The armed men seemed more intent on playing cards than guarding their prisoners.

"My mother's eye is charged again. If we got hold of the Wi-Fi password, she could use the in-built wireless link to connect to the outside world and get a message out."

"And how are we going to find that out?"

"As I see it, there are two people who might have it. One is Doctor Kubar. The other is sitting right there." Jason's gaze flicked towards the general and his daughter. "Do you think we can trust him?"

"Like I said, they had to follow orders, or they would've been killed."

"He didn't have to execute his own man though, did he? Judging by what he told us a few days ago, he wants to get out as much as we do. Even if we escape from this building, we'll need his help to reach the border."

Antimone studied Jason's face. "I think we should ask him."

"Okay, but we have to play this carefully. We mustn't tell him why we want the code."

As Shaladi turned with a full plate in his hand, Jason spoke in a low voice. "General, would you like to join us?"

The general shrugged and sat opposite Jason and Antimone. He leant forwards and rested his elbows on the table. "Do you have a plan?" he whispered.

Jason moved his head closer to Shaladi's. "Maybe. Do you know the Wi-Fi password?"

A glint of excitement sparkled in the general's eyes. "Why? Did you find a phone?"

"No, but we may have a way to link to the Internet."

"Oh." Shaladi's body seemed to deflate. "I am sorry, but I do not have this information. If you do discover the password, I must send a message to my people so they can help us once we are out."

"What are you talking about?" Aya Shaladi asked, sitting beside her father.

"Our friends have found a way to communicate with the outside world, but they need the Wi-Fi password."

Jason exchanged a glance with Antimone at the mention of the term *friend.*

"Could you ask one of the scientists?" Aya said. "They may know it. They must realise they are also prisoners."

"Why don't you just announce it to the guards?" came Rosalind Baxter's petulant voice from behind them. "Try to keep your voices down. And by the way, you need my help to do this."

A guilty silence fell over the group. Antimone glanced towards the glass window of the office. Their minders were engrossed in a card game and seemed oblivious to the conversation taking place on the other side of the room. Her gaze swung to the figure of Max Perrin. He was staring in their direction. As their eyes met, he looked away.

"Actually," Jason said, his voice now a whisper, "there may still be a way you can help us. Do you have access to any of your government databases?"

The general gave a low laugh. "There are many different systems. What do you require?"

"Is there one to track down a missing person?"

"Yes, but a lot of people in this country disappear with no trace. If the government has knowledge of a citizen, then I can check their status. At least, I could before this. I do not know if I still have permission. Why do you ask?"

"I may be able to get the Wi-Fi password in exchange for finding out what happened to a specific person."

"So, you want me to tell you how to access this site?" Shaladi asked. He rubbed the back of his neck. "And how well can you read Arabic?"

"Not at all," Jason replied

"That is a problem. How will you understand the words?"

"Um… I don't know."

"If they find out that I gave you this information, it is not like in the West. There will be no trial. They will kill me."

Antimone sighed. "I hate to break this to you, but isn't there a good chance they might do that anyway? You already told us they probably executed your men."

Once again, silence descended, broken only by the muffled laughter of the guards in the nearby office. The general sat with his head lowered.

Finally, he raised his eyes and stared at Jason. "You may be right. I will give you my decision in the morning."

50

Saturday 26th July 2036

Tripoli Infectious Diseases Hospital, Republic of North Africa
12 days until the deadline

The next morning, Jason was reading the Harry Potter paperback when General Shaladi settled down on the bench beside him. Antimone was washing Paul in the bathroom.

"I have given your proposal much thought," the general said. "You need four pieces of information to access the website containing details of our citizens: the site address, a username, a password and a military service number. Before I give this to you, I must understand how you will use it."

Jason took his time placing the book on the table as he thought. What should he reveal? Could he really trust the general? "Okay," he said, drawing out the last syllable. "Somebody is worried about a family member. If we discover what happened to her, he may give us what we want."

"You mean Doctor Kubar?"

Jason felt the blood rush to his face. *So much for not revealing anything.* "Yeah," he murmured.

Shaladi's lips curved into a smirk. "I thought so. If you find the information for his daughter, he will help us? If the authorities are holding her, it is unlikely he will risk her safety. This is how they work. They make threats to keep the people in order."

"I don't know."

"It is true. You better hope she is not alive."

Jason turned sideways towards the general.

"Do not look at me," Shaladi hissed. "If I was a gambling man," he continued in a conciliatory tone, "I would bet that she is dead. Many women have died in this country. You will need the doctor's help to access the database—unless you have learned to speak Arabic overnight."

"So, you'll give me the information?" Jason said. A prod on the thigh provided the response.

"Take it," Shaladi whispered. "Put it in your pocket. Do not let the guards see."

Jason's fingers closed around a scrap of paper. His gaze flicked towards the two men in the glass-fronted office. They sat with half-open eyes, staring at a screen. Neither seemed to be paying any attention to their prisoners. He slipped the note into the pocket of his jeans. "Thanks," he replied.

"It is extremely dangerous for me to give you this information. As I told you yesterday, if they discover what I have done, they will execute me immediately. Only use the database if you are confident you can do so without being discovered."

"How are we going to escape from here with all these guards?"

Shaladi tapped the table with a fingernail. "I do not know yet, but we will not get far unless we have outside help. And remember, I can only take you to the border. You must find your own way home from there. Now, do not let them see us talking, so please sit somewhere else."

Jason opened his mouth to object. Why should he be the one to move? But maybe this wasn't the time for an argument. He picked up the book and shuffled down the bench away from the general. He opened the pages but found he could no longer concentrate on the words. Moments later, Antimone and Paul returned from the bathroom.

"Shaladi has given me his login details," he whispered as he leant over to lift his son off Antimone's lap.

"Good luck," she replied. "Be careful."

He tried to entertain his son with made-up stories, but his mind kept wandering much to Paul's annoyance. It was another forty minutes before Kubar arrived.

Jason lowered his face to kiss Antimone and patted Paul on the head. "Sorry, but Daddy's got to go to work."

"Please," the doctor said. "Come with me." Unlike the previous day, his features were set in a sombre expression.

"Is something wrong?" Jason asked.

Kubar didn't reply. He watched Rosalind as she put on her shoes. "I'm ready," she announced. "I thought we were going to have an early start."

The doctor ignored her statement and marched towards the door. Jason and Rosalind exchanged a glance as they hurried to keep up. They entered the lift and rode up a floor in silence. They passed through the dining area, once again running the gauntlet of cold stares from the few scientists who were still eating. Kubar led them down the corridors and into the laboratory. The group of three crossed the room to the workstations they had occupied the previous day.

Rosalind settled into a chair. Her eyes surveyed the work surface, looking for the cap and improvised charger. "Where's it gone?" she asked, glancing up sharply. "I left it here."

Kubar pointed at the small, circular bin beside the desk. "It is in there."

"What? You've thrown it away?" Rosalind asked in astonishment.

"Yes," the doctor replied, "but it is of no use to you now."

She leant forwards and reached inside to retrieve the contents. A piece of tape still attached the charging pad to the hat, but the black slab now comprised two parts, each with a jagged edge where it had snapped in half. A thin strand of wire connected the halves. Somebody had also hacked off the power cable.

"Who did this?" Rosalind asked, glowering at the doctor.

Kubar shrugged. "I do not know."

"There's some writing on the front of the cap," Jason said in a low voice.

Rosalind rotated the material in her hand and read the single word: *Murderer*. Her face drained of colour except for the bright-red circles forming on each cheek. An uncomfortable stillness settled on the room. Rosalind raised her head. All conversation ceased around them. Her eyes darted from one group of scientists to another as she tried to identify the culprit. The onlookers, who had been watching the exchange with keen interest, looked away under the fierce coldness of her gaze.

She turned her focus to Kubar. "Are you going to do something about this?" she asked, her voice trembling with barely suppressed fury.

The doctor cleared his throat. "Unfortunately, we do not know who is responsible."

"And you still expect me to work with these people?" A speck of saliva flew from her mouth as she spat out the last word.

"I agree this is unacceptable," Kubar said. "I will arrange for somebody to buy the parts so we can make a replacement."

"That's hardly the point though, is it? How can I trust my colleagues when this sort of immature behaviour takes place as soon as my back is turned?"

"It will not happen again."

"This whole exercise is futile. You pull together—or in cases like mine, kidnap—a team of misfits and mavericks who have never worked with each other before, then you prevent them from leaving the site or communicating with the outside world. Yet somehow, in a few weeks, you expect them to deliver the solution to a hugely complex problem. Frankly, it's ludicrous."

Kubar drew in a deep breath. He seemed about to say something when the direction of his gaze shifted.

Jason turned. "It looks like we've got company," he murmured.

Professor Halfon strode towards them purposefully. He stopped a pace away and surveyed the group of three. "Good morning," he said. "I trust everything is fine."

"Yeah," Rosalind replied, her voice dripping in sarcasm. "Just fantastic." She opened her fingers and allowed the broken contraption to drop into the bin.

If the director detected the simmering tension, he chose to ignore it. He cleared his throat. "There is something I want to show you. Please come with me."

Rosalind rose to her feet with exaggerated slowness. "What is it?"

"You will see."

Jason, Rosalind and Kubar trailed after the professor as he led them towards the enclosure in the centre of the room and peered through the clear panels.

Jason's pulse quickened. His mother had told him about the previous experiment they forced her to watch. With a surge of relief, he realised the area was empty. "What are you going to do?"

Halfon didn't reply. Instead, he tapped on the glass. The door at the end of the enclosed space opened. A man in a white protective suit entered, pushing a hospital trolley. A naked three- or four-year-old boy lay on top, his ribs prominent against the skin of his chest. Straps extended over his thin body, preventing him from moving. The child's eyes gazed listlessly at his surroundings.

Rosalind turned sideways and grasped Halfon's forearm. "What is this?"

The professor lowered his gaze to her hand. After a second, she took the hint and released her grip. Halfon focused his attention back on the boy. He nodded to the suited attendant and spoke without turning his head. "The child is conscious but has been sedated. The doctor in there is about to inject him with the compound you designed yesterday."

Rosalind's mouth opened in shock. "What? That was just an idea. We haven't even run any simulations yet. You have to stop this."

Halfon's eyes stayed locked on the restrained boy. "There are many test subjects but little time. Doctor Brandt programmed the molecular synthesiser last night."

"What effect will it have?" Jason asked, staring intently at Rosalind.

"I have no idea," she replied. "Anything could happen."

The white-suited figure picked up a syringe gun from the table at the side of the room and fitted a small vial of clear liquid.

Jason hammered his fists on the glass. "Hey! Leave him alone."

Rosalind joined in, slamming both palms against the window.

Halfon held up a hand and dragged his attention away from the trolley "Enough!"

A rifle barrel jabbed into the centre of Jason's back. A second guard pointed his weapon at Rosalind.

"If you cannot watch in silence," Halfon said, "I will have you bound and gagged."

The Westerners fell silent, although both still rested their hands on the glass. The man inside the room placed the syringe against the boy's upper arm and depressed the trigger. A low whimper emerged from the child's throat. Outside, the observers held their breath, waiting to see what would happen next. The suited doctor picked up a torch and directed the beam at the site of the injection. He leant over the boy and peered through his facemask.

Seconds passed in silence. Halfon withdrew a mobile device from the inner pocket of his jacket, tapped a few icons and stared at the screen. "Excellent. All his vital signs are stable. There is no immediate adverse reaction. We will observe him for twenty-four hours before performing further tests. Now, I suggest you get back to work."

Jason released the breath he had been holding and turned to Rosalind. “We can’t allow that to happen again,” he whispered.

51

Saturday 26th July 2036

Tripoli Infectious Diseases Hospital, Republic of North Africa
12 days until the deadline

The group returned to their workstations. Rosalind stared at the display for several seconds, then turned to Dr Kubar. "Did you know he was planning to do that?" she asked, her voice trembling with fury.

"No, he did not tell me," the doctor replied. "He must have looked at our work last night."

"This is totally unacceptable. Is he going to test every compound we come up with on a live subject before we've even had time to model it or test it in cell cultures?"

Kubar sighed. "I will talk to Professor Halfon."

"And what about Brandt? Aren't you in charge of him now? Doesn't he work for you?"

"Yes, but if the professor tells him to do something, he must obey. Everybody is under much pressure to deliver a solution."

"So, what happens next? Do they intend to expose that boy to a pregnant woman?"

"I do not know, but I think so."

"But that's ridiculous. The chances of it working are miniscule. The child will die needlessly."

"I am sorry, but there is little I can do."

The breath rasped in Rosalind's throat, and her pulse raced. "I'm going to delete the work from the machine at the end of every day."

"That would not be wise," Kubar said. "The professor will punish us if we do not deliver."

Rosalind slapped the surface of the desk. "How am I supposed to perform at my best under these conditions?"

Kubar shot an anxious glance towards the guards. "Please. You must remain calm."

Rosalind's eyes stared at the screen but took nothing in.

Several seconds passed until Jason broke the silence. "Have you given any more thought to helping us get out of here?" he asked, turning to the doctor.

Kubar looked away for a moment, then turned back. "I told you," he replied in a low voice, "I cannot leave until I learn about my daughter."

"What if we could access the database and find out?"

Kubar's gaze locked onto Jason. "How can you do this?"

Jason lowered his head. "I've got a username and password," he whispered.

"Where did this information come from?"

"I'll tell you when you agree to help us."

"It will not work," Kubar said. "The guards have taken all the mobile phones, and they monitor all the workstations."

"We may have a way around that too, but we don't have the Wi-Fi password. Do you know what it is?"

Kubar's eyes widened in surprise. "You have a phone?"

Rosalind's hand touched Jason's thigh. He met her gaze as she gave an almost imperceptible shake of the head.

"Something like that," he replied. "All we need is the password for the wireless network."

Kubar went still. He remained silent for several seconds. When he spoke, his voice was subdued. "I am not sure I want to find out."

Jason frowned in puzzlement. "Why not?"

"For now, there is hope. If I discover she is dead, then it is gone."

"But isn't it better to know one way or the other?"

"Perhaps." Kubar hung his head for a moment, then seemed to come to a decision. He looked up. "You are right. I will tell you the Wi-Fi password. In return, you will find out about my daughter. But we must be careful. They are always watching."

"Will they be able to detect a connection?"

"If they are looking, perhaps. I am not an expert in such matters. You should disconnect when you are not using the link."

"Can they tell what sites we've logged into?"

"Maybe. I do not know."

"Could you write the password down?"

Kubar's eyes flashed to the nearest guard. Satisfied the man was paying them no special attention, he grabbed a pen and scribbled a series of letters and digits on a piece of paper. "I cannot be sure it still works," he said.

Rosalind's face took on a blank expression. She touched her earlobe and muttered a few words. Moments later, she smiled. "It does work."

Kubar stared at her in surprise. "But… ah, of course, your eye."

"There's one other small problem," Jason said. "I assume the website is in Arabic, and my mother doesn't speak the language."

"Actually, I may have a solution for that," Rosalind said. "After the doctors installed my implant, they wanted to test it was working correctly, so they linked it wirelessly to a computer display to check out the quality of the image. I'm assuming we can do the same. That way you'd be able to see the same as me, and Doctor Kubar could tell me what to type in."

"You mean casting," Jason said. "These computers look fairly up to date. That should work." He tapped some keys on the virtual keyboard floating in front of the screen. "If you find the right menu option, you should be able to connect now."

A blank expression returned to Rosalind's face. The background hum of the machines filled the silence. Eventually, she turned to Jason. "There, I think I've set it up correctly."

A circular image of Jason's features appeared on the display. The contents jerked about as she changed the point of her focus.

"Now all we have to do is pull up a browser," she added. A rectangular window overlaid the central third of the picture.

"Can you show a keyboard, preferably with Arabic characters?" Kubar asked.

While Rosalind concentrated on responding to his request, Jason glanced surreptitiously around the room, then retrieved the scrap of paper from his pocket. He placed it on the work surface. After a few seconds, an array of keys materialised at the bottom of the screen.

"So, your secret helper is General Shaladi," Kubar said, studying the Arabic words.

"How did you—?" Jason started. Then realisation dawned. "Ah, of course: the username. Yeah, he told us he'd help us to escape."

As they watched the display, a series of characters appeared in the address bar. Moments later, a form popped up with three empty text boxes. Kubar showed the letters he wanted in each field.

"Come on," Jason said. "This is taking too long."

"That is the last one," Kubar replied. "Now click the button."

A list containing three results in Arabic script appeared on the page. The doctor leant forwards. He pointed to the middle entry. "This is my daughter."

The image changed once again. None of the characters meant anything to the two Westerners. Jason turned his attention to Kubar, watching as the doctor's gaze tracked down the rows of text.

"What does it say?" Jason asked.

Kubar did not respond at first. Then he leant back in his chair, his expression devoid of emotion. "You can turn it off now."

The image from Rosalind's eye disappeared from the screen. "I've disconnected from the wireless network," she said. "Is your daughter still alive?"

Kubar sat motionless, staring straight ahead. Rosalind shot a glance at Jason. He shrugged. Finally, the doctor turned his head slowly towards them.

"She died five years ago."

52

Saturday 26th July 2036

Tripoli Infectious Diseases Hospital, Republic of North Africa
12 days until the deadline

Max Perrin walked one pace ahead of his escort, standing to the side whenever they reached a locked door to allow the armed man to present his identity card to the reader. His mind raced. A week had gone by since striking the deal with Professor Halfon. What could he tell the administrator about the other prisoners? In truth, he had little to report, but if he didn't provide anything, he knew he would soon find himself sleeping in the cells.

When they arrived at the final set of doors before the professor's office, the lock refused to operate. The guard raised both hands in a petulant gesture as he glared up at the camera lens.

Perrin's gaze strayed to the holstered pistol on the guard's hip. The man subconsciously detected the focus of his prisoner's attention and moved his fingers down to the strap. After presenting the identification a second time, the mechanism operated with a loud clunk. The guard shoved Perrin down the carpeted corridor ahead of him, muttering curses under his breath.

"Easy, tiger," Perrin said, glancing backwards. "I think your boss will be interested in what I have to say."

His reward was another push in the back. They stopped at a door decorated with a large sign in Arabic script. His escort knocked once. A voice called out from inside, and the armed man turned the handle before ushering Perrin forwards.

"Please take a seat," Halfon said, gesturing towards an uncomfortable looking wooden chair. He uttered a brisk command to the guard, who departed without another word. "Can I get you anything? Tea? Water?"

"No, I'm fine," Perrin replied.

"I trust your accommodation is acceptable."

"Yeah, it's okay." Every evening, somebody came to collect Max from the communal prisoner area under the pretence of taking him to the cells. In fact, he spent the night in the relative comfort of his old room before they returned him to the other detainees in the morning.

"It is a week since we last talked. The deal was that you agreed to spy on the others for me. In exchange, I gave you certain privileges. There is still plenty of space in the basement. I hope you bring some news."

Perrin nodded.

Halfon placed his hands on the wooden surface of the desk. "So, tell me, are they planning anything?"

"Well… they're careful about discussing things in front of me, but something's definitely going on."

"What do you mean?"

Perrin leant forwards. "General Shaladi and his daughter kidnapped the rest of them, yet now everyone's acting like best buddies."

Halfon glowered at his prisoner. "Explain."

"Um… okay. Last night, the general sat beside Floyd while they ate. The girl joined them. I've never really seen them together before yesterday. They talked for a few minutes."

"What did they talk about?"

"Right, well the thing is, I didn't catch very much. They don't seem to trust me. I heard them mention the word *friends*."

"Hmph," Halfon said with a sneer. "This is hardly proof of a conspiracy. Maybe they have agreed to forget their differences."

"No, I'm sure it's not that. They were definitely planning something. They also mentioned the other scientists."

"Do you expect me to be impressed by this? I should throw you in the cells. That may concentrate your mind."

"Actually, there's more." Perrin lowered his voice. "The English group seems very friendly with that doctor."

"Kubar?"

"Yeah, that's him."

Halfon crossed his arms, his face set in a thoughtful expression. "This is perhaps not surprising. They work together. Did you hear what they were discussing?"

"Not really, at least nothing interesting beyond the usual everyday stuff."

"So, all you have brought me is your suspicions with no real evidence to back it up. I have heard enough. It is time for you to—"

"Look, I've done what you asked. I'll see if I can get closer to them. As soon as I hear anything at all, I'll tell you about it."

Halfon splayed his fingers, took a breath and held it for a moment. "All right. I will give you one last chance. I believe you are still motivated. Do not let me down."

53

Saturday 26th July 2036

Tripoli Infectious Diseases Hospital, Republic of North Africa
12 days until the deadline

Rosalind glanced towards Dr Kubar. He had barely spoken a word since learning of his daughter's death that morning. Both Jason and Rosalind tried to engage him as they explored possible approaches using the powerful molecular modelling software. Despite her initial reservations, Rosalind had to admit the tools at her disposal exceeded the capabilities of those at Ilithyia Biotechnology, the company she had once owned.

"Let's set this simulation going," she said, pointing to the screen. They had reviewed several compounds over the day, but the most promising candidate remained the same one Halfon had given to the boy earlier that morning. Even with the latest quantum algorithms, the program predicted the job would take at least seven hours to run. "What do you think?"

Kubar didn't reply. He stared sightlessly at the three-dimensional image.

"Doctor Kubar?"

The doctor's eyes regained focus. He turned to Rosalind. "I am sorry. Please repeat your question."

"It doesn't matter," Rosalind said. "You've not really been paying attention all afternoon." Her tone softened. "Not that I blame you in the circumstances. It must be a big shock."

Kubar took a deep breath and exhaled slowly. "I always feared she might not be alive. It is still hard for me to hear it confirmed." He lapsed once again into silence.

Jason cleared his throat. "I know this is a difficult time, but now that you've found out what happened to her, will you help us get out of here?"

The doctor's face tightened in anger. "I have lost a daughter, and all you care about is escaping."

"I have a child as well," Jason replied. "Unless we escape, he'll probably die too."

Kubar's angry expression morphed into one of remorse. "I am sorry. You are correct. The work they are doing here is wrong. I have—how do you say?—turned an unseeing eye for too long."

"Blind," Jason said.

"Yes, a blind eye," Kubar continued. "So many people have died. So many terrible things have happened, it starts to become normal. Now, they use children like test animals." He twisted to Rosalind. "You told me you will try to find a job for me in the West. Is this true?"

Rosalind looked away. She forced herself to turn back and meet the doctor's questioning expression. She spoke in a subdued voice. "I'll do what I can, but you saw the television pictures. I'm not exactly the world's most popular person at the moment."

Kubar stared up at the ceiling, then focused his gaze on Jason. "I will help you escape, but you must take as many of the children with you as possible. You tell me your son will die if he stays here; the same is true for them."

"That sounds like a fair deal," Jason agreed. "How do you plan to get us out?"

"Let me think about it," Kubar replied. "We will discuss this tomorrow."

"I propose we finish for the day," Rosalind said. "If we start the simulation now, it'll be done by morning. Will you please persuade Halfon to hold off testing on the boy?"

The doctor gave a resigned sigh. "You know what the professor is like. He will not listen to me, but I will try."

Rosalind reached out a finger and started the analysis. "At least there's nothing new today for that bastard to trial on one of those kids."

Kubar stood and led the two Westerners towards the exit under the watchful eyes of the guards. As before, a sudden hush in the conversation greeted their entry into the dining area. The doctor hurried past the seated scientists, ignoring the hostile glances cast in their direction. Moments later, he deposited his charges in the living quarters a floor down.

"I'm sorry once again for… you know," Jason said to Kubar. He glanced towards the general, whose gaze lasered in on him.

"Thank you. I will see you in the morning."

***

Dr Kubar turned around and retraced his steps, his mind a mass of conflicting emotions. He had agreed to help the Westerners escape, but was that the right decision? He had little left to live for following confirmation of his daughter's death. His own life counted for little in the grand scheme of things, but was he prepared to gamble everything on the chance of a new start in the West?

Maybe he should stay and continue to lead the efforts to develop a cure. Using children to test possible treatments turned his stomach, but if they were successful, how many more lives would be saved? What would his daughter want him to do?

Dr Kubar found himself outside Professor Halfon's door with no recollection of how he had arrived there. He wiped his damp palms on the white lab coat and knocked.

"Udkhul," came a shout from within. *Come in.*

Halfon looked up from his desk as the doctor entered. "Ah, Doctor Kubar. This is fortuitous. I wanted to speak to you. Please take a seat."

Kubar lowered himself into the wooden chair and found himself looking upwards slightly at his superior.

"There is good news," Halfon said, leaning forwards. "I checked on the status of your daughter this afternoon. She is alive and well, living in Alzintan, a town a few miles outside Tripoli. I contacted the local military commander, and he has agreed to bring her here in a few weeks."

"But…" Kubar stopped. He desperately wanted the professor's words to be true. But he had seen the entry with his own eyes. "Are you sure?" Every square inch of his face felt numb.

"Yes, of course. I checked it myself."

"She was born in two thousand and six."

Halfon tutted impatiently. "I know this. I spoke to the commander just a few hours ago. Your daughter is definitely alive. A group of rebels were holding her prisoner. The army discovered her during a raid last week. Unfortunately, it is not possible for you to see her until you finish your work here. I am sure you are very excited, but we must deliver on time. We cannot afford to lose even one day. It will be a double celebration when we come up with a cure."

The blood rushed in Kubar's ears. Could it be true? Had he examined the wrong entry earlier that morning? No, he had confirmed the date of birth… unless there was another woman with the same name and an identical birthday. But there had been only three entries, and the other two were considerably older than his daughter.

"You don't seem pleased." Halfon's words intruded on his thoughts.

"I am just surprised. I didn't expect after all this time…"

"You should be grateful. Now you can be reunited with your daughter."

"Could I speak to her on the phone?"

"Do you think it would be fair if we had one rule for you and another for everybody else?"

"Well—"

"I share your frustration, but I cannot make an exception. When you finish this work, you will be able to talk to her for as long as you like. Now, was there some other matter you wished to discuss with me?"

Kubar scratched his head as he tried to place his thoughts in order. "Actually, there was another thing. The boy who you gave the drug—"

Halfon drummed his fingers on the desk. "You need not worry. He has shown no adverse reaction."

"Yes, but we never even modelled the behaviour of this substance. Anything could have happened."

"But it didn't, did it? You should have more faith in your own work."

"I have faith in the scientific process. That means we run simulations, we test on cell cultures, we perform animal tests and only then do we consider conducting human trials."

Halfon banged the table with the palm of his hand. "You have not been listening. There is a deadline. If we do not deliver on time… well, I dare not think of the consequences. I gave a personal assurance to Mullah Awad that we would prepare a treatment within three weeks, and I intend to keep that promise. More than a week has already passed. You have been freed from the restrictions of conventional medical ethics so we can meet this commitment. This was a difficult decision, but we must sacrifice the lives of the few to benefit the many. Do you understand?"

"I..."

Halfon rose from his seat and leant over the desk, glaring down at the man sitting opposite. "I asked if you understood."

"Yes, Professor."

"Excellent. We will study the child's blood count over the coming days. In one week, the subject will be placed in a room with a heavily pregnant woman. I expect your full cooperation in analysing the results. Now, if there is nothing else, I have much work to do."

Kubar stood and nodded his head. Without another word, he turned and let himself out. He walked a few paces down the corridor, leant against the wall and exhaled a deep breath. If there had been any doubts before entering the professor's office, there were none now.

Whatever the consequences, his mind was made up.

54

Saturday 2nd August 2036

Tripoli Infectious Diseases Hospital, Republic of North Africa
5 days until the deadline

Jason raised his eyes from where he sat alongside his mother and the general, picking listlessly at the food on his plate. Another week had passed, and the research efforts had still brought them no closer to developing a treatment for the virus. Nor had the doctor come up with any proposals for how to get past the armed guards and break out of the facility. In five days, Paul would become a test subject. Luckily, his son was blissfully unaware of the looming deadline as Antimone dressed him by the bed.

Max Perrin occupied a spot at the opposite end of the table. Like every other morning, a guard had escorted him to the communal area to eat breakfast with the other prisoners. The rest of the detainees reserved any discussions about escape plans for times when he wasn't present. Max had attempted to engage them in conversation on the topic, but the other members of the group mostly ignored him.

The clunk of the electronic lock echoed through the room holding the prisoners. The door leading to the elevators opened, and Dr Kubar crossed to the wooden table. "Are you not ready?" he asked, folding his arms.

"I'll just be a second," Jason replied, cramming a piece of bread into his mouth.

Rosalind made no attempt to hurry as she sipped tea from a clear glass.

Kubar's gaze lowered to a piece of paper on the table. "What is this?"

"It's one of Paul's masterpieces."

The doctor picked up the drawing and studied the crude interlocking circles drawn with different coloured pencils.

"What's so interesting about it?" Jason asked.

"It reminds me a little of the compound we are working on. But come. We must go. Professor Halfon will start the test on the boy in fifteen minutes," Kubar said, putting down the picture and glancing at his wrist.

Rosalind glanced up sharply. "What test?"

"It is as we feared. He will put a pregnant woman in the same room."

"I thought you were going to talk to him out of that."

A flush crept into Kubar's cheeks. "I tried, but unfortunately, the professor chose not to listen to my advice."

Rosalind slammed the almost empty glass down on the table. "This is ridiculous. I'll tell him myself."

"I would not do that."

"We'll see." She rose and stormed towards the exit.

Kubar's eyebrows rose. "Your mother is a difficult woman," he said, addressing Jason.

"Yeah, but on this occasion, she's right."

"Still, it is not a good idea to confront the people with power."

"That's just the way she is."

"Come. Let us go before the guards decide there is a problem."

Jason followed a pace behind as Kubar approached the locked door.

"What does he hope to achieve?" Rosalind asked as they drew alongside, her face a thunderous mask of anger.

"He is under much pressure," Kubar replied. "He has made a promise to our leader, and now he must deliver, or there will be serious consequences." The lock clunked as he raised his card.

"Well, he's a fool if he thinks this problem can be solved by trialling random compounds on live subjects."

"But if what I have heard is correct, did you not perform human trials at Ilithyia?"

A vein throbbed at Rosalind's temple. "That was totally different. We researched everything thoroughly before we went to that stage, and we never tested on children."

The rest of the short journey passed in silence.

"Shall we have a look at the latest simulation results?" Jason asked as they neared the workstation.

"What's the point?" Rosalind replied. "It seems Halfon is intent on testing anything we develop on a live subject."

Ignoring Rosalind's negative attitude, Jason sat in the chair and studied the screen. "Well, it ran to completion." He scrolled through several graphs. "But there's no discernible effect on the simulated virus activation rate from what I can see."

"Just like all the others then," Rosalind said, leaning over Jason's shoulder.

"What if we modified this area?" Kubar asked, pointing at a part of the molecular structure. "That might alter the absorption factor."

Despite her initial reluctance, Rosalind drew up a chair of her own and peered at the three-dimensional image. An intense debate between the British scientist and the North African doctor ensued. On average, Jason understood about every other word.

As they argued, other researchers congregated around the glass-encased room in the centre of the laboratory. Halfon's voice rose above the hubbub. "Are the cameras recording? What about the telemetry links?"

Rosalind sprang up from her seat and marched towards the professor. Kubar tried to grab her arm, but she shook off his grip.

She placed a hand on the professor's shoulder and spun him around. "This is a total waste of time. I can tell you now, this won't work. You'll be killing a child for nothing."

Halfon took a step back, his eyes blazing with fury. "How dare you touch me? Are you forgetting that you are a prisoner here?"

The blood drained from Rosalind's face and pooled in two bright red spots in the centre of her cheeks. "How could I possibly forget? You treat us as slaves without even a day off. Now, you're about to expose a four-year-old boy to a trigger that will cause his certain death. For God's sake, we've run the simulation. We already know this compound won't protect him."

Halfon spoke in a low, menacing voice. "This test will happen whether you like it or not. There is no time for the cautious approach to medical research you follow in the West. We must be bold and push the boundaries."

"You can't—"

"ENOUGH!" bellowed Halfon. His hand reached into the pocket of his white coat. It emerged holding a black cylinder. He jabbed the tip against Rosalind's shoulder and depressed the button with his thumb. She cried out and dropped to the floor, writhing in agony. But the professor wasn't finished. He leant over her and delivered another jolt of electricity to her midriff. An inhuman scream tore from her throat.

Halfon barked a command in Arabic. Two guards stepped forwards. They hesitated for a moment as if unsure whether the agonised thrashing of the prostrate woman was somehow contagious, then each grabbed hold of one of Rosalind's arms. They dragged her still-convulsing body upright and hauled her across the floor.

Halfon turned to the small crowd of scientists, brandishing the stun baton. "Does anybody else have any objections?" Silence greeted his question. "Good. Shall we continue?"

A low murmur rose from the group as most of the eyes in the room, including Jason's, followed the two men and their incapacitated prisoner. Somebody grabbed him by the arm.

"Do not do anything stupid," Kubar hissed in his ear.

Jason nodded, and the doctor released his grip. A movement behind the glass panels snapped his attention back to the enclosed space. A trolley emerged through the doors at the far end, pushed by a man in a white protective suit. Held down by straps, the same boy they had seen a week earlier gazed blearily at the onlookers.

The suited medic applied the wheel locks and retreated the way he had come. Moments later, he returned, pulling a woman by the arm. She wore a headscarf and a black dress, which reached the floor and protruded around her belly. A deathly hush descended on the spectators as the man dragged the reluctant mother-to-be closer. She spotted the trolley holding the test subject and tried to pull back. The man's grip tightened. She cried out in pain, but still, he moved forwards, stopping only when they stood a yard away from the foot of the metal frame.

The woman stared at the young child, the whites of her eyes reflecting the bright overhead lighting. She muttered something under her breath.

Nothing happened for several seconds. The murmur of conversation rose from the group of spectators. Then a thin trail of blood flowed from the boy's left nostril, rolling across his cheek onto the white sheet. He tried to raise a hand to brush it off, but the straps prevented any movement. Similar streams emerged from his ears. A tremor ran through his body, and his eyes rolled up in his head.

Jason could no longer watch. The pointless death sickened him to the core of his being. He turned away and meandered back to the workstation. There, he dropped into the chair and buried his face in his hands. In a few days, his son, Paul, would be strapped to the trolley: another innocent sacrificed to the goals of the ruthless men running this country. A rushing sound whooshed in his ears. His throat tightened up. He tried to inhale, but it felt like he was breathing through a straw.

A gentle hand brushed his shoulder. Jason recoiled at the touch.

"Your mother was right," Kubar said as he dropped into the adjacent seat. "She predicted the drug would not work."

"That bastard doesn't care about that though, does he?"

"No."

Both men sat in silence, each lost in their own thoughts. Finally, Jason spoke. "We have to get out of here. Have you had any ideas?"

Kubar flashed an anxious glance at the nearest guard, who stood ten yards away, leaning against the wall. "Actually, yes."

"Well?"

"A lightbulb in my room failed yesterday, and it reminded me. Two or three months ago, we had a power cut. When that happened, all the lights turned off, the electronic doors opened, and I heard Professor Halfon complain that the cameras no longer worked either. There is a backup generator, but it only provides electricity to the isolation areas. It is not powerful enough for the entire building."

"So, how does that help us?"

"When the power fails, it will go dark for a moment before the emergency lighting comes on. Perhaps we can overpower the guards and take their weapons."

Jason turned to Kubar. "That might just work. But how do we turn the supply off?"

"Yes," the doctor said. "That is a problem. There are probably fuses somewhere, but I do not know where they are. I think they are in another part of this hospital. Unfortunately, they will not allow me to leave this section."

Jason's eyes narrowed in thought. "General Shaladi has people on the outside who are prepared to help him. They might be able to cause a power cut."

Kubar leant forwards. "This is good. How do we contact them?"

"That could be an issue. The one person with the means to get a message out of here is currently in the cells, recovering from an electric shock."

55

Saturday 2nd August 2036

Tripoli Infectious Diseases Hospital, Republic of North Africa
5 days until the deadline

For the rest of the day, Jason and Kubar worked with the molecular modelling software. Much of what the doctor proposed was beyond Jason's grasp, even if he had been able to concentrate fully. As it was, his mind kept wandering to plans for escape. Key to everything was getting a message to the outside world.

"There, that might work," Kubar said as he jabbed a finger at the save icon.

Jason forced himself to focus on the screen. "What? Oh, yeah. Have you set up another simulation?"

"Yes. The circles on your son's drawing gave me a new idea to try. This one will take nine hours because the compound is more complex."

"How do we stop Professor Halfon from manufacturing it and testing it on some other poor child while we aren't here?"

"When the software is running, he cannot access the model without stopping the job."

Jason glanced towards the nearest guard. "Good. I've been thinking about how we could send a message to Shaladi's people."

"Go on."

"Tonight, I'll ask him for their contact details. Tomorrow, I'll give them to you."

"I do not understand. I have no phone. How will this work?"

"You tell the professor that you need my mother's help with some technical questions. Assuming he agrees, you visit her in the cells and pass her a note. Then she uses the wireless interface in her eye to send the message. If he releases her beforehand, I can ask her myself."

Kubar ran a hand through his hair. "I fear she may have pushed Professor Halfon too far this time. Perhaps I will talk to him again tonight and tell him I need her support to continue this work."

"Why don't you go and see him now? It's a little early to stop, but while the simulation's running, there's not much else we can do."

The doctor hesitated for a moment. "Yes. That is a good idea."

***

Professor Halfon glared at Dr Kubar from the other side of the desk. He desperately wanted to grab the scientist by the neck and crush his windpipe. Despite the hammering of his heart, he forced himself to breathe slowly and maintain an outwardly calm demeanour. "If you cannot control your staff, I must reconsider whether you deserve this position of responsibility."

Kubar shifted uncomfortably on the wooden chair. "I understand, Professor. She is a difficult woman, but her expertise is vital to our success."

"That may be so, but her behaviour cannot go unpunished. I will not tolerate insubordination in my people."

"I agree. But hasn't she already suffered considerable pain?" Kubar's gaze tracked to the slight bulge in the pocket of Halfon's jacket. "What further punishment do you propose? It cannot be anything that prevents her from working."

Halfon steepled his fingers and glowered at his subordinate through narrowed eyes. "You definitely need her help?"

"Yes. She is not easy to work with, but she is an expert in her field. Is that not why you kidnapped her?"

Halfon tamped down his rage. Unfortunately, the doctor made sense. He released a deep sigh. "Very well. She can stay with you during the day, but she will spend the night in the cells. If she delivers what we need, I may allow her to return to the others."

"That is generous of you, Professor. I will make sure nothing like this ever happens again."

Halfon leant forwards and lowered his voice to a growl. "Let me tell you something, which I trust you will keep to yourself. When we develop a treatment that works, she will be punished for her crimes. She has caused many thousands of deaths. Our people will demand justice."

"I know."

Halfon sat back. "What about her son?"

Kubar stared at the director in confusion. "I do not understand your question."

The professor tapped the desk impatiently. "Mr Floyd. Is he proving useful? I have not seen him performing any technician's work."

"He is inexperienced, but he has a good brain. He shows much promise."

"Despite their past, I think the woman is still fond of him. Maybe we can use that to our advantage."

"What do you mean?" Kubar asked.

"He may provide leverage."

"But…"

"I hope you are not becoming too attached to the prisoners. They are here for one purpose and one purpose alone: to help us develop a cure. Once we have accomplished that, we have no further uses for them."

"Of course, sir," Kubar replied.

"So, how is the research progressing?"

"We are running a simulation tonight. We should know by tomorrow morning whether it is worth pursuing further."

"Shall I get Dr Brandt to work on synthesising it?"

"I suggest we wait until we see the results."

"Very well. Just remember that time is short. We cannot afford to fail or we will all suffer the consequences."

"Thank you, Professor."

"There is one more thing. We must think about preparing the child."

Kubar's face blanched. "You mean Paul Lessing?"

Halfon leant closer to study his subordinate's reaction. "Yes. Who else?"

"So, you really intend to perform a test on the boy?"

"Is that going to be a problem?"

Kubar looked down at his shoes, then raised his eyes to meet those of the professor. "No, of course not. I just thought perhaps—"

The blood pounded in Halfon's veins. Why did this man always query his decisions? He slammed a fist down on the desk, causing the doctor to recoil at the sudden impact. "This is something that is already decided. You will not question my orders. Ever."

"Yes, sir. Sorry."

"Good. Take the child to the isolation area now. On second thoughts, I will do it myself. You need to get back to work."

Kubar rose. "Right away. Thank you for your time."

Halfon's gaze followed the scientist as he crossed the room to the door. He waited a few seconds, then raised his hand in front of the computer screen and selected a name from the contact list. The face of his head of security filled the display.

"Good evening, sir. How may I help you?"

"I am concerned about Doctor Kubar. I want you to monitor him. He is getting far too close to the prisoners. Also, I am not sure your idea to inform him that his daughter is still alive is working. He seems... unsettled. I expected him to be much more enthusiastic."

"Of course, Professor. I will tell my men to watch him closely."

56

Saturday 2nd August 2036

Tripoli Infectious Diseases Hospital, Republic of North Africa
5 days until the deadline

Antimone lifted the plastic fork to her son's mouth. "Please, Paul. Eat this for Mummy."

The three-year-old angled his head away, his lips tightly sealed.

She raised her eyes in exasperation. With nothing to occupy her except childcare duties, she felt her mind and body atrophying. "I've really had enough of this. Can you try?"

Jason, who had returned from the laboratory earlier than usual, lifted his son off Antimone's wheelchair and placed him on his lap. "Come on, buddy. This is yummy. Let's drive the car into the garage. Beep! Beep!"

Paul giggled and allowed the food to pass through what had moments earlier been an impenetrable barrier.

Antimone picked at the contents of her own plate.

"What's wrong?" Jason asked, his face etched with concern. "I mean apart from the obvious."

"This is driving me nuts," she replied. "Every day is the same. I love being with Paul, but it's just so boring. My brain is turning to mush."

Jason leant forwards and lowered his voice. "We'll find a way to escape. I promise."

Antimone shot a glance towards the general and his daughter, sitting at the other end of the table. "Do you really trust those two?"

"I don't see we have much of a choice. We all need to work together." Jason lifted another forkful of food to his son's mouth. By now, the novelty had worn off, and Paul pushed his father's hand away.

Antimone gave a wry smile. "Not so easy after all, is it?"

Jason continued his half-hearted attempts to force nutrition past Paul's lips while he spoke. "We need Shaladi's people to knock out the power. To do that, my mother—I mean Baxter—has to get a message out to them, and she can't do that while she's stuck in the cells. Dr Kubar said he'd tell Halfon the research couldn't progress without her, but who knows whether that bastard will listen."

"Speak of the devil. Here he comes now," Antimone said, staring at the entrance.

Jason's head swivelled. "What the hell does he want?" he murmured.

Professor Halfon strode towards them, trailed by a pair of armed guards. He stopped a pace away. "Good evening."

Neither Jason nor Antimone responded.

"I hope the food is to your liking. "This"—he pointed to a piece of dough on Antimone's plate—"is Zummeeta. You should dip it in the sauce."

"I'm not hungry."

"Very well. I am not here to engage in—how do you say?—chitchat. I must take your son."

Antimone's blood froze in her veins. "What do you mean?"

"Are my words not clear? He will come with me."

"No way," Jason said, pushing the bench back as he stood. "He stays with us." He clutched Paul tightly to his chest.

Halfon's eyes narrowed. "I think you misunderstand your situation, Mr Floyd." He beckoned the armed guard closer. The man raised his weapon. "You are in no position to make demands."

"Is this for the test?" Antimone asked. The roaring sound in her ears made her voice seem distant. "There are still five days to go."

"If you behave, you may visit him. If there is any trouble, you will not see him again."

A shiver ran through Antimone's body. "Tell me what you're going to do to him."

"Miss Lessing, I am losing patience. If I wanted to, I could just take him with no discussion. My men are armed. There is nothing you can do to stop me. I would prefer to do this without causing the boy distress, but understand that I will use whatever means are necessary."

Antimone could barely breathe. A prickly sensation ran across her scalp and down her neck. She trembled uncontrollably. Her lips moved, but no words came out.

Halfon glared at Jason. "Now, I must insist that you hand the child to me, or I will have no alternative but to use force."

Jason met the professor's stare for a moment, then kissed Paul on the forehead and placed him on the ground. "This man is going to take you to meet some new friends," he whispered. "You be good." He turned to Halfon and spoke in a low voice. "I swear, if any harm comes to him..."

Halfon's brows drew together in a frown. "Be very careful what you say next." He reached down, grasped the three-year-old's tiny hand and walked towards the exit.

Paul tried to pull away, casting an uncertain backward glance. Despite the terror clawing at Antimone's insides, she forced a smile and gave him a reassuring wave. "Have fun," she said. Her son held her gaze for a second, then continued to walk alongside the professor.

As Halfon and the boy passed through the door, she slumped onto the table, deep sobs wracking her body.

57

Sunday 3rd August 2036

Tripoli Infectious Diseases Hospital, Republic of North Africa
4 days until the deadline

Antimone propelled herself after the tall scientist in the white coat, her heart pounding in her chest. Black spots danced in front of her eyes after a sleepless night. The professor had tasked the man with escorting her to visit her son.

"What's your name again?" she asked. He had told her a few minutes earlier, but in the excitement at being allowed to see Paul, it had already slipped her mind.

"Doctor Fernando," the man replied. He was in his early forties with tight-cropped, short hair and expressive brown eyes.

"Is he all right? Did he eat any breakfast? Did he sleep well?" She knew she was babbling but couldn't stop herself.

"I am sorry. I do not know." The doctor's voice carried a slight Spanish accent. "My expertise is cell cultures. I do not look after the children."

"So, you're a scientist?"

"Si."

"And you think it's okay to murder young kids and kidnap people?"

The doctor cleared his throat. Just when Antimone thought he wouldn't reply, he spoke. "I have made some mistakes in the past which I do not wish to talk about. They will not let me work in my own country. The other European countries and America are the same. Here, they allow me to do what I love, and they also pay me well. I do not agree with some things they do, but if I want to stay, I must follow orders."

"So, you just turn a blind eye to kidnap and murder and get on with your job?"

This time, Fernando remained silent. They followed the corridor until they came to a sealed double door. The doctor fumbled in his pocket for the key card. "One moment," he mumbled, staring up at the black circle of the camera lens.

The light turned green, and the deadbolts slid back with a metallic clunk. Fernando pushed through the swing doors. Antimone raised her arms just in time to prevent the edges from banging into her.

They entered an open-plan laboratory area. An array of large, complicated-looking machines occupied the floor space. A group of scientists in lab coats stared at them in silence as they passed. Fernando didn't acknowledge his colleagues. He led Antimone to another set of doors and repeated the procedure to pass through.

"Here we are," he announced.

The room was five metres square with white walls. Directly opposite, a row of yellow hazmat suits hung from a metal rail. Two separate sliding doors, each containing a rectangular glass window, took up most of the left wall. Mounted between them at chest height was a large green button. A sign in Arabic occupied the space above the button.

"What's that?" Antimone asked, pointing at the twin mechanisms.

"Those are airlocks," Fernando replied. "This side is the entrance. The right is the exit. Before we can go through, we must wear protective clothing."

Antimone pointed to the rack. "I assume you mean one of those? How am I supposed to put that on?"

The doctor picked up a hazmat suit and glanced down at her. "We need some help." He stepped towards a small speaker grill set into the wall beside the left door, pressed the pushbutton and spoke in a low voice. Several seconds passed, then a hissing sound emerged from the right side. Moments later, a figure covered in yellow plastic stepped out, dripping water. A harsh chemical smell permeated the room.

Antimone coughed at the acrid scent. Fernando and the newcomer exchanged a few words. Peering through the curved glass of his faceplate, she identified the suited person as a middle-aged man with receding, black hair. She had never seen him before. The Spaniard unzipped the front, and between them, the two men manipulated her body into the hazmat suit. She experienced a moment of claustrophobia as the zip closed, sealing her inside.

"I will leave you with Doctor Gregg," Fernando said, his voice muffled by the thin material. "The airlock is not wide enough for the wheelchair. There is another one on the other side. My colleague will take you through."

The suited figure grunted as he lifted Antimone in his arms, then carried her to the leftmost door. Fernando prodded the green button. The man shuffled into the enclosed space sideways. Antimone's legs scraped against the wall. A rattling noise filled the small chamber, and her ears popped with the sudden change in air pressure.

The sound stopped abruptly, and the panel ahead slid open. Gregg staggered out into a brightly lit foyer area. A wheelchair sat to one side, and he lowered Antimone into the seat. She turned her attention to her surroundings.

A huge expanse of glass lined the entire right wall of the long corridor. The rectangular outlines of doors broke the smooth surface. Behind the floor to ceiling window, white partitions divided the space into separate rooms. A green button mounted beside each door apparently controlled access. She peered past her reflection into the first room and saw the interior contained a pair of empty beds. There was no other source of entry or exit.

"Is this where they're keeping Paul?" Antimone asked.

"It's this way," Gregg replied, striding ahead. He spoke with an American accent. When they reached the next glass-walled chamber, a woman wearing a black robe stared at them from where she perched on the edge of the bed. Her hands rested on top of her stomach. She was either obese or heavily pregnant. Antimone guessed the latter based on what Jason had told her.

The doctor passed another empty room, then stopped. Antimone rolled up behind him. Three young boys sat on the floor with their backs to the window. They chattered to each other happily as they played with a variety of cheap plastic toys. None of the children had noticed the adults yet. Antimone's heart lurched as her gaze settled on the child in the centre of the group with the palest skin: Paul.

She leant forwards, placing her palms on the glass. Tears streamed from her eyes and rolled down her cheeks. She raised a hand to brush them away but came up against the thin plastic of the hazmat suit. She choked a little as she inhaled. The sound must have carried inside the room because the boy on the left turned. He stared open-mouthed at the strange-looking people on the other side of the window.

Paul was the last to turn. His gaze settled on the wheelchair and tracked up to the features behind the transparent headgear. Their eyes met. He scrambled to his feet and rushed to the glass, screaming, "Mummy!" at the top of his voice.

Without a second thought, Antimone spun the wheels of her chair and slammed her palm against the green button. The door swung open towards her. Paul raced through the gap and flung himself into his mother's arms. He grasped her around the neck and nestled his head beneath her chin.

Antimone pulled her son's tiny body into her chest and lowered her face to kiss his hair, but instead, her lips came up against the smooth surface of the polycarbonate facemask. "Paul," she murmured in a strangled voice.

"Be careful," an alarmed Dr Gregg said, stepping forwards. "You must not break the seal."

Gregg's words of warning penetrated to Antimone's unconscious but had the opposite effect to what he intended. Maternal instincts took over. She could no longer remain separated from her child. Her fingers lifted and grasped the pull tab of the zip. She yanked downwards. The rasp of the zipper sounded incredibly loud in her ears.

The doctor lunged to stop her, but the years of athletic training had given her tremendous upper body strength. She shoved him away and pulled the seams apart. Seconds later, she had thrown the hood back over her head and released one arm.

As she embraced her son tightly, tears dripped from her chin and mingled with his.

58

Sunday 3rd August 2036

Tripoli Infectious Diseases Hospital, Republic of North Africa
4 days until the deadline

Jason sat at the table as he waited for Dr Kubar to arrive. He pushed the food around his plate. His appetite had deserted him. Neither he nor Antimone had slept at all during the previous night. She had departed ten minutes earlier with the Spanish doctor. Despite their protests, Dr Fernando was adamant only one parent at a time could visit their son.

General Shaladi approached the bench with a half-filled plate and sat on the same side, a metre away to Jason's left. Jason had explained Kubar's proposal to him the previous night. Shaladi's mouth barely moved as he spoke. "Do not look at me. Just listen. Now take this."

Jason glanced down. Something white lay on the wooden seat. He stretched out an arm and closed his fingers around a tightly folded piece of paper.

"Put it in your pocket," Shaladi commanded. "It contains a web address and some English text. You must comment on the first article using the words exactly as written. The website is in Arabic and appears to be for a company selling deep sea fishing trips. The top line is a code to tell my people it is from me and that nobody is forcing me to write the message. This is why you cannot make a mistake when you enter it on the page. Do you understand?"

Jason continued to stare straight ahead, but he tilted his head downwards.

"Good. My men check all comments. They delete everything so nothing appears on the site. If they wish to send information back to me, they comment on the second article. If you want to reply to them, you must do so on the same page and include the phrase *fishing boat*. This is important. Do you have any questions? Cover your mouth so they cannot see you talking."

Jason leant forwards, resting his chin on his right hand to conceal his lips from the guards in the office. "Won't they be expecting you to write in Arabic?" he asked in a low voice.

"Yes, this is true, but they will understand as long as the correct phrases are present."

"Right, I think I've got all that."

"Good luck."

Jason rose and deposited his plate at the end of the table, then strolled back to his bed. He removed his shoes and lay down with his hands behind his head.

The entire plan depended upon his mother being able to access the website. It would be hard to explain to her the instructions for using the site unless they could spend a few minutes together in private. He grasped the tightly folded paper in his clenched fist. Despite the setbacks, they were finally taking action to get out of this place.

***

The door at the end of the room opened. Jason shoved the note into the pocket of his trousers as Dr Kubar entered. He swung his legs onto the floor and tied his laces.

"How's my son?" Jason asked, looking up as Kubar drew nearer.

"He is well," the doctor replied. "I am sorry they have taken him from you."

"Yeah. If they hurt him in any way… What's happening about my mother?"

"I spoke to Professor Halfon yesterday. I told him she was vital to our research. He agreed to let her work with us during the day, but she will return to the cells at night."

Jason breathed a sigh of relief. *That would certainly make things easier.* He caught the eye of the general who was still sitting at the table and nodded.

"Shall we go?" Kubar asked.

Jason followed him across the room. When they arrived at the lifts, the green numbers on the control panel indicated that the car was one level up. Moments later, the doors parted to reveal Max Perrin, accompanied by a guard. Jason stepped back to allow the two men to pass. Neither Westerner acknowledged the other.

Jason and Kubar rode up in silence. When they emerged into the corridor, Jason turned to the doctor. "They told us he was spending the night in the cells."

Kubar stared at him in confusion. "I am sorry. Who?"

"Max Perrin. The lift started on the floor above. If he was in the basement, he should've been going up not down."

"He sleeps up there," Kubar replied. "I thought you knew that. Is there a problem?"

"No," Jason said. "It's nothing. Never mind." Perrin was definitely up to something. This served only to confirm his deep mistrust of his former classmate.

The doctor led him to the workstation, then strolled over to the nearest guard. A brief conversation ensued. He returned moments later. "They will bring Mrs Baxter up."

Kubar sank down on the seat beside Jason and studied the display. "The simulation is complete." He waved a hand in front of the screen and peered at the tables of results.

Jason tried to interpret the data, but much of it was beyond him. He waited for the doctor to reach the end.

"Hmm," Kubar murmured.

"What does that mean? Is it good news or bad?"

"We should wait until Mrs Baxter arrives, or I will have to explain twice. Ah, here she is."

A guard pushed the dishevelled form of Rosalind Baxter forwards. From her appearance, it seemed she hadn't slept much the night before. She flopped into a chair, saying nothing.

"Are you okay?" Jason asked.

She turned her head sideways and glared at him. "Do I look okay to you?"

"Um... not particularly, no."

She rubbed her shoulder. "Well, that's not surprising. If you thought conditions were primitive in that shared room, it's palatial by comparison. The cells are crawling with rats and insects. I barely slept a wink with all the scratching and squeaking. Something big even ran over my leg in the night."

Jason shuddered. "That sounds bad."

"You have no idea." Rosalind rotated her chair. "Anyway, what's going on here?"

Kubar pointed at the screen. "I started with the molecule we worked on a few days ago."

"The one Halfon gave to that poor kid?"

"Yes. I modified it here and here." He jabbed a finger at the display. "The simulations show that it may be effective."

"No doubt that bastard will inject another child with it before we've run any more tests."

"I hope not. We should trial it on a cell culture."

"Let me have a look."

Kubar rolled his chair back.

Rosalind moved closer to the screen. She brought up the molecular model, then used her fingers to manipulate the images and examined them from several directions. Finally, she studied the simulation report. "Yes, this all looks very promising, but before you get too excited, there's a long way to go. However, I agree it's worth taking further."

"Doctor Fernando is our expert on cell cultures. Doctor Brandt can synthesise the compound. I will ask them both to start now. If there are no problems, we should be able to begin testing in one or two days."

Kubar pushed back his chair and strolled towards a tall man with close-cropped hair. Soon, they were deep in conversation.

"Is the battery in your eye still charged?" Jason whispered.

Rosalind's expression went blank for a second. "Just over thirty percent. Remember to ask Kubar for the bits to build another charger. Why are you asking?"

Jason flashed a glance at the guard, then turned back to his mother. "Shaladi is planning to get us out of here. We need you to send a message to his people."

Jason explained how the secret messaging system worked and the general's plan.

"What happens when the power goes down?" Rosalind asked.

"All the doors open, and we overpower the guards. He reckons only six or seven of them work at night. After nine o'clock, most of them will be off duty."

"I'll be in the cells by then. You aren't thinking of leaving me behind, are you?"

Jason met her gaze. "No, of course not. You have my word, we'll get you out of there. That reminds me, Kubar only agreed to help if we promise to rescue the other kids as well."

Rosalind massaged her temples. "Talk about trying to make this as difficult as possible. How many of them are there?"

"I'll have to ask him when he gets back, but I don't think they keep more than a few on site at any one time."

"When do I need to send the message?"

Jason's eyes surveyed the room. Nobody was paying them any attention. "How about now?" he said. He dug his fingers into his pocket, retrieved the folded piece of paper and, with another surreptitious glance at the nearest guard, pushed it across the surface of the desk.

Rosalind unfolded the note. She studied it for a moment. "I look forward to meeting you beneath the blue sky on your fishing boat; that hardly sounds like a comment you'd leave on a website, does it?"

"What does it matter? You have to get the first part exactly right," Jason said.

"I know that," Rosalind snapped. "Fetch me one of those equipment manuals from the shelf over there."

"Why? What do you need it for?"

Rosalind raised an eyebrow. "You still can't help questioning every request I make, can you?"

"Apparently not."

"I'm going to use it to hide the note in case anybody comes."

"Oh, I see." Jason strolled across to the row of books and selected one at random. The guard's eyes tracked him all the way back to the desk. He allowed the manual to fall open and pretended to study the contents. Then he passed it to his mother.

After a few seconds, the armed man lost interest and looked away. Rosalind placed the note between the pages and stared at the dense writing. Jason read over her shoulder. He scanned the second line written on the paper.

Tripoli IDH. Cut power at night. Urgent. Confirm date and time.

"What's happening?" he asked.

"Be quiet. I'm trying to concentrate." Rosalind shook her head. "Damn, there's an error message."

"Did you type it in correctly?"

"Just checking. I'll try again."

More seconds ticked by. "I'm in."

Jason exhaled the breath he had been holding. "Thank God for that."

"There are photographs of people with fish they've caught."

"That sounds about right."

"I'm clicking the link. Everything's in Arabic. There are photos of boats. There's a button at the bottom of the page. That must be for the comments... Yes, a text box has opened."

A frown of concentration formed on Rosalind's forehead. A bead of perspiration rolled down her temple.

"The first line's done."

"Have you checked it?"

"For Christ's sake, will you let me do this without nagging me every few seconds?"

Jason bit his tongue. He jiggled a leg in nervous anticipation.

"That's it. Everything looks good. There are two buttons. I assume one must be okay and the other cancel. The button on the right is highlighted."

"Perhaps we should wait for Dr Kubar."

"I'm going to click it. The box has disappeared."

"Make sure you disconnect from the network."

"Hang on. I've done that, too." Rosalind closed the manual with the note still between the pages. "What now?"

"We give it an hour or two and see whether they've replied."

59

Sunday 3rd August 2036

Tripoli Infectious Diseases Hospital, Republic of North Africa
4 days until the deadline

"Shit! She did what?" Jason asked.

Dr Kubar sighed. Moments earlier, he had returned from a brief meeting with the head of security. "When she saw your son, she pulled off the hazmat suit to embrace him."

"That's just typical," Rosalind said.

Jason ignored the acerbic comment. "So, now both Paul and Antimone are infected with the virus?"

"Yes, I am afraid so," Kubar replied. "It is very infectious."

"Damn it."

The doctor raised an eyebrow. "It seems you are surrounded by impetuous women."

"Yeah, tell me about it." Jason sank into a morose silence. This would only complicate the escape.

The morning had passed in a state of nervous tension. An air of purpose filled the scientists as they set about the tasks required to test the new compound. Jason had overheard two of them discussing what they would do when they were allowed to leave. Of the science team, only Dr Kubar seemed withdrawn.

When the doctor departed to attend a staff meeting, Jason and Rosalind found themselves alone at the workstation.

"Shall we check for a reply?" Jason asked.

Rosalind shot a glance at the nearest guard. He was leaning against the wall, gazing aimlessly at the ceiling. "Okay. Let's do it."

"Don't forget to connect to the network first."

Rosalind let out a sigh of irritation. A moment later, she muttered, "I've connected. I'm just reopening the website."

Time seemed to slow down for Jason. His heart thumped in his chest. It took all his self-control not to ask his mother what was happening.

Several seconds passed before she spoke again. "Right, I'm in. So, I need to look at the second article. More pictures of boats. I'm scrolling to the bottom of the page. Yes, there's a comment."

"What does it say?"

"The next fishing trip starts—"

"So, should we start another simulation?" Jason asked, raising his voice.

Rosalind turned, frowning at the unexpected interruption.

A cheerful-looking Professor Halfon stepped up behind them. "I hear we are preparing a new compound for test. Have you seen Doctor Kubar?"

Both Jason and Rosalind shook their heads.

"Never mind," Halfon said. "I am sure he will be back soon." He reached across and picked up the thick manual in which Rosalind had hidden the note. "I did not know you planned to use the mass spectrometer. What do you want to analyse?"

"Oh, it was nothing," Jason replied. "There's a machine like this at the university. I was just curious to see if it was the same model." He had to consciously force himself to breathe until Halfon replaced the manual without opening it. *That was close.*

"Very good. We will talk again when the compound is ready."

Rosalind scowled at the director. "You aren't going to test it on a human subject ahead of the cell culture trials, are you?"

Halfon's eyes narrowed as he met Rosalind's gaze. He remained silent for a moment before replying. "Doctor Kubar has persuaded me we should follow the scientific method more closely. But remember, we will still place a pregnant woman in the same room as your grandson in a few days. If the treatment is not ready, he will die."

"I'm well aware of that," Rosalind snapped.

"I am glad you understand. Now, when the doctor returns, please tell him I wish to speak to him."

"We'll do that," Jason said, keen to defuse the situation.

Halfon turned and headed towards the exit.

"Do you always have to wind him up?" Jason asked when the professor was out of earshot.

"He's a pompous idiot," Rosalind replied. "He wouldn't recognise scientific method if it bit him on the arse."

"I still don't think you should antagonise him. I was sure he'd find the note."

Rosalind rolled her eyes. "You really thought I'd be stupid enough to leave it in the manual, did you? What sort of moron do you take me for? I flushed it down the toilet when I went a few hours ago. It's just as well one of us is on the ball."

Jason bit back on his retort. "So, what does the message say?"

"The next fishing trip starts at ten o'clock on the sixth of August."

"That means they're going ahead with the plan. Did you reply?"

"I was about to when we were interrupted. What shall I write?"

"How about *we'll be ready*? Actually, I nearly forgot. We've got to include the phrase *fishing boat*."

"Okay, so *we'll be ready for the fishing boat*? Just a sec… Right, that's done."

"Don't forget to disconnect."

Rosalind's jaw muscles clenched. "Everything's sorted. How does the general propose to overpower the guards?"

"He hasn't mentioned that yet. I'll try to discuss it with him tonight. The only other question is, who else do we tell?"

"Good point. We should only inform people we trust."

"Does that include Doctor Kubar?"

"I think so," Rosalind replied. "He's the only one of us who has free run of the place. We might need his help. If he was going to turn us in, he would've done so already."

"We have a few days to come up with the plan. I'll talk to the general tonight and discuss it with the doctor tomorrow. But there is another thing we need to sort out."

"What's that?"

"Assuming we escape from here, we still have to get home. Shaladi said he could take us as far as the border, but everything after that is down to us. We can hardly call a taxi and tell it to drive us back to England. Maybe we could contact somebody in the government."

Rosalind folded her arms. "The Prime Minister and I aren't on the best of terms. They had the chance to rescue us on the ship, but they backed off. Why would they help us now? And another thing—after what we saw on the news, I must be top of the most hated people in the world list at the moment. Apart from anything else, my picture is all over the media."

"Yeah, that could be a problem. You might need to disguise yourself. But surely you still have some contacts."

"I can't think of anyone," Rosalind said. "I've been somewhat cut off since… well, since the sale of the company. Pretty much everyone I knew was related in some way to the business."

"But I remember you being friends with some important people."

"Yes, but none of them would lift a finger to help me now."

"So, it'll have to be somebody I know, then. If we emailed the Lessings, I'm sure they'd pass it on."

Rosalind scowled at Jason. "*Her* parents?" She stared at him for a moment. "I suppose beggars can't be choosers. I'll connect to my webmail and send them a message." Once again, her features took on a distant look. "That's strange."

"What?"

"There's what looks like an error box. It's in Arabic."

"I've got a CommsHub mail account. Why don't you try that?"

"Give me a second… No, I'm getting the same thing."

"I haven't given you their email address yet."

"No," Rosalind said. "You don't understand. I can't access the site at all. It seems to be blocked for some reason. What do we do now?"

"I'll see if the general has any ideas when I talk to him later. Actually, there is something else you could do; leave a message on the fishing website and ask them to pass the information to the British government. It has to be worth trying. Remember to include the words *fishing boat*."

Rosalind's face froze in concentration. A minute passed in silence. Eventually, she said, "At least that site works. I've left another comment on the second article. Their previous one has disappeared, so they definitely got my acknowledgement."

***

Professor Halfon was working in his office when the screen signalled an incoming call from his head of security.

"Yes, what is it?" he asked.

"Sorry to disturb you, sir, but I have received a report that somebody has tried to access the CommsHub webmail site."

"Who was it?"

"Unfortunately, I do not have that information, sir. A device logged into the wireless network, then disappeared after a few minutes."

"I bet one of those damned scientists still has a phone. You better hope Mullah Awad doesn't get to hear about this. I told you to confiscate all their devices."

"We did that, sir, but whoever it is must have hidden it from my men."

Halfon glared at his subordinate. "This is not acceptable. I want the culprit found. Turn off the Wi-Fi immediately. You have my permission to perform a strip search of every member of the science team."

"I'll get on it right away, sir."

"Let me know when you have identified the person."

60

Monday 4th August 2036

Tripoli Infectious Diseases Hospital, Republic of North Africa
3 days until the deadline

"How are Antimone and Paul?" Jason asked with a yawn as he trailed behind Dr Kubar. It had been a strange night, sleeping beside two empty beds. Three days to go. The looming deadline had occupied centre stage in his mind as he tossed and turned throughout the hours of darkness.

"I have not seen them," Kubar replied, "but I heard they are both fine."

"That bastard, Halfon, wouldn't let me visit them."

"This does not surprise me. They do not want to risk you trying to join them."

A series of sulky scowls followed the pair through the dining area. The science team's positive attitude of the previous days seemed to have evaporated.

"What's going on?" he asked the doctor as they arrived at the workstation. "Why does everybody look so angry?"

"The security people have searched for a mobile phone. The scientists are not happy because they were forced to remove their clothes."

"You mean a strip search?"

"Yes."

Jason's heart sank with a premonition of bad news, but he had to ask. "What triggered that?"

"Professor Halfon told me they detected an unauthorised device on the network. I take it Mrs Baxter has tried to log in to a CommsHub account."

"Oh, shit! Do they know it was her?"

"Not yet, but they will keep searching. In this country, they block access to most Western websites. In any case, now they have turned off the wireless link."

Jason's head spun as he considered the implications. It seemed their actions in trying to contact the outside world had triggered a security alert. Had Shaladi's people received their request to send a message to the British government? Would the North African authorities be able to read the comments from the fishing website?

"What will they do next?" he asked.

"I do not know," Kubar replied. "Why is she sending messages?"

Jason performed a surreptitious inspection of their watchers. They seemed more alert than on the previous few days, but none of them was paying particular attention. "If everything goes to plan, there'll be a power cut at ten o'clock on Wednesday night."

"So, the doors will unlock. What will happen after that?"

"The general intends to overpower the guards. He has people on the outside who will help us escape."

"But he is only one man, and he has no weapons. There are many armed men here."

"He didn't tell me any more than that. He said he'd provide more details closer to the time."

"It is important that Professor Halfon does not call for support. Although the computers will not be available, he still has a mobile phone."

"How do we stop him using it?"

Kubar hesitated before replying. "There is only one solution. I will ask him for a meeting. When the lights go out, I must prevent him from contacting anybody."

"What does that mean?"

Kubar's jaw set in a tight line. "Whatever is necessary."

"It sounds like it could be dangerous."

"There is no other option. Will your government send help to you?"

"We can't be sure. That's why we were trying to access the CommsHub website."

"So, you failed."

"Yes, but we left a message with Shaladi's people to contact the British authorities. Unfortunately, we can't tell whether they received our request."

Kubar took a deep breath. "There are many things that could go wrong. We must hope they do not. Now, if you wait here, I will fetch Mrs Baxter."

Jason stared sightlessly at the screen while he waited for the doctor to return. It was clear whatever Shaladi proposed would be dangerous. Somehow, he had to release Antimone and Paul from the isolation unit. Would the scientists stand with or against them? There was no way of knowing without asking, and that was a risk he couldn't afford to take before the power cut.

He heard Rosalind before he saw her. Her voice resounded through the laboratory. "How the hell am I supposed to do a day's work after being kept in those conditions? I barely slept a wink, and there's nowhere to wash properly." She limped forwards, flopping into the adjacent office chair. The sharp tang of body odour assaulted Jason's nostrils.

Kubar glanced nervously at the guards. "Please keep your voice down. I will talk to the professor again, but do not give them an opportunity to punish you further."

"Bloody barbaric savages," Rosalind muttered.

"Is there any news on the drug trials?" Jason asked, trying to change the subject.

Kubar dragged up another seat and sat beside them. "We applied the compound to the cell cultures yesterday. So far there is no adverse reaction. We have not yet tested whether it has any effect on the new strain of virus."

"When are they going to do that?"

"The test is due to start tomorrow."

Rosalind drummed her fingers on the surface of the desk. "Don't expect me to get excited. I plan on being out of here before we finish testing it."

"About that," Jason said. "Doctor Kubar was just telling me they noticed an unauthorised device on the network yesterday. They detected us trying to access the CommsHub site."

Rosalind leant forwards, biting her lip. "What are they doing about it?"

"They are hunting for a hidden mobile phone," Kubar replied. "They have searched all the scientists, a—how do you say?"

"Strip search," Jason reminded him. "Apparently, they've also turned off the Wi-Fi network."

"So, there's no way to tell whether our last message got through?" Rosalind asked.

"No," Jason said. "Unfortunately, not."

"Damn. I take it they don't know about the interface in my eye?"

"No, I do not think so," Kubar replied. "We must hope that they do not find out."

61

Monday 4th August 2036

Tripoli Infectious Diseases Hospital, Republic of North Africa
3 days until the deadline

Jason stood beside Rosalind. She had tried to freshen up in the small toilet adjoining the laboratory, but the acrid scent of body odour signalled she had only been partially successful. They waited alongside the other scientists for Halfon to arrive. Seven or eight armed guards studied the group from the periphery of the room. Jason wiped his palms on his trousers. This had to be something to do with the unauthorised access to the website.

The professor had called a stand-up meeting of the scientific staff just five minutes earlier. As they awaited his arrival, ripples of nervous conversation rose and fell. One topic dominated: the most recent indignity inflicted by the guards. If there were doubts beforehand, the scientists now understood their situation. For most, what had started out as an opportunity to benefit from lucrative, tax-free contracts had transformed into a prison sentence with little hope of release.

The low murmur of conversation died as Halfon made his way to the front.

"Good afternoon, everybody. I must first apologise for the searches you were forced to endure this morning. Please let me explain why this happened. The work we are performing here is vital, and we cannot afford for another organisation to gain an advantage by stealing our intellectual property. For this reason, we took the difficult decision to confiscate all personal communication devices. I realise it is hard for you to be out of contact with your friends and family, but it is only for a few weeks.

"Unfortunately, we discovered yesterday that somebody did not hand over their phone. That same person attempted to communicate with the outside world and sell our secrets. I am sure I need not remind you that this contravenes your contracts. I am pleased to tell you that today we have identified this individual."

Several whispered conversations broke out around the room. Jason shot Rosalind a sideways glance, but she continued to stare straight ahead. His gaze wandered to the armed men. They would shoot anybody who tried to escape before they covered two paces.

Halfon raised his hands. "Please let me finish. This person has betrayed us all. It is because of them that you have been forced to suffer the indignity of a strip search. Instead of working with you to complete this important work, your colleague has worked against you. I cannot tell you how disappointed this makes me.

"However, I am feeling generous this afternoon, so I will give the culprit one last opportunity to confess and apologise to their fellow scientists. If this person steps forwards now, I guarantee there will be no further repercussions. For the rest, to compensate for your efforts and the restrictions on your ability to communicate with the outside world, I will pay a bonus of six months wages when we demonstrate a successful treatment."

Rosalind leant into Jason as the buzz of voices once again rose from the gathered scientists. "What are they waiting for?" she whispered.

Moments later, Halfon beckoned a pair of armed guards forwards until one stood on either side of him. He raised a hand and pointed in Rosalind's direction. The men strode towards her. She closed her eyes, but they barged past and seized a rake-thin man standing behind her. Jason recognised him as a member of the team working with Dr Fernando on the cell cultures. They had never spoken, but he recalled Dr Kubar mentioning that he was Italian.

The guards dragged the scientist towards the exit, each holding an arm.

The man tried to twist around. "I never used it," he yelled. "It was in my bag. I forgot I had it."

"Quiet!" Halfon boomed. His eyes tracked the men as they left with their prisoner. He turned back to the shocked scientists. "An hour ago, we discovered a hidden mobile phone in Dr Rossi's room. I am sure you will agree I gave him every opportunity to confess."

"What will happen to him now?" a voice called out from the rear of the assembled group.

"We will terminate his contract with immediate effect. He will be held in a secure location, at least until our work here is done. In this country, industrial espionage is a serious offence. If any others of you have hidden communications devices, provided you hand them in today, I promise no further action will be taken.

"Now, we are making excellent progress, but I need you all to apply your best efforts to the challenge ahead. The sooner we complete this task, the sooner you may leave and spend your bonus. Let us get back to work."

***

"Shit. That was close," Jason said to Rosalind as they sat at the workstation. "I'm still shaking."

"They're not the sharpest tools in the box," she replied. "Let's just hope they don't figure it out." She seemed calm, but the pair of dark sweat patches extending out from her armpits told a different story.

Dr Kubar's face pinched in worry. "It is not over yet. When they examine the phone, they will see he did not connect to the network."

"So, what do we do now?" Jason asked.

"We keep working and hope they do not discover what really happened."

"But we don't know whether the general's people passed on the message. It's no good if we get out of here and nobody is waiting at the border to help us."

"There's no point worrying about something you can't control," Rosalind said.

Jason scowled back at her. "That's easy to say, but I really don't want to spend the rest of my life in this prison."

"Believe me, none of us want to stay here," Kubar added.

62

Tuesday 5th August 2036

Prime Minister's Office, 10 Downing Street, London
2 days until the deadline

Andrew Jacobs settled himself behind the polished mahogany desk. Charles Moreland sat opposite. A man in his early sixties with a dome-shaped bald patch, wearing a military uniform, perched nervously on his seat alongside the head of MI6. Admiral David Trent was responsible for British naval operations in the Mediterranean.

"You asked for a meeting, Charles," Jacobs said. "And I see you've invited the Admiralty."

"Yes, Prime Minister."

"We can do without the formalities in here," the premier said with a half-smile to his former university colleague. "What's this about?"

"Well… you know we agreed to try to locate our people in The Republic of North Africa."

"Has there been any progress?"

Moreland interlaced his fingers across his stomach. "Maybe."

Jacobs sat forwards, his interest piqued. "Go on, then."

"Last night we received a message through somewhat unorthodox channels."

"What does that mean?"

"An anonymous caller phoned our embassy in Tunis from Tripoli."

"And…?"

"If we can believe this person, they belong to a faction inside the Reponan army."

Jacobs frowned. "That *is* strange. Why would somebody in their military be contacting us?"

"They claimed that General Shaladi is being held against his will. They plan to break him out in a day or two."

"Sorry, I'm not following. Is this the same Shaladi who was behind the kidnappings at the Olympics?"

"Correct," Moreland replied. "It seems they might be holding him in the same place as our people."

"Why would they be keeping their own man in captivity?"

"Good question. I've had various teams working on it through the night. The prevailing theory is that because they're denying responsibility for the attack, they can't allow him or his daughter—assuming both are still alive—to be seen in public."

Jacobs placed his elbows on the polished surface of the desk. "That sounds plausible. It wouldn't surprise me to hear those shifty bastards rewarded their man for a successful mission by imprisoning him. Are you sure this isn't a hoax?"

"No, Andrew. We can't believe a word they tell us."

"What would be in it for them? What are they expecting us to do?"

"The caller spoke to a member of the night staff. All he told her was that our people would be freed tomorrow at ten o'clock in the evening local time. That doesn't give us long to plan anything. He also said he couldn't or wouldn't escort them out of the country. When our officer called back, the number was dead."

"Why would they bother to contact us?"

"Well, as I see it, there are two possibilities. One, they're rattling our cage, trying to get us to respond. Who knows why? If we send in a team to pull our people out, they could have a welcoming committee waiting for us. Then they go bleating to the international community about us invading a sovereign country. They'd love to prove to the rest of the world that we're the bad guys, especially if they can cause some damage to our armed forces in the process."

"And the alternative?"

"It's genuine, and this group really is trying to help us. If I had to guess, I'd say it was the latter. There are several other ways they could pick a fight if they wanted to."

"So, that's why you invited Admiral Trent."

"Yes," Moreland replied. "If the intelligence is correct, the best way to evacuate the hostages would be from a ship-based helicopter launch."

Jacobs pinched the bridge of his nose between two fingers. "If we get this wrong, we might be putting our navy personnel in serious danger."

"The alternative is that we abandon our people."

"How quickly could we move a ship to the coast of North Africa?"

Trent cleared his throat. "We have a cruiser near Malta. It'll only take them three or four hours to reach Tripoli."

"That's all very well," Jacobs said, "but what happens after that?"

"Just before the appointed time, we perform low-level aerial reconnaissance to see what's happening," the admiral replied. "Whatever we send in will have to be small, or the Reponans will spot it. They may not have the latest gear, but their air defence systems are quite advanced. The problem with using miniature drones is the reduced range compared to the larger ones: four or five miles at most, depending upon the conditions.

"International waters extend to twelve miles. We could bring the ship in to fifteen miles—so it doesn't look like we're deliberately issuing a challenge—then use the marines and an inflatable to go the rest of the way. They'll see our cruiser, but they shouldn't be able to detect a small landing craft. Once ashore, the team would launch the drones and provide backup if required. We'd pull out both the prisoners and our men by helicopter."

Moreland rubbed his chin. "If this goes wrong, we might end up embarrassing ourselves again."

Jacobs offered a wry smile. "Things can't get much worse than they already are, can they? On the plus side, if we can get our people out, it'll show the rest of the world that the Reponans are the lying bastards we know them to be."

"Good point."

"If you're in agreement, Prime Minister," Trent said, "I'll give orders to move that cruiser. We don't want to tip off their military, so I suggest we proceed slowly and make it look like a routine patrol. Then at the last minute, we set a different course and divert towards Tripoli. Our inflatables can do about fifty knots in calm conditions, so once they launch, it won't take long for them to get to shore."

Jacobs narrowed his eyes in thought. After a few seconds, he nodded. "Let's do it. What happens when they land?"

"It'll be dark, but the landing area could be populated. If that's the case, they may need to put ashore elsewhere. According to the intel, the hospital where they're being held is just over a mile from the coast. The team will launch the drones from the beach and travel by foot to the extraction point."

"No meeting place has been arranged," Moreland said. "As I mentioned earlier, we haven't been able to contact our source to agree that level of detail."

The admiral folded his arms. "I'm well aware of that, but we do know roughly where they're holding our people, so my men will set out in that direction."

"That's if the information is correct," the head of MI6 replied. "Why don't you wait until you get confirmation the escape has been successful before launching?"

"It may be too late by then. What if the inflatable approaches to within two or three hundred metres of the shore and holds station there?"

Moreland studied the admiral for a moment. "All right, that sounds like a sensible compromise. There is one other thing we need to consider; we don't know who is infected with this new strain of the virus. If the hostages or any of the locals are carrying the infection, we can't afford for them to pass it on to anybody else."

Trent scratched his head. "That complicates things a bit."

"He's right though," Jacobs said. "We're trying to keep it from the press, but there've already been some nasty incidents over the past few days where pregnant women have been abused, and in one case, even attacked. There's a lot of fear among the general public. The last thing we need is to pass this disease on to your crew."

"I'll ensure the marines are equipped with protective gear," the admiral replied. "We also need to instigate full quarantine measures for everybody we bring back on board the ship until we can test them."

"So, are we all agreed on the plan?" Jacobs asked.

Both men on the other side of the desk responded in the affirmative.

"Good work, gentlemen. Let's keep the circle on this small, just to make sure there aren't any leaks. And please apprise me of any progress."

63

Wednesday 6th August 2036

Tripoli Infectious Diseases Hospital, Republic of North Africa
1 day until the deadline

Jason leant forwards to study the computer screen beside Dr Kubar and his mother. A cough came from behind them. Jason twisted around to see the tall, white-coated figure of Dr Fernando. The doctor remained impassive as he shifted from one foot to the other.

"I must apologise once again for my colleague," he said. "I had no idea he had hidden a phone."

"It is not your fault," Kubar replied.

"Still, he worked on my team, and I feel partially responsible for the discomfort we have all suffered."

"Don't worry about it," Jason said. He didn't want to explain that they had been spared from the strip search.

A slow smile rose on the Spanish doctor's face. "Thank you. Now, I have some good news. These are only preliminary results, but it seems the compound you created has prevented the activation of the virus, at least in the cell cultures."

A stunned silence greeted the scientist's announcement. Then Kubar pushed back his chair and jumped to his feet. "Are you sure?"

Fernando nodded. "We must perform more tests, but yes, from the work we have done so far, there is no evidence of a transition to the lytic stage."

"Have you told the professor yet?" Kubar asked.

"No, I thought you should be the first to know. After all, you were the one to design it."

Kubar beamed as he placed a hand on Jason's and Rosalind's shoulders. "It was not just me. I had a lot of help from my colleagues here."

"Do you want to see the analysis?"

"Of course."

Fernando led the threesome towards the glass-walled room. He pointed to a two-metre high beige cabinet standing on the other side of the window. "That is the machine where we performed the tests."

"Not particularly exciting," Rosalind muttered.

"Let me show you the results," Fernando said, his enthusiasm undimmed. He crossed to a nearby desk and lowered himself into the chair. He waved a hand in front of the computer screen as the others gathered behind him. The display lit up, showing an array of slightly distorted circles.

"These are untreated human lung cells from a juvenile," he explained. "They are infected with the virus, but it is in its dormant phase. Watch what happens when we introduce the activation agent."

He poked a finger at the image. A time-lapse video played. For the first few seconds, nothing happened. Then one circle collapsed in on itself, followed moments later by another. The rest rapidly did the same until not a single intact cell remained.

"What you saw there took place over a period of approximately four minutes. There is no point in showing you what happens when we bathe the cells in your new compound and repeat the experiment because there is no apparent change. Let me show you instead some numerical data."

He waved his hand sideways in front of the screen. A three-dimensional graph appeared.

"This is the control," he said. "You can see this drop in the cell count for the lytic stage here. This is what you observed on the display just now." He pointed at a part of the single red line where the gradient decreased rapidly.

"Let me show you what happens with the compound you designed." He reached out a finger and flicked it to the left. A second plot appeared, containing six differently coloured lines.

"What are we looking at here?" Rosalind asked, leaning forwards.

"Each line is a different concentration."

Two of the lines showed a slight decrease halfway along the horizontal axis, but the rest remained level.

"And if I superimpose the control on the same axes…" Fernando flicked his finger to introduce a third graph. In this one, the red line fell steeply as before, but the others merged into a single flat trace. The doctor extended his hand and twisted his wrist in front of the screen. The image rotated, showing six horizontal lines running across the top of the display alongside each other.

"Even at the lowest concentration, there is almost no decrease in the healthy cell count. Congratulations. I think we have found a treatment that will protect against the virus."

Kubar and Jason grinned as they accepted Fernando's handshake. Rosalind continued to stare at the screen. After a few moments, she raised her eyes and met the Spanish doctor's puzzled gaze. "Halfon will want to test this on a live subject. You better be absolutely sure it'll work before you inform him."

"Of course. I will run more tests before I tell him, but I don't expect the results to change. From what I understand, the molecular structure is very similar to the one we trialled on the child a few days ago—"

"And look how that ended up," Rosalind interrupted.

Fernando flushed. She gestured towards Jason. "Tomorrow, the test subject will be his son."

"I think we would all prefer to delay any more human trials until we have more information," Kubar said. "I will discuss this with Professor Halfon tonight. Please do what you can to confirm the results. Thank you for telling us first."

"You're welcome," Fernando replied.

Kubar led Jason and Rosalind back towards their workstations. In silence, he sat in the chair and waved his hand in front of the screen to wake up the computer. Then he navigated several menus.

"What are you doing?" Jason asked.

A low whirring sound came from a few feet away. Kubar rose, strolled to a nearby printer and picked up the sheets of paper that emerged.

"It is my insurance policy," he replied as he folded them and placed them in the back pocket of his trousers.

Part Four: Evacuation

64

Wednesday 6th August 2036

Tripoli Infectious Diseases Hospital, Republic of North Africa
5 minutes before the planned power cut

Jason glanced at his watch band: 21:55. Only five minutes to go. A guard had collected Perrin half an hour earlier, leaving Jason and the Shaladis as the only prisoners in the room. At the end of that day's shift, Dr Kubar had informed him that Professor Halfon planned to conduct the test on Paul at eleven o'clock the following morning. If this escape attempt failed, his son would be sedated and strapped to a trolley, then placed in close proximity to a pregnant woman. Despite the success of the cell culture trials, he had no intention of risking his son's life on a compound yet to be proven in human subjects. Now he straddled the wooden bench, his legs jiggling up and down with nervous tension.

The general flicked a glance in Jason's direction from the opposite side of the table where he sat alongside his daughter, Aya. "It would not be possible for you to look more tense," he whispered without turning his head.

"Oh, right," Jason replied. "Sorry." He studied the digits on his watch band again. No change.

"And stop checking the time," Shaladi hissed. "You will alert the guards."

He muttered a few words in Arabic to Aya. She stood, then strolled towards the guard station. The two men inside watched her approach through a haze of grey cigarette smoke. One rose and ambled through the doorway to question her. She pointed at the door to the bathroom. He shrugged and returned to his colleague. He let out a brief bark of laughter, then raised his hand to his mouth and took a long drag of his cigarette, causing the tip to turn a bright cherry-red.

"Two minutes," Shaladi whispered. "Move to the end of the table, but do not look at them."

Jason followed the command, sitting with his legs astride the bench. Despite the general's earlier instructions, he checked his watch again: 21:58. His pulse rate soared as he tried to remember the tasks he had been assigned. He ran over the first part of the plan in his head. *Do not move until the lights go out.* It was about ten metres to the office. How long would it take him to cover the distance?

Shaladi's voice intruded on his thoughts. "Any moment now. Be ready."

Jason twisted around and risked a glance at the guards. The two men seemed relaxed as they chatted and smoked. Another quick check of the time: 22:01. Was anything going to happen? "They're late," he whispered.

Shaladi lifted one leg and placed it on the other side of the bench, matching Jason's stance. Despite the general's calm outward appearance, a bead of sweat ran down the man's temple. He raised his hand and brushed it away.

Jason drummed his fingers on the wooden surface of the table. He could barely breathe. Another surreptitious glance at the watch band: 22:02. His gaze drifted across to the general. Their eyes locked onto each other. Shaladi's lips moved in silence. *Wait.*

A burst of laughter came from the office. Both prisoners turned their heads towards the noise. How much longer? Jason focused his attention on the glowing digits, making no attempt to disguise his actions. 22:03. They weren't coming. "Nothing is—"

A dull thud. The lights flickered, then died. Shaladi's urgent command: "Run!"

Jason shoved himself off the bench and ran in a low crouch with his hands out in front of him towards the office. The red tips of the two cigarettes provided the only guidance. The clamour of somebody hammering on a door rose above the harsh sound of his breathing. A series of shrill screams followed moments later.

Jason bumped into the wall and immediately dropped flat. He inched his way to the right until he came to the corner. A figure brushed past him in the darkness. Suddenly, the room brightened a little. *Shit! Emergency lighting.*

A quick glance confirmed Shaladi squatting beside him. The general raised a finger to his lips in a shushing gesture. The banging sounds continued unabated. A guard emerged through the office doorway. He held a pistol in his hand. The man crept towards the source of the noise. He yelled some words in Arabic.

The guard's focus remained on the door to the female bathroom. With a yell of fury, Shaladi rose from his crouch and charged. He barrelled into his target, slamming him against the wall. The pistol dropped to the floor and skittered away from the struggling pair. Jason flung himself forwards. Two shots rang out, throwing up splinters where the bullets smashed into the tiles, inches from his head. He scooped up the weapon and spun around just as another shot punched into the stained plaster behind him.

Jason extended his arm without thinking and squeezed the trigger. The bullet struck the guard in the shoulder, spinning him sideways.

"Give it to me," Shaladi barked. His opponent lay dazed, blood streaming from a cut to his forehead. Jason handed him the weapon. The general raised the barrel. Jason flinched at the impossibly loud bang. He turned away in horror at the sight of the gore and brain matter splattered against the wall.

A groan came from inside the office. Shaladi took a pace forwards, extended his arm and fired another two shots. Moments later, he emerged with a cigarette dangling from his mouth and a pistol in each hand. He handed one weapon to Jason and placed the other in the waistband of his trousers. "Well done. Now hold this. We have more work to do."

"You didn't have to kill them."

The general took a deep drag, then dropped the butt and ground it beneath his heel. He blew out the smoke he had been holding in his lungs. "We do not have time to take prisoners. They would have killed you without a second thought. Just be thankful they are dead and you are not. Let me fetch my daughter, then we can get out of here."

Jason stared at the pistol. "I don't think I can use this."

Shaladi shook his head in disgust. "The man you wounded would have died in a few minutes anyway. It is too late for regrets." He strode towards the bathroom and called out in Arabic. The door inched open, and a terrified Aya Shaladi peered out. A short conversation followed.

Jason stared at the dead body. He had shot somebody. The smooth black shape of the gun suddenly felt heavy in his hand. His stomach heaved. Thin bile splattered on the dirty tiles. He spat to remove the acidic taste from his mouth.

Shaladi jogged to the exit. "Quick, we must hurry. Let us hope the doctor's information was correct, and the doors are unlocked."

The general pulled the handle towards him and grinned as the door swung open. "Good, he was right."

"We need to get my mother from the cells," Jason said as he hurried to catch up.

Shaladi's face darkened. "Why do you want to rescue this woman? Did she not kill your biological mother and millions of other women? We should leave her here to suffer."

"I made a promise."

"We have a saying; promises are like eggs: fragile and easily broken."

"Look, if you aren't going to help, I'll do it by myself."

The general's eyes narrowed. "I will never understand you Westerners. Fine, let us go and free the most hated person in the world."

65

Wednesday 6th August 2036

Tripoli Infectious Diseases Hospital, Republic of North Africa
3 minutes before the planned power cut

Dr Kubar stood outside Halfon's office. He glanced at his watch for the third time in the last two minutes: 21:57. He was a little early, but he needed to be with the director when the power failed. His fingers closed around the object in the pocket of his white medical coat. He wondered whether he could summon the courage to use it.

Initially, the professor had been reluctant to meet him at this late hour. What had finally convinced him was Kubar's promise of important news. The scientist had persuaded his colleague, Dr Fernando, to hold off on revealing the promising results of the trials. Despite his treasonous intentions and more to keep his mind from what lay ahead, he had spent the last three hours poring through the test data looking for holes. Everything seemed to indicate the conclusions were correct.

Kubar knocked on the professor's door. He turned the handle upon hearing the muffled call to enter.

Halfon glanced up from the screen he was studying. "Sit, sit," he said, waving the doctor to a seat. "This must be important if you want to see me this late in the day."

"It is," Kubar replied. "There is some good news. We have developed a new compound, and it is effective in preventing the virus from activating in cell cultures."

Halfon's brows knitted together in a frown. "Why has nobody told me about this before now?"

"I wanted to check the results myself."

"And let me guess; you wished to delay testing on a live subject until you had done so?"

Kubar met the professor's piercing gaze. "That is correct."

Halfon rested his elbows on the desk and steepled his fingers. "I see. It is indeed good news, but I am disappointed you did not tell me sooner."

"I did not want to give you false hope."

A venomous look flitted across Halfon's face. "Or perhaps you have allowed the attitudes of the Westerners to rub off on you. Actually, Dr Brandt showed me the results a few hours ago."

Kubar flushed. "If this treatment works on a human subject, will you allow me to talk to my daughter?"

"Yes, I have already told you this."

"And you are sure she is well? May I view the records? You could access the database now."

Halfon's eyes narrowed. "You do not believe me?"

"I would like to see the information for myself."

Halfon leant back in his chair, studying the doctor. "I am beginning to think you know more than you are telling me."

"What do you mean?"

"The security people have been checking Dr Rossi's phone. There is no evidence it ever connected to the Wi-Fi. In addition, the network logs confirm the unauthorised device accessed one of our government sites: the same site you are asking me to show you now."

"I just want to know whether my daughter is alive."

"Whoever the person is, they would need the wireless password. Unless I am mistaken, you are among the people with this knowledge."

Kubar remained silent. He glanced at his watch: 21:59.

Halfon continued. "We may not be able to see from our logs what information was requested from the database, but the system maintains full records of all queries. We have the exact time the request took place, so we can use the timestamp to identify the query at their end. I have passed this along to our government's internal security agency, and I am expecting a reply shortly, although I suspect the answer will not surprise me. I do not believe in coincidences. So, I ask again; do you know something about this?"

Kubar closed his fingers around the object in his pocket. Still, he said nothing.

"How did you get the login credentials?" Halfon asked. "Did you steal mine?" He opened the top drawer and reached inside. His hand emerged holding a black cylinder. He placed it on the desk in front of him.

Kubar's eyes locked onto the shape of the stun baton. He tore his gaze away to check the time: 22:01. *Is this power cut going to happen?*

The professor glared at his subordinate. "I must say, I am disappointed in you. As one of our most talented scientists and the inventor of a cure for this virus, you could have been a national or perhaps even an international celebrity. But instead, you have betrayed your country. I will summon the security guards here in a few seconds to arrest you."

"I found out my daughter died years ago. You lied to me."

Halfon stared at his subordinate. "I did what was necessary. Get over it. Did you really think she was still alive after so long?"

Kubar pushed back his chair.

"You cannot escape," the professor said. He grasped the baton and stood.

Suddenly, the lights flickered. A moment later, the room plunged into darkness. Kubar grabbed the syringe gun from his pocket. He launched himself towards the spot where Halfon had been standing. The two men collided and crashed to the floor. Kubar was the first to react. He pressed the nozzle against the professor's body and pulled the trigger. A short hiss signalled the device had delivered its payload. He rolled away before Halfon could recover sufficiently to use his own weapon. He pushed himself upright, using the edge of the desk for support.

A second later, the dim glow of the emergency lighting clicked on to reveal the prostrate form of the director. "What did you—?"

"It is a muscle relaxant," Kubar said. "You will soon find yourself unable to move at all. Before you ask, there is not enough to kill you."

"They will torture you for this. You will die a painful death."

"They have to catch me first."

"You are a traitor. I hope your daughter died in agony." The stun baton dropped from Halfon's grasp and rolled a short distance along the carpet. Despite his situation, his features twisted into a sneer. "You lack the courage to do what needs to be done. You are too afraid to sacrifice a life for the greater good." His eyes followed the doctor as he leant forwards and scooped up the weapon.

Kubar depressed the circular button. A blue spark crackled across the tip. Wordlessly, he knelt over Halfon's incapacitated body. Kubar reached inside the professor's jacket, removed his mobile phone and key card, then slipped them into his own pocket.

Kubar moved his mouth close to the director's ear. "Oh, I am prepared to do what must be done—just not to sacrifice the lives of innocent children."

Then he placed the end of the device on the man's chest above his heart and pushed down with his thumb. Halfon's body spasmed. He pressed the button again. After three further jolts of high voltage electricity, the professor's eyes remained open, staring sightlessly at the ceiling.

66

Wednesday 6th August 2036

Tripoli Infectious Diseases Hospital, Republic of North Africa
2 minutes after the power cut

Jason followed the general and his daughter through the doorway. The dim emergency lighting cast a ghostly glow over the cracked walls. Their footsteps echoed as they jogged towards the staircase. Jason stopped and listened when they reached the door. A stillness seemed to have settled over the building. For a moment, he wondered whether he was imagining things, but then he identified the cause—the ever-present background hum of machinery had ceased.

"Are you coming?" Shaladi hissed.

Jason stepped into the stairwell. A dank, musty smell assaulted his nostrils. Here, the emergency lights were more widely spaced, throwing long shadows as they descended the concrete steps. Two flights down, they arrived at the ground floor and another door.

Shaladi held up a hand. "There is sure to be a guard. He will be armed. He may have heard us already, so we need to be ready. Aya, you have no weapon. You must wait here. I will go first. Do not make any sound." He pushed the handle and slid sideways through the gap, then beckoned Jason forward.

"Be careful," Aya whispered as the door closed behind them.

A narrow corridor stretched ahead. Dim strip lights extended along the ceiling. The black, circular lens of a camera pointed towards them, but it showed no signs of being active. Dark patches stained the concrete floor and walls. The musty odour was worse here. They crept forwards. A flash of movement.

Jason swung the pistol, then removed his finger from the trigger. "Only a mouse," he murmured, his heart racing.

"Or a rat," Shaladi added with a low chuckle.

"Shit. I hate rats."

"They are more scared of you than you are of them."

"I wouldn't be so sure."

Shaladi stopped. "Shh! Listen."

Jason tilted his head, his ears straining to pick up what the general had heard. The muted sound of a female voice came from the other side of the rusty metal door ahead. "My mother is trying to distract the guard," he whispered. "What's the plan?"

"There is only one route forward. We must surprise him before he has time to react." He studied the hinges. "It opens this way, but I think he will hear us before we can enter."

"So, what do we do?"

Shaladi scratched his cheek. "I will pull the door towards us. You go in and shoot him."

"What? I just step inside and—"

"No. You stay low. It gives him less of a target."

"Why can't you do the shooting?"

Shaladi stared hard at his co-conspirator. "You are the one who wants to free her. We can leave her here if you wish."

Jason met the general's gaze. "All right. I'll do it."

"Remember. Aim for the centre of the body and squeeze the trigger."

Jason drew in a deep breath. A whooshing sound rushed in his ears.

"Are you ready?" Shaladi asked. "I will count up, and on three, I will open it."

"Okay." Jason crouched and nodded at the general. "Let's go."

"One… Two… Three!"

The hinges squealed in protest as Shaladi heaved the heavy metal door towards him. Jason scuttled forwards, his arm outstretched. A concrete corridor extended away to his left. Five equally-spaced rusty doors lined the right wall. A guard was peering through the hatch at the far end. The man turned his head in surprise at the sudden interruption.

In the dim light, Jason raised the pistol and sighted along the barrel. His finger started to squeeze the trigger. The breath caught in his throat. A wave of dizziness swept over him. He swallowed hard. The guard reached towards his holster. The weapon wavered in Jason's hand. He couldn't do it. He closed his eyes, waiting for the bullets to rip through his body.

An incredibly loud bang boomed inches from his head. His own gun leapt as he inadvertently pulled the trigger. When he dared to look along the corridor, the guard lay on his side, moaning in pain. Two more thunderous bangs followed. The man jerked twice and stopped moving.

Jason dropped the weapon. He twisted around to see Shaladi's angry stare.

"Why did you not shoot?" the general yelled.

"I…"

"Do you want to die?"

"I'm sorry. I just couldn't…"

Shaladi spat on the floor and muttered a curse. He stepped forwards, scooped up Jason's pistol and hurried along the corridor. When he reached the pool of blood, he stretched out a leg and prodded the guard's body with his foot. Satisfied with the lack of response, he bent down, unfastened the man's holster and removed his gun. After placing the weapon in the waistband of his trousers, he peered through the hatch, then hauled down on the lever and pulled the heavy door towards him.

Jason crept up behind him, taking care to avoid stepping in the expanding crimson puddle. Rosalind Baxter cowered against the back wall.

"Are you coming," Shaladi said, his voice laced with disdain, "or do you like it here?"

"Is the guard dead?" she asked, unable to hide a quiver in her words.

The general rolled his eyes. "You are the doctor, no? I am not an expert, but I think so."

"Did the plan work?"

"So far, yes—no thanks to your son—but we still have much to do."

"What do you mean?"

"He could not shoot the gun."

Jason lowered his head in shame.

Rosalind grabbed his hand. "Well, I'm grateful you came for me. What now?"

"We return to my daughter and disarm the other guards," Shaladi replied. "After that, we fetch the girl and their child and get out of here."

"Okay, lead on."

The general turned and jogged back the way they had come. Both Jason and Rosalind cast nervous glances at the dead body before following. Shaladi called out in Arabic before opening the door into the stairwell. Aya's anxious face greeted them. They exchanged a few more words, then the general removed a pistol from his waistband and handed it to her.

He fixed Jason with a stare. "Unlike you, I trust my daughter to follow instructions," he said. He turned to Rosalind. "Can you use one of these?"

She nodded.

"But will you fire it if necessary?"

She flashed a sympathetic glance at Jason. "Yes."

Shaladi handed Rosalind the second spare weapon. "Good. Let us go and get the others. My men will be waiting outside."

67

Wednesday 6th August 2036

Tripoli Infectious Diseases Hospital, Republic of North Africa
4 minutes after the power cut

The general led them up the staircase, trailed by his daughter. Rosalind came next, with Jason bringing up the rear. His ears still burned with humiliation at his inability to use the weapon when required. As he plodded up the stairs, his brain whirled in an internal conflict. He was reluctant to take a life, but the people holding them prisoner would show no such mercy. His inaction could easily have led not only to his own demise but also the deaths of those depending upon him to escape. Next time, if there was one, he would do whatever needed to be done.

Jason was so lost in thought he nearly bumped into his mother when she stopped behind the others, two floors up from the basement.

"I will go first," Shaladi whispered. "If you see any guards, you must shoot them." He stared pointedly at Jason, then focused his attention back on the women. "When they are down, take their guns. It is possible some of the scientists remain loyal to the professor. None of them can be allowed to have weapons. Is everybody ready?"

The general didn't wait for a response. He pushed the door open, hesitated a second, then slipped through the gap. The three others followed his lead. He led them along the dimly lit corridor as far as the entrance to the dining area. The sound of angry voices penetrated from the other side.

Shaladi raised a hand and crouched down. "Keep low and do not fire until I do." He reached for the handle and twisted it slowly. The noise level rose as a crack opened. He eased his way in. Aya followed him. Rosalind turned back before entering. "Good luck," she murmured.

Jason opened his mouth to reply, but she was already moving, the gun stretched out ahead of her. He trailed her into the room. Several scientists milled about under the gloomy lighting. A guard shuffled nervously from foot to foot in the far corner, his weapon drawn. Another man stood to one side, talking into a radio as his eyes anxiously scanned the small crowd.

Jason's gaze followed the three other members of his group as they crept along the wall, their movement hidden from the guards by the intervening bodies.

A voice called out in a thick Arabic accent. "Return to your rooms."

"Why are the lights out?" came a shout from the gathering.

"You must go back to your rooms," the man repeated. Now, the second guard also drew his pistol.

"We're not moving until you tell us what's happening," somebody yelled. A murmur of approval accompanied the challenge.

A shot rang out as the nearest guard fired above the heads of the crowd. Instinctively, they flinched and dropped down, providing the opportunity for which the general had been waiting.

Another gunshot boomed from Jason's left, followed swiftly by two more. The pair of armed guards jerked backwards, then lay unmoving. The scientists scattered in panic. Jason ignored the commotion and scuttled towards the closest fallen man. He scanned the floor, searching for the dropped pistol. A glint of light on metal reflected from beneath the dead body's legs. He reached out a hand and snatched up the weapon. His gaze rose inadvertently to the blooming patch of red in the centre of the man's chest, then to the blank stare of the wide-open eyes.

Swallowing hard, he turned his attention towards the second corpse, but Aya was already crouching beside it.

Shaladi strode to the middle of the room and stood with his gun pointing downwards. "Please stay calm," he yelled. Frightened stares greeted his statement. "We mean you no harm. We are leaving this place tonight. You are free to go too."

"Why are you doing this?" a man asked. "They told us we could leave when they developed a cure, and we have done that." Jason recognised him as the Spanish doctor, Fernando.

The general barked out a laugh. "You think they will honour this agreement? You do not know these people like I do."

"What happens when we get out of here?" a different voice called. "Can you help with transport?"

"I am sorry, but no. You must arrange your own travel."

"We'll never make it across the border," another man replied. "I don't know about you, but I'm staying here. Apart from anything else, I want to get paid before I leave."

"That is your decision."

Jason tuned out the conversation. He had more important things to attend to. Before he could think about leaving, he needed to free Antimone and his son, Paul.

68

Wednesday 6th August 2036

Tripoli Infectious Diseases Hospital, Republic of North Africa
6 minutes after the power cut

Jason jogged across the dining area and along the corridor to the laboratory entrance. He eased the door open. The gun he had recovered from the dead guard pointed ahead of him. He exhaled the breath he had been holding; the room was deserted. The space looked different in the dim emergency lighting. Hulking machines stood like monoliths, creating patches of shadow that didn't exist when the mains power was on. The unfamiliar silence added to the threatening atmosphere of the place.

He buried his anxiety and crept towards the entry to the isolation area in which Antimone and Paul were being held. As he passed by the glass-walled observation chamber, he spotted a bright light penetrating through the frosted window in the door. It seemed Dr Kubar was right; the electricity supply continued to function here.

He pushed through the unlocked swing doors and found himself in a room, approximately five metres square, with white walls. Straight ahead, several yellow hazmat suits hung on hangers. To his left, a solitary green button occupied a position between two sets of sliding partitions. Mounted above it was a sign in Arabic script. An empty wheelchair sat in the corner.

Jason flashed a glance at his watch. Already, seven minutes had passed since the start of the escape attempt. How much time did he have before they restored power? It couldn't be long. Putting on the protective suit would waste valuable seconds. If he got Antimone and Paul out and they were infected, they would pass on the virus, anyway. *Damn it!* He'd have to take the risk. He shoved the pistol into the waistband of his trousers and slammed his palm against the button.

The left partition opened, revealing a chamber one metre wide by two long. Jason stepped forwards. The panel closed behind him, sealing him inside. The dim sound of machinery penetrated the walls. His ears popped. For a horrible moment, he wondered whether the pumps would suck out all the air and suffocate him, but after a few seconds, the door in front slid back.

Jason emerged into a foyer area. He blinked as his eyes acclimatised to the sudden increase in brightness from the overhead lighting. Antimone and Paul were in here somewhere. A passageway extended thirty or forty metres ahead. A series of rooms occupied the right side. Solid partitions separated each room from the next. Full-height windows bordered the corridor, allowing those outside to look in. Conventional white plastic doors lined the opposite wall. Halfway down, one door contained a frosted-glass panel. He identified it as the entrance to the observation chamber.

Jason crept forwards. He couldn't be sure whether anybody was still working, and he had no wish to use the pistol unless absolutely necessary. The first room was empty apart from two unoccupied beds. In the next, a bed lay against the back wall. The outline beneath the sheets belonged to an adult. The sleeping figure moved, revealing the face of the pregnant woman he had last seen in the observation area.

Jason continued along the corridor. His breath caught in his throat when he peered through the window of the third room. Antimone sat in a wheelchair, her eyes closed and her chin resting on her chest. He tapped on the glass. She jerked her head upright, and her mouth opened in shock. She gestured towards the panel mounted beside the door.

The only control was a single green button. Jason pressed it with his finger. A metallic click signalled the opening of the lock.

Antimone wheeled herself forwards, wearing a huge grin on her face. Then, just as quickly, it faded. "What are you doing? Don't you know I'm infected?"

Jason placed a foot against the door to prevent it from closing. "We're getting out of here," he whispered. "Shaladi arranged a power cut. He shot the guards. I haven't got time to explain it all. We need to find Paul."

"You don't understand. Both of us have the new strain. You'll be infecting everybody we come into contact with."

Jason glanced at his watch. "Dr Kubar and my mother came up with a cure—at least we think it is."

"What does that mean?"

"They haven't run any human trials yet, but it works in a cell culture."

Antimone's features clouded in doubt.

Jason leant forwards, placed a hand behind her head to draw her nearer and kissed her. "Look, I love you and our son. We may not be doing the right thing, but unless you want to spend the rest of your life in here, we need to leave now."

"I'm not—"

"There's no time. Do you honestly think these people will share any drug they develop with other countries? We both know the answer to that. If we get out of here, we can publish the formula and make sure everybody gets it. But that won't happen unless we go immediately."

"All right. Paul's in the next room."

Jason stood back for Antimone. She wheeled herself out and turned right. When she reached the adjacent door, she pressed the green button on the panel. "You wait here. I'll get him."

Jason's heart fluttered at the sight of the tiny figure in the single cot. "Paul," he murmured. He watched as Antimone leant forwards, scooped up the sleeping child, still wrapped in the bedsheet, and held him against her chest.

She spun the wheelchair around and headed back. "Let's go," she whispered.

Jason hesitated. "Actually, I promised Dr Kubar I'd get the other kids out as well."

"They're in the next room."

"How many are there?"

"Just two, I think."

Jason jogged further along the corridor and peered through the window. Four cots lay against the right wall, separated from each other by a gap of half a metre. The two furthermost beds held the sleeping forms of children. Antimone moved up behind him.

"I'll fetch them," Jason said. He pushed the button, crossed the small room and crouched beside the nearest occupied bed. He reached out a hand and shook the shoulder of the unconscious child.

"We haven't got time for this," Antimone hissed. "Just grab them."

Jason pulled back the thin sheet. The boy was maybe four-years-old. He wore a brightly coloured T-shirt and shorts. A mewl of protest escaped his lips when Jason picked him up. Moments later, Jason bent down and lifted the second child. The boy's eyelids fluttered open for a moment, then closed once again.

With a child resting against each shoulder, Jason hurried back towards Antimone. "Let's get out of here," he said. He took one step into the corridor, then stopped. Antimone twisted her head and gasped.

Fifteen metres away, between the escapees and the airlock, stood the pregnant woman. A figure in a white hazmat suit stayed behind her. The reflection of a scalpel blade held to the woman's throat glinted in the bright overhead lighting. She resisted, but the person pushed her forwards.

69

Wednesday 6th August 2036

Tripoli Infectious Diseases Hospital, Republic of North Africa
8 minutes after the power cut

Jason retreated a pace. “Is there another way out of here?” he asked.

“I don’t think so,” Antimone replied. “I’ve only ever seen them come in through that entrance.”

“We might be able to get out from the observation room. I can use my gun to break the glass.”

“Can’t you just shoot him?”

“Not without hitting her.”

The man in the hazmat suit pushed the pregnant woman forwards again. He called out something in Arabic.

Jason twisted his head and glanced behind him. The door with the frosted window was five metres away. “Come on. We have to go.”

Antimone spun her wheelchair around and covered the short distance in two shoves. Jason followed, casting another backward glance. The North African pair continued to shuffle closer.

Jason shoved the swing doors open with his foot and edged through the gap. He stepped to one side to allow Antimone to pass. “I’ll have to put these two down,” he said. Compared to the bright illumination of the corridor, the gloomy lighting gave the observation area an oppressive feel. Jason strode to the far end and gently lowered the pair of children to the floor. Antimone manoeuvred the wheelchair alongside them.

Jason removed the pistol from his waistband. “This is going to be loud.” He moved back towards the door and pointed the weapon at the window. “Are you ready?”

Antimone nodded, clutching Paul more tightly.

Jason squeezed the trigger. A deafening boom rang out in the enclosed space. The glass remained intact apart from a splinter pattern extending from the point of impact. Immediately, the three children woke and started to cry.

“Shit, it’s reinforced,” he said.

“Try again,” Antimone replied, glancing anxiously at the door.

Jason aimed at the same spot and fired a second time. Despite the incredibly loud bang, there was still no discernible difference to the window. On the far side of the room, one of the terrified African boys screamed in fright. He leapt up and ran towards the only way out. He reached the swing doors at the same moment as the man in the hazmat suit shoved his hostage through in the opposite direction. The impact knocked the boy off his feet. He landed on his back, staring up in terror at the equally petrified woman standing over him. His arms and legs scrambled in panic as he tried to move backwards.

Jason stood rooted to the spot. Suddenly, he remembered he was holding the gun. He swung his arm towards the doors. The woman cowered as the weapon pointed in her direction. There was no sign of the man. The sound of running footsteps echoed from the corridor.

"Get back," Jason yelled, taking a forward step.

The woman backed away with hands extended, a jumbled stream of words spilling from her mouth.

"Go," he shouted, gesturing with the pistol. She needed no second invitation. She whirled around and barged through the swing doors. Jason stuck his head through the gap and checked both ways along the corridor. Other than the retreating figure of the woman, nobody was there.

A wet cough drew Jason's attention back to the room. The closest African boy sprawled on the floor, blood streaming from his nose and mouth. He twisted onto his side and coughed again, spraying bloody droplets over the white tiles. Seconds later, his whole body convulsed. Jason shoved the pistol into the waistband of his trousers and knelt beside him. The boy shuddered once more, then his eyes rolled up, and he lay still.

"Is he—?" Antimone's voice quivered as she asked the question.

A bang on the window from behind Jason saved him from having to answer. He whirled around. Rosalind Baxter stood on the other side of the glass. She gesticulated at the table and mouthed something. Jason turned, trying to identify the object of her attention.

"Oh, no, no, no." Antimone's panicked words cut through Jason like a knife. A thin trickle of blood ran from the second African boy's nose down his chin. When he opened his mouth to cry, crimson streaks stained his tiny white teeth.

The hammering on the window grew more frantic. "What?" Jason mouthed.

He studied his mother's lips as she enunciated the words more slowly. What was she trying to tell him? She jabbed a finger. "This?" Jason asked, pointing to a stack of papers. She shook her head in frustration. He pointed to another item. Rosalind gave an exaggerated nod. Jason picked up the object: a syringe gun.

Finally, he understood: the drug. He grabbed the tray of clear vials. This time, he got the single word she mouthed: *yes*. With fumbling fingers, he snatched up a sealed capsule. Rosalind gestured again. He turned the cylinder upside down: a thumbs up. *How did the damned thing fit?* He pushed a lever on the medical instrument, and a slot opened. He shoved the glass tube home. Rosalind nodded in encouragement.

Jason grabbed a couple more vials from the tray and sprinted to the end of the room. He hesitated. Who should he give it to first? The African boy coughed.

Specks of blood landed on the floor. Paul wiped a hand over his nose. A thin trail of red smeared his cheek.

"Just do it," Antimone screamed.

Jason placed the syringe gun against the foreign child's upper arm and pressed the trigger. The boy stopped crying for a second, then restarted with renewed vigour before falling silent. Jason flipped out the empty vial. It bounced across the floor in a series of clinks. He slotted home a full one and held the device to his son's shoulder. A short hiss signalled the entry of the drug into Paul's body. He slid the medical instrument into his belt alongside the pistol.

Antimone cradled her son. "Is it going to work?" she asked, her voice barely a whisper.

Jason studied Paul for a moment. "We can't stay here."

"You didn't answer my question."

"I don't know."

Antimone locked eyes on Jason. Unable to meet the ferocity of her glare, he looked away. "Come on," he said. He bent down and picked up the now unconscious African boy, then headed towards the swing doors. As he passed the table, he scooped up a handful of the vials and put them in his pocket.

Holding the weapon out ahead of him, Jason stepped around the dead child and stuck his head into the corridor. Empty. He jogged, retracing his footsteps to the exit. Antimone followed, grasping Paul in a tight, one-armed embrace as she powered the wheelchair with her free arm. Jason's gaze strayed to the left as they came to the pregnant woman's room. She sat on the bed, her face buried in her hands. She didn't even look up as they rushed past.

They arrived at the airlock without further incident. Jason studied the boy in his arms. His eyes were closed, but his breathing was deep and regular. Jason glanced back towards Antimone. Paul's head rested on her shoulder.

"How is he?" Jason asked.

"The bleeding seems to have stopped," she replied. "I think he's asleep."

"Thank God for that," Jason murmured. He pushed the solitary green button. The door opened immediately.

"I can't fit through in this thing," Antimone said. "You'll have to lift me out."

"There's no way I can carry all three of you."

"Put the kids in first, then come back for me."

Jason backed inside the chamber with the African boy and gently placed him on the floor. "Block the gap with your chair."

Antimone rolled forwards until one wheel rested against the door. She handed Paul to Jason, who positioned his son beside the other unconscious child. Finally, Jason lifted Antimone and kicked the wheelchair away. The panel slid shut almost immediately. A moment later, a foul-smelling chemical mist filled the small compartment.

The ordeal lasted only a few seconds, but both adults emerged coughing. The two children remained unaware throughout.

General Shaladi awaited them.

"Can you get the kids?" Jason asked, blocking the door with his foot.

The general stepped inside the chamber and came out moments later with a child under each arm.

"At least my wheelchair's still here," Antimone said, pointing to the device in the corner.

Jason hurried over and lowered her into the seat. He took Paul from the general and placed him on Antimone's lap, then returned for the African boy. "I'd prefer you to be the one holding the gun," he said to Shaladi with a wry grin.

They followed the general through the doors into the laboratory area. To the left, a blood-soaked figure in a hazmat suit lay crumpled on the ground. Seeing the focus of Jason's attention, Shaladi growled, "He deserved to die." His expression softened. "How is your son?"

Jason shot a glance at Antimone. "I think he's going to be okay."

"And the other child?"

Jason transferred his gaze to the boy in his arms. "It looks like he'll be all right as well."

"Excellent. Now, it is already too long. We must leave. Follow me."

Rosalind fell in alongside as they passed through the dimly lit laboratory. "It seems the drug works."

Jason flashed a tense smile at her. "Yeah. Thanks for your help."

"One good turn deserves another. I'm just glad my grandson survived."

As the group approached the exit leading into the dining area, an armed figure stepped out from the shadows. "Where do you think you're going? Stop right there."

70

Wednesday 6th August 2036

Tripoli Infectious Diseases Hospital, Republic of North Africa
11 minutes after the power cut

A gunshot punctured the silence. The four adults flinched as a chunk of plaster exploded from the wall inches above their heads. Both the children remained unconscious.

"That was to demonstrate I'm armed, and I know how to use this. Now, place your weapons on the ground and push them towards me with your feet... and no sudden movements."

The general and Rosalind both did as instructed.

Jason still held the African boy. "I can't—"

"Put him down."

Jason laid the sleeping child on the floor, then straightened up slowly.

"Now, remove the gun from your waistband. That's it. Toss it away." Jason followed the order. The pistol landed with a metallic clatter. "And the other thing too." Something inside shattered as the syringe hit the ground and skittered over the white tiles. "Good. Now, all of you put your hands behind your head and interlock your fingers."

Max's eyes glittered in the dim illumination cast by the emergency lighting as he watched the escapees comply. All the while, the dark circle of a gun barrel pointed at Jason's stomach.

"Well, well. My four least favourite people, all together in one place. And in such a hurry to leave."

"Please let us go," Antimone said, still clutching Paul to her chest.

"Oh, I don't think that'll happen."

"You could come with us."

"It's kind of you to invite me, but you've left the invitation a little late. I wondered what you were cooking up. I must have asked you quite a few times, but you wouldn't tell me."

"Because you were working with Halfon, weren't you?"

"I might have been."

"Which just goes to prove we were right not to trust you," Antimone replied.

Jason cleared his throat. "So, what are you going to do?"

Max's lips twitched in a smirk. "I could wait for more guards to arrive. I'm sure somebody will be here any minute. With a bit of luck, they'll pay my fee.

They might even give me a bonus for stopping you from escaping. But I've got a better idea. I think I might just shoot you all. I'll say you tried to jump me. There won't be any witnesses to contradict me. The only question is who goes first."

He swung the barrel to point at Shaladi. "Maybe I'll start with you. We had a deal. I delivered exactly what we agreed upon, but instead of receiving the money, my reward was to be beaten up and treated as a prisoner just like the others."

The general muttered a curse.

"Yeah, whatever." The gun pivoted towards Antimone. "And what about you, Trike Queen? If you hadn't tripped me, none of this would have happened, the police would never have been brought in, and my father would still be alive."

Antimone let out a gasp of outrage. "How many times have I got to tell you, the thing at the track was a bloody accident? Even if it wasn't, how can you justify raping me? And that's not to mention—"

"Enough!" Max bellowed. "Do you want me to shoot you now?" He glowered at her for a moment then transferred his aim to Jason. "And what about the boy scout? You're as bad as her. Do you fancy trying to beat me up again, tough guy?"

"Put the gun down," Jason growled, "and I'll gladly take you on."

Max's face darkened. "Tempting though it is, I think I'll keep hold of this." He aimed the pistol at Rosalind. "That brings me to you. You killed my father in front of me. And that's on top of the millions of other deaths you caused. I'd be doing the world a favour by pulling the trigger."

Rosalind met his angry gaze. "If he hadn't caved in and tried to confess, I wouldn't have been forced to take such drastic action. I can see you have your father's genes. You're a pussy just like him."

Max stepped forwards, his face knotted in fury. He swung his fist in a vicious arc, catching Rosalind across the cheek. She let out a cry of pain as she staggered backwards, clutching the point of impact. When she lifted her fingers, they came away smeared with blood. She glowered back at him with a look of pure hatred.

Max retreated to his original position before anybody could react. His breathing was harsh and ragged, and his pupils had reduced to pinpricks. "The next person to talk will receive a bullet for their trouble. So I need to decide. Get down on your knees."

Antimone glared at Max from her wheelchair and gestured towards her legs. "I think you're forgetting something."

"Just stay there and don't move," he snarled.

Rosalind and Shaladi slowly lowered themselves one knee at a time.

Jason was about to follow suit when he detected motion behind Max in the shadows. "No," he said. "If you want to shoot me, you can do it while I'm standing."

The movement resolved into a person creeping forwards. As the figure moved into a patch of light, Jason recognised the outline of Dr Kubar. But he was still ten metres away and seemed to be unarmed.

Max stepped up to Jason and jabbed the pistol into his chest. "I won't tell you again. Down on your knees."

Jason went down on one knee. Five metres to go. Now he could see the approaching doctor held something in his hand.

Max took a step back. His gaze landed on Rosalind. Jason studied his captor's features. A decision formed in Max's eyes. His gun arm swung to the right. His finger tightened as he exerted pressure on the trigger.

Jason lunged. The pistol boomed. Kubar closed the final few paces. A sharp crack of electricity filled the air. Max Perrin dropped to the floor, his body convulsing. Silence fell on the room. Time seemed to stand still.

Then Antimone's voice shattered the calm with a piercing scream.

71

Wednesday 6th August 2036

Prime Minister's Office, 10 Downing Street, London
12 minutes after the power cut

Andrew Jacobs glanced out of the window at the night sky. He removed a handkerchief from his pocket and mopped at his brow. The underlying cause of his perspiration was the tension of waiting to hear from the forces stationed just off the Tripoli coastline rather than the temperature in the air-conditioned room. Admiral Trent and Charles Moreland sat beside him, staring at the blank screen. Both looked equally uncomfortable.

Trent's phone rang. He snatched it off the desk and held it to his ear.

"Where are they?" the Prime Minister asked.

"I'm patching the pictures through now," the admiral replied. Moments later, a jerky image consisting mostly of greys and blacks appeared on the monitor. The sound of splashing water mingled with the low murmur of male voices. "The team is still holding at a distance of three-hundred metres offshore. There's no sign the North Africans have any idea they're there. The beach looks deserted. You're seeing the view through a bodycam."

The video brightened as somebody turned on an infrared light, then settled to show six figures crouching in an inflatable. One of the occupants twisted towards the camera. Dark material shrouded the man's head and body. A mask containing two large lenses covered his face, giving him the appearance of a huge insect. He muttered a few words, then resumed his original position.

The minutes stretched out as the three men in the Prime Minister's office waited for something to happen. Finally, the admiral sat forwards, the phone still held to his ear. "Yes, I understand," he said.

"What's going on?" Jacobs asked.

"We're getting reports of a power failure near the Tripoli Infectious Diseases Hospital. There's nothing yet about any shots being fired."

"That must be them."

"I agree," the admiral replied. "Do we have permission to launch?"

The head of MI6 glanced towards the Prime Minister. "You have my agreement. What do you think, Andrew?"

Jacobs paused in thought for a second, then nodded. "Let's go for it. But for heaven's sake, keep it quiet. We don't want to start a shooting match with the Reponan military if we can help it."

Trent barked a few words into the phone. Almost immediately, the figures on the screen hunched down. A low buzz replaced the sound of lapping water as the bow of the inflatable lifted. Moments later, a scraping noise signalled that the craft had reached the shore. All the occupants bar one jumped out. The man operating the camera and three of his colleagues grabbed the rope running along the gunwale of the boat and spun it around. When it faced back the way they had come, the group gave it a coordinated shove towards deeper water. The note of the engine rose and a white wake followed the vessel as it raced out of sight.

"What's happening?" Jacobs asked.

"It's returning to the ship," the admiral replied. "We don't want to leave it where somebody will spot it and call in their military."

The three marines in front of the camera feed launched themselves forwards, splashing through the last few metres of the Mediterranean Sea to join the pair on the beach. Ahead of the camera, a man crouched down, raised his weapon and stared down the sights. The hiss of two suppressed shots followed one another in quick succession. The tinkle of broken glass carried faintly to the microphone.

"What are they doing now?" Jacobs asked, his voice a whisper.

"Taking out the nearby streetlights," Trent replied without diverting his attention from the screen.

The grainy pictures showed a marine removing his backpack. He withdrew a sphere the size of a tennis ball, pressed a button on its side and tossed it into the air. He repeated the process with a further two of the devices.

"Those are the drones," the admiral explained. "They'll be directed to the target."

The image bounced up and down as the men broke into a jog. Soon, they cleared the beach and ran across a deserted road.

"Won't somebody see them?" the Prime Minister asked.

Trent pointed to the display. "May I?"

Jacobs leant back from the screen.

The admiral moved his hands in front of the monitor, reduced the video to a small window and brought up a map.

"This is the hospital," he said, pointing to a red circle in the bottom right containing a white letter H. "That's where the drones are heading as we speak. At the moment, the team is here. They'll be following this route." He drew a line with his finger from the shore across a green shaded area. "It takes them through the National Park and the Al Nasr Forest. The Reponans have established a night time curfew, and both these areas are relatively unpopulated, so there's less chance of them being spotted."

"What about the last section?" Jacobs asked, pointing to the streets between the forested region and the H symbol.

Trent turned to the Prime Minister. "There's a lot of construction work going on in the vicinity, but you're right; they will stick out if they have to cross that area. Let's just hope our mysterious benefactors come through and give the local forces something else to keep them occupied. Once we set eyes on the hostages, we'll send in a chopper and lift them out along with the marines."

"If there are two different groups out there, how will we know who's on our side and who isn't?"

"I think I can answer that," Moreland replied, his mouth set in a grim line. "If they shoot at our people, they're probably the bad guys."

72

Wednesday 6th August 2036

Tripoli Infectious Diseases Hospital, Republic of North Africa
13 minutes after the power cut

Antimone's scream echoed through the darkened laboratory until her lungs ran out of air. Suddenly, she seemed to notice the unconscious child clasped in her arms. A series of choking sobs wracked her body. She couldn't drag her eyes away from the figure lying still on the floor. Blood dripped from the head wound. The slowly expanding pool appeared almost black in the dim lighting.

She forced her lips to move. "Is he…?" She barely recognised her own voice. The words emerged as if somebody else was operating her vocal cords. Her breathing hastened. A wave of dizziness swept over her as she hyperventilated.

General Shaladi made a gesture towards his daughter. It took Aya a moment to catch on, but then she stepped forwards and lifted Paul from Antimone's chest.

Antimone rolled her wheelchair alongside Jason's body. Awkwardly, she leant over and gently touched his cheek. *He can't be dead.* Any second now, he would stand up and dust himself down. "Come on. Get up," she whispered.

She flinched at the hand on her shoulder. "There's nothing we can do for him," Dr Kubar murmured.

Antimone whirled around. "Why didn't you stop him sooner?" she screamed. "Couldn't you tell he was about to shoot?"

The doctor stared at her, then turned away, unable to meet the expression of pain and anger in her eyes. "I tried to get there as soon as I could. I thought I would reach him in time."

Antimone's gaze flicked down to Jason's lifeless body. "Why did he have to sacrifice himself for her? Why couldn't he just let her die? That psycho was happy to kill both of us when we were stopping her from getting what she wanted."

"I am sorry," Kubar said. "I do not have an answer. Perhaps he still thinks of her as his mother."

"Not thinks," Antimone corrected. "Thought. He's dead because of her." She closed her eyes and breathed through clenched teeth.

Shaladi crouched in front of her. "Please, we have to go. If we do not leave now, his sacrifice will be for nothing. I know you are in pain, but you must continue for your son."

The tears dripped from Antimone's chin onto her lap. Then she looked up. She wiped her cheeks with the palms of her hands. She checked to her right, then to her left. "Where is that bastard? And where's that bloody woman? They were both here a minute ago."

A gunshot boomed from the other side of the laboratory. Shaladi immediately darted towards the corner where he had kicked his gun. Antimone didn't hesitate. She propelled herself in the direction of the gunfire.

"Wait!" the general called from behind her.

Antimone ignored his call. She raced past a towering machine, then clamped her hands down against the shiny hand rings, relishing the sharp sting as it burned her palms. She skidded to a halt. At first, the dim lighting made it hard to interpret what her eyes were telling her. Max Perrin lay on a workbench. One strap ran over his neck, another across his feet. His arms were bound together in front of him by a length of electrical cable. There was no evidence of any wounds. He seemed to be unconscious. His chest rose and fell in slow, regular movements.

Rosalind stood at an adjacent table, her back to Antimone. To her right, the door of one of the metal cabinets was open. The handle dangled at an oblique angle. That explained the gunshot, but what was she doing?

Antimone scanned the contents. Labelled bottles and jars filled the shelves. A circular stain identified where something had been removed. Behind her, the sound of Shaladi's footsteps drew nearer. "What's going on?" she asked.

Rosalind spun around, her face an unreadable mask. "I'm ending this once and for all."

"Ending what?"

"His miserable life."

Rosalind turned away and picked up an object from the table. Antimone moved closer. Rosalind held a brown bottle. Its size matched the empty space on the shelf. She twisted the top and placed the stopper down. An acrid smell accompanied the thin cloud of vapour that curled upwards.

Antimone squinted at the label. The writing was mostly in Arabic, but she recognised several letters: H_2SO_4. She wracked her brains, trying to identify the compound. It sounded familiar somehow. Then, in a flash, it came to her: sulphuric acid.

Rosalind reached out a hand and grabbed a glass syringe with a long metal needle. She inserted the tip inside the open neck of the bottle and withdrew the plunger. Careful not to spill any of the corrosive substance on herself, she crossed to where Max Perrin lay restrained on the workbench.

"Hold this," she said, handing the loaded instrument to Antimone. "I want him to be awake for this. And don't drop any on yourself. It might sting a bit."

Rosalind leant forwards and slapped Max hard on the cheek. "Come on, wake up."

Her captive opened a bleary eye and stared around in confusion for a moment. Finally, his gaze settled on Rosalind. As it did so, he bucked, trying to break free from his bonds.

"Don't bother," she said. "You aren't getting out of those knots any time soon."

Max tried again with the same results. His body relaxed. "So, you're still alive. That's a shame. I thought I'd done the world a favour."

"No," Rosalind replied. "You killed my son instead. And now you're about to pay for that."

Max's eyes flicked towards the end of the laboratory leading to the rest of the hospital. "As I recall, you were only too keen to kill him yourself a year or two back."

A harsh coldness settled on Rosalind's face. "You won't be quite so talkative when I've finished with you. What is it the Bible says? An eye for an eye? This will hurt—a lot."

She held out a hand towards Antimone. Max's gaze followed the movement and landed on the syringe. His eyes widened as they locked onto the point of the needle. He blinked rapidly in the first real sign of fear. He looked up at Antimone's scowling features. "You don't have to do this," he said, his voice trembling. "Please. You're not really going to stand there and watch her stab me, are you? You'll be no better than she is."

"Oh, stabbing you in the eye is only the beginning," Rosalind said. "The concentrated acid I inject might be more of an issue."

Max's mouth opened in shock. Once more, he struggled against the knots in a vain attempt to free himself.

"You killed him," Antimone muttered.

Max dragged his attention from the syringe to her face. "I didn't mean to. I was trying to shoot her."

Antimone's tone rose as she spat the words out. Her pulse thundered in her ears. "You raped me. You forced Jason to rape me. I would have died but for a fluke of genetics."

"But you lived. Look, I'm sorry. I may have overreacted. But it was all years ago. We were still kids." Desperation edged Max's voice.

"Then you sold us out to this bunch of savages."

"I needed the money. If they ever pay me, you can have it."

"I don't want your money. Finally, you murdered Jason. Together with my son, he was one of the few good things to come out of all this."

"I told you. It was an accident." Panic laced every word.

Antimone spoke through gritted teeth. "Now he's lying back there, dead on the floor. And all because I accidentally collided with you in a stupid, meaningless race."

Tears rolled down Max's cheeks. "Please. I'm begging you. I'll do whatever you want."

"Come on, give it to me," Rosalind said, impatiently.

Antimone stared at Jason's mother for a moment, then lowered her gaze to Max. As she stretched out the hand holding the syringe, the whir of machinery started up, and bright light flooded the room.

73

Wednesday 6th August 2036

Tripoli Infectious Diseases Hospital, Republic of North Africa
16 minutes after the power cut

Antimone blinked in the sudden brightness. Without thinking, she withdrew the hand still holding the charged syringe.

"Let me have it," Rosalind insisted. Antimone hesitated.

Shaladi glanced towards the far end of the laboratory with a worried expression. "If the power is back on, they know it is no accident. They will be here soon. We must leave now."

As if to emphasise his warning, the creak of an opening door reached their ears, followed seconds later by a man's voice, calling out in Arabic. The general raised one finger in a shushing gesture and jabbed his gun barrel towards the exit.

Antimone started to move, then stopped. She turned her wheelchair around. A look of relief had replaced Max Perrin's abject terror. Their eyes met. "By the way, Princess," he whispered, "I'm glad I killed your boyfriend." His mouth curved in a smirk. "Over here!" he called out aloud.

A flash of molten fury surged through Antimone's veins. Her mind filled with pent up rage, obscuring all conscious thought. She lunged forwards, jabbed the needle into Max's upper arm and rammed the plunger down as far as it would go.

His lips drew back in a howl of agony. The tendons in his neck contracted like cords. He stared down in horror as the skin blackened and shrivelled in a slowly expanding circle. Wisps of smoke rose from the site of the injection. His whole body rocked and bucked against the straps holding him down. Another inhuman shriek escaped his throat.

Antimone dropped the syringe. The glass shattered on impact. Vapour rose from the floor, twisting upwards in coils. She held a hand to her mouth as she studied the effects of her handiwork in horrified fascination. A pair of rapid gunshots boomed nearby, jolting her attention from the writhing form strapped to the workbench. Two men in dark uniforms sprawled on the ground twenty metres away, their limbs twisted in death. Somebody grabbed her wheelchair from behind, spun it around and shoved her towards the exit.

Another shot rang out. Antimone accelerated under her own power. Up ahead, Paul and the African boy lay side-by-side on the floor. Aya knelt over Jason's body. *What the hell is she doing?* As Antimone drew nearer, his left foot twitched. Her mouth fell open in shock. *Is he still alive? How is that possible?* She had seen the head wound with her own eyes.

"Jason?" she murmured, her voice barely above a whisper.

Aya twisted around, revealing Jason's face. Dried blood streaked his forehead and right ear. She dabbed a white handkerchief against his scalp. His gaze rose, and he blinked at Antimone.

"But... you were..." The words stumbled out of Antimone's mouth as she struggled to form a coherent sentence. Tears of relief flooded down her cheeks. She darted forwards. "My God, you're alive."

Jason raised a shaky arm. Antimone stretched down. His skin felt cold as their fingers intertwined. "But how?" she asked.

"The bullet shaved his skull," Aya replied. "It knocked him out. Doctor Kubar said the scalp bleeds very much. He has gone to fetch—"

A gunshot cracked from nearby. Both Antimone and Aya instinctively ducked. Rosalind and the general sprinted around the corner. Shaladi crouched and turned. The gun in his hand jumped, accompanied by another deafening boom. He cursed in Arabic, then switched to English. "The power is on, so the doors are locked," he growled. "I told you before, we must leave. Now we will die here."

Before anybody could respond, the lock clunked, and Dr Kubar emerged through the swing door, pushing an empty wheelchair. "Quick," he said, "help me lift him."

"How did you—?"

The doctor held up a rectangle of plastic. "I have the professor's key card," he interrupted. "It opens all the doors in this place."

"That may buy us some time," Shaladi grunted, "but we must go immediately." He pointed the pistol around the corner and loosed off another two shots towards their unseen attackers.

Rosalind helped Kubar load Jason into the newly arrived chair. "I'll push him."

Jason's body slumped to the side as he gazed listlessly at his surroundings. Aya scooped up Paul from the floor and deposited him in Antimone's arms. "I may need to shoot," she said.

Aya handed a gun to Rosalind and offered another one to Antimone, who declined with a raised palm. The general's daughter shrugged and passed the spare to her father. Kubar crouched beside the African boy and gently lifted him.

Shaladi twisted around. "I will fire some covering shots. Move when I start shooting." Two loud bangs followed in quick succession.

The doctor held the card up to the reader and barged through the swing door, trailed closely by the others. He rushed through the dining area, clutching the unconscious child in his arms. A group of ten scientists huddled in a corner, glancing fearfully towards the escapees.

"What's happening?" one called out.

The general slowed. "The guards are coming. You should come with us or go to your rooms."

Several separate conversations broke out. A crash erupted from the other side of the door through which they had just passed.

"You must decide now," Shaladi yelled over the babble of voices. The small crowd scattered.

A solitary man remained: Dr Fernando. He flashed a nervous glance towards the general's gun. "Do you mind if I join you?"

"Can you shoot?" Shaladi asked.

The scientist swallowed hard. "Well, I have never tried."

The general handed him the spare pistol. "We do not have time for lessons. This is the safety. Point and pull the trigger."

"Okay," Fernando replied. "That sounds easy."

Shaladi turned away. "Come. We must go."

They passed into the reception area where Kubar waited for them by the same doors through which they had entered the facility three weeks earlier.

"Move to the side," Shaladi said, pointing to the walls. He took the card from Kubar and held it to the reader. The lock clicked. He crouched down and inched the door open. When no shots were fired, he edged through the gap with his gun raised, surveying the area for hostile forces. Satisfied they were alone, he beckoned the others forwards.

"Where are your people?" Rosalind asked as she pushed Jason's wheelchair onto the rough concrete. The sudden heat and humidity enveloped them like a damp rag.

Shaladi filled his lungs with the warm air before replying. "I do not know, but they will find us."

Rosalind rolled her eyes. "This is a really great plan."

The general ignored the sarcastic remark. "Aya, I want you to protect our rear. Mrs Baxter, you and I will lead." He pointed at the Spanish scientist. "You, push the boy's wheelchair. If you see somebody with a gun, do not ask; shoot. If anybody fires at us, you must take cover. Is everything clear?"

Shaladi didn't wait for a reply. He turned away and hurried along the centre of the road in a low crouch. They had covered approximately fifty metres when the sound of a revving engine and the screech of tyres echoed from the walls.

The general scuttled to the side and pointed to a concrete pillar on the other. Kubar was slow to react, weighed down by the child he was carrying. Before he could reach cover, a pair of blazing headlights from a rapidly approaching car picked him out. The vehicle screeched to a halt and four men in dark uniforms emerged, one from each door. Moments later, the sound of automatic weapons immersed the underground tunnel in a cacophony of noise.

The escapees returned fire, but the disparity in firepower put them at a significant disadvantage. The attackers used their superiority to advance in a pincer movement. Antimone clutched Paul to her chest as the bullets dug holes into the walls around her and showered her with sharp fragments of concrete.

Fernando crouched to her left. A pillar provided cover for both the scientist and Jason's wheelchair. He held the gun in trembling hands but hadn't yet fired a shot. Suddenly, he dropped the weapon on the floor and sprinted back towards the hospital. He had covered less than ten metres when a group of three rounds found their mark and slammed him forwards into the concrete.

Just when it seemed there was no hope, the sound of a second approaching vehicle rose above the cascade of gunfire. The intensity of shots increased. Antimone dared not look out from behind the cover of the pillar, but after another thirty seconds, silence fell over the battle scene.

Shaladi stood from his crouching position on the opposite side of the roadway. He strode forwards and embraced a man wielding an automatic rifle. The newcomer wore camouflaged army trousers and a green T-shirt that accented his bulging bicep. A beard and moustache covered the lower parts of his face. The pair separated, clapped each other on the back and continued a rapid-fire conversation in Arabic.

"Come," Shaladi shouted. "This is my friend, Major Halim. We must leave now. More of our enemies will be here soon."

74

Wednesday 6th August 2036

Prime Minister's Office, 10 Downing Street, London
17 minutes after the power cut

"What's happening?" Andrew Jacobs asked.

Admiral Trent was holding the mobile phone to his ear. He lowered it before speaking. "We still don't have eyes on the hostages. We're picking up reports of a gun battle near the hospital, but the drones have spotted nothing so far."

"So, we can't even be sure it's anything to do with our people," the Prime Minister said.

"Where are the marines now?" Moreland asked.

"They're waiting at the edge of the forest, about half a mile from the hospital." The images from the camera showed the dark outlines of a few straggly trees growing between the shattered stumps of their predecessors, destroyed during the long years of civil war. The men crouched at the rim of a shell crater. "There's no point in breaking cover until they know their destination."

"So, all we can do is wait and hope for the best."

"Yes," Trent agreed. "I'm afraid that's right."

Silence settled on the room as the three pairs of eyes watched the screen intently, waiting for something to happen. The sudden ringing of the phone on the Prime Minister's desk made them all jump.

Jacobs snatched up the handset. "Yes," he barked.

A female voice came down the line. "We've just received a call from the British embassy in Tunis. There has been contact with somebody from The Republic of North Africa. I'll patch you through now."

A click followed. Jacobs pressed a button and replaced the receiver. "Hello, this is the Prime Minister speaking," he said. "I've put you on speaker phone. With me are Admiral Trent and Charles Moreland of MI6. What's going on?"

"Good evening, sir," a man replied. "I'm John Doyle, the duty officer on call tonight. Someone called a minute ago, claiming to be in Tripoli. He told me he had met up with our people and wanted to know the rendezvous point. He's still on the line if you want to talk to him."

"Put him through."

The muted sound of a revving engine emerged from the speaker.

Jacobs exchanged a sideways glance with his two colleagues, then leant forwards. “Hello, you’re speaking to the British Prime Minister. I believe you have contacted some of my countrymen who were being held hostage.”

“Yes, this is Major Halim. I—”

In the background, a man’s voice yelled in Arabic. A series of bangs and a muffled scream accompanied the words. The man spoke again. “Sorry, but somebody is shooting at us. I have your people. Where shall we take them?”

“We have a team at the edge of the Al Nasr Forest,” Trent replied, “where it meets the Second Ring Road. Do you know where I mean?”

“I am familiar with the location. We will be there in a few minutes.” Halim paused for a second before speaking again. “If I do this for you, I will require something in exchange, however.”

“What do you want?” Jacobs asked.

The major explained his request.

Trent was already on his feet, speaking urgently into his mobile phone. “I don’t care. Make it happen,” he yelled into the handset. He turned and nodded to the Prime Minister.

“Yes, we can do that,” Jacobs said.

“Excellent,” Halim replied.

The line went quiet.

“Hello. Are you still there?” Doyle asked. He repeated the question. “Sorry, sir. He just hung up.”

“Thanks,” Jacobs said. “If anything else comes through, please call us back.”

“Right away, sir.”

Trent continued to talk into his handset.

“Well?” Jacobs asked with a questioning look.

The admiral lowered the phone from his ear for a second. “The helicopter is already in the air and will be there in five minutes. They’ll land close to the ring road. The marines will provide covering fire from the ground if necessary.”

The images on the computer screen shifted as the armed men directed their weapons from the rim of the crater towards the potholed strip of concrete.

“Just make sure you get them out safely,” Jacobs muttered.

75

Wednesday 6th August 2036

Outside Tripoli Infectious Diseases Hospital, Republic of North Africa

18 minutes after the power cut

The bearded major directed a reassuring grin at the group of frightened Westerners. "More of them will be here soon," he said, his baritone voice a mixture of Mediterranean and American accents. "We must hurry."

"Where are you taking us?" Rosalind asked.

"I will call now. Please get in." He pointed at the black van, straddling the road fifty metres nearer the exit. Three other armed men in military fatigues approached and shook General Shaladi by the hand. One took the child from Dr Kubar and jogged to the waiting transport. Another crouched beside Fernando's body, holding a finger to his neck. The man rose with a shake of the head, then jogged towards Jason, who lay barely conscious in his wheelchair. The third member of the rescue team slid back a door on the side of the vehicle and, with the help of the others, lifted Antimone's and Jason's wheelchairs inside.

Halim was still talking into his phone. Shaladi and the driver joined him as he climbed into the front seats. The van moved off with a squeal of tyres. The major's voice rose above the roar of the engine as they raced along the narrow roadway. A minute later, they arrived at the exit from the underground garage. The barrier was down, and a handful of men stood waiting with weapons raised.

"Everybody down!" Shaladi yelled. The driver jammed his foot down on the accelerator and ducked. One of Halim's team put an arm around Jason's shoulders, pushing him forwards so his body folded in two. Only the man's strong grip prevented Jason from toppling out of the wheelchair. The van surged towards the blockade. Immediately, all hell broke loose as the armed guards outside opened fire. Bullets ripped through the windscreen and punched holes in the roof's lining. Aya screamed as the side window shattered and showered the occupants on that side of the vehicle with fragments of glass.

Within seconds, the van smashed through the barricade and hurtled down the road. The major continued to talk on his phone. He directed the driver with a point of his finger.

"Is everyone all right?" the general called, looking behind at the pale-faced passengers. A series of nods greeted his question.

Antimone straightened up from the position she had held, shielding Paul with her own body. She brushed a strand of hair from her son's forehead. To her relief, his breathing was calm and regular. Next, she checked on Jason. Halim's man helped him to sit upright, but it was clear from the glazed look in his eyes that he was still largely oblivious to his surroundings. Antimone's gaze rose to the view ahead as she fought down the fear that threatened to overwhelm her.

Several bullets had punctured the windscreen, leaving small circular holes surrounded by a spiderweb of cracks. The van navigated a slip road and emerged onto a two-lane carriageway. Ruts and potholes peppered the uneven surface. Antimone glanced towards the speedometer: a fraction over forty miles an hour. The driver tried to steer around the obstacles, causing the occupants to sway from side to side. Only a handful of cars kept them company as they jolted along the neglected roadway.

Halim lowered the phone and twisted in his seat, his cheerful expression undiminished by the recent conflict. "It will take two or three minutes to reach the rendezvous point. Your people are waiting there."

Shaladi spoke in a low voice to the major. A rapid-fire conversation in Arabic followed. It was clear from the tone that they were having a vigorous argument. Brake lights in the road ahead brought an end to the debate. The general muttered a curse as the van slowed. A pair of black cars, parked sideways on, blocked both lanes. As they drew nearer, nine armed men in total emerged from the doors and took up position behind the barricade.

***

"Shit," a marine said, lowering his binoculars. "They're setting up a roadblock. Range is two hundred and fifty metres."

"What's the ETA on the bird?" the leader of the group asked, speaking urgently into his radio.

"Still a few minutes out," a man's voice replied.

"Permission to engage?"

"Please hold."

"Look, I don't mean to hurry you, but unless we do something quickly, the only hostages we'll be taking out of here will be in body bags."

The seconds ticked by in silence as all eyes studied the slowing traffic on the carriageway below. Finally, the radio crackled into life. "Engage at your discretion."

The sergeant breathed a sigh of relief. "Okay, guys, wait for my command. Make sure you don't hit any civilians." He peered down the sights of his automatic rifle. Below them, the men in dark uniforms crouched behind the pair of vehicles, unaware of the threat to their rear.

"Fire!"

The hiss of suppressed weapons filled the air. Five of the enemy dropped in the first volley. Three more followed in quick succession. The final soldier had identified the direction of the incoming rounds before his colleagues and flung himself over the bonnet.

"One still in play," the sergeant said.

The man to his left picked up the binoculars again. He watched through the lenses as the panicked drivers at the front of the short queue of traffic turned their cars around and tried to head back against the flow, drawing a cacophony of beeps from those behind.

The doors of the black van opened, and the three members of Major Halim's team surged out. Their bullets quickly found the sole survivor from the roadblock, but not before he had gabbled a desperate plea for help into his radio.

With no ability to manoeuvre out of the jam and facing a group of heavily armed men, the civilian occupants of the trapped vehicles jumped out and fled, leaving the carriageway completely blocked.

***

"It is impossible to get past these cars quickly," Shaladi said to the major, stepping down onto the cracked concrete. "We must go on foot."

"More troops will be here any minute," Halim replied. "I hope the helicopter arrives soon. They told me it has enough seats for all of us."

"We already discussed this," Shaladi said, referring to their earlier heated discussion. "Why could you not find our own transport?"

"I am sorry. It was not possible to organise an aircraft in such a short time. They would stop us quickly if we stayed on the road."

"I cannot go with you. Look after my daughter. Explain to the British that they would have executed both of us if we had not followed orders."

The major stared at his former commanding officer. "But what you say is true. You should tell them yourself."

"I am the man who organised the attack at the Olympics. They will never allow me to be free. I do not want to spend the rest of my life in prison, no matter that British prisons are far more comfortable than any in this country."

"So, this was all for nothing?"

"No, my friend. You have helped to save my beautiful Aya. I am trusting you to make sure she survives. You must let them know she had no part in this. I forced her to help me."

"I will do my best, General. It has been an honour serving with you."

Shaladi clapped his colleague on the shoulder. "We still have much to do—and I am not dead yet."

Two men lifted Antimone's wheelchair, then Jason's down from the van. When everybody was on the concrete, Halim led them towards the barricade. Rosalind pushed Jason. Kubar clutched the unconscious African boy to his chest. Drivers on the other side of the road slowed to rubberneck the carnage. Several took pictures or spoke into mobile phones.

"Come on," the major said. "We must hurry."

Antimone stared at the dead bodies as they skirted around the two military vehicles. The sight no longer scared her. Three weeks of random cruelty and a disdain for human life had dulled her senses to the point where death seemed commonplace. She cast an anxious downward glance to the unconscious child on her lap. To her relief, Paul continued to sleep, ignorant of the horror surrounding him.

"Over there," she called as a flashlight from a raised embankment on the right signalled the position of the marines. Every weapon in the group pointed in the direction she had indicated until a man stood up and waved back at them. The hostages picked up the pace as they raced to close the distance to the support team.

A low buzzing sound rose above the rumble of vehicle engines. Antimone raised her eyes. A dark shape blotted out a patch of stars overhead: the helicopter at last. It banked sharply and settled into a hover.

A cry drew her attention back to the ground. Three sets of headlights approached on the wrong side of the carriageway.

"Get to cover," Shaladi yelled, gesticulating towards the shrubs adjoining the cracked concrete. Moments later, gunfire erupted from the nearest vehicle, catching one of Halim's men in the open and throwing him backwards. At almost the same time, the second and third armoured cars opened up. Bullets tore up the concrete to Antimone's left. She shoved down hard on the metal ring, accelerating out of the incoming fire with milliseconds to spare. She skidded to a halt alongside Rosalind, who crouched beside Jason's wheelchair, protected from the enemy troops by a large boulder at the side of the road. Their eyes locked in fear.

Shots from the marines silenced one gunner, but the two remaining vehicles targeted another of Halim's team who was too slow in reaching cover. The rounds spun him around as they found their mark.

The battle would have been over in seconds if the helicopter hadn't joined the fray. It pivoted in mid-air and directed a hail of thirty-millimetre shells towards the three armoured vehicles. The first two disintegrated in balls of flame. The occupants of the third flung themselves out of the doors moments before it too exploded. Shots from the marines targeted the survivors, keeping them pinned down behind the burning wreckage.

The electric motors driving the huge blades of the flying weapons platform reduced in pitch. The sleek black shape flared six feet above the road surface, then settled down in the centre of the carriageway, fifty metres from the terrified escapees. A panel on the side hinged open, and a man dressed in a plastic-coated uniform with full facemask leant out, beckoning the group towards him.

Dr Kubar was the first to break cover, still carrying the African boy. Shots erupted from behind the destroyed vehicles, but the marines returned fire, silencing the source of the gunfire within moments. Strong hands reached down and hauled the child up. Rosalind rose from her hiding place, pushing Jason. Between the two of them, the doctor and Rosalind struggled to lift Jason's barely conscious body onto the lip of the aircraft's entryway.

Antimone followed Rosalind's lead and raced to the open door. A moan of protest escaped Paul's mouth as she raised him up to the helicopter's hold.

The man grabbed the three-year-old and returned almost immediately. "I'm afraid you'll have to leave that here, Miss," he said, his voice muffled by the mask as he pointed to the wheelchair.

By now, the major's only surviving team member had arrived, leading Aya by the hand. He lifted Antimone out of the chair and placed her in the waiting arms of the crewman. Seconds later, she found herself unceremoniously dumped into a cushioned seat beside the two children and Jason.

"Let's move it, people," the man shouted. "We're vulnerable on the ground."

The general's daughter was next to embark, then came Rosalind, followed by Dr Kubar.

"Another group of hostiles," a voice yelled from outside. Antimone spotted the approach of more headlights through the curved windscreen above the array of flashing dials. The haste to board the aircraft intensified as two marines trailed Halim's man through the open hatch. The noise from the electric motors rose in pitch.

Bullets pinged harmlessly against the armoured glass of the cockpit. The remaining members of the British team sprinted across the concrete. The one at the back staggered and let out a yell of pain. His colleagues grabbed him by the arms and hauled him aboard, leaving a streak of blood on the floor of the cabin. Halim was the last to arrive.

"Come on," the crewman shouted, holding out a hand to haul him in. The aircraft lifted off the ground before the major was fully inside. He scrambled aboard as the floor tilted.

"Wait!" Aya screamed. "Where is my father?"

Muzzle flash from the side of the road answered her question.

"No," she yelled, hurling herself forwards as the panel slid shut.

The thirty-millimetre cannons opened up again, shaking the whole interior as they spat out a stream of shells towards the approaching vehicles.

Halim put an arm around her shoulder and whispered into her ear.

"He didn't have to stay," she cried, pushing him away.

"Your father is a brave man," he replied. "His last command to me was to protect you. I will look after you like my own daughter."

Tears streamed down Aya's cheeks as she stared at the ground out of the window.

The helicopter banked in a tight curve and raced across the night sky towards the waiting cruiser.

***

The three men in the Prime Minister's office embraced at the news that the aircraft had landed safely on the deck of the warship.

Admiral Trent broke away to continue a hushed conversation. "All the hostages who made it out of the hospital are onboard," he announced, lowering the handset. "That includes Rosalind Baxter and the three British people abducted at the Olympics: the Lessing girl, her partner and their child. We also picked up five Reponan nationals, including their missing athlete and a four-year-old boy."

"How are they?"

"The two young children are receiving medical attention, as is Jason Floyd who was shot. But all are expected to survive."

"Any news on Perrin?"

"No," Trent said. "He wasn't among the evacuees, but I have no information on what happened to him."

"What about the marines?" Jacobs asked.

"One relatively minor bullet wound, but otherwise all fine."

"Good. Has there been any response from the Reponan military?"

"Not so far, but we're keeping a close eye on things. The Reponans don't have much of a navy. As we speak, the ship is making full speed towards Malta. They should be there in just over four hours."

"Congratulations on a job well done, gentlemen," Jacobs said.

76

Wednesday 27th August 2036

Tripoli Infectious Diseases Hospital, Republic of North Africa
Three weeks later

The first thing to register on his senses was the rhythmic beeping sound. The piercing electronic tone wormed its way inside his skull. He groaned. The use of his vocal cords triggered a gag reflex as he registered the object jammed down his throat. His right hand rose instinctively and grasped the flexible tubing. He tugged, but something held it in place. In mounting panic, he pulled harder. The adhesive strips surrendered their grip, and the plastic tube slid out of his mouth, provoking a coughing fit.

The rate of the beeps increased in time with his thrashing heart. A female voice spoke in a foreign language. He tried to open his eyes, but they seemed to be gummed shut.

The woman switched to strongly accented English. "Please be calm. Somebody is coming."

He raised his head, but a gentle hand pressed him back onto the pillow.

"Where…?" The attempt to speak sent a sharp pain shooting down his trachea. More coughs followed.

The sound of rapidly approaching footsteps mingled with the shrill bleeps. A rapid-fire conversation took place between the new arrival and the woman, although he still couldn't understand any of the words exchanged between the pair. Moments later, the electronic beeping stopped.

Fingers touched his face and removed the tape from his eyelids. He blinked his eyes open and immediately screwed them shut again in the bright glare from the overhead lights.

"Welcome back, Mr Perrin," the man said. "My name is Doctor Ahmed." He didn't bother to introduce the woman.

Max squinted at the medic through lowered lids. "Where am I?" he rasped.

"You are in a hospital in Tripoli. What do you remember?"

Max wracked his brain. His head seemed to be full of sawdust. "Not much."

"After a traumatic episode like the one you have recently suffered, it is natural that you will be a little disorientated."

"Can you tell me what happened?"

Ahmed hesitated before replying. "You have been in a medically induced coma for the last three weeks. There is no easy way to say this to you. Unfortunately, we could not save your left arm."

For the first time, Max opened his eyes fully and glanced down at where the limb should have been. His shoulder ended in a short stump covered by white bandages. Now the memories returned: the acid, the expanding circle of blackening skin, the unbearable pain. A scream erupted from his throat.

"Please," the doctor said. "You must conserve your energy for your recovery." He turned and spoke rapidly in Arabic to the nurse. She returned moments later with a syringe.

Max shrank back in terror. "No, no, no," he yelled. "Not again."

Ahmed quickly realised his mistake. "Do not worry. It is only a sedative."

Max twisted away and tumbled off the mattress onto the floor, toppling the drip stand, which was still attached by plastic tubing to his right hand. He scrabbled backwards to evade his carers. With only one arm to support him, he unbalanced and collapsed on his side.

The doctor rushed forwards and shoved the needle into his patient's thigh, then depressed the plunger with his thumb.

Max's panicked movements gradually subsided. Over the next few seconds, a fuzziness filled his head, sending him back to the welcoming darkness.

***

Somebody tapped him gently on the cheek. His second return to consciousness was less confusing than the first. Perhaps it had all been a bad dream. Before trying to identify who had woken him, he glanced down at his left arm. But no, the limb was still missing.

He raised his eyes. Four other people occupied the small hospital room. Among them was the doctor who had tended him earlier. Two wore dark uniforms and carried automatic weapons. The last had a thick beard and wore black robes. He looked vaguely familiar, but Max couldn't place him. Judging by their submissive body language, the others deferred to him. The man's lips moved behind his wiry facial hair. He spoke in Arabic.

"Mullah Awad is glad you are awake," Ahmed translated. "Do you know who did this to you?"

Max blinked as his sluggish brain stirred into action. Awad—of course, he was the leader of this country. Now it made sense. "It was the girl," he rasped.

Another brief exchange took place between the mullah and his translator.

"Which girl?" the doctor asked.

"That cripple, Antimone Lessing," Max replied. He detected surprise on the faces of his interrogators.

"So, it was not Mrs Baxter?" the mullah said in accented English, raising a hand to wave off Ahmed before he could translate.

"No, she was going to inject acid in my eye, but the cripple refused to give her the syringe. Your men arrived, and I called out to warn them because some of the prisoners had guns. She injected me in the arm just before they left."

"I do not understand. Why did she do this to you?"

"I shot her precious boyfriend dead. He tried to jump me. Then somebody got me from behind with that damned stun baton."

The mullah and the doctor exchanged more words in Arabic.

"You did not kill Mr Floyd," Awad said. "He survived and escaped to the UK."

"What? He's alive? So, that bitch did this to me for no good reason."

"You were lucky it happened in a hospital," the doctor added.

The words tugged at something in Max's memory. Then it came to him. "Wait. What about the virus? Weren't they all carrying it? Have I got it?"

"Yes. You, me, almost everybody in this country now. When the woman and her child escaped from isolation, they allowed this new form of the disease to escape with them."

The mullah took over. "They infected too many other people to limit the spread. But we will manufacture drugs to protect the children."

"Did the rest of them get away?" Max asked.

"Unfortunately, most did. They had outside help from the rebels and the British military. They killed at least thirty of my countrymen, including Professor Halfon. All are now in Britain. They are being held in quarantine apart from the Baxter woman, who is in prison. They keep her location secret. We requested her extradition, but I do not think they will give her to us." He let out a short, humourless laugh. "Many others also want to try her for her crimes."

"What about that bastard, Shaladi, and his daughter?"

The mullah's tongue protruded from his mouth, moistening his lips before he spoke. "That coward is dead. He shot himself as our armed forces closed in to capture him. Aya Shaladi is now in England with the other traitors. We demanded their return to face judgement, but again, it is unlikely the British authorities will comply."

"Did Dr Kubar escape with them?"

"Yes, another person who betrayed his country and this establishment. He has provided their scientists with the formula he stole from us."

"I tried to warn Professor Halfon they were planning something, but he wouldn't take me seriously."

"I see." The mullah turned to the rest of his entourage and barked a series of curt instructions in Arabic. The three other men filed out of the room. "You realise we spent much money to keep you alive?" he asked when he and Max were alone.

"Yeah, thanks."

"Now there is something you can do for me."

Max's voice took on a wary tone. "Okay. What's that?"

"We cannot allow these traitors to go unpunished. They murdered many citizens of this country and caused you serious harm."

"So, what do you need from me?"

"We have few operatives in Britain. If we send more, they do not know your customs. They... ah... stick out. You, however, are a native. You fit in. I want you to work with my men to eliminate those who have betrayed us. You will be well paid for your efforts."

"You still owe me for the last job."

The mullah stared at Max, his eyes unblinking. After a few seconds, he gave a single, slow nod. "I will ensure you receive everything you are owed, and we will transfer the money for this assignment in advance."

"I have one other condition."

Awad glared back at him. "You are in no position to make demands. Nobody outside this facility knows you are alive."

"You're right, but I think you'll like my proposal. I want payback. I want those who've hurt me to suffer. If you help me with this, I'll do whatever you ask."

"You are referring to the prisoners who escaped from here?"

"Yes." Max stared into the dark pits of the bearded man's eyes. "Do we have a deal?"

"Perhaps," the mullah replied. "As long as our objectives align, I will provide you with all the support you need to have your revenge."

"Good," Max growled. "I'm going to make them pay for what they've done."

The End of Termination: The Boy Who Died

Book Three

ANNIHILATION: ORIGINS AND ENDINGS

Part One: Retaliation

1

Monday 23rd March 2037

Compton Majestic Hotel, Northstowe

Antimone Lessing drew back the curtain and peered down onto the street below. The clamour of voices rose to greet her, only partially muted by the one-way glass.

"Bloody vultures," Jason Floyd, her partner, murmured from behind her. "How are you feeling?"

She flinched as his hand touched her shoulder. Ever since their escape from the Tripoli Infectious Diseases Hospital in The Republic of North Africa, she had felt tired and irritated, a condition not aided by her family's constant questions about her state of mind. She knew they meant well, but she wanted to scream at them to leave her in peace.

"I'm fine," she muttered between clenched teeth.

Jason let out an exasperated sigh. "Clearly you're not. I wish you'd just talk to me about it."

She spun the wheelchair around, scowling at him. "All right, if you really need me to spell out what's bothering me, I haven't had a good night's sleep since we were rescued. I murdered a man by injecting him with acid for Christ's sake. Every time I close my eyes, I hear his screams, and I see the smoke rising from his arm. How am I supposed to move past that?"

"It wasn't your fault," Jason replied gently. "Max Perrin got everything he deserved."

"Don't you think I'm aware of that?" Antimone snapped. "That bastard was going to kill us all. I thought he'd killed you. Unfortunately, none of that makes the slightest difference to how I feel. He taunted me, and I lost control. I allowed my anger to get the better of me. There isn't a minute that goes by when it's not on my mind."

She paused and drew breath. Her voice rose again as she ploughed on. "Then there's Paul. I can barely function myself, let alone give a four-year-old child the love and attention he needs and deserves. I understand that everybody's only trying to help, but sometimes I wish you'd all just leave me be."

"Look, I know it's hard," Jason said, "but we'll get through this."

"Will we, though? Now, there are paparazzi camped outside on the pavement. I can't even go to the toilet without worrying that some arsehole is watching me through the camera lens of a drone.

"And if that's not enough, we've been cooped up in a hotel room for the past two months. I haven't been able to get down to the track for fear of all the nutjobs and lunatics who might want to hurt me simply because I was the first woman in twenty years to survive childbirth. It's the one thing I love doing, and I can't even train at the moment, let alone compete. Everywhere we go, we have to be accompanied by a bodyguard. I feel like a prisoner with our bloody warders camped out in the hall." She waved a hand towards the door.

Finally, the dam burst. Tears flooded down Antimone's face. "I've had enough," she sobbed. "Now tell me, how could this get any worse? I just want it all to end."

Jason grabbed a box of tissues from the nearby table and crouched down beside her. "Here," he said, handing them to her. "There's something you need to remember. We all love you. Me, Paul, your parents; we're all looking out for you. One day, everything will go back to normal. But you can't bottle it up. You have to talk to us about it. Isn't that what the shrink with the caterpillar eyebrows told you?"

Antimone let out a sound between a sob and a laugh. The psychiatrist appointed to help with her recovery had advised her to discuss her feelings with close members of the family—and he *did* have bushy eyebrows that seemed to move with a life of their own.

"Yes, you're right," she said, drying her tears. "But it's far harder to put into practice."

"I'm here for you."

"I know."

A silence descended, punctuated only by the sniffles as Antimone dabbed at her face. Paul was spending the afternoon with his grandparents. The press interest in them had waned over the past few months, and earlier that day, a car had whisked him the short distance across town to her parents' house.

A light knock came at the door. Jason rose and took a step towards the heavy wooden frame. "Who is it?" he called.

"Derek Walker, sir. Could we have a chat? Today's codeword is dinosaur."

Somebody from the Prime Minister's office had assigned Walker the task of ensuring their safety. Every morning he selected a new password that progressed by one letter from the day before. If any member of the protection detail failed to provide the correct security code, his clients were under strict instructions to stay well away from the door and raise the alarm. It was a simple precaution, but Walker insisted they follow his directive.

Jason twisted the handle.

"Hello, sir," Walker said. "May I come in?"

"Yeah, sure."

The tall figure stepped inside the room and performed a quick surveillance of the interior. Apparently satisfied with what he saw, he turned to Antimone. "Good evening, madam."

She rolled her eyes. Ever since taking on the role and despite numerous attempts to get him to use their first names, Walker had clung to the practice of using formal terms of address when speaking to the family.

"Evening, Derek," Jason said with a slight smile. He knew addressing their protector in this way would irritate the man, but he couldn't help himself. "What can we do for you?"

"You've probably noticed members of the press occupying the pavement outside," Walker replied, his face an impassive mask. No trace of colour remained in his hair, leaving it almost totally white, but his skin displayed few signs of ageing, making it hard to estimate his age. His everyday work attire comprised a grey suit with highly polished, lace-up shoes.

He carried himself with military precision, was immensely organised and took no nonsense from his subordinates. To cap it all, he appeared to lack any sense of humour; none of his clients had ever witnessed a single smile from him, let alone a laugh. When asked, he always deflected questions about his career or background.

"Yes, we had spotted that," Antimone said. "How did they find out?"

"I imagine one of the hotel staff must've talked. I intend to discover who it was. They're all signed up to a strict non-disclosure agreement."

"What does it mean for us?" Antimone asked.

"I'm afraid we're going to have to move you. It'll take a few days to sort something out. In the meantime, we'll strengthen the security detail. You'll have to stay in your room."

Jason released a deep sigh.

Walker carried on regardless. "The glass at the front of the building is fitted with a reflective film, so nobody can see inside, and the mesh fence will block any drones. Even so, I advise you to keep away from the windows."

The thin netting had been developed a few years earlier to protect privacy. It was extremely durable, almost invisible and designed to be impenetrable to the small flying machines frequently used by the paparazzi to capture footage of unsuspecting victims. Even if they managed to sneak a drone through this barrier, the interference emitted by the material blocked the outward transmission of any unauthorised radio signals.

"Where will you take us?" Antimone asked.

"We haven't decided yet, but it'll be somewhere we can keep you safe."

"Sounds like another prison," she muttered under her breath.

If Walker heard her comment, he gave nothing away.

***

On the pavement outside, a figure stood apart from the other journalists. He held a pair of high magnification binoculars, which he pointed at the reflective windows. He might not be able to see inside the building, but at last, he had discovered where they were hiding. Earlier that day, he had watched as a man escorted the wheelchair bitch's four-year-old son to a waiting car. He and his team had tracked the family down once and would do so again wherever they hid. And the next time, they would get to them before the press.

Max Perrin lowered his hands. A loose component rattled as the servo motors in his left arm moved the limb. He could have asked the scientists to rectify the problem before the start of this mission, but he had chosen not to. The irritating noise served as a constant reminder of his new goal in life.

The familiar surge of hatred flared in his chest. He would make her pay for what she had done to him. He would make them all pay.

2

Tuesday 24th March 2037

New Dawn Immigration Centre, Dover

Major Ibrahim Halim lay on the single bed, watching the television screen: a current affairs programme about the political situation in the Middle East. He wasn't listening to the bearded male reporter as he spoke to camera—the sound was turned down low—but the dusty backdrop in the three-dimensional image filled him with a sense of nostalgia. He desperately missed the country of his birth. This place he found himself in was comfortable enough, but the featureless room, the bland, functional architecture of the facility and the perpetually grey skies left him yearning for home.

He had been held with the two surviving members of his team in the New Dawn Immigration Centre since leading the operation four months earlier to free his old commander, General Shaladi. In doing so, he had ended any chance of returning to his birthplace. The leaders of The Republic of North Africa had long memories and would never pardon somebody who had so blatantly opposed their brutal regime.

And that single factor was what made his appeal to remain in Britain so vital. Despite rescuing four British nationals including their celebrity Olympic wheelchair champion, Antimone Lessing, the immigration authorities had yet to decide whether he could stay. If they deported him, he would almost certainly die within a few days; if he was unlucky, his life would extend for much longer under the tender ministrations of the torturers in his former homeland.

His court-appointed lawyer had assured him the authorities would allow him to stay, but a niggling worry never left his mind. The second hearing wasn't due for another fortnight, and in the meantime, he remained a guest of the British government.

The immigration centre lay somewhere in the spectrum between prison and refugee camp. Living standards were higher than he had expected, and he maintained a modicum of freedom; he could come and go from his bedroom whenever he pleased, and he had free access to the communal facilities, including a canteen and well-equipped games room. But the tall metal fence topped with razor-wire that surrounded the facility left little doubt as to his true status.

The inmates, as he thought of them, originated from a variety of trouble spots around the world. Rising temperatures and a shortage of fresh water had rendered vast tracts of land across the globe uninhabitable, triggering a rapid increase in the flow of immigrants to more temperate climes. As far as he knew, none of the other refugees were fellow countrymen, but new people arrived all the time.

Many had travelled in dangerously overcrowded boats, only to be picked up by the fast patrol vessels off the British south coast. A significant proportion of those who set out either drowned or ended up being deported to their countries of origin. And of course, there were no refunds. Despite decades of trying to stop the traffickers, it was still a lucrative business that attracted the criminal fraternity like pigs to a trough.

A tapping sound drew him back from his thoughts. He slid off the bed and padded across the room in bare feet. He hauled open the door to discover a solidly built man he didn't recognise, blocking out the view of the corridor.

"Yes?" Halim said in English, his gaze running up and down the muscular figure standing before him. The man scratched at the armpit of his plain yellow T-shirt. Halim's eyes shifted to a rust-brown stain around the neck. A second, slightly shorter man stood to the side and behind his colleague.

The visitor lowered his head in greeting. "As-Salaamu Alaikum."

"Wa-alaikum As-salaam," Halim responded automatically.

"May we come in?" the first man continued in the major's native Arabic. The speaker's familiar accent identified him as a fellow countryman and placed his origins somewhere in the region between Tripoli and Misrata.

Halim gestured the men inside. "Where are you two from?" he asked.

"We are from The Republic of North Africa, just like you."

"It is a pleasure to see some new people from our beautiful country. When did you arrive?"

"They intercepted our boat and brought us here yesterday," the newcomer replied. "We have travelled a long way to meet you, Major Halim."

The mention of his rank and family name triggered a spike of adrenaline in Halim's bloodstream. Nobody at the immigration centre outside the members of his team knew his true identity. He instantly transitioned to a state of high alert. His attention switched momentarily to the second shorter man who hadn't spoken yet. The major's gaze drifted down to a dark patch on the left knee of the visitor's jeans. *Is that blood?*

Their eyes met, but there was no friendship in his countryman's hard expression.

"I have a message from Mullah Awad," the taller man said.

Too late, Halim spotted an object protruding from the man's clenched fist. The man lunged. The major swerved sideways to avoid the weapon's trajectory. Despite evading the main force of the surprise strike, he sensed the slightest of impacts.

There was no pain yet, but his fingers came back tinged with red when he dabbed them against the site of the contact, just above his right kidney. His eyes darted across the room, desperately searching for anything with which to defend himself. *Nothing obvious*. His only chance was to get out and call for help.

As if reading his thoughts, the two men stepped forwards and closed the door behind them. Each grasped a wooden handle with a protruding shaft. Halim immediately recognised the objects as narrow-bladed screwdrivers. And the way the pair bounced lightly on their feet advertised their training in close-quarters combat.

The shorter man bared his teeth in a snarl. "You are a traitor to your country. You deserve to die."

Halim backed up. "Punish me if you must, but my men had nothing to do with the mission. Leave them alone. They were only following orders."

"It is too late. They are already dead. They squealed like pigs."

A surge of anger burned in the pit of the major's stomach. Bellowing in rage, he hurled himself at the taller of his two assailants. He locked his grip on the man's wrist as they tumbled onto the floor. The sole of a boot slammed into his chin, dazing him. A sharp pain in the back shocked him out of his momentary disorientation. He scrambled to the door on all fours and reached for the handle.

A heavy weight hammered into him from behind, sending him crashing face-first into the solid panelling and closing his only avenue of escape. He staggered upright, shaking his head to clear the dizziness. As he did so, the shorter of the two darted in from the side, stabbing him once again with the makeshift weapon.

Halim groaned and lowered a hand to cover the new wound. The taller man feigned to his right, jabbing his blade in the air to drive him away from the door. The major backed along the wall. Behind him, the display continued to show images of a region he had once called home. A sudden idea burst into his brain.

He moved a little further, then whirled around and seized both sides of the screen. One sharp tug and the fixings gave way, leaving a bulky rectangle of plastic in his hands, still attached to the plug socket by a length of wire. He could feel his strength waning. In a few seconds, he would no longer have the ability to resist.

Holding the display panel under his left arm, he wrapped the electrical cable around his right hand and yanked it free. Without releasing the white cord, he once again grasped both sides and held the screen out in front of his body as a shield. He waited for his nearest assailant to move a step closer, then flung the chunk of electronics at his opponent's head.

The man raised an arm and ducked. The television narrowly missed its target and smashed into the wall behind. Several components detached during the impact and scattered over the carpet. The assassin advanced another pace, focusing his gaze on the face of his victim in quiet concentration.

Halim waited until the distance separating them was less than a metre. Then he lunged. The bared ends of the electrified wire touched the taller man's skin, causing him to yelp in pain and drop his weapon. The major dived to retrieve it. But the smaller of the two was on him in a flash. The thin shaft penetrated Halim's back three more times. He rolled over and raised his arms to protect himself, but the jabs rained down on him.

Finally, one struck him in the neck. The blood welled between the major's fingers. Now the assassins backed away, their job done, watching as the life ebbed from their target.

Major Halim's chest rose for the final time. He let out a final juddering breath and was still. A crimson stain soaked into the fibres of the carpet beneath his body. The two killers tossed their weapons on the floor as the shorter man leant forwards and spat on the corpse.

"That is what happens to traitors. You will pay for your sins in hell."

3

Wednesday 25th March 2037

Acorn Guest House, Northstowe

Mohammed Abadi pushed the wafer-thin screen towards Max Perrin. "Have you seen?" he said. "They killed the traitor Halim and his two men. There is a news article here about it."

Max didn't respond. He stared into space, scratching absent-mindedly at his prosthetic left forearm.

A puzzled frown materialised on the forehead of the North African. "Are you not pleased? It was your plan to get the killers into the immigration centre. It worked perfectly."

"Huh? What?" Max's gaze transferred to the diminutive figure with the sun-bronzed skin and tightly curled black hair.

"I said the traitors are dead."

"Yeah, good, Mo," Max replied distractedly.

The man exchanged a glance with the third member of the team, Omar Hijazi. If Mo was a featherweight and the brightest person in the room, Omar was more of a heavyweight and provided the brawn. At just over six feet in height, he carried himself with a gracefulness that defied his sturdy frame. He kept his head shaved, the stubble forming a dark ring on his polished scalp. The material of the black T-shirt he wore showed off the pronounced muscle structure of his arms and chest.

"Unfortunately, there is nothing about the Shaladi girl," Mo added. "It seems they must be keeping her somewhere else."

"Hmm," Max replied. "That's not much of a surprise. She may have helped the British prisoners to escape, but she and her father played a huge part in the attack at the Olympics. He's lying in an unmarked grave in Tripoli, so they need somebody else to prosecute. He led the mission, but as far as the authorities here are concerned, she was a crucial member of the team. She's all they've got. They'll be holding her in a high security location while they decide what to do with her. It shouldn't be too hard to track her down, but we won't be able to reach her until they release her, and I can't see that happening anytime soon."

"And that traitor, Kubar?"

"The intelligence from higher up is that he's working at Porton Down. I expect he'll be under close guard with his background and what he knows, but we have more chance of getting to him. I want you to find out where he's staying."

"What about the Baxter woman?" Omar asked.

Max's breath caught in his throat at the mention of the person he had witnessed murdering his father. "We know exactly where that bitch is, but we're not the only ones who'd like to see her dead. It's no secret she's being held at Bronzefield prison. There's no way we can reach her in there. Normally, I'd suggest the same approach as at the immigration centre: arrange for somebody on the inside to do it. But they're bound to be keeping her in solitary, so nobody would ever get close enough."

Omar rose and paced backwards and forwards, rhythmically clenching his fist. "So, at the moment, there is nothing we can do about the traitors from our country or the woman who started this disease. How will we kill the wheelchair girl and her boyfriend?"

Max raised his head and studied the weapons expert. "I'm thinking about it."

"I admit your plan for the immigration centre was effective, but sometimes there is a simple answer to a problem."

"In that case, there was an obvious solution. You don't have to be a genius to work out that they send most immigrants they pick up crossing the channel into a nearby detention facility. The only challenge was to make sure our assassination team got sent to the same place. By now, the British authorities will probably be on high alert."

"This time, we should just go in and shoot them all."

Max rolled his eyes. "That's why I'm the one planning this mission. If they went to the trouble of hiding them, don't you think they'd also arrange protection? It's not like we have an army at our disposal. There are only three of us."

"Blow them up, then. That worked well at the Olympics."

"And how do you propose to get close enough to plant a bomb? No, this requires careful thought. We can't just blindly rush in."

"So, what *is* your master plan?"

Max bit down on his irritation. The team had been selected for their specialised skills and aptitude at speaking English, not their ability to organise a mission. Mo was there for his expertise in Information Technology, and Omar for his proficiency in killing people. They had travelled separately on fake Algerian passports, arriving in the UK on different days and only meeting up the day before at this guest house, where they had rented all the free rooms for the next week.

"We know where they're staying," Max said, forcing himself to speak calmly. "The only problem is so does everybody else. They're bound to move them to another location. We have to track them down and complete our mission before the press find them again."

"How do we do that?"

Max turned to Mo. “That’s where you come in. Mullah Awad told me you were the best hacker in Africa. I need you to use your skills to discover where they’re taking them.”

The IT expert puffed out his thin chest in a show of pride. “Don’t worry. I’ll get on it right away. I have a few ideas.”

4

Thursday 26th March 2037

Solitary Isolation Wing, Bronzefield Women's Prison, Near London

The bolts shot back with a metallic clank. The door swung open to reveal the stocky figure of the female prison guard. A second male warder remained in the corridor. The all-in-one blue uniform did the woman no favours, emphasising her bulging waistline. Her lank, greasy hair hung down in a basin cut. A kink on the bridge of her nose told of some past altercation with a belligerent inmate. She carried a cloth in her hand.

"Not feeling hungry?" she asked with a malicious grin.

Rosalind Baxter's gaze rose to the newcomer, but she remained silent. She pushed the barely touched plate of food across the scuffed surface of the moulded plastic table.

"What a shame," the woman continued. "The chef worked hard on that." She poked a finger into the centre of the grey-coloured mashed potatoes. "Who knows what he puts in to make it so creamy?"

Rosalind's eyes narrowed. "You'll be hearing from my lawyer."

"Ooh!" the guard cooed. "I'm really scared." Her tone hardened. "You might have been able to threaten people when you ran that big company of yours, but things have changed. In here, I'm the one setting the rules."

In truth, Rosalind's threat was worthless. Her lawyers were far too busy fighting to uphold the terms of the amnesty document she had negotiated with Andrew Jacobs four years earlier to be concerned with the conditions of her incarceration. That and the numerous requests for extradition from foreign governments.

Rosalind rose from the table and perched herself on the edge of the narrow bed. The thin mattress provided little cushioning. Whenever she lay down, she could feel the lumpy padding through the stained material of the covering.

But that wasn't the only thing to keep her awake at night. In addition to the persistent bangs and clanks during the hours of darkness—many of which she believed to be deliberate attempts to deprive her of sleep—her mind continually played back Max Perrin's last moments. Her subconscious mingled the vivid images with those of her own agony as she had pushed the tip of the pen into her eye. Most nights, she would throw off her blankets, unsure whether the screams that woke her were real or just part of her dreams.

Not that she had any regrets about Max's demise. It was only what he deserved. Apart from anything else, he had tried to murder her adopted son. What mother wouldn't do the same to her son's would-be killer? The irony that she had also threatened Jason's life was not lost on her. But that was just the heat of the moment; she would never have gone through with it. At least that's what she kept telling herself.

"Don't get too comfortable," the female guard said, jamming the plastic knife and fork into the mountain of mash. "You've got an important visitor. I'll be back in a minute."

Rosalind raised her head sharply. Other than her lawyers, visitors were rare. "Who is it?"

The woman ignored the question. She placed the paper plate on the bolted-down chair and wiped down the metal surface of the table with the damp cloth, filling the cell with the acrid stench of disinfectant. When she had finished the task, she scooped up the remains of the meal and headed to the door.

Moments later, she returned with her male colleague, carrying a clinking bundle of cuffs and chains. Dressed in the same style of blue uniform, the man was an inch shorter than the female warder and probably weighed a third less. He had a narrow face and thinning brown hair. He carried a second chair, which he deposited on the opposite side of the table to the other.

Rosalind groaned. "Is this really necessary?"

"It is if I say so," the woman replied. "Come here."

Rosalind rose stiffly and ambled towards her.

"Put out your hands."

Rosalind complied. The guard slipped the handcuffs over her wrists and ratcheted them down tightly.

"Now, sit."

The female warder lowered herself to one knee and fitted a set of ankle restraints. Next, she looped the chain through the loop in the floor beside Rosalind's feet, then both sets of cuffs, before securing the arrangement with a bulky padlock. She checked the bonds, then invited her colleague to repeat the inspection.

"All secure," he agreed.

The woman grinned down at the prisoner. "It's a shame we can't shackle you like this all the time." She turned to her fellow warder. "Come on. We better not keep them waiting."

The cell door clanged shut behind the two guards. Rosalind stared at the wall, wondering about the identity of her surprise visitor. Several minutes passed, and her fingers lost feeling as the cuffs restricted the blood supply to her hands.

Eventually, the clang of bolts signalled the wait was over. The solid steel barrier swung open, and two men wearing dark suits entered. Rosalind had never seen the pair before, but she immediately recognised the body language as they surveyed the room for threats. They finished their inspection, and one of them returned to the man waiting in the shadows outside. Andrew Jacobs stepped forwards, confirming Rosalind's suspicions. The bodyguards took up position by the wall behind her.

She rolled her eyes. "I might have guessed. As you can see, I can't shake your hand—not that I'd particularly want to. Is it really necessary to keep me trussed up like this?"

The Prime Minister raised an eyebrow. "Unfortunately, Rosalind, you have past form. You murdered your partner in front of several witnesses. My people insisted you remain under lock and key during my visit."

"What's wrong with an interview room? If you're so worried about what a danger I am to you, why not talk to me from the other side of a Perspex screen?"

"I wanted to see the conditions they're keeping you in." Jacobs surveyed the cramped surroundings and the narrow bed. "Not exactly the Ritz, is it?"

Rosalind scowled back at him. "Have you come here to gloat? Because this is unlawful imprisonment. Need I remind you that you signed an amnesty four years ago. Why am I stuck in this hole?"

The British leader shook his head. "We're keeping you in protective custody for your own safety. If I let you out, you'd be lynched in five minutes flat. The taxpayers would strongly object to footing the bill for your protection on the outside. Unpleasant though it is, you're far safer here than anywhere else."

"Surely, that's my decision to make."

"Maybe, but then there're the dozens of extradition requests we've received from around the world. Several of those countries still have the death penalty, so you should be grateful I haven't handed you over to any of them yet. Even those bastards from The Republic of North Africa had the gall to ask for you back, if you can believe it."

"What are you doing about those savages? I've heard nothing on the news about any retaliatory attacks."

Jacobs sighed. "It's complicated. I shouldn't really be telling you this, but there's been a lot of debate at cabinet level about a suitable response. We submitted a report to the United Nations. Getting the Europeans, Chinese, Russians and Americans to agree on a course of military action is like herding cats, so I don't expect much progress there. The US are thinking about going it alone, but Congress is very nervous about being drawn into another ground war. The best we've been able to achieve is a strengthening of sanctions. Needless to say, nobody wants to be associated with a terrorist state, so they're holding for now."

Rosalind lifted her arms as far as the chains allowed. Immediately, both the Prime Minister's bodyguards placed their right hands inside their jackets and took a forward step. "Relax," she said with a sigh. "I'm just trying to get some blood flowing. How's my grandson?"

Jacobs blinked in surprise. "He was traumatised by the whole affair, but all the members of the family have been receiving counselling. Miss Lessing is taking it the worst. The experience affected her badly, coming so soon after the last episode. But then, you'd know all about that. That girl has been through a lot in her life."

Rosalind strongly suspected Antimone's current state of distress derived more from the part she had played in Max Perrin's final moments than any carryover from their incarceration in Tripoli. Only four people knew about Max's fate. During the journey back to England, Rosalind and Antimone had agreed to keep the details to themselves, telling anybody who asked that a stray shot had killed him in the gunfight while they were trying to escape.

"It's been hard on the entire family," Jacobs continued. "They've gone into hiding to avoid the press and the lunatics who still think she had something to do with the virus."

"What happened to the rest of the people who escaped with us?"

"The young African boy has been adopted. Unfortunately, last week somebody murdered Major Halim and his men in the immigration centre where they were being held. They'd all requested asylum, and we were processing their applications. We booked them in under false names on the paperwork, but sadly it seems that wasn't enough to protect them. We caught the killers; they said they were from Algeria and claimed they got into a fight when one of Halim's group insulted the prophet, but the Algerian authorities have no record of them. Our people suspect they're actually operatives from The Republic of North Africa.

"We can't decide what to do with Aya Shaladi. We're holding her somewhere secure, much like this. Her father led the operation, and there's no doubt she knew what was going to happen. She's claiming she took no part in the planning. According to her account, the Reponan authorities threatened both of them with death if they didn't follow orders. I don't suppose you can shed any light on matters."

Rosalind met his gaze and held it. "I'm sorry. All I know is that she helped with the escape, but by then she was a prisoner, just like the rest of us. From what I heard, the only part she played in the original attack was getting the Lessing girl out of the stadium after the blasts. What happened to Dr Kubar?"

"Ah, yes. The good doctor. He brought details of the drug he developed for this new strain of the virus with him."

"You mean *we* developed, Andrew. He didn't do it alone. It was a joint effort between the two of us."

"If you say so. He used the formula as a bargaining chip. It seems he learned that trick from somebody else I know. We agreed to grant him immediate asylum. He's now working at one of our government research labs. The first human drug trials started a week ago."

"Let me correct you again, Andrew. I think you'll find the first trial took place in Tripoli. My grandson was among the test subjects. Why did you decide to stop quarantining people with the new strain?"

Jacobs stood and paced a few steps in each direction. "It must have been about six weeks back. By then, it was clear there was nothing we could do to halt the spread. We couldn't afford to implement strict social isolation. The last occasion we tried that, it practically bankrupted the country. We took the decision that it was easier to isolate all expectant mothers from the population. I won't disagree there have been some unpleasant incidents—it's not a good time to be overweight and mistaken for being pregnant, for example—but it seemed like the lesser of two evils."

Rosalind tried to stretch her legs but found her movements restricted by the chains binding her ankles to the floor. "Look, Andrew, nice though it is to have somebody vaguely intelligent to talk to, these cuffs are cutting off my circulation. I'm sure you didn't come here just for a chat or to tell me how generous you are in not handing me over to the countries requesting my extradition. Why exactly are you here?"

Jacobs stopped pacing and sat down again. "Vaguely intelligent: that was almost a compliment. But you're correct. I have a proposition to make to you."

Rosalind leant forwards. "I'm all ears."

"My scientific advisors tell me it's only a matter of time before there's another mutation of this virus."

Rosalind tilted her head in agreement. "They're probably right."

"And the next one could be far worse. Nothing actually kills this thing inside the body. The best we can hope for with current treatments is to prevent the activation phase."

"Unfortunately, also correct."

"So, I've attended a series of high-level discussions with other world leaders, and we've reached an agreement to set up an international research effort with the brightest minds we can bring together. Unlike previous initiatives, we plan to collocate the team at one location. As you can imagine, arranging all the equipment and facilities will be very expensive. While the other countries have agreed to help with some of the funding, they feel we are responsible for creating this mess and should pay more."

"What do you want from me, Andrew?"

"After much debate, we have reached consensus on establishing this research centre in Britain. Specifically, at your old company, Ilithyia Biotechnology. They recently went into receivership, and we're keen to retain a major interest in the global pharmaceutical industry. I'd like you to join the new team."

"What's in it for me?"

Jacobs made a point of staring around the small cell. "Well, for a start, we'd move you out of here. It would also delay any extradition arrangements. You'd have to live on site under lock and key, but that would be more for your protection than anything else. You wouldn't receive any salary, only food and board."

"And if we succeed in beating this thing?"

Jacobs's eyes locked onto Rosalind's face. "I'm not making any promises, but let's just say I might oppose any attempts to extradite you."

"No, that's not enough. I want your personal guarantee that you'll deny any extradition requests."

"I'm sorry, Rosalind. I can't give you that assurance. In any case, I won't remain in office forever. I'm thinking of retiring before the next election."

Rosalind continued to stare back at the British Prime Minister.

Finally, she conceded with a sigh. "All right, you have a deal. When do I start?"

5

Friday 27th March 2037

Ilithyia Biotechnology, Northstowe

The man stopped in the open doorway and turned to Rosalind. "I'll be back to pick you up in half an hour. I expect you to be ready"

He had informed her he was responsible for security at the Ilithyia site, but she had already forgotten his name. Before she could reply, the door closed behind him, and the lock clicked home. "That doesn't exactly give me long," she called anyway.

In a supreme act of irony, her new custodians had allocated her the room which was once her own office. During her absence, they had converted the area her secretary previously occupied into a bathroom, as she discovered when she pushed the door open.

They had come for her at five o'clock that morning, allowing her to change into the garments she wore during the escape from The Republic of North Africa before bundling her into a prison van. A pair of guards sat up front as the autonomous driver whisked them from Bronzefield on the west side of London to the site of her former company in Northstowe, a few miles north-west of Cambridge. The journey took the better part of ninety minutes. By the time her escorts guided her through the security gates and inside the chrome and glass building, another hour had passed.

Upon entering the foyer, she had stared around at the sweeping arch of the ceiling. Until recently, she and Nigel Perrin had owned everything she saw. It was a far cry from the poky little two-storey unit she and her business partner rented on the Cambridge Science Park during the first few years of the company's existence.

Between them, they had built the organisation into a multi-billion-pound enterprise. The British Prime Minister had forced her to sell off her stake as part of the deal for her immunity from prosecution, and she received only a fraction of its true worth. Even then, she pocketed a staggeringly huge sum of money, not that there had been much chance to benefit from her burgeoning bank balance over the past eight months.

The early start combined with a sleepless night, had left her with a headache, pulsing at the back of her skull. She rubbed her temples, then returned to the narrow hallway and entered what was now the bedroom. A single bed lay along one wall, and a simple wooden desk, a quarter the size of the massive expanse of wood she had previously sat behind, rested against the opposite side. A small wardrobe butted up to the desk.

She strolled to the floor to ceiling plate-glass window and looked down. The neatly tended flowerbeds were as she remembered them, but a high metal fence, topped by razor wire, marred the aesthetic qualities of the grounds. Another recent addition was the presence of the man in the dark uniform, patrolling the barrier alongside the large German Shepherd guard dog, which he kept on a short leash.

Perhaps sensing the movement behind the glass, the man glanced upwards. Rosalind stepped back out of his view and surveyed the rest of the room. A cream-coloured towel, a toiletry bag and a small suitcase lay on the bed. She undid the zip of the case, lifted the lid and studied the contents: several sets of plain underwear, a supermarket-branded pair of jeans, a white blouse and a thin, pale-blue jumper.

She checked the labels; at least they had bought the right sizes for her. A click drew her attention to the dial of the wall clock. In a little over twenty minutes, somebody would come by to introduce her new colleagues. If she was going to freshen up, now was the time.

She had brought nothing with her apart from the clothes she stood in. She raised an arm and sniffed the back of her hand: a musty, faintly metallic odour, overlaid with a hint of sweat. Before meeting her new colleagues, she wanted to remove the prison smell from her skin. It would come as a welcome relief to shower without a warder carefully watching her every movement.

She grabbed the towel and sponge bag and headed to the bathroom. The light and a fan came on automatically as she entered. Moments later, she was standing under the shower. She felt the soul-sapping crust of prison life washing off as she luxuriated under the stream of hot water. Even though she remained a prisoner, she could at least avail herself of a few home comforts.

She emerged from the cubicle feeling refreshed and towelled herself dry. A quick search of the sponge bag turned up a plastic toothbrush and a tube of mint toothpaste. She wrapped the towel over her chest and hummed to herself as she brushed her teeth in front of the misted over mirror.

A metallic thunk interrupted her musical interlude. She rinsed the brush head under the tap and opened the bathroom door. The same man who had escorted her to the room stood in the open doorway to the corridor. He was in his mid-fifties with short-cut grey hair. A cheap suit hung off his trim frame. His face carried a frown. Try as she might, she couldn't remember his name.

"I thought I told you I'd be back in half an hour, Mrs Baxter," he said.

Rosalind self-consciously checked the overlap of the towel. "Yeah, sorry. I lost track of time."

The man's scowl deepened. "May I remind you, this isn't a holiday camp. If I had my way, you'd still be rotting in prison."

Rosalind glared at the man, then looked away. "I'll be ready in two minutes. Tell me again, what did you say your name was?"

His eyes lasered in on her as if he could determine simply by staring at her whether her words intended a lack of respect. "My name's Nick Butler, and when I ask you to do something, I expect you to follow my instructions. Is that clear?"

"Yes, sir." Rosalind couldn't resist putting a slight emphasis on the second word.

Butler glared at her for a moment longer, then said, "Two minutes."

"I take it you don't plan to stand there and watch me get dressed."

A vein pulsed at the man's temple. He spun around and stormed out of the open door, slamming it behind him.

Rosalind padded back to the bedroom in bare feet. "Windows, darken," she commanded.

The outside world took on a darker shade. It seemed the previous owners had retained the same system from her time in this office. One of her last acts before leaving the company was to update all the executive offices to use voice control. "Windows, opaque."

The overhead light turned on, and the view disappeared as the glass transitioned into a matte black. She allowed the towel to drop and quickly slipped on a pair of knickers and a bra. She was pulling on the jumper when the outer door opened again.

"Christ," she muttered. "Is there no privacy in this place?"

"Time to leave now, Mrs Baxter," Butler announced, marching into the room.

"Don't you know it's rude to enter a lady's bedroom without knocking?"

Butler ignored the question and studied the band on his wrist. "We're already late. Do I have to carry you out of here?"

"All right. Calm down. Just lead the way."

Butler spun around and marched towards the corridor. Rosalind had to jog a little to keep up. "Where are we going?" she asked.

Once again, the man refused to answer. She followed him to the lift. He pressed the button and entered as soon as the doors parted. He jabbed the letter G before Rosalind was even inside.

"You're not really one for conversation, are you?" she said.

Butler's eyes narrowed, and the muscles of his jaw spasmed. He raised a hand, grabbed her by the neck and pushed her back against the metal side of the compartment. He thrust his face within a few inches of hers, so close that spittle flecked her skin when he spoke.

"This might not look like a prison, but make no mistake, you're still a prisoner. For my sins, I'm responsible for you in here. You may have run this place once, but as far as I'm concerned, you're just a mass murderer, who should be made to suffer for your crimes. My wife died from the virus you created. I can't for the life of me understand why anybody would choose to let you out. If it was up to me, I'd put you against a wall and shoot you."

Rosalind tried to inhale, but the fingers around her throat prevented her from breathing. A gurgle escaped her mouth. Just when she thought she was about to pass out, the panels slid apart. With a grunt of disgust, the man released his grip.

"Now, no more talking," Butler growled. He marched ahead without checking to see whether Rosalind followed. She stumbled along the carpeted corridor behind him as she tried to catch up, the breath rasping in her throat as she filled her oxygen-starved lungs.

"Here," Butler announced, slowing as they approached the door of what had once been the boardroom.

A man stood outside, leaning against the wall with a coffee cup in his hand and seemingly deep in thought. He raised his eyes and stared at the two newcomers, but his gaze focused on Rosalind as they drew closer. "Mrs Baxter?"

Butler greeted the man with a nod. "Good morning, Dr Hendrick."

Rosalind blinked in surprise. She hadn't recognised her former employee. She had last seen him about twenty years ago when Ilithyia Biotechnology was still a fledgling startup on the Cambridge Science Park. His face was rounder and his sandy hair thinner, but now she clearly remembered the scientist she had let go two decades earlier.

"Martin, it's been a while," she said.

"I take it the pair of you know each other," Butler said.

"Yes, we met in a previous life," Hendrick replied. "I can escort Mrs Baxter in and introduce her to the others."

Butler stepped away from the doctor and beckoned Rosalind closer. He lowered his head to her ear and spoke in a hoarse whisper. "I'll be along later to take you to your room. If any of the people in there ask you to do something, you follow their instructions immediately and without question. If you fail to do so, I will personally drag you back to prison before your feet can touch the floor. And don't even think about trying to leave this building—it wouldn't be good for my career, but it would give me great pleasure to see one of my men taser you and send several thousand volts arcing through your body."

He spun on his heel and marched back the way he had come without a backward glance.

Rosalind rubbed her throat and glared at the departing figure. "What are you doing here?" she asked, turning to her former employee.

"The same as you, I imagine. Christine mentioned that somebody else would be joining the team. I had no idea it would be you."

"Are you talking about Christine Harris?"

"Yes," Hendrick replied. "Do you know her?"

"We've met a few times over the years. She's a fairly competent virologist."

"More than competent. One of the best, I'd say."

"So, what have you been working on for the last two decades, Martin? I haven't seen your name mentioned in any of the journals."

"I've become something of an expert in cross-species viral transmission, but I've stayed out of the limelight for the past few years. They've pulled together a pretty diverse group here. Let's go in, and I'll introduce you."

Hendrick's hand stopped halfway to the door handle. He turned back to his former boss. "Just one last thing: I haven't told anybody that I worked at Ilithyia. I'd prefer they didn't know."

"Fine. I won't mention it."

Hendrick's blue eyes locked on Rosalind's. "You have no need to worry," he said with a glint. "I don't hold anything against you. In fact, I'm looking forward to working with you once again."

Part Two: Disinformation

6

Friday 14th August 2015

Ilithyia Biotechnology, Cambridge Science Park

Twenty-one years ago

Martin Hendrick swallowed, then raised a hand and knocked on the office door.

A female voice from inside shouted, "Come."

He twisted the handle and stepped into the small room. A window in the back wall looked out onto a car park. Behind the solitary desk sat the CEO and co-owner of the company, Rosalind Baxter. Nigel Perrin, who formed the other half of the company's ownership, stood beside her.

Several frames adorned the walls. They held a variety of certificates, awards and group photographs. From a preliminary inspection, they gave little personal information away about the occupier of this space.

Hendrick focused his attention on the woman. She was elegantly dressed in a dark skirt, white blouse and matching jacket. Her straight blonde hair fell to shoulder length and framed an attractive face. From his research into her background before joining the company, he knew she was in her early thirties. For all her good looks, there was a coolness about her, a barrier through which little emotion leaked, and which made her hard to like.

Her partner was more approachable. Dr Nigel Perrin was a year or two older and held the title of Chief Scientist. His appearance—the thinning hair, dark-rimmed glasses and white medical coat—combined with his earnest manner gave him the air of an eccentric professor, but beneath the stereotypical exterior lurked a razor-sharp brain. His infectious enthusiasm helped him to motivate the twenty members of the science team who worked under his management.

Mrs Baxter also came from a scientific background, having studied Biochemistry at Cambridge University, but had gravitated towards the commercial side of the business. Both had to be convinced if the company was to take on a new project, but ultimately, the CEO held the purse strings. And releasing them was Hendrick's motivation for calling this meeting.

"Good morning, Martin. Please sit." Rosalind gestured towards one of two empty chairs on the opposite side of her desk. Perrin moved around and took the remaining vacant seat.

"Now," she continued, "you mentioned in your email that you have a potential new project you wanted to discuss with us. I'm not sure why you felt you couldn't document your proposal like everybody else, but here we are. So, what's this all about?"

Hendrick had spent a lot of time preparing his pitch, but under the attentive gaze of the company owners, he suddenly couldn't remember how he planned to start. He took a calming breath, then cleared his throat. "Ah, right."

Perrin pulled a ballpoint pen from the top pocket of his medical coat and clicked the point in and out. Most of the staff joked about the boss's nervous tic, but rather than distracting the Belgian scientist, the repetitive action helped him to focus.

"Do you know what the most common notifiable disease is in the West?" Hendrick began.

"Measles?" Rosalind said.

"Mumps?" Perrin suggested.

"No," Hendrick replied. "It's actually Chlamydia trachomatis. It's also the most prevalent of all the sexually transmitted diseases. In America alone, over one and a half million cases were reported to the CDC last year. In the UK, the figure is around a third of that. Across the developed world, the average notification rate is somewhere around one in every three hundred people."

"That's a lot of cases," Rosalind said, "but aren't antibiotics commonly used to treat that sort of thing? Azithromycin and doxycycline as I recall."

"Correct," Hendrick replied, getting into his stride, "but they're typically only ninety-five per cent effective."

Perrin wrinkled his forehead in concentration. "So, if we took just the US and UK together, that would be around one hundred thousand patients per year who don't respond to conventional treatments."

"Yes," Hendrick said, leaning back slightly as his message hit home. "But I'm thinking bigger. Much bigger."

Rosalind rested her chin on her left hand. "What do you propose? I take it you don't have a miracle cure up your sleeve."

The Belgian researcher let out a low chuckle. "Well... no. That's true." He hesitated. *Would they take the bait?*

Perrin clicked the pen in and out faster. "What if we could develop a vaccine?" he asked. "The market would be colossal."

Hendrick waited a moment in silence to allow the words to sink in. *Good.* The Chief Scientist had taken the first nibble. "My thoughts exactly. The main problem would be generating adequate levels of mucosal T-cell and antibody responses to provide long-term immunity." Once again, he paused.

Perrin returned the pen to the top pocket of his medical coat. "You'd need a vector to target the right cells—like a virus."

Hendrick recalled something he had heard at university; if you want something approved, allow the boss to think it's at least partially their own idea. *Time to attempt the strike.* He had stacked the deck by leaving printouts of an article around the office and in the printer output tray. The paper described the work of a research group, who had used flu viruses for exactly this purpose.

"Yes," he said, gaining momentum as he reached the critical part of his pitch. "I was reading a paper only last week about using an attenuated influenza A virus to target specific cells."

Perrin jumped to his feet. "Yes, I saw something about that recently. That's a fantastic idea. I'll need to do some reading, but the potential is huge. We should definitely look into this one, Rosalind."

Hendrick released the breath he had been holding. *Hook, line and sinker.*

Rosalind drummed her fingers on the desk. "I'll admit it sounds promising. The only problem is we'd require a lab with biosafety level two to work with a live flu virus, whether attenuated or not, and I don't need to tell you that cash is tight at the moment. We couldn't afford to update the facilities in this building without a considerable cash injection. And who would perform the research? It's not as if we have a spare team sitting around twiddling their thumbs."

Hendrick's face flushed. Just as this was looking like a done deal, it was slipping away from him. "We could rent space at another lab with the facilities we require."

Rosalind shook her head. "Didn't you hear what I said? We don't have the capital to engage in unfunded research, let alone what it would cost to hire lab space from a third party. We can barely make ends meet as it is."

"I could do the research here," Hendrick blurted out.

A stunned silence greeted his statement. Eventually, Perrin spoke in a hushed voice. "You know as well as we do that this building is only suitable for biosafety level one. We'd lose everything if anybody ever found out."

Rosalind let out a humourless laugh. "That may happen anyway the way things are going."

Perrin grabbed the pen from his top pocket, subconsciously clicking it in and out at a furious rate. "Mrs Baxter and I could end up in prison if the authorities ever got wind of something like that."

"I'll be careful and take all the right precautions." Hendrick could hear the wheedling tone in his voice. "You can trust me to keep quiet about this."

"And what about the jobs you're already working on?" Rosalind asked. "They bring in the revenue that we need to survive."

"I'd continue with the paid contracts during the day and work on this in my own time during evenings and weekends. If it's the money that's the problem, you don't need to worry about paying me overtime; I'm happy to do this unpaid. I could do the preliminary tests here. If everything pans out, we could rent the external lab space to confirm the results. We'd have to repeat everything, but we'd already have all the answers."

"Dr Perrin and I will think about it," Rosalind said. "A professor of mine once told me you should never perform an experiment when you don't already have an expectation of what the results will be. I'm not sure he had this sort of thing in mind though."

Perrin turned to Rosalind, his face tight with shock. "You aren't seriously considering doing this work here, are you?"

Hendrick stood. It was time to try to land the fish. “This is something I’d really like to explore. If I can’t do it here, I’ll have to seriously consider finding somewhere else I can pursue this avenue of research.”

7

Friday 14th August 2015

Ilithyia Biotechnology, Cambridge Science Park

Twenty-one years ago

The door to the small office closed behind Martin Hendrick as he left.

The CEO and Chief Scientist sat on opposite sides of the desk without speaking. The only sound came from the clicking of the pen in the latter's hand.

"For Christ's sake, Nigel, will you stop that?" Rosalind snapped.

"Right, sorry." Perrin returned the ballpoint to his top pocket.

Rosalind's brown eyes locked onto Perrin's. "So, what do you think of Dr Hendrick's proposal?"

"I can't believe you're considering this. It's a fantastic idea, but like I said a minute ago, the authorities could shut us down if they ever found out we were working with live viruses without the right biosafety precautions. We might even end up in prison."

"Come on, Nigel. I'm not for one moment suggesting that we wouldn't enforce sensible safety measures. All I'm saying is that we can't afford to upgrade the labs to pass a level two assessment. We both know the rules are set by a bunch of old men who are afraid of their own shadows. Didn't you hear him say that he proposes to use an attenuated influenza virus? We all take far greater risks when we venture outside our homes. You're a lot more likely to pick up a dangerous bug in a shop or a pub."

"I'm more worried about being caught. Even if we don't end up in jail, the company would be finished."

Rosalind tapped the desk with a manicured fingernail. "Clearly you haven't been looking at the spreadsheets I send over every month. It's time to face facts; if nothing else changes, we'll be forced into administration in around twelve months, eighteen at tops. The rent on the building is due in three weeks, the overdraft is close to its limit, and we're on hold with a significant proportion of our suppliers.

"Our purchasing people are using the company credit card to pay for the essentials. We have a couple of outstanding customer invoices, but most of those funds will go to paying the salaries. We're operating hand to mouth and have been doing for the last year. It's possible we may be able to find another investor, but we both know it dilutes our shares every time we bring somebody new on board."

"Yes, but—"

Rosalind cut him off before he could continue. "Dr Hendrick is on one month's notice. If he resigns and leaves, we'd never get anybody else up to speed on his projects quickly enough. Both would miss the deadlines, and the late delivery penalties would leave us even shorter of cash."

Perrin shot his partner an angry scowl. "I was against accepting those terms in the first place. Anyway, how does letting him take on more work help us?"

Rosalind's expression softened. "You know I didn't want to accept those penalty clauses, but we discussed it at the time, and it was either that or lose the contracts. As for increasing Martin's workload, he said he's happy to put in the extra hours for no additional salary. And what if he manages to pull it off?"

"Don't get me wrong. I'd love to start researching this area, but doesn't it worry you, gambling on the company's future?"

"Look, I'll be honest. It would place both of us in a risky situation, but we could take a few precautions. We'd have to make sure that any work he does on this project is off the books: no emails about it, no research notes on the company file servers, no meeting minutes. Absolutely everything would have to be stored offline. That way, it's all deniable. If the Health and Safety Executive ever caught wind, we could claim we knew nothing about it. It would be Martin's word against ours."

"Bloody hell, Rosalind. You'd throw him under the bus?"

"I'm sure he'd do the same to us. But think about the upside. This could be worth billions."

"Where would we even get a live influenza virus from? It's not as if you can just walk into the local chemist and buy a bottle off the shelf."

"We'd have to keep that off the books too. I'm betting the good doctor has a way of getting hold of a sample. He seems to have thought of everything else. If not, we could probably obtain some off the dark web from a part of the world where the regulations are somewhat less strict."

"Christ, Rosalind. I can't believe what I'm hearing." Perrin's hand moved towards his top pocket again, but a scowl from Rosalind stopped him before it reached the pen. "I still find it hard to understand how this is going to improve our cash-flow problem. Approval for a new vaccine takes years. From what you've said, we'll run out of money long before then."

"We don't have to get it approved ourselves. Hell, we don't even have to complete the research. Once we have something solid, we rent some lab space and repeat the work. Then all we need to do is show the results of early tests to one of the big pharma companies. We license any vaccine to them and arrange for them to rerun the trials.

"Alternatively, we sell them the company. They're not stupid; they'd offer a fortune to own the rights for a treatment to eradicate Chlamydia. It would be worth looking into who owns the antibiotics commonly used today; they might even pay us big money to drop our research."

Perrin shook his head. "I'm pretty sure you'll find the patents for azithromycin and doxycycline both expired a long time ago."

Rosalind forced a tight smile. "I bow to your superior knowledge, Nigel, but it doesn't really matter. A vaccine for the most common sexually transmitted disease on the planet is a pharmaceutical company's wet dream."

"I'm not sure about this, Rosalind."

"Do you have any other bright ideas to increase funding over the next few months? Because if you don't and you say no to this, we may as well cut our losses and fold the company right now. Who can tell what chance Martin has of delivering, but surely it's better than nothing? If we decline his proposal, there's a strong possibility he'll leave and find somebody else who will allow him to pursue this research. They'll reap the rewards, and it'll bring about the end here even sooner. I know you're not comfortable with all this, but I think we should take the gamble and go for it."

Perrin closed his eyes and took a deep breath. He remained still for a few seconds, then exhaled and met Rosalind's questioning stare.

"All right," he said. "You win. We've put too much in to give up now. Let's do this."

8

Friday 14th August 2015

Ilithyia Biotechnology, Cambridge Science Park

Twenty-one years ago

Eileen Floyd sat on the toilet seat, staring intently at the white strip. *Five minutes*, the instructions said. She had planned to take the pregnancy test when she got home, but her impatience to know the results whittled away at her resolve throughout the day. Her manager's request to work late again had finally cracked her resistance. He could hardly begrudge her the short time required to learn whether such a life-changing event lay in her near-term future.

Is that a line? Her heart beat faster as she moved the plastic closer to her face. Yes, there was definitely something there. As she watched, the thin band grew darker. It was as she suspected; she was pregnant.

Her immediate reaction was to call her husband, Daniel. Two things prevented that: first, company rules prohibited employees from bringing mobile phones onto the premises, and second, the father of the recently conceived child was on the other side of the Atlantic and occupied in a series of business meetings.

She performed a quick calculation in her head; five hours behind, so that would make it one o'clock in the afternoon over there. Daniel had told her he expected a long day with his potential new customers. The earliest she would be able to share her news was at least ten at night UK time.

They had been trying to start a family for the past six months, mainly at Daniel's instigation. She was more than happy to wait a while, but he claimed he wanted to be a youthful parent as their offspring grew up, unlike his own father, who had been in his mid-forties when his only son was born. Sadly, Eileen's child would never get to meet their paternal grandfather; the man had passed away five years earlier from a heart attack.

Anyway, this wasn't the sort of information to send in a text message. She wanted to see her husband's face when she told him. A smile formed on her lips as an idea occurred to her. When he arrived back home the following morning, she would tell him she thought she *might* be pregnant without revealing that she already knew the result. Then she would repeat the test with him present to watch his reaction.

Pleased with her decision, Eileen pulled up her panties and flushed the toilet. She took one last look at the strip of white plastic to confirm the presence of the solid line, then tossed it in the bin together with the packaging. The face that stared back at her from the mirror as she washed her hands glowed with happiness.

Eileen pushed through the swing door and followed the corridor to the laboratory in which she worked. As she entered, she spotted her boss, Alan Hastings, bent over a computer screen alongside the third member of their small team, Natalie Stevens.

The former was in his mid-thirties and, according to the office rumour mill, still single. His thick-framed glasses accentuated his narrow face. He was the only researcher to wear a shirt and tie to work every day. The latter was an attractive black woman who had only been with the company for a few weeks. She was quick to find humour in a situation and possessed a bright and bubbly personality.

"You need to reword this sentence," Alan said, jabbing a finger at the display. "Oh, and this one, too. Um... if you don't mind."

The door closed behind Eileen with a click. Her manager spun around. "Ah, there you are. I was beginning to think you'd gone home already. We have to get this report submitted tonight, and there're still some results to format. Apologies for keeping you late again."

Eileen hid the huge grin that threatened to burst out. It wouldn't be appropriate to reveal her exciting news to her co-workers before telling her husband.

Alan misread her facial expression. "Is everything okay?"

She felt sorry for the poor man. He really wasn't cut out for leadership and struggled to set the right tone managing the two women who worked for him. It was clear that members of the fairer sex made him deeply uncomfortable. He would certainly have no idea how to react if she told him what was on her mind.

"I'm fine. Better than fine actually."

Natalie stopped typing and shot a curious glance at Eileen before resuming her work. The pair had become friendly after being thrown together on their latest project, although they had never met up outside the workplace.

"What can I do to help?" Eileen asked.

Alan thrust his hands in his pocket. "Those graphs aren't good enough for a printed report. Would it be possible to include the units on the axes and export them as JPEGs at a higher resolution? If that's okay with you."

"Sure." As Eileen moved towards her workstation, she spotted a reagent bottle perched on the edge of her desk. "Do you want me to put that away?"

"Uh... yes, please. There's no room in our refrigerator at the moment though. Could you ask Dr Hendrick if we can store it in his lab just for tonight? I think he's working late again. I'll rearrange everything tomorrow to make more space."

Eileen picked up the chemical container. Natalie turned sideways in her chair and flashed a brief smile.

A sudden impulse came to Eileen. She could do with some company while her husband was out of the country. She didn't plan to discuss her pregnancy, but it would be good to share some girl talk. "Hey, do you fancy going out for a drink after we finish tonight?" she asked.

Alan's gaze jerked towards her. He turned away, embarrassed, as he realised she was directing the question at Natalie.

"I'd love to," the woman replied, "but I've arranged to go into Cambridge with my boyfriend. Definitely some other night though."

"No problem. I'll take this over now, then I can sort out those graphs."

Eileen headed across the room. Her boss rushed to get the door for her. "Thanks," she murmured as she entered the corridor. Hendrick's lab was three doors down on the right. As she drew nearer, she spotted a square of light coming through the small window. She peered inside and saw the doctor sitting at a workstation with his back to her. Good. He was still working.

Eileen rapped on the glass with her knuckles. He didn't move, continuing to stare intently at the screen. At that point, she noticed the pair of thin white wires leading up to his ears.

She turned the handle and stuck her head through the gap. "Excuse me, Dr Hendrick."

Once again, he failed to acknowledge her presence.

"Dr Hendrick," she said a second time, raising her voice.

Eileen entered the room and took a tentative step towards the seated scientist. Unaware that he was no longer alone, Hendrick reached a finger out and tapped a key.

The screen contents changed. Eileen advanced another pace, now close enough that she could read several words. Two immediately caught her attention: *virus* and *influenza*.

"Hello, Dr Hendrick," she called, practically shouting.

The doctor jerked his head around at the unexpected intrusion. His hand shot out. Moments later, the display went blank. He tugged the right earbud out.

"What the hell are you doing in here?" he yelled angrily.

Eileen took a backward step at the vehemence of his reaction. "I'm sorry," she replied, her voice shaking. "I knocked and called out several times, but you didn't hear me."

"Yeah, I had the music on." He gestured towards his ear, then offered her an apologetic smile. "Look, I didn't mean to shout. You gave me a fright. So, what can I do for you?"

"Um... we don't have enough room in our fridge. Alan wanted to know if he could store this in yours until tomorrow."

"Okay, no problem. Just put it on the bottom shelf."

As Eileen approached the glass-fronted cabinet, a flash of yellow caught her attention. On the workbench to the side of Hendrick's desk rested a sealed metal flask with a bright triangular label. Beside it sat a petri dish.

Hendrick spotted the direction of her gaze. He leapt from his seat and stood in front of the bench, blocking Eileen's view. She studied his face, but he retained an impassive mask. Her eyes lowered to the slight tremble in his left hand. The Belgian doctor thrust his fingers under his armpit.

"Right, I'll just put it in," Eileen said, mystified by his nervous reaction. She pulled the handle, releasing a puff of condensation as the door swung towards her. Her knees creaked as she knelt and placed the bottle in the empty space.

She rose to her feet and was about to close the cabinet when a second identical flask marked with a yellow triangle drew her eye. The breath caught in her throat at the biohazard symbol of four overlapping rings and the text below: *Danger Biological Hazard.* Another word stood out in smaller black letters on a white background: *influenza.*

What the hell is something like that doing in here? She opened her mouth to ask Hendrick the question, then thought better of it. The doctor watched her carefully as the seal closed with a gentle thud. Still, he blocked her view of the workbench.

"Thank you," she muttered. She crossed to the door and shut it behind her. When she turned and stared through the small glass windows, Hendrick remained stationary, his gaze fixed upon her.

As she made her way back to her boss, all thoughts of her pregnancy fled her mind, leaving one abiding question; why was Martin Hendrick working with what appeared to be an influenza virus with no evident safety precautions?

9

Friday 14th August 2015

Ilithyia Biotechnology, Cambridge Science Park

Twenty-one years ago

Nigel Perrin frowned as the phone on his desk rang. The caller ID signalled the call originated from Alan Hastings's laboratory. He wasn't expecting the report to be finished for at least an hour, so it probably meant yet another problem had arisen. And he certainly didn't need anything else to deal with right now.

"Yes," he snapped, picking up the handset.

"Um... good evening, Dr Perrin. It's Eileen Floyd. I wonder if you could spare a few minutes. There's something I'd like to discuss with you."

Perrin stifled a groan. In his experience, when an employee asked for a meeting late in the day, it normally played out in one of two ways: they either demanded a salary increase or handed in their notice. Or sometimes one followed the other.

"Yes, fine, Eileen," he said despondently. "I plan to be here for at least the next thirty minutes."

"Thanks, Dr Perrin. I'll come up in a second."

Perrin lowered the phone to its cradle. What could this be about? Another thought occurred to him: perhaps she planned to tell him she was pregnant. He knew she was married with no children, and she was around the right age to start a family. That was all they needed when cash was tight and the workload heavy. But surely she would discuss something like that with her manager first. He sighed. There was no point trying to second guess the subject of her request. All would become clear shortly.

Moments later, a gentle tap came from the door. "Come in," he called.

The handle turned, and Eileen Floyd's head appeared in the gap. A worried expression clouded her face. "Can I...?"

"Yes, take a seat," Perrin replied impatiently, gesturing towards the empty chair on the other side of his desk. Her demeanour suggested whatever she planned to reveal wouldn't be good news. He studied her carefully as she crossed the carpet. Up close, he saw she wore little makeup, not that she needed any. She was an attractive woman, with dark wavy hair, flawless skin and an open face. At around five feet six in her flat-heeled shoes, she carried herself with a precise elegance. She sat and folded her hands on her lap.

"How's the report going?" Perrin asked.

"Oh, fine," she replied, glancing down. "It should be done tonight."

He waited for a second to allow her to speak, but she remained silent. It seemed he would have to tease out the reason for her meeting request.

"Well, thanks for staying late. What can I do for you?"

She looked up and met his gaze for a moment before looking away. "Um... I don't know if I'm doing the right thing. I wasn't sure who to talk to."

"What's the problem, Eileen?"

She raised her head slowly. "Is this company working with a live influenza virus?"

Oh, God! That's what this was about. Perrin feigned ignorance. "I don't understand what you're asking."

"I saw a colleague with a flask on his bench. It appeared to be a viral sample. There was a biohazard sign on the container. I didn't think we were set up to perform that sort of research."

"Are you sure it wasn't something else? There's no way anybody here is authorised to undertake any work like that."

Eileen scowled at Perrin's attempt to brush off her question. "There was also an article about viruses on his monitor."

"Do you mind if I ask who it was?" he asked.

"I'd rather not say."

"But Eileen, this is a serious accusation. There must be a good explanation. Are you certain it wasn't a hazardous substance label?"

Her chin jutted out. "Yes, I am aware of the difference between a biohazard and a hazardous substance label."

Maybe she wasn't quite as meek and mild as he had thought.

Perrin placed his palms flat on his desk. "I'm not sure what you expect me to do if you won't tell me who it was."

"What's the procedure if I want to take this further?"

The first real sense of alarm sent Perrin's pulse racing. "You're thinking about taking this further?" His eyes locked onto hers.

"I haven't decided yet."

Perrin let out an inner sigh of relief. There was still hope she would drop the matter. "I guess you'd need to consult the whistleblower policy, but I have to say, that's a big step to take. Once you set the process in motion, it becomes very hard to stop. People end up losing their jobs."

"I know that. I'll sleep on it and let you have my decision in the morning."

"Great. I'm sure it's all just a misunderstanding."

Eileen stood, then crossed the room and stopped in the doorway. She turned back to Perrin. "Thanks for your time. See you tomorrow."

"Goodnight."

When the latch clicked into place, Perrin rose from his desk and padded across the carpeted floor. He placed his ear to the door for a few seconds, then pulled the handle and stuck his head into the corridor. She had gone. His next act was to return to the phone and dial a three-digit internal number.

Martin Hendrick answered after two rings. "Hello, Dr Perrin."

Perrin's voice trembled with barely suppressed fury. "What the hell did she see?"

"Sorry, what are we talking about?"

"Eileen Floyd," he spat. "She spotted the virus in your fridge. For heaven's sake, why did you even let her in your room?"

"Ah, that. There was no refrigerated space in their lab, so she asked whether she could store some chemical solutions in mine."

"Well, she saw enough to ask me about the whistleblower policy."

A pause. Then Hendrick whispered a single word: "Shit."

"Yes, shit indeed. She hasn't decided what to do yet. She said she's going to sleep on it. I need you to remove anything that shouldn't be there immediately. And delete your browser history. She also spotted something related on your screen."

"Sorry, I had my headphones in when she came in. I'll get on it right away."

"Let's hope she doesn't take it any further. I should never have agreed to let you do this research."

"I'm making good progress. In a few weeks, I should be ready to start some trials with mice."

"It better be worth it. Just make sure there's nothing in your lab that will incriminate anybody."

Perrin slammed down the handset.

He tapped in the sequence of digits for his next call from memory. The ringing tone repeated twice before a female voice answered.

"Yes, Nigel."

"Rosalind, we have a serious problem."

10

Friday 14th August 2015

Ilithyia Biotechnology, Cambridge Science Park

Twenty-one years ago

Rosalind Baxter returned the mobile phone to her handbag. *Bloody typical.* The one night in the week she left work early to eat at a decent restaurant, events conspired to drag her back to the office. Not that she was overly worried. Eileen Floyd was no match for her, except perhaps in the affairs of the heart.

Rosalind knew Eileen's husband, Daniel—intimately—having dated him whilst both were students at Cambridge University. The sex had been good, but she realised fairly quickly that they weren't compatible enough for a long-term future together. The relationship drifted along for a while, but after six months, they agreed to separate. Until relatively recently, they hadn't talked for over ten years.

When Eileen joined Ilithyia, Rosalind had been unaware that her new employee was married to her onetime boyfriend until they became reacquainted at last year's company Christmas party. Everything remained amicable, but Rosalind couldn't help wondering how much Eileen knew about her husband's previous love life. Maybe this was nothing but a fit of jealousy.

She took another mouthful of the tuna steak, then summoned the waiter and asked for the bill. While she waited for him to return, she picked up the half bottle of red wine and inspected the label: a twenty-thirteen Bordeaux. She had certainly tasted better. She raised her glass with the other hand and drained it.

"Was everything all right, madame?" he asked, speaking with a slight French accent as he eyed the remains of the meal on her plate.

"Yes, fine thanks," she replied, handing him her bank card. "Although the vin rouge left a little to be desired."

"Oh, I'm sorry," the man said, any trace of his alleged heritage now missing from his voice. "Would you like me to fetch the manager?"

"No, don't bother. I'm in a bit of a hurry."

She inserted her card in the reader and entered the PIN. His eyes tracked her movements as she removed a ten-pound note and placed it on the crisp, white tablecloth.

The note disappeared into his back pocket within seconds. "Thank you, madame," he said, the accent returning. "Bonsoir. Have a good evening."

Rosalind strode down Bridge Street to the car park on Castle Street. There, she climbed into the driver's seat of the white, year-old BMW three series. Ten minutes later, she rolled up in front of the squat, two-storey Ilithyia building. Lights blazed from both the ground and first-floor windows. Despite the relatively late hour—just after eight o'clock—half a dozen cars remained in the marked spaces outside. She rummaged in her bag for her access card.

She looked around as she passed through the empty reception area. It was strange to think she had invested her financial future in such an ugly structure. At the top of the stairs, she knocked on the door of Nigel Perrin's office and entered without waiting for a reply.

Perrin glanced up from behind his desk. "Thanks for coming back in, Rosalind."

She lowered herself into the chair opposite. "What's this all about?"

Perrin peered over his glasses at her, a worried frown creasing his forehead. "Eileen Floyd saw something she shouldn't have in Martin Hendrick's lab."

"What the hell was she doing in there, anyway? I thought we told him to keep the door locked while he was working on his secret project."

"Well, obviously he didn't. She also spotted some related virus research material on his screen."

Rosalind shook her head. "It never ceases to amaze me how somebody, who is so intelligent in some ways, could be so stupid in others. Has he left yet?"

Perrin turned and peered out of the window. "His car's still down there. Let me call him."

Rosalind stood and paced over the worn carpet while they waited for their errant employee to arrive. A sharp knock signalled the doctor's arrival. She pulled the door open. Hendrick failed to hide the worried expression on his face as the CEO directed him to the second chair opposite the Chief Scientist. He glanced anxiously from one to the other.

Rosalind stared down at him for a moment, then took the remaining free seat. A red spot formed on each of her cheeks. "What the hell do you think you're playing at?" she yelled.

Hendrick shrank back at the ferocity of her words.

"Well?" she continued. "I wasted an expensive meal because of this. I'd like an explanation."

The researcher swallowed, then spoke in a subdued voice, refusing to meet her gaze. "I was wearing my earphones, so I didn't hear her come in. She caught me off guard. I totally forgot about the virus samples in the fridge."

"You know she asked about the whistleblower policy?"

Hendrick raised his head sharply. "Yes, Dr Perrin mentioned that earlier. Is she planning to go ahead with a complaint?"

Rosalind ignored his question. "I hope you've hidden away anything that shouldn't be in your lab. There better not be any incriminating files on the server either."

"Um, yeah. There's nothing to find."

"If she takes this further, deny it all. Tell her she was mistaken, that it was just hazardous chemicals."

"She seemed pretty insistent to me," Perrin said in a low voice. "She made a point about knowing the difference between a hazardous material label and a biohazard one."

Rosalind's head snapped towards her partner. "I'm sure I don't need to remind you what might happen if this escalates, Nigel. They could shut this place down. We could all go to prison. At the very least, the company will be prosecuted and fined. We'd become pariahs. Nobody would even consider putting more work our way. I've put in far too much to let it fail now, and that's not to mention losing my house and every penny of the money I—make that we—have invested in this business."

Perrin removed a pen from his top pocket and started clicking the tip in and out. "I think you're forgetting that I was the one who argued against this project. We all knew the risks. Anyway, none of that matters now. The big question is what we do next."

The sound of the ballpoint was the only noise to disturb the silence. Perrin glanced down at his hand as if seeing the pen for the first time, then placed it on his desk.

"Perhaps we should go on the attack," Rosalind said after a few seconds.

"What do you mean?" Perrin asked.

"We inform her she was breaking company rules. There's something in one of our policy documents about entry to unauthorised areas. What if we put a sign up on the door to Dr Hendrick's lab? Nobody ever reads those things, so we could claim it was there all along. From what you mentioned before, she never received permission to enter. We can always get Anders to play bad cop and raise the subject of disciplinary action."

Anders Grolby had joined the company a year earlier. The blond-haired Swede led the IT team and doubled as the head of security. His background in the Swedish military had given him a unique blend of skills. Amongst his initiatives was a ban on the use of mobile phones and memory sticks inside the premises. He argued that both posed a severe risk to the protection of intellectual property, which provided a core part of the company's value.

"I'm not sure that'll work, Rosalind," Perrin said, a look of uncertainty etched on his face. "If we get all heavy-handed with her, it might push her the wrong way."

"So, you're suggesting we play nice? She shouldn't have been there in the first place. She'll probably change her tune if we threaten her with the sack."

The worry lines on Perrin's forehead deepened. "I really don't think that's the right approach."

Rosalind stood. "If all else fails, remind her she signed a non-disclosure agreement. Let me give Grolby a call and brief him."

Hendrick followed her lead. "If there's nothing else, I'll get back to my work."

Nigel Perrin sat, absent-mindedly clicking his pen.

"See you both tomorrow," Rosalind said, brightly, but she wasn't smiling.

11

Friday 14th August 2015

33 Willow Drive, Cambridge

Twenty-one years ago

Eileen Floyd arrived home shortly after eight o'clock. She had completed the tasks assigned to her but found it hard to concentrate on work after the discovery in Dr Hendrick's laboratory. She shoved all thoughts of her recently confirmed pregnancy to the back of her mind. What could he be working on? The biohazard warning labels, combined with his angry reaction when he realised what she had seen, set the alarm bells ringing inside her head. Dr Perrin's attempts to downplay her concerns were equally baffling.

She felt fairly sure of her ground but decided to check the guidance on biosafety anyway. Using her phone, she pulled up a search window and browsed through the results. Her findings confirmed her original suspicions; influenza viruses fell under the Hazard Group two classification, which meant any work should be carried out at Containment Level two or higher.

All new employees received a safety briefing during induction, but she was certain there had been no mention of working with potentially dangerous pathogens. Neither did she remember any reference to viral materials during the audits many of the company's customers demanded before placing a contract. Even if she was mistaken, what was the flask doing out on the bench and not inside a biosafety cabinet?

Dr Perrin had mentioned a whistleblower policy. She didn't want to get anybody in trouble, but if Dr Hendrick wasn't taking the correct safety precautions, she owed it to her colleagues to escalate the matter. If he was recklessly endangering his fellow employees, she had a duty to act. And it no longer just affected her; she now had another life, growing inside her, to think about.

Eileen performed a second search using the words biosafety and whistleblower. The topmost hit pointed to a page at the *hse.gov.uk* domain. She opened the link to discover an article about whistleblowers on the Health and Safety Executive website. It advised employees with a serious concern to take the issue up with a senior manager in the first instance. But hadn't she already done that?

She followed several more links. From what she read, if an employer didn't deal with the complaint to the employee's satisfaction, the recommended next stage was to contact the Advisory, Conciliation and Arbitration Service, otherwise known as ACAS. She strongly suspected the owners of the company would try to sweep her concerns under the carpet.

Daniel would know what to do. She glanced at her watch and performed a quick calculation in her head. It was still only mid-afternoon in the States. Perhaps the meeting had finished early, and he was free to give her advice.

She selected his name from the recent contacts list and pressed the dial icon. Several seconds of silence went by, then her husband's familiar voice emerged from the speaker. "Sorry, I'm not available. Leave a message."

She hesitated for a moment, unsure what to say. She needed time to organise her thoughts, and answer machines always flustered her. Should she tell him first about the pregnancy or her worries at work? *Damn.* She lowered the phone and stabbed the disconnect button.

Maybe a text was the right approach. She tapped at the screen with her thumbs.

"Please call when free. E xxx."

***

Daniel Floyd pulled back the sleeve of his jacket below the table and glanced at his watch. The purchasing director of the electronic measurement equipment distributor they were visiting droned on in his brash New York accent: something to do with volumes and profit margins. Daniel turned off; this was the domain of his colleague, Trevor Taylor, who had joined him on this trip to cover the sales side.

"That's great, Trev," the large American sitting opposite said, eventually. "Let's do this deal. If you can update those figures, I'll send the order through tomorrow."

Daniel breathed a silent sigh of relief. *Finally.* It had taken an entire morning discussing the technical details and most of the afternoon on the commercial side, but at last, they had reached an agreement. The long hours on the plane in economy class might be worth it after all.

The four men in the spacious boardroom stood. Trevor rounded the expanse of polished wood and grasped his new customer's hand. "Thanks, Randy. I look forward to receiving your business."

Daniel stifled a smirk. He could never understand why anybody given the name Randolph would abbreviate it to Randy. Perhaps the word didn't have the same connotations on the other side of the pond. Moments later, he found his own fingers crushed by the American's meaty paw. As if that wasn't punishment enough, he received a hearty slap on the back from the man. "I want you technical guys to keep talking to each other, Dan."

"Sure thing," he replied in an American accent, suddenly worried that the new clients might think he was parodying their way of speaking. Randy didn't seem to notice as he turned to Trevor and resumed an enthusiastic conversation.

The fourth meeting attendee and the more subdued of the two customers came up and also shook hands. Mike Peters headed up their technical sales support team. Daniel found himself liking his opposite number. They had established a good rapport over the phone, but this was the first opportunity to meet in person.

"Great to finally get together," Mike said. "You should come for longer next time. We could see a few of the sights. It's quite a city."

"I might just do that," Daniel replied with a smile. "I'm sure we'll be seeing plenty more of each other if this deal is as successful as we both hope. Let me know if you're visiting the UK anytime, and I'll show you around Cambridge. London's less than sixty minutes away by train too."

"Thanks. What time's your flight?"

"Seven fifty."

Mike consulted his watch. "You probably need to get moving. You've got over two-and-a-half hours before take-off, but traffic is hell during rush hour. What time do you land?"

"That's easy. Exactly twelve hours later."

"A real red eye then."

Daniel laughed. "You're right. Travelling cattle class doesn't help either. I better go and drag Trevor away."

***

Mike Peters hadn't been lying about the trip to the airport. After a journey that combined long stretches of sitting stationary in traffic with an adrenaline-filled dash at the mercy of a lunatic cab driver, Daniel and Trevor Taylor arrived at JFK with seventy minutes to spare before take-off.

They rushed through passport control and reached the gate just as boarding started. Finally, they sank into their cramped seats near the back of the plane, a quarter of an hour ahead of the scheduled departure time.

Daniel pulled his mobile phone from his jacket pocket and remembered he had set it to silent to avoid being disturbed during the meeting. Half a dozen emails, two missed calls and a text message awaited him. He started with the calls, checking the caller ID: both from Eileen. The message also originated from his wife. "Please call when free."

He did a quick calculation. The UK was five hours ahead, making it close to one o'clock in the morning. Would she really want him to wake her? She had called him twice, so he reasoned she probably wouldn't mind being woken in the middle of the night. He selected the contacts and was about to click the call button when the stewardess came down the aisle, checking that everybody had fastened their seatbelts and placed their seats in the upright position. The embossed name tag identified her as Barbara.

Her gaze landed on the phone in his hand. "Excuse me, sir," she said, speaking in a clipped British accent. "I'm afraid passengers need to turn off all electronic devices for take-off."

Daniel hesitated for a second. Five minutes still remained before departure. He was about to ask whether he could make a quick call, but the stern expression staring back at him signalled it would be a pointless request.

He pulled down the settings menu and set the phone to flight mode. "Okay, Barbara."

She flashed a false smile in return and waited until he returned the device to his pocket before continuing her journey down the aisle.

Daniel turned sideways in his seat to Trevor, but his colleague already had his earphones in with his eyes glued to the video on his laptop screen.

12

Friday 14th August 2015

33 Willow Drive, Cambridge

Twenty-one years ago

The harsh jangling of the alarm clock jolted Eileen from a deep sleep. Reaching out a hand, she slapped the mute button. She lifted her wrist and checked the time on her watch through bleary eyes: six-thirty.

She had lain awake most of the night, only drifting off around four in the morning. A pounding headache throbbed at the base of her skull. Her body felt like she had spent the previous evening drinking heavily, but not a single drop of alcohol had passed her lips.

She threw back the covers and lowered her feet to the carpet. A wave of nausea washed over her. *It couldn't be morning sickness already, could it?* She sat with her face in her hands for several seconds, waiting for the sensation to pass. A sudden thought penetrated her sluggish brain; had Daniel tried to call?

She staggered upright and crossed to where her mobile lay on the dresser, connected to the mains charger through a coiled black wire. She pulled the cable free and unlocked the screen: two junk emails but no missed calls or texts and nothing from her husband.

Cursing silently, she tossed the phone on the bed and padded to the en suite bathroom. After standing under the jet of hot water for over ten minutes, she felt vaguely human again. She brushed her teeth, then returned to the bedroom.

What time had Daniel told her the plane was landing? She wracked her brains: around eight o'clock if she remembered correctly. It would be at least another half hour before he cleared passport control, but she planned to be at work long before then. She would leave the building during a coffee break and call him from the car park—unless he called her first on the office line.

She hurried down a breakfast of tea and toast and was on the road before seven-fifteen. At this time of the morning, the drive would be much quicker than her usual forty-minute commute. She rolled into a parking space twenty minutes later, remembering little about the journey. A final check of her phone confirmed no recent messages before she locked it in the glovebox.

Despite the early hour, she wasn't the first to arrive, judging by the three cars parked near the entrance. The two-year-old blue Toyota Prius belonged to Nigel Perrin. She immediately recognised the new Ford Focus with red metallic paint as Dr Hendrick's. Had he been here all night? Whatever he was working on, he was certainly putting in long hours. Her heart lurched in her chest at the prospect of jeopardising his career if she decided to proceed with her complaint.

The last car, a battered white Saab 93, took longer to identify. She glanced inside as she passed and spotted a paperback on the passenger seat. The cover depicted an armed man holding a machine gun. The title, in a foreign language, contained several accented letters. Of course; the vehicle had to belong to Anders Grolby.

She recalled hearing about the man's background in the Swedish military. He was perfectly friendly around the other employees, but something about him made her uncomfortable in his presence. She had tried to place the cause of her uneasiness but failed. The closest she came was a sense that he was weighing her up as a potential opponent.

She raised her identity card to the reader and pushed through the front door into the building. She headed past the empty reception desk and down the corridor towards her workplace. Her footsteps slowed as she approached Dr Hendrick's laboratory. Unconsciously, she inhaled deeply and held her breath as she drew nearer the doorway. A piece of white paper covered the small window, preventing a view of the interior. Beneath it, a laminated notice in inch-high letters read, *No Unauthorised Entry*.

Neither had been there yesterday. Their presence sent a shiver of apprehension deep within her core. She quickened her pace and shoved through the door into the area she shared with her two colleagues. On any other day, she would have brewed herself a cup of tea before settling down at her workstation, but her mind was on other things.

Her boss, Alan Hastings, had spent most of the previous night watching over her shoulder as she corrected the graphs, making it impossible to study the whistleblower policy. She navigated the network to the company folder and pulled up the document on her PC screen. On the first pass, she scrolled down quickly, skimming through just the headings: *Introduction*, *Scope*, *Safeguards* and *Procedures for Making a Disclosure*. Two pages in total.

She started again at the top. Ten minutes later, she had digested the contents. The process obligated the company to treat any complaint in a sensitive and confidential manner. It made the directors responsible for investigating any grievance unless they were the target of the allegation, in which case they would nominate a senior manager as the investigative officer. In the final stage, the assigned investigator was required to acknowledge the issue in writing and keep the complainant apprised of any progress.

Eileen closed the file and leant back in her chair. The new notice outside Dr Hendrick's laboratory implied that somebody must have already discussed the issue with him. That meant confidentiality was now a moot point. The Belgian researcher would have little doubt as to the identity of the whistleblower if she chose to go ahead.

She cursed her stupidity. Why hadn't she waited to discuss the matter with Daniel before raising it with Dr Perrin? Her husband would know what to do.

She checked her watch: still five minutes until the plane's scheduled landing time.

***

Seventy miles away, a British Airways Boeing 747 completed the long flight from New York as its wheels touched down on the northernmost runway at Heathrow Airport.

The captain's voice came across the tannoy. "Would all passengers please remain seated until the aeroplane reaches the gate and the seatbelt signs are extinguished."

Despite the instructions, frantic movement broke out around Daniel Floyd. Unlike many of his fellow flyers, he remained in his seat. A wave of exhaustion swept over him. The man sitting in the row behind had sneezed and coughed throughout the flight, not only spreading his germs throughout the cabin but also ensuring nobody in his vicinity got any sleep.

Daniel removed the phone from the top pocket of his creased white shirt. After unlocking the screen, he navigated to the settings menu and cancelled flight mode. Almost immediately, his mobile added to the hubbub, pinging as a flurry of emails arrived in the inbox. He brought up his contacts and selected Eileen's name from the list. The ringing tone repeated eight times, then his wife's voice spoke in his ear. "Sorry, I'm not available now, but if you leave a message, I'll try to get back to you as soon as I can."

Daniel waited for the beep. "I've just landed. You're not still in bed, are you? I'll ring again later."

Next, he selected the text message icon and tapped in a few words. "Arrived in the UK. Will call when through customs."

He put the mobile away and sat patiently as the stewardesses urged the passengers to remain seated. After what seemed an age, the plane eventually stopped moving, and the seatbelt lights turned off with an accompanying ping.

Daniel watched his fellow travellers leap back to their feet and haul their cases out of the overhead lockers as if their lives depended upon it. "Cabin crew, doors to manual," came the captain's voice over the tannoy.

Five minutes later, a mechanical whirring sound set off a fresh frenzy of movement as the occupants of the plane packed closer together to get nearer to the exits. When the crowd began to disembark, he collected his overnight case from the locker above and followed them down the aisle. His colleague, Trevor, had already departed in the first crush after a hurried farewell. The stewardess named Barbara waited by the rear door.

"Goodbye," he said.

She flashed an insincere smile at him. "Thanks for flying British Airways. Have a safe onward journey."

It took another fifty minutes before he had cleared customs and stood on the pavement, waiting for the airport shuttle bus to arrive. As he stared along the road, the familiar notes of his ring tone emerged from his shirt pocket. Caller ID told him the call originated from Eileen's work number.

He tapped the green answer icon. "Hello, gorgeous. Have you missed me?"

"Thank God, you're back." Her voice sounded breathless. "Where are you?"

"I'm at the bus stop for the car park. Ah, here it comes now."

"How long will it be until you get home?"

Daniel consulted his watch. "I don't know. It's rush hour, so probably anything between two and three hours. Why?"

"There's something I need to discuss with you. I'll tell them I'm feeling unwell. Hang on."

A bang in the background. She stopped speaking. The faint sound of a man talking came down the line. Eileen's reply was also severely attenuated, but he picked out the word "see".

"I'll be back around eleven—"

A click cut off his wife's voice.

He lowered the mobile and checked the signal strength: three bars. His fingers tapped the screen as he selected the recent contacts option and returned the call. The phone rang six times before an automated female recording took over. "You have reached the number of..." A pause, then a man spoke. "Alan Hastings." Another brief delay followed by the computerised voice. "Please leave a message after the beep. To re-record your message, press the hash key."

The bus door remained open. "Are you getting on, mate?" the driver called.

Daniel returned the phone to his pocket and climbed the steps. If it was important, she'd call him back. But when he slumped into a free seat, he couldn't put the sense of uneasiness out of his mind.

13

Friday 14th August 2015

Ilithyia Biotechnology, Cambridge Science Park

Twenty-one years ago

Anders Grolby logged into the administrator account and pulled up the activity history from Eileen Floyd's workstation. His actions fell into a grey area; the standard contract of employment at Ilithyia contained a clause which gave the company the right to monitor computer usage but tracking an employee's access to network files probably crossed the line between reasonable and excessive behaviour.

If circumstances dictated, he could also activate the keylogging software installed on all the company's computers, but the current situation didn't yet warrant that level of intrusion. Not even the senior management knew about this capability. In addition, there was no mention in the terms of employment, making it illegal.

Dr Perrin had warned him she was considering invoking the whistleblower policy. He had been half tempted to remove the file from the server but decided that doing so would probably have a detrimental effect and only raise her level of suspicion. A brief inspection of the log from her computer confirmed she had opened the document.

Next, he downloaded her internet browsing history. Her mobile phone and desktop machine both used the Chrome browser, and she had set the options to synchronise data. A quick check informed him she had recently viewed several pages related to whistleblowing and consulted the Health and Safety Executive site.

It seemed she was intent on going ahead with a complaint. Dr Perrin had explained the possible repercussions. In the worst case, the company could be closed down. Alternatively, the authorities might issue a fine, resulting in the loss of most of their customers. If that happened, the inevitable closure of the business would follow shortly afterwards.

Grolby needed this job. Opportunities for an ex-soldier with a dishonourable discharge from the Swedish army were few and far between. There had been insufficient proof to convict him of murdering the Iraqi family of four—not that they didn't deserve it—but he had stayed out of prison only due to the skill of his lawyer.

While on tour in Iraq, Grolby's unit had come under attack during a routine patrol. During the battle, he recognised one of the attackers, a local shopkeeper, who it turned out doubled as an insurgent outside business hours. The army arrested him at his shop the next morning but released him after several days of intense questioning, believing it to be a case of mistaken identity. After all, didn't the locals all look the same?

But Grolby possessed a knack for remembering faces and knew what he had seen. A few days later, he followed the man home and gunned down the entire family, including the wife and two teenage sons. No eyewitnesses to the slaughter came forward, but several neighbours reported seeing a tall, blond Westerner fleeing the scene. At the court-martial, Grolby's alibi had been exposed as a lie, but the defence lawyer successfully argued there was insufficient evidence to return a conviction.

Fortunately, the directors at Ilithyia had been satisfied with his recently gained IT qualifications and omitted to request references from the Swedish military, thereby failing to uncover his chequered past. But the chances were slim his luck would hold for a second time if the closure of the company forced him to seek new employment. Anything that threatened the future of Ilithyia Biotechnology was also a threat to Anders Grolby—and that included Eileen Floyd.

If his army career had taught him one important lesson, it was to take the fight to the enemy. Rather than sitting back and waiting for an attack, the better approach was to go on the offensive and strike aggressively. And that's what he intended to do.

He logged off his machine and moved to the window to check the car park. *Good. Only four cars present.* He descended the stairs leading to the ground floor laboratories at a jog and strode along the corridor to the door at the end.

As he entered the room, she sat with her back to him with the telephone to her ear. She spun around in her seat. "Hang on," she said, raising a finger.

"Mrs Floyd, there's a serious matter we need to discuss," Grolby said.

She tried to mask the consternation on her face. She placed her left hand over the mouthpiece. "Can't you see I'm on the phone?"

She carried on speaking to the person on the line. "I'll be back around eleven—"

He crossed the floor in two strides and pressed the button to end the call. "This is more important. Who were you calling?

Her mouth dropped open in shock for a moment before she regained control of her facial features. "Uh... my husband. Anyway, what's that got to do with you?" She rose from her chair and glared at him. The ex-soldier stepped half a pace closer, towering over her.

"A disciplinary issue has come up," Grolby said. "We should go somewhere more private. Please follow me."

The first sign of fear flickered in her eyes.

The head of security returned to the door and marched down the corridor without checking to see whether she was following. The sound of hurried footsteps trailed after him. He smiled inwardly. *Good. Keep her off balance.*

He proceeded up the steps and into the boardroom. Six chairs lined the opposite sides of the long table. A projector hung from the ceiling, aimed at the large screen affixed to the end wall. A variety of framed certificates broke up the monotonous pattern of the striped wallpaper.

Grolby waited in the open doorway and gestured to a chair where she would have her back to the only door. She stood uncertainly for a moment but followed his lead when he lowered himself into the seat on the other side.

"What's all this about?" Eileen asked, unable to hide the quiver from her voice.

"Are you aware of the company's health and safety policy?"

"Um... well, I know it exists, and I have a rough idea of the contents."

Grolby clasped his hands together and leant forwards. "Yesterday, you committed a serious breach of that policy by entering an area you weren't authorised to go into."

"This is about Martin Hendrick's lab, isn't it? A better question might be why he's working on an influenza virus when we aren't set up to deal with materials of that kind."

"What takes place in Dr Hendrick's laboratory is highly confidential, and you had no business going in there without prior authorisation."

Eileen folded her arms. "Really? Firstly, I was told to go there. My manager, Alan Hastings, suggested I ask Dr Hendrick whether we could use the fridge in his lab. Secondly, there was no notice on his door yesterday. Somebody must have put that up last night after I talked to Dr Perrin about what I'd seen. I asked him about the whistleblower policy, which *you* should be familiar with. There's a clear statement in there that all complaints should be handled confidentially. But the new sign and your presence here suggests that isn't the case, is it?"

Grolby leant across the table. "I am well aware of the whistleblower policy, and it clearly states that the complaint must be submitted in writing. To the best of my knowledge, you haven't actually done that, have you? And if that's true, the confidentiality clause is irrelevant, don't you think? When I came in, if I'm not mistaken, you were engaged on a personal call. Need I also point out that discussing company business with another person contravenes the terms of your employment contract."

Eileen's eyes blazed with fury. "I was trying to talk to my husband who's been away with his work until this morning, but I didn't get the chance to say anything much before you so rudely ended the call."

Grolby's voice took on a conciliatory tone. "Look. I don't want to go to all the trouble of instigating disciplinary proceedings, and I guess you'd rather not have the stress of going through that either."

"What are you saying?" she asked, barely above a whisper.

"If you drop the whistleblower complaint, we'll forget the other thing."

Eileen pushed the chair back and jumped to her feet. She slapped the table with her palm. Her face flushed with anger. “I’m not the one in the wrong here. Do you think you can intimidate me? Dr Hendrick is performing dangerous research without adequate safety precautions. If the people at this company aren’t prepared to take my complaint seriously, then you leave me no option but to discuss my concerns with somebody else.”

14

Friday 14th August 2015

Ilithyia Biotechnology, Cambridge Science Park

Twenty-one years ago

Nigel Perrin sat at his desk, the pen clicking furiously in his hand. Anders Grolby occupied the seat opposite.

"I'm sorry," the Swede said. "I may have misread the situation."

"Where is she now?"

"She's still in the boardroom. I don't think we can change her mind. If anything, she seems more adamant than before. Perhaps you should try to talk to her again."

"What am I going to say? Yeah, you caught us doing something we shouldn't?"

Grolby grimaced. "Apologise and tell her you had no knowledge of what Dr Hendrick was working on. Let her know you plan to start disciplinary proceedings against him."

Perrin gave an exasperated shake of the head. "We can't afford to lose him. He's vital to at least two different projects. Damn. I should never have allowed Rosalind to talk me into this."

Grolby splayed his fingers on the desk. "You don't have to fire him. Tell Mrs Floyd you issued him with a final warning. She has no right to see his records. How many people know about this work on the flu virus?"

"Only Rosalind and me. And whomever Eileen has talked to. Why do you ask?"

"Just an idea. Anyway, I'm fairly sure she hasn't discussed the matter with anybody else. From what she told me, her husband has been away on business and only landed a few minutes ago. They were on the phone together when I went into her lab."

"Okay," Perrin said. "Maybe I'll have another chat with her. See if I can salvage the situation."

"Do you want me to come in with you?"

The doctor bit his lip, mired in a moment of indecision. "Yeah, why not?" he replied eventually, returning the pen to his pocket. The two men rose from their chairs and headed down the corridor.

Perrin pushed open the door to the boardroom and entered first. Eileen Floyd paced backwards and forwards at the far end of the room. She whipped around to the new arrivals.

"Good morning, Eileen," Perrin said, lowering himself into a seat. Grolby dropped into the chair beside him.

Eileen took up a position on the opposite side of the table to the men but remained standing. She shot back an angry reply. "Is it?"

Not a great start. This was clearly going to be a difficult sell. "Look, I'm sorry if you don't think we're taking your concerns seriously."

"I came to see you yesterday evening to discuss a serious matter in confidence. It's obvious you relayed our conversation to Dr Hendrick because I arrived at work this morning to discover new signs outside his lab. And then he..." She jabbed a finger towards the Swedish ex-soldier. "... threatens me with disciplinary action for entering an unauthorised area. You're treating me like I'm the one in the wrong when in fact you should be investigating Dr Hendrick."

Perrin forced a reassuring smile onto his face. "You're absolutely right, Eileen. I had a long conversation with Dr Hendrick last night. I wasn't aware he was doing research with a flu virus, but he assures me it's perfectly safe. He's an experienced researcher, and he would never consciously do anything to endanger his colleagues or anybody else for that matter."

Eileen raised her eyebrows, incredulous. "You're telling me you don't know what your own employees are working on? I find that hard to believe. Aren't you supposed to be the Chief Scientist here? Dr Hendrick's reaction when he realised what I'd seen only confirmed that my concerns are valid. And what about the threat to discipline me for not following our health and safety guidelines? You've admitted the signs weren't even there yesterday."

Perrin nodded sympathetically. "It was a mistake to mention disciplinary action. Mr Grolby wasn't aware the notice was only recently put up. I can assure you we'll take any complaint seriously. In fact, after our discussion and my chat with Dr Hendrick, I've started an internal investigation."

Eileen leant forwards and placed her hands on the table. "Why should I believe you? I reckon you already knew about Dr Hendrick's work. And as for you." She glowered at Grolby. "I don't appreciate your attempts to intimidate me. And I certainly don't respond well to threats."

The Swede stared at her, stony-faced.

"So, where do we go from here?" Perrin asked.

Eileen sat and folded her arms. She opened her mouth to speak, then closed it again.

"Look, tensions are a little high at the moment," the doctor said. "We don't want anybody to say something they'll regret later. I suggest we all take some time to calm down. I'd just like you to consider that your actions could have severe repercussions for the future of this company and its employees. We're already on a financial precipice, and it wouldn't require much to push it over the edge."

Eileen's fierce gaze bored into him. "What? Now you're applying the emotional blackmail as well to keep me quiet?"

Grolby stood. "Dr Perrin, may I have a word outside?" he asked.

The Chief Scientist followed the head of security into the corridor, pulling the door closed behind him. "What is it, Anders?" he whispered.

"She's not going to back down. You shouldn't have pushed her at the end."

"Christ, what a mess," Perrin said. "What should we do?"

"That depends upon how badly you want this problem to go away."

The doctor regarded him hopefully. "What do you have in mind?"

Grolby explained the outline of his plan.

When he had finished, Perrin stared back at the door of the boardroom in horror. "You've got to be joking."

Grolby's eyes glittered with venom. "Believe me. This is not something I would joke about."

"But... but you can't expect me to make a decision like that."

"In that case I suggest you either kiss goodbye to this company or call somebody who can give the go ahead."

"I'll need to speak to Mrs Baxter," an ashen-faced Nigel Perrin replied. "There has to be another way."

"Well, you better hurry. There isn't much time. The office will soon start filling up. Actually, may I make a suggestion? Do we have any chemicals in stores that would keep people out of the building?"

"What do you mean?"

"Perhaps something that smells bad and would deter them from coming in."

"Oh... I see. Ammonium hydroxide is very unpleasant."

"Good," Grolby said. "Get a bottle and drop it as close to reception as you can. Pretend it was an accident. Dr Hendrick's here, isn't he? Put him in charge of keeping everybody outside while we organise the clean-up. Tell the employees to go home for the day."

"I'm not sure—"

"Time is running out, Dr Perrin. Soon, we'll be out of options."

"Um... right." Perrin hurried down the stairs and headed to the chemicals storeroom, situated in a secured area off the corridor on the ground floor.

Despite the relatively cool temperature, beads of sweat rolled down his forehead. His mind roiled in turmoil.

This is a total nightmare. What I have got myself involved in?

15

Friday 14th August 2015

Ilithyia Biotechnology, Cambridge Science Park

Twenty-one years ago

Rosalind opened the car door and stared at the small group of workers standing outside Ilithyia Biotechnology. She clicked the button on the key fob and marched towards the entrance. Dr Hendrick stood with his back to the doors, explaining something to the gathering. *What the hell is going on?*

Hendrick's expression brightened at her approach. "Ah, Mrs Baxter. I was just saying there's been an ammonium hydroxide spillage, and it isn't safe to enter. Dr Perrin asked me to close the building and tell everybody to go home."

Rosalind glowered at the researcher. "Where is he?"

"Upstairs. He told me to let you in. He wants to see you as soon as possible."

She turned around. "You heard the man. We can't allow any of you inside until we get this sorted. We'll let you know when it's safe to come in. Watch your email."

"We won't have to book it as holiday, will we?" a woman asked. Laura Brewer. She worked in accounts.

"No, of course not," Rosalind snapped. She waited until the group dispersed and she and Hendrick were alone. "Lock the doors and put a sign up. You better add something for any deliveries that arrive. Get the drivers to call reception. Now, what happened?"

"Dr Perrin dropped a bottle of ammonium hydroxide in the corridor outside my lab. We've shut the door into the reception area to contain the smell, but I'm not sure what good it's doing."

"Damn. We could do without losing another day with all these bloody deadlines looming. Has anyone been brought in for the clean-up?"

"Ah... I don't know. I've been standing here since the accident."

"Okay. Put the notice up and for Christ's sake open all the windows. Then you can go home too."

Hendrick's face creased in worry. "We've already opened the windows, but I'd still hold my breath in there if I were you. It's pretty unpleasant."

Rosalind applied her card to the reader, then inhaled deeply and pushed inside. Despite the precaution, the harsh stench, reminiscent of decaying fish, still invaded her senses. She hurried up the stairs and barged through the door at the top before exhaling. Even here, the pungent reek permeated the air.

The agitated figure of Dr Perrin waited in the corridor. He spun around at her arrival. He greeted her with an anxious frown.

"Christ, Nigel. What the hell have you done?" she asked.

"We need to talk—urgently."

She followed in silence as he led her to his office. He dropped into his chair and covered his face with his hands.

Rosalind closed the door behind her and sat on the opposite side of the desk. "I hope you're about to explain what's going on."

Perrin glanced up with haunted eyes. "It was Anders's idea. We needed to clear the building."

"Whoa, slow down. Are you saying the spillage wasn't an accident?"

"She's sitting in the boardroom. I don't know what to do."

"Who's—? Oh, this is about Eileen Floyd, isn't it? You better start at the beginning."

Perrin met her gaze for a second, then looked away. His hands shook as he placed them on the wooden surface. He seemed to notice the trembling and lowered them to his thighs. It was a measure of his distress that the pen remained in his pocket.

"Anders had a talk to her this morning, but she took it the wrong way. I wasn't there, but it sounds like he tried to threaten her. He told her she'd breached our health and safety policy by entering Hendrick's lab without permission. Then he said he'd forget all about it if she dropped the complaint against Dr Hendrick. Needless to say, she didn't respond well."

"Go on."

"I went in and apologised to her. She accused me of breaking her trust by talking to Martin about her concerns. I tried to reassure her by telling her he wouldn't do anything to jeopardise the safety of his fellow employees, but she didn't believe me. I may've mentioned that she could bring the company down if she decided to go public with her accusation. She responded badly to that too, told me it was emotional blackmail."

"Right," Rosalind said. "None of this sounds good."

"It gets worse." A shiver ran through Perrin's body. For a moment, it seemed he was about to burst into tears. "Anders offered to make the problem go away."

A frisson of dread rippled down Rosalind's spine. She had a strong premonition this was the key factor that had her partner so rattled. "And how did he propose to do that?"

"He said he could arrange for her to disappear."

The two partners in Ilithyia Biotechnology stared at each other in silence for several seconds.

Rosalind lowered her voice when she spoke. "Disappear? How?"

"He didn't say, but that's when he told me to drop the ammonium hydroxide to keep people out of the building."

"Where are Anders and Floyd now?"

"He's still with her in the boardroom."

Rosalind stood. "I better try to sort this out."

"Would you like me to join you?" Perrin asked. The pleading look in his eyes gave away his preferred response.

"No, I can manage by myself."

Perrin's body sagged with relief. "Okay. I'll be in here if you need me."

"If you want to be useful, you could start by finding somebody to clear up the spillage. And send a message to all staff telling them not to come in."

"Leave it with me," he replied enthusiastically. "I'll get right on it."

Rosalind stepped into the corridor. The stench hit her again. No doubt the building would reek for weeks afterwards. *Why did that bloody idiot Hendrick not keep his laboratory locked? And what the hell was Grolby proposing?*

She pushed into the boardroom. The Swedish ex-soldier stood by the large projector screen, leaning against the wall. Eileen Floyd paced anxiously at the far end.

"Can you give us a minute, Anders?" Rosalind asked. She waited for the door to close behind him before continuing. "I have to apologise," she said. "Mr Grolby likes to follow rules. I guess it's his army background."

"He wouldn't let me out of this room," Eileen replied, folding her arms.

"Yes, I'm afraid there's been a spillage as you can probably tell from the smell of ammonia."

"But you still came into the building. If you're allowed to come in, why can't I leave?"

Rosalind pointed to a chair. "Why don't you sit down? I wanted to have a chat, just between the two of us. This whole thing has been handled very badly, and I want to stop it blowing up out of all proportion. What can I do to resolve the situation?"

Eileen reluctantly sat. "I think it's too late for that. Dr Perrin seems more concerned with protecting Dr Hendrick than he does about taking me seriously. I mean he had a flask containing an influenza virus just sitting there on his bench. You know as well as I do that we're not set up for that kind of work. But when I told Dr Perrin what I'd seen, he went straight to Dr Hendrick and discussed it with him. When I came in this morning, there were signs outside his lab, and that arsehole Grolby threatened me with disciplinary action for entering an unauthorised area."

Rosalind offered a sympathetic smile. "That was all a mistake, and I can only apologise again. You have my word; we'll investigate Dr Hendrick's activities. The safety of the workforce is our primary concern."

Eileen shook her head. "I'm sorry, but I just don't believe you. Dr Perrin brought up the financial security of the company. If it comes to a choice between doing what's safe and preserving the company's future, well... I have no faith you'll do the right thing. And I have to consider others as well as myself now."

Rosalind maintained a calm exterior, but her pulse rushed in her ears. To which others was she referring? "It's a shame you feel that way. If I may ask, what do you propose to do next?"

Eileen lowered her eyes to the table for a moment, then looked up to meet Rosalind's gaze. "I don't see any option but to raise my concerns outside the company. Both you and Dr Perrin are too involved to be objective. It's not something I want to do, but it seems to me you've left me with little choice but to escalate the matter."

Rosalind stared at her employee as a flurry of conflicting thoughts tumbled through her head. "What if we were to offer you a substantial pay rise? You're on what? Forty-five thousand a year? What if we raised it to sixty? That's more than generous."

Eileen sat back. "You've tried threats and emotional blackmail, so now I get the bribery angle."

The blood drained from Rosalind's face, pooling in a pink spot on each cheek. Her voice trembled with suppressed fury as she spoke. "I've made every attempt to be reasonable, but it seems you're intent on this foolish course of action. Have it your way. We'll begin an immediate internal investigation into your flagrant disregard of the company's health and safety policy. Until we reach a conclusion, you'll be suspended on full pay. I'll arrange for a formal letter of suspension to be sent today."

"Then we have nothing more to say to each other," Eileen said, rising to her feet.

"And may I also remind you about the strict non-disclosure agreement you signed when you joined this company. If you discuss anything you have seen while working here with an outside entity, you will be in breach of that contract. Let me assure you, we treat such matters with the utmost gravity and won't be shy about using the courts to protect the company's interests."

"Can I go now?"

Rosalind stood. "You better remain here until I check whether it's safe for you to leave."

16

Friday 14th August 2015

Ilithyia Biotechnology, Cambridge Science Park

Twenty-one years ago

Nigel Perrin rushed up to Rosalind as soon as she emerged from the boardroom. "Did you manage to convince her to drop this thing?"

"No," she said, "quite the opposite, in fact. I told her she's suspended while we investigate her breach of the health and safety policy."

"But I thought you were going to—"

"She made her decision. I tried to be reasonable, but she wouldn't change her mind. So, now she'll have to suffer the consequences."

Perrin's gaze left Rosalind's face and drifted to Anders Grolby, who stood by the door to the stairs, just out of earshot. "What do you mean?"

"Okay. Let me explain. The legal aspects of her case don't worry me in the slightest."

His eyes snapped back. "I don't understand."

"If she takes it to an industrial tribunal or the Health and Safety Executive, it'll look like sour grapes. We instigate disciplinary proceedings against her, so she retaliates with a claim of unsafe practice. There's no documentary evidence of her complaint, so she has no proof whatsoever. It's her word against ours."

Rosalind paused for a moment, then continued. "But what does give me serious cause for concern is the potential damage to our reputation. We need to win new contracts to survive. If there's the slightest whiff of a scandal, our customers will run a mile. She'd lose if she brought a case against us, and we could also sue her for damages, but by then it would be too late."

Perrin frowned in puzzlement. Why was his partner so calm when everything they had worked so hard for rested on the edge of a precipice? "Why can't we just pay her off?" he asked.

"I tried that approach. I offered her a substantial salary rise, but she threw it back in my face and accused me of bribery. Even if she were to drop her complaint now, there's a risk she might use any documented financial incentive we offer her as proof we have something to cover up."

"So, what happens next?"

"I plan to talk to Anders about his thoughts on the matter."

A cold flood of terror swept over Perrin. "You can't seriously..."

"I don't have the details of what he's proposing yet, so the first step is to ask him."

Perrin's eyes followed her as she approached Grolby, who waited impassively, blocking the only way out. The doctor watched on while they spoke for several minutes, their voices low enough not to be heard. Then the Swede turned away, opened the door and trotted down the stairs, an arm over his mouth to fend off the vile stench. Meanwhile, Rosalind retraced her steps.

Perrin thrust his hands deep into his trouser pockets to stop them shaking. "What did he say?" he asked.

"He's going to deal with it."

"What? How?"

"It's probably best you don't know."

"Christ, Rosalind. You can't be serious. You're not really... Just let her go. We've survived worse situations in the past."

"No, Nigel. She's brought this on herself. Did you arrange for somebody to clean up the mess downstairs?"

Perrin stared at her for a second. "Yes," he replied weakly. "I found a company that specialises in chemical spillages. They told me they'd be here around ten o'clock. And I sent an all-staff email telling them not to come in today." He swayed on his feet, his face deathly pale. "Actually, I think I'm going to be sick."

He turned and bolted for the entrance to the toilets. There, he barged into a cubicle and emptied his stomach into the white porcelain bowl. After tearing off a few sheets of toilet paper to wipe his mouth, he staggered to the sinks and inspected his reflection in the mirror. He had joined the medical profession to save lives. Was the face of a murderer staring back at him?

Out of habit, he rinsed his hands under the cold tap, dried them under the hot air dryer and stumbled to the exit. Perrin emerged into the corridor at the same moment as Grolby returned from downstairs. A second pungent smell accompanied the Swede, merging with the stench of ammonia. He held a cloth in his left hand as he shoved open the door to the boardroom. A cry followed by the sound of a brief struggle escaped from inside the room.

Perrin almost fled straight back the way he had come. Instead, he forced himself to approach Rosalind and grabbed her by the arm. "He's not..."

His partner turned to him, her complexion pale. "No, he wanted to know where we stored the chloroform we use for euthanising the laboratory animals. He told me he's just going to knock her out."

"For the love of God, Rosalind, you've got to stop him. I didn't sign up for this."

"So, you'd rather be bankrupt and in prison?"

"Prison? I haven't done anything."

"It's too late to back out now, Nigel. What would we say to her? 'Oh, sorry, we never meant to drug you. It was all a big mistake.' Somehow, I don't think she'd believe us."

"I never agreed to any of it. We could call the police. Tell them it was all Grolby's doing."

"No, Nigel. Anders assures me he can make her disappear without leaving a trail."

"So, you're happy to commit murder?"

Rosalind blinked at the question. "Of course not. But like I said, she brought this on herself."

"She's not dead yet. There's still time to call it off."

"Pull yourself together, Nigel. We're committed now."

The ringing of the telephone interrupted the conversation.

"I better answer that," Rosalind said. "It might be a delivery."

"Are you two just going to stand there arguing?" Grolby called. Neither of the business partners had noticed him emerge from the boardroom. "Perhaps one of you could help me."

Perrin took a tentative step towards the tall Swede. The terrified expression on his face signalled he'd rather be sprinting in the opposite direction. "What do you want me to do?" he croaked.

"We'll hold her in here for the moment. The police will be suspicious if they find traces of chloroform on her, so we need to leave sufficient time for it to wear off. And there are some questions I want to ask her. Have you got anything I can use to restrain her, like duct tape or something?"

"There's some Sellotape in the stationery cupboard. I'll fetch it now."

Perrin turned towards the open plan office, but Grolby shot out a hand and grabbed him by the upper arm.

"One other thing," he said. "I couldn't help overhearing your little conversation with Mrs Baxter. Just so we're absolutely clear, if either of you gets cold feet and confesses to the police, I'll let them know it was all your idea. If I go down for this, you can be sure I'll take you both with me."

17

Friday 14th August 2015

Ilithyia Biotechnology, Cambridge Science Park

Twenty-one years ago

Daniel Floyd applied the handbrake of the BMW 1 series, turned off the engine and leant back in the driver's seat with his eyes closed. A sudden bout of dizziness greyed the edges of his vision. He never slept well on aeroplanes, and the sneezing man sitting behind hadn't helped. The lack of rest, coupled with the stress of navigating rush hour traffic, had pushed him to the point where his main goal was to fall into bed for a few hours and catch up on his lost sleep.

A hint of worry nagged at the back of his brain. He had called Eileen's number twice from the shuttle bus at the airport, receiving an automated response on both calls. He knew her company prohibited the use of mobile phones on the premises, so it didn't come as a big surprise when she failed to answer. But several times in the past, when she wanted to talk during working hours, she had slipped out of the building and sat in the privacy of her car. He had sent a text message, asking her to contact him when she was free, but his phone remained silent during the entire journey home.

He had also tried her work number several times, recording a request to return his call on the third occasion. Eileen often joked with him about her manager, Alan Hastings, and his struggles to be assertive with his team, but from her description, he didn't seem the type to disregard a message.

Daniel levered himself out of the car and pulled open the rear door to retrieve his overnight case from the back seat. He dragged it up the short drive and let himself into the house. The familiar smell of Eileen's perfume lingered in the air. He dropped the bag in the hall and slumped onto the sofa in the lounge. Once again, he called her mobile and office line, receiving the same machine responses to both. *Strange.* It was now over two hours since she had broken off her call in mid-conversation.

He pulled up a browser window on his phone and performed a search for Ilithyia Biotechnology. The details appeared on the screen. He clicked the listed number to dial the company switchboard. Surely a human would still be there to answer incoming calls.

He was about to give up after six iterations of the ringing tone when a woman's voice answered brusquely. "Yes."

Great telephone manner.

"Hello. This is Daniel Floyd. I wonder if it would be possible to put me through to my wife, Eileen."

"I'm afraid she's not available at the moment. We've had a chemical spill on site, and we sent everybody home for the day."

"So, she isn't at work?"

"No, in fact I don't remember seeing her today."

"Well, she called me from her lab earlier this morning, around eight o'clock."

"I'm sorry, Dan, but I can't help you. There's nobody here."

Wait. Dan? The woman's voice suddenly sounded familiar. "That's not you, is it, Rosalind?"

"Yes, but we're very busy, trying to organise the clean-up. I haven't really got time to chat at the moment."

"Okay, it'd be good to catch up at some point. One last thing: when did this accident occur?"

"I... um. I'm not sure. Earlier this morning. Why?"

"Eileen's not home yet. I just wondered where she is."

"Oh. Well perhaps she did some shopping or went to see a friend or something."

"Possibly, but she's not answering her mobile."

"Look, I'm sorry, Dan. I don't know where your wife is. I've got to go now."

A click signalled she'd hung up. Daniel lowered the phone, a puzzled frown creasing his forehead. If Eileen wasn't at work, where was she? Perhaps she was stuck in traffic. But her car was fitted with a hands-free set. Why didn't she answer? Maybe it was turned off.

Another possibility sprang to mind; had she been injured in the spillage? No. Surely Rosalind Baxter would have let him know if that was the case. He hadn't thought about his former girlfriend for years. It came as quite a shock to bump into her at last year's company Christmas party and discover she was Eileen's overall boss. Eileen hadn't mentioned her before. She told him afterwards most of her dealings at senior management level were with the other partner, Nigel Perrin.

What if his wife had been involved in a car crash? An escalating series of wild thoughts spun through his brain. He clamped down on his panic. *No, she's fine. There has to be a logical explanation.* They'd have a good laugh about his overreaction when she arrived home.

Daniel forced the uneasiness from his mind. The exhaustion engulfing his body made it hard to think rationally. He rubbed his Adam's apple absent-mindedly at the first hints of a sore throat. A cold was the last thing he needed in his current state of fatigue. Maybe he would feel better after a short lie-down. He trudged up the stairs and along the hall to the master bedroom, then threw himself down onto the king-sized bed. He lay on top of the covers, still in his shoes and fully clothed.

Minutes later, he succumbed to the tiredness tugging at his eyelids and fell into a dreamless sleep.

18

Friday 14th August 2015

Ilithyia Biotechnology, Cambridge Science Park

Twenty-one years ago

Anders Grolby grabbed the roll of Sellotape from Nigel Perrin and re-entered the boardroom. The co-owner remained outside. The ex-soldier ran a hand over the back of his neck as he analysed the situation. *The Chief Scientist might become a liability.* He would need to maintain a careful watch on that one. The first doubts crept into his mind. Could he hold all the strands together? Perhaps he had allowed his worries about the company's future and the threat this woman posed to cloud his judgement. But it was far too late to turn back now.

She lay on her side, still wearing the white lab coat. Beneath the laboratory-wear, a dark skirt and a cream-coloured jumper were visible. One black shoe had come off in the brief struggle before she had succumbed to the chloroform-soaked cloth. A strand of hair partially obscured her face. Her chest rose and fell in slow, even breaths.

He knelt beside her, checking for anything about her person she could use as a weapon or to free herself. Now was not the time for carelessness. A quick search of her pockets turned up nothing of interest.

He pulled off a long strip of tape and bound her wrists together behind her back. He repeated the process with her feet, wrapping multiple layers around her ankles. Finally, he taped several shorter segments over her mouth, taking care to ensure she could still breathe. Despite the absence of people in the office, he couldn't risk a passerby hearing her screams if she regained consciousness before he explained the consequences to her of making any sound.

Now that his prisoner was secure, he turned his attention to other priorities. The presence of her car in a parking space outside the building would serve as a big pointer for anybody trying to find her. He would have to move it somewhere else as soon as possible.

Her black leather handbag lay on the table where she had been sitting. He opened the clasp and rummaged inside: a set of keys including one bearing the Mini logo, some loose tampons, a pen, a small pack of tissues and a fluorescent-blue packet with a pink stripe. He pocketed the car key, then grabbed the brightly coloured box: Clearblue Pregnancy Test. The seal was broken. He studied the cardboard box. A pink rectangle in the corner contained the words '5 tests' in white letters. A quick inspection of the contents confirmed only four remained.

Shit. Was she pregnant?

Grolby snapped his head up as the door opened. He let out a sigh of relief: Rosalind Baxter.

"Where's Dr Perrin?" he asked, his heart still racing in his chest.

"He's sitting in his office. I have to say he's not taking this at all well."

"Is he going to be a problem?"

"No, I don't think so. If it hasn't already sunk in, he'll soon realise he's in this as deep as we are."

"I hope so. I made the situation quite clear to him a few minutes ago."

"He won't like it, but he'll come round in the end," Rosalind said, staring down at the unconscious researcher. "Is she still alive?"

"Yeah," Grolby replied. "I think she'll be out for a while."

"I just spoke to her husband on the phone. He wanted to know where she was."

"What did you tell him?"

"I told him there was a chemical spill, and that I haven't seen her today, but he knows she was here. Apparently, she called him from her lab this morning."

"That's right," Grolby agreed. "They were talking to each other just before I brought her up here. She mentioned that he's been away on business, and his flight only landed a few hours ago. It won't be long before he comes here looking for her when she doesn't arrive home."

"So, what do we do when that happens?"

"To start with, we have to move her car. We can use the spillage as an excuse to keep him out of the building."

"There's something else you should be aware of." Rosalind slumped into a chair. "There's some past history between us. He and I were students at the same university. We even went out together for a bit until I dumped him. I hadn't seen him for years, and I didn't realise they were married until I bumped into him at last year's Christmas party."

"I don't see how that changes things."

"Maybe it doesn't. I was just making sure you knew."

"Okay. Thanks."

Rosalind's gaze slipped to the blue and pink packet in Grolby's hand. "What's that?"

"It was in her handbag," he replied, holding the small box up and showing her the label. "It only contains four strips. There should be five."

"So, she might be—"

"Yes, it's possible she's pregnant."

"Oh. That might explain her comment earlier today about considering others."

"I'll find out from her when she comes round."

"And if she is?" Rosalind's question hung in the air, unanswered.

After a long pause, Grolby spoke again. "When the police realise she's missing, they're bound to come here and ask you a lot of questions. We need something to throw them off the scent. What if we provided them with a readymade suspect?"

"I don't follow."

"I saw this true crime documentary. It stated that in around fifty per cent of female homicides, the culprit is a close relative of the victim. That means the investigating officers always take a good look at the husband. If we make him the target of their investigation, it'll focus attention away from us."

"How do you propose we do that?" Rosalind asked.

"We frame him for her murder. I assume you have syringes here to draw blood?"

"We have cupboards full of them down in the laboratories."

"Okay," Grolby said. "I want you to fetch one and take a sample from her."

"How much do you need?"

"I don't know. Enough to fill a test tube. We're running out of time. You better get on with it."

The Swedish ex-soldier watched her leave, a plan forming in his head. If everything played out how he hoped, the police would soon be looking in the wrong direction.

19

Friday 14th August 2015

33 Willow Drive, Cambridge

Twenty-one years ago

Daniel Floyd jerked awake. Bright light streamed through the open curtains. A grainy fuzziness filled his head. His throat ached from the onset of a cold, gifted him by the ill passenger sitting in the row behind on the plane. For a moment, his brain struggled to catch up with his body. He rubbed both hands across his face. As his gaze roamed over the familiar surroundings, the events of the previous twenty-four hours tumbled into place.

He lifted his wrist and studied the dial of his watch through bleary eyes: half-past one. Was it morning or night-time? He cursed his stupidity. The sunlight streaming through the window told him all he needed to know. He had only intended to close his eyes for a few moments. He performed a quick calculation in his head. Despite his unintended sleep, he had still gained less than four hours' rest.

"Eileen," he called. A distant click from the boiler was the only sound to break the silence. He repeated her name, louder this time, and listened carefully. Nothing. The house had a stillness about it that suggested he was alone.

He swung his legs off the bed and onto the bedroom carpet. He tried to stand, but a bout of wooziness drove him back to a sitting position. His head throbbed, and his sinuses felt like they were filled with cotton wool. Shuffling sideways along the mattress, he scooped up his phone from the bedside table: no calls, no messages, just three unread emails. He unlocked the screen and clicked the mail icon. The first was a memo from the human resources team at his workplace; the other two were clearly spam.

Where the hell was Eileen? Why hadn't she contacted him? Hadn't she seen his missed calls and texts? He pulled up the contacts and selected her name. Several seconds of silence passed without a ringing tone, then his wife's familiar voice asked him to leave a message. That had to mean she had either turned off her phone or there was no signal.

"Uh, Eileen," he said, "I don't know where you are. I heard there was an accident at your work, some sort of chemical spillage. They told me everybody's been sent home. I'm really worried. Call me when you receive this."

Maybe she was downstairs or in the garden. He pushed himself upright a second time. He swayed a little but soon recovered his balance. Running one hand along the wall to support himself, he shuffled across to the window. A quick glance down to the short drive confirmed the absence of her car. He descended the stairs and checked all the rooms. No signs of his wife.

Perhaps she had broken down, but that didn't explain why she wasn't answering her phone. An accident then? Once again, his mind ran wild, considering all the mishaps that might have befallen her.

Eileen often teased him about the way he always feared the worst outcome in any situation. Three months earlier, he had received a terse email from his boss, requesting a meeting the following morning. Despite Eileen's reassurances, he didn't sleep at all that night, convinced he was about to receive a redundancy notice. It turned out his worries were groundless; his manager had in fact offered him a promotion and a pay rise.

He forced himself to calm down. There was probably a rational explanation, but he couldn't just sit at home and wait. He had to do something. He started by redialling the switchboard at Ilithyia Biotechnology. The ringing tone sounded eight times before an automated response told him his call was important and requested that he leave a message. He hung up without speaking.

Who could he phone to check whether she had been involved in a road accident? Addenbrooke's Hospital provided the only emergency department in the city. He looked up the number and dialled.

After navigating several multiple-choice options, he eventually selected one that led to a human operator.

"Good morning," a cheery female voice greeted him. "Addenbrooke's Hospital. How may I help you?"

Daniel hesitated. He hadn't thought through what he planned to say.

"Hello," the woman said, her tone becoming more impatient.

"Ah, yes. I'm worried about my wife. I wondered if perhaps she might have been transferred to—"

"If you could provide me with a name, sir, I can check the system."

"Floyd. Eileen Floyd."

The rapid tapping of keys came down the line. The receptionist asked him to confirm the spelling of his wife's surname. Another tap.

"I'm sorry, sir. There's no patient with that name in our care at the moment."

A faint click, followed by silence.

"Is it possible she—?" Daniel trailed off as he realised he no longer had an audience.

What next? It seemed premature to dial 999. He pulled up a browser and searched for a non-emergency number for the police.

After a brief message, informing him that all conversations were recorded, an automated man's voice said, "Thank you for calling one oh one. We are connecting you to..." A slight pause. "... Cambridgeshire police."

Several seconds of another ringing tone. "Parkside Police Station, Cambridge," a man answered. "What can I do for you?"

"I'm concerned about my wife," Daniel replied. "She left work over five hours ago and hasn't come home yet. She's not answering her phone either. I didn't know who to contact."

"Right, sir. Let me start by taking your name and address."

Once again, Daniel provided the details. He had half expected the call handler to tell him to wait until at least a full day had elapsed since Eileen's disappearance, but the man seemed unconcerned by her relatively short period of absence.

"Now, you say your wife is missing. What's her name?"

"Eileen Floyd."

"Her date of birth?"

"Twentieth of June, nineteen eighty-eight."

"And the last time you had any contact with her was five hours ago?" The note of scepticism in the call handler's voice came through loud and clear.

"Yes. The journey shouldn't take more than twenty minutes. I was abroad, and I spoke to her just after I landed early this morning, but she hasn't been answering her phone since."

"Right, sir. I understand. Can you describe her appearance? What was she wearing?"

"Um," Daniel said. "I have no idea what she had on. As I told you, I've been away on business, and I haven't seen her today. As for a description, she's around five foot six, brown hair, brown eyes, slim build, attractive."

"And does she share the same address with you?"

"Yes."

"This may seem obvious to you, sir, but have you carefully checked your home? Are you absolutely certain she's not there?"

Daniel bit back on his irritation. "Her car's not here and neither is she."

"And are you sure she hasn't left you a message or voicemail?"

"Yes, I'm positive."

"You mentioned she was working. Have you called her place of work?"

"I did that four or five hours ago. They told me there was a chemical spillage this morning, and they'd sent everybody home. And no, she wasn't injured in the accident from what they said. I tried again a few minutes back, but nobody's picking up."

"Was that her last known location?" the man asked.

"Yes."

"The address?"

"Ilithyia Biotechnology on the science park."

"And that would be the Cambridge Science Park, right?"

"It is," Daniel replied.

"May I take her car registration?"

Daniel dictated the number plate. The distant sound of tapping keys came through from the background.

"So, the records are telling me that's a red Mini Cooper? Is that correct?"

"Yes."

"Does she have a mobile, sir?"

"Yeah. Like I said. She isn't answering. Do you want the number?"

The call handler responded affirmatively, and Daniel read out the digits.

"Just a few more questions. Are there any relatives she might have visited?"

"Nobody who lives anywhere near here."

"Have you noticed any recent changes in her behaviour? Has she been withdrawn? Worried by something maybe?"

"No."

"Does she have any medical problems?"

"No."

"What about financial issues?"

"No, nothing at all like that."

"I know this is a sensitive question, but is it possible she's been seeing somebody else?"

"You mean an affair? Not as far as I'm aware. We've been trying to start a family, so I think that's very unlikely."

"And what about you, sir?"

"Are you asking whether I've been unfaithful?"

"I'm sorry, but we have to ask these questions." The man's voice sounded apologetic.

"The answer's no."

"Has she suffered from depression in the past? Drugs or alcohol dependency? Suicidal thoughts?"

"No to all of those."

"Is there any reason you can think of why somebody might have abducted her?"

"Christ. Abducted? Absolutely not."

"Do you have any other information that might help to find her?"

"No, nothing."

"Right, sir. I've got everything I need. Let me give you a reference for the case. Do you have something to write this down?"

Daniel reached out and snatched a pen and a magazine off the coffee table. "I'm ready." He recorded the details as the man read out the ten digits, then repeated them.

"One final thing. Is this phone number the best to reach you on, Mr Floyd?"

"Yes."

"That's everything. I'm sure there's no need to worry. It's rare for people to go missing for more than a day; the vast majority turn up within the first twenty-four hours. I'll be in touch if we receive any news. And of course, if you hear from Mrs Floyd, please let us know."

Daniel ended the call and blew out his cheeks. The man had said nothing to assuage his fears and had, in fact, provided him with several more possibilities to add to his over-active imagination.

As he tried to decide what to do next, another avenue of approach for tracking down his wife sprang to mind. The last time he spoke to her, she was at work, but now nobody was answering the phone.

Hopefully, if somebody was still there, they could provide him with more information about his wife's whereabouts.

20

Friday 14th August 2015

Ilithyia Biotechnology, Cambridge Science Park

Twenty-one years ago

Anders Grolby sank down on his haunches beside Eileen Floyd. Her chest rose and fell in a regular rhythm. He leant over and gently tapped her cheek. Her skin felt warm to the touch.

"Come on," he said. "Wake up."

She groaned, and her eyelids fluttered. Her eyes blinked open. Her gaze wandered to the ceiling in confusion, then locked onto his face. She attempted to move and bucked as the sudden realisation hit that both hands and feet were bound. She tried to talk, but the only noise to emerge was a series of grunts. Her nostrils flared rapidly as her respiration rate increased.

Grolby moved closer so that his head filled her vision. "Mrs Floyd," he said. "I need you to remain calm. Can you do that for me?"

Eileen nodded, but the panic in her eyes told a different story.

"Now, I'm going to remove the tape over your mouth. If you scream or make any other sound, I'll put it straight back on. Then I will hurt you. Badly. Is that clear?"

She made a noise that could have been either a yes or a no.

He reached a hand out. She flinched as he picked at the edge of the strip of adhesive material. With a single sharp tug, he ripped it free.

Eileen let out a cry of pain.

"Ah-ah. Remember what I said, Mrs Floyd."

"Where am I?" she croaked.

"You're in the boardroom at Ilithyia."

"What did you do to me?"

"I knocked you out with chloroform."

Silence greeted Grolby's admission.

"But why?" Eileen continued after a long pause.

"I'm afraid we had to stop you from talking to the authorities and risking the future of this company."

Confusion clouded Eileen's face. "What?"

"You threatened to raise your concerns about Dr Hendrick's work with people outside this organisation. We can't allow that to happen."

"So, you drugged me and tied me up? What the hell is wrong with you?"

"You brought this on yourself."

Another long gap while Eileen processed his words. "So, what are you going to do to me?"

"Well, that depends upon whether you cooperate or not."

"I promise if you let me go, I won't tell anyone."

Grolby chuckled. "Unfortunately, I don't believe you. Now, it would make things easier all round if you answer some questions for me. There was an open pregnancy kit in your handbag. Are you?"

"Am I what?"

"What do you think? Pregnant of course."

Eileen stared at him.

"Do you want me to hurt you, Mrs Floyd?" Grolby asked in a low voice.

"No. I mean yes. I only discovered this morning."

"How far along are you?"

"I... a month, maybe six weeks."

"Good. That wasn't so hard, was it? Now, who have you spoken to today?"

"My husband, but you already know that. You cut him off when you came into my lab downstairs."

"Anybody else?"

"Nobody apart from you, Mrs Baxter and Dr Perrin."

"All right," Grolby said. "What did you discuss with Mr Floyd? Your husband's name is Daniel, isn't it?"

Eileen hesitated.

He could almost hear her brain whirring. "Do you remember me warning you about what would happen if you don't cooperate?" he asked. "Or perhaps I could turn my attention to your partner instead."

"Leave my husband out of this. He told me his flight from America had just landed. That's as far as we got before you ended the call."

"Did you discuss your concerns about this company?"

"No. I said I'd be home early, but I didn't tell him why. I wanted to ask for his advice."

"And you haven't talked to anybody else about Dr Hendrick's work?"

"No. Who would I talk to?"

Grolby's expression tightened. "I don't know. That's why I'm asking."

"I already told you. I haven't spoken to a soul."

"Okay. I believe you."

Eileen shifted her position and winced in pain. She twisted her head sideways and lifted her arm as far as the knots would allow, only now spotting that her sleeve was rolled up above the elbow. "What else did you do to me?" she asked, studying the site from which Rosalind Baxter had drawn blood a few minutes earlier.

"Not your concern. I have one last question. Do you have a mobile phone?"

"Yes."

"Where is it?"

"In the glovebox of my car."

"And what make is it?"

"A Microsoft Lumia."

"What's the unlock code?"

Eileen glared at her captor. "Why do you want to know?"

"I'm told it's a very painful experience when somebody crushes a finger with a pair of pliers. Would you like to find out how it feels?"

"All right. Two, zero, zero, six, eight, eight."

"Thank you. See. You can be helpful when you try."

"Now what?" Her gaze focused on his face as she whispered the words, "Are you going to kill me?"

Grolby didn't answer. He grabbed the roll of tape from the table and tore off a strip. She tried to avert her head, but his left hand held her jaw in a vice-like grip as his right taped over her mouth. He added a couple of extra layers for good measure. Her eyes jittered in panic. A series of frightened squeaks emerged through the muzzle. Her breathing whistled through her nose.

"You'll find it far easier to breathe if you stop struggling and take long slow breaths," he said.

Gradually, her panicked expression faded as it transitioned to one of despair.

Grolby stood. "I'm going to leave you alone for a while now. Don't do anything stupid. Stay still and keep quiet." He leant forwards and stroked her cheek, but there was no warmth in the gesture. "Follow my instructions, or I'll punish you."

The ex-soldier opened the boardroom door and followed the corridor to the Chief Scientist's office. He raised his hand to knock but thought better of it and turned the handle. Perrin sat behind the desk, his face in his hands. Rosalind stood on the other side, looking out of the window. Both stared at him as he entered.

Grolby pointed to the vial of dark red liquid resting beside the keyboard. "I assume that's the blood sample you took from her."

"Yes," Rosalind replied. "Is it enough?"

"I'm sure it'll be fine." He snatched up the glass tube and dropped it in his trouser pocket.

"What will you do to her?" Perrin asked, a pleading look in his eyes.

"She has to disappear. If we let her go now, we'll all be arrested and end up in prison on charges of kidnap and false imprisonment. That's probably a sentence of between ten and fifteen years."

"God. You mean you're going to kill her?"

Grolby folded his arms. "Unless you can think of another way of making somebody vanish indefinitely without killing them. But frankly, I can't."

"What about the pregnancy test?" Rosalind asked.

"She reckons she's somewhere between four and six weeks."

Perrin's mouth dropped open, aghast. "You're planning to murder a pregnant woman? I haven't told you yet, Rosalind, but we're expecting our first child in a few months. Whatever she's done to bring this on herself, you can't take her child's life."

"Yes, on this occasion I'm inclined to agree," Rosalind added, pacing between the walls of the small room.

Grolby's gaze alternated between the other two. "Seriously? Women have abortions all the time, and many are far more advanced than just a few weeks."

"It's not the same thing," Perrin replied. "I can't let you do this."

"So, what do you propose we do instead?" Grolby asked.

Silence greeted his question.

"You won't have to be involved in the..." the Swede continued. "I'll handle all that by myself."

Rosalind stopped moving and turned to face him. "What if we wait until she has the baby?"

"Where the hell would she stay?"

"We could keep her here. I'm sure we could create a soundproof space somewhere. What if we adapted the storage room? If we moved the mice nearby, that would help to mask any sounds. They're noisy little buggers."

Grolby shook his head. "That's a crazy idea. What if somebody hears her? We'd have to feed her and provide toilet facilities."

Perrin raised his chin. "I'm with Rosalind on this. We can make it work."

"What happens after the child's born? Who'll look after it?"

"We drop it off at a hospital or something."

"And what do we do with her?"

"Whatever you were planning on doing before. If you don't agree, I'm going to the police to confess."

"It seems Nigel and I are in agreement," Rosalind said. "Are you with us, Anders?"

"It appears as if I don't have a choice in the matter," Grolby replied. "It would be far simpler just to dispose of her now."

"So, what next?" Rosalind asked.

"You can start by giving me a pay rise. If you're going to ignore my advice, it comes at a price. Unless you'd prefer me to be the one making the confession."

Rosalind scowled at her employee. "How much?"

"What did you offer her? Fifteen grand, wasn't it? Let's say twenty grand then."

"There's no way we could go that high," Perrin said.

"Agreed," his co-owner snapped, glaring at the Swede. "Now what else?"

Grolby forced his face to remain impassive. *Perhaps I should have requested more. But that could always come later.* "First, we need to make sure the police have a suspect. If you insist on keeping her alive, we can't have them searching too hard for her here. I'll take her car and set it up." He stared belligerently at the two company owners. "If that's all right with you." His voice dripped with sarcasm.

"By the way," he continued, "if anybody comes looking for her, make sure you don't let them inside the building. Tell them it's unsafe. Whatever it takes. And you better inform the staff the place is closed for another day or two if you seriously plan on keeping her here. I'll be back in an hour or so."

"Right," Rosalind said. "Got that. Basically, don't allow anybody in."

"Exactly. And just so we're clear, neither of you can breathe a word of this to anyone else. That includes close family. Do you understand?"

"I get it," Rosalind replied with a frown. Her partner stared down at the surface of the desk.

"Do you understand, Dr Perrin?"

The doctor looked up sharply. "Yes, I heard you."

"Good."

Grolby left the room and strode to the main entrance. He unlocked the door, then relocked it behind him, glad to see no other employees loitering outside. He jogged across the tarmac to his own car and grabbed a pair of thin driving gloves from the side pocket before pressing the button on the key fob to let him into the red Mini Cooper. *Not exactly inconspicuous.*

Fortuitously, despite the security cameras on the side of the building, none directed their gaze at the car park. He lowered himself into the driver's seat and pushed the lever to slide his seating position backwards by a few inches. The faint smell of her perfume permeated the interior.

He opened the glovebox. Her Microsoft Lumia phone lay on top of the car's service booklet. Within moments, he had prised the back off the mobile and detached the battery. He dropped the parts into his pocket. A further search uncovered a loose pair of sunglasses. *Good.* He slipped them on. They were slightly too small, but they would hide his face from any prying eyes.

He started the engine and followed the grid of roads out of the science park. He could have taken the main road to his destination and saved time, but there was a chance a traffic camera might pick up and record his progress. Instead, he navigated the narrow country lanes, avoiding any busy routes. Twenty-five minutes later, he parked on a patch of scrubby grass beside a gate leading into a field. The distinctive smell of running water reached his nostrils from the nearby river.

After checking for potential observers, he removed the parts of Eileen Floyd's phone from his pocket and reattached the battery. The screen flashed the manufacturer's logo. After a few seconds, the display showed the time. He swiped up and entered the six digits she had given him. Next, he tapped the texts icon and selected Daniel Floyd from the list of contacts.

He thought for a moment, typed in a brief message and hit send, then tossed the phone in the glovebox. After a final survey of the interior, he locked the car and returned the keys to his pocket.

The plan was in motion. The countdown had begun. Everything was at stake.

21

Friday 14th August 2015

Ilithyia Biotechnology, Cambridge Science Park

Twenty-one years ago

Daniel Floyd rolled to a stop beside the Ilithyia Biotechnology sign. The summer cold he had picked up on the plane was getting worse. The scratchiness at the back of his throat had worsened. He sneezed and wiped his nose on a handkerchief before exiting his vehicle.

Only three cars, a blue Toyota Prius, an almost new white BMW 3 series and a battered Saab 93, occupied the spaces in front of the building. He twisted in his seat but could see no trace of Eileen's red Mini. He hadn't expected to find her here, but a surge of disappointment at her absence still hit him in the stomach.

Where was she? Hopefully, somebody inside would help him answer that question. He left the car parked sideways across two parking bays and strode to the entrance. A hand-written note was attached to the inner surface of the glass.

Building closed today due to accidental spillage. Check email for more details. All deliveries, please ring the bell.

A shiny metal box occupied a space on the wall to the left of the door. The top half contained a square of black plastic etched with the image of a hand holding an access card. Beneath that sat a call button and a speaker.

He pressed the button. Several seconds passed with no response. He repeated the action. Still, nothing happened. He glanced up and spotted a small camera, mounted high up on the red bricks above the reader and directed downwards at the entrance.

"Come on," he shouted, waving his arms at the lens. "Open up." He jammed his thumb against the pushbutton and held it down.

Perhaps the switch was broken. He switched his attention to the door on his right. The rectangle of paper masked his view, and the reflections of the blue sky flecked with white clouds made it hard to see inside. He cupped his hands and peered through at the interior: an empty reception desk, lights off, two doors leading elsewhere. Raising both fists, he hammered on the glass.

Rosalind Baxter had answered the phone. She had to own one of the three cars.

"I know you're in there, Rosalind," he shouted, increasing the intensity of his banging.

A strong sense of being observed tickled the base of his neck. He spun around. A woman stood in the centre of the road outside the entrance to the car park, staring at him. She held his gaze for a moment, then continued over to the pavement, casting a single sideways glance in his direction.

Daniel directed his focus back to the building. The pattern of light shifted inside. Somebody emerged through the doorway behind the reception desk. The person masked their face with an elbow as they hurried to the entrance. Fumbling fingers twisted the lock. Daniel stood aside to allow room for the door to open. A wave of foul-smelling air, carrying the stench of rotting fish, washed over him. He sneezed as the stink made his eyes water. Clearly, they hadn't been lying about the spillage.

"Christ, what the hell happened?" he asked.

The woman lowered her arm: Rosalind Baxter.

"Hello, Daniel," she said. "Somebody dropped a bottle of ammonium hydroxide. I think you can see—or should I say smell—why we sent everybody home."

"I'm looking for my wife, Eileen."

"Yes, I gathered that from your earlier call. Unfortunately, I can't help you. She was here, but she left."

"What time that was?"

Rosalind's eyes lifted to the right, returned to his face, then looked away. "I don't know. Maybe eight o'clock. I wasn't actually in the building myself when it happened."

"But Eileen was here this morning?"

"Yes, I already told you that on the phone. She must have gone shortly afterwards."

"So, she wasn't injured in the spillage or anything?"

"No, she was in her lab. She came in early to finish a report that's due today. That'll probably be late now with all this going on. I was rather hoping she'd complete the work at home."

"Well, she isn't there. You're sure you have no idea where she could be?"

"Sorry, Daniel. All I can tell you is she's definitely not here. Look, nice as it is to chat, I really have to get back to sorting out this mess."

A slight movement drew Daniel's attention. A muscle in her jaw twitched rhythmically, and she refused to make eye contact. Something was making her nervous.

"I want to come inside and check for myself," he said.

A flash of anger clouded Rosalind's face. "We evacuated the building immediately after the accident and then swept it to make sure nobody was left behind. I can assure you there's no chance we missed her. Anyway, even if she was here, why isn't her car in the car park? She has a red Mini, doesn't she? I don't see one. Do you?"

Daniel turned. Only the other three cars and his own. But now a yellow delivery van, emblazoned with the red DHL logo, swung off the road outside. He watched as it sped across the tarmac towards them. A man, wearing a T-shirt in the same colours as his vehicle, jumped out and hurried to the rear doors. Moments later, he approached the pair, carrying a parcel.

Daniel refocused his attention on Rosalind. "I'm really worried about her. Just let me have a look around inside, so I can confirm with my own eyes she's not here."

"That's not going to happen," she replied. "I've already told you she's not there. Now, please leave."

The delivery man's gaze switched from one to the other and back, clearly uncomfortable at having intruded upon an argument. "Um… I have a package for a Dr Hendrick at Ilithyia Biotechnology," he said. "I need a signature."

Rosalind held out a hand. "Give it to me."

The man handed her a terminal with a plastic stylus attached by a short cord.

She scribbled on the screen and returned it to him, then accepted the cardboard box. She turned away, extended the lanyard hanging from her neck and lifted her card to the reader. The lock clicked. As she grabbed the handle, Daniel placed a hand on her shoulder.

"Get your hands off me," she yelled, spinning around in fury.

He released his grip and took a step backwards. His gaze shifted to the delivery driver, watching through the windscreen of the cab.

Daniel raised his palms to Rosalind in apology. "Sorry, I'm just—"

The phone in his pocket pinged, announcing the receipt of a text. He grabbed the device and inspected the screen. A band across the top of the display displayed a speech bubble icon, the sender's name and the start of the message. Any thought of entering the building to search for his missing wife dissipated as the first two words registered on his brain.

Eileen Floyd.

22

Friday 14th August 2015

Fen Ditton village, Cambridge

Twenty-one years ago

Anders Grolby jogged down the country lane. Luckily, few people were about. He passed a church to his left and continued along the road into the village of Fen Ditton, then turned right. He had done his research in advance and headed down a side street to the offices of a small taxi company. Streaks of rust ran down from the two screws affixing the dilapidated sign to the brick wall.

He pushed through the door and found himself in a cramped room containing a pair of brown plastic visitor chairs. A variety of framed certificates and a photograph of the outside of the building adorned the tatty walls. A woman sat behind the solitary desk. She wore a headset and tapped at the keys of an ancient computer as she peered at the screen.

She looked up in surprise at his entry. "Oh. Can I help you?"

"I need a taxi into Cambridge."

"Right. Um... most people just phone."

"I saw your sign and thought I'd save myself the trouble."

"Okay. Hang on a sec, I've got another call. Fenn Ditton Taxis."

Grolby sank into the scratched chair. The woman listened for a few seconds then said, "So that's Mr Evans on Milton Road, Cambridge, by the Church, to Histon. A car will be with you in around a quarter of an hour. Thank you for your business." She tapped on the keyboard, then turned back to Grolby. "You were saying. Whereabouts do you need to go?"

"The Science... actually, make that Cowley Road."

"It'll be about twenty-five minutes. Is that all right?"

"Fine. I'll wait outside." He would have preferred to return to Ilithyia sooner, but he didn't want to raise attention by making a fuss. He pulled the door handle and stepped into the warm afternoon air. A billboard advertising fresh ice cream occupied the pavement alongside the entrance to the newsagent shop thirty yards down the road.

It was good to be involved in something exciting again. Information Technology paid better than a career in the Swedish army, but he missed the occasional adrenaline surges that accompanied life in the military. This job would provide the first genuine excitement he had encountered in the past three years.

His only worry was whether his accomplices would hold together under the stress. Dr Perrin was the greater liability of the pair. In some ways, it would be easier to dispose of him like the woman, but he reminded himself that without the Chief Scientist, the company would fold even quicker than if he had allowed the whistleblower to proceed. And two disappearances among the company's workforce would raise far too many suspicions. No, he would simply have to keep the man in check.

He strolled down the street to the newsagent and bought himself a can of Coke. After taking a long chug, he crossed to a wooden bench on the opposite side of the road. There, he sat, jingling Eileen Floyd's car keys in his pocket as he pondered the next phase of his plan. It was a shame his co-conspirators wanted to keep her alive. Far simpler to dispose of her now, but they were adamant she should live, at least until after she gave birth.

Was it feasible to imprison her on the premises? If everything worked out as planned, the police would be searching elsewhere. The only risk lay in somebody discovering her by accident. He would have to ensure the room in which they kept her was soundproof, but it could work. Thanks to his quick thinking, at least they had the perfect opportunity to keep the building closed while they prepared a place to hold her.

He checked his watch. The damned taxi was late. He rose and crossed the road. He was about to re-enter the office to ask where it was when the sound of an approaching engine reached his ears. The small white sign on the roof identified the car as the one he was waiting for.

As soon as it pulled over to the kerb, he grabbed the rear passenger door.

"Did you order this, mate?" the driver asked through an open window.

"Yeah. I booked it from the office. Cowley Road please."

"That's all right, then. Jump in." The lock clicked, and Grolby settled himself on the back seat. A floral air freshener scent overlaid the lingering smell of fresh cigarette smoke. He debated whether to say something but chose to stay silent; today of all days, he needed to blend in.

Fifteen minutes later, they drew up fifty yards from the turning into the Science Park. He paid the cabbie and added a ten per cent tip. After a five-minute walk, he arrived back at Ilithyia. Besides the three cars he expected to find, a white van sat in a space by the entrance. A large sign on the side identified the owner as *Chem Response*. The second line read, "24-hour Chemical Spill Clean-up".

He used his card to enter the building, holding his breath so he didn't have to inhale the foul-smelling fumes as he jogged up the stairs.

Rosalind Baxter greeted him as he emerged into the corridor on the first floor. "Thank God you're back. I was beginning to worry."

"Nothing to be concerned about on my end. Is everything all right here?"

"Yes, she's still in the boardroom. I assume you saw the cleaners' van when you arrived. They're sorting out the spillage now, but they did say it would take a few days for the smell to go altogether."

"That may not be a bad thing. If you really want to keep her here, we'll need a day or two to set things up. Did anything else happen while I was away?"

"Her husband came by. He tried to get in the building to look for her."

Grolby jerked his head towards her in alarm. "You didn't—"

"No. He received a message and rushed off. I take it that was your doing?"

"Yes. I'll do a quick check on her, then I need to go out for another hour. Can you give me her home address? I suggest one of you stays with the workmen so they don't come up here."

"I'll send Dr Perrin to keep an eye on them. He's not handling this well."

Grolby lowered his voice. "Has he mentioned going to the police again?"

"No, but he's driving me mad clicking that damned pen like his life depends upon it."

"Perhaps you could have another chat with him. Explain the situation to him once more."

"Leave it to me. I'll just get her address for you." Rosalind headed to her office. The sound of low voices carried into the corridor. Moments later, she returned and handed him a folded piece of paper, which he placed in his back pocket.

Grolby opened the door to the boardroom. Eileen Floyd's frightened face greeted his entry. He leant over her and checked that the tape binding her hands and feet remained intact. She emitted a series of muffled grunts through the adhesive strips across her mouth.

"I have to go out again," he said. "I have just one question before I leave. Does your house have a burglar alarm?"

Eileen's eyes widened in fear.

"Don't worry, I'm not planning to hurt your husband, but I may have to if you won't answer me."

She studied his face for a moment, then shook her head.

"Okay. We'll talk when I get back. If you've lied to me or you try to escape while I'm away, there'll be serious consequences." Satisfied that everything was under control, he headed down the stairs and out to his car.

Fifteen minutes later, he pulled up at the address Rosalind Baxter had given him. The short driveway was empty. *Good.* The husband was still following the false trail. He withdrew the pair of leather driving gloves from the glovebox and slipped them on. After checking that no neighbours were watching, he used Eileen Floyd's keys to let himself in through the front door. No alarm. The same brand of perfume he had detected in her car greeted him. He found what he was looking for almost immediately and dropped the item into his pocket.

Only one task left to complete. That would have to wait until it was dark.

23

Friday 14th August 2015

St Mary The Virgin Church, Fen Ditton, Cambridge

Twenty-one years ago

Daniel Floyd's white BMW coasted to a stop beside the church at the edge of the village of Fenn Ditton. He pulled his mobile phone off the screen mount and switched to the text application. Once again, he read the brief message.

We need to talk. Meet me at St Mary The Virgin Church in Fen Ditton.

That was it. No explanation, just the two sentences. The last thing she had said before their conversation ended earlier that morning was that she would be back around eleven o'clock. But that was presumably before the spillage. Why on earth did she want to meet here? For the life of him, he couldn't think of any good reason for this meeting place. He had called her several times since receiving the text, but every time the call went straight to voicemail.

He got out of the car. The church lay at the junction between two narrow country lanes. If she was nearby, surely he would spot her red Mini, but the only vehicles he could see occupied private driveways.

He pushed through the gates and followed the gravel path towards the building. Several worn gravestones sat on the short-cropped grass. He passed through an arch into a stone porch set in the long edge of the structure. At the solid wooden door, he twisted the brass handle. It swung open with a metallic clank, accompanied by the squeal of ancient hinges.

A wave of cooler air washed over him, carrying a faint, musty odour infused with the scent of hot candles. Benches carved from a dark wood sat on either side of the aisle beneath a vaulted ceiling. Stained glass windows added a colourful hue to the darker shades of the pews and the tiled floor. But the only occupant was a man scraping excess wax from around the edges of a large candle. As he drew nearer, Daniel spotted the white dog's collar encircling the man's neck.

A sneeze erupted from Daniel's mouth.

The vicar looked up and flashed a warm smile. "Bless you. It sounds like you might be getting a cold. I always find summer colds are the worst."

"Sorry to bother you," Daniel said, "but I'm looking for my wife. She sent a message to meet here."

"Well, your wife has excellent taste in meeting places," the man replied, "but unfortunately I haven't seen anybody here for the last hour or so. Are you sure you've got the right place?"

"This is St Mary's Church, isn't it?"

"Yes, indeed. Perhaps she's in the grounds somewhere."

"Okay."

"What's her name?"

"Eileen. Why do you ask?"

The vicar grinned. "Well, if someone called Eileen comes in looking lost, I can tell her that somebody by the name of, uh…"

"Daniel."

"Right. That Daniel was trying to find her. It's been nice meeting you. If I have the good fortune to meet your wife, I'll let her know you were here."

"Thanks."

Daniel's eyes performed a quick scan of the interior before he retraced his path into the bright sunlight. He completed a route around the perimeter of the church but found no sign of his wife. Where could she be? He pivoted on the spot. Feeling slightly foolish, he shouted her name. No reply.

He returned to the gate by the entrance to the grounds. An elderly man wearing baggy dark trousers and a too-large beige jumper limped along the pavement.

"Excuse me," Daniel called.

The pensioner stopped and, without rotating his neck, shuffled his whole body around. "Yes."

"Um… my wife sent me a message asking me to meet her here, but there's no sign of her. You haven't spotted a woman about my age, looking lost, have you?"

A pair of rheumy blue eyes studied him through thick lenses. "No, can't say I have."

"She's driving a red Mini. Maybe you've seen that."

The man adjusted his glasses. "Now you mention it, I did see a car like that down the lane near the footpath leading to the river. I always try to walk for at least an hour a day to keep fit. At my age, I can't move too fast anymore. It's not really a parking place. Sometimes at weekends, there're two or three cars there."

"How far is it?"

The man stuck out a gnarled finger. "Oh, just a short distance that way. Go to that junction and turn right. It's on the corner where the road bends sharply to the left. It's a dead end. If the car's still there, you can't miss it."

"Thanks."

Daniel was already running in the direction his guide had pointed. The tarmac narrowed to the width of a single vehicle. Up ahead, the lane curved leftwards. He slowed as he approached the bend. *There!* A red Mini sat on a gravelly patch of ground beside a black waste bin. His heart thudded in his chest as he studied the number plate. It was definitely hers.

He performed a circuit of the car. "Eileen," he called. The only sound was the rumble of a tractor in the adjacent field. He cupped his hands and peered through the glass. No sign of her bag on the seat or in the floor well. Perhaps if she was somewhere nearby, he would hear the ringing of her phone. He selected her number from the recent contacts list. The ringing tone repeated eight times, then his wife's voice asked him to leave a message.

He ended the call without speaking and hit the redial button. The clattering of the tractor engine suddenly stopped, and the faint strains of an old-fashioned telephone ringtone reached his ears. He lowered the handset and blocked the speaker with a finger. Was the sound coming from the interior?

When the voicemail prompt repeated, he placed his ear against the window and dialled a third time. Her mobile was definitely inside the car, but where was she? Surely, she couldn't have gone far. He tried the doors but found them all locked.

He jumped over the metal barred gate beside the layby and yelled, "Eileen!" After twenty metres, the path opened out onto a patch of grassland bordering the river. He jogged across the meadow, the grass swishing against his legs as he ran. No trace of his wife.

Once again, he called her name. The only response was the gentle gurgle of running water. He retraced his steps, following the darker band of flattened greenery back to his starting point. *This makes no sense.* Why would she ask to meet him at the church, then abandon her car nearby and disappear?

The narrow lane turned into a gravelly track as it continued around to the left, past a high brick wall. He covered the distance in a few strides and discovered a footpath sign. He passed through a wooden gate and followed the path to the riverbank, calling her name as he went until his voice was hoarse. Two hundred metres later, he came across a footbridge that spanned the slow-moving water.

What now? If she had reached this spot, she could have continued in at least three different directions. *This is hopeless.* Perhaps her phone contained a clue to her whereabouts. He navigated back the way he had come until he arrived at the red Mini. It would take over an hour for him to drive home and return with the spare keys. What if he broke a window to get in?

He rolled the idea around inside his head. Eileen would be furious if he damaged her precious car. But he was seriously concerned about her wellbeing. Better he should incur her wrath than risk her safety. He lowered his gaze to the ground, searching for a suitable implement. All the nearby stones were far too small.

He walked back along the grassy verge, eyes downcast. Eventually, he spotted a potential candidate. He levered the rock out of the soil and brushed off a layer of mud. It fit snugly in the palm of his hand. He would have preferred something weightier, but it would have to do.

"Eileen," he yelled one last time. He strained his ears to pick up any sound above the rattle of the tractor's engine, which had started up again. Nothing.

He returned to the car. After a furtive glance at his surroundings, he stood to the side of the passenger door. He looked away and swung his fist at the window. A shockwave rocketed up his arm, but when he inspected his handiwork, the only evidence of his endeavour was a small chip in the otherwise flat surface.

He put more effort into the second swing. This time, an inch-long crack formed. The third attempt had the desired effect as the glass frosted into a patchwork pattern, and a sizeable chunk fell in onto the passenger seat. He reached inside and felt around for the door handle. The moment he operated the mechanism, the ear-splitting screech of a car alarm filled the afternoon air.

Ignoring the deafening noise, he pulled open the glovebox and retrieved the phone. As he turned to head back to his own vehicle, he spotted a figure. The man, wearing a helmet and garishly coloured cycling gear, stood astride a mountain bike, twenty yards away. He held up a mobile with one hand and tapped the screen with the other.

Then, without a word, the cyclist spun in a semi-circle, stepped on the pedals and raced past the church.

24

Friday 14th August 2015

Ilithyia Biotechnology, Cambridge Science Park

Twenty-one years ago

Anders Grolby pulled up outside the main entrance to Ilithyia Biotechnology. A quick survey confirmed only two cars in the car park, one belonging to Rosalind Baxter, the other to Nigel Perrin. It seemed the company hired to sort out the spillage had completed the job.

He unlocked the front door with a key, used his access card to operate the electronic mechanism, then locked up once again behind himself. Despite the clean-up, the foul stench of ammonia still lingered in the air as he jogged up the stairs. At the top, he found the corridor empty. A quick check of the boardroom confirmed that Eileen Floyd remained trussed on the floor. She tried to say something through the tape, but he ignored her. He hurried to the CEO's office. Rosalind whipped around as he entered.

"Is everything all right?" he asked.

"Yeah. They cleaned up the mess. They left half an hour ago."

"You wouldn't know judging by the smell."

Rosalind let out a humourless laugh. "They said it would take a few days for the stink to die down. Nigel's having a meltdown, but apart from that, there've been no additional problems. How about you?"

"It's nearly all set up. I have one more task to complete, and it'll be done."

"So, her husband..."

"By the time I finish, all the evidence will point to him as the prime suspect. You told me earlier he came here. Did anybody else see him?"

"Yeah, a van driver dropped off a parcel while he was talking to me outside the building. Daniel Floyd was insistent on getting in and was becoming quite aggressive. He only left when he received a message on his phone."

"And the delivery man saw all this?"

"I think so."

"Good," Grolby said. "We can use that. The police will still want to talk to you. You mentioned earlier that you went out with him at university. I want you to inform them that he came onto you, but that you rejected his advances."

Rosalind's face paled. "But then he'll know I'm lying."

"That doesn't matter. It'll be your word against his. The best lies contain an element of truth. When the police question you, make sure you tell them you were a couple in your student days. You didn't realise his wife was an employee. When you met at the Christmas party, he had too much to drink and tried to kiss you. He became obsessed and attempted to rekindle the relationship, but you rejected him. He came here today, telling you that he was planning to finish with her. You told him you weren't interested, and he got aggressive. Do you think you can carry that off?"

"I suppose."

"I'll get an unregistered phone and send you some text messages. Show them to the police, but only when they ask. Appear reluctant to divulge the information, as if you're still fond of him. Don't seem too eager to drop him in the shit. Did anybody else see her this morning before the spillage?"

"No, only Nigel, you and me as far as I know."

"Right. It's probably best if you keep it quiet that she came in earlier."

"I already told him she was here," Rosalind said. "And what about the phone records? Didn't you say she rang her husband from her lab?"

"Good point." Grolby scratched his cheek. "She was working on an important report, wasn't she?"

"Yes."

"Okay, so you lie. She promised to come in early but didn't show up. You—actually it's probably better if we make that Dr Perrin given the story we're trying to sell—called his number to see if he knew where she was."

A worried frown creased Rosalind's forehead. "Nigel's in no fit state to have a conversation with the police at the moment."

"Hmm. Do you think we can settle him down?"

"I'm not sure."

"We could tell them Mrs Floyd's disappearance coupled with the spillage has left him so shocked and upset that he's in no condition to do an interview, but he'll have to talk to them in the end. If you don't believe he's capable of holding it together, it may be time to consider other options."

"What does that mean?"

Grolby's piercing stare cut through his employer. "If we can't trust him to keep his mouth shut, we could resolve the situation through alternative means. It's not something I want to do, but he may leave us no choice."

"No, he's vital to the future of this company. Let me have another chat with him."

"Okay. And you're still determined to let the woman live until she gives birth?"

Rosalind took a deep breath, then nodded. "Yes."

Grolby sighed. "I think that's the wrong decision, but if you insist. So, we'll keep her at the back of the storeroom. We have to get that set up quickly. We'll need some builders."

"I'll sort that out."

"The building will have to remain closed until the work is done. Ensure they use some top-quality sound-proofing material. Tell whoever does the job it's because of the noise made by the test animals. We'll have to make sure the room is totally secure and that none of the employees can get in."

"Assuming the police search the premises for her, how do we stop them from searching there?"

Grolby rubbed the back of his neck. "Put some shelving in front of the area where we keep her so they can't see it. Stick a big biohazard sign on the doors outside. That way, they won't want to go in. Hopefully, they'll be looking hard at Daniel Floyd by then, anyway."

"Okay, so what happens next?"

"I'm feeling hungry, and our prisoner probably needs something to eat and drink. Oh, and she'll need a toilet break. You'll have to accompany her."

"Me?" Rosalind asked.

"Unless you plan to untie her and wait outside, but I wouldn't recommend it. I suggest we free her legs but keep her hands tied and the gag on. Why don't we do that now, then I'll go out and get some sandwiches and the new phone?"

"Right."

Rosalind followed Grolby as he returned to the boardroom. He knelt and loosened the knot around their prisoner's ankles.

"We're taking you to the toilet," he said.

Eileen made a muffled grunt through the tape binding her mouth.

Grolby grabbed her by the arm and hauled her upright. She almost toppled over, but he tightened his grip and half dragged her along the corridor to the ladies' washroom. When they reached the door, he turned to Rosalind. "Go in with her. If you need help, just shout."

Five minutes later, the two women emerged. Eileen's frightened gaze focused on Grolby's face. He ignored her silent pleas, placed a hand on her shoulder and guided her back to the boardroom. As he grabbed the handle, Nigel Perrin burst from his office and rushed towards them.

"There's a police car outside," he said, his eyes wide with alarm.

Grolby shoved Eileen through the open doorway. "Stay with her," he barked to Rosalind. "Tie her up again and keep her quiet. I'll deal with this."

Moments later, the doorbell sounded. He slipped a cotton facemask over his face, then took a calming breath and descended the stairs. A middle-aged policeman in a dark uniform stood outside with hands cupped around his face, peering in.

Grolby crossed the reception area, unlocked the door with the key and pressed the access button. "Yes, can I help you?"

The man opened his mouth to speak, then stopped and held a hand over his nose. "Christ, what's that smell?"

Grolby pointed to the sign. "We had a spillage and had to close the building while we sorted out the mess. If you think this is bad, you should have been here earlier. Why don't we talk outside?"

The policeman stepped back, and Grolby followed him out.

"We're looking for an Eileen Floyd," the man said. "Her husband reported her missing this morning. I understand she works here."

Grolby folded his arms. "Yes, she does, but I haven't seen her in the office today. We sent everybody home after the accident, but luckily there were only a handful of people here at the time, and she wasn't among them. We followed our company procedures, and I personally performed a full sweep of the building after the spill. I can assure you she's definitely not inside. I hope she's all right."

"Do you have any idea where she might be?"

"Sorry, I'm afraid not. What do you think has happened to her?"

"It's probably nothing," the policeman said. "I'm sure she'll turn up soon. What's your job here?"

"I head up the IT department and look after site security."

"Well, thanks for your time Mr..."

"Grolby. Anders Grolby."

"We'll be in touch again if we can't track her down. If you hear from her, could you please call me on this number?" The policeman handed over a business card.

"No problem," Grolby replied, pocketing the card. He watched as the man returned to the white police car. He raised a hand as the car swept out onto the main road. When he glanced back at the building, the silhouettes of two people stared down at him from an upstairs window.

"Damn," he muttered to himself. "We don't have as much time as I first thought."

25

Friday 14th August 2015

33 Willow Drive, Cambridge

Twenty-one years ago

Daniel Floyd navigated the quiet residential road and approached the small three-bedroom semi-detached property where he and his wife had lived for the past two-and-a-half years. He parked on the short driveway and got out.

He knew it was irrational, but his spirits sank at the sight of the empty space normally occupied by his wife's Mini. Perhaps she was inside. Maybe she had abandoned her car after breaking down and taken a taxi to get home. But why would she leave her phone in the glovebox? And why hadn't she called to tell him?

He had checked her mobile before returning to the house. They both used the same system for their unlock codes: the date of the other's birthday. The list of emails contained nothing of interest. When he switched to texts, the only item of any note was her message requesting the meeting. She had sent no other messages that day. Neither had she made any outgoing calls, and the only entries in the incoming calls log were his own unanswered ones.

He twisted the key in the lock, strode inside and called her name. Silence greeted his shouts. He climbed the stairs and checked the upstairs rooms. More in hope than expectation, he opened the back door and stepped through into the compact garden. No sign of her there, either. *Where the hell could she be?*

He re-entered the house, made his way to the lounge and sank onto the sofa. The faint trail of his muddy footprints led towards the kitchen. Eileen would have been furious with him for tracking in mud across the beige carpet. He would have gladly traded a few moments of her anger for the relief of discovering she was well.

He pulled out his own mobile and checked for messages. Other than a few work-related emails, nothing. Without thinking, he selected his wife's number from the list of contacts and tapped the dial button. For a moment, hope surged at the old-fashioned ring tone. Just as quickly, despair returned at the realisation the sound originated from his back pocket. Of course. He cursed his stupidity.

Perhaps the police would have some news. Apart from anything else, he needed to tell them about the strange message and finding her car. He dialled 101 and waited for the call to connect to the police station. When a man with a deep baritone voice replied, he gave his name and quoted the reference number he had been given.

"One second, sir," the call handler said. "Right, yes. A Mrs Eileen Floyd, missing since this morning. What can I do for you?"

"I received a text from her, asking to meet me at the church in Fen Ditton."

"So, you've found her then?"

"No, she wasn't there. I discovered her car a short distance down the road. Her phone was in the glovebox."

A keyboard tapped in the background. Several seconds passed in silence. Eventually, the man spoke again. "We've received reports of a theft from a vehicle matching your wife's."

"Yes, that was probably me. I heard her mobile ringing inside, and the doors were locked. I didn't have a spare set of keys, so I broke the window. A cyclist saw me."

"Okay, I'll make a note of that. But there was no sign of your wife?"

"No. The car was in a layby by the entrance to a field. I searched around the area, but she wasn't there. Has there been any other news? Do you have any leads?"

More tapping sounds. "I checked the road cameras and spotted her vehicle on the A14 around seven-thirty, but we have no coverage from junction thirty-three to the science park. We visited her workplace, but apparently nobody has seen her today."

Daniel's breath hitched. A shiver ran across his scalp. "That can't be right. She called me from her lab this morning."

"I'm sorry, sir. I can only tell you what it says here."

"None of this makes any sense. I was talking to her when the call cut off, so she was definitely there. She said she'd see me around eleven o'clock. And why would she send me a message to meet her in Fen Ditton? I don't think either of us have ever been there before. Something's happened to her."

"I'm sure it's just a misunderstanding, sir, but I'll get somebody to check out her car."

"Right," Daniel replied. "Thanks."

"If you hear from her, please contact us on this number. Are you at home now?"

"Yes. I arrived back a few minutes ago, but like I said, she isn't here."

"It's probably best if you stay there for the moment," the man said. "We'll let you know if we find anything."

"I'm really worried. Please find her."

A click signalled the end of the call.

What the hell was going on? Why did the person at Ilithyia claim she hadn't been there that morning?

He searched for the company name and clicked the link to dial the number. After a few seconds, a female voice answered. "Yes."

"Is that you, Rosalind?" he asked.

"Look, Daniel. Like I told you earlier, I'm sorry, but I have no idea where your wife is."

"I've just finished talking to the police. They claim they spoke to somebody at Ilithyia who said she hadn't been in today. She called me using a company phone number while I was at the airport, so I know she was in the building. And when we talked this morning, you told me she'd recently left."

The line went quiet.

Daniel moved the handset away from his face and checked the status. Still connected. "Are you there?"

"I didn't say anything about your wife being here. I haven't seen her today. Now, please stop calling. I can't help you."

A click. The call had ended.

26

Saturday 15th August 2015

33 Willow Drive, Cambridge

Twenty-one years ago

Anders Grolby lifted his wrist and glanced at his watch: just after two o'clock in the morning. He raised his eyes to the curtained upstairs window. No lights. *Good.* Daniel Floyd's white BMW sat on the drive.

A quick survey of the quiet residential neighbourhood confirmed nobody else was about. He had parked his own vehicle a quarter of a mile away and walked the short distance to his target's address. One couldn't be too careful; people tended to remember unfamiliar cars when questioned.

Grolby slipped on his leather gloves and removed from his pocket the spare set of car keys he had taken from the house the previous day. He tapped the unlock button. A loud click echoed through the stillness of the night. He held his breath, but nothing stirred. He moved to the back of Daniel Floyd's vehicle and pressed the BMW badge. The rear door swung upwards with a quiet hiss of air from the struts.

Withdrawing the vial of blood from his pocket, he removed the stopper from the glass tube and sprinkled several drops over the coarse carpeting. The burgundy liquid quickly seeped into the material, leaving barely visible, darkened spots where it landed. He reached up and carefully pulled the tailgate down, taking care to close the mechanism with the minimum of noise.

Next, he withdrew the cheap mobile phone from his trouser pocket and pressed the power button. His fingers tapped out the PIN: 1234. Obvious, but he wanted the police to have no trouble unlocking the device when they discovered it later. He opened the text application and selected the sole contact, Rosalind Baxter. He scrolled down the list of sent messages, all just a few words long.

I love you. Please call me. D x

I told her about us. She didn't take it well.

I'm free of her. Now we can be together. D xxx

I need to see you.

You know I can't live without you.

One more couldn't hurt. Grolby deliberated for a moment, then hit the compose icon and typed in the message.

I'm sorry I lost my temper earlier. Let me make it up to you. D xxx

He tapped the send button, opened the passenger door and dropped the phone in the side pocket. A second low clunk disturbed the silence as he locked the car with the key fob. He listened for a few seconds, but the only sound to emerge from the darkness was a dog barking in the distance.

One task remained. He shrugged the rucksack off his back and withdrew Eileen Floyd's housekeys. After another brief survey of his surroundings, he approached the house and let himself in through the front door. He stood in the hallway, inhaled a deep breath, then released it slowly.

Grolby returned Daniel's car keys to the same hook from which he had removed them the previous day. As he turned to leave, a handle rattled upstairs. Footsteps moved across the landing. He backed up to the open doorway. A pair of bare legs appeared, coming down the stairs.

Grolby eased the door closed behind him, then sprinted over the grass and flung himself to the ground on the far side of the low hedge surrounding the property. He lay on the hard pavement, desperately trying to control his laboured breathing. A quick glance through the dense foliage confirmed a figure in a white T-shirt and dark shorts, standing on the doorstep.

"Eileen?" a man's voice called.

If Floyd came out as far as the road, he couldn't fail to spot Grolby.

The Swedish ex-soldier remained stock-still. He watched as the man looked left and right, then turned and re-entered the house. The loud whoosh of exhaled breath accompanied the sound of the front door closing. *Christ, that was close.*

He maintained the same position for several more minutes. The decision to move was a balancing act; if he broke cover too soon, there was a risk Floyd would spot him. If he stayed where he was, a car might drive past and raise the alarm at his suspicious behaviour. Finally, he rose to a low crouch and cast an anxious glance towards the house. Nothing moved. Nobody called out. He set off, hunched over until he was out of sight of the upstairs windows.

He jogged back to his Saab and sank into the driver's seat. A wry grin formed on his face. The past few moments had been stressful, but it was a long time since he had experienced the adrenaline rush and nerve-jangling thrill of surviving a close encounter with the enemy.

Even though he wouldn't know it yet, Daniel Floyd was well and truly caught in the snare. Later that day, the next phase of the plan would begin.

All it would take to spring the trap was one anonymous phone call.

27

Saturday 15th August 2015

33 Willow Drive, Cambridge

Twenty-one years ago

Daniel Floyd threw back the bedcovers and swung his legs onto the thick carpet. He glanced at the bedside clock: six forty-five in the morning. It didn't feel right to sleep while Eileen was still missing, but he had been unable to keep his eyes open as his body fought off the cold and struggled to recover from the jet lag of his transatlantic trip. Overnight, his sore throat had developed to the point where it felt like he had swallowed a roll of barbed wire. The previous night's disturbance had certainly done nothing to aid his recovery.

He cast his mind back. A noise had woken him just after two o'clock. For a hopeful moment, he wondered if it was Eileen returning home. He could swear he had heard the click of the latch, but when he descended the stairs, he discovered the front door unlocked but nobody there. Try as he might, he couldn't recall whether he had locked up before going to bed. Lack of sleep and the effects of his cold had turned everything from the previous evening into a blur. Perhaps a gust of wind had made the sound.

A quick search of the house confirmed she hadn't returned. Afterwards, he had lain awake until exhaustion dragged him back to a succession of disturbing nightmares featuring his absent partner. Normally, Saturday mornings were filled with reading in bed—or if she was in the mood, activities with his wife of a more intimate nature—followed by a late breakfast. Today, he desperately missed their normal routine.

He snatched up his mobile and checked for messages. Nothing other than the usual emails. A sense of helplessness overwhelmed him. What could he do to find her? Maybe he should search again around the area where he had discovered her car. Perhaps she had been injured or collapsed from some undiagnosed illness. She might be lying somewhere nearby, unable to move and desperately waiting for help to arrive. A spiral of increasingly morbid thoughts spun through his brain. No matter how ill he felt, he couldn't just sit here, waiting for her to come home.

He padded to the en-suite bathroom in bare feet and slipped into the shower cubicle. He raised the water temperature, twisting and turning under the jets until his skin turned a shade of pink. After brushing his teeth, he dressed in a short-sleeved shirt and beige chinos before descending the stairs to brew the first coffee of the day. He needed a powerful jolt of caffeine to survive the coming hours, so heaped twice the usual quantity of grounds into the cafetiere.

While he waited for the water to boil, he strolled aimlessly from room to room. Was there a clue here? Was he missing something? His mind turned to Rosalind Baxter. Her reaction puzzled him. The first time he called the switchboard, she seemed unsure whether Eileen had arrived for work earlier that day. But later, when he visited the company in person, she told him his wife had left following the spillage. During his final call, she contradicted herself by flat out denying Eileen's presence in the building that morning.

The ring of the doorbell interrupted his thoughts. Was it her? Perhaps she had lost her keys. He rushed to the front door but slowed as he drew nearer. The blurred outlines of two figures stood silhouetted on the other side of the frosted glass. He pulled the handle and held up a hand to shield his face from the harsh glare of the early morning sun.

A pair of policemen stared at him with serious expressions.

His heart sank. "Oh, God. Have you found her? Where is she? Is she all right?"

"Mr Floyd?" the taller man asked.

"Yes. What is it? Why are you here?"

"Please stay calm. We haven't discovered your wife's whereabouts yet. May we come in?"

Daniel stepped back and beckoned them inside. Conflicting emotions raced through his brain: relief that the policemen weren't there to report what he feared most, but despair that they hadn't located Eileen either. He led them into the lounge, lowered himself into an armchair and perched on the edge. The two men sat at opposite ends of the sofa.

"When did you last see your wife?" the man sitting nearest asked.

Daniel shook his head in confusion. "As I already told the person at the police station, I've been abroad for a couple of days. I haven't seen her since I left on Wednesday morning."

"Okay. Would you tell us about finding her car?"

"I'd been calling her all day yesterday with no success. Then, out of the blue, I received a text message from her, asking me to meet her at St Mary the Virgin Church in Fen Ditton."

"Did you speak to her?"

"No, she wasn't there when I arrived."

The scratch of a pen on paper drew Daniel's attention to the second policeman. He scribbled something in a notebook.

The other man cleared his throat and leant forwards. "What I meant was, did you try to call her?"

"Yes, of course, but she didn't answer."

"Okay, so you drove to the place she identified, this church, but you didn't find her there. What did you do next?"

"I went in and talked to the vicar. He told me he would let her know I'd been there if she showed up looking for me. Then I searched the grounds. When I came out, an old man was walking up the road. I asked him whether he'd seen my wife. He said he hadn't, but he had noticed a car matching hers in a nearby layby. I followed his directions and discovered my wife's Mini. Anyway, I spoke to the call handler yesterday and mentioned all this to him. Why are you asking me again?"

The policeman ignored Daniel's question. "What happened after that?"

"Her phone was in the glovebox."

"How did you know that?"

"I heard it ringing. So, I searched in the adjacent field and along the footpath, but I couldn't find any trace of her."

"Are you sure about that, sir?"

Daniel jerked his head towards his questioner. "What's that supposed to mean? Of course I'm sure."

The policeman studied him with suspicious eyes. "We received an anonymous call last night. The caller told us they saw a couple having a violent argument by the river bank. The man was yelling the woman's name. It was a very distinctive name: Eileen. The man's description sounds very similar to yours. So, I'll ask you again. Did you or did you not meet your wife at Fen Ditton yesterday?"

A prickle of apprehension rippled across Daniel's scalp. "How many times do I have to repeat myself? We never met. Yes, I was shouting her name, but that was because I was trying to find her. But if she was having an argument with another man, you should be looking for him instead of wasting time asking me questions I've already answered."

"Let us worry about that, sir. Now, tell me about the car."

"Like I said, she wasn't there. I knew the phone was inside the glovebox because I could hear it ringing through the glass. I thought it might give me a clue where she was, so I found a stone and broke in."

"Or perhaps you were so angry with her, you wanted to get back at her by damaging something she valued."

Daniel gasped. "What? I love my wife. I'd never do anything to hurt her."

"And did you find any useful information on her mobile?"

Daniel's head lowered. "No. There were no outgoing messages other than the one asking to meet me."

"Where is it now?"

Daniel pointed to the coffee table where he'd put the phone the previous night.

"Do you mind if we check it ourselves, sir?"

"If you think it might help to find out where she is, go ahead, but I didn't see anything to explain her disappearance on there."

The policeman with the notepad pulled a clear plastic bag from his pocket and nudged the mobile inside, using the top of his pen.

"I take it you know the unlock code then?" his partner said.

"Yes." Daniel dictated the digits. "It's the date of my birthday," he explained.

"We'd like to have a look around the house, if that's okay with you."

"Do you have a search warrant?"

Both men studied him carefully for a moment before the nearest officer spoke. "No. Do we need to arrange one?"

Daniel gave a brief shake of the head. "Sorry, of course not."

The policemen stood. As Daniel followed their example, the taller man raised a hand. "It's probably best if you remain here, sir. This shouldn't take long. Is it all right if we check inside your car too? While we're at it, do you have the keys for your wife's car?"

Daniel gestured towards the door. "The spares for both our cars are hanging on hooks in the hallway." The two men left him alone. He leant back in his chair. His hands tapped out an irregular rhythm to accompany the jiggling of his legs. Floorboards shifted above as somebody moved about upstairs.

After a few minutes, the stairs creaked as the policemen descended. The familiar click of the door-latch followed. A gust of air blew in from outside, shifting the lounge door slightly on its hinges. A short blip from the car alarm. The distant clunk of opening car doors. Several seconds of silence. Hurried footsteps.

The two police officers burst into the room.

"Daniel Floyd, we are arresting you for the suspected murder of your wife, Eileen Floyd."

The nearest officer pulled a set of handcuffs from the pouch on his belt.

"What did—?" Before Daniel could finish his question, the second policeman grabbed him by his upper arm, hauled him out of the chair and yanked his hands behind his back. The cold metal embraced his wrists.

"You do not have to say anything," the other man intoned, "but it may harm your defence if you do not mention when questioned, something that you later rely on in court. Anything you do say may be given in evidence."

28

Monday 17th August 2015

Ilithyia Biotechnology, Cambridge Science Park

Twenty-one years ago

Rosalind Baxter stared through the glass at the two people waiting outside. Their visit wasn't unexpected. Detective Sergeant James Roberts had called an hour earlier, requesting an interview. Beside him stood his female boss, Detective Inspector Veronica Turner. Rosalind pressed the access button to open the door.

Both police officers turned away in disgust as the faint lingering stench of ammonia washed over them.

"Christ, what the hell is that smell?" Turner asked, placing a hand over her nose.

"Yeah, sorry about that," Rosalind replied, stepping back to allow them to enter. "We had a chemical spillage a few days ago. We called in a clean-up company, but it will take a while before all the fumes dissipate. It was far worse last week. It's slightly better upstairs. Please follow me."

She led them up to the boardroom.

"How do you work in these conditions?" Roberts asked, lowering himself into a chair.

Rosalind sat on the opposite side of the long table. "To be honest, I've become acclimatised. I don't really notice it anymore. Now, you mentioned on the phone this was about one of our employees. What can I do to help?"

Turner withdrew a file from the briefcase she had been carrying. "I believe an Eileen Floyd works here."

"Yes. Has something happened to her?"

The policewoman ignored the question. "When did you last see her?"

Rosalind shook her head. "Do you mean me personally, or anybody here? I vaguely recall seeing her on Tuesday or Wednesday, but she spends most of her time in the labs, and I don't go down there every day. I can check with her manager when she was in."

"If you wouldn't mind, Mrs Baxter."

"Now?"

"We'll wait."

Rosalind rose and covered the short distance along the corridor to her office. Anders Grolby waited inside.

"They want to know when she was last in the building," she said.

"Obviously don't tell them she was here on Friday," the Swede replied. "Have they asked any other questions?"

"Not yet. I'll give it a few minutes, then I'll go back. Can you print out the attendance logs in case they ask?"

"No problem. I've already been in the system to modify the records for that day. May I use your computer?"

Rosalind nodded. She paced backwards and forwards while he tapped at the keys. Eventually, the printer unit by the wall spat out three sheets of paper. She scanned the report. "Thanks," she said, heading back into the boardroom.

The two detectives occupied the same positions as when Rosalind had left them. "Here we are. She was last in on Thursday, but we told everybody to stay at home on Friday after the accident. This data comes from the key cards the employees carry to get through the front door." She placed the printout on the table.

"Is it possible she followed somebody else in and didn't actually use her own card?" Turner asked, picking up the sheets of paper.

"I suppose so, but one of our conditions of employment is that everybody has to present their ID on entry to the building. It's a serious disciplinary offence if they don't. The information is used to check who's here in case we ever need to evacuate, for example during a fire drill."

"Or a chemical spillage," Roberts added.

"Yes, exactly."

Turner studied the report. "So according to this, the only people here last Friday morning were Martin Hendrick, Nigel Perrin, Anders Grolby and Rosalind Baxter—you."

"That sounds about right. May I ask what this is about?"

"Eileen Floyd's husband reported her missing on Friday. He claims she called him from here, and his phone records support that. But now you're telling me she wasn't here that day."

"No, I don't remember seeing her, but I didn't arrive until after the spillage."

"So, it's possible she was here."

"Only if she didn't use her card, and all the people you just mentioned are senior members of staff who know better than to let somebody else bypass the system."

"How do you explain the call, then?" Roberts asked.

Rosalind feigned a look of puzzlement. "Maybe it was Dr Perrin. He's my partner by the way. We had an important report to deliver on Friday. Now you mention it, he was complaining to me earlier this morning that she hadn't shown up. Perhaps he was calling to find out where she was."

"In that case, why would he call her husband's mobile instead of hers?"

"You'd have to ask him that—if it actually was him. We keep several phone numbers on record for each employee. Whoever it was probably chose the wrong one. Or it's possible they tried hers first and called his when nobody answered."

"All right. Can you bring Dr Perrin here? While you're at it, we'd also like to talk to the other people who were present last Friday morning."

Rosalind stood. "I think they're all in today. I'll just go and fetch them." She felt the suspicious stares of the two police officers on her back as she crossed to the door. Moments later, she barged into her partner's office.

Perrin sat at his desk, his head in his hands. He looked up as she entered, revealing the pair of dark half-crescents beneath his eyes.

"They've asked to see you," Rosalind announced without preamble.

The expression of fatigue on his face morphed into one of panic. "What do they want to know?"

"They have Daniel Floyd's phone records, which show a call made from this building to his mobile on Friday morning."

"Christ, what do I say to them?"

"Tell them you needed her to complete an important report. She didn't turn up as promised, so you wanted to track her down. You dialled the first number you came across, which happened to be his."

Perrin's shoulders slumped. "I can't do this, Rosalind."

"You can and you will... unless you want all of us to spend the next ten to fifteen years of our lives in prison. I have to fetch the others, so you've got a few minutes to pull yourself together. The police are in the boardroom."

Rosalind left the room and crossed to her own office. Grolby stood at the window, looking out at the cloudless blue sky.

"What's going on?" he asked, turning around.

"They want to see you, Nigel and Martin," she replied. "Can you fetch Dr Hendrick from his lab? And make sure he doesn't mention anything about the work he's been doing. They know about the outgoing phone call. I told Nigel to say he was the one who made it."

"How's he holding up? He's not about to drop us in it, is he?"

Rosalind let out a sigh. "It's impossible to tell. I had a few words with him. Perhaps you should have a quick chat too."

"Fine. I'll do that. Give me a couple of minutes."

Rosalind turned and headed back to the boardroom. She returned to her seat. "Somebody's just getting them. They'll be here in a minute." The tension grew as she and the pair of police officers waited in uncomfortable silence.

Eventually, the door opened and the three Ilithyia employees trooped in. When everyone had taken their seats, Rosalind introduced her colleagues.

Turner, the female DI, spoke. "As you're probably already aware, we're trying to trace the whereabouts of Eileen Floyd. Nobody has seen her since last Thursday night. Her husband claims she made a call from here on Friday morning. The attendance records show she wasn't in the building that day. So, first of all, did anybody see her?"

A series of head shakes greeted the question.

"Is it possible she didn't use her access card?"

Nobody responded immediately. Grolby filled the silence. "The only way that could happen is if she entered with somebody else. I know for a fact it's impossible that she came in with me."

"Me neither," Hendrick added.

"What about you, Dr Perrin?" Turner asked.

No reply.

"Doctor Perr—"

"No, I don't recall seeing her at work at all that day," Perrin replied.

The detectives both studied the bespectacled scientist for a moment.

"Okay," Roberts said. "Did anybody call her husband?"

Again, an uncomfortable silence.

"I think it was probably me," Grolby said.

"Probably? Surely you would know whether or not you called him."

The Swede cleared his throat. "Dr Perrin mentioned that Mrs Floyd had promised to come in early on Friday morning to finish an important report. When she didn't show up, I offered to talk to her and find out why she wasn't here. I pulled up her file but must have selected the wrong number."

"So, you spoke to her husband, Mr Floyd, then?"

"I assume it was him. He told me his flight had just landed, and he didn't know where she was. I quickly realised my mistake, so I ended the call."

"But after that, you tried her mobile?"

"No," Grolby replied. "The chemical spillage happened before I had the opportunity. My chief priority was keeping people out of the building until we could clean up the mess."

"What exactly is the process when something like that happens?"

"We respond in the same way we would to a fire alarm. We evacuate the premises and perform a name check to confirm everybody present is accounted for. There were only four of us here, so that was quick. After that, I did a room by room sweep to make sure nobody else was still inside."

"So, if she had been in the building, you would have known?" Turner said.

"Yes."

"What exactly is your role in the company, Mr Grolby?" the female detective asked, consulting her notes.

"I head up the IT team, and I also look after site security."

She scribbled a few words in her notepad. "How did this spillage happen?"

All eyes turned to Perrin. "I... I accidentally dropped a bottle of ammonium hydroxide in the corridor downstairs. It was a stupid mistake."

"And what about the report?"

"What report?"

"The one Mr Grolby just mentioned. Apparently, it was of high enough importance to call Mrs Floyd about when she didn't turn up."

"Oh, that. I ended up finishing it off by myself."

"Okay. Have you tried to locate her today?"

Perrin glanced at his watch.

"I'm sorry, Dr Perrin," Turner said, her voice laced with sarcasm. "Do you have somewhere more important to be?"

"No, no, it's not that," he replied hurriedly. "I was just checking the time. Employees have to phone their manager before ten o'clock if they can't work. It's ten fifteen, so she should've called in by now."

"And I take it she hasn't?"

Perrin shrugged. "I don't know. She doesn't report directly to me."

The two police officers exchanged a glance. "Okay," Roberts said. "I think that's all for the time being. Mr Grolby, perhaps you could show us where Mrs Floyd worked. We'd also like to speak to her manager. The rest of you are free to go although we'll probably need you all to make a statement at some point. Thanks for answering our questions."

Nigel Perrin and Rosalind Baxter remained seated while the remainder of the group left the room. Rosalind waited several seconds after the door closed before speaking.

"It's over for now, Nigel. I think that went as well as we could have hoped."

The Chief Scientist raised his elbows onto the table and lowered his face into his hands. The sound of low sobs emerged from between his fingers.

29

Monday 22nd February 2016

Belmarsh Prison, Thamesmead, London

Six months later

The only sound inside the cramped cell was the scrape of plastic on plastic. Daniel Floyd sat hunched over on the bottom bunk. He held a tray on his knees as he picked at the unappetising fare. This was officially his first day as a convicted felon, although he had spent the past six months behind bars here awaiting trial. The case had been high profile, catching the attention of the public for obvious reasons: a well-educated man murders his beautiful wife and refuses to identify the location of her body.

Another prisoner with short-cropped grey hair and wearing the ubiquitous drab prison clothes occupied the sole chair in the small room.

Daniel looked over at him. "Food all right, Victor?" he asked.

"Same crap as usual," the man replied in a Russian accent. "You enjoy your first day as a convict?" That morning, the two men had become cellmates following Daniel's sentencing.

"Things could be better. Somebody abducted and murdered my wife. Meanwhile, I'm stuck in this place for the next fifteen years at least, paying for that crime."

"You should probably not tell people you are innocent. Many here say this, but nobody is interested. It only marks you as weak."

"You may be right," Daniel replied, "but some bastard set me up. They found her blood in the boot of my car. I've no idea how it got there, but it was certainly nothing to do with me. I'm sure those bastards she used to work with had something to do with it. My wife called me from there the day she disappeared, for Christ's sake, but they claimed it was somebody from the company, trying to find out where she was. That bitch, Rosalind Baxter, also lied. She told the court I came onto her. I was happily married. She and I went out together for a while years ago, but I wouldn't sleep with her now if she was the last woman on earth."

"There is nothing you can do," Victor said. "Once they convict you, it is too late."

"I could always appeal."

"Perhaps you get lucky, and they find new evidence. But I advise you to accept your situation. You will go mad if you do not adapt."

"Thanks for the advice," Daniel replied, piling his plastic fork with peas. Their consistency bore more resemblance to green ball bearings than anything edible. The two men ate in silence for a moment. "How did you end up in here, Victor?" he asked.

The Russian let out a low laugh. "This is something else you should not say to people." He turned serious. "But now we live together, so for you, I will answer. For many years, I work in Soviet army. Much equipment goes missing. Everybody takes it. Pay is bad, but I have good business, and I make much money. When Soviet Union break up, I come to England for new life. Work is hard to find, so I do what I know best; I sell things on the black market."

"What sort of things?"

Victor frowned at the question, then relaxed his features. "Oh, anything a person cannot buy easily: weapons, drugs, women. Anyway, soon others think I take sales from them. They interfere. They hurt my people. So, I do something else I am good at. I start war."

"War?"

"Yes, not like tanks and rockets, but guns and knives. After a short time, nobody messes with me. Most are dead." Another chuckle. "Everything is good for a few years, but then things go wrong. I make too much money. The men who work for me want more. They get greedy and try to take my place."

"So, what happened?"

"Somebody betrayed me. I receive order for weapons. Good money. Very good money. When we deliver to buyer, armed police are waiting. They arrest us all. But I find out who it is. He is already dead along with his close family."

"Um... All right. I appreciate you telling me."

A wide grin cracked the Russian's face. "But perhaps I just tell you this story so you fear me, yes?"

Daniel laughed uneasily.

"Do not worry. They will not bother you in here if you stay near to me. Nobody messes with Victor Yahontov. I see you are good man. We become friends."

"Sure. I'd like that. How much longer have you got inside?"

Victor shrugged. "I don't know. Eight years, ten years maybe. It makes no difference. It is long time in future. I try to make the most of my life even though this is not palace." He gestured towards the discoloured walls.

Daniel resumed his meal.

After a few seconds of silence, the Russian spoke again. "I continue business in here. If you need anything, you come to me. For you, I give good discount. I get whatever you request. But maybe not girls. This is too difficult."

"Cheers, Victor."

"And when we are both out, if you want weapons or drugs or other illegal things, you know who to ask."

"Thanks, I appreciate it, but I don't think that's ever likely to happen."

Daniel Floyd smiled politely at his new cellmate, but a part of him wondered whether he would ever have cause to take up the Russian's offer.

30

Monday 22nd February 2016

Ilithyia Biotechnology, Cambridge Science Park

Twenty-one years ago

Eileen Floyd stared listlessly around the cramped room. Barely ten feet square, it contained a narrow bed, a washbasin, a toilet, a solitary bare lightbulb dangling from the ceiling and nothing else. No windows, just a single locked door. She would have lost count of how long she had been here were it not for the marks she scratched every day on the beige walls with a fingernail: a little over six months.

She ran a hand over her belly. The rounded bump of her baby pushed out the material of her T-shirt. That bastard, Grolby, had brought her a variety of clothing during the first week, but she had quickly resorted to the cotton top and baggy jogging bottoms as her standard attire. Every few days, one of her three jailers—the Swede, Baxter and Perrin—took away her used clothes and returned them a short while later, cleaned.

Food came only twice a day, once early in the morning—although she could only discern the time from the yawns and tired expressions—and once at night. She had learned to save some of her breakfast to stave off the hunger pangs at lunchtime. The only visitors she received were Rosalind Baxter, Nigel Perrin and Anders Grolby. Presumably, they were the only ones who knew she was here—wherever here was.

Six months earlier, they had drugged her again. When she regained consciousness, she found herself in this tiny space and hadn't been out since. She guessed she was somewhere on the Ilithyia premises, but the soundproofed walls gave no clues as to her whereabouts. For the first few days, she had screamed and hammered her fists against the sides of her prison, but nobody came to her rescue. After a while, they threatened to keep her tied up and gagged if she didn't stay quiet.

As the weeks turned into months, her resolve wavered. The initial fury at her imprisonment transformed into grim acceptance. Now, she almost relished the twice-daily human contact as a respite from the crushing boredom. At her request, they had brought her books and even a handheld gaming console, but neither source of entertainment did anything to drag her from her hopeless lethargy.

She had considered trying to end it all. On at least one occasion, she had removed the bulb and, in the absolute darkness that pressed on her like a physical force, debated whether to plunge her fingers into the exposed pins of the socket. But every time, her thoughts turned to her unborn child. The only reason they were keeping her alive was to allow her baby the gift of life. She couldn't bear to think about what that future might entail, but neither could she bring herself to take it away.

As she lay on the thin mattress awaiting the arrival of her evening meal, she tried to picture her husband's face. What was he doing now? He had to be sick with worry. A few days ago, Grolby let slip that they had framed Daniel for her abduction. At the thought, a surge of molten rage ran through her veins. She couldn't give up. She had to make them pay for what they had done. *I have to get out of here. But how?*

For the past three months, she had been docile and followed her captors' instructions to the letter. Perhaps they had become complacent. She sat up. For the umpteenth time, she surveyed the small room. As on every previous occasion, no obvious weapon caught her eye. She placed her bare feet on the floor. They wouldn't be expecting her to resist after so long. Was there a chance she could catch whoever came tonight by surprise?

Her gaze rose to the lens of the infrared camera. She had to act her usual lethargic self or they would be prepared. At the first click of the lock, she lowered her head and placed her face in her hands. The door swung inwards a few inches.

"I've brought you some food, Eileen," a voice called.

Good. Perrin. The doctor was probably the least physically capable of her three captors. He pushed into the room, carrying a plastic tray holding a pack of garage sandwiches and a can of coke. He approached the bed and placed it beside her on the mattress.

"Are you okay?" he asked.

Still, she maintained the same position.

"Eileen?"

Slowly, she raised her head. With a sudden yell of fury, she launched herself at her captor. He staggered backwards and collided with the wall. His hand reached down for the baton tied to his belt, but she was already past him. Her bare feet slapped against the cold tiles as she sprinted through the doorway. She emerged into another narrow room and, in her haste, barged into a stack of mouse cages with wire mesh fronts. A flurry of movement greeted her arrival as the occupants sought whatever cover they could find inside their own prisons.

She swore under her breath and scrambled along the row towards the only way out. Already her breathing was becoming laboured; six months of confinement had left her unaccustomed to physical exercise. She slipped through the open door and found herself in a storeroom. Locked cabinets filled all the available wall space. Just a few feet away lay the exit. A large yellow sign displayed a prominent message:

Remember to lock up when you leave

She lunged for the handle and twisted. It refused to turn. With increasing desperation, she rattled it up and down.

"Help," she screamed. "Let me out of here."

Footsteps rushed up behind her. A hand landed on her shoulder and spun her around.

Nigel Perrin stood, holding a black baton, hair dishevelled and glasses askew. A bead of sweat rolled down his right temple.

"I don't want to hurt you, Eileen," he said, "but I will if you force me to."

"Please let me go. I won't say a word to anybody." She sank down on her haunches with her spine against the wall. Tears of despair stained her cheeks.

"Come on, back to your room. I'm not going to ask again."

With weary resignation, she forced herself upright and trudged past the caged rodents. She hesitated as she neared the threshold to her cell, but a shove between the shoulder blades pushed her inside. The door slammed shut behind her with a heavy thud. The rattle of the lock followed a moment later.

She crossed to the bed and curled up on her side in the foetal position.

***

In the corridor, Nigel Perrin ran a trembling hand through his hair. If he hadn't locked the door to the storeroom, she would have escaped. How could he have been so careless? The others would be furious if they found out. It was probably for the best if he kept the incident to himself.

After six months, he had finally come to terms with their actions in keeping her a prisoner, but he still dreaded what was to follow after she gave birth. Grolby had said he would be the one to deal with her, but that didn't make it any easier to accept.

He drew a shaky breath and headed back towards the reception area. A square of light leached around the sign, filling the window to Dr Hendrick's laboratory. Perrin failed to notice as the door behind him opened.

A pair of curious eyes tracked his progress.

31

Wednesday 30th March 2016

Ilithyia Biotechnology, Cambridge Science Park

Two days later

Martin Hendrick glanced at his watch. Five minutes to eight in the evening. If tonight followed the normal pattern, somebody would come down the corridor and enter the storeroom shortly. Ever since the ammonium hydroxide spillage six months earlier, access to the chemical storage cupboards had been restricted to three people: the two company directors, Rosalind Baxter and Nigel Perrin, and the head of IT and security, Anders Grolby.

It made no sense. Why were these senior members of staff performing the role of storeman? What did they do in there every night? Perhaps he should just ask one of them. But that was a problem to solve later. For now, he turned back to his computer screen.

For the past few months, Hendrick had been using CRISPR technology to edit the RNA of the influenza virus. The technique enabled him to alter the building blocks of the organism and insert fragments of modified genetic material. After several ups and downs, his research was finally nearing completion of the first stage. The next step would be to trial his creation on laboratory animals. He had deliberately downplayed the level of progress to his bosses, but the early signs were that he would achieve his goals.

The sound of footsteps in the corridor outside dragged his attention away from the display. *Right on time.* He crossed the room and peeled back the edge of the sign that blocked the small square window. It seemed it was Anders Grolby's turn tonight. Hendrick eased open the door a fraction and watched through the gap as the Swede withdrew a set of keys from his pocket and let himself into the storeroom.

Hendrick waited a moment, then crept after the security chief. If past form was anything to go by, it would be several minutes before he emerged. The scientist placed his ear against the cold, white plastic and strained his ears to pick up any sounds from within. Silence.

With slow, deliberate movements, he twisted the handle. To his surprise, the mechanism turned, and the door clicked open. He hesitated for a second, scanning the interior, then stepped through the doorway. The room seemed much smaller than he recalled. Locked cabinets butted up against the walls. A narrow passageway led off from the right side of the opposite wall. That hadn't been there before.

The characteristic, musty smell of laboratory animals hung in the air. A flurry of movement rattled the bars of their metal cages. So that's what Grolby was doing here. It still didn't make sense why the senior management had taken responsibility for feeding duties, but it did explain the nightly visits.

Hendrick turned away and retraced his steps. He reached for the handle and pulled it towards him. The door was an inch from closing when a new sound emerged from the other side of the room. Were those voices? Had more than one person come in? Surely, he would have noticed.

Caught in a moment of indecision, he stood stationary and strained to hear the words. He was too far away to understand what was being said, but it sounded like a man and a woman. Taking a deep breath, he re-entered the storeroom. He moved cautiously, treading carefully to avoid making any noise.

Grolby's voice rose above the scurrying of animals. "I don't care whether you hate cheese and onion or not, that's all they had. You should be grateful we feed you twice a day."

"Yeah, thanks a million."

Definitely a female, but who could it be?

"Somebody will be back tomorrow morning. It's Rosalind's turn, I think."

"Can't wait."

The sound of a door slamming emerged from the narrow passageway, followed by the rattle of keys. Hendrick turned and sprinted across the floor, counting on the renewed scuttling of the caged animals to mask his retreat. He slipped through the open doorway, pulling the door shut behind him. He raced along the corridor back to his workspace. Once inside, he slumped against the wall and sank down on his haunches.

The click of footsteps drew nearer and stopped outside his room. Hendrick froze. After a few seconds, they resumed. There could be no doubt; only one person had passed by. As the scientist returned to his workstation, a single inescapable conclusion rattled through his head.

Grolby, Perrin and Baxter were holding a woman prisoner somewhere behind the storeroom.

***

Martin Hendrick had been unable to concentrate for the past half hour. His mind kept wandering; who were they keeping in the room? He flinched as a tapping sound came from the corridor.

He rose from his seat, twisted the latch and pulled the door open.

Grolby stood outside. "Everything all right?" he asked.

Hendrick could barely meet the man's gaze. "Yeah," he mumbled.

"Everything's locked upstairs. You only need to lock up here and set the alarm when you leave."

"Fine."

"See you tomorrow. Don't stay too late."

The scientist shot him a weak smile. "I'm just wrapping things up. I won't be much longer. Goodnight." He closed the door as the head of security headed down the corridor.

There was no point trying to continue. Hendrick shut down the computer and tidied his work surface. He grabbed his bright-green winter jacket from the coat stand and strolled towards the reception area. Only one car remained in the parking spaces outside: his own red Ford Focus. He approached the beige box on the wall beside the entrance and reached out a hand to tap in the arming code.

His finger hovered over the first digit. Who was the woman? He had to try to find out. With a surreptitious backward glance, he tramped up the stairs. At the top, he turned on the lights at the master switch and followed the corridor to Rosalind Baxter's office. He pushed the door open, stepped inside and crossed to the window in darkness. After peering down at the solitary vehicle, he flicked the light on, squinting against the sudden brightness.

The desk drawers were unlocked, and he spent a fruitless two minutes rummaging through the contents. Maybe he would have more luck in Nigel Perrin's office. He rearranged the items and pushed the drawer closed.

The Chief Scientist's room was the same size as the CEO's, but the interior was fastidiously neat and uncluttered. He lowered himself into the swivel chair and tried the right side first. A desk tidy held an assortment of pencils and several identical ballpoint pens. He lifted the tray out, but nothing occupied the space beneath.

Next, he turned his attention to the left drawer. A pile of post-it pads in a variety of fluorescent colours lay stacked neatly towards the front. At the back was a jam jar filled with paperclips. He picked up the container and peered at the contents. Two silver keys on a ring stood out against the brass colour of the clips.

Hendrick reached in and retrieved the set. Could these be the right ones? He hurried down the stairs, turning off the lights behind him. At the bottom, he barged through the swing doors and jogged to the storeroom door. With trembling fingers, he fitted the first key in the lock, but it wouldn't turn. He removed it and inserted the second. This time, the mechanism rotated with no effort. He pushed his way inside.

Once again, the distinctive odour of laboratory animals assaulted his nostrils. He switched on the light, triggering a sudden bout of activity. His heart mimicked the behaviour of the frightened rodents as he crossed to the narrow passageway. A small amount of illumination penetrated an area approximately three feet wide. A variety of cages lay stacked against the left wall. To the right was a solitary door.

This was where they must be keeping her. His gaze settled on a tiny circle of glass at head height: a peephole. He placed his face up against the white plastic surface and peered inside.

An involuntary gasp of shock escaped his lips as he identified the sole occupant: Eileen Floyd.

Part Three: Relocation

32

Friday 27th March 2037

Compton Majestic Hotel, Northstowe

Antimone was half-watching an animated film about a baby giraffe when a light knock sounded at the door to their room. "Pause TV," she said.

Paul shifted impatiently on her lap. "Oh, Mummy. I want to watch this."

She ignored her son's complaint. "Jason, somebody's here. Can you get it?"

Jason put down the e-book reader. After a moment, the screen automatically dimmed as the device's sensors detected the focus of his eyes were no longer on the words. He swung his legs off the bed and ambled across the carpeted floor. "Yes, who's there?"

"An important visitor would like to see you, sir," a muffled voice replied from the opposite side of the thick layer of wood.

Jason shot Antimone a worried look and backed away.

"Ah… sorry, sir, I should have said, today's password is hamster."

Jason breathed a sigh of relief and turned the handle. A flustered looking Derek Walker waited in the corridor. A pair of men in dark suits stood behind him. One placed a finger on his left earlobe and muttered a few words.

"If you could just step back, please," the other said.

Jason moved to the side as Walker led the group of three into the room.

The man who had issued the command crossed to the bathroom and peered inside. "Clear."

Moments later, the smartly dressed figure of Andrew Jacobs, the British Prime Minister, appeared in the doorway, flanked by another two sombre-faced men.

"Good afternoon," he said. "Sorry to turn up unannounced like this. I hope I'm not disturbing you."

Jason glanced down at his bare feet. "It's no problem at all, sir."

"I'll catch up with you later," Walker said, retreating from the room and closing the door behind him.

"So, how are you all?" Jacobs asked. "Oh, and please call me AJ."

"We're fine, um… AJ," Jason replied.

"You're probably wondering what I'm doing here," the Prime Minister continued. "You must have noticed the members of the press outside, so clearly your presence in this place is no longer a secret. It's not safe for you to stay here anymore. I have a proposal to make, and I wanted to put it to you in person."

Antimone wheeled her chair closer. From his mother's lap, Paul stared open-mouthed at the four men accompanying the leader of the country.

"Well," Jacobs said after a brief pause, "my advisers tell me there's a high chance another dangerous mutation of this virus will take place before too long, so we've agreed to set up an international research effort. We're bringing in scientists from around the world to try to beat this thing once and for all. Given the original source of this pandemic, it was the least we could do."

He cleared his throat. "Now, as you may have heard, Ilithyia Biotechnology has recently gone into administration. We plan to establish this new science centre on the site. The building already has all the facilities we need, so it's perfect from that perspective. You're probably asking yourselves what this has to do with you. Well, we'd like to move you there too. I know you've been through a lot, and I'm sure it'll bring back some bad memories, but it would be a big help to the team if you could spend some time with them."

Antimone scowled at the Prime Minister. "Let me get this straight. You're proposing to return us to the place where they held me prisoner and where we all nearly died."

"Look, I'm aware it's not ideal from that point of view, but it does have some major advantages. For starters, the location is secure. What's more, it happens to be close to where you used to live, so if you want to pick anything up from home, it won't take long to make the trip. And your parents can visit whenever they like. Not only will you be safe and away from the press, but also the researchers would really appreciate your presence there to assist with their work."

"What help could they possibly need from us?"

Jacobs offered a weak smile. "You're still the only person to survive childbirth without taking drugs to prevent the activation of the virus."

Antimone folded her arms. "Yeah, sometimes I wish that wasn't the case. I don't mind helping, but I'll be the one to choose what tests they run on me and my son."

"Of course. I wouldn't expect anything less."

"Where would we stay?" Antimone asked.

"They've already converted some of the old office space to luxury apartments so the scientists can live on site. I've seen photographs, and it's really quite comfortable. On top of that, you'll be well protected."

"Will anybody else we know be there?"

"I forgot to mention. Dr Kubar has joined the team. He was very enthusiastic about seeing you again."

"So, you've already discussed our situation with him?" Jason said.

"Yes. He and I spoke last week. In fact, he was the person who suggested it would be a good place for you to stay."

"What aren't you telling us?" Antimone asked.

Jacobs glanced anxiously from one to the other. "Right, well I suppose I should mention beforehand that Mrs Baxter will also be on site—not that either of you need to see her if you don't want to."

"What?" Jason said, raising his eyebrows in surprise. "You're going to release her from prison?"

"Yes. In fact, she's already moved to the Ilithyia building. We kept it out of the press for obvious reasons. She wants to help undo some of the damage she has caused. I know the situation may be awkward for you, and I can't force you to go, but I honestly think it's the best solution all round."

"I'm not worried about her," Antimone said. "She's still not my favourite person, but she did save Paul's life in Tripoli. Will there be armed guards? I don't want my son living around people carrying guns."

Jacobs's face cracked in a wry grin. "I'm afraid some of us have to put up with that all the time." His smile faded at the impassive response from his audience. "Given the company's history and the high-value individuals staying on-site, hopefully yourselves included, we need to maintain a significant security presence. It's a balancing act, but we're keen the place doesn't feel like a prison, so we're trying to keep everything low key. The compound is protected by an electrified fence, and we've provided the team with a variety of non-lethal weapons, such as tasers, and sonic cannons, that sort of thing."

"And what about schooling for Paul?"

"How old is your son now? Four? I'm sure we can arrange for somebody to come in and teach him."

"If we do agree to go, how long would we have to stay?" Jason asked.

"Unfortunately, that's a question for which I don't yet have an answer. I have experts to advise me on subjects like that, but my guess is that after we've defeated this virus once and for all, people will be less interested in you and your family. I don't want you to feel that I'm applying undue pressure, but your presence on site may reduce the time needed to come up with a solution."

Jason turned to Antimone. "What do you think?"

She met his gaze for a moment before replying. "It seems there aren't many other options."

Jason refocused his attention on the Prime Minister. "Okay, AJ. We'll do it."

33

Friday 27th March 2037

Ilithyia Biotechnology, Northstowe

Rosalind Baxter followed Martin Hendrick into the boardroom. A thin woman with shoulder-length brown hair stepped forwards. "Welcome, Mrs Baxter. Glad you could join us."

Professor Christine Harris spoke with a precise British accent. Her clothes, a matching navy-blue jacket and skirt, were clearly expensive and clung to her slim body. Rosalind knew this scientist was over fifty years old, but she could easily pass for somebody a decade younger. She might have the appearance of an ageing model, but she possessed an incisive mind and was a world-renowned expert in viral science. "Obviously, we've met many times before, so I don't need to describe my background," she said. "I'll be leading the team and coordinating the different work packages."

Harris extended an arm to introduce the next scientist. "This is Herr Professor Jacob Fischer. Once again, I'm sure you're already well acquainted." The man with the open-necked, flowery shirt, stood and bowed. As he did so, his floppy white hair fell across his face. He swept it back with his right hand. Fischer, like the woman who introduced him, had established himself as one of the foremost experts in viral research.

Harris moved on to the next team member. "You may have less familiarity with the work of Professor Armand Allard."

"No, I don't think we've met before," Rosalind said, studying the overweight man in the dark suit. She estimated he was in his early sixties, although his hair remained jet black. *Probably from a bottle.*

"Bonjour, Mrs Baxter," he replied, speaking with a heavily accented French accent. "My expertise lies in the subject of nanomachines. I look forward to discussing my research with you."

Rosalind flashed a brief smile.

"That brings me to Dr Rachel Miller. Rachel joins us from Johns Hopkins University in Baltimore. She has spent many years in the biomedical field and is an authority in drug synthesis." The woman on the other side of the table rose from her seat, displaying her full height. Rosalind estimated she stood at least an inch over six feet tall. Her hair was tied back in a ponytail, and she was dressed casually in blue jeans and a white shirt. She tilted her head at Rosalind without smiling.

"I know you are well acquainted with our next team member, Dr Naeem Kubar. He has made quite a name for himself by developing a treatment for the new strain of the Orestes virus although he is very modest and claims you should receive much of the credit. It is mainly down to his insistence that we have asked you to join our group."

Kubar jumped up from his chair, grinning from ear to ear. "It is so good to see you again, Rosalind. I hope we will have another successful collaboration."

"And it seems you've already met, Dr Martin Hendrick. Martin joins us from the Oslo Medical Research Centre and is an expert in the field of cross-species viral transmission."

Rosalind nodded to her former employee. If he wanted to keep his past association with Ilithyia secret, she would play along—for now. Nine months earlier, an employment history at the company that developed the first treatment for the Orestes virus would have been considered a positive, but ever since the revelation about the source of the outbreak, she imagined it counted as a significant black mark within the scientific community.

Harris pointed to an empty chair. "Would you like to take a seat, Mrs Baxter?"

Rosalind headed around the large circular table to the only unoccupied space.

"Right, now that everybody's here, let's begin. I appreciate you joining me on this vital project. You are all world-renowned experts in your chosen field. In the past, we have all worked in our separate groups, and to some extent, in competition with each other. From this point forwards, we have to work together. It's no coincidence that you come from diverse backgrounds. Hopefully, the different skill sets you bring will help us to be more productive and generate innovative solutions to the challenges we face.

"Now, several of you have brought your teams with you. I expect those of you who are alone—that includes Mrs Baxter, Dr Hendrick and Dr Kubar—to spread your time between the specialities. Your experience and insights will help to engender the cross-functional cooperation I believe we need to make a difference and find a solution where we have previously failed. In essence, you will be the glue that binds the separate work packages together. Are there any question so far?"

Allard, the French nanomachine expert, raised his hand. "Madame 'Arris, what is our budget?"

"I have been assured by the people who hold the purse strings that they will not refuse any reasonable request," the professor replied. "If you can justify the expenditure, I'll ensure you get the funds."

Kubar spoke next. "You propose that I spend my time across the groups. May I also perform my own research?"

"Of course. If you would prefer to establish your own group, provided it aligns with our goals, I will do my best to make it happen. Now, if there are no more questions, I suggest each of you gives a fifteen- or twenty-minute synopsis of how you plan to address the problem facing us."

Rosalind listened as each of the scientists described their area of expertise and their thoughts on how to tackle the challenge. She was familiar with the work of most of the attendees other than the Frenchman, Armand Allard. His team of researchers had developed microscopic machines that could be programmed to perform operations at the molecular level. Despite her lack of knowledge, she found herself fascinated by his radically new approach.

When he ended his short presentation, she raised her hand.

"Oui, Mrs Baxter," he said.

"What you've told us is really interesting, Monsieur Allard."

"Thank you. And please call me Armand."

"Okay, Armand. What's stopping your nanomachines from ignoring their programming and running out of control? What would happen if they malfunctioned, and you couldn't stop them?"

The French scientist rolled his eyes.

"I'm sorry if that sounds like a stupid question," Rosalind said, glancing around at the other meeting attendees.

"I blame science fiction," he replied. "They call this the grey goo scenario, or to use a more technical term, ecophagy."

"I don't understand."

"Many writers have written stories about self-replicating microscopic machines that multiply uncontrollably to the point where all matter on this planet is broken down to produce more and more copies until nothing remains other than a sea of nanomachines. The so-called grey goo."

"Right."

"But this cannot happen here. Firstly, my devices do not have the capability to self-replicate. We use specialised machines to manufacture them in a separate process. Secondly, in order to function, we must first send them a signal. This can take several forms, such as light or magnetic fields, but they will not turn on until they are instructed to do so. Thirdly, they are all programmed to shut down upon receipt of the appropriate command. This uses a similar mechanism to the one used to activate them. Finally, the power source contained inside each device has a limited life. When it is exhausted, they stop."

"So, you have no worries about them malfunctioning in a dangerous way?"

Allard clasped his hands over his stomach. "No, Madame Baxter... Rosalind. Twenty years ago, people had similar concerns about artificial intelligence taking over the world. Now, we cannot live without that technology. This is the same thing."

Harris glanced at her watch. "Well, it's nearly twelve thirty, so that's good timing. Lunch is available in the canteen. That was an interesting session. I propose we meet here daily at nine o'clock for a fifteen-minute stand-up, so that everybody can keep abreast of progress. Every Monday morning, we will hold a longer meeting like this. With your wide-ranging expertise, I anticipate a fruitful collaboration. Together we're going to beat this virus once and for all."

Rosalind pushed back her chair and rose to her feet with the others. As she trailed after her fellow scientists, a hand landed on her forearm. She whirled around to meet Christine Harris's stern gaze.

"If you wouldn't mind staying behind for a moment, Mrs Baxter," the professor said. "I'd like a quiet word." She waited until the other attendees had left, then pushed the door closed.

Rosalind pulled up the nearest seat. Harris crossed to the opposite side of the table and followed suit.

"What can I do for you, Christine?"

For many years, the two women had maintained a professional rivalry. Over that time, they had met at several conferences and often found themselves on the same expert panel. On more than one occasion, they had argued about the best way to approach the pandemic.

Harris leant forwards with a slight frown on her face. "Before I say anything else, I want to make it clear it wasn't my idea to include you in this project. I have been instructed to utilise every resource at my disposal, but your presence here is not something I asked for. As I mentioned earlier, Dr Kubar is one of your biggest supporters. I am not alone in believing you should remain in prison for what you did."

Rosalind met the woman's gaze. "Well, it's nice to receive a vote of confidence. They offered me a choice between staying in my cell or returning to this place. I chose to come here, but it was a close-run decision."

Harris's frown deepened. "If I must have you on-site, I want you to assume a role acting across all the different research teams. Despite my objections to your being here, I still value your scientific opinion. Make sure you keep up to date with what's happening."

"Fine."

"Oh, one last thing. If you cause any trouble, or I feel you aren't making a significant contribution to the work we're doing, I'll request your immediate removal from the team."

34

Sunday 29th March 2037

Ilithyia Biotechnology, Northstowe

Antimone shuddered as she rolled through the entrance to the Ilithyia Biotechnology facility. The last time she came this way, she had been trying to rescue her son. It all turned out well in the end, but she, Jason and Jason's father, Daniel Floyd, had come within moments of losing their lives, and the place still gave her the creeps.

The building had a different look and feel about it from what she remembered. For a start, the foyer was far quieter. Five years ago, the bustle of patients and scientists had filled the space with noise. Now, most of the people present were security staff. The curved reception desk had gone, replaced by a ten-foot-high barricade incorporating a pair of barriers, one side for entry, the other for exit. Antimone's gaze focused on the two unsmiling men in pale-blue uniforms, who stood guard beside the electronically operated gates, blocking access to the area beyond.

She gave a start as Jason's hand landed on her shoulder.

"Are you okay?" he asked.

"Yeah, fine," she replied in a flat monotone.

He glanced down at Paul, whose tiny fingers intertwined with his father's. "And how about you, buddy?"

"Why does it smell funny in here, Dad?"

The air carried the strong odour of disinfectant.

"Oh, it's only the stuff they use to keep this place clean," Jason said.

Antimone twisted in her wheelchair and directed her attention to Derek Walker. The man assigned to their security over the last few months approached the two guards, and they conducted a conversation in low voices.

After a few seconds, Walker beckoned them forwards. "They're expecting us. You'll have to pass through a scanner to check for concealed weapons. Once we're inside, they'll show you to your rooms. They're just waiting for somebody called Nick Butler to turn up. Apparently, he's in charge of site security."

"Is this the only way in and out?" Antimone asked. "Will we be safe here?"

"From what I understand, there's a goods entrance as well, but that's equally secure. There's absolutely no chance the press, or anybody else for that matter, is getting in without permission. You saw the barrier across the road when we came in. And if that isn't enough, there's also the electric fence around the building. This place is locked down tighter than a duck's arse."

"Right. Do you think we'll be allowed to go outside?"

"You'll have to discuss that with Mr Butler."

A man with short-cropped grey hair stepped through the exit barrier. "Did I hear somebody mention my name?" he asked.

Walker and Butler introduced themselves. Knuckles cracked as they shook hands, but neither signalled weakness by displaying any discomfort. The former was three inches taller than the latter, but Butler's heavily muscled frame more than compensated for his lack of height. Antimone watched on as the two men sized each other up. If it came to a fight between the pair, she couldn't decide who she would put her money on.

The person responsible for ensuring their security from this point on passed from one member of the family to another, crushing their fingers in his powerful grip.

When he got to Paul, he patted him on the head. "Hello, big boy."

"Hello, little man," the four-year-old replied with a cheeky grin.

Butler raised an eyebrow, unsure how to respond.

Walker maintained a deadpan expression. "I'll say my goodbyes now," he said, turning to Jason and Antimone. "It's been a pleasure working with you." He spun on his heel and headed back to the exit without a backwards glance.

Butler waited for their former protector to depart through the rotating doors. He gestured towards the entrance gate. "Good afternoon, everybody. If you'd like to go through, we'll run through a brief induction session."

Butler went first, followed by Jason and Paul, then Antimone. As each of the adults passed through the barrier, one of the uniformed guards handed them a laminated card bearing a 3D hologram of the holder and instructed them to hang it around their neck. Antimone studied the image on her badge. Judging by the background, the camera must have taken the picture as she entered the building. The people running this place were definitely leaving nothing to chance.

"But I want one too," Paul said.

"Perhaps when you're a bit bigger," Butler replied.

Antimone slipped hers over her son's head. "You can wear mine for now." The plastic rectangle dwarfed Paul's body.

Butler flashed an irritated glance at her. He clasped his hands behind his back and addressed the family of three. "Welcome to the Ilithyia facility. When you are on-site, you must keep your identity card on show at all times. Please do not leave your rooms without it. It gives you access to all the areas you are permitted to visit and will operate lifts and doors as appropriate, including entry to your room. There is a canteen, which remains open twenty-four hours a day. We have a gymnasium with all the latest equipment for those of you who want to exercise. The laboratories are off-limits to everybody apart from the scientific staff.

"All the rooms are well equipped with state-of-the-art entertainment systems. The building provides free Wi-Fi access, but I need to warn you that we monitor all network links. Maid service will come in every morning between ten and eleven o'clock. Please hang a sign on your door handle if you don't want to be disturbed. Now, are there any questions?"

"Can we go outside?" Antimone asked.

"I'd rather you didn't, but if you're determined to leave the building, then one or more of my men will escort you at all times."

"What about leaving the site?"

Butler chuckled. "You've only recently arrived, and you want to go already? Look, the reason for transferring you here is to keep you safe. We can't spare the resources to protect you outside the fence. If you can find somebody else to guarantee your safety, then I don't see why not, but it's not something my team is able to support. The scientists operate under the same restrictions. They all live on site too."

"I heard that Mrs Baxter is staying here," Jason said. "Is that true?"

Butler's forehead creased in a frown. "I suppose you'll find out for yourselves pretty soon anyway, so there's no point denying it. Yes, she's helping out the research teams."

"Will we be allowed to visit her?"

Butler stared at him with an incredulous expression. When he saw Jason wasn't joking, he said, "You can't go in her room, and nor can she enter yours. However, if you wish, you may meet up in the canteen. Just be aware, a member of the security staff will be sitting close by all the time. Now, if there are no more questions, I'll leave you here, and one of my team will take you to your accommodation."

The three new arrivals trailed after the man in the pale-blue uniform, who had been assigned to their group. The card around his neck identified him as John Griffin. He led them across the foyer and prodded the call button when they reached the lifts. Moments later, the elevator doors parted. The others moved forwards to enter, but Antimone froze. A sudden sense of déjà vu overwhelmed her. For the past four years, she had tried to forget what had happened here, but now the memories of her failed escape attempt and the subsequent mistreatment came crashing back into her mind.

"What's wrong?" Jason asked, turning around and inserting a foot into the gap to prevent the panels from closing.

"I... I'm... It's nothing." She forced her hands to keep the wheelchair moving forwards. She closed her eyes and held her breath until the swish of the opening doors signalled their arrival. With trembling arms, she backed out into the corridor.

"This looks familiar," Jason said, lowering his voice. "This used to be where my mother had her office."

"I wouldn't know," Antimone snapped. "They kept me in the basement where they could study me like a lab rat."

"I'm sorry. This must be hard for you."

"Yeah. I would probably have died down there if you hadn't rescued me."

Jason had freed her using knockout gas grenades that his father, Daniel Floyd, obtained through a former prison cellmate.

Jason took her hand and squeezed it. They followed the guard in the blue uniform down the corridor until he stopped outside a door. He pulled a mobile device from his pocket and studied the screen. "Miss Lessing, Mr Floyd and your son are in here," he said. "Just hold your card to the reader to get in." He pointed at a small box mounted to the wall. "There's a fire escape that way, and the main stairs are over there."

"Thanks. Who's next door?" Jason asked.

"We've put some of the scientists on this floor."

"What are their names?"

The man shuffled uncertainly from foot to foot but didn't answer.

"Oh well, I suppose we'll find out soon enough," Jason continued.

"All right. That side is Mrs Baxter and the other room is Professor Fischer's. If you're worried about Mrs Baxter, you're perfectly safe. She can't come or go without one of the security team to open the door."

Jason's and Antimone's eyes locked for a moment. Jason shrugged. "Fine. Thanks for letting us know."

"I'll leave you to it," the guard said. "You can come and go as you please. Just remember to make sure your identity badges are visible at all times."

Jason held up his card. A green light flashed, accompanied by the click of the lock. He went first, holding the door open for Antimone and Paul. The overhead lighting immediately came on, illuminating a short hallway.

"I think this was Nigel Perrin's old office," he said. He stuck his head in the doorway on the right. "Bathroom," he announced. "This is where his secretary used to sit." He carried on down the narrow passageway, opening the pair of slatted doors. "Built-in wardrobe." He pushed through into the bedroom. "Oh, this is different."

The beds took up the floor space along the back wall. A bedside table separated a child's bed from a full-sized double, both covered with matching, brightly coloured covers. The person responsible for the room's decor had crammed in several items of wooden furniture, including two chests of drawers and a desk. A pair of armchairs sat beside the large window at the far end.

Antimone pushed herself forwards and looked out onto the gardens below, bordered by an electric fence. A man held a massive German Shepherd on a tight leash as he patrolled the perimeter.

She turned back to Jason. "It's comfortable enough here, but it still feels like a prison."

He stood beside her and stared down. "Maybe, but nobody's getting in with all that security. At least we'll be safe here."

Once again, a strong feeling of déjà vu descended on Antimone.

"I certainly hope so," she replied.

35

Sunday 5th April 2037

27 Boxworth Road, Northstowe

Max Perrin paced backwards and forwards. "So, now we know Baxter and Kubar are at the old Ilithyia building," he said.

The three-man team had moved into the rented house a week earlier. The two-bedroom semi-detached property provided a far superior base of operations, well away from the prying eyes of the landlady at the guest house. It also had the advantage of a long-distance view across the fields to where the aforementioned targets were staying. Max had a bedroom to himself, while his two colleagues shared a room.

"What about the others?" he asked. "Do we have any idea where they've gone?"

Mohammed Abadi glanced up from the screen. "I am still looking for them. There are some rumours on the net they may be in the same place."

"What?" Max moved over and stood behind him. "Show me."

The diminutive North African reached out a hand and dragged a window to the front. "Here. The information on this forum is usually fairly reliable."

Max lowered his head and studied the posts. "It would certainly make life easier if they were all together. We still have to figure out a way to get to them. The place is bound to be heavily guarded."

Omar Hijazi looked up from the virtual reality computer game he was playing. "As I said before, we should just go in and shoot them all."

Max rolled his eyes. "There are only three of us. We wouldn't even get inside the building, let alone any further than that. And getting the sort of weapons we'd need to complete the job would be difficult to organise."

A support team in The Republic of North Africa had been set up to supply them with any equipment they requested for the mission. Their handlers dealt with a list of local suppliers who arranged delivery and asked no questions about the intended purpose of the items they provided.

"Yes," Mo agreed. "And they use dogs. Look." He flicked his wrist and brought up a picture of the security fence surrounding the facility. In the photograph a man stood beside the meshed barrier, leading a huge black and tan dog. "The fencing is probably also electrified," he added.

Omar shook his head. "The British police do not carry guns. They will have no defence if we shoot them."

"I wouldn't be so sure," Max replied. "They won't be using ordinary policemen to guard somewhere like that. I'm not ready to sacrifice my life for this."

"That is where we are different. I would gladly die if I could take those traitors with me."

"I want them dead as much as you, but there has to be a better way. There are some important people on site, so they're bound to have some fairly serious protection. This requires a more subtle approach. We need to prepare properly."

"Okay," Omar said, returning to his game. "You are the boss. I am sure you know best."

"Before we proceed, we must confirm who's in there."

Mo flicked the picture off the screen. "Leave it with me. I am already on it."

"What about those microbots you brought with you? Can't you get one of those past the fence?"

"Perhaps, but I think they will have radio detection and EM blocking," Mo replied.

The tiny robots carried a camera and could be remotely controlled, but if electromagnetic interference blocked the signal to control them, as seemed likely, they were useless. As an added downside, if the guards discovered one of the machines within the grounds, that would raise the alert level, and the operation would become much more difficult.

"We've already set up long-range surveillance," Max said, referring to the telescope upstairs, targeted at the entrance. "Can't we use that?"

"The glass on the building is reflective. This is common to stop industrial espionage, so it is not possible to see inside. But if they come outside..."

"You're telling me there's no easy way to tell who's there, then?"

"Yes." Mo focused his attention back on the computer. After a few seconds, he turned around again. "Did you not say your father worked at Ilithyia?" he asked.

"Yeah, but that was four or five years ago. The company has changed ownership since then."

"But maybe the systems are the same?"

"What are you getting at, Mo?"

"I am thinking perhaps if you know your father's password, we can break into their computers."

"Unfortunately, I've no idea what it might've been."

"Oh, well. It was just a suggestion."

Max tapped his teeth. "Actually, now you mention it, my dad was useless at remembering details. He always wrote things like passwords down. He used to keep them in a notebook he kept locked in his desk drawer."

"If I could see that, I might be able to use the information to get inside their systems."

"Wouldn't the new owners just delete his account?"

"Yes, that is likely, but it is worth a try." Mo leant closer. "Do you know where this book is?"

"Yeah, I may have an idea. As long as my mother hasn't thrown it away, it's probably still at her house."

"Can you get it?"

The motors in Max's arm whined as he repeatedly clenched and unclenched the fingers of his artificial hand. "I haven't been in contact with her for many years. Let's just say we didn't part on the best of terms. She stole my father's inheritance from me. I've been meaning to pay her a visit for a while."

"Is there not a risk she will tell the British authorities she has seen you?"

Max's face took on a thoughtful expression. "No, I don't think so. She won't say a word."

36

Sunday 5th April 2037

Ilithyia Biotechnology, Northstowe

Rosalind Baxter read the label on the door: BioNEMS. The fact she had no idea what the letters stood for summed up her lack of knowledge when it came to nanomachines. She had arranged a two-hour meeting with the French leader of the team, Armand Allard, to rectify the situation.

She held her card to the reader. A red light glowed for a moment, then turned off. Clearly, they didn't trust her enough to permit access to the laboratory. She raised her hand and knocked.

A guard in the ubiquitous pale-blue uniform strolled down the corridor in her direction, glaring at her suspiciously. When he was still a few paces away, the door swung open.

"Ah, there you are," the rotund Frenchman said. "Please come in."

Rosalind followed him into a room fifteen metres long by ten wide. When she had been the CEO of the company, this was one of the operating theatres. Now computer workstations had replaced the surgical tables. Four people sat in front of the screens. None of them looked up at her entry.

"This isn't what I was expecting," Rosalind said.

"No," Allard replied, "but this is the future of medical research. We use nanomachines to do the work once performed by drugs. But somebody has to tell these machines what functions to perform. We do this using computers."

"Surely, you must still carry out tests and experiments."

"Yes, of course. We have small-scale production capabilities here. That happens in there." He pointed towards the room where the surgeons had once scrubbed up before an operation. "The researchers only go in when they want to run an experiment. We take precautions to ensure none of our creations can escape."

"Pardon my ignorance, but what do the letters on the door outside stand for?"

"You mean BioNEMS? Bio-nanoelectromechanical systems. Shall we sit down?"

Rosalind followed Allard to an unoccupied workstation. He grabbed an empty chair and pulled it up alongside the one already there. Both sat.

"Now," the Frenchman said, "what would you like to know?"

"I guess, the first thing to discuss is how you think these nanomachines could destroy the virus."

"Okay. Put simply, we can program them to latch onto particular molecular sequences. They have the means to travel through the body, but we must tell them when they are in the right place. There are several ways to do this, but the two principal methods are magnetic fields and light."

"So," Rosalind said, "if I understand you correctly, you can design them to home in on and attack a specific pattern of molecules."

"Yes, but they can also be used to build. For example, one area of research for this technology is the reconstruction of severed nerves, such as those that occur in spinal cord injuries. However, this is not the focus of our work here."

"How do you program them?" Rosalind asked.

Allard spent the next hour taking her through the process of design and manufacture. The subject changed to the application of the technology for another thirty minutes. When he had finished, he turned to Rosalind. "Well, what do you think?"

She leant back and steepled her fingers. "If everything you've told me is right, I agree this could be the future of medicine. The biggest problem will be in convincing the public and scientific community that it's safe."

"I know this. It is so frustrating. I blame Eric Drexler."

"Who?"

"Many regard him as one of the main pioneers of nanotechnology. He wrote a book called the Engines of Creation in the nineteen-eighties. Over fifty years have passed since then, but still, people talk about grey goo. I have already told you all the precautions we take to prevent such a scenario from happening.

"I worry that the ignorant and the uneducated will always hold this technology back. The press love to sell fear, and it is a good theme for science fiction writers. Scientists have the capability to manufacture biological organisms today that are far more dangerous than anything I can create with my machines. In fact, the Orestes virus itself was artificially created."

Rosalind stiffened. "It was an accident."

Allard raised his hands apologetically. "I am sorry. I was not trying to say..."

"Let's move on. I'd rather not talk about it. An experiment went badly wrong, that's all."

"Fine. Do you have any ideas about how we can apply nanomachines to this question?"

Rosalind ran her fingers through her hair. She described the techniques they had used to prevent the activation of the virus. "The big problem," she added after finishing her explanation, "is that the approach I've just gone through doesn't address the underlying latent infection. Every living person already has this viral material inside their cells."

"I agree. We need to target both the lytic and the latent phases."

"Ideally, yes."

"And how do you propose we do that?"

"Well," Rosalind replied, "that's the billion-dollar question. Let me have a think about it. I have a meeting with one of the other teams now."

Allard rose from his chair and shook her hand. "That was a very interesting discussion. I look forward to working with you."

"The same here. I'm sure this technology will help us find a solution. That is, if it doesn't turn everybody into grey goo first."

The slightest hint of a humourless smile persisted on the French scientist's face as Rosalind left the room.

37

Sunday 6th April 2037

23 Daffodil Drive, Northstowe

Max Perrin pushed through the narrow gate and approached the house he had lived in for the first sixteen years of his life. He knelt and picked up a rock from the ornamental feature to the left of the front door. He turned it over and pressed with his thumb. The hidden lid sprung open. Some things never changed. After all this time, his mother still kept a spare key in the same place.

He removed the key from its hiding spot and slid it into the door lock. With a final surreptitious glance behind, he let himself in. Where was she? Her car occupied its normal position in front of the double garage, so the chances were she was somewhere inside. He stood still and held his breath, listening for a clue to her whereabouts.

The faint sound of voices carried from the living room. He crept down the hall. It seemed she had splashed out on a new carpet. The expensive weave in a shade of dark-green muffled his footsteps. He stopped and placed his ear against the door. A sudden burst of clapping emanated from the other side: a daytime chat show.

"What do you want?"

Max spun around at his mother's tense voice. The blade of a large kitchen knife glinted in her hand.

Her mouth dropped open in shock as recognition dawned. "Max?"

"Hello, Mum."

She placed the makeshift weapon on the hall table. "What are you doing here? I thought you'd disappeared off the face of the planet. Where have you been all this time?"

"That's a lot of questions," Max said. "I've been abroad. Shall we go through and sit down?"

As he reached for the doorknob, her gaze settled on his arm. "Did something happen to—"

"Yes, I lost it... in an accident. But they've done a good job with this prosthetic, don't you agree?"

Max stepped through the doorway into the lounge. More new carpets. His mother bustled in after him, snatched up the remote control and switched off the television. He studied her more carefully in the light streaming through the windows from the tidily kept garden. Her hair had turned totally grey, and her waistline had filled out a little. She wore a loose-fitting pair of cream trousers and a chequered shirt. She lowered herself into an armchair.

"Why didn't you ring the doorbell?" she asked.

Max sat on the sofa, perching on the edge. "I wanted to surprise you."

"Well, you certainly did that. I thought you were a burglar. You're lucky I didn't stab you."

"You really shouldn't leave the key in the fake rock."

"To be honest, I'd totally forgotten about it. So, you say you've been abroad? Where?"

"It doesn't matter."

"What was this accident?"

Max shook his head but remained silent.

"The police came here asking about you."

Max frowned. "When did this happen? What did they want?"

"It must have been nine months ago, maybe a year. They just asked me whether I knew where you were. I told them I had no idea. Do you know what that was about?"

"Yes."

Max's mother waited for him to expand on his answer. When he didn't, she continued. "So, what've you been up to for the last four years? An email or a phone call to tell me you were okay would've been nice."

"I was working because you wouldn't give me the money Dad left me in his will."

"It was for your own good. You were too young to have that sort of cash. I'm sure I can let you have some now if you need it."

"It's too late for that," Max said. "Did you keep Dad's things?"

"I gave away most of his clothes. I didn't think they were really your style."

Max remained impassive at his mother's failed attempt at humour. "What about his desk?"

Her face clouded in confusion. "I got rid of the medical books in his study, but I've left everything else as it was."

"So, you haven't been through the drawers?"

"No. Why are you asking?"

"I need a notebook Dad kept in the top drawer. Did you know, the day he died he called me and told me to pack a bag. We were going to leave together. This was before that bitch, Rosalind Baxter, killed him."

His mother lifted a hand to her mouth. "What are you talking about?"

"You thought he was the victim of a freak accident at work. They spun you some story about how he was holding a pen when an explosion sent it flying into his brain. But that was all a lie. Baxter stabbed him in the eye."

"Max, why would you say such a thing? I realise it affected you badly at the time, but—"

"You don't know the half of it. They made me sign the Official Secrets Act. They threatened to send me to prison if I ever spoke about what really happened. The Prime Minister himself was in on it."

"I don't believe you."

Max's face flushed. "For Christ's sake, listen to me, you stupid cow. Dad wasn't the man you thought he was. He was a mass murderer. Between them, Rosalind Baxter and my father created the Orestes virus. He's no longer with us, but it doesn't change the facts."

"I was married to him for over twenty years. He may have spent all his time at that damned company, neglecting his family, but I know what he was capable of, and he could never kill anybody."

"Well, you're wrong on that count. Unlike you, I was there. He was about to confess when she rammed a pen into his eye to prevent him from saying more. But I got my revenge on her. I broke into her house and slipped a mind control drug into her drink. Then I forced her to do the same thing to herself. I even used one of Dad's old pens. I should've stayed to watch until the end because somehow she regained enough willpower to stop."

"What happened to you, Max? What's made you like this? Your father didn't create the virus; he died in a terrible accident. If he was responsible, why would they allow us to keep the money when they sold the company?"

"Do I really have to explain? Rosalind Baxter pressured them into a deal—she agreed to complete development of the drug if they kept it all quiet and let her go. She also had to give up ninety percent of her stock. They could hardly hang on to Dad's shares without telling you why. You received all that cash because the woman who killed my father blackmailed the Prime Minister of this country into a pardon for her crimes."

"I'm sorry. I don't believe any of this. You need help, Max."

"That's why I've come back."

His mother shot him a puzzled look before continuing. "You were always a difficult child. Nothing made you happy. You never smiled as a baby. Just a few weeks after you were born, your father had to work on an urgent problem at the company and didn't return home for a few days. You cried day and night. You nearly drove me mad. The doctors examined you but couldn't find anything physically wrong with you.

"You became worse as you got older. They banned you from kindergarten for continually biting the other children. You almost killed another boy in primary school. The child psychologist told us afterwards that you lacked empathy. Your father thought having a pet might help. The gerbil lasted less than a week. I can still remember the blood coming out of its mouth. You crushed it to death in your hand because it nipped you.

"We spent thousands on counselling. They warned us you might suffer from mental health issues later in life. Things got better when you went to Oakington Manor. We thought we'd seen the back of your problems, but now this. I don't know where you've been for the last few years, whether you've been taking drugs or something, but it's clearly caused some sort of—"

"Stop." The quiet tone of Max's voice was more chilling than if he had shouted. "I didn't come here to listen to you list my faults. Do you still use CommsHub?"

"CommsHub? Why on earth are you asking about that?"

Max stood. "Just answer the question."

"Yes. I post the occasional status update."

"Can you log in?"

"I... I don't understand."

Max turned and spotted the tablet computer on the coffee table. He strode across, picked it up and handed it to his mother in silence. She stared at him for a moment, then held it up to her face as the iris scanner did its work. "There."

The familiar logo filled the 3D screen. Max flicked his finger and scrolled through her recent posts.

"What're you doing? You're frightening me."

Max tapped at the keyboard floating above the display. A few moments later, he clicked the off button. "Thanks." He tossed the device onto the sofa.

"What did you just type?" she asked.

"Oh, I posted an update to your account, saying you were planning to go away for a few weeks and that you wouldn't be able to log in."

"But I'm not going anywhere."

"I know."

"Um... how long are you staying?" His mother's voice trembled with fear.

"I'll be leaving shortly. But it's time to say goodbye now."

Max stood over her armchair and stared down at her. She leant forwards to rise, but he pushed her back. Then he clambered on top of her and wrapped his fingers around her throat. She tried to bat him away, but he avoided her feeble attempts with ease. The motors in his left arm whirred as he tightened his grip. Within moments, the light faded from her eyes, and her struggles stopped.

He pulled his mobile from his back pocket and dialled a number from contacts. "It's done. Make sure nobody sees you coming in."

The other team members were waiting at a kid's playground half a mile away. He turned and headed for the hall. Other than the mostly empty bookshelves, his father's study looked the same as when he had last been here four years earlier. He rounded the large wooden desk and lowered himself into the leather office chair. He tugged at the drawer on the right side. *Damn! Locked.*

A quick inspection of the room didn't reveal a matching key. The solution would require brute force. A pot containing pens and other items sat on one of the shelves. He got up and emptied it onto the desk's surface. A sturdy, brass letter opener spilt out along with the assorted writing implements. Max snatched it up and forced the shaft into the gap. A sharp jerk and the drawer shifted with a splintering sound.

Max rummaged inside and discovered a small leather-bound notebook hidden beneath various items of paperwork. He flipped the cover open. His father's neat handwriting filled the page with usernames and passwords.

He scooped up the pens and returned them to the pot except for one, which he placed in his shirt pocket. After a final check of the room, he closed the door behind him. Moments later, a light tapping sound came from the front door. He peered through the peephole and twisted the latch, stepping back to allow the other two members of the team to enter.

"She's in there," he said, pointing. "You'll find tools in the shed outside. Take her out through the patio doors, then bury her in the flower bed. It's a private garden so the neighbours won't see you."

"What are you doing, boss?" Mo asked.

"I just want one last look around this place," Max replied. He removed the pen and clicked the tip in and out a few times. "Thanks, Dad," he said, glancing down at the notebook.

38

Monday 7th April 2037

Ilithyia Biotechnology, Northstowe

Rosalind sat alone in the cafeteria. A burst of laughter came from the other side of the room. She stared across at the family of three. The boy she had raised—a man now—held a spoon to his son's lips in what appeared to be a game to get the child to eat. Judging by the state of Paul's face, more food had landed on the table than in his mouth. Surely, at four years old, he could feed himself.

She cast her mind back, trying to remember how Jason compared at the same age. The memories all blurred into one another. It had been a hectic period, and in those days, she spent most of her time in the office. The live-in nanny probably had a better recollection than she did.

As she dredged the recesses of her brain, she recalled an occasion—it must have been at a weekend—when they visited the seaside at Hunstanton. Jason was three, maybe four, and managed to get ice cream all over his face, his clothes and even in his hair. It took an entire pack of tissues to clean him up, and for weeks afterwards, the car seats remained sticky. Like father, like son.

Perhaps sensing the weight of her stare, Jason turned his head towards her. He flashed a brief smile. She raised a hand in return, then quickly lowered it again. Despite the promise to visit her after she had saved his son's life in Tripoli, he and his partner had only met up with her twice in the last two months. Like almost everybody else in this place, they kept her at arm's length, although the restrictions imposed on her movements didn't help when it came to arranging time together.

She twisted in her seat. Sure enough, the ever-present security guard occupied the next table over, half-watching her with a disinterested expression. Whenever she left the laboratories, somebody always accompanied her. What did they expect her to do? Make a bid for freedom? She would have to circumvent at least two checkpoints and numerous patrols to reach as far as the fence surrounding the compound. And what would she do then? Anybody who hadn't been living under a stone for the past year would recognise her immediately.

This was the best she could hope for from now on. The conditions of her confinement were massively better than the cell at Bronzefield Women's Prison, but nonetheless, she remained an inmate. At the end of every workday after eating her evening meal, one of the security team escorted her back to her former office. The other residents had free access to the on-site facilities, but she had no such opportunities. She spent more time between the four walls of her room than anywhere else.

The babble of voices dragged her from her thoughts. A group of scientists entered the canteen, the tall figure of Rachel Miller towering over the others. The French tones of Armand Allard rose above the rest as he shared a joke with Martin Hendrick. Christine Harris glanced across at Rosalind, then quickly looked away. The senior members of the leadership team queued at the serving hatch. When Naeem Kubar spotted her, he waved. A few moments later, he pulled up a chair on the opposite side of the table, a huge grin on his face.

"Hello, Rosalind. How are you?"

"Fine, Naeem. And you?"

"Good. Good. That was a very interesting meeting. I thought you would have attended."

"Nobody invited me," Rosalind replied in a monotone voice.

The doctor's cheerful demeanour lost some of its shine. "Oh, I am sorry. I did not know."

The majority of the scientists treated Rosalind with suspicion and shunned her company. Meetings often took place without her receiving an invitation, despite her official position as a cross-functional coordinator.

By contrast, Martin Hendrick had seemingly integrated into his role with little problem. He spent much of his time with Armand Allard and his microscopic machines but also mingled with the other researchers. Whenever she asked to become more involved, the French professor and his team found a convenient excuse to deny her request.

Dr Kubar was one of the few who went out of his way to keep her in the loop.

"What did you talk about?" Rosalind said.

"The nanotechnology research is going extremely well. They are making excellent progress."

Rosalind's interest perked up. "Yeah, it's got real potential to make a difference. They've developed an exciting technology if they can work out how to apply it to this problem."

"That is true. It is a shame the others waste time at meetings with Professor Allard. It is like a game. Whenever they mention grey goo, he always responds. They think it is a big joke when he becomes excited on this matter."

Rosalind stifled a smile. She had observed that the other team leaders loved to wind up the Frenchman. "Yes, I've noticed he's a bit sensitive about the whole subject, isn't he? So, what's new?"

Kubar tore off a piece of bread and popped it in his mouth. He took a sip of water before replying. "Dr Hendrick works most of the time with the nanotechnology group. He has presented some useful ideas on how to target the virus. They have set him up with a workstation in their laboratory."

"Well, he's certainly an expert in virology and a very gifted scientist. If anybody can cross the divide between the two disciplines, it's him."

"I had not heard of him before coming here. Did you know him in the past?"

Rosalind hesitated a moment before replying. "Yes, we worked together about twenty years ago."

"It is strange. He has not talked about this."

"No."

Kubar waited for her to say more. When it became clear she had nothing to add, he continued. "I will try to make sure they invite you to more meetings. We collaborated well before, and I know you have much to contribute. They should not waste your talents. I will send you the reports they presented at today's session."

"Thanks, I appreciate it." The security team had severely restricted Rosalind's online access. They prevented all outgoing links, including ones from the entertainment system in her room. With little else to occupy her time, she spent long hours reading through the technical papers written by the on-site scientists. If she wanted to read an external paper, she had to ask one of the other researchers to send her a copy. Plenty of good ideas occurred to her, if only somebody would listen.

Kubar's attention returned to the food on his plate, and the pair ate in silence. When he finished, he pushed the chair back and stood. "Well, it was nice to talk to you, Rosalind. Good evening."

"Yeah, you too."

She turned and stared at the security guard. He made a point of studying the face of his watch. When she left the canteen, he would accompany her to her room, where she would remain until morning.

Was this her future, spending her remaining years as a prisoner, if not here, then behind bars, but constantly under somebody else's control? Even if they allowed her to go free, she would always be looking over her shoulder. What was there to look forwards to?

For the first time in her life, she questioned whether she had made the right choices.

39

Wednesday 8th April 2037

27 Boxworth Road, Northstowe

Mo flung himself back in his chair. "Yes!" he yelled.

Max Perrin peered over his fellow conspirator's shoulder. "What is it?" he asked. "Have you found a way in?"

The North African hacker's fingers twitched and jerked above the surface of the desk. The focused ultrasonic waves generated by the advanced haptic technology created the sensation of tapping physical keys, but only he could see the keyboard floating in mid-air.

Mo stopped typing and twisted around, a wide grin on his face. "There is some good news. I have just received confirmation that Jason Floyd, Antimone Lessing and their son are staying at the Ilithyia building."

"Excellent. So, they're all together. That makes life—or perhaps I should say death—easier. What about gaining access?"

"Nothing so far. The systems where they keep the medical research all seem very secure."

"So, we wasted our time getting the book from my mother's house?"

Mo's grin faded. "It is too soon to say. I still have much to try."

"All right. Well, don't give up."

The diminutive figure refocused his attention on the computer. He picked up the notebook that had once belonged to Max's father and turned the page.

Omar looked up from the sofa, where he was playing a shooting game on a handheld console. "Is it time for guns yet?"

"No, we're not quite at that stage," Max replied. "You just keep practicing." He flashed his team member a slight smile.

"Fine, but I would rather shoot real people."

Max headed out of the lounge and up the stairs. He opened the window, drew the curtains together and pressed the button to power up the telescope. He pulled up a wooden chair and squinted into the twin lenses of the eyepiece. A three-dimensional boot message hung before his eyes. He could have used any screen in the house to view the images and orientate the instrument, but he preferred the immediacy of using the built-in display. A picture of the Ilithyia car park filled his vision. He tapped the control box and adjusted the direction until the fence surrounding the building came into focus. The image was crystal clear despite the two-mile range to the target. As he zoomed in, he discovered he could read the letters on the manufacturer's sign affixed to the barrier.

He widened the viewing angle and pressed a button to select the identification mode. After a few seconds, a thin red line appeared around the outline of a man and the large dog who patrolled beside him. He panned across the area in front of the building. Another guard rounded the corner, highlighted by the instrument's target acquisition system in the same way.

Once again, Max narrowed the field of view, focusing on the man's face. The guard's mouth moved as he called out a greeting to his colleague. The sharpness of the images made it seem as if the men were standing just a few feet away. Despite the distance, the advanced video technology allowed an observer to read the speaker's lips. Max's jaw muscles tightened in frustration; he knew the approximate location of the targets, but there was no way to get to them. Everything depended on the hacker.

As if responding to his thoughts, Mo's excited voice called out from downstairs. "Come. Come quick."

Max rose and hurried down the stairs. He arrived in the lounge to discover Mo pointing at the screen. Omar stood behind him. They exchanged a few words in their native Arabic. When the muscular soldier spotted Max's approach, he stepped back. "I do not understand any of this."

Max drew up a chair and settled beside Mo. "What've you got?"

"I have a way in."

"So, you can get into their systems?"

"Um, no. Not all of them. Only one. As I said earlier, the areas where they store research data and other important information are well secured."

"Okay, so what can you access?"

"It is the system that controls building maintenance. There is a single admin user. They must log into this account for all tasks. The software is at least fifteen years old. It is not tied to their directory services."

"And how does that help us?" Max asked.

Mo hesitated a moment before replying. "We can control things like the heating."

"Is that it?"

"Perhaps I could access the other systems from there."

"Won't that raise alarms or something?"

Mo bobbed his head in agreement like a small bird pecking a worm. "Yes, that may happen."

"So, you're saying you have the ability to adjust the temperature, and that's about it."

"I must do more work to see what is possible."

"What if you made it too hot for them?" Omar said from his position on the sofa.

Max let out a sigh of frustration. "What difference would that make? It's not as if... Wait a minute. If we get the heating controller to pump out so much heat that it becomes too uncomfortable in the building, they'll have to come outside."

"Yes, and then we shoot them."

"Actually, for once, that's not a bad idea."

Omar blinked in surprise at Max's response. "Really?"

"See what else you can discover about this system, Mo. And be careful. We don't want to trigger any alarms."

The North African hacker turned back to the computer.

Max paced across the carpet, deep in thought. A moment later, he stopped. "You mentioned the software is around fifteen years old. I find it hard to believe no parts have worn out in all that time."

"I do not know," Mo replied. "Why do you ask?"

"What if we make it appear like something has failed, then disguise ourselves as the maintenance team that's come to fix it?"

"Let me check the settings," Mo said. Once again, his fingers whirled over an invisible keyboard. Max resumed his pacing while the hacker worked.

Two minutes later, Mo twisted around, a satisfied grin on his face. "Yes, it is possible to set the temperatures inside the building remotely."

"So, you can make it look like there's a problem?"

"I think so."

"Won't that leave a trail behind?"

Mo shook his head. "It is easy to delete the logs, but if I do this, they can tell. Maybe I change the password. If I do that, they cannot see what is happening. They will probably call the maintenance company. The contact details are stored on the system."

"And after that, we pretend to be the engineers coming to fix the problem," Max said excitedly.

"But how do we stop them from sending their own people?"

"Ring them back immediately afterwards and tell them it's a false alarm. This might work."

Omar rose from the sofa. "Good. I am tired of waiting. But please explain the plan again."

Max ran his fingers through his hair. "Okay. Mo goes into the controller and adjusts the temperature settings inside the building to make it uncomfortably hot—or cold for that matter. At the same time, he changes any passwords on the control system so nobody else can access it. Somebody at Ilithyia will contact the maintenance company to ask them to fix the issue. We know who the firm is, so we wait a bit, then place another call, pretending to be from Ilithyia, and cancel the job. We turn up dressed as the repair engineers, and they let us in."

"Then we shoot the targets?" Omar asked hopefully.

"We have to find out where they are in the building, but yes. Quietly if possible. I, for one, don't want to get caught. We'll also need uniforms, identity cards and a vehicle."

"I can print the identity cards," Mo said. "That is easy."

"We could steal a van and the uniforms," Omar added.

"Actually, I'm not sure that's such a good idea," Max replied. "We can't afford to raise any suspicions ahead of time. It's better if we make replicas. I suspect they'll have scanners to detect explosives and hidden weapons, so we'll also have to find a way to conceal anything we bring in with us. I'll contact our handlers and get them to put together everything we need."

The room buzzed with renewed enthusiasm.

Max draped an arm around the shoulders of his two colleagues. "Well done, guys. I think this'll work."

40

Friday 10th April 2037

Ilithyia Biotechnology, Northstowe

Martin Hendrick scrolled through the scientific paper with a flick of his finger. The more he read on the subject, the more convinced he became that nanotechnology was the way forward for medicine. Fusing together the worlds of computing and biochemistry, the possibilities were endless.

He glanced at his watch: just after eight-fifteen. His stomach rumbled. Maybe he should grab a bite to eat. The others had left ninety minutes earlier, so he was alone in the laboratory. He stood and stretched out his arms, working out the kinks from a long day staring at a computer screen.

"You are here late, I see," a voice said behind him.

He whirled around to discover Professor Allard standing by the door with a slight smile on his face.

"Yes, I was just thinking about heading to the canteen. I might come back later... if that's all right with you."

"Of course. I wish the rest of my team demonstrated the same levels of enthusiasm. So, what do you think of our little machines?"

Hendrick sat again. "They show a great deal of potential. While you're here, do you mind if I ask a few questions?"

"Be my guest," Allard replied, pulling up a seat.

"I understand what the technology is capable of, but not how you go about programming them."

"Well, let me explain. Each nanomachine has a set of instructions. We create those instructions with a computer. It is not like a microprocessor, which interprets code to decide what to do next. Once we have manufactured these devices, their function cannot be changed. It is fixed. The software compiles our designs into a format the manufacturing machines understand."

"I've had a play with the models generated by your group. We've had a few discussions about how to adapt the nanomachines to target the virus."

"Yes, I am told your input has been extremely useful."

"Thanks. If possible, I'd like to learn more about the programming side."

Allard patted Hendrick on the arm. "I will ask one of my team to show you."

"How do you design in the safety features?"

Allard's smile vanished. His shoulders tensed. "I hope you are not going to mention grey goo."

"No... It's not that. I just want to understand how the functions are built in."

The professor relaxed. "I am sorry if I seem overly sensitive. Whenever I discuss the technology, there is always someone who mentions ecophagy. It drives me mad. There is so much potential, but everybody only sees the negatives. I cannot remember the last time I spoke at a conference and somebody did not ask me about this. The audience think they are so clever, as if we have never even considered the dangers. But to answer your question, we created a standard platform on which we build the functions we require. This is common to all our designs."

"So, you can't edit this core?"

"No, and nor would we wish to. It is what we term a library component. Technically, it is possible to change the base model, but we would never do this. Why do you ask?"

"I was just curious. So, how do you manufacture the machines?"

"As I have already said, the compiler translates the instructions to a format understood by the manufacturing units. These use a combination of lithography and what we call molecular tweezers to manipulate individual atoms. In the same way that software engineers do not need to know how computers are manufactured to create code, most of my group have little knowledge of this side of the process and work on the application of these nanomachines rather than the production."

"Fascinating. I wonder if it would be possible for me to try out some of my own ideas."

"Of course," Allard replied. "But you already have access to all the tools for simulation."

"Yes, thanks for that. As I mentioned earlier, I've been having a play with the simulators, and I'm really impressed. But I was thinking about trialling something on some cell cultures."

"I will arrange for somebody to have a discussion with you about your suggestions. I am sure we can manufacture some samples for you."

"Actually, I'd prefer to operate alone."

"Hmm," the professor said. "We are not here to take credit or score points. We have come together to cooperate. What belongs to one belongs to all."

Hendrick nodded in agreement. "Yes, I understand that. It's just... well, I suppose my brain works slightly differently to other peoples'. If I have to stop to explain what I'm doing to somebody else, I find the thought often fades away. I guess you could say I'm easily distracted. I'm at my most productive when I'm in the groove."

Allard pondered the request for a moment. "Fine. I will allow you to do this, but I expect a weekly report on your progress. And any findings belong to the entire team. We need Christine's approval. If she is happy, I will set up the required privileges to access the manufacturing process. I trust you to be careful and adhere to all safety guidelines."

"What's different about the precautions for nanomachines?"

Allard's lips compressed into a thin smile. "Must I really go over this again? The other teams do not have anything like this level of scrutiny, even though this terrible disease came out of a laboratory."

"Oh, I see. No problem. You don't need to worry about that."

"May I ask you a question now?"

"Feel free," Hendrick replied.

"Where did you work before this? I thought I knew everybody in this business, but I am sorry to say I had not heard of you."

"I spent many years in Norway at the Oslo Medical Research Centre. Our group didn't publish a lot of papers. My particular area of study was cross-species viral transmission. The Orestes virus has had a terrible impact on human reproduction, but if it ever jumped to other species, the results would be catastrophic. Imagine a world where all creatures died when they gave birth. The majority would become extinct within a generation or two. Humans consume vast quantities of meat and dairy. If farm animals became susceptible to this virus, millions across the planet would starve."

"Frightening indeed," Allard said. "This is clearly a vitally important area of study, so why did you choose to come here?"

"I guess I wanted a change of scenery. I also enjoy a challenge. When I heard about this project, I jumped at the chance. Luckily, they accepted me."

"Well, from my point of view, you are a very valuable addition. I look forward to hearing more of your ideas."

"Thank you," Hendrick replied. "I am sure we'll achieve our goals together."

41

Monday 13th April 2037

Ilithyia Biotechnology, Northstowe

Max Perrin tried on the blue coveralls. The fit was a little tight across the shoulders, but they would do the job. He sat on the bed and slipped his feet into the safety shoes. Just the right size. He strolled to the adjacent bedroom, pushing open the door without knocking.

Mo and Omar stood together, buttoning up the front of their identical overalls.

Max cast a critical eye over the replicated uniforms. "Are they okay?"

"Good," Omar replied. "Now we look like British workmen. You have explained how we get into the building. But what happens after?"

"We repair the heating system," Max said. "By that, I mean we restore the original settings."

Mo frowned in puzzlement. "I do not understand. We create a problem then fix it?"

"We have at least four targets: Baxter, Kubar, the wheelchair girl and her partner. I want all of them. We'll only get the one chance once we show our hand, so we have to prepare properly. We don't know where they are inside the building, which means we have to track them down before anything else. Think of it as a scouting mission."

"So, we find out their location, then we complete the operation?"

"Exactly. During the first visit, we'll be unarmed. I want to get a good look at their security systems before we make a move. After that, we return with weapons and finish the job. If everything's ready at this end, Mo, access the system and set the temperature really high. Change the password, so they can't adjust it back. When we see people coming outside, we can safely assume somebody at Ilithyia has placed the call. That's when I contact the maintenance company. I tell them a junior trainee accidentally modified the settings and cancel the callout. At the same time, we jump in the van, turn up at the building, then restore everything to how it was. They'll think we fixed it."

"I will get on it right away," Mo said, hurrying out of the room.

"Finally, we are doing something," Omar added. "I am tired of all this waiting."

Max moved across to where the telescope poked out between the curtains and lowered himself into the chair. He could have watched from any computer screen in the house, but somehow it gave him a sense of greater involvement to observe the Ilithyia building through the control unit.

A few moments later, Mo ascended the stairs. "It is done."

"Make sure you put the ID badge around your neck. We're leaving as soon as people start coming out."

Max stared at the image of the chrome and glass structure. Several minutes passed with no change. The only signs of movement behind the fence came from the routine patrols of guards and their canine companions. Suddenly, a group of three white-coated scientists emerged through the rotating door. The trickle turned into a surge as more people hurried through the exit and gathered in front of the building.

"That's it. Let's go," Max called. He grabbed his mobile and selected the number he had stored in the contacts. The ringing tone echoed in his ear.

After a few seconds, a woman's voice answered. "Beechwood Environmental Systems. Please state the nature of your call, and I'll put you through."

"Um, yes, this is Nick Butler at Ilithyia Biotechnology." He had checked the name of Ilithyia's site manager the previous night. "I'm just calling up to let you know the callout from our building was a mistake. One of our trainees was messing with the heating system and adjusted the settings by accident. Sorry for any inconvenience. If you need to contact me again for any reason, you can reach me on this number."

"No worries," the woman replied. "I'll make sure our maintenance team gets the message. Thanks for contacting Beechwood."

Max ended the call and strode towards the front door, where his companions waited. The group of three left the house and hurried down the quiet residential road. They had parked the van fifty metres away. The distinctive Beechwood logo of a green tree adorned the sides. Max jumped into the driver's seat and pressed the start button. The support team had disengaged the vehicle's navigation system before delivering it two days earlier. They had also tinkered with the wiring of the onboard transponder to make it appear like it had become accidentally disconnected.

Max swung the wheel and pulled out. The roads were quiet, and it took less than five minutes before they slowed at the gates to the Ilithyia site. A smattering of journalists waited outside on the pavement. The arrival of the van generated some initial excitement, but their interest soon waned when the sign on the side panel became apparent.

Two men emerged from a booth to the left of the barrier. One held a large black and tan Rottweiler on a tight leash. The other approached the driver's door. Max wound down the window.

"What are you doing here, gentlemen?" the guard asked, peering inside.

"We're from Beechwood Environmental Systems. We've just received an urgent callout," Max replied. "Apparently, the heating system is on the blink."

The man stepped back and held a phone to his ear. He spoke for a few seconds, then beckoned them forwards. "Fine, they're expecting you."

Max breathed a sigh of relief as he drove the vehicle beneath the raised barrier. Moments later, they drew up outside the building. He snatched the baseball cap off the dashboard and pulled it down low over his eyes. At the van's arrival, a muted cheer rose from the group of people milling about beside the entrance.

Keeping his head lowered, Max got out, moved to the back of the van and grabbed the toolbox. He handed it to Omar. "Here, you carry this."

The large North African accepted the heavy metal box in silence. The three men approached the rotating door and pushed through, accompanied by a smattering of applause. As soon as they stepped inside, a wave of heat washed over them.

"What did you set the temperature to?" Max whispered to Mo.

"Thirty-five degrees," the diminutive hacker replied.

"Maybe not so high next time. Remember we've got to work here for a while."

Sweat already beaded on Max's forehead. He strode to the barricade, where a stressed-looking guard waited.

Dark patches stained the underarms of the man's pale-blue uniform. "I'm certainly glad to see you guys," he said with a grin. "It's like a furnace in here."

"We'll sort out the problem as quickly as we can," Max replied.

"I need to put your toolbox through the scanners if you don't mind." The man reached out a hand and grabbed the handle of the metal case. He passed it to a colleague, who appeared equally flustered in the intense heat. "Please step through the gate."

Max stood back and beckoned his two men to go first. His eyes surveyed the foyer for cameras while he waited. As he stepped through the arch, a shrill beeping sound rang out.

The guard's friendly expression vanished in an instant. He lowered his hand to a beige plastic device clipped to his belt. "Please stand still with your arms outstretched."

From the corner of his eye, Max noticed Omar's shoulders tense. "That'll be my prosthetic arm," he said loudly, following the man's instructions. "I should have mentioned it earlier. I lost it a few years ago in an industrial accident."

The second man approached, carrying a portable scanning device approximately the same size as an empty toilet roll. He ran it over Max's body. The scanner emitted a loud beep as it passed across his left arm.

The two men relaxed. "Sorry about that," the first said. "There're a lot of important stuff going on here, so we can't be too careful. Here are your security passes. Please wear them at all times. I'll let you get to work."

"Where's the heating control system?" Max asked.

The guard frowned. "Don't you guys know where it is?"

Max offered the man an apologetic smile. "We've only recently started at the company," he said. "Our manager told us you'd show us where to go."

"Fine. I'll ask my colleague to take you. I hope you know what you're doing."

"Yeah, no problem. We've all done training on this type of system. It's just that none of us has been here before."

Moments later, the man who had used the portable scanner led them across the foyer. He raised the card hanging around his neck to a reader. A light on the wall changed from red to green, and the electronic lock clicked.

Before the guard's hand reached the handle, the door swung open. Three people waited in the doorway: a man, a woman and a young boy. The woman sat in a wheelchair with the child perched on her lap. The Lessing girl, Floyd and their brat.

Max looked away, averting his face. Had they recognised him?

The guard stepped back and gestured for the group to come through. The family moved past, showing no signs of recognition. Max's gaze followed them as they headed towards the barrier across the foyer. Just as they reached the checkpoint, the boy turned and peered over his mother's shoulder.

Max quickly raised his hand to the brim of his cap.

"Are you coming, then?" the guard asked.

Max jerked his head around, realising that the others were waiting for him. "Sorry," he said. "I was miles away. By the way, do our cards open the doors too?"

"Yeah," the man replied. "They'll let you in anywhere you need to go."

"What if we find there's a problem elsewhere?"

"Come back to reception, and I'll get somebody to escort you. Right, we're here. That's the control room. I'd really appreciate it if you could sort the issue out as quickly as you can. Everybody's melting, and they won't allow us security guys to leave the building."

"We'll do our best."

"The canteen's that way if you need any refreshments."

"Thanks."

Max pushed open the door. A light flickered on, illuminating a five-metre square area containing an old-fashioned flatscreen terminal and an assortment of other equipment scattered around the walls. Although slightly cooler than the corridor outside, oppressively warm air enveloped the three men as they entered.

"What now?" Mo asked.

"Before we do anything else," Max snapped, "you can start by lowering the bloody temperature."

42

Monday 13th April 2037

Ilithyia Biotechnology, Northstowe

A tap came from the corridor outside the room.

"That'll be Paul," Antimone said. "Would you mind letting him in, Jason?"

The young family had been staying at the Ilithyia building for a fortnight and had quickly settled into a routine, which for Paul comprised five hours of education per day at the on-site kindergarten.

During the first week, the scientists took blood samples from Antimone and Jason, but the reason for Antimone's survival four years earlier—her body contained both male and female DNA resulting from the fusing of two foetuses in her mother's womb—was already common knowledge. The sight of needles terrified their son, and he resisted every attempt to draw blood. As Andrew Jacobs had promised, the science team didn't press the issue.

"Pause TV," Jason said. The highlights of the football match on the large three-dimensional screen stopped in mid-action. He swung his legs off the bed and padded across the carpet in bare feet. He twisted the handle and pulled the door open.

"Look what I did, Daddy," his son said, proudly holding up a rectangle of paper splattered with several blobs of brightly coloured paint.

"That's very good. What is it?"

Paul giggled. "It's a dog, silly."

"Why don't you show it to mummy?" The four-year-old skipped past him. "Thanks for bringing him up here," he said, addressing the guard. Most days, somebody called the parents when it was time to collect their offspring, but if the security guards weren't overly busy, they sometimes accompanied the children back to their rooms.

The man smiled. "No problem. You're lucky. He's a cute kid. My wife and I are trying for one of our own."

"Well, um... good luck."

"I'll see you around then."

Paul was the eldest child in his class of five by nearly a year. The other pupils had parents who worked as part of the science or security teams. Every weekday morning, a local preschool schoolteacher came in to educate the children. Paul had become attached to the woman. She reminded Jason a little of the old photographs he had seen of his biological mother with her dark hair and heart-shaped face.

Earlier that day, the teacher had been forced to abandon her lessons when the heating system failed, causing the temperature inside the building to rocket. The security team contacted the parents, advising them to collect their children and evacuate the facility while the maintenance company fixed the problem. Within an hour, the energy-sapping heat dissipated sufficiently to allow Paul to return to his classroom.

Jason closed the door and followed his son back into the room. Paul perched on Antimone's lap, explaining the features of his artwork.

"And there's his collar. Look, he's got a big pink tongue."

"You're an excellent artist," Antimone said. "I'm really proud of you. We'll have to stick it up on the wall. So, what have you been doing at school today other than painting?"

Paul climbed off her legs and hopped onto his bed, his eyes lifting to the television screen. "I want to watch cartoons."

"Fine, but I'd like you to tell me about your day first."

Paul shook his head.

Jason lowered himself onto the mattress beside his son. "Come on, buddy. What else did you do in school?"

The boy turned to his father. "I had a hundred babies today," he said.

Jason flashed a grin at Antimone. "Really? I thought only girls could have babies."

"No, boys can too," Paul replied confidently.

"If you say so. Did you learn any other interesting things?"

"We watched a programme about penguins. I want to be a penguin when I grow up."

Jason stifled a laugh. "You'd look good in black and white, but penguins live at the North Pole, and it's really cold up there."

"I don't mind. I like it in the snow. Can I watch cartoons now?"

"All right. TV, show me a list of cartoon programmes suitable for a child of four."

They had configured the entertainment system so that it listened only to the adults' voices. The built-in software monitored the amount of screen time every day. If left to Paul's whims, the device would have been displaying a constant stream of children's material from dawn until dusk.

"I want Peppa Pig," Paul announced

"Just for a few minutes," Antimone said. The ancient cartoon was her son's favourite programme. She could remember watching the same thing as a child, although in those days, the animated images had been flat instead of the more recent three-dimensional technology.

After two episodes, Antimone instructed the television to turn off.

"Another one," Paul said, jutting out his chin.

"If you're going to be like that, young man, you won't get to watch TV at all in future. Now, tell me what else happened in school today."

The four-year-old jiggled his leg. "It was very hot. We went outside."

"Yeah, I know. We came to collect you if you remember."

"I saw the bad man."

"The bad man?" Jason asked, putting down the book he had been reading.

"Yes."

"Which bad man?"

"He was with us."

"What do you mean? Where?"

"In that nasty place."

Antimone and Jason exchanged a confused look.

She reached forwards and placed her hand on Paul's back. "Are you talking about Africa?"

Paul didn't answer. He jumped off the bed and moved to the window, where he stood, staring down at the well-kept gardens bordered by the metal fence.

They hadn't really discussed the events of the previous year with their son. A group from the Republic of North Africa had kidnapped the family of three, together with Rosalind Baxter, after setting off a series of bombs at the Olympic stadium in Glasgow. The terrorists, led by a general in the North African military, transported them to a hospital in Tripoli where a team of scientists studied their biology, in the hope of developing a cure for a mutation of the Orestes virus that was killing children.

General Shaladi soon found himself held prisoner with the other captives, along with his daughter, Aya. They only escaped when Rosalind Baxter got a message out to one of the general's former colleagues, who mounted a rescue operation. This was the first time Paul had mentioned anything relating to their abduction. The child psychologists had advised Jason and Antimone not to mention their experiences unless their son raised the topic.

"Do you mean the place we went on the boat, buddy?" Jason asked.

Paul nodded silently.

Antimone steered her wheelchair over, stopping alongside him. "You're not talking about Dr Kubar, are you? He was with us in Africa, but he's not a bad man. He helped us all to get home."

Paul placed his hands against the glass.

Jason rose from the bed and squatted down beside his son. "What did this bad man look like?"

Paul shrugged.

"What colour was he wearing?"

"Blue."

"What, like the guards?"

Paul shook his head again.

"You don't need to worry about any bad men," Jason said. "We're safe here."

He stood and shot a puzzled glance at Antimone. He stepped away from the window and waited for her to join him.

"Who do you think he's talking about?" he asked in a whisper.

"I've no idea," Antimone replied. "I can't see how anybody from North Africa could be over here apart from Dr Kubar, and Paul has seen him loads of times since we arrived."

"Maybe he just saw somebody who reminded him of a person we met over there."

"He's really into his stories at the moment. Remember he told us a few minutes ago that he had a hundred babies today."

Jason let out a laugh. "Yeah, there is that. It's probably nothing. Who knows how the mind of a four-year-old works?"

"I'm worried though. He's never said anything like this before. I know we're all praying that what happened over there hasn't affected him too badly, but what if it's a delayed reaction?"

Jason placed a hand on her shoulder. "Let's wait and see. If he mentions it again, we'll contact the child psychologists."

"I suppose."

A shiver ran through Antimone's body. Despite Jason's assurances, something didn't feel right.

"Okay," Jason said, clapping his hands. "Who's hungry?"

43

Tuesday 14th April 2037

Ilithyia Biotechnology, Northstowe

"Come on," Max Perrin said with a leer. "You know you want to go out with me, don't you, trike queen?" He held a gun. The unwavering barrel pointed at her chest.

Antimone reached down to the hand rings of her wheelchair and tried to move backwards. No matter how hard she pushed, the wheels refused to turn.

"Mummy, are you coming?"

She turned and stared at her son. He stood beside her and seemed to be oblivious to the danger.

"Run!" she screamed, but no sound came out.

Paul tugged at her elbow. "I want to go now, Mummy."

She attempted to position herself between her son's body and the gun, but once again, she couldn't shift the wheelchair. Perrin took another step closer. Smoke rose from his arm as his flesh puckered, turned black and dripped on the floor. He swung the pistol to point at Paul's head.

"No, please," she begged.

Her gaze focused on Perrin's finger as, in exaggerated slow motion, he squeezed the trigger.

"No!"

Antimone jerked awake, the cry still fading in her throat. Her heart hammered in her chest. The white T-shirt she wore for sleeping clung damply to her skin. She reached for the bedside light, wincing at the sudden increase in brightness. Beside her, Jason groaned and rolled over to face the other way. Using her elbows, she levered her body up from the mattress. Paul lay asleep in the adjacent single bed, his head and shoulders protruding from the covers. With a sigh of relief, she sank back into the pillow and tapped the base of the lamp.

"Thank God," she whispered into the darkness.

Nearly a year had passed since the events that triggered her recurring nightmare. Even after all this time, the memories of the blackening skin on Max Perrin's arm and the accompanying inhuman screams escaping from his throat were never far from her thoughts. After several late-night discussions with Jason, they had agreed she should arrange some sessions with a psychiatrist.

The man had been sympathetic, but she found herself unable to tell him what truly happened in the Tripoli hospital. How could she confess to killing a man by injecting him with concentrated sulphuric acid?

After diagnosing her with Post-Traumatic Stress Disorder, the doctor had taught her a range of techniques to manage her anxiety and help her relax. Despite his best efforts, the burden of maintaining her secret prevented her from gaining maximum benefit from the treatment. On several occasions she came close to confessing what she had done but always held back from revealing the full story.

She reached out an arm in the darkness and felt for the reassuring warmth of Jason's body. He stirred at her touch and rolled to face her.

"Is everything all right?" he asked, his voice heavy with sleep.

"Just a nightmare," she replied.

"Oh. First Paul this afternoon and now you."

"I keep seeing him." She didn't have to explain to whom she was referring.

"Do you think we should arrange more sessions with the shrink?"

Antimone held her breath for a moment before replying. "I'm not sure it'll help."

In the silence, the sheets rustled as Jason adjusted his position. "We both need to be doing something constructive with our time. I've offered to assist in the labs, but none of the scientists seem interested. I suspect it's related to my mother; nobody really trusts her. Dr Kubar would let me join him, but he doesn't have a team of his own. He suggested distance learning, so I'm thinking about starting an Open University degree. Have you thought about returning to education? It might take your mind off things."

The administrators at King's College in London, where he had been studying biochemistry before being abducted by the terrorists from The Republic of North African, had agreed to defer his course for a year, but without a security team to watch over him, it seemed unlikely he would be able to accept their offer.

"There's only one thing I want to do," Antimone said, "and you know what that is. I really miss my wheelchair racing."

"Why don't you ask Butler? He's bound to complain, but I'm sure he can spare some of his men to keep an eye on you at the athletics track for an hour or two. It would do you good to get out of here."

"You could come with me and practice your javelin throwing."

"What about Paul?"

"We could go while he's at his lessons."

Jason remained silent as he considered her suggestion. "All right then. Let's ask him. If he says yes, you should give John Marshall a call. I'm sure he'd be delighted to see you."

"That's not a bad idea. I might just do that."

Part Four: Activation

44

Wednesday 6th April 2016

Ilithyia Biotechnology, Cambridge Science Park

Twenty-one years ago

A week had gone by since Martin Hendrick first identified the woman they were detaining in the newly created space behind the storeroom. He hadn't spoken to anybody about his discovery.

He could hardly ask the CEO and Chief Scientist why they had taken the drastic move to imprison an employee. How would that conversation go? If he contacted the police, the investigation was bound to focus on the reasons for her incarceration. When they questioned her, Eileen Floyd was sure to reveal the reason for her abduction.

His work would play a pivotal role in the subsequent inquiry just as his project was nearing completion. What's more, he would certainly lose his job when the company folded, as it was certain to do when the courts convicted the two co-owners of false imprisonment.

Hendrick quickly deduced what must have happened. He already knew about her complaint concerning the viral research he was performing. No doubt, Rosalind Baxter and Nigel Perrin had tried to talk her out of becoming a whistleblower. When she refused, they took the unthinkable step of taking her prisoner. Her husband, Daniel Floyd, was now in prison, serving a life sentence for her murder. Clearly, somebody had framed him, and there was only one person Hendrick could think of who might possess that particular skillset: the third partner in the conspiracy, Anders Grolby.

If the trio were prepared to go that far to protect the company, the primary unanswered question was why she remained alive. If they ever released her, she would quickly report them to the authorities. Something else had to be going on. He could think of no rational reason for allowing her to live.

Hendrick had spent several sleepless nights pondering what to do next. Whatever course he chose would have negative consequences. He would have to play this carefully. It seemed certain they would monitor her through CCTV. If he tried to establish communications with her, there was a good chance the three conspirators would learn of his actions. And that would place him firmly in their sights. There had to be a better way.

Finally, he had come up with a plan. It certainly contained elements of risk, but it had the potential to resolve all his problems. Now was the time to put the first phase into action. He sat at his workstation, his legs jiggling with tension.

Footsteps echoed down the corridor. At long last, somebody was coming. Hendrick glanced at his watch: 20:03. Rising to his feet, he waited for the person to pass, then inched open the door and spotted Dr Perrin's departing back as he headed to the storeroom. It seemed it was the Chief Scientist's turn to feed the prisoner that night.

The Belgian researcher returned to his seat. Five minutes passed until the sound of shoes scuffing on the floor resumed, travelling in the opposite direction. A knock from outside the laboratory. He hurried across the room and pulled the handle.

"It looks like you're the last one again tonight," Perrin said. "You're certainly putting in the hours. I found the preliminary research very interesting. I'm looking forward to seeing the results and reading the final report on this little project of yours."

"It's nearly ready," Hendrick replied. "Just a week or two more."

"Good. Would you mind locking up this evening?"

"No problem."

"Well, don't work too late."

"I'll probably only hang around for another half an hour. Goodnight, Nigel."

"Yeah, see you in the morning, Martin."

Hendrick waited until his boss reached the exit leading to the reception area, then returned to his workstation. Grabbing a pad of paper and a pen, he chewed the end as he thought about what to write. He scrunched up the first two attempts after a few words and stuffed them in his trouser pocket. He couldn't afford to leave clues lying around to be discovered later. The third version turned out more successful.

Somebody will unlock your room three nights from now one hour after they bring food. Make no attempt to open the door before then. You will find a key to the building in the first lab on the right. Under no circumstances tell anybody about my involvement. Do not let them see you reading this note. When you have read this, destroy it. Chew and swallow it. If this doesn't work, I will try again, but it is vital you do not mention that you received help.

Good luck,

A friend.

Hendrick scanned the words a second time. It wasn't perfect, but it would have to do. He folded the paper in half and placed it in his shirt pocket. In three days, it would be a Saturday. If they followed the same pattern as before, somebody would come to feed her around eight in the evening. By then, hopefully the building and the science park would be deserted.

Before proceeding with the plan, he needed to retrieve the key from Dr Perrin's office. He headed out of his laboratory towards the reception area. *Good.* The floor above lay shrouded in darkness. He climbed the stairs and flicked on the master switch. The lights flickered into life as he made his way down the corridor.

The door to the Chief Scientist's room stood open. He moved to the desk, opened the draw and retrieved the keys from the jar of paperclips. A sudden thought crossed his mind; what if Perrin started locking his office at night? Ideally, he would have preferred to get a replica set made, but the doctor might notice their absence. No, he had no option but to hope for the best and return the keys to their storage place after delivering the note.

He retraced his steps and headed back to the storeroom. By now, he knew which key to use. He let himself in and turned on the light. The familiar scratching sounds penetrated through the closed door on the far side. He hurried past the shelves stacked with chemicals and pushed his way into the cramped room beyond. The frantic scrabbling of startled animals set the bars of the cages ringing. As before, the stink of the rodents permeated the confined space. He approached the spyhole, placed his eye to the glass and peered inside.

Eileen Floyd lay on the bed, reading a paperback. She wore a white T-shirt and black leggings. Feeling like a peeping Tom, Hendrick studied the woman. Something seemed different about her. Maybe it was her casual attire or her unkempt hair. Perhaps sensing his eyes upon her, she lowered the book. That was when he noticed the rounded bump of her stomach. Christ, she was pregnant.

He stepped back. This changed everything. His mind spun as he considered the options. *No, the plan would still work.* He withdrew the note with trembling fingers. The key turned in the lock, and he opened the door a fraction. He crouched, slipping the folded paper in the narrow crack. Before she had time to react, he shut the door again. He rose and placed his eye against the peephole. Her forehead creased in a frown. She stared at the floor and swung her feet off the bed. Satisfied she had spotted his message, Hendrick backed away.

He retraced his route, turning off the light and locking the storeroom behind him. Two minutes later, he had returned the keys to the drawer in Nigel Perrin's office and stood beside the alarm panel by the entrance to the building, ready to arm the system.

There was no going back now. The wheels were in motion.

45

Saturday 9th April 2016

Ilithyia Biotechnology, Cambridge Science Park

Twenty-one years ago

Martin Hendrick glanced at his watch: 18:21. He had wedged the door to his laboratory open with a bin shortly after arriving that morning. Now, the distant sound of somebody entering the reception area echoed down the corridor. Whoever had just arrived was an hour and a half earlier than he had expected. He crossed the room and shoved the makeshift doorstop with his foot, allowing the gap to close.

He picked up a journal and flicked through the pages while he waited. After a few minutes, somebody hurried past his laboratory. A short while later, the person returned, coming in the opposite direction. A light tap broke the silence. Hendrick opened the door.

Nigel Perrin stood in the corridor. "I saw your car was still outside," he said. "I hope you're not working too hard. Is everything okay?"

"Yeah, fine, thanks. I'm just about to pack up for the evening. Actually, while you're here, I wonder if you could arrange for somebody to take a look at the light." He pointed to the fluorescent strip running along the ceiling. "It took ages to come on this morning. I think the starter must be on the way out."

"I'll try to remember, but remind me again on Monday."

"Right. I'll do that."

"Well, I thought I'd just finish off some paperwork," Perrin said. "I can lock up for a change tonight if you like."

Hendrick's stomach lurched. "No, it's fine. I don't mind doing it."

Perrin studied him curiously. "I'll be in my office. I'll let you know when I leave if you're still here."

"Likewise." Hendrick cursed inwardly. The clock was already ticking.

"Okay, catch you—"

The shrill tone of Perrin's mobile phone blared from his jacket pocket. He pulled it out and rolled his eyes. He stepped away and spoke in a low voice.

"Yes, darling. What is it?"

"... I'm sure it's nothing."

"... No, I can leave now.

"... Fine, I'll be home in a few minutes."

He turned back to the Belgian researcher and smiled apologetically. "Sorry. Change of plan. The baby won't stop crying, and my wife is worried. He kept us up most of last night as well. I've got to go. Is it okay if you lock up after all?"

A surge of relief flowed through Hendrick's body. "No problem."

"Thanks. Have a good weekend."

Hendrick blew out his cheeks. He still had much to do. He waited a moment before following Perrin's steps to the end of the corridor, where he remained, peering through the rectangle of glass into the reception area. A few seconds later, the Chief Scientist reappeared, emerging from the doorway to the upstairs offices. He hurried across the foyer and out into the car park, locking the outside door behind him.

Hendrick stayed where he was in case Perrin returned, then, deciding he had left it long enough, headed towards the stairs. He didn't bother to turn on the lights; the overcast evening sky, penetrating through the open doors, provided all the illumination he needed. When he reached Perrin's office, he opened the drawer and retrieved the keys. A quick glance at his watch confirmed twenty-five minutes had already passed since the woman had received her second and final meal of the day.

He jogged down the steps and along the corridor to the storeroom, where he let himself in. After unlocking the next door, he stood outside the woman's cell. He lowered his eye to the peephole and peered inside. Eileen Floyd paced across the narrow width of the room, the pre-packed sandwich and soft drink resting untouched on the bed.

Hendrick slid the key carefully into the lock. He twisted the head. Despite his attempts at stealth, the mechanism clicked. Cursing his clumsiness, he completed the revolution. For a second time, he studied her through the fish-eye lens. The woman stood still, staring back at him as if she could see right through the reinforced barrier. Would she follow his instructions and wait the full hour before attempting to leave?

After a few seconds, she sat on the bed and placed her face in her hands. Hendrick breathed a sigh of relief. He turned and retraced his footsteps through the storage room.

46

Saturday 9th April 2016

Ilithyia Biotechnology, Cambridge Science Park

Twenty-one years ago

Eileen Floyd took the three paces to cross the room. She spun about and returned to her starting point. She maintained a count in her head with every step. *Wait one hour*, the note had said. How was she supposed to do that without a watch? She had no idea of the time of day. She assumed it was sometime in the evening.

Two weeks earlier, Dr Perrin had brought her meal. Normally, he emptied the contents and used the empty bag to store the waste from the previous night. On this occasion, he was clearly in a hurry and simply deposited the thin plastic bag on the floor before beating a hasty retreat. Inside was not only the food but also a petrol station receipt. The slip of paper contained details of the amount paid together with the date, and more significantly, the time of the transaction—six twenty in the evening.

Forty-seven minutes. One second, two second. *This is ridiculous. What am I waiting for?* Surely, she had left it long enough. She stopped and glanced up at the camera, out of reach on the ceiling in the corner above the bed. *Is anybody watching? Is this some cruel trick?*

Eileen halted when she reached the wall and stood still. She inhaled deeply. Hiding the camera's view with her back, she extended a hand and pulled the handle gently towards her. It moved. Her mysterious helper had come through for her. With a final backward glance, she hauled the door open the rest of the way and darted through the doorway.

The stack of animal cages greeted her. She rushed past without a glance. Her heart sank at the sight of the closed door to her left. She approached and twisted the latch, expecting to find it locked. To her relief, the mechanism turned. The band of illumination coming from behind her cast long shadows on the shelves of the unlit storeroom. The only way out lay on the opposite wall. That was where her previous escape attempt had ended. She rushed across to the far side. Panic engulfed her as the wedge of light narrowed and disappeared altogether, plunging the room into darkness.

The inky blackness pressed in on her like a physical force. She could barely breathe. Her hands felt along the rough wall until she touched a large area of smooth plastic. She clawed desperately for the mechanism. Finally, her fingertips brushed against something cold and metallic. She twisted the knob and stumbled out.

In the dim twilight penetrating through the small window at the end of the corridor, she recognised her surroundings. Her old laboratory lay to the left. In the other direction was the exit to reception, but she would need the front door key to get out—or to shatter the glass. She recalled the words from the note; *You will find a key to the building in the first lab on the right.*

That had been Dr Hendrick's workspace. A stab of pain shot through her stomach. *No, please, not now.* She waited for the spasm to abate, then staggered the short distance to the next doorway, using her hand to support herself against the wall. She pushed inside and reached for the light switch. Nothing happened. Apart from the occasional abrupt click accompanying the flickering of the fluorescent tube, the room remained in near darkness. As she drew a ragged breath, a pungent chemical smell registered on her senses.

Her eyes picked out a waste bin by the open door. She wedged it in the gap and edged forwards. The further in she moved, the worse the stench became. Broken glass crunched beneath her feet. She almost tripped over the computer base unit lying on the floor. What the hell was going on? Somebody had trashed the place. But why? She ran her hands over the top of the work surface but came up empty. She cursed in frustration. Where was the damned key?

She would just have to find another way out of the building. Maybe she could call Daniel from reception. But no, she remembered Grolby boasting about how he had framed her husband. The ex-soldier wouldn't be quite so smug when she escaped, and they arrested him for her abduction. Perhaps she should phone the emergency services. Whatever option she chose, she couldn't afford to stay here.

Using the dim wedge of light to guide her, she retraced her steps. She followed the corridor and pushed through into the foyer. Immediately, more signs of damage drew her gaze. A beige computer unit and matching monitor, the display screen fractured in a criss-cross pattern, lay strewn across the floor beside the receptionist's desk. The fragmented parts of a two-piece telephone rested nearby. A breath of cool air dragged her attention to the entrance. The lower pane was missing. Fragments of glass glinted in the overcast twilight.

What should she do? Somebody had apparently broken into the building, leaving a trail of destruction behind them. Should she try to find a different phone? The nearest was probably in the boardroom, just a short distance up the stairs.

Surely, the intruder had set off the alarm, so why wasn't it sounding? She vaguely recalled her manager telling her that the system stayed silent for ten minutes before triggering the siren in the building to allow time for backup to get there and apprehend the criminals. That meant the break-in must have occurred very recently. Somebody would be along soon. Perhaps she should sit tight and wait for help to arrive. But what if the intruders hadn't left and remained on the premises? Worse still, what if her captors were the ones to respond to the alert?

No, she had to leave. She would flag down a car or find a building where someone was working late and try to catch their attention. She hurried to the front door and crouched down to clamber through the broken frame. Had she not been pregnant, she would have fitted through the gap with ease, but the bulge in her stomach made it hard to fold her body small enough. As she twisted sideways, her shoulder caught on a shard protruding from the top edge. She cried out in pain.

Tears welled in her eyes. She had to keep going, if not for herself, then for her unborn child. She tried again, earning another gash on the upper arm for her trouble. Finally, she rose on unsteady legs beneath an overcast sky and considered her next course of action. Her heart almost stopped in fright at the sudden wail of the siren on the side of the building above her head.

Eileen set off across the car park at a half jog. Lack of exercise and the advanced stage of her pregnancy meant she had to stop every few paces to regain her breath. The ear-splitting screech of the alarm cut through the evening air and trailed her to the pavement. She stopped and considered her options. To the right lay the main road leading out of the science park. There, she could flag down a car. If she turned left, it would lead her deeper into the maze of industrial units. That route offered the greater chance of discovering somebody working late in one of the adjacent buildings.

She stood still, caught in a moment of uncertainty. The headlights approaching from the right decided for her. She staggered into the road, waving her arms above her head.

"Help!" she screamed, silhouetted by the twin beams.

The car slowed and stopped. A deep sob escaped her throat. Her sense of relief lasted just long enough for the driver to open the door of the battered white Saab and step out onto the tarmac.

"Planning on going somewhere, Eileen?" he asked.

47

Saturday 9th April 2016

Ilithyia Biotechnology, Cambridge Science Park

Twenty-one years ago

Anders Grolby tapped the button to end the call. He muttered a curse under his breath. Martin Hendrick had just called to let him know about two suspicious men he had seen loitering outside the Ilithyia premises after locking up for the night. It seemed the scientist's suspicions were well-founded because only five minutes earlier, Grolby had received an automated intruder alert from the building's alarm system.

Now he was on his way there to check the place out. More often than not, such call-outs were false alarms. Most likely, the idiot scientist had forgotten to close a door properly, but in his role as head of security, he couldn't afford to take the chance. For the life of him, he didn't understand why the owners allowed Martin Hendrick to work in the building alone when his laboratory was mere metres from the room in which they were holding their secret prisoner.

Grolby was particularly irritated because the call from the alarm system had interrupted the World War II movie he was watching on the huge 3D television in his flat. The story had been entertaining enough, but he found the fighting scenes somewhat unrealistic. In his experience, warfare was much dirtier and far more violent than the action portrayed on the silver screen.

Still, it could have been worse. At this time of night on a weekend, he could cover the five miles to Ilithyia in less than ten minutes. As he turned into the science park, the faint screech of a siren penetrated the old Saab's interior. If that was the alarm on the side of the building, any intruders would be long gone. He just hoped they hadn't caused too much damage. He really didn't want to hang around for hours while he waited for the maintenance company to arrive and board up any broken windows.

As he rounded a left-hand bend, a woman wearing a white T-shirt and black leggings leapt out into the road, waving her arms above her head. He jammed on the brakes and slowed to a halt. It was a bit early for the usual half-dressed Saturday night partygoers to be staggering about on the street, and she was more than a little off the beaten track. Still, nothing surprised him these days.

This girl seemed to be carrying a lot of excess weight. Or perhaps she was pregnant. *Shit!* With a jolt of recognition, he identified the figure as Eileen Floyd.

What the hell was she doing here? He flung open the door and levered himself out of the leather driver's seat.

"Planning on going somewhere, Eileen?" he called.

Immediately, she turned and ran down the centre of the road in the opposite direction. Within ten paces, he caught up to her. He put an arm around her neck and hauled her back.

"Come on, now. We can't have you roaming the streets in your condition, can we?"

"Get off me!" she screamed. "Help!"

He clamped a hand over her mouth and frogmarched her to his car. After a quick scan of his surroundings, he opened the boot, lifted her and bundled her inside.

"No!"

Her cry cut off as the lid slammed shut. Grolby breathed a sigh of relief. Two minutes later and she would have been clean away. He navigated the short distance to the Ilithyia building and parked beside the entrance. This close, the screech of the siren was deafening. It would take real balls to stay around with that racket blaring in the background, but he should check anyway before returning her to the cell.

He got out of the car. *Damn.* It would be a long night after all; the bitch had smashed the lower pane of the front door to escape. Or had she? Most fragments lay inside, implying somebody had shattered the glass from the outside. The large rock, lying by the wall a few feet away, confirmed his hypothesis.

He selected the key for the building and let himself in. His first action was to silence the alarm. His next step was to open the flick knife he kept in his trouser pocket. He advanced cautiously, blade extended, towards the reception desk. As he drew nearer, he spotted the broken computer equipment on the floor. Had she done this or the intruder?

Should he check upstairs or downstairs first? He pondered for a moment, then headed for the steps. All the lights remained off. In the darkness, he pushed through the door to the boardroom and reached for the spot where he knew the light switch resided. The sudden brightness revealed nothing out of the ordinary.

He moved along to the toilets, checking the gents first, and then the ladies. Both empty. The open-plan office proved equally undisturbed, as did the offices of the two bosses, Nigel Perrin and Rosalind Baxter. The last place he checked was his own domain, the server room. A wash of cool air passed over him as he stepped inside, but like everywhere else, there was no trace of an intruder.

He retraced his steps and descended the stairs. At the bottom, he navigated around the damaged equipment and turned left towards the laboratories. Broken glassware and another wrecked computer greeted him in the first laboratory. When it came to Martin Hendrick's space, a bin jammed the door open. He flicked the switch, but the light refused to come on. With knife drawn, he slid inside and waited for his eyes to acclimatise to the darkness. The powerful stench of chemicals washed over him. As the room slowly took shape, he spotted the pile of shattered glass, the toppled chair and the computer base unit lying on the floor. When he was sure nobody lurked in the shadows, he moved on.

He twisted the handle to the storeroom. It turned without the use of a key. His hand reached inside and flicked on the lights. There was no sign of a disturbance. He crossed the room and tried the next door. Also open. The lab animals scuttled in their cages as he stepped through the doorway. Light flooded out of Eileen Floyd's cell. How the hell had she got out? Somebody must have helped her.

Unless... Dr Perrin had been on feeding duty that night. Could he have forgotten to lock up behind him? That didn't explain the destruction and the broken glass inside the reception area. He planned to have a quiet chat with the woman when she was safely back in her cell.

There were still a few places to check. He retraced his route to the corridor and inspected both male and female toilets, coming up empty on both counts. The laboratory at the end, where Floyd had worked months earlier, also seemed undisturbed. Time to get her in the building and ask a few questions.

When Grolby returned to the car, a series of muffled screams emerged from inside the boot. He slammed his palm down three times on the top before opening it.

"If you make another sound, I'll hurt you," he growled. "Is that clear?"

Tear-stained eyes glared up at him.

"Good, let's get you into your little room." Grolby reached down and helped Eileen out. He wrapped an arm around her waist and steered her across the lobby. "Looks like you've picked up some nasty cuts there," he said, studying the rips in her T-shirt and the lacerations to her shoulder beneath.

As they passed through the reception area, she pulled away. "Just let me go," she pleaded. "Please. I won't say a word to anyone."

"I'll think about it if you explain how you escaped."

"There was a noise outside the room. I tried the door, and it opened. I didn't break anything. The glass at the entrance was already broken by the time I got there."

Grolby studied the discoloured stains on her trainers. "Why did you go in the laboratories, then? There's no point denying it. The chemicals are all over your shoes. I can smell them from here. If you didn't smash all that stuff, who did?"

"I don't know, but it wasn't me. I thought I might be able to find a key in there to get out."

"Hmm, I'm not sure I buy that. You expect me to believe somebody entered the building, caused all that damage, and it had nothing at all to do with your escape."

"Yes, I swear that's the truth."

"Fine. We'll talk about this again in the morning."

"No, no, no. You said—"

The slap across the face stopped Eileen in mid-sentence. She tried to pull away, but Grolby's rough hold tightened around her upper arm as he dragged her along the corridor. When they reached the storeroom, he relaxed his grip to put the key in the lock.

Halfway through the door, she staggered and grasped the frame for support. She stopped and glanced down; a puddle expanded around her feet.

"What—?" The question died in Grolby's throat as he took in the damp patch on her leggings.

She squatted on her haunches. "But it isn't due for another two weeks."

"Let's get you inside," Grolby said, once again taking her by the arm. He guided her to the small room, where she sank onto the bed. "I'll make a call. Try to remain calm."

He removed the mobile from his pocket and dialled the first number on speed dial.

"We had a close thing tonight," he replied after receiving a peremptory greeting. "The woman nearly escaped, and she almost certainly had help."

He listened patiently to the barrage of questions, then spoke again.

"Before I answer any of that, there's something else you should know; her waters have broken. You better come in straight away."

48

Sunday 10th April 2016

Ilithyia Biotechnology, Cambridge Science Park

Twenty-one years ago

Rosalind Baxter sank into the chair as exhaustion crept up on her. She lowered her eyes and stared down at the front of the once white laboratory coat, now stained a dark, almost black, shade of red. So much blood. She raised her sleeve with trembling fingers and studied the dial of her watch: 3:34. She clamped her right hand with the left.

On the opposite side sat Nigel Perrin, his face deathly pale. Anders Grolby stood by the door. Even the Swedish ex-soldier looked shaken.

"What the hell just happened?" Rosalind said, lifting her head.

Neither of the other two replied.

"I've never seen anything like it," she continued. "Everything seemed to be going well..." Her voice trailed off into silence.

"What do you want to do with the body?" Grolby asked.

"I never wanted to kill her," Perrin said in a dull monotone.

"Technically, we didn't," Rosalind snapped. "But to answer Anders's question, in my opinion we should perform a post mortem before deciding what to do next."

Perrin removed a pen from his pocket and clicked the tip in and out. "Why? What's the point? She's dead now, and there's nothing we can do about it."

"Well, apart from anything else," Rosalind replied, "we need to know if whatever killed her is infectious." She gestured to the brightly coloured box on the floor, and the tiny face that peeked through the blankets. "We also have the child to consider."

The lightweight plastic container was the best solution they could improvise at short notice.

"He's not our problem," Grolby said. "We can leave him somewhere safe, and I'll call the police on an unregistered phone to tell them I heard a baby crying."

"You think she might have infected us?" Perrin asked, his face creased in alarm.

Rosalind sighed. "I really have no idea. The symptoms she exhibited had all the hallmarks of a haemorrhagic fever or something similar."

"Christ!" Perrin exclaimed. "You mean like Ebola or Marburg? If that's the case, we should stay well away from the body."

"Don't you think it's a little late for that?" Rosalind replied, pointing at the stains on her white coat. "Whatever she had, if it's infectious, we've already got it by now. What's weird is that she seemed okay right up to the point she gave birth. Normally, with those types of disease, the patient suffers aches and pains before progressing to the later stages over the course of several days. You'd expect to see diarrhoea and vomiting too, but she never complained about anything like that. The symptoms developed extremely rapidly. If we do a post mortem, we might learn more about what this is."

"How would she catch this illness?" Grolby asked. "The only three people she came into contact with over the past few months are in this room."

"We should go to a hospital," Perrin said. "Get them to check us over."

Rosalind rolled her eyes. "Don't be ridiculous, Nigel," she snorted. "You can hardly wander in to A&E and say, 'I think I may have contracted a haemorrhagic fever'. The first question they'd ask would be why you suspected that to be the case. It's not as if you've been abroad recently."

"I'm not single like you two. There's more at stake for me. I have a son of my own and a wife. I can't take the risk I might pass something on to them."

"Look, it's highly unlikely to be Ebola. If any of us start exhibiting symptoms, that's a different story, but for now, the one thing we need to do is learn what we're dealing with. If you're worried, tell your family you can't come home because you have to attend to some urgent business. Then self-isolate somewhere. You could make yourself useful by staying here and looking after the baby."

"I'm not going to stay in the same room she died in."

"Okay, just relax. All of us have been in regular contact with her. I don't know about you two, but I certainly haven't suffered any fever-like symptoms."

"So, what do we do now?" Grolby asked.

"I suggest Nigel and I examine the body while you clean up the mess," Rosalind replied.

"We aren't equipped for this," Perrin said. "We don't have any of the right protective gear."

She pushed back the chair, stood and leant forwards. She slammed her fist down on the table. "For crying out loud, will you stop whining and pull yourself together? If she died of something transmissible, it's likely we're already infected. We can't change that. Let's just get this done, and then we can decide on our next course of action."

"Fine," Perrin muttered.

"Anders, any chance you could find some of those large black bin liners?"

"Yeah, I know where they're stored."

"When everything's finished, we'll wrap the body up. We'll need to do a thorough clean of the room afterwards to sterilise it and remove any signs she was there. How are you going to dispose of her?"

"I've already given that some thought," Grolby replied. "There are some lakes just off the A14, near St Ives. I bought an inflatable dinghy; it's in the boot of my car. I'll row out to the middle, weigh her down with stones, then dump her. There are no houses nearby, so I shouldn't be disturbed."

"Good. While we're busy, I suggest you start cleaning up the two labs."

"Who's going to look after the baby?"

"When he wakes, we'll have to feed him. There's formula milk in her room. Nigel and I will take him with us now. We need to get a move on. It may be the weekend, but everything has to be finished by the morning in case Martin comes in to work on his pet project."

Armed with a roll of bin bags, Rosalind entered the small cell. Both she and Perrin wore facemasks and thin plastic gloves. Eileen Floyd's body lay on the bed where she had died. A mass of red stained the bedding. Rosalind placed a towel over the dead woman's face.

"We don't have the right tools for this," Perrin said.

"I agree, but let's do the best we can. We should be able to examine the internal organs at least."

The pair worked in silence for several minutes.

Rosalind blew out a deep breath. "Take a look at this. The kidneys and liver are both liquified. It's no wonder she died so quickly." She removed the towel. "Check out her eyes. See these burst blood vessels."

"It definitely looks like a haemorrhagic disease. What the hell could've caused this?"

"I've no idea. I suggest we keep some tissue samples. After we've done that, we'll bag the rest." She glanced at her watch. "It's too late to dispose of the body today. It'll be light soon. Anders can do it tonight."

"My wife will wonder what I've been up to," Perrin said.

"Tell her about the break in. Say we had to clean up afterwards."

"What excuse do I give her for not going home?"

"Maybe explain that the intruders spilled some dangerous chemicals. You're staying here to keep your family safe. I mean, it's half true, isn't it?"

"I never wanted any of this, Rosalind."

"That may be the case, Nigel, but we can't go back now."

49

Sunday 10th April 2016

Ilithyia Biotechnology, Cambridge Science Park

Twenty-one years ago

Rosalind Baxter drummed her fingers on the boardroom table. On the opposite side, Nigel Perrin clicked a pen in and out. Both glanced up as the door opened, and Anders Grolby entered.

It had taken until after nine o'clock to clean up all the mess and remove all traces of Eileen Floyd's presence. Her body, together with the bedding, lay in bin bags in the boot of Grolby's car. They had fed the baby twice already. He remained in his makeshift crib on the floor of the room in which his mother had died. The failed light in Martin Hendrick's area hadn't made Grolby's task any easier. In the end, after clearing the adjacent laboratory, the Swede borrowed the fluorescent tube starter from there and replaced the faulty one.

"Is everybody still feeling all right?" Rosalind asked.

"Yeah," Grolby replied. "Just a bit tired."

"I'm okay," Perrin said.

Rosalind ran a hand over her face. "We haven't yet discussed how she got out. What do you think happened?"

"She couldn't have opened the door by herself," Grolby said, stifling a yawn. "That leaves two possibilities." His gaze fixed on Perrin. "Either Nigel forgot to lock up, or somebody else released her."

"I'm sure I didn't leave her room open," Perrin protested. "I definitely remember turning the key before I left."

"You mentioned receiving a call last night from your wife, asking you to come home. Is it possible you were distracted?"

"That came after I'd already locked her up. I was in Martin Hendrick's lab at the time. I was going to finish up some work in my office, so I offered to lock the building."

"Well, if it wasn't you, she must have received outside help."

"What about the break in?" Rosalind asked.

"Yes," Grolby said. "That's puzzling. Somebody apparently smashed the front door, came in, caused a load of damage, then left without taking anything. If they were intent on smashing stuff, why only target two laboratories and not the third?"

Rosalind shrugged. "Perhaps they planned to trash that too, but the sound of the siren disturbed them."

"Or maybe Eileen Floyd did it," Perrin added.

"So, somehow she gets out of her room and hangs around wrecking things instead of escaping or calling for help," Grolby replied. "Sorry, but that doesn't seem likely to me. I checked the time of the alarm. Martin called me five minutes after the silent alert had already gone off. He told me he saw a pair of suspicious men on the road outside."

"What if the intruders let her out?" Rosalind asked.

"Again, that seems pretty unlikely. How would they know she was there? Where did they get the keys from? She claimed she didn't see who released her. Why didn't they talk to her after opening the door?"

"Perhaps they expected the building to be empty," Perrin said. "If they broke in, they'd worry she might be able to identify them later."

"But that still doesn't explain the other two points."

"Could it have been Martin?" Rosalind asked.

Silence descended on the room. After a few seconds, Grolby spoke. "We have to consider the possibility. He spends a lot of time here, working by himself. His laboratory is a short distance down the corridor from the storeroom. Perhaps he found out about her."

"Christ, that's all we need," Perrin muttered.

"It still doesn't make sense. If it was him, why smash up his own area? Why not just contact the police? They haven't come knocking, so we have to assume he didn't call anybody. And if he was going to release her, he could've done it at any time. Where did he get the key to open her door?"

"I keep mine on me at all times," Rosalind said.

"Me too," Grolby added. "Nigel?"

"I hide a set in my office, in the desk drawer."

Grolby folded his arms. "Could somebody have borrowed them to let her out?"

Perrin shook his head. "How would they know where to look? Anyway, if the intruders were criminals, they'd probably have the expertise to pick a lock."

"This is getting us nowhere," Rosalind said. "So, what do we do now?"

"I suggest we call Martin Hendrick in and have a chat with him," Grolby replied.

"What?" Perrin's forehead creased in confusion. "We can't ask whether he was the one to release her."

"I don't plan to, but I'd like to question him about the two men he spotted outside. He might be able to provide additional information."

"If we're infected, there's a chance we could pass it on to him."

"When I asked a minute ago, you both told me you're feeling fine," Rosalind said. "We've all had regular contact with her, and none of us is showing any symptoms. I reckon the risk is low." She stood and retrieved the phone from her bag. "If past performance is anything to go by, he's probably planning to come in today anyway, but I'll call him now." She stepped into the corridor and spoke in a hushed voice. Moments later, she returned. "He'll be here in twenty minutes."

"What are you going to say to him?" Perrin asked.

"I'll tell him about the break in," Grolby replied, "then get him to describe the men. I also want to clear up the sequence of events around the time he left."

"How will we find out whether he knew about the girl?"

"Well, obviously we can't ask him directly. Leave the questions to me."

"I'll be in my office," Rosalind said. "Call me when he gets here."

She strolled down the corridor, sank into the leather executive chair and placed her face in her hands. *What a mess*. Eileen Floyd's unexpected death had saved them from one unpleasant task, even though they still had to dispose of her body. But if Grolby had arrived a minute or two later, she would have got away, and all three of them would be facing a long jail term. There were too many coincidences; Martin Hendrick had to be involved somehow, but she could hardly accuse him outright.

The financial situation at Ilithyia was far stronger than when she had agreed to support his pet project. Several major contracts had landed in the last six months. Whilst the rewards of Hendrick's research were potentially huge, everything was at risk if anybody ever found out about the work he was performing. He had yet to demonstrate any meaningful progress. Maybe it was time to pull the plug.

She logged into her computer and sighed at the long list of emails in her inbox. She scrolled down the page, deleting all of them unread, apart from three sent by important clients. Her vision shimmered as she tried to focus on the screen. A headache pulsed just behind her eyes. Unable to concentrate, she signed out. They would have to wait for a response until Monday.

She stood and stared out of the window. When she had founded the business with Nigel Perrin, she had imagined developing Ilithyia into a global pharmaceutical company. The struggle to make ends meet and the constant battle to find new customers were factors she hadn't really considered.

After three tension-filled years, all they had to show for the long hours and continual stress was contained within these four walls, and even then, they didn't own the building. She had invested too much time and money to fail now. Whatever it took, she wouldn't allow anybody to take away her life's work.

The arrival of a red Ford Focus in the car park below dragged her back from her thoughts. She strode out of her office and down the stairs. She arrived at the bottom just as Martin Hendrick came through the entrance.

"Hello, Rosalind. What happened here?" he asked, pointing at the empty lower pane in the door.

"Somebody broke in last night. I've spent most of the time since then cleaning up the mess they made."

"Oh. I called Anders about a pair of men behaving suspiciously outside. He said the alarm had gone off. I offered to come back, but he told me to go home. Did they take anything?"

"No, but there was considerable damage in two of the laboratories, including yours."

"What sort of damage?"

"They emptied the contents of the refrigerator onto the floor and smashed up your computer."

"Shit!"

Rosalind followed the scientist as he jogged towards his workspace. If he was the instigator of the events that had taken place over the previous night, he was doing a good job of disguising his involvement. She stepped through the doorway to discover Hendrick staring at the bare shelves of the fridge.

"What did you do with it all?" he asked, turning as she entered.

"They broke everything. We bagged it and threw it into the industrial waste bin."

"What about the metal flasks?"

"Empty. Why?"

"That's where I kept the virus samples I was working on."

Alarm bells went off in Rosalind's head. "What? I didn't see any biohazard labels. We would have taken more precautions if we'd known."

"You asked me to keep anything like that out of sight."

Rosalind clenched her fists and took a deep breath. "Is there any risk of infection?"

"No, it's perfectly safe. There's nothing to worry about."

"Right. Where did you store the data?"

"I backed up all my regular work to the network, but I kept the stuff for the other project on the hard drive. If you remember, you told me not to put it on the file servers."

"You better see if it still works."

Hendrick crossed to his workstation. The beige unit exhibited several dents and scratches. He pressed the power switch. After a short beep, followed by the manufacturer's logo, a line of white text appeared on a black background.

DISK BOOT FAILURE - INSERT SYSTEM DISK AND PRESS ENTER

He tried a second time with the same result. He turned to Rosalind, his face pale. "It looks like it's gone. There aren't any backups. Everything was on there."

She studied him for a moment before speaking. "I'll get Anders to take a look and see if he can fix it. He wants to talk to you, anyway."

Hendrick trailed her up the stairs and into the boardroom. Perrin and Grolby already sat on the far side of the table.

"Hello, Martin," the Swede said when everyone was seated. "You called me last night about two men you spotted outside the building."

"Yeah, they were standing on the pavement by the main road just past the entrance. I thought they looked suspicious."

"What makes you say that?"

"They didn't seem to be going anywhere, and they turned away from me as I drove by."

"Can you describe them?"

"No, sorry. Like I said, I didn't get a look at their faces."

"What were they wearing?" Grolby asked.

"Oh, uh... dark clothes, I think. I can't really remember. One of them wore white trainers. I should've mentioned it last night, but I heard some strange sounds outside just before locking up."

Rosalind's gaze met Perrin's. "What sort of sounds?" she asked, focusing back on Hendrick.

"Um... banging. There was also some shouting. It sounded like kids. It seemed to be coming from the rear of the building."

"Let's return to these men you saw," Grolby said. "Why did you wait until you were nearly home before calling me?"

"I didn't want to disturb you unnecessarily. Then I thought about it some more and decided to phone you."

"You set the alarm last night."

"Yes, as I do most nights."

"I checked the logs. The silent alert went off two minutes after it was armed. How do you explain that?"

Hendrick scowled at the Swede. "What? Are you suggesting I had something to do with this?"

"I didn't say that. I'm just trying to find out what happened."

"Well, obviously you believe I am involved, otherwise you wouldn't be asking these questions. Why would I smash up my own lab? I've spent months on this project. What possible reason could I have for destroying my research?"

"This work of yours," Rosalind said. "Is there any way it could cause disease?"

"Of course not. You know what the goals were—to provide a vaccination for Chlamydia. Why do you ask?"

"Just curious."

"So, back to the break in. Was it you?" Grolby asked.

Hendrick slammed his palms down on the desk. "Seriously?"

Perrin raised his hand in a placating gesture "Calm down, Martin."

"Why should I?" He poked a finger first at Rosalind, then at Perrin. "After all the unpaid overtime I put into this company, you sit there and let him accuse me of something like this. Well, I've had enough. If that's the way you want to play it, you can have my immediate resignation. The only reason I stayed here these past few months was to finish this work, and now it's all gone, destroyed by some mindless vandals. I'm really not interested in any of the other crap jobs you give me."

Stunned silence greeted Hendrick's outburst.

"Look, Martin..." Perrin began.

"No, I've had enough. You never wanted me to take on this project in the first place."

"Actually, I—"

"I trust you'll at least have the decency to pay my wages up to today. I'm leaving right now."

Hendrick pushed back his chair and strode through the door, slamming it behind him.

"That went well," Rosalind said, drily.

50

Saturday 23rd April 2016

North Middlesex University Hospital, London

Twenty-one years ago

"Breathe," the man said.

"As opposed to what?" his wife replied through clenched teeth.

"Remember the techniques they talked about at the NCT sessions."

"Oh, piss off, will you?"

He reached over to brush aside a strand of sweaty hair that had fallen across her face.

She slapped his hand away. "Don't touch me."

He glanced at the door. Where the hell was the midwife? Just before departing, she had told them his wife's cervix was nearly at the full ten centimetres dilation. The woman had received a call on her pager and promised to return soon after helping with the final stages of another birth. That had been fifteen minutes ago.

A piercing scream echoed through the thin walls from the adjacent room. The man winced. *Was that normal?*

As if in sympathy with the other expectant mother, his wife clenched her fist, digging her fingers into his palm. He tried to pull away, but she tightened her grip.

"Ow, you're hurting me," he said.

"Good, you bastard," she replied, her face twisting in agony.

A moment later, the contraction ended and the pressure on his hand relaxed.

"I need more gas," she mumbled between short pants of breath.

He lifted the transparent facemask, which was attached to the wall via a white tube, and handed it to her. "The midwife said not to overdo it."

His wife ignored him and continued to breathe deeply. After twenty seconds, her arm dropped to the side. Her grip loosened on the mask, and he gently removed it from her hand before replacing it on the stand beside the hospital bed.

"Why didn't you get back sooner?" she whispered.

"Sorry, but I got the first flight I could," he replied. "I drove here straight from the airport."

"You should've told them you couldn't go. It was your second trip this week."

"It's part of the job, but I've booked a fortnight off now, so I can stay at home and look after you and the baby."

She pushed herself up on her elbows as another contraction surged through her body. Thirty seconds later, she sank back onto the pillows, her face beaded with sweat. "Where is that bloody woman?"

"Shall I try to find her?"

"Yes, but be quick. I don't want to go through this by myself."

The man rose and let himself out of the door. As he stepped into the corridor, a white-coated doctor jogged towards him.

"Excuse me."

The medic ignored him, ran past and barged into the adjacent room. Moments later, a woman in similar attire rounded the corner and rushed in the same direction.

"My wife is—"

"Somebody will be with you shortly," she interrupted without breaking stride.

The man stood in bewilderment. After a few seconds, the midwife, who had been assisting with the birth of their child until she was called away, emerged from the adjacent delivery room.

Finally. "Ah, Marie..."

His voice trailed off as he took in the dark crimson stains splashed across her uniform, contrasting with the paleness of her face. She staggered and leant against the wall for support.

"Is everything all right?"

She shook her head.

"Can I do anything? Only, my wife—"

"Give me a minute to clean up, Mr Gowan," she said.

"Is the woman in there okay?"

"I'm sorry, I can't talk about it." She turned away and headed in the opposite direction.

The man returned to his wife's room. A shiver of apprehension ran through him. Something bad must have happened to cause that much blood.

His wife lay on the pillows, her hair straggled in damp clumps. "Is the midwife coming?" she asked in a hoarse voice.

"Yeah, she'll be here shortly," he replied, lowering himself into the chair beside the bed. He didn't want to alarm her by telling her what he had seen. He took her hand in his own. "It'll soon be over."

"I can feel another contraction on the way."

"Breathe in through your nose and sigh out through your mouth."

His wife scowled. "I don't need you to tell me that. I was at the course—ah." Her teeth clamped together, and her hands grasped her stomach. "More gas," she groaned.

She snatched the mask out of his hand as he offered it to her.

At that moment, the door opened, and the midwife burst in. She had changed into a fresh uniform. "Sorry to leave you like that, Sarah. How are we doing?" She raised the maternity gown. "You're crowning. I can see the baby's head. Not long to go now."

Minutes went by, and the intensity of the contractions increased.

"One final push," the midwife urged. "The baby's almost out."

His wife groaned. All her muscles seemed to tense at the same time. The man watched as the midwife's hands caught the slippery bundle. She placed the child on a clean towel and wiped the blood and mucus from the tiny body. A reedy wail filled the room.

"It's a boy. Would you like to cut the umbilical cord, Mark?"

He glanced nervously at the twisted white tube and grasped the offered surgical scissors. "Here?" he asked.

"Yes, just by the clamp."

The razor-sharp blades severed the coiled link with little effort.

The new mother accepted the bundled child and clasped him to her chest. Her lips curved in an exhausted smile as her husband gently touched her cheek. "He's..."

A look of confusion clouded her face. Her right hand moved to her throat as a wet cough shook her body. The midwife snatched up the baby and deposited him in a cot at the end of the bed.

"What's wrong?" the man asked.

The coughing intensified. His wife hacked up a gobbet of bloody fluid. Her lips bared, revealing bloodstained teeth as she opened her mouth to scream. A patchwork of broken blood vessels discoloured the once white sclera of her eyes.

"What's happening?" the man shouted.

"No, not another one," the midwife muttered. She rushed to the wall and pressed the large red emergency button.

Moments later, the sound of urgent footsteps echoed down the corridor outside the room. The doctor, who had hurried past a few minutes earlier, burst through the door. His gaze immediately focused on the patient. "Status?" he asked.

"She's haemorrhaging," the midwife replied, "just like the other two."

Choking sounds emerged from the new mother's throat. Convulsions shook her body. Her stomach heaved, and a thick, dark-red fluid spouted from her mouth, leaving a Rorschach ink blot pattern splattered over the doctor's white coat. With a final gasp, the woman's movements ceased, and she lay still.

The doctor placed a finger to her neck and frowned with concentration. A moment later, he raised his eyes and met the man's desperate gaze. "I'm sorry," he murmured.

The new father shoved him out of the way. "This can't be happening." He leant over and shook his wife's shoulders. "Come on, Sarah, please wake up."

The midwife's hand landed gently on his back. "There's nothing we can do for her. She's gone, Mark."

Unseen by the grieving husband, the female doctor entered the room. She took in the scene with a single glance. Her male colleague gave a surreptitious shake of the head.

“That’s the third today,” she said, her grim expression hidden by a surgical mask. “It has to be more than a coincidence. I’m afraid we’re going to have to quarantine the building. We have a nightmare scenario on our hands.”

51

Monday 25th April 2016

Ilithyia Biotechnology, Cambridge Science Park

Twenty-one years ago

Rosalind Baxter knocked on the door. For once, she waited for a reply before striding into Nigel Perrin's office. She carried a newspaper beneath her arm. Perrin glanced up from behind his desk.

"Good morning, Rosalind. How's the boy doing?"

"Fine. The nanny is costing me a bloody fortune though."

"You're using a company, aren't you? What did you tell them?"

"I said he belongs to a niece who's still at school. Her family wants to keep the birth quiet, so I offered to look after him. The agency claims to be discreet. Let's just hope they're true to their word."

"He's not showing any symptoms, then?"

"No. And by the way, his name is Jason."

Perrin peered over his glasses. "You're not growing attached to him, are you?"

"No, but we all agreed it was a good idea to keep an eye on him. I can hardly do that as well as running the company. His mother told me that's what she wanted to call him. I didn't see the harm in following her wishes."

"I understand. Anyway, I'm assuming you haven't popped in for a social chat. What can I do for you?"

"I take it you've seen this," she said, dropping the folded newspaper on his desk.

Perrin opened out the front page and read the headline.

New Virus Strikes Recent Mothers. In-Depth Feature Inside.

"Yes, I've been following the news reports."

"And?"

"And what?"

"Doesn't any of it sound familiar?" Rosalind asked. She snatched up the paper and rustled through the pages. "Here," she said, jabbing a finger at the newsprint. "Victims die within minutes of giving birth."

"Right."

"And here. Doctors say the symptoms are similar to those seen in patients suffering from haemorrhagic fevers, such as Ebola. That sounds exactly like what Eileen Floyd died from."

Perrin removed his glasses and peered at the page. "Well, I'll admit there are similarities."

"No, Nigel, it's more than that. The cases are identical. And it's not just a few. I checked Yahoo News on the Internet this morning. There have been numerous deaths across the world. It says here, the first reported case was a week ago. I'm sure I don't need to remind you that Eileen Floyd died two weeks ago."

Grolby's disposal of Eileen's body had gone as planned. Her final resting place was the bottom of a lake near St Ives.

"So, you really think she had this disease?" Perrin said.

"I do," Rosalind replied.

"What are the newspapers calling it? The Orestes virus?"

"Yeah, apparently Orestes was some character from Greek Mythology who killed his mother when he discovered she had murdered his father. It was something to do with the Trojan War. Anyway, it doesn't matter what the press have called it. I read this morning that the medical authorities have quarantined a number of maternity units across the world, including one in north London. The report said there have been several deaths at the site."

"But you can't possibly think it started here."

"For Christ's sake, Nigel, open your eyes. Eileen Floyd suffered exactly the same symptoms a week before anybody else. The evidence is staring us in the face."

"But if she did contract this virus, how did she get infected?"

"That's the million-dollar question. As I see it, there are only two possibilities; either you, me or Anders gave it to her or..."

"Or what?"

"Anders mentioned that she went into one of the labs after she escaped from her room. She had chemical stains on her trainers. She told him afterwards that she was looking for keys to open the front door to the building. What if she picked up the infection in there?"

"How could that happen?" Perrin asked.

"Let's face it, neither of us really has a clue what Martin Hendrick was working on. We know it was based on the flu virus, but that's all. We don't have any notes from his research; the contents of his computer were destroyed during the break-in. Anders was only able to retrieve a few file fragments. It gives us some clues, but it's not enough.

"The intruders also smashed everything in his refrigerator. He told us he was storing the organisms he was working on in unmarked containers. Is it possible that when all that material got mixed together, it somehow combined into a new strain?"

Perrin's face turned pale. He snatched up the pen from his desk and began clicking. "Shit. I hadn't thought of that. So, what do we do next?"

"I guess the first step is to try to get hold of Martin."

"If he'll even talk to us. I have his personal mobile number on record. But what do I say to him?"

"I suggest you grovel a bit and ask him to come in for a chat."

"And if he refuses?"

Rosalind chewed a fingernail. "I don't know. We've still got the autopsy samples."

"I suppose we could send them off for analysis, but that might raise a few unwanted questions. Look, I'll try him now."

Rosalind paced while Perrin tapped the keys of his phone. He held the device to his ear. Moments later, he lowered it again. "I'm getting number unobtainable."

"I assume you have his address. Why don't we pay him a visit?"

"What, right this minute?"

"Well, I'd say this is more important than anything else we've got on at the moment."

"Fine. Your car or mine?"

"We'll take mine," Rosalind replied. She marched along the corridor, down the stairs and past the reception desk, ignoring the receptionist's greeting as she passed. Perrin trailed behind her, hurrying to keep up.

Twenty minutes later, after riding in silence, they drew up outside the address they held on record.

"That's the one," Perrin said, pointing at the small semi-detached house. A large to-let sign dominated the front garden. The two business partners emerged from the car and approached the bright-red front door. Nobody responded to the ringing of the bell. A stack of post lay on the doormat.

Rosalind pointed at the pile of unopened mail. "It looks like we might be too late. Why don't you call the letting agent and try to find out where he's gone?"

Perrin read the number off the board and tapped in the digits. He spoke for a few minutes, then clicked the button to disconnect. "She said he moved out two days ago. They don't have a forwarding address."

Rosalind returned to the car. When her partner had buckled himself in, she turned sideways in the driver's seat. "Somehow, I don't think we're going to be having that chat with Martin Hendrick after all."

52

Friday 20th May 2016

33 Apple Tree Drive, Cambridge

Twenty-one years ago

A groan of pain came from inside the room. Dominic Lessing placed his hands against the wood panelling. His wife, Helen, had gone into labour five hours earlier.

"Are you all right?" he asked from the other side of the bedroom door. "What's going on?"

"The last two contractions were two minutes apart," she replied in a shaky voice. "I think I'm getting close."

Despite the barrier between them, Dominic still wore a surgical facemask. "Are you sure you don't want me in there to help?"

"No, we can't take the risk. I'll manage."

He desperately wanted to sit by his wife and support her as she gave birth, but ever since news broke of the Orestes virus and its devastating effect on recent mothers, Helen had isolated herself in the master en-suite bedroom of their home. Stacked against the wall with her were a pile of disinfectant wipes and several bottles of hand sanitiser.

Over the same period, Dominic had instigated a similar isolation policy, confining himself to the house throughout. He booked all his annual vacation allowance in one go, so he didn't have to leave the building. He ordered all food and groceries online, wiping down anything that would come into contact with his wife.

Despite all the precautions, there was no guarantee Helen would survive the birth of their child. After numerous deaths, maternity wards across the country had closed. Blanket television coverage encouraged expectant mothers to self-isolate, but many succumbed to the desire to be with loved ones or medical staff when the baby was born—resulting in a near one-hundred per cent mortality rate.

There was still no test yet to determine whether a woman had contracted the Orestes virus. Those who were infected died without exception. The scientists had determined that provided the mother survived the first few minutes after severing the umbilical cord, the chances of dying reduced to practically zero.

Another cry of pain came through the door, followed by the sound of several short, sharp breaths. Dominic sank down with his back to the wall and buried his face in his hands. A feeling of helplessness washed over him. Giving birth was supposed to be one of life's greatest moments for a parent, but a surge of dread ran through him. Could she do this alone? Would she survive long enough to hold her baby? The ultrasound scans had confirmed it would be a girl; he had wanted to wait to discover the gender when the child was born, but Helen preferred to know in advance.

They had spent many hours discussing a name. They agreed it should be something unique that would stand out but without being too alternative. After much deliberation, they settled on Antimone. *Like the metal*, he had joked. Four syllables: in some ways similar to the main female character in the Harry Potter books, Hermione Granger.

Another scream jolted him from his memories.

"Is everything okay?"

Several seconds of silence passed. What was happening?

Then his wife's voice. "I think it's—"

Her words morphed into a long shriek of agony.

"Helen, please talk to me."

The cry ceased, sending an icy shiver of apprehension racing through his body.

"Helen!" he yelled, pressing his face against the door.

Nothing.

He was about to barge in despite their previous agreement when his wife spoke in a weak voice. "I'm holding her. She's beautiful. I'm going to cut the cord."

A thin, reedy wail penetrated from inside the room.

"Please tell me what's happening," Dominic called.

"It's done."

"Keep talking. Describe her to me."

"She has wispy brown hair. Her eyes are dark, almost black. Her face is..."

"What is it?" He tried to hide the note of desperation in his voice, but it came through loud and clear.

His wife continued in little more than a whisper. He pressed his ear against the cold wood to hear. "Her face is all scrunched up. She's definitely not happy." The wailing sound intensified.

Dominic exhaled the breath he had been holding. "Can I come in yet?"

"Just give it a while longer. She's started feeding. She seems to be hungry."

Each second seemed like an hour as he waited. Finally, she said, "I think it's probably safe by now."

Dominic turned the handle and pushed open the door. His wife lay on the floor in the centre of the room. She greeted him with an exhausted smile, clutching a small bundle to her breast.

"Come and meet your daughter," she whispered.

His gaze lowered to the blood-soaked towels beneath her. The glint of the surgical scissors caught his attention.

"Is everything okay?" he asked, crouching beside her. "Are you all right?"

Helen glanced down at their child, then met his eyes. “I’m tired, and I hurt like hell, but apart from that, I’m fine.”

Dominic placed his little finger against his daughter’s tiny palm. Her fingers closed around his. “I promise I won’t let anything bad happen to you,” he murmured in Antimone’s ear.

Part Five: Revelation

53

Tuesday 21st April 2037

23 Daffodil Drive, Northstowe

The two North Africans sat on the sofa. Max Perrin paced backwards and forwards, holding a thin metal object. He rotated the sealed tube and examined it carefully.

"It doesn't look anything special, does it?" he said.

Omar held out a hand. "Let me see."

"Don't open it, will you?"

The muscled soldier rolled his eyes. "Do not worry. I am not stupid." He raised it to the light. "I cannot detect a join." He passed the item to Mo.

The diminutive hacker studied the cylinder for a moment before handing it back to Max. "No. It should not appear out of place in a toolbox."

Two days earlier, Max had requested a supply of firearms from their handlers. The metal object contained one of the components, which, when combined with the other pieces, would form a gun. It was designed to pass through the scanners at the Ilithyia entrance without triggering an alert. The weapons dealer had sent through a demonstration video showing the assembly process and a test-firing of the assembled item. After thoroughly cleaning the exterior surfaces of all gunshot residue that might trigger the sensitive sensors, the anonymous supplier had shipped the parts using three different couriers.

"So," Max said, "we know we can get inside by adjusting the thermostat setting. We have a gun. That leaves one remaining issue; how to locate our four targets. None of them ever leave the building, but we must reach them all without being discovered."

"If we raise the temperature high enough," Mo said, "they will come outside again. Yes, we have asked for a handgun, but maybe we could use a sniper rifle to shoot them from distance."

"No, that would never work. We're too far away. As soon as the first one went down, the rest would all scatter. Anyway, I want them to know who's pulling the trigger. I want to look them in the eyes when I do it."

"The last time we adjusted the temperature, they all waited by the entrance," Omar said. "So, we turn up the heat inside, arrive in the van and shoot them at close range."

"I didn't sign up for a suicide mission. Anyway, what about the guards?"

"I did not see one gun. They carry only non-lethal weapons."

"Too risky," Max replied. "Even if they aren't carrying guns, there are too many of them. They'd quickly disable us if we just opened fire. And don't forget the dogs."

"So, you want to do this inside," Mo said. "How do we find the traitors and kill them?"

"Okay, what about this? We start by reassembling the weapon in the control room. Then we take a member of the security team prisoner and force him to reveal their location. Those guys should know where everybody is in the building."

"Yes, this could work," Omar said. "The best time to do this is at night. Our targets will be in their rooms, and we can kill them quietly one by one without raising the alarm."

Max nodded. "Good suggestion. We can't leave it too late in the day, though. We'll stand out too much if we're wandering about when all the people who live there are tucked up in bed. I suggest we access their system and raise the temperature sometime in the early evening, then hang around out of sight in the control room pretending to fix the problem until later. That will allow everybody time to get back inside. When we're ready, we grab a guard and force him to take us to the targets. If anybody asks what we're doing, we tell them the sensors are giving out faulty readings, and we need to replace them. That should enable us to go where we want."

"This sounds a good plan," Omar said. "How do you say? It is like shooting fish in a box."

"You mean a barrel," Max replied with a slight smile.

"Right. When do we do this?"

"Why not today? It's just after eleven o'clock now. Let's do it this evening. Is everything else ready?"

"Let me check I can still access the system," Mo said. He rose and sat in front of the computer screen. His fingers moved in a blur of motion. After a few seconds, he turned around with a grin on his face. "Yes, it all works well."

Max placed the metal tube in the toolbox, which lay open on the floor. "Excellent. At four o'clock, I want you to raise the temperature again. I'll call their site manager, Nick Butler, at ten past, telling him we've been monitoring the system and have spotted a problem. As soon as I've done that, we'll head over there.

"When we arrive, we go to the control room and lower the setting to normal. Then, we just hang around for three or four hours, pretending to be working on a fix. When the place is quiet enough, we grab the guard and find out where they're keeping the traitors. If necessary, we get him to open the doors to their rooms. Once we've killed them all, I call Mr Butler, inform him the problem's fixed, and we leave. By the time they discover the bodies, we'll be long gone and on our way back to Tripoli."

"How will we travel?" Mo asked.

"There's too much security at the airports," Max replied. "I'll book us some train tickets. We can't sit together because it might draw attention. It's less than an hour from Cambridge to London and a little longer from there to Paris. We can decide on the rest later. If all goes well, we should be home in a couple of days."

"Good," Omar said. "I hate this miserable country. I will be glad to return to the desert."

"Right. Before we go, we have to remove all evidence of our presence here. We need to ensure we leave nothing for the police to find. Let's get to work."

54

Tuesday 21st April 2037

Ilithyia Biotechnology, Northstowe

Antimone pulled the door shut behind her and propelled herself towards the lift. Moments earlier, she had received the call that Paul was ready to be picked up from his classes. It was half an hour before the usual five o'clock finish, but the flustered sounding receptionist had offered no explanation. Whatever the reason, it seemed no members of the security staff were available to escort him back to his room, so the responsibility fell to his parents.

She pushed the button. As she waited, she allowed her mind to wander. Jason had suggested she restart her athletics training. Two days ago, she had followed her partner's advice and called her former coach, John Marshall. The conversation was awkward at first, but in the end, he agreed to an initial trial session after she promised to answer his questions concerning the events surrounding the previous summer's Olympic wheelchair final. Now, all she had to do was persuade the security team to let her leave the building.

She shivered slightly at the thought of the agony she would have to endure to get back to her former fitness level, but if she wanted to compete again, there was no alternative. As her coach was fond of saying, *no pain, no gain.* The prospect of appearing in public now that everybody knew the details of her past filled her with trepidation. Some still blamed her for not revealing the facts following the birth of her son. But what did they expect her to do?

The ding of the bell drew her back to the present. The doors slid apart, and she wheeled herself inside. Moments later, a wall of warm air swept over her as she emerged into the foyer. Surely the heating system wasn't on the blink again? She hadn't noticed any significant temperature rise in the room, but here the heat was oppressive. That would explain the early finish to Paul's day.

A few people milled about, mostly scientists judging by the white medical coats. A group of security staff stood in a huddle by the scanners, deep in conversation. She turned right and headed towards the classroom. She arrived moments later to find the teacher, Mrs Prendergast, waiting with the last two of her students.

"Sorry," the woman said at Antimone's arrival. "We had to wrap up early because it was getting too hot for the children. One of the other parents mentioned that at least the maintenance engineers have already arrived to fix the problem. You'd think with all the money they spend on this place, they could sort out the heating system."

"How's he doing?" Antimone asked.

"Oh, he's a little star. Have you got your drawing to show your mum, Paul?"

The four-year-old placed the paper he was holding in his hand on the table. Antimone's smile faded slightly as her gaze took in her son's artwork. The picture depicted a crude stick man, drawn in blue crayon. The face comprised two wonky eyes and a disproportionately large downturned mouth. Dark hair rose in jagged lines from the top of the head. The figure oozed menace.

"Um, no, I meant the painting you did earlier," the teacher said. She turned to Antimone. "We let them draw while they're waiting."

Paul placed a second sheet over the first. This one showed several trees and what appeared to be an animal in front.

"It's a dog," he announced. "Can we get a dog, Mummy?"

The two women exchanged a glance.

"Maybe when you're a bit older," Antimone replied. "We can't really keep a pet here, though." She reached out a hand and uncovered the second picture. "Who's this then?"

"It's the bad man."

A shiver ran through Antimone's body despite the temperature. "Which bad man?"

"The one in blue."

"Have you seen him?"

Paul nodded.

Mrs Prendergast shrugged. "I'm not sure where that could have been. Nobody else has been in the classroom all day."

"I saw him when I went for a wee-wee."

The teacher shot Antimone a worried look. "We let the older ones go to the toilet by themselves. It's just down the hall. I have to say Paul has an especially well-developed imagination. It's probably nothing."

"He mentioned the same thing a few days ago," Antimone said, frowning. "Paul, have you seen this man before?"

"Yes."

"You mean while we've been here?"

Another nod.

"Was he alone?"

"No."

"How many were there?"

Paul pondered the question for a moment. "A hundred."

The teacher squatted beside the boy. "Remember, we've done counting. What comes after one?"

"Two."

"Good."

"Three, four, five, six..."

"That's excellent, Paul. So, can you tell us how many men you saw?"

A look of concentration occupied Paul's face. "Three," he announced, proudly.

Mrs Prendergast straightened her legs. "I wouldn't worry about it. Like I said, I'm sure it's nothing."

"Yeah," Antimone replied, a frown creasing her forehead. "Paul, this is important. Are you saying you've seen one of these men before when we were in that place in Africa, you know, after we went on the sailing boat?"

"Can we go now, Mummy?"

"Did you recognise the man from our time in the hospital, Paul?"

"I'm hot. I want to watch television."

Antimone shrugged at the other woman. "Fine. Would you like a ride?"

Paul clambered onto his mother's lap with no hesitation.

"Say goodbye to Mrs Prendergast," Antimone said.

"Bye."

"See you tomorrow," the teacher replied.

Antimone steered her wheelchair through the doorway, then stopped. "Where were the men when you saw them?"

Paul pointed a finger. "Just there."

"What were they doing?"

"I don't know. Can we go and watch Peppa Pig now?"

"You said these people were wearing blue?"

"Please, Mummy."

Antimone shook her head. "Fine, but only for a few minutes. Then we need to take you down for tea."

55

Tuesday 21st April 2037

Ilithyia Biotechnology, Northstowe

Max Perrin glanced at the band on his wrist: a few minutes before six o'clock. The site manager, Nick Butler, had greeted them upon arrival and expressed his displeasure at the second disruption to the facility in a week. Max promised to resolve the issue that day, no matter how long it took. Mo had already adjusted the temperature back to the regular setting. Now, they just had to sit tight, pretending to fix the underlying problem, until the time came to carry out the next stage of the mission.

"I am bored," Omar said, inspecting the assembled weapon he held in his hands. "How much longer do we need to wait?"

"We've already been over this," Max replied. "We have to stay here for another two hours at least."

"But I hate waiting. Also, I am hungry."

"Bloody hell. It's like babysitting a bunch of children. You knew the plan, and I reminded you to bring food with you."

"Yes," Omar said sulkily, "but it is all gone. The man told us we could eat in the canteen."

When they had arrived, Nick Butler offered them use of the building amenities and handed them a card, which they could use to order meals.

Max shrugged his shoulders in resignation. "All right. If you must, but I'm staying here. There are too many people about who might recognise me. Don't be long. And for God's sake, don't do anything to attract attention."

Omar grinned and placed the reassembled pistol in the toolbox. "Good. Are you coming, Mo?"

"No, I am not hungry."

The muscular North African crossed to the door. "Fine. I will be back soon."

"I do not know how he can eat at a time like this," Mo said when his colleague had left.

"Yeah." Max rose from his seat and bent down to pick up the weapon. He turned it in his hands. It looked totally unlike a conventional gun, but the purpose was clear from the shiny barrel and simple trigger mechanism. Although only a single-shot pistol, it was deadly at close quarters. Re-arming required the user to unscrew the parts before inserting a new bullet. Another metal tube held a supply of ammunition.

"What do you plan to do after the mission is over and we have reached Paris?" Mo asked.

"I don't know. I haven't really given it much thought. One thing's for sure; I can't stay here. Maybe I'll spend some time on a beach. How about you?"

"Oh, I will return to my family. They live in Tripoli."

The conversation lapsed into silence. Neither man had anything in common with the other. Mo returned to the computer screen and navigated the menu options for the heating system. Max paced across the room with the gun in his hand. Both men spun around at a sound from the door.

The handle turned, and Nick Butler entered. Despite the heat, he still wore a suit. The acrid scent of body odour followed him inside. He loosened the red tie at his neck, then ran his fingers through his short, grey hair.

"How's it going?" he asked. "The temperature seems to be returning to normal, so I assume you're making progress."

Max moved against the wall, hiding the pistol behind his back. "We're still not quite to the bottom of things," he replied. "We suspect there could be a sensor fault, so we may need to track the faulty part down. But don't worry, we'll get it done tonight."

"Good. We can't afford any more disruption." Butler's attention settled on the screen. "Could you show me where to find the readings on the system in case this happens again?"

Mo shifted uneasily on his seat. "Um..."

"We're pretty busy just at the moment," Max said. "Perhaps we can run you through it when we've finished."

"Oh." A frown developed on the site manager's forehead. "I suppose so. I'll catch you later." His gaze tracked to Max's right arm. He turned away, then seemed to reconsider his decision. "Actually, do you mind if I ask what you're holding behind your back?"

Max withdrew his hidden hand and pointed the pistol barrel at the man's chest. "You probably shouldn't have asked that."

Butler's face turned pale. "Is that a...?"

"Yes, it's a gun. It doesn't look like a conventional weapon because we had to disguise the parts to get it through the scanners."

"But, what—?"

"I'm sorry," Max said in little more than a whisper. He squeezed the trigger.

The bang wasn't as loud as he had expected. Even so, Butler staggered backwards. A crimson stain expanded rapidly across his white shirt on the left side of his chest. He coughed, and a trickle of blood dribbled from his mouth. He extended his right arm, then toppled silently onto the floor and lay still.

Mo leapt back from his chair. "What are you doing?"

"We can't afford to take a prisoner now," Max replied.

"I... I thought that was the plan."

"Yes, but there are only the two of us. If somebody else came in, we wouldn't be able to control the situation."

"What if someone heard the bang?"

"Hopefully nobody noticed. I guess we'll find out soon enough."

"But they may look for him when he does not return."

"That's a risk we're going to have to take. Help me move the body."

Mo stared at Max wordlessly for a moment, then moved to the side of the dead man. "Where shall we put him?"

"We need to get him out of sight. Can we shift that cabinet?"

"Yes, but it will not hide him for long."

"I'm aware of that," Max snapped. "We just have to make sure he's not visible to anyone coming in."

The pair manoeuvred the heavy metal unit away from the wall. Between them, they dragged Butler's corpse across the floor, leaving a streak of red behind in their path.

"What about that?" Mo asked, pointing at the bloodstain.

"There are some rags in the toolbox. You clean up the mess while I reload the gun."

The hacker looked like he was about to argue, but after a moment's deliberation, he followed the instructions.

Max grabbed the shiny cylinder and unscrewed the end. The metal cap escaped his grip and bounced across the floor in a series of metallic tings. With trembling fingers, he extracted a bullet from the tube, removed the barrel and reloaded the weapon.

As he reassembled the final part, the rattle of the handle drew his attention. Both men in the room froze as the door swung open.

Omar appeared in the doorway, a wide grin on his face. "I feel better now," he said. "Did I miss anything?"

56

Tuesday 21st April 2037

Ilithyia Biotechnology, Northstowe

Paul skipped ahead of Antimone into the canteen. She had allowed him to watch two episodes of Peppa Pig in their room, but now it was time for him to eat. A variety of tantalising food smells set her stomach rumbling as she followed her son through the swing doors.

At a quarter past six, the canteen was mostly empty. Most people at the site ate their evening meal later. A handful of scientists in white coats congregated around one table, engaged in a vigorous conversation. A security guard, identifiable from his pale-blue uniform, occupied another by himself. He picked at the contents of his plate while he stared into the screen of a mobile device. The schoolteacher, Mrs Prendergast, also sat alone. Paul hadn't spotted her yet, or he would have rushed up to greet her.

Antimone followed her son to the serving area. "What do you fancy tonight?" she asked.

"Turkey dinosaurs and chips," he replied.

"You had that yesterday. How about the beef stew?"

"But I don't like stew. I want ketchup too."

Antimone debated with herself whether to hold her ground or concede. Getting Paul to eat healthily was a constant battle. Jason was far better at persuading their son to vary his diet, but her partner wasn't here.

"All right," she said after a short pause. "But tomorrow you have to try something else."

The woman behind the counter flashed her a sympathetic look. "Is there anything in particular you'd like us to get in? I'm on this shift for the rest of the week. I can probably arrange for the chef to make a special meal for you."

Antimone's mind went blank for a moment. Every food her son enjoyed seemed to have some unhealthy aspect. "Um, I don't know. Actually, he likes macaroni cheese."

"No problem. I'm sure we can manage that."

"Thanks."

"And what about you? What would you like?"

"Oh, nothing, thank you. My partner and I will be eating later."

"Right, see you then."

Antimone placed the payment card against the reader, perched the tray on her knees and steered herself towards an empty table.

At that moment, Paul spotted his teacher. "Can we sit with Mrs Prendergast?"

Antimone tried to steer him away. "We don't really want to bother her. You've been with her all day. I'm sure she needs some time alone. You can see her again tomorrow."

The woman turned in her seat and flashed a smile. "It's all right. I don't mind."

Paul ran over and perched on the edge of a chair. "I watched Peppa Pig," he announced.

"That sounds exciting."

"Peppa made a friend. It was a cat."

Antimone placed the food in front of him. He reached out a hand. "Knife and fork, please," she said.

The teacher sipped from her drink, then put the glass down. "Thank goodness the place has cooled down."

Antimone helped her son to hold the cutlery. "Yeah," she replied. "It's ironic that with all this advanced technology and all these scientists on site, they still can't manage to keep the temperature under control."

Mrs Prendergast hesitated a moment before speaking. "You mentioned a trip on a boat to Africa earlier. Do you mind if I ask what that was about? Paul has talked about bad men a few times. It seems whatever happened had a big impact on him."

The rescue of four British citizens from Tripoli had been front-page news for many weeks, but most of the details concerning the abduction from the Glasgow Olympics stadium and the subsequent journey by ship stayed out of the press.

Antimone pondered how to reply. Paul spent several hours a day with this woman. If her son's experiences were having a bearing on his behaviour, his teacher deserved to know the basic facts.

Antimone leant forwards and lowered her voice. "You must have heard that I'm Paul's birth mother. Despite what you may have read, Anna Mayfield wasn't actually the first to survive childbirth. I was."

"Yes, I already knew that."

"Well, it seems some other people found out before it became public knowledge. They kidnapped the three of us and transferred us by boat to Tripoli so they could study our biological makeup. They would be the bad men Paul talks about."

"Did they hurt him?"

"They extracted blood and tissue samples. He's terrified of needles now. They also deliberately infected him with the modified strain of the Orestes virus."

"I can't imagine what that must have been like."

"Most people have the new variant, so that's no longer such a big deal. What affected him—and me—most was when they separated us. They took him away from me and planned to put him in a room with a pregnant woman. They were trying to coerce members of our group into developing a cure."

"You mean Mrs Baxter?" the teacher asked.

"Correct."

"It must have been awful."

"It was."

"I've seen her in here a few times," Mrs Prendergast said. "I don't understand why she isn't rotting in prison. She caused this whole thing."

"Yes, I'm certainly not a fan of hers, but she did save Paul's life. Luckily, she and Dr Kubar came up with a drug that protected my son from the virus. She's working here with the other scientists to develop a cure, but a guard escorts her everywhere, and they lock her up every night. By the way, she claims the original outbreak was an accident."

"Even if that's true, she still kept quiet about it. As far as I'm concerned, they should put her behind bars and throw away the key."

Paul continued to eat his food, resorting to fingers now that his mother was distracted by the conversation. He looked up as another person entered the canteen.

"A blue man," he announced.

The two women twisted in their seats and stared at the new arrival. The newcomer wore a set of dark-blue, one-piece overalls. Standing at over six feet tall, the fabric of his uniform stretched tightly around his upper body. The tanned skin of his clean-shaven scalp glistened under the bright ceiling lights.

"Is he the bad man you saw earlier?" Antimone asked, watching as the workman approached the counter.

"No, silly," Paul replied.

"Oh." Antimone turned back to Mrs Prendergast. "Well, I've never seen him before."

"Me neither," the teacher said.

"He has the tree logo on his chest. That's Beechwood, the maintenance company, isn't it? I remember seeing the van outside the first time it got too hot. He must be one of the engineers who've come to fix the heating system."

"You're right. He does look like he might be from North Africa though."

Antimone twisted her neck and surreptitiously studied the engineer. "Yeah, possibly."

Paul lifted a chip to his mouth and wiped his fingers on his T-shirt. Patches of tomato ketchup stained his face.

"The bad man was with him," he said, pointing.

57

Tuesday 21st April 2037

Ilithyia Biotechnology, Northstowe

Paul chattered away as he finished his meal. Most evenings, Antimone would have chivvied him along, telling him to spend less time talking and more time eating, but she sat in distracted silence, mulling over what her son had said about the bad man. Soon, the teacher, Mrs Prendergast, made her excuses and departed. Every few seconds, Antimone glanced over at the workman in the blue coveralls. He seemed oblivious to her scrutiny as he worked his way through a mounded plate of food.

"I'm finished."

Antimone dragged her attention back to her son and pointed at the last half-eaten turkey dinosaur. "Aren't you going to eat that?"

"No."

"So, you don't want anything else?"

"I'm hungry for jelly and ice-cream."

"So, you're too full to finish your main course, but you can still fit in some pudding?"

"Please."

"Fine." Some battles just weren't worth fighting.

Antimone steered her wheelchair to the counter and returned moments later carrying a small bowl. Paul rapidly consumed the contents, although a fair proportion landed on the tabletop. She wiped his mouth, despite her son's vigorous attempts to avoid the paper napkin. When her attention shifted back to the maintenance man, he was no longer sitting at the table. She glimpsed a flash of blue as the doors swung closed.

"Come on, we're going now," she said. "Jump on."

Paul needed no second invitation. He scrambled onto his mother's lap. With a pang of guilt, Antimone headed to the exit. On any other occasion, she would have followed the notice on the wall and taken the dirty crockery to the return station, but she wanted to see where the man went.

She emerged from the canteen and spotted the distinctive uniform thirty metres away to her left. She pushed down on the hand rim and accelerated after the departing figure. He rounded a corner as Antimone hurried to catch up. She reached the point where he had disappeared from view and stopped. Other than a group of three security guards standing by a water cooler further down the corridor, the place was empty. Where had he gone?

A slight movement drew her gaze as a door set in the wall to her right clicked shut. The man must have entered the room beyond. What should she do? She was probably worrying unnecessarily. As Mrs Prendergast had said, Paul possessed a vivid imagination. More than likely, the man's appearance had reminded her son of somebody he had seen during their time in North Africa. But she had to be sure.

She glanced across to the pale-blue uniforms, gathered approximately forty metres away. If she discovered anything untoward, she could always call for help. Her heart rate crept up as she wheeled herself nearer. Should she knock or just go in?

"Can I watch television when we get back?" Paul asked, shifting his position.

"We'll see," Antimone replied, distractedly. "I want to have a peek in here."

Her son's presence cemented her decision. She would open the door, take a quick look, then shout to the security guards if necessary. She reached out a hand and turned the handle. A wave of cooler air washed over her, tainted by a faint oily smell. The gap widened to reveal a control room of some sort, with metal cabinets containing electrical equipment lining the walls. Three male figures stood together, all wearing dark-blue coveralls embossed with the Beechwood logo. The men stared at her in surprise.

Antimone's gaze darted from one to the next. Her mouth gaped as her eyes locked onto the third maintenance man with the paler skin.

"Max?" she croaked.

Paul's arms wrapped tightly around her neck. "Mummy, it's the bad man. I'm scared."

Antimone glanced down at her son. A scrabble of movement from inside the room snapped her attention back. When she looked up, the burly, shaven-headed workman she had followed from the canteen was pointing a shiny metallic cylinder at her face.

"Don't," Max barked.

The barrel of the weapon wavered in the other man's hand for a moment.

"If you make a sound, both you and your son will die," Max continued in a quieter tone. "Come in slowly and pull the door closed behind you."

The maintenance man holding the pistol scowled at Antimone. "We should just shoot her," he said.

"Not now," Max hissed. "Not with the door open. There are probably security guards out there. They'd be onto us in a flash."

Every muscle in Antimone's body froze. "But I thought you were—"

"I won't ask you again," Max interrupted. "It may not look like much, but believe me, that gun is deadly at close range. And my colleague here is more than willing to use it."

Antimone edged forwards. How could she have been so stupid? A swirl of conflicting emotions spun through her brain. For months, she had believed herself to be a murderess, but here was her victim, alive and well. But what the hell was he doing in this building? What would they do if she called for help?

The cold eyes glaring back at her left her in no doubt that the man holding the weapon would shoot if ordered to do so. She moved into the room and pulled the door closed behind her.

"Good," Max said. "Much as I'd enjoy watching you die here and now, it would jeopardise the rest of our mission."

"But your arm..." Antimone's gaze locked onto the spot where she had inserted the needle. "The acid..."

"Yes, this is all artificial thanks to what you did to me." The fingers of his right hand tapped his left shoulder with a solid sounding clunk. The low whir of motors accompanied the movement as he rotated the prosthetic limb.

"I never meant... How did you survive?"

"Luckily, they have some decent doctors in Tripoli. They tell me it was touch and go, but I'm still alive."

"But what are you doing here?"

"Enough with the questions. If you don't do what you're told, the boy will be the first to suffer. Now, move over there away from the door."

Antimone could barely tear her eyes from Max's left arm as she navigated across the room—until her gaze lowered to the faint streaks of blood on the tiled floor and tracked them to their destination. A leg protruded from behind the cabinet. She gasped and held her hand to her mouth. "Is he—?"

"Yes, he's dead."

"Who is it?"

"Somebody who didn't do what he was told."

Antimone clutched her son tightly to her chest. "Please don't hurt us."

"That depends upon whether you follow my instructions."

"What do you want?"

"You can start by telling me where the others are."

"Which others?" Antimone's voice quivered as she asked the question.

"You know exactly who I mean. Kubar, Baxter and that arsehole boyfriend of yours."

"What are you going to do to them?"

"Let me worry about that. Now, where are they?"

"I don't—"

"Shoot the boy."

The barrel of the pistol moved. Antimone tried to wrap her arms around her son to cover his body. "No, please. I'll tell you."

Max directed a slight shake of the head to his subordinate. "Go on, then."

"The rooms are all along the corridor on the second floor. Jason said the one we're in is where his mother used to have her office."

"You better not be lying."

"I'm not, I swear. But they keep Mrs Baxter's room locked. Nobody can get in or out without a key."

"That figures. The bitch should be behind bars. Will she be there now?"

"I don't know. Most of the scientists will already have finished for the day, but she's probably still working. We were going to eat with her tonight, but that's not until eight o'clock."

"Quite the happy family. I can't believe either of you has anything to do with her. If the police hadn't turned up when they did four years ago, she would've incinerated both of you."

"I don't want to spend time with her, but Jason agreed to let her be part of our lives if she saved Paul when we were in Tripoli."

"You'll take us to her workplace. If anybody asks, you're showing us the way so we can repair the sensors for the heating system. If you make any attempt to raise the alarm, I'll shoot your boy first."

"Please. Leave him out of this. He's only four years old for God's sake."

"No, he's coming with us. Omar, you take the gun. As for you, trike queen, if anything goes wrong, you'll watch your son die. Then it'll be your turn. Is that clear?"

Antimone stifled a sob. "Yes."

"Right. Let's go."

58

Tuesday 21st April 2037

Ilithyia Biotechnology, Northstowe

Max opened the door to the control room. He surveyed the area outside before beckoning Antimone forward. “Remember, if you do anything to alert the guards, well... you know what will happen.”

Paul clung tightly around her neck. She sensed the trembling of his body as he buried his face against her chest. She clasped him to her and lowered her lips to his ear. “It’ll be all right,” she murmured.

Max trailed behind her, his hands resting on the back of her wheelchair. The big man she had followed from the canteen stood to the side, carrying a toolbox. She had watched as he placed the pistol on top of the other tools. The smallest of the three brought up the rear.

As soon as they emerged into the corridor, Antimone’s gaze settled on the group of guards, still standing by the water cooler. One of them said something to his colleagues, and a peal of laughter carried across. They paid no attention to the workmen in the blue coveralls or their reluctant companions.

“Which way is it?” Max whispered.

She turned away from her potential rescuers and pointed. “The labs are down there.”

“Lead on, then.”

Antimone reached down to the hand rings and propelled herself to the left. Thoughts of escape rattled through her brain. If she accelerated at top speed, could she put enough distance between them before the big North African retrieved the gun from the toolbox and took a shot? Had she been alone, she might have taken the chance, but having her son on her lap made it too risky. No, she would wait for a better opportunity.

“Don’t even think about it,” Max said from behind as if reading her mind. She felt a vibration through her back as he grabbed the handles. They followed the corridor to a pair of swing doors. Max stepped forwards and placed his card against the reader. A red light shone briefly, accompanied by a buzzer. He tried a second time with the same result.

“What’s going on? Why won’t it open?”

“You obviously don’t have the correct access rights,” Antimone snapped.

“What about yours?”

Before she could reply, Max ripped the laminated rectangle from around her neck and repeated the process. Once again, the lock refused to release.

"If you'd bothered to ask," Antimone said, "I could've told you mine wouldn't work either. Only the scientists can get through here."

"So, how…?"

Max's voice trailed off as a security guard turned the corner and strode towards them. The man drew nearer, a scowl on his face. He was of medium build with short brown hair. The pale-blue uniform was at least one size too large for him. Antimone hadn't seen him before. His hand reached down to a plastic object on his belt.

To her left, she watched as the muscular North African placed the toolbox on the ground.

"What's going on here?" the guard asked.

"We're from Beechwood Environmental Systems," Max replied. "We're here to repair the heating system."

"But why are you trying to get through this door? The control room's back that way."

"Yeah, we know. The computer's telling us there's a faulty sensor in one of the laboratories. I thought the card we were given would allow us in."

"Right. Well, clearly it doesn't. And what's this young lady doing with you? She should be aware access to this area is restricted."

Antimone's wheelchair jolted slightly as somebody gently kicked a wheel from behind. The man Max had referred to as Omar crouched over the toolbox with his hand on the lid. Their eyes met.

"Um…" she said. "They asked me where the labs were, so I was just showing them the way."

"Wait a sec," the guard said, his face lighting up with excitement. "You're that wheelchair racer, Antimone something, aren't you? I was watching the Olympic final on the television. I couldn't believe what happened when the bombs went off and everything. You were definitely going to win though."

"Yeah."

"Hey, would you mind signing an autograph for me?"

"Actually, we're in a bit of a hurry," Max said. "It's late, and we're already on overtime. The boss won't be pleased if this takes too long. He's a real cheapskate. Time is money and all that."

"Oh, sure," the guard replied, his face falling in disappointment. "I'll catch you later, Antimone. I haven't got a pen or paper on me at the moment, anyway. Perhaps you could sign something when I'm on duty again tomorrow. Hang on a sec, sir, and I'll get the office to update your pass. Can I just have the number?"

Max removed the rectangle of plastic from around his neck and handed it to the other man. The guard stepped a few paces away, unclipped the walkie talkie from his belt and spoke in a low voice.

"Right, that's sorted," he said a moment later, handing the card back. "You should be able to pass through all the doors leading to the laboratory area now, but you'll have to find a scientist to accompany you if you need to get inside any of the labs. Even the security guards aren't allowed in there alone. I'm afraid most of the science team have already knocked off for the night. I think Dr Hendrick is still working, though. He's normally one of the last to leave."

"What about Mrs Baxter?"

The guard shot Max a curious look. "Why are you asking about her?"

"It's just, um... somebody mentioned that she works in the same lab as the faulty sensor."

"Okay. I don't know if anyone's there now. If you find Dr Hendrick, he can let you into anywhere you need to go."

"Thanks," Max replied. "You've been a big help."

"No problem. Happy to be of assistance. I'll catch up with you for that autograph tomorrow, Antimone."

The guard returned in the direction from which he had come. He turned and threw a wave before turning the corner and disappearing out of sight.

"There, that wasn't too hard, was it?" Max said. "You're quite the celebrity, aren't you? And by the way, you just saved fan boy's life." His gaze flicked across to the burly North African, who straightened up and tapped the toolbox lid. Max held his pass against the reader. This time, the light flashed green, accompanied by a clunk as the lock released.

"Please," Antimone said, "let my son go. I did what you asked."

"Sorry, I can't do that," Max replied, his lips curling into a smirk. "We've barely started yet. Now, let's find that murderous bitch. I have a score to settle with her."

59

Tuesday 21st April 2037

Ilithyia Biotechnology, Northstowe

Martin Hendrick stretched out his arms and cracked his knuckles. He checked the time: 18:28. The other scientists left a quarter of an hour earlier, and once again, he was alone in the nanomachine laboratory. He hit save, navigated the menu options, then selected the compile command. It would take at least five minutes for the complex software to convert his program into a format understood by the manufacturing machines in the room next door.

He had studied his colleagues' creations and now felt competent enough to undertake his own. It had taken him a while to adapt to this new methodology, but the technology was hugely powerful and would definitely change the face of medical research. In a few minutes, all being well, he would be ready to perform the first trials on a tissue sample. His design was relatively simple and an order of magnitude larger in size than the machines the team were developing to treat the Orestes virus, but he was still excited to transfer a simulation from the computer screen to the real world.

As he waited for the compilation to finish, his thoughts returned to his final days at Ilithyia twenty years earlier. If he had stayed, he would have become immensely wealthy alongside the two founders of the company. He didn't regret the way things turned out. The science interested him far more than wealth or fame. When it all went wrong—as it had—celebrity could just as quickly switch to notoriety. He was lucky to have kept his name out of the headlines when the story about the company's involvement broke in the press nine months ago.

A beep from the terminal signalled the end of the job. Hendrick leant forwards to study the compilation report: no errors and only one warning. He reached out a finger and prodded the information button to provide more details. Apparently, he had omitted an initialisation, but it seemed the software was intelligent enough to substitute a default value.

Ever the perfectionist, Hendrick switched back to the development screen and corrected the issue. He waited impatiently for the process to complete a second time. When the message box appeared, he studied the display and sighed with satisfaction: no warnings at all on this pass.

The next step was to manufacture samples of his design. Professor Allard has asked him to ensure somebody peer-reviewed his work before the manufacturing stage, but nobody was around. He decided to proceed. If anybody queried his actions, he would claim he'd become so wrapped up in the excitement of the moment that the professor's instructions had slipped his mind.

Operating procedure required a full decontamination of the machine's assembly chamber before activation to prevent cross-contamination between samples. Hendrick knew the machine had remained inactive all day, so it was ready to accept his project. Afterwards, if he set the cleaning process in motion before leaving that night, the operation would complete long before the scientists arrived to start the following day's shift.

He pulled up the manufacturing screen and loaded the job. The software worked through a list of questions, starting with the quantity to manufacture. Hendrick selected five grammes. That would be more than enough to prove out this initial batch. Finally, a message box popped up, informing him the operation would take fifty-four minutes to complete. He clicked the accept button. A timer appeared, the digits counting down every second.

He knew there would be little to see, but he wanted to witness the birth of his first creation with this technology. Rising from his workstation, he rolled his neck. He strolled across the room to the archway separating the manufacturing area from the rest of the laboratory.

A prominent sign on the wall warned about the presence of high-strength magnetic fields that remained energised at all times. Professor Allard had explained that the purpose of the field was to deactivate any nanomachines that might accidentally transfer from within on a worker's body or clothing. The devices were so small that even a gentle breeze could carry them in the air like dust. A red glow shone around the doorframe, serving as a secondary warning.

Hendrick felt no discernible difference as he strolled inside. The overhead strip light flickered on, bathing the room in harsh illumination. A hulking, obsidian-black machine occupied the whole of the back wall. A series of winking multi-coloured lights broke up the flat surfaces on the front. Set in the centre was a display panel. It showed the number of his job and the estimated time remaining: 52:04.

As Hendrick approached the mechanism, he picked up a low humming noise. He stretched out a hand and touched the matt surface. A faint vibration ran through his fingertips. A sudden feeling of déjà vu flashed through his mind. He recalled the same sense of fascination when, as a young man, he had spent hours studying his 3D printer as it built up his creations, one wafer-thin layer at a time. He imagined the inner workings of this machine putting together his design in a similar way but at a significantly smaller scale.

After watching the countdown for a few minutes, he tore himself away. There was still much to do if he intended to perform the initial tests of his work that night. He grabbed a pair of disposable gloves from the dispenser mounted on the wall, slipped his fingers inside, then crossed to the refrigerator, where he had placed the thin sections of defrosted skin cells a few hours earlier.

Picking up the plastic case, he carried it to the workbench on which the biocontainment unit rested. The sealed, glass-fronted cabinet allowed researchers to work without fear of contamination from whatever they were testing.

Unlike his previous time at Ilithyia, he had no intention of cutting corners and taking risks. He removed a pre-prepared slide from the box and mounted it inside the unit. After sealing the exterior, he manoeuvred the sample beneath the high-power microscope and adjusted the focus until the regular pattern of the cells showed up clearly.

Satisfied with his preparations, Hendrick strolled over to the manufacturing machine. Still just over ten minutes to go. He paced the width of the room as the timer counted down to zero. After what seemed an age, a loud beep emerged. The screen displayed a *Job Complete* message. He slid back the hatch and removed a glass vial. A tiny printed label on the side indicated the batch number, date of manufacture and a bright yellow biohazard symbol. He held it up to the light and studied the contents; the thin layer of grey powder at the bottom of the tube looked unremarkable in the harsh glare.

His heart beat faster as he returned to the biocontainment cabinet and slotted the vial into the sliding drawer. Now to activate the nanomachines. He pressed the button to switch on the ultraviolet light. Everything inside the sealed box took on a purple-blue tinge. After a few seconds, the lamp turned off.

He placed his hands in the two slots and confirmed the robotic actuators followed his exact movements. With great care, he unscrewed the vial and inserted a plastic rod until the tip touched the contents. It would take only a tiny amount of the substance to prove its operation.

He moved the stick to the sample and dabbed the end against the wafer-thin layer of cells, then dropped it inside the yellow biohazard bin in the corner of the cabinet. The maintenance team would remove the container later and pass it through an array of high-strength magnets before a furnace incinerated the contents.

He resealed the vial and opened the drawer in the side of the unit. He retrieved the glass tube and fitted it into the foam insert inside the small metal box he had placed on the bench earlier, then slipped it into his pocket.

Turning back to the microscope controls, he performed a few minor adjustments until the screen displayed a razor-sharp image of the test sample. Ten seconds passed. Nothing appeared to be happening. Twenty seconds. Still no activity. What had he done wrong? He tweaked the knobs to adjust the horizontal position of the lens. As the view moved sideways, all the cells seemed perfectly normal.

Then a movement at the edge of the display caught his eye. The regular shape of the cell wall collapsed into a thin oval. An adjacent cell did the same, followed by several more. When he peered closely, he spotted a handful of tiny black dots, barely visible even under maximum magnification, drifting across the image ahead of the wave of destruction.

"Yes," he murmured in triumph, as the pattern radiated outwards. He continued to watch until every circle had collapsed. He stood and rotated his shoulders to ease out the kinks. The experiment was a success, but now came the clean-up.

He re-inserted his hands in the slots at the front of the cabinet and directed the robotic fingers to deposit the test sample into the disposal bin. The next task was to set the manufacturing machine to a decontamination cycle. He strode to the control screen and selected the command. A few seconds later, a low hum emerged from deep inside the mechanism, accompanied by a countdown timer on the display.

Satisfied with his day's work, he crossed the room and stepped through the glowing red doorframe into the outer part of the laboratory. Sensing his presence, the overhead lights, which had turned off due to a lack of activity, burst into life, throwing a bright illumination over the workstations.

One job remained. Hendrick returned to his seat and entered his login credentials into the system. At that moment, the sound of knocking on the outside door disturbed the silence. The other scientists who worked in the laboratory would use their access card to enter. That meant the visitor had to be somebody without the necessary permissions. He debated whether to respond. Unfortunately, the lighting gave away his presence.

If he failed to answer, there was a good chance the person might think the occupant had suffered an accident and raise the alarm. And that would entail answering some awkward questions.

"Just a minute," he called.

He hurriedly navigated through the menu options until he found the setting he wanted. A few clicks later, he finished the task and logged out.

The knock repeated.

60

Tuesday 21st April 2037

Ilithyia Biotechnology, Northstowe

Antimone steered the wheelchair behind the two North Africans. Paul had stopped trembling, but his arms still clung to her like a limpet to a rock. Max brought up the rear, his hands resting on the back of Antimone's seat. The group progressed without talking, the silence broken only by the click of footsteps and the low hiss of wheels on the tiled floor. They approached another sealed door.

Max strolled forwards and used his card to let them through. A long corridor stretched ahead. Doors lay at regular intervals along both walls, each carrying a sign with white letters on a black background. Frosted glass obstructed a view of the interior of each laboratory, but the darkness from behind the windows of all but one suggested the majority of scientists had already left for the day.

Max strode towards the only brightly lit area and studied the label: BioNEMS.

"What the hell does that stand for?" he said.

Nobody answered.

He glowered at Antimone. "I asked you a question."

She stared back at him for a moment before replying. "I've no idea, but Dr Hendrick is focusing on nanomachines or something like that."

"Who's Dr Hendrick?"

"He's one of the scientists. From what Jason told me, he used to work for Rosalind Baxter, so he must have worked with your father, too. The guard we spoke to earlier mentioned he'd probably be working late."

"So, this guy had a job at Ilithyia?"

"Isn't that what I just said?"

Max scowled at Antimone. "Which lab would Baxter be in?"

"I don't know. I've never been in this part of the building before."

"What do we do next, boss?" the thin North African asked.

"I'm thinking, Mo," Max replied. After a moment, he continued. "Right. Get the gun out. We knock on the door. When he opens it, we force our way in. You've got the tie wraps in the toolbox, haven't you, Omar? Then we ask him where that bitch is."

"What if he doesn't know?"

"Well, if she isn't here, she'll probably be in her room." He turned to Antimone. "What time did you say you were eating with her?"

"Eight o'clock," she said.

"That's twenty-five minutes from now. Let's find out if she's still working first."

Max waited for Omar to retrieve the gun, then approached the door. He knocked.

After a short delay, a muffled male voice responded from inside. "Just a minute."

Max shifted impatiently from foot to foot as several seconds ticked by. He repeated the action, knocking a little louder the second time.

A few seconds later, a figure moved behind the frosted glass. A gap opened, revealing a man with thinning sandy hair and wearing a white medical coat. He stared at the three men in blue uniforms for a moment, then lowered his eyes to Antimone and her son.

"Yes, what can I do for you?"

Omar raised the pistol, aimed it at the man's chest with his right hand and pushed him back into the room with his left.

The scientist turned pale at the sight of the weapon. "What do you want?"

The other members of the group followed the pair inside. Max closed the door behind them. "I could tell you we've come to fix the heating system, but that would be a lie."

Hendrick's gaze settled on the Oaktree logo, then returned to Max's face. "Sorry, I don't understand."

"We're looking for someone. Do you know where Mrs Baxter is?"

"I haven't seen her all day."

"Doesn't she work in here?"

"Sometimes, but not today. Who are you?"

"That's not important."

"This is Max Perrin," Antimone interjected. "You probably knew his father."

"What?" Hendrick said. "Not Nigel Perrin's boy? It must be over two decades since I last saw him."

"Well," Max replied, "he's been dead for four years, so you've missed your chance. Anyway, we're not here to catch up on old times. Where would I find the bitch?"

"Like I said, I haven't seen her. If she's not in one of the other labs, she'll be in the canteen or back in her room."

"This is the only lab with the lights still on. Whereabouts is her room?"

"It's on the second floor."

"Didn't I just tell you that?" Antimone said, scowling.

Max glared at her. "It doesn't hurt to be sure." He turned to Omar. "Secure his wrists and gag him."

"Wait. What're you going to do to me?"

"If you keep quiet, nothing will happen to you. But if you make a noise or try to escape... well, all you really need to know is that my friend here is an expert in causing pain."

Max waited as Omar restrained their prisoner, then beckoned his men towards him.

"What now?" Mo asked.

"People will be eating. We should sit tight for an hour or two until they're all back in their rooms."

Omar scratched the thin layer of stubble on his scalp. "What if a guard comes in?"

"Didn't you hear what the other guy said? They can't get inside the labs. If we turn off the lights, nobody will know we're here."

The North African scanned the wall beside the door. "I do not see a switch."

"They must be automatic," Max said. "Look for a master switch." He spotted a likely candidate above a workbench. "Here we are." The laboratory plunged into darkness, lit only by the red glow of the archway leading into the manufacturing area. Another click and the brightness returned to its previous level. "Good. That's sorted."

"What about the body of the man you shot?" Omar asked.

"They won't find him unless they go in the control room."

"But will somebody not look for the wheelchair girl and her son?"

"Maybe, but there's nothing we can do about that."

"Okay," Mo said. "So, we wait in the dark, then we come out and finish the mission. When do we kill her?"

"I'll deal with her after the others," Max replied. "I want to save the best for last."

61

Tuesday 21st April 2037

Ilithyia Biotechnology, Northstowe

Jason paced backwards and forwards across the bedroom. Where were Antimone and Paul? The site administration manager had provided him with a desk and a computer in one of the offices for the day so he could prepare his application for the Open University. He had expected to find his partner and son waiting for him when he returned to their room an hour earlier, but nobody was there. He performed a brief search but didn't uncover a note.

They were due to eat with Rosalind Baxter that night. Most of the other people on site shunned the company of the person universally blamed for the release of the Orestes virus. He knew Antimone would prefer to be among that majority, but he had made a promise eight months ago in Tripoli; he agreed to visit his adoptive mother if she saved Paul's life by developing a drug to protect his son against a new strain of the disease that was attacking children. It had been touch and go, but the woman who had raised him for sixteen years succeeded in achieving that goal with the help of Dr Kubar.

The first tendrils of worry burrowed through his stomach. It was unlike Antimone not to contact him or leave a message. They had planned to feed Paul early, but when Jason had checked the canteen half an hour earlier, there were no signs of either mother or son. The serving staff remembered them coming in but knew nothing about their movements afterwards.

He whirled around as somebody knocked at the door. Had Antimone and Paul returned? But if that was the case, why didn't they use the key card? He rushed across the room and twisted the lock without checking through the peephole. A security guard stood beside Rosalind Baxter.

"Are you ready?" she asked.

Jason failed to hide the disappointment on his face. "Um... no. Sorry, but we're going to have to reschedule. Antimone and Paul seem to have vanished. You haven't seen them around, have you?"

"No, I'm afraid not. But it's not as if they can go far. I guess I'll have to eat alone—again."

"Look, if they turn up, we'll come down and join you later."

"Fine." Rosalind turned to the man standing beside her. "I suppose you better take me down then."

Jason watched as the pair headed to the lifts. What should he do? He couldn't just wait in the room. Grabbing a pen, he scrawled a quick note and left it on the bed. He stepped into the corridor, allowing the door to close behind him. But where to start? He had already checked the canteen, but it wouldn't hurt to check again. He jogged in the direction his mother had taken, but the numbers above the lift signalled that both cars were on the ground floor.

Unwilling to wait, he descended the stairs two at a time and emerged into the foyer area. A quick survey confirmed no sign of Antimone or Paul. Fifty yards ahead, Rosalind and the guard disappeared through a pair of swing doors. Jason followed them. The hubbub of raised voices and clinking cutlery greeted his ears as he shoved through and rushed to catch up.

His mother turned in surprise as they reached the entrance at the same instant. "I thought you weren't going to join me."

"Yeah, I just wanted to make sure they're not waiting here."

Rosalind joined Jason in inspecting the diners. "Well, I can't see them."

"No, neither can I."

"Why don't you contact the security team?"

Jason addressed the guard, who was standing a few feet away. "Excuse me. Have you seen my partner this evening? She goes around in a wheelchair."

The man shook his head. "Sorry. I only started my shift half an hour ago. You'd be better asking somebody over by the front of the building. Do you want me to call them on the radio?"

"No, it's all right. I'll go there now and talk to them."

He said goodbye to his mother and jogged back the way he had come. Moments later, he arrived at the row of barriers by the entrance. Still out of breath, he approached one of the two men on duty.

"Sorry to bother you, but I'm looking for my partner. She and my son have disappeared. She's in a wheelchair."

"Yeah, I know who you're talking about," the man replied. "I'm afraid I haven't seen her. What about you, Dave?"

The second guard scratched his head for a moment, then his face brightened. "You mean the girl with the young child? I remember seeing her earlier with those maintenance men."

Jason frowned. "Which maintenance men?"

"The crew who are here to fix the heating system."

"What was she doing with them?"

"I've no idea. I just saw them walking together. There was a boy of about three or four sitting on her lap. They went through that door over there."

"Do you know where they were going?"

"Sorry, no."

Something Paul had said a few days earlier tugged at Jason's unconscious. What was it? *That's right.* His son talked about seeing a bad man.

"What were they wearing?" Jason asked.

"Who are we talking about now?" the guard called Dave replied with a puzzled expression.

"The maintenance men."

"Oh, they work for Beechwood. They wear dark-blue coveralls with a tree logo on the front."

Paul told them the bad man wore the same colour. Was it a coincidence? "Are they still here?" Jason asked.

"I haven't seen them."

"Can you check the visitor log?"

"Why?"

"It's something my boy said a day or two back. Are these maintenance men the same ones who visited earlier in the week?"

"I'm afraid the visitor log is confidential, sir."

"Okay. Will you at least tell me whether they've checked out tonight? And while you're at it, could you please confirm that my partner and our son haven't left the site? She's called Antimone Lessing."

The two men moved away and conversed in low voices. One of them removed an electronic device from his pocket and tapped at the screen. After a few moments, both returned.

"There's no record of Miss Lessing or your son leaving the building," the guard said. "The maintenance team are still on the premises, and I can confirm they're the same guys who visited earlier. What was it your boy said that's got you so worried?"

"He told us he'd seen the bad man. He's only four and has a vivid imagination, so we thought it was just a story or something. When we asked him what he meant, he said this person was in Tripoli with us. And he was wearing blue."

"Tripoli? You and your partner were mixed up in that whole bomb thing at the Olympics, weren't you?"

"Yeah."

"So, you think these guys might be linked back to that?"

"It's possible."

"All right," the guard said. "I'll put out an alert on the radio to let us know if anybody spots either the maintenance men or Miss Lessing. I'll also arrange a quick sweep of the building. We'll call you if anything comes up. I suggest you go and wait in your room until you hear from us or in case she turns up."

"Okay, thanks."

Jason turned away. What he had learned in the last few seconds had transformed his initial worries into gut-wrenching fear.

62

Tuesday 21st April 2037

Ilithyia Biotechnology, Northstowe

Max glanced at his watch band again in the red glow cast by the archway. Just after nine o'clock. His two men sat on the floor, conversing in low voices. Beside them, the scientist lay curled on his side, his arms bound behind his back. The girl was still in her wheelchair, holding her son. The irritating brat had nearly revealed their presence when a guard came down the corridor outside the room an hour earlier. Only the threat of violence had persuaded her to silence her child. Even now, he clung to his mother, making small sniffling sounds.

Max rose to his feet, yawned and stretched his arms. The lack of activity after the initial surge of adrenaline, combined with the muted lighting, had made him feel sleepy. But the time had come for the mission to continue. He strolled over to his two colleagues and kicked the larger man's shoe.

"Let's get going."

The men stood. "Where do we go first?" Omar asked.

Max replied in a low voice. "From what she's told us, their rooms are all together. We'll start with Baxter, then Kubar and finally, her boyfriend. Somebody will have to remain here to guard the scientist."

The North Africans exchanged a glance. "I'll come with you," Omar said.

Max narrowed his eyes in thought. "No, I'm sorry, but you should stay. If anybody discovers you here, I'd rate your chances higher than Mo's in unarmed combat. We'll take the gun and the girl."

Omar glared at his boss. "We should have brought more guns."

"That would have increased the risk of discovery when they scanned the toolbox. Anyway, we can't do anything about it now."

"We could just kill the scientist, then we can all go."

Max considered the suggestion for a moment, then shook his head. "No, we may need a hostage later. We keep him alive for the time being."

"What about her boy?" Mo asked.

"He's the only reason she's doing what we tell her. If she sees a chance, she'll try to escape with him. We should leave him here."

"But he will make much noise."

"If he won't stay quiet, we gag him."

"She will not like that."

"So what? We're the ones in charge. Right, let's do it."

Max strolled across to Antimone. Her eyes glinted in the red glow of the archway as she stared up at him.

"It's time for you to take us to Baxter's room," Max said. "Your son stays here."

"No way. You're not separating us."

"I give the orders. Do you want me to hurt him?"

"If you—"

The sound of Paul's shrill crying interrupted her words.

"Shut him up," Max barked.

"He's four years old, for Christ's sake. What do you expect me to do?"

The wailing grew louder.

"I swear, if he doesn't keep quiet, I'll silence him myself."

A flurry of movement on the floor drew Max's attention. The scientist made several muffled grunts through the gag.

Max crouched by the prisoner and lowered the damp cloth from the man's mouth. "What the hell do you want?"

"I'll show you the way to Mrs Baxter's room," Hendrick said, his voice cracking. He directed his gaze at Antimone. "She can stay here."

Max stared at him for a moment before replying. "All right." He turned back to Antimone. "We'll take him instead. But if you cause any trouble at all, the kid dies. Got it?"

A slight nod signalled Antimone's agreement. She murmured into her son's ear and stroked his head. Paul's cries reduced to a series of muted sniffles.

Max stretched upright. "Mo, get the toolbox. Omar, grab whatever you want to keep as a weapon and untie Dr Hendrick. He's coming with us. If she doesn't follow your instructions, you have my permission to hurt both of them."

Moments later, the three men stood by the door.

"We'll be back soon," Max said. "If anything happens, contact me by phone."

A dishevelled Martin Hendrick followed him through the doorway, rubbing his wrists as he tried to restore circulation. The skinny North African came last, carrying the toolbox.

"Um... How do you plan to get into her room?" the doctor asked.

"What do you mean?" Max replied.

"She's under house arrest. The only people who can open her door are the guards. She can't do it by herself."

"We'll worry about that later. Which way do we go?"

"Follow me."

Hendrick started moving, but Max placed a restraining hand on his shoulder and spun him around. "Not so fast. Just in case you've forgotten, my colleague is armed. Make any attempt to alert somebody and you'll be the first to die, but the girl and her brat will be next. If anyone stops us, we're trying to track down a faulty sensor for the heating system. We asked for directions, and you're showing us where to go."

The scientist nodded. "Yes, I understand."

"Right. Let's get going."

Hendrick turned left and used his card to open the door at the end of the corridor. Mo trailed behind, toolbox in hand. Max brought up the rear. They passed by several more darkened laboratories until eventually they emerged into the brightly lit foyer area. A few people milled about. On the far side, a couple of guards stood, deep in discussion, facing the opposite way. Nobody paid any attention to the group of three as they headed towards the lifts.

Hendrick reached out a hand to press the call button. The leftmost doors slid apart almost immediately.

Max glanced nervously behind him. "No, let's take the stairs. We can't be sure who might be there when we get out."

"Suit yourself," Hendrick replied. "The staircase is just over here."

They climbed the carpeted steps in silence. At the second floor, Max held out an arm. "Hang on. Which room is Kubar in?"

"Dr Kubar? Why do you want to know that? I thought we were going to pay Mrs Baxter a visit."

Max's artificial left hand shot out, and his fingers closed around the scientist's throat. "Just answer the question," he growled.

Hendrick tried in vain to prise the grip loose. He drew a deep, gasping breath when Max released him a second later. "It's four down on the right. I'm not sure what the number is. Actually, it's two oh nine, I think."

"Okay. That wasn't so hard. Now, do the doors have peepholes to check visitors or anything like that?"

"Yeah, they do."

"This is what's going to happen. You knock. We'll stand to the side so he can't see us. When he opens the door, we all go inside. And remember, any attempt to raise the alarm, you, the girl and her son all die. Clear?"

"Understood."

"Good."

Max eased the door open and stuck his head through the gap. The corridor beyond was deserted. He stepped through the doorway and headed to the right, counting off the rooms as he went. The thick carpeting muffled their footsteps. He stopped outside the fourth. The sign on the wall matched the number Hendrick had provided.

"You're sure this is the one?" Max asked.

The scientist swallowed hard. "Yes."

Mo placed the toolbox on the floor and retrieved the assembled pistol. His eyes met Max's, then he handed the weapon over to his team leader.

The two men stood, one on either side of the frame.

Max pointed at Hendrick. "Go ahead and knock," he whispered.

Hendrick's first attempt was barely audible. The second was louder. A muffled call, followed by a rattling sound, came from inside. The door swung inwards. Immediately, Max barged through and shoved Kubar hard in the chest with his left hand.

The North African doctor stumbled, lost his balance and fell backwards in the narrow passageway leading to the main part of the room. When he looked up in shock at the intruders, the barrel of a gun pointed at his head. He opened his mouth, but no words came out.

"Well, well," Max said, his lips twisting in a malicious grin. "Finally, we meet again."

"What... what do you want?" Kubar stammered.

"We'll come to that. What's through there?"

Kubar scrambled back on all fours as Max advanced towards him. "It is the bedroom."

"Go in, sit on the bed and shut up."

Mo pushed Hendrick forwards as all three followed Kubar into the room. The African doctor's eyes remained fixed on the pistol as he lowered himself to the mattress.

Max turned to Hendrick and gestured to an armchair by the darkened window. "Over there. If you move, you'll be next." He refocused his attention on Kubar. "A nice place you have here. Much better than that shit hole in Tripoli they kept us in."

"I... I thought you were dead. The acid..."

"Well, I lost the arm, but as you can see, I'm still alive—unfortunately for you."

"Traitor," Mo spat. He muttered a curse in Arabic.

"They would never have shared the work," Kubar said, his voice quivering with fear. "Many more children would have died without the drug I created."

"I don't care about any of that," Max replied. "You helped the prisoners to escape. You used that damned stun baton on me. When I woke up, the Baxter bitch had me tied down. You knew she intended to inject the acid into my eye, didn't you? There's no way I could've survived something like that."

"I had nothing to do with it. Anyway, you were going to shoot them."

"Maybe, but you're still the main reason I lost my arm."

"If I had stayed, they would have executed me," Kubar protested.

"You deserved it," Mo added. "You betrayed your country."

"They planned to kill all the Western hostages when they had a cure," the North African doctor said, "including you." His gaze flicked to the gun barrel and back to Max's face. "And they lied to me about my daughter. They told me she was still alive, even though they knew she was dead. Those bearded fanatics do not care about anybody but themselves. Can you not see that?"

"All I see is a traitor who deserves to die," Mo snarled.

"Enough," Max said. "It's time to end this. Do you want to do the honours, Mo?"

Nationalistic pride glinted in the diminutive hacker's eyes as he reached out to accept the weapon. "It would be my pleasure."

Kubar raised his hands. "No, please. Do not—"

The subdued pop stopped the doctor in mid-sentence. His body slammed backwards onto the mattress. A small round hole lay in the centre of his forehead. He stared sightlessly at the ceiling.

A crimson stain expanded from behind the dead man's head, darkening the floral-patterned bed cover.

63

Tuesday 21st April 2037

Ilithyia Biotechnology, Northstowe

Jason put his eyes to the peephole. The knock a few seconds earlier had startled him. A guard in a pale-blue uniform stood in the corridor. Jason's pulse raced. Something was badly wrong. Where could Antimone and Paul have got to? By now they had been missing for nearly two hours. Why was a member of the security team here?

He yanked on the handle and pulled the door open. "What is it? Have you found them?"

"May I come in, sir?" the man asked. Acne scars disfigured both his cheeks and his forehead. He looked little older than Jason.

"Yeah, sure. Is there any news?"

"Not at the moment, but I wanted to ask you a few questions."

Jason ran a hand through his hair. "Fine." He led the way past the bathroom into the bedroom and plonked himself on Paul's bed. He gestured towards the other bed, and the guard settled down opposite.

"So, what's this about?"

"First of all, I want you to know we're taking this very seriously."

"Good."

"When did you last see your partner and your boy?"

"We met up for lunch, but I haven't seen them since. My son has been in school all afternoon."

"Yes, we checked all that," the man said. "We confirmed that they visited the canteen after lessons finished, and they were spotted a short while later with the guys from Beechwood Maintenance. They were heading to the laboratory area. When one of our team asked what they were doing, they told him they were looking for a faulty sensor. Unfortunately, there's no sign of them there, although I should say we can't actually get into any of the labs."

"What? You're saying that even in a situation like this, you aren't allowed in to perform a search?"

"The site manager, Nick Butler, has the authority, but he seems to have disappeared as well. Nobody else in the building is senior enough to override the regulations. We're trying to track down Christine Harris, but she's apparently eating out in Cambridge tonight. Unfortunately, we haven't been able to find out which restaurant she's at, and she isn't answering her phone."

Jason's face screwed up in puzzlement. "But any of the scientists could let you in. They all have key cards."

"In theory, yes, but most can only access their own areas. We'd also need permission first or at least evidence that something serious has happened. Some of the work that goes on here is top secret, and that's not to mention the dangerous bugs they're working on, so security is very tight."

Jason blew out his cheeks. "Bloody hell, my partner and son are missing. Isn't that serious enough for you?"

"I'm sorry, sir, but they're very strict on process."

"And you're absolutely positive they haven't left the building?"

"That seems highly unlikely. The only ways in and out are through the checkpoints, and everybody is logged as they come in and leave."

"So, you're saying they're here somewhere, but you don't know where?"

"As I mentioned earlier, we're doing our best to find them. There was something else I needed to discuss with you."

"What's that?" Jason replied.

The man shifted uncomfortably. "Look, we're supposed to keep the visitor logs confidential, but in the circumstances… The guys you talked to downstairs said you suspected your son might have recognised somebody on the Beechwood team. Would you mind checking out their photos to see if you can identify any of them?"

"Yeah, no problem."

The guard handed over a portable device. "Just swipe to the left to move onto the next picture. There are three of them."

Jason scanned the first image. It showed the head and upper body of a well-built man with broad shoulders. The man's face expressed no emotion. The bright overhead lighting reflected off his shaved scalp. His skin tone matched that of the people he had come across in The Republic of North Africa. Jason could see why Paul might think he had seen this person before, but he was certain they had never met.

"Not him."

He moved onto the next photo. If the first man was muscular, the second had almost the exact opposite body shape. The only similarity was in the Mediterranean cast to the man's skin. His shoulders hunched slightly, and his face seemed pinched with worry.

Jason shook his head. "No."

He swiped to the third image. His heart leapt into his throat, and he dropped the device on the carpet. "Max," he whispered.

The guard leant forwards and inspected the screen. "You recognise this man?"

Jason stared straight ahead without answering. He reached out a trembling hand. "Let me see." He studied the picture for a second time. There was no doubt. "Yeah, I do. His name is Max Perrin. He was in Tripoli with us, but we left him behind when we escaped. We thought he was dead. He tried to shoot me."

"Do you have any idea what he might be doing here?"

"His father used to be a co-owner of this place, but if he's inside the building now, it's certainly nothing good. If I had to guess, I'd say he's here to get revenge on a few people. That includes Mrs Baxter, Antimone and me. Oh, and maybe Dr Kubar too."

The guard jumped to his feet, a panicked look etched on his face. "Shit, all their rooms are on this floor. I better go check them out. Stay here, and don't let anybody in unless it's somebody you know."

The man jogged towards the door, slamming it shut behind him.

Jason put his head in his hands. A sense of dread ate through his chest. Max Perrin: how the hell had he survived? Jason had been unconscious, suffering from a gunshot wound, but Antimone told him later how, in a fit of uncontrolled rage, she had emptied a syringe of concentrated sulphuric acid into Max's upper arm. Now she was missing along with their son, and the victim of her actions was somewhere in the same building. The two events had to be related.

"Please God, let them be safe," he whispered.

64

Tuesday 21st April 2037

Ilithyia Biotechnology, Northstowe

Max was the first out of the door. Martin Hendrick came next, followed by Mo. Max's heart thundered in his chest. Finally, he was getting payback for what they had done to him in Tripoli. But how could he get to Rosalind Baxter?

"Where do we go now?" Mo asked.

"I'm thinking." Max turned to Hendrick. "You're saying there's no way into Baxter's room without a special key card? So, she can't open the door from the inside?"

"Yeah, that's correct."

"And only the security guards have access?"

"Yes."

"Maybe we should kill Floyd first," Mo said.

"Which room is he in?" Max asked.

Hendrick shook his head.

Max grabbed the gun off his partner and jammed it under Hendrick's chin. "Do you want to die right here? Now, I won't ask again. Which one is Floyd's room?"

"Will you let me go if I help you?"

"You have my word. I don't have any quarrel with you."

Hendrick stared into Max's face for a second, as if his gaze could pierce through to his captor's thoughts and determine his true intentions. He swallowed hard and dropped his eyes to the deep carpet. "All right," he said, quietly. "It's that one." He pointed to a door on the opposite side of the corridor.

Max lowered the gun. "Good. I want you to do the same thing you did before. Knock until he lets us in."

"Okay."

Max pushed Hendrick forwards. At that moment, a rattle followed by the click of a lock broke the silence. "Wait," he hissed.

A guard emerged from Jason's room. The man spoke into a radio. "Yeah, it's Sam. I've just spoken to him and showed him the photos from when the Beechwood team checked in." His eyes rose. He blinked in surprise as he took in the three men standing ten feet away.

Max immediately identified the topic of the conversation. He raised the gun and pointed the barrel at the guard's torso. In four quick paces, he was at the man's side. "If you want to live past the next second," he whispered, "tell them he didn't recognise any of us."

"Say again, Sam," the voice at the other end said. "I missed that. Has he seen any of them before?"

"Ah... no. He thinks his son mistook one of them for somebody they met in North Africa."

"Well, it was worth a go. We should still try to find them. Get back down here as soon as you can."

"Okay."

Max gestured for the man to hand over the radio. "Give me your key card and any weapons you're carrying too."

The guard withdrew the rectangle of plastic from his shirt pocket, his eyes never leaving the pistol directed at his chest. Next, he unclipped a grey, cylindrical object from his belt.

Max took the item and studied it. Two buttons protruded from the side. A rectangular slot occupied one end of the cylinder. "What does this do?"

"It's a non-lethal stun weapon."

"You mean like a taser?"

"Yeah, except it uses a small dart instead of wires."

"How does it work?"

"Press and hold the red button to arm it. The green one makes it fire."

"Is it single shot?"

"Yes."

Max pocketed the device. "You," he said, turning to Hendrick. "Come over here and stand next to him." He stepped a few paces away from the two prisoners and beckoned his partner closer.

"Who do we do first, Baxter or Floyd?" he whispered.

"If this man has spoken to the boy, he will know we are here. We may not have much time. Who do you wish to see dead more?"

"That's easy: Baxter, of course. That bitch murdered my father and tried to kill me too."

"Well then, you have your answer."

"What do we do with him?" Max gestured towards the guard, who stared fearfully back, clearly aware that he was the subject of the discussion but too far away to decipher the words.

"We do not need another hostage, and there is only one gun."

"Two, if you count this," Max replied, removing the object from his pocket. "Take it. Did you hear what he said about how it works?"

"Yes. Red to arm, green to shoot."

"But you still think we should get rid of him?"

"That is what I would do, but you are the boss."

"Okay. I'll let us into her room. You go at the back. As soon as we're inside, use that to incapacitate him. We can't leave him lying in the corridor for the other guards to find, and I don't want to have to drag him anywhere."

Mo nodded. "Fine."

"I've been waiting a long time for this. Let's not mess it up." He returned to the captives. "Right. Which room is Baxter in?"

Hendrick pointed to the next door down. "That one."

"Good," Max said. There's been a slight change of plan. We're going to pay her a surprise visit first. I'll lead, you two follow. My colleague will be at the back. If either of you tries anything, you'll die too. Got that?"

Both men's heads bobbed in acknowledgement.

Max strode forwards and raised the stolen key card. The lock clicked, and he pushed his way in. An overhead light automatically switched on, illuminating a narrow passageway. The open doorway to the right led into a white-tiled bathroom. A floral scent of female toiletries drifted out. He progressed to the closed door straight ahead, his feet scuffing through the deep pile of the carpet. He turned and waited until the others were out of the corridor before turning the handle.

Extending the gun in front of him, he eased into the main part of the room. A sense of déjà vu washed over him. The décor was different, but the wide window looking down onto the gardens and car park outside awoke memories of the times he had visited his father's office.

He whirled around at the sudden cry of pain behind him. The guard writhed on the floor. Mo stood over the prostrate man, holding the grey plastic object in the palm of his hand. As Max turned back, a rapid movement at the periphery of his vision caught his eye. A picture frame spiralled through the air, striking his upper arm. The weapon flew from his grip, hit the wall and landed six feet away.

A lamp followed immediately afterwards, glancing off his skull. He raised his arms to ward off the barrage of objects raining down on him and advanced into the room. Rosalind Baxter stood beside the bed, her face twisted in fury. A drawer from the bedside cabinet arced towards him. He ducked at the last moment as the sharp edges sailed past his head and smashed harmlessly into the wall.

Max took another pace, his lips drawn back in a savage grin. Rosalind's eyes cast about, searching for more ammunition. In desperation, she lifted the empty unit from beside the bed and tossed it in his direction. It fell short but tumbled over the thick carpet and caught him on the shin. He let out a grunt of pain, but it didn't stop his advance.

Rosalind scrambled over the bed to escape. Max lunged after her, grabbing at her legs. A shoe came away in his hand. She lashed out and struck his cheekbone with the sole of her bare foot. Momentarily dazed by the blow, he rolled off the mattress and landed on all fours. Another kick smashed into his stomach, winding him.

Slowly, he rose to his feet. "I'm going to enjoy killing you," he growled.

Rosalind backed away. “I should have finished the job in Tripoli when I had the chance.”

With a scream of fury, Max leapt forwards and swung his left arm in a vicious arc. The clang of metal on the bone of her skull reverberated through the room. She staggered backwards, blood already welling from the cut on her temple. Her feet tripped over each other, and she fell to the floor in an undignified tumble.

Max stood over her, his breath coming thick and fast. “I lost my left arm because of you,” he said, tapping his shoulder. “And now I’m going to make you pay.”

“Stop!” a voice yelled from a few metres away.

Max turned slowly. Martin Hendrick held the pistol. The barrel pointed at Max's chest.

“Stop,” the doctor repeated, quietly.

Max’s gaze slid across to where Mo stood in the open doorway, the useless weapon still clutched in his hand. Behind him, the unconscious guard lay sprawled on the carpet.

Hendrick’s aim alternated between the two men in the dark-blue overalls.

“You can’t shoot both of us,” Max said.

“But I can take one of you. Who’s going to try first?”

Rosalind pushed her upper body upright. A bruised knee protruded from the rip in her cream trousers.

“You piece of shit,” she snarled, glaring at Max. “How come you’re still alive? Did you plan all this just to get your revenge?”

“You killed my father, and you came within an inch of killing me. And that’s not to mention the millions of women who died because of what you did. Somebody should’ve put you down ages ago.”

Rosalind let out a bark of laughter. “Don’t forget, your dear departed daddy was as much to blame as me. We were in it together. Anyway, it looks like you failed, doesn’t it?” She reached out a hand to the edge of the bed to steady herself as she prepared to stand.

“No, stay down there,” Hendrick said, transferring his aim.

“Oh, come on, Martin. You’re not listening to what he says, are you? I mean, you were there back then. It was an accident. We didn’t intend for it to turn out like that.”

“Yes, I was, Rosalind. By the way, I know about Eileen Floyd. Who do you think let her out?”

Rosalind’s eyes locked onto her former employee. “What? That was you?”

“I called Grolby a few minutes later to tell him that she’d escaped.”

“What the hell’s going on here?” Max asked. “What are you two talking about?”

“I don’t understand,” Rosalind said, ignoring Max’s question. “You freed her, but then you phoned Anders Grolby?”

"Never mind," Hendrick replied. "It all happened a long time ago." He stepped forwards, extended his arm and handed the pistol to Max. "This is yours, I believe."

"What the hell are you doing?" Rosalind yelled.

Max accepted the gun. His fingers closed around the grip. "Does it still work?"

Hendrick shrugged. "I haven't done anything to it, so I expect it does."

"Right... thanks." Max's forehead creased in a puzzled frown. He turned back towards Rosalind. "I made a big error four years ago when I left before you were dead. I won't make the same mistake a second time."

He raised his arm and aimed the barrel at her head.

65

Saturday 9th April 2016

Ilithyia Biotechnology, Northstowe

Twenty-one years ago

Martin Hendrick studied Eileen Floyd through the fisheye lens. He had just twisted the key to unlock her room. She must have heard him because she stopped pacing and stared at the door as if she could see him standing on the other side. A moment later, she sat on the bed and placed her face in her hands. It seemed she would follow his instructions to wait an hour, after all. He turned and sprinted back to his laboratory, where he once again wedged the door open.

He had spent the earlier part of the day backing up the data on his hard disk to a USB stick. After a final check, he shut the computer down. Next, he removed the side from the base unit and ran the powerful magnet he had retrieved from his pocket over the thin casing of the internal drive before replacing the cover. Nobody would retrieve anything useful from this machine.

He replaced the side panel, raised the metal-sided box above his head and hurled it downwards with all his strength. It hit the ground with a clatter as something inside broke loose. He moved to the refrigerator. Hauling open the door, he swept the contents of the top shelf onto the hard flooring. The glassware smashed with a satisfying crash. Within seconds, the acrid stink of chemicals filled the air. He turned his attention to the lower shelves, removed the lids from the unmarked steel flasks and emptied out the liquid. The empty containers landed on the floor with a reverberating clang.

After a final survey of his destruction, he moved a chair to the centre of the room, then stood precariously balanced on the seat. His fingers grasped the small white cylinder of the starter in the light fitting and removed it. The laboratory plunged immediately into darkness, lit only by the narrow band of brightness penetrating from the corridor. He reached into his pocket, grabbed the faulty replacement part he had brought with him and twisted it into the slot.

The fluorescent tube clicked intermittently but, other than the occasional flicker, provided no illumination. He returned the chair to its original spot and tipped it over on its side. Grabbing the notebook off his desk, he raced back towards the reception area. He hesitated by the door to the adjacent laboratory. Time was short, but it would arouse suspicion if his room was the only one targeted. He dropped the book, barged inside and flicked on the light. After a moment's thought, he emptied the fridge contents onto the floor and shoved the nearest computer off the work surface. That would have to do.

He retrieved his notebook, rushed up the stairs to Nigel Perrin's office and returned the storeroom keys to their hiding place in the desk drawer. He descended the staircase at a more sedate pace and strode towards the alarm panel. There, he tapped in the arming code, followed by the button labelled with a green tick. The shrill warning tone rang out, transitioning to a series of rapid beeps as the timer ran down.

Finally, the sound stopped. Hendrick studied the face of his watch: 19:01. It had been forty minutes since Perrin had brought the woman her meal. He didn't expect her to wait the full hour, but she would surely take action when she heard the siren. Now was the time to leave. Before he did so, he returned to the door leading to the laboratories and pulled it open. After a few seconds, he let it swing shut. A final thought occurred to him as he surveyed the reception area. He marched to the receptionist's desk and shoved the contents, including the computer monitor, base unit and telephone, onto the tiled floor.

Satisfied that he hadn't missed anything, he crossed to the entrance. A brief inspection of the alarm panel confirmed a flashing icon, signalling the countdown of the silent alert. He let himself out and locked the door behind him.

He stood in the cool evening air and inhaled deeply. One more task remained. He strode to the side of the building and picked up the large stone he had left there upon arriving that morning. After a surreptitious examination of his surroundings to make sure nobody was watching, he angled his head away and swung the rock at the glass panel. It took three further blows to clear the shards from the lower half of the frame.

The red Ford Focus chirped as he pressed the unlock button. He sank into the driver's seat and started the engine. He couldn't be here when the next stage of his plan unfolded, but he wanted to observe. The spot he had identified earlier was in the car park for the industrial unit on the opposite side of the road. He navigated the short distance and sighed with relief when he found all the spaces empty. He parked in a space invisible from the Ilithyia building and retrieved his phone. The ringing tone sounded once before a male voice answered.

"Hi, Anders, it's Martin Hendrick."

"I'm in the car. What can I do for you?"

"When I locked up tonight, there were a couple of suspicious men on the pavement outside. It's probably nothing, but I thought I should let you know just in case."

"Actually, I'm on the way to the office right now. The silent alarm went off about five minutes ago. Where are you?"

"Oh, sorry, Anders. I should have called you sooner. I'm nearly home."

"Okay, don't worry about it. I'll be there in a minute or two, anyway."

"Do you want me to come back in?"

"No, it'll be fine. I'll ring you if I need you. Goodnight."

Hendrick ended the call and got out of his car. He moved behind the cover of a bush and waited for the action to start.

66

Tuesday 21st April 2037

Ilithyia Biotechnology, Northstowe

Max opened the door and stuck his head into the corridor. *Good.* Nobody was about. He strode through the doorway and waited for the others to emerge behind him. He tried to calm his rapid breathing. Two down, two to go. Despite achieving the goal he had dreamed about for the past four years, a sense of satisfaction still eluded him. So many times, he had pictured how it would end, but now it was over, he felt nothing. Rosalind Baxter was dead.

He tried to examine his feelings. Perhaps it was the way she had stared back at him. She seemed resigned to her fate. There was no sign of fear in her eyes. She didn't beg for her life. In fact, she actively encouraged him to finish the job. "Go on. Do it then." Her final words still reverberated inside his skull. He had expected a buzz of euphoria as he pulled the trigger, but instead, the completion of his goal left him feeling strangely empty.

Perhaps he had enjoyed the thrill of the chase more than the achievement of his ambition. Now that his nemesis lay dead on the floor, what came next? The girl and her boyfriend remained alive. She was the person who had destroyed his arm, even if the woman whom he had recently murdered was the instigator. It seemed that Antimone regretted injecting him with concentrated acid. Had he seen a look of relief on her face when she first recognised him?

Maybe it was time to leave while he still had the chance. The North Africans would be satisfied with the execution of the traitor, Kubar. They didn't really care about the three Westerners. Was it worth risking his freedom to gain his revenge?

He cast his mind back to the beginning. Everything had started at the athletics track. If he was being honest with himself, he *had* overreacted a little. Perhaps she hadn't intentionally tripped him after all. What irked him most though, was the disrespect they demonstrated afterwards when they showed him up in front of his friends.

He could forgive an accident, but they had humiliated him. To add insult to injury, her boyfriend had assaulted him. He couldn't allow that to pass. He shook his head. No, he had promised himself he would get payback. He would only regret it if he backed down and let them live. Now was not the time for weakness.

But one mystery still remained; why did the scientist hand him the pistol? After Max shot Baxter, the man had stayed stationary, watching on impassively while he reloaded the weapon.

Max beckoned Hendrick closer. "Why did you do it?"

The researcher shrugged. "You promised you would let me go. I decided to trust you."

"But you had the gun. Why didn't you ask her to call security?"

"Are you saying you'd rather I had you arrested than hand it back?"

"No, I'm just curious. And what about that stuff with Eileen Floyd?"

"As I mentioned earlier, it all happened a long time ago—twenty years, if I'm not mistaken. Mrs Baxter, Mrs Floyd, your father and I all worked for the same company. Mrs Floyd threatened to become a whistleblower, so Mrs Baxter kidnapped her and held her prisoner, even though she was pregnant. I found out and released her, although Mrs Baxter didn't learn about that until just now."

"Wait. I've heard this before."

"I doubt it, Hendrick," replied. "Nobody else knows I was the one to release her."

"No, not that; I meant the whistleblower part. You must be talking about Jason's mother."

"Yes."

Max scratched the ridge of skin between his forefinger and thumb. "You mentioned something about Grolby too."

"Yeah, he was the head of security."

"I know who he was, but you said you phoned him when Eileen Floyd escaped."

Hendrick folded his arms but didn't reply.

Max's gaze settled on the clear surgical gloves covering Hendrick's hands. "Why are you wearing those?"

"Oh, I had them on when you came into the lab. I never took them off."

Max scowled at the scientist. "I'm sure I would've remembered that."

"I thought you mentioned you were running short of time."

"Right. Wait there."

Max stepped a few paces away and gestured for Mo to join him. The North African stood nervously, shifting from foot to foot. He carried the toolbox in his hand.

"Are you ready for the next one?" Max asked.

Mo responded with a silent nod.

"We're nearly done," Max said. "Only two more, and then we can leave."

Mo leant forwards and spoke in a hushed voice. "I do not understand why he gave you the gun."

"Well, I'm not about to complain."

"Something is wrong. Why did he help us? I do not trust him."

"From what I can tell, there was prior history between him and Baxter. But it worked out for us, didn't it?"

"I suppose so, but it is still very strange."

"Right. Let's do this. We'll make this one a quick in and out. I'll use the card to open the door. Once I'm inside, I'll locate him and put a bullet in him. After that we'll go down to Omar, finish off the girl, and then we can all get out of here. You wait here with Hendrick. I don't think he'll cause you any trouble."

"Fine."

Max strode a few paces down the corridor and raised the rectangle of plastic. The lock released with a click.

67

Tuesday 21st April 2037

Ilithyia Biotechnology, Northstowe

Jason sat on the edge of the bed, tapping his knees. Max Perrin was in the building and nobody had seen Antimone and Paul for hours. Surely, it was no coincidence; the two events had to be related in some way.

Only five minutes had passed since the guard left. The man had told him to remain in this room and not to open the door to anybody he didn't know. But waiting here by himself was sheer torture. Perhaps he should call security and ask whether they had tracked down the intruders yet. No, they would be busy enough as it was without added distractions. There was nothing he could do to help but wait.

A thud reverberated through the wall from next door. His mother occupied that room. Neither he nor Antimone had ever heard any disturbance from her before. Jason held his breath and cocked his head to listen. Another bump. He leapt to his feet and placed his palms against the coolness of the plaster. What the hell was going on? More banging sounds followed.

The noise stopped as abruptly as it had started. He strained his ears to pick up any repetition of the previous commotion. Silence. His eyes strayed to the telephone on the bedside table. Should he alert the security team? He turned his head sideways and placed his ear against the partition. Were those voices? The sounds were too faint to work out who was talking and what was being said.

Jason's heart stopped pumping as a muffled pop penetrated from the other side. Had somebody fired a shot? Who was the target? Were the walls thick enough to stop a bullet? He ducked down and crouched behind the bed. A flurry of hundred-mile-an-hour thoughts rattled through his brain. Was his mother still alive? Should he run or hide? Should he call security now or wait until he had reached a safe place first?

If Max Perrin and his two accomplices were in the adjoining room, they would probably come here next. And if that was the case, he needed to get out as soon as possible. Staying low, Jason scrambled across to the passageway leading past the bathroom to the door. The overhead light clicked on automatically. He crept towards the peephole and raised his eye to the spyhole.

The lens restricted his view to a narrow band, but from what he could see, the corridor seemed empty. He passed this way every day, but in the stress of the moment, he struggled to remember the layout of the floor. How far was it to the staircase? How long would it take him to cover the distance? His hand reached for the handle. A sound penetrated from outside.

Jason froze. He shifted his head to the side and tried to identify the source. A shape moved at the periphery of his vision. The murmur of low voices came from the same direction. A figure in dark-blue overalls crossed into the edge of the frame, the outline distorted by the curvature of the glass.

Shit! There was no way to escape now without being spotted. If they had managed to get into his mother's room, they would certainly be able to enter his. He turned. His eyes darted frantically along the narrow passageway, searching for somewhere to hide.

The bathroom? No, he would be far too exposed.

The bedroom? Perhaps he should take cover on the opposite side of the bed, out of sight from anybody entering the room. But if they did come in, they would spot him almost immediately.

The blood rushed in his ears. Seconds remained.

The in-built wardrobe to his right? It might work. He yanked it open and eased his way in. If he crouched a little, he could just about fit inside. His fingertips scrabbled against the smooth surface as he desperately attempted to close it from within. After a moment of panic, his nails snagged a seam with sufficient purchase to pull the door closed. The clothes hangers clinked gently as they swayed around his head. In the confined space, the scent of Antimone's deodorant tickled his nostrils.

A muffled click came from outside. Somebody had let themselves in. Jason tried to slow his rapid breathing. He fought the desperate urge to release his bladder. The floor vibrated slightly as the intruder moved, then stopped. He tensed every muscle, ready to burst out at the slightest hint the person had discovered his hiding place.

The door to the wardrobe shifted and tapped against its frame, disturbed by the airflow from the main part of the room. Jason prayed it wouldn't swing open. The seconds crawled past. After what seemed an age, the footsteps returned.

"Did you kill him?" The speaker's words carried a slight Arabic accent.

"No, he's not there." Jason immediately recognised Max Perrin's voice. "We'll have to leave him. Let's go and deal with the girl, then we can get out of here."

Jason breathed a huge sigh of relief; Antimone was still alive. Moments later, another click signalled Perrin and the other man had left. He remained in his hiding place for a few seconds longer, then emerged.

He rushed back into the bedroom and snatched up the phone. His hands shook as he tapped the zero key and waited impatiently for somebody to answer. A female voice spoke. "Hello, reception. How may I—?"

Before she could complete the sentence, he gabbled out his message.

"This is Jason Floyd. There are at least three intruders on site. They're wearing dark-blue uniforms and are disguised as maintenance men. They have weapons. One of them is Max Perrin. I overheard them talking, and they're holding my partner, Antimone Lessing, and my son hostage. They plan to kill her. I need you to call security. I'm going after them. Did you get all that?"

"Um... is this a joke?"

"No, I'm deadly serious. Tell them Max Perrin is here, and he's armed. They'll know who I mean. I'll try to make contact again when I find out where they're keeping my family."

"Well, I..."

"Please just do it." Jason slammed the handset down. He didn't have time to argue. Hopefully, the receptionist would pass the information on to the security guards. He rushed back to the peephole and stared out. Satisfied nobody lingered outside, he eased into the corridor. Which way had they gone? A quick glance at the panel above the lifts confirmed both were still on this floor, so they must have taken the stairs. The door to his mother's room was closed, and he had no means to let himself in and check on her status. For now, his first priority was to find Antimone and their son.

He rushed to the staircase in a few strides. The distant click of footsteps reached his ears from below. He slipped off his shoes, leaving them where they fell, and set off in pursuit. His bare feet made barely any noise as he dashed down the steps. He arrived at the bottom, already panting from the exertion. It seemed unlikely they would cross the foyer, especially if they suspected the guards were searching for them. Only two choices remained: right or left.

The doorway on the left led past rows of offices to the entrance, the one on the right to more offices and towards the wing containing the laboratories. He selected the latter and peered through the glass panel. Fifty yards away, three people strode down the corridor. Two wore dark-blue overalls, the third a white doctor's coat.

Jason waited for them to pass through the next set of doors, then followed at a jog.

68

Tuesday 21st April 2037

Ilithyia Biotechnology, Northstowe

Max Perrin hurried along the corridor. The clock was ticking down. Somebody might have heard the shots that killed Kubar and Baxter. The weapon was designed to make minimal noise, but the sound was still loud enough to carry through the walls. It was clear from the guard's overheard radio conversation that the security team already harboured suspicions about the identities of Max and his two men. It was only a matter of time before someone either found the bodies or called the maintenance company and discovered the truth.

Max increased his pace. This route would take longer, but it avoided the foyer, where somebody was sure to spot them. It was a shame he had failed to kill Jason Floyd. The only consolation was that his former classmate would still suffer from the loss of his precious girlfriend. Perhaps he should shoot the kid too. That would really screw Floyd up.

They reached a set of swing doors. Max barged through and waited for the others to join him. Hendrick came last. The doctor hunched forwards with his hands on his knees as he gasped for breath. "Sorry," he puffed between breaths, "I'm not as fit as I once was."

"We can't stop," Max said. "How much farther is it?"

Hendrick gulped a lungful of air before replying. "Just down there and to the left."

"Let's get going then. You go first."

Hendrick straightened up and set off at a fast walk. Mo trailed a pace behind. The toolbox clanked with every step.

Max transferred the gun to his pocket and scratched distractedly at the ball of his right thumb. The itch was getting worse. He rubbed his palm on the trousers of his overalls, then jogged to catch up. At this time of night, the corridor was deserted, and they reached the sealed door to the laboratory area without encountering another person.

"Give your card to Mo," Max said to Hendrick.

"I thought they gave you one."

"They did, but if they're suspicious about us, they might be tracking its usage or maybe even have disabled it by now."

Hendrick fumbled in the breast pocket of his shirt and handed over the rectangle of plastic to the small North African. A green light flashed, and the lock clicked.

Max followed as Hendrick and Mo passed through the doorway. The ceiling lights sprang into life, illuminating a corridor with darkened laboratories on both sides. "Which way is it?" he asked.

Hendrick pointed. "It's the third on the left. We're coming at it from the opposite direction to when we set off."

"Okay."

Max strode forwards. He reached the door labelled *BioNEMS* and let them in.

A muffled scream emerged from the corner. As Max's eyes adjusted to the gloomy red glow, he picked out the form of Antimone Lessing sitting in a wheelchair with her child clinging to her neck. A muscular figure crouched behind them. A blade glinted in the dim light.

"It's all right, Omar. We're back."

The burly North African rose to his feet and lowered the knife. "You have been gone a long time. Did you kill the traitors?"

"Yeah. I shot Kubar and Baxter. They're both dead."

"Good."

"What happened to Jason?" Antimone's voice trembled with fear.

Max hesitated a moment before replying. His mouth twisted in a thin-lipped smile. "I killed him too."

Silence settled over the room. He stared at her, trying to gauge her reaction.

"You're lying," Antimone whispered.

"Why would I lie?"

Antimone's words grew in strength. "You mentioned Dr Kubar and Mrs Baxter straight away, but you only said something about Jason when I asked."

"I missed by a millimetre or two in Tripoli, but this time, the bullet ended up here." Max tapped the centre of his forehead.

"I don't believe you."

"I don't care whether you believe me or not. It's your turn now. Any last words?"

"Screw you."

"Not the most eloquent I've ever heard. Omar, grab the child."

Paul screamed as the man peeled him off his mother and carried him under his arm.

"Close your eyes, Paul," Antimone shouted to her son. "Don't watch."

Max raised the pistol and aimed at Antimone's head.

69

Tuesday 21st April 2037

Ilithyia Biotechnology, Northstowe

Jason stopped at the door leading to the laboratory area. He peered through the square of glass but could see no signs of the three men he trailed here. At one point, he got so close he could hear them talking on the other side of the swing doors. From the brief conversation he overheard, he identified the man in the white doctor's coat as Dr Hendrick. Realising it would only take a single unlucky glance for them to spot him, he held back after that. But where had they gone now?

The overhead lights were on, signalling that they must have passed this way a short time earlier. He raised his key card and let himself in. The security staff had given him access to this part of the building when he was helping some of the scientists with their administrative work, but his privileges didn't extend to permitting entry into any of the laboratories.

All the frosted windows on both sides lay in darkness. He crept down the corridor, straining his ears to pick up any clue to his targets' whereabouts. He stopped outside the first doorway he came to. One of the virology labs. No sounds emanated from within. He moved on to the adjacent laboratory. Also silent. This was taking too long.

He continued forwards in a low shuffle, crouching to keep his body below the level of the glass. He crossed to the opposite side to listen at the next door on the right. A click. His head snapped around as he picked up a sudden movement at the periphery of his vision. A group of five men, wearing the pale-blue security uniform, filed through behind him.

The leader of the group pointed the barrel of what, at first glance, looked like an oversized water pistol at Jason's torso.

Jason shook his head and raised a finger to his lips. The guard shot him a puzzled stare, then edged closer.

"Who are you?" the man whispered when he was close enough. He kept his weapon up.

"I'm Jason Floyd. I take it the receptionist contacted you. They must be in here somewhere. I followed them this far, but I didn't see where they went after that."

"We got your message and tracked your key card. The system also reported that Dr Hendrick's card opened the door to the nanotechnology lab a minute ago, but the lights are off, so we think they're probably hiding out in there. Do you know who might be with them?"

"My partner, Antimone Lessing, and our son, Paul. I saw Dr Hendrick with them, so it seems they must be holding him hostage as well. We've got to hurry."

"Were they carrying any weapons?"

"Max Perrin had what looked like a gun in his hand. I heard a gunshot earlier."

"Right, sir. I need you to move back." The man beckoned his colleagues closer.

"How are you going to get in?" Jason asked. "The guard I spoke to before said your guys didn't have access to the labs."

"They finally tracked down where Dr Harris was eating, and she elevated our privilege levels. Now, please sir, move back and let us do our job."

A child's piercing scream broke the stillness.

Jason's heart lurched in his chest: Paul.

The group of guards hurtled towards the door. The leader raised a card to the lock mechanism. Antimone's voice rose above the sounds of movement. "Close your eyes, Paul. Don't watch."

The men surged through the opening. Several low thuds reverberated from within. A single gunshot rang out. Then silence.

Jason didn't wait for the all-clear. He jumped up from his crouch and sprinted towards the open doorway. At first glance, his brain couldn't make sense of what his eyes were telling him. A dim red glow illuminated what appeared to be a collection of grotesque statues.

As he entered, somebody flicked on the master light switch. The three men in dark-blue overalls stood draped in what appeared to be loops of grey foam. Judging by the grunts and straining muscles, they were trying to escape, but the tubular folds of material held them tight. The gun lay on the floor at Max's feet. He attempted to move his leg, but a brief squirt from the nozzle of the nearest guard's weapon cemented his foot in place.

Jason's gaze immediately transferred to Antimone. He rushed to her side. "Are you all right?"

"Yes. He missed."

"Thank God for that. Where's Paul?"

Antimone pointed at the tiny figure, cowering in the corner. Jason stepped forwards and scooped up his son.

"It's over. I've got you," he murmured into the four-year-old's ear, clutching him tightly to his chest.

Dr Hendrick stood to the side, a blank look on his face. Suddenly, his mouth curved in a smile. He took a pace towards Antimone and patted her wrist. "I'm so glad you're okay." He turned to the security guards. "Thank you so much for saving us. I thought they were going to kill us. Let me shake your hands." The bemused men accepted his outstretched palm as Hendrick moved from one to the next.

A cry of agony brought an abrupt end to the celebrations. All the occupants of the room, who still retained the ability to move, turned to stare at Max Perrin. He squirmed in the grey material's embrace.

"My hand," he screamed.

Jason winced in shock as he stepped closer to study the reason for Max's anguished cries.

Blood dripped from a deep hole of exposed, weeping flesh, forming a ring in the centre of his former schoolmate's right palm.

70

Tuesday 21st April 2037

Ilithyia Biotechnology, Northstowe

"What's wrong with him?" Antimone asked. "Is it the foam?"

The guard standing beside her shrugged. "He won't be able to move until somebody sprays him with the release agent, but that's all it does."

"So, why's he complaining so much?"

The man didn't answer. Instead, he stepped closer to Max and studied the dripping wound. His face crinkled in confusion. "Something is eating away at his hand."

Max stared in horror at what remained of his palm. His gaze swung to the doctor. "He did this to me. It was him."

"Who?" the guard asked.

"Hendrick."

The scientist raised his eyebrows. "I've no idea what he's talking about."

"I dropped the pistol, but he gave it back to me." Max let out a groan of agony. "He could've stopped us, but he didn't. It made no sense. He must have put something on the grip. You've got to help me."

Antimone rolled nearer to the smallest of the three restrained intruders. "You were with them. Is he telling the truth?"

"Yes, it is true," Mo said. "He picked up the gun and returned it. Why is he wearing those gloves?"

Hendrick thrust his hands into the pockets of the white lab coat. "They took me prisoner. They told me if I failed to do what they asked, they'd kill me. And you too." He angled his head towards Antimone. "You were there. You heard them."

Antimone folded her arms. "They did threaten us, but that doesn't explain why you've still got the gloves on. Or what's happening to him."

Hendrick frowned. "Look, this has been a very stressful evening. Why would you listen to them? You can't believe a word they say. I've done nothing wrong. I'm a victim of all this, just like you. As for the gloves, I was wearing them when these terrorists burst in here and took me hostage. I have no idea what's affecting his hand, and frankly, I don't much care. He forced me to watch as he murdered two people in cold blood. He deserves to suffer after what he did. It's probably an allergic reaction or something. You seem to have the situation well under control, so I'm going back to my room now. If you have any questions, you can ask them in the morning."

He turned and strode towards the door. The guards exchanged glances but didn't move to stop him. As Hendrick reached for the exit button, an anguished cry erupted from behind him. Every eye in the laboratory locked onto Max Perrin. His index finger dangled by a thread of skin, then dropped to the floor, followed moments later by his thumb. The bones of his hand showed through the exposed flesh. The drips developed into a steady flow. A red pool expanded around his feet.

The parts of his body that could move writhed against the bonds of the solidified foam. Suddenly, a jet arced from Max's wrist and splattered the white wall with blood. The tendons in his neck thickened into tight bands as his lips drew back from his teeth in a shriek of agony. The shocked guards took a hurried step backwards to avoid being splashed.

Jason clutched Paul tightly to his chest, blocking his son's view.

A thin trail of smoke accompanied the whine of the electric motor as Max's left arm fought against his bindings. With a splintering crack, he wrenched it free. The limb gyrated in wild circles. The artificial fingers sliced through the material of his overalls and gouged a deep wound in his leg, adding to the haemorrhage.

"Help me!" he screamed.

Antimone tore her focus away from the horrific sight. She scratched absentmindedly at an itch on her wrist. She glanced down and spotted a band of inflamed skin. The patch of redness spread over the same area where the scientist had patted her moments earlier.

Her gaze settled on Martin Hendrick. He stood watching like the rest of them. She couldn't read his expression—somewhere between fascination and... something else. Satisfaction maybe.

He turned his head towards her. Their eyes met. A slight smile played at his lips. He tapped the button, and the lock released with a click.

"Stop him!" Antimone yelled.

The two nearest guards whirled around in surprise, weapons raised.

"Perrin was telling the truth," she said. "Dr Hendrick has infected us all with something. I've got a rash where he touched me."

The men flashed a glance towards the writhing figure. Max's features had become much paler, and his struggles seemed to be waning. One guard lifted his hand. He gasped as he took in the inflamed skin of his palm. "It's true. Stay right there and don't move."

Hendrick slowly raised his hands, revealing the thin white gloves he still wore. "It must be something you touched in here. I had nothing to do with this."

Fear was etched into the faces of the security team. "They make those tiny machines in this lab," the nearest man said. "What the hell have you done to us?"

"I just told you. It wasn't me. I'm the victim here."

Max Perrin groaned, and his head slumped onto his chest. The flow of blood had reduced to a trickle. All attention switched from his limp body to the scientist in the white coat.

"He is lying," the smaller of the two North Africans babbled, panic lacing his voice. His eyes flicked to the fingers of his right hand.

"Shut up," the guard beside him snapped, "unless you want another shot of this stuff in your face."

"No, let him speak," Jason said, clutching Paul tightly to his chest. "What's your name?"

"Mohammed Abadi, but people call me Mo. First, he handed over the gun that killed Mrs Baxter. He gave me his key card to open the door. Where I touched it, my fingers are burning."

"Why are you listening to this terrorist?" Hendrick asked, glaring at his former captor.

"He knew Mrs Baxter from before," Mo continued. "She was very surprised when he said he set free a person called Eileen."

"You're not talking about Eileen Floyd, are you?"

"Yes, yes. This man here worked with Mrs Baxter many years ago. He told her he released this Floyd woman. Then he made a call to somebody else. I cannot remember the name. Gral—"

"Anders Grolby?" Jason asked.

"Yes. That is right."

"But my biological mother was the first to die of the virus. My mother—I mean Mrs Baxter—always claimed it was an accident. If he was the one to let her go... But why tell Grolby? He handled security."

"Yes, I admit I was a researcher at Ilithyia," Hendrick said, "but I left before the pandemic started. I worked with Eileen Floyd. She threatened to become a whistleblower. It would've destroyed the company, so they kidnapped her and kept her in a cell behind the storeroom. The courts convicted her husband for killing her. I only found out about the kidnapping later when I heard a noise from the place where they were keeping her locked up, so I tried to help her escape."

"Why didn't you just call the police when you discovered what they were doing?"

"It was complicated."

"I don't see... Oh, I get it. You were involved in developing the virus."

Hendrick stared at Jason. His forehead creased in a scowl. "I'm leaving now."

"It was you, wasn't it? You were the one performing the dangerous research. You couldn't allow my biological mother to escape because she would've implicated you, so you told Grolby. But why let her go in the first place? It doesn't make sense unless... My God. You wanted her to spread the virus."

"That's all conjecture," Hendrick said. "You can't prove any of it."

"Maybe, but there's plenty of evidence of what you've done here. What is this stuff?"

Hendrick's gaze fixed on Jason as he contemplated his response. After a moment, he shook his head. "Not so bright after all, are you? You're in a nanotechnology lab. What do you think it is?"

"But why?"

"Don't you see that humanity is causing the annihilation of the planet? We rape and pillage the natural world for resources. Humans worry about new viruses and pandemics, but *we* are the disease. *We* are the ones killing the earth. Mankind is the greatest threat to the future of life. Do you know how many species we have driven to extinction? It's well over a million and still counting. If we keep going like this, soon nothing will remain."

A pious light lit up Hendrick's eyes. "Yes, I created the Orestes virus, and the irony is, Mrs Baxter and his father..." He pointed at Max Perrin's now limp body. "... funded my research. I designed it to save the world. When I discovered they were holding your mother, it provided an excellent opportunity to initiate the pandemic and deflect blame all in one go.

"I had no inkling how successful my plan would be. I always thought somebody would find a cure within the first few months, but as time went by and the virus kept mutating, I realised I'd created the perfect solution to curb mankind's destruction. No woman in their right mind would get pregnant, knowing it would cause their own death. The global population has been declining for over twenty years, and nature is finally making a recovery.

"When the opportunity to join this research effort came up, I jumped at the chance. I wanted to learn what the brightest minds in the world were working on. The old methods of antivirals are doomed to failure, but nanotechnology has the potential to cure all human diseases. I couldn't let that happen and destroy all my previous good work.

"Ironically, it was Professor Allard who sowed the first seeds of an idea. He can't stop talking about grey goo. What better way to put an end to this area of research than to turn his worst nightmare into reality? Yes, I placed a small quantity of these nanomachines on my gloves. They're designed to attack human tissue. I've touched most of you. They'll also transfer to anybody who touches a surface I've come into contact with.

"Before you worry too much about them spreading across the world and killing everybody on earth, that's not my intention. I only want to prevent this technology from becoming widely adopted and undoing my previous efforts. Their power source will run out of juice after a few hours. By then it'll be far too late for any of you. But if you allow me to go, I'll tell you how to stop them."

Stunned silence greeted Hendrick's confession.

"So, you were just going to leave and let us die?" Jason said.

"That's no longer necessary. The authorities won't be able to cover this up. Once word gets out about the real-world dangers of nanotechnology, the public will complain so loudly that they'll have no option but to stop all development."

"How much time have we got?" a guard asked, studying the reddening skin on his palm

"Not long. I'd say about ten or fifteen minutes before it starts getting really painful."

The man frantically rubbed his hand against the trousers of his uniform.

"I wouldn't do that if I were you," Hendrick said. "You'll only drive them in deeper. Oh, and by now, soap and water will have no effect. They've already worked their way below the surface of the skin. They're remarkable little machines."

"If we do let you go," another guard asked, "how do we know you'll keep your word?"

"Well, you don't, I suppose. You have no alternative but to trust me."

"I'm sure Professor Allard knows how to stop them," Antimone said.

"Perhaps eventually, but not in time to save any of you I've touched. The only way to deactivate these little critters is by using the magnetic field built into the archway over there." He gestured towards the section of the lab where the manufacturing machine sat. "I deactivated the magnetic field earlier tonight and changed the code. Not even the professor will be able to bypass my changes before it's too late. I'm leaving now. I'll call in a few minutes with instructions on how to reactivate it. It's been nice meeting you all, but I really must dash before the police arrive."

71

Tuesday 21st April 2037

Ilithyia Biotechnology, Northstowe

The five guards remained motionless, watching as Hendrick strode through the open doorway. Jason placed Paul on Antimone's lap.

"What are you doing?" she asked, her face creased in concern.

He lowered his lips to her ear and whispered, "Saving your life, I hope."

She held their son in an awkward embrace as she tried to prevent the inflamed patch of skin on her wrist from touching him.

Jason dashed after the scientist. "Wait!" he yelled.

Hendrick flashed a backward glance, and his pace quickened from a fast walk to a jog.

Jason broke into a sprint. His hand landed on the fugitive's shoulder and spun him around.

"If you don't let me go, they'll all die," Hendrick said between deep breaths.

"I'm guessing you have no intention of telling us how to stop the machines, so the chances are all of them will die, anyway."

"Well, you'll just have to trust me."

"Rosalind Baxter was vilified for the deaths of all those millions of women, but it was you all along. Why should I believe anything a mass murderer has to say?"

Hendrick's face twisted into a grin. "You really have little choice. Now, back off unless you want me to touch you too." He raised a gloved hand.

Rather than backing away, Jason lunged forwards. He seized both of Hendrick's hands in his own. The thin latex felt cool beneath his fingers.

Hendrick frowned in confusion. "What the hell are you doing?"

"This," Jason replied, releasing his grip and sliding a palm down each side of the scientist's face. Next, he spun the bewildered man around and forced his right arm behind his back.

Hendrick yelped in pain. "You're hurting me."

Jason ignored the doctor's protestations and, grabbing him by the neck, frogmarched him to the laboratory. Neither had a key card on their person that would permit entry, so he rapped a knuckle on the smooth surface. Moments later, the door slid open, revealing Antimone's worried face. He shoved the scientist inside.

"Do those guns still work?" Jason asked the nearest guard.

"Um... yes," the man replied.

"Well, what are you waiting for? Shoot him. Make sure you immobilise his hands and legs."

Jason stepped back from his prisoner, and a squirt of grey material jetted from the nozzle of the guard's gun. Within a second, Hendrick could no longer move, locked in place by several loops of foam.

"Right," Jason said. "As I see it, you have two choices; you can either explain how to deactivate the nanomachines, or you can die with us."

"I told you earlier, release me and I'll let you know what to do."

"No deal. I should think your cheeks might be starting to itch a bit by now. They do look a little red."

Antimone shot Jason a questioning glance.

"The good doctor has some of his own creations on his face," he said.

"But how did you...?"

Jason held up his hands. "It's possible I accidentally touched his gloves and smeared a few nanomachines over his skin."

Antimone stared at him incredulously. "That means you're infected too."

"Yes, we're all in the same boat now. I imagine it might turn more than a little messy as they munch through to his brain."

Hendrick's eyes widened in panic as he tried to pull his arm free. "If you release me and promise to let me go afterwards," he said, "I'll tell you what to do."

"I don't think so," Jason said.

"This is blackmail."

"Call it what you like." Jason stepped closer to Hendrick and placed his hand on the man's forehead. "Oh, you're feeling warm. Oops, I may have spread a few more by doing that."

"All right," Hendrick gabbled. "I'll tell you how to disable the nanomachines, but you have to put me through first."

"Okay," Jason replied.

"Log in to my account on that computer over there. The username is M dot Hendrick, and the password is *save the earth* but using numbers for the S and E."

"What do you mean?"

"For Christ's sake. Five, lower case A, lower case V, three, capital T..."

"Oh, I get it."

Jason moved to the terminal and tapped the keys, floating in mid-air before his eyes. "Right, I'm in. What next?"

Hendrick navigated him through the options to access the controls for the powerful electromagnets built into the archway. After several more entries, a message box appeared: *Settings Updated.*

"Is that it?"

"Yes."

The red glow around the arch seemed unchanged. "Are you sure?" Jason asked, doubtfully.

"Of course I'm sure. Please hurry."

"Okay. Who's first?"

"Wait," Hendrick yelled. "You promised it would be me."

"Sorry, I forgot. Just walk through when you're ready."

The man struggled ineffectually against the grey loops of material.

"Oh dear. It looks like you missed your turn."

Hendrick screamed in rage. "You lied to me."

Jason ignored the increasingly vociferous protests and stood aside to allow the five guards to file through the glowing archway, one after the other. Antimone waited at the back of the line with Paul on her knee, shielding him from the grisly sight of Max Perrin's body. The four-year-old buried his face against her chest. She kept her wrist outstretched to prevent herself from transferring the nanomachines to her son.

"Come on, buddy," Jason said. "I need you to be a big boy and walk through by yourself." After a moment's more cajoling, Paul released his grip and stepped through to the adjacent room.

Jason leant over and picked up Antimone. "There's a strong magnetic field, so it's probably best not to go through in your wheelchair."

"What are we going to do about them?" she asked, nodding towards the three remaining live captives.

"We'll call for a decontamination team in a second, but quite frankly, I'm not in any great hurry. Let them sweat for a while. They deserve everything they get."

Jason shuffled sideways through the archway. "This reminds me of that time on the beach in Hunstanton."

"Could you assist me to the ground, sir knight?" Antimone said with a smile.

"Yes, my lady."

"But perhaps you would do me the honour of a kiss first."

Their lips met as they clung to each other for a brief moment, then he knelt on one knee and lowered her gently to the floor.

Epilogue

72

Tuesday 23rd June 2037

The Royal Palace of Tripoli, Tripoli, North Africa
Six months later

The aroma of spicy food drifted on the steamy air. Pots and saucepans clanged in a frenzy of activity as the army of cooks scurried about preparing the feast. The meal would feed fifty times the number of people who would actually be in attendance. Most would be wasted despite a significant proportion of the population in The Republic of North Africa suffering from malnutrition.

The cook bowed to his supervisor. "I am very sorry, sir, but I need to go to the toilet."

"Well, do not take too long about it," the sous-chef snapped. "We still have much work to do. Everything must be perfect for Mullah Awad. Only ten minutes remain until we must start serving. And make sure you wash your hands before returning."

"I will be as quick as I can, sir," the cook replied.

He turned and hurried from the kitchen. As he pushed through the doors into the men's washroom, the stench of faeces and stale urine provided a stomach-churning contrast to the enticing smells of cooking. The cook covered his face with his elbow and breathed through his mouth. He passed down the row of stalls, looking for one with clear water in the bowl of the stained white porcelain.

Finally, he settled on a cubicle marginally cleaner than the others. There was no toilet paper on the roll, but he wouldn't be needing any. He locked the door behind him and dropped the lid before settling down on the plastic cover. His pulse raced as he lowered his head to the floor to confirm the absence of any fellow workers. No, he was alone.

He removed his left shoe and turned it over, wrinkling his nose in distaste at the ingrained dirt staining the sole. His fingers grasped the heel and twisted. The bottom ten millimetres rotated with a click, revealing a tiny circuit board fitted with a small pushbutton at the centre. His handler had assured him the device was undetectable by the scanners used to check the workers before they were allowed in the vicinity of the ruling elite. So far, the promise had held true.

The mullah's movements were a closely guarded secret. This was the sixth time the cook had worked in the kitchens, preparing food for important dignitaries, but the first occasion the leader of the country had attended in person.

The calls from the agency always came at short notice. The humourless security staff confiscated all electronic devices before they even allowed the workers on the bus to take them to the venue.

They paid him barely enough to survive, but he had little to live for after his wife and teenage daughter had died within the space of a few months of each other. The authorities forced the two most important people in his life to bear children to replenish the population lost to the Orestes virus. And of course, without the drugs to protect them, death followed moments after the multiple births. They hadn't even allowed him to see his twin daughters or four granddaughters before the bearded men in dark robes whisked them away to be raised by the state.

The operative had approached the cook when he left the hospital for the second time as a recently created widower with no surviving dependents. The agent kept his face covered. He offered to create the paperwork to get the cook to neighbouring Algeria and pay him enough money to live out the rest of his days in comfort. All he had to do in return was press the button when Mullah Awad was somewhere nearby.

He didn't know what would happen after that. The agent had promised that the people he worked for would spare him from any attack, provided he maintained a distance of at least fifty metres from the intended target. The cook didn't care whether he lived or died. All that mattered was that the man responsible for the deaths of his wife and daughter paid the price for his actions.

A satisfied smile occupied the cook's face as he pressed the button. Nothing happened, but he didn't expect it to. At least, not immediately. He planned to stay where he was for the next few minutes. If they came looking for him, he would claim he was suffering from diarrhoea. Judging by the foul stench lingering in the air and the state of the toilet bowls, he wasn't the only one.

He sat on the toilet seat, waiting for retribution.

***

Across the border in Algeria, an automated listening post picked up the radio signal. Within two minutes, a dozen human operators pored over a map, studying the location of the source. They pulled up satellite imagery and soon spotted the dark outlines of the heavily armoured vehicles used to transport the mullah and his entourage. The Reponan military frequently used decoys to mask the mullah's movements, but this was a confirmed sighting.

Next, they checked the name of the operative and confirmed he was a cook. There were several spots inside the recently restored Royal Palace where the ruler of The Republic of North Africa might be dining. But that didn't matter. After a short confirmatory phone call, the British Prime Minister and the American President gave their approvals for the mission to proceed.

Thirty-six thousand kilometres overhead, the geostationary satellite released three of its array of kinetic bombardment weapons. The dart-shaped projectiles fell towards the surface of the earth. With nothing to oppose the force of gravity, they accelerated rapidly to a speed of eight kilometres per second. At a height of four hundred kilometres, the fins on the exterior began to interact with the thin atmosphere, guiding the warheads to their target. As the air grew thicker, the resistance increased, slowing the rate of descent. The noses of the bombs punched through the troposphere, glowing a bright cherry red.

A few seconds later, they carved through the sky above the Royal Palace in Tripoli. The metre-long tungsten rods carried no explosive charge, but they didn't need to. The kinetic energy they carried, as they neared the earth's surface, was equivalent to that contained in many times their weight of conventional explosives.

A sonic boom trailed behind the weapons, but if their targets registered the sound, it was far too late to react. The warheads were still travelling at over three kilometres per second when they reached the ground. They hit almost simultaneously, instantly vaporising everything within the immediate vicinity. The bodies of Mullah Awad and his entourage disintegrated into their constituent atoms in less time than it took to blink an eye.

Afterwards, the intelligence reports confirmed the deaths of over seventy people. Among the few survivors was a cook who had the good fortune to leave the kitchens due to a bout of diarrhoea moments before the bombardment began.

73

Saturday 7th July 2040

New York Olympic Stadium, USA

Three years later

Antimone rounded the final bend onto the home straight. She risked a quick backward glance. Her nearest competitor trailed by at least thirty metres. She drove down hard against the shiny hand rings of her wheelchair to accelerate towards the finish.

She tuned out the deafening roar of the crowd as she neared the end of the race. Almost every person in the stadium chanted her name. Five metres short of the finishing line, she allowed herself the luxury of raising her arms. That raised an even louder cheer from the enthusiastic spectators.

Out of instinct, she lifted her eyes to the electronic scoreboard to check her time: half a second outside the world record, but that didn't matter. She already held the achievement of being the fastest woman ever to cover fifteen hundred metres in a wheelchair. There would be plenty of opportunity in the future to improve upon her lifetime best.

The most significant factor in this race was that she had smashed the field, leading from start to finish, and had finally achieved her goal of winning a gold medal at the Olympics. The letters 'OR' after the time signalled another major accomplishment: a new Olympic record.

She cruised to a halt. Shielding her eyes from the blazing sun with her left hand, she completed a three-hundred-and-sixty-degree rotation, waving to the packed arena with her right. Every seat seemed to be occupied, and not one facemask in sight. The recent rapid advances in nanotechnology had all but eradicated the Orestes virus, rendering protective face coverings a thing of the past. Strict guidelines regulated the use of the new miracle technology, but by now, few diseases remained that the tiny machines couldn't cure.

A figure jumped over the barrier at the edge of the track. Immediately, half a dozen law enforcement officers raised their weapons. They relaxed when they spotted the security badge hanging on the lanyard around the man's neck.

"It's all right, guys," the man called. "I'm her trainer."

John Marshall jogged over, his craggy face cracking in a wide grin. He draped a Union Jack flag over Antimone's shoulders. "I always knew you'd do it. Congratulations."

"Thanks, Coach," Antimone replied. "I couldn't have done it without you."

"Enjoy the occasion. You've earned it. I'll catch up with you afterwards."

Her gaze followed him as he retraced his steps.

She looked up to the giant screens mounted between the four stands. Every corner of the stadium showed three-dimensional images of the last few seconds of the race. The shot changed to one of her family. Her parents sat side by side at the centre of a group of people wearing the red, white and blue colours of the British flag. Her father hugged her mother as both wiped tears of happiness from their cheeks. The three adjacent seats were empty.

Where was Jason? Her eyes tracked down the rows of seating to where the cheering crowd parted to allow somebody to descend the steps. Then she saw him. One hand grasped their son, Paul, now seven years old. The other arm held their fifteen-month-old daughter, Eileen. Antimone and Jason had married shortly after their last brush with death. The three surviving men who had threatened their lives, including the notorious creator of the Orestes virus, Martin Hendrick, were all serving life sentences without hope of parole. Max Perrin had suffered too much blood loss by the time the medical team arrived and was beyond help. Rosalind Baxter, Naeem Kubar and Nick Butler were also pronounced dead at the scene.

None of the leaders in The Republic of North Africa responsible for instigating the plot had survived the aerial bombardment of the Royal Palace in Tripoli. In the leadership vacuum following the bombing, free elections took place for the first time in over a decade. Under pressure from the world's superpowers, the new government adopted a more moderate stance. They no longer forced women to bear children and benefitted from the subsequent influx of medical aid.

Behind the three members of her family stood Antimone's onetime competitor, Aya Shaladi. The North African woman had applied for permission to remain in Britain after being released from the asylum centre. The authorities had believed her when she told them she was coerced by her government, under fear of death, into assisting her father in the attack at the 2034 Olympics in Glasgow. Antimone had agreed to speak on her behalf, and Aya's assistance in helping the Westerners escape from Tripoli counted in her favour at the adjudication.

Aya had become an unlikely friend and was now Antimone's main training partner. In a few months' time, she planned to apply for British citizenship, which would enable her to compete for her new country. Antimone attributed much of her recent success to the friendly competition offered by her former rival.

Antimone guided her wheelchair to the side of the track. Jason passed Paul over the barrier, then handed Eileen to Aya before clambering over himself. He accepted his daughter back and leant down to kiss his wife. Raucous cheers, interspersed with several oohs and ahs, greeted the embrace. Paul ran up to his mother and wrapped his arms around her neck. He held her for a moment, then released his grip and grabbed his father's hand.

The girl who survived the Orestes virus waved to the crowd as the three most important people in her life accompanied her on a lap of honour.

The End of Annihilation: Origins and Endings

Author's Notes

I sincerely hope you enjoyed reading this trilogy. Writing is a solitary activity, and it takes several hundred hours of effort to complete a novel. What makes it all worthwhile for me (and I suspect almost all other writers) is when people enjoy what I have written. If that is the case, I would be immensely grateful if you could spread the word by leaving a review on Amazon, Goodreads or preferably both. Good reviews are a significant factor when readers are searching for their next book and are especially important for independent authors, who often struggle to raise awareness of their work in a crowded market. I pay particular attention to all review comments and use them to improve my writing.

Little did I know when I started work on Decimation in 2016, and the sequel, Termination, in 2019, that we would soon be living in a world where viruses play such a huge part in people's lives. When I first wrote about the fictional Orestes virus, nobody had even heard of COVID-19. I can only hope that fact follows fiction, and scientists discover ways to prevent this and other, as yet unknown, illnesses in the future.

If you enjoyed this series, you can learn about my new releases early by signing up to the mailing list on my website at www.rjne.uk. You'll also receive a link to a free short story. I hate unsolicited emails with a passion, and I promise that I will never spam you. You can change your mind at any time by clicking the unsubscribe link in the footer of any email you receive from me.

You can also follow me on:
Facebook: www.facebook.com/RichardTBurkeBooks and
Goodreads: www.goodreads.com/author/show/14731743.Richard_T_Burke

Thanks for reading my work.
Richard T. Burke November 2022

Printed in Great Britain
by Amazon

36431133R00456